HORSE HEAVEN

JANE SMILEY

HORSE
HEAVEN

ALFRED A. KNOPF   NEW YORK   2000

THIS IS A BORZOI BOOK
PUBLISHED BY ALFRED A. KNOPF

Copyright © 2000 by Jane Smiley
Photographs copyright © 2000 by Norman Mauskopf

All rights reserved under International and Pan-American Copyright
Conventions. Published in the United States by Alfred A. Knopf,
a division of Random House, Inc., New York, and simultaneously
in Canada by Random House of Canada Limited, Toronto.
Distributed by Random House, Inc., New York.

www.aaknopf.com

Knopf, Borzoi Books, and the colophon are registered
trademarks of Random House, Inc.

Library of Congress Cataloging-in-Publication Data
Smiley, Jane.
Horse heaven / Jane Smiley.
p.   cm.
ISBN 0-375-40600-X
1. Horsemen and horsewomen—United States—Fiction.
2. Horse racing—Fiction.   I. Title.
PS3569.M39 H67 2000
813'.54—dc21   99-052728
Manufactured in the United States of America
Published April 6, 2000
Second Printing Before Publication

The gentle reader of this "comic epic poem in prose" is hereby
reminded that all locations, characters and events mentioned
herein, including those whose names seem familiar, are
figments of the author's imaginings, and their characteristics
as represented bear no relationship to real life.

To the memory of TERSON (Ger.), by Luciano out of Templeogue, by Prodomo (fifty-two starts, seven wins, eight seconds, and three thirds in France and the United States), this novel is dedicated with love and gratitude.

And to Jack Canning, likewise.

Thank you, especially, to Dr. Gregory L. Ferraro, D.V.M., of Davis, California, and to Jim Squires, of Lexington, Kentucky, for their endless patience, help, and kindness; and to Dave Hofmans, Eddie Gregson, Dr. Mike Fling, Dr. Gary Deter, Roy and Andre Forzani, Benjamin Bycel, Bea and Derek DiGrazia, John Grassi, Nana Faridany, Rick Moss, Ray Berta, Tara Baker, Stefano Cacace, Bob Armstead, and countless others who gave of their time, their expertise, and, best of all, their wit.

In no other department of human knowledge has there been such a universal and persistent habit of misrepresenting the truth of history as in matters relating to the horse.

—JOHN H. WALLACE, *The Horse in America*

I recognized with despair that I was about to be compelled to buy a horse.

—*Some Experiences of an Irish R.M.*, SOMERVILLE AND ROSS

I never heard of a great thing done yet but it was done by a thorough-bred horse.

—English steeplechase jockey DICK CHRISTIAN, 1820s

CAST OF CHARACTERS

New York and Florida (Aqueduct, Belmont, Saratoga, Calder, Gulfstream)

Alexander P. Maybrick: owner, industrialist
Rosalind Maybrick: socialite, connoisseur
Eileen: Rosalind's Jack Russell terrier
Dick Winterson: Al and Rosalind's horse-trainer
Luciano: Dick's horse masseur

Tiffany Morse: checker at Wal-Mart
Ho Ho Ice Chill: Tiffany's boyfriend, rap singer
Dagoberto Gomez: Tiffany's horse-trainer
Herman Newman: toy magnate, racehorse owner

Maryland (Pimlico, Laurel, Delaware Park, the New Jersey and Philadelphia tracks)

Krista Magnelli: breeder, owner of a small studfarm
Pete and Maia Magnelli: Krista's husband and baby daughter
Sam the vet: Krista's equine practitioner

Skippy Hollister: owner, lawyer, Washington powerbroker
Mary Lynn Hollister: Skippy's wife, dragon of good works
Deirdre Donohue: The Hollisters' horse-trainer
George Donohue: Deirdre's cousin, assistant trainer
Ellen: Deirdre's old friend, owner of hunter-jumper stable and riding school

Chicago and New Orleans (Hawthorne, Arlington Park, Sportsman's Park, Louisiana Downs)

William Vance: horse-trainer

California (Santa Anita, Hollywood Park, Del Mar, Golden Gate Fields, Bay Meadows)

Kyle Tompkins: owner of a vast Thoroughbred breeding farm and much else
Jason Clark Kingston: software magnate

Andrea Melanie Kingston: Jason's wife
Azalea Warren: virgin, racehorse owner, old California money
Joy Gorham: mare manager at Tompkins Ranch
Elizabeth Zada: Joy's friend, author, animal communicator
Plato Theodorakis: Elizabeth's boyfriend, futurologist
Farley Jones: Kyle Tompkins' horse-trainer
Oliver: Farley's assistant trainer

Buddy Crawford: Jason Clark Kingston's horse-trainer
Leon: Buddy's assistant trainer
Deedee: exercise rider for Buddy
Curtis Doheny: Buddy's equine practitioner
Roberto Acevedo: apprentice jockey
Marvelous Martha: exercise rider and legend

Lin Jay "the Pisser" Hwang: small-time owner, former Red Guard
The Round Pebble: the Pisser's mother

Leo: racetrack afficionado, theorist of track life
Jesse: Leo's son, aged nine

Texas

R. T. Favor: horse-trainer and suspicious character
Angel Smith: owner of a small horse-boarding establishment
Horacio Delagarza: Angel's friend

France

Audrey Schmidt: youthful horse enthusiast
Florence Schmidt: Audrey's mother

Everywhere

Sir Michael Ordway: horse agent, peer of the realm

Horses

Mr. T.: gray gelding, stakes winner in France, bred in Germany
Justa Bob: brown gelding, bred in California
Residual: chestnut filly, bred in Kentucky
Limitless: bay colt, bred in Maryland
Froney's Sis: gray or roan filly, bred in California
Epic Steam: dark-bay or brown colt, bred in Kentucky

BOOK ONE

1997

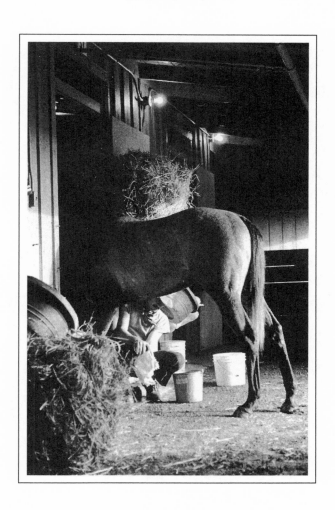

WHO THEY ARE

A LL THE JOCKEY CLUB knows about them is parentage, color, markings:

Residual, by Storm Trumpet, out of Baba Yaya, by Key to the Mint, chestnut, born January 23, 1996. White star, three white stockings that end below the knee. Kentucky-bred.

Epic Steam, by Land of Magic, out of Pure Money, by Mr. Prospector, dark-bay or brown colt, February 18, 1996, would be called black if there were any true black Thoroughbreds. He has no white at all anywhere on his body. Kentucky-bred.

Froney's Sis, by Mr. Miracles, out of My Deelite, by Cee's Tizzy, gray or roan filly, March 21, 1996. Now almost black, but flecked with white hairs, she has a star and a snip between her nostrils, as well as one white sock, but these markings will disappear over the years, enveloped like tide pools by the encroaching sea of white that will spread over her body from her face and her shoulders and her haunches. She has a clockwise whorl on her chest around which the rest of her seems to orbit like a galaxy. Cal-bred.

Bay colt, by Lake of the Woods, out of Wayward, by Independence, May 5, 1996. This is the commonest color in Thoroughbreds. He has a tiny star on his forehead, symmetrical cowlicks on either side of his neck, and a little white triangle on the inside of his right hind fetlock. Maryland-bred.

All their markings are described on their registration papers, and all have numbers and files. Their live births have been noted, their blood has been taken and tested to be sure they descend from whom their owners say they descend, their births have been recorded under the names of their sires in a num-

3

ber of documents, and published in the *Thoroughbred Times*. Already they are successful, having gotten conceived, gestated, born, nursed, weaned, halter-broken, shod, transported, and taught some basic manners with some misadventure but nothing fatal.

They are all related to one another. Every one of them carries the blood of the Darley Arabian, and Eclipse. You could hardly have a Thoroughbred who did not. Every one of them, too, carries the blood of Stockwell and of Nearco. Three of them carry the blood of Rock Sand. Two descend from the great female progenitor Pocahontas. Two are more American than English, going back to Lexington. The lucky ones carry St. Simon. Hyperion appears here and there, a dot of sunlight in any pedigree. The four great broodmare sires—War Admiral, Princequillo, Mahmoud, Blue Larkspur—appear, too, even though no one around any of these foals is old enough to have actually seen them race.

As Thoroughbreds, Residual, Epic Steam, Froney's Sis, and the as-yet-unnamed bay colt share some characteristics. They are active and inquisitive. They would rather move than not. Easing into a gallop is as natural to all of them as breathing. When they run, they look ahead, about four strides, and their tails stream out straight behind them. They are born to go forward, nose aligned with neck aligned with back aligned with tail, as a border collie is born to follow the heels of sheep, or a cat is born to toy with a mouse. All are evidently intelligent and inquisitive. They will follow after anything that wanders through the pasture, noses down, investigating. They are exuberant. They are sensitive. They have opinions. They in general have too much of every lively quality rather than too little. On average, they are more closely related to one another than cheetahs.

Nevertheless, even if they were all the same color, you could readily tell them apart. They say of Epic Steam, Well, *he* knows who *he* is! Yeah, he knows he's a son of a bitch, or, rather, the son of a son of a bitch! He's a big burly colt. The farrier doesn't like to trim him and no one else likes to do much with him, either. He's resisted haltering, resisted grooming, resisted worming and shots. He always gets saved for last, even though last is when everyone is tired and irritable. It just puts you in such a bad mood to deal with him that it's bad for the other horses if he goes first, that's the justification. You can't approach him with affection, kindness, gentleness, but, then, neither can you approach him with firmness, dominance, aggression.

He is worth a lot of money: his dam cost her owner $567,000 (though she has amortized that expenditure with the three of her seven foals who sold as yearlings for two to five hundred thousand dollars). Land of Magic's stud fee was sixty thousand dollars. Epic Steam himself brought $450,000 at the yearling sale in Keeneland last July. Epic Steam is easily offended. He has high standards of behavior with regard to his own person, and every human he has met so far has offended them. Other horses aren't so bad—they have been capable of learning, and so they don't offend him, and he isn't mean with them, only bossy. It's the people who are blind and stubborn. Epic Steam would like to see a person, just one, who can pay attention and meet his standard. Almost two now, he is frequently termed "a monster," sixteen hands, with a great arching neck and ribs that spring away from his lungs and his oversized heart. His haunches are a county of their own; his tail streams like a black banner almost to the ground.

Residual knows who she is, too. She is the one who is always walking around the pasture, stopping, lifting her head, having a look, walking on. She is the one with the meditative air. When they handle her, they've learned from her to wait just a second. The farrier asks her to lift her foot—there's a momentary pause, and then it's clear that she has decided, and she lifts her foot. They say that she is easy to get along with, and so she is. When she runs around with the other fillies, she doesn't barge to the front, but instead hangs back for a second and waits for an opening, then flows into it. She is fifteen hands two inches, well developed and nicely built for two-year-old racing. She has big haunches, a graceful neck, and an attractive head that is short but beautifully molded. She has pretty, mobile ears. Her chestnut coat is richly colored, preternaturally fine. Her right knee turns out, like her sire's. At the Saratoga sale, she brought a disappointing twenty-four thousand dollars.

The bay colt knows who he is, too, and so does his breeder, who simply calls him "Wow." The youngest of the four, he has not left home yet, so every day his handlers see that he has inherited from his grandsire, Independence, a gallop that is easier for him than standing still. His idea of relaxing is galloping around the pasture, speeding up, slowing down, turning, sweeping around a large curve. He works on his stride and pacing every day while others are sleeping, play-fighting each other, eating, except that it isn't work, it is his natural activity, his default option. He gallops in response to every stimulus. He isn't as big or as pretty as some other yearlings, and his conformation isn't perfect, either. He has a long back, slightly swayed, and long hind legs. His neck is skinny. His head is a bit common, until you look at his eyes, soulful, long-lashed. He is pleasant to handle but distracted, half ignoring you, waiting, always, to go back outside. He was too young and undeveloped in the summer to go to a sale, and his owner is thinking of racing him.

Froney's Sis is the only one who isn't sure who she is. Orphaned at a month old, when her dam colicked in the night and died, she was put in with a mini-horse for companionship, and fed milk from a bucket, because she was too old to go to a nurse mare. The mini-horse was a patient fellow. He stood quietly near her, moved away from the feed bucket when she wanted to eat, grazed almost underneath her, even trotted around companionably while she romped and kicked up and galloped, but he wasn't matter-of-fact about things, the way a mare would be. He didn't nuzzle her much, and he wasn't possessed of that throaty, loving nicker that is a specialty of mares. Most of all, his interest in her wasn't the compelling element of his existence, as a mare's interest in her foal would be. A mare would be pushy and interfering and attentive. A mare would call out and trot over; a mare's body language would be telling the filly what to think and how to behave twenty-four hours a day. But the mini-horse didn't have a mare's body language. Already culture has interfered with nature in the case of Froney's Sis—the twigs of her personality are like the shoots of an espaliered apricot tree; however nice she becomes, she may never know who she is.

Her owner, Mr. Kyle Tompkins, seems to own everything else in central California, too. On a hot, sunny piece of land so vast and featureless that it offers no limits or resistance, Mr. Tompkins grows cattle, apricots, grapes, cotton, wheat, rice, and alfalfa, manufactures cosmetics, runs restaurants, a resort, a horse-training center, a horse-breeding center, a trucking company, a holding company, an asset-management company, an insurance company, and a company that underwrites insurance companies, but he takes a personal interest in the racehorses. Froney's Sis he has named after Bob Froney's sister. Bob Froney is the guy down the road who developed the special formula for Tompkins Perfection Almond and Aloe Skin Revitalizer, Tompkins Perfection Skin Nurturing Kindness Cosmetics' best seller. Bob has recently mentioned to Mr. Tompkins that his sister Dorcas was the first tester of the formula and guided them toward the greaseless product that Bob finally came up with in his kitchen. In a fit of gratitude Mr. Tompkins spent a day trying to decide between "Dorcas," "Bob's Baby Sister," and "Froney's Sis." One year, he named a filly "Chemolita" and a colt "Radiation Baby," because his mother was undergoing chemotherapy. His names are so odd that no one else ever wants them, and the Jockey Club seems always to give him what he wants. He names nearly a hundred foals a year, and races mostly his own stock.

The filly has not been easy to train, and Jack Perkins, who manages the training farm, is thinking of throwing her out in the pasture for another six months. Tompkins Worldwide Thoroughbred Breeding and Racing—Only the Best has plenty of pasture and plenty of water to keep it green.

Everything about them now is speculative, mysterious, potential. On the first of January, when they all turn two simultaneously, who they are, who they will become, how they will be known and remembered, or not, will begin to take form. In a couple more years, everything will have been revealed—how they raced as two-year-olds, how they raced as three-year-olds, whether they manifested the hidden bonuses in their DNA or the hidden deficits, whether they deserve to reproduce or not, what they made of those who trained them and cared for them and rode them and owned them, and what those trainers, grooms, jockeys, and owners made of them. They are about to enter upon lives as public as any human life, lives as active and maybe as profitable, lives about which they will certainly have opinions, though they will never speak to the press, even off the record.

Jack decides, as he always does, that there's plenty of time.

NOVEMBER

1 / JACK RUSSELL

ON THE SECOND Sunday morning in November, the day after the Breeders' Cup at Hollywood Park (which he did not get to this year, because the trek to the West Coast seemed a long one from Westchester County and he didn't have a runner, had never had a runner, how could this possibly be his fault, hadn't he spent millions breeding, training, and running horses? Wasn't it time he had a runner in the Breeders' Cup or got out of the game altogether, one or the other?), Alexander P. Maybrick arose from his marriage bed at 6:00 a.m., put on his robe and slippers, and exited the master suite he shared with his wife, Rosalind. On the way to the kitchen, he passed the library, his office that adjoined the library, the weight room, the guest bathroom, the living room, and the dining room. In every room his wife had laid a Persian carpet of exceptional quality—his wife had an eye for quality in all things—and it seemed like every Persian carpet in every room every morning was adorned with tiny dark, dense turds deposited there by Eileen, the Jack Russell terrier. Eileen herself was nestled up in bed with his wife, apparently sleeping, since she didn't raise even her head when Mr. Maybrick arose, but Mr. Maybrick knew she was faking. No Jack Russell sleeps though movement of any kind except as a ruse.

Mr. Maybrick had discussed this issue with Rosalind on many levels. It was not as though he didn't know what a Jack Russell was all about when Rosalind brought the dog home. A Jack Russell was about making noise, killing small animals and dragging their carcasses into the house, attacking much larger dogs, refusing to be house-trained, and in all other ways living a primitive life. Rosalind had promised to start the puppy off properly, with a kennel and a trainer and a strict routine and a book about Jack Russells, and every other thing that worked with golden retrievers and great Danes and mastiffs, and dogs in general. But Eileen wasn't a dog, she was a beast, and the trainer had been able to do only one thing with her, which was stop her from barking. And thank God for that, because if the trainer had not stopped Eileen from

9

barking Mr. Maybrick would have had to strangle her. Rosalind, who sent her underwear to the cleaners and had the windows washed every two weeks and kept the oven spotless enough to sterilize surgical instruments, tried to take the position that the turds were small and harmless, and that the carpets could handle them, but really she just thought the dog was cute, even after Eileen learned to jump from the floor to the kitchen counters, and then walked around on them with her primevally dirty feet, click click click, right in front of Mr. Maybrick, even after Eileen began to sleep under the covers, pushing her wiry, unsoft coat right into Mr. Maybrick's nose in the middle of the night. "Do you know where this dog has been?" Mr. Maybrick would say to Rosalind, and Rosalind would reply, "I don't want to think about that."

Mr. Maybrick was a wealthy and powerful man, and in the end, that was what stopped him. He knew that, in the larger scheme of things, he had been so successful, and, in many ways, so unpleasant about it all (he was a screamer and a bully, tough on everyone), that Eileen had come into his life as a corrective. She weighed one-twentieth of what he did. He could crush her between his two fists. He could also get rid of her, either by yelling at his wife or by sending her off to the SPCA on his own, but he dared not. There was some abyss of megalomania that Eileen guarded the edge of for Mr. Maybrick, and in the mornings, when he walked to the kitchen to get his coffee, he tried to remember that.

The first thing Mr. Maybrick did after he poured his coffee was to call his horse-trainer. When the trainer answered with his usual "Hey, there!," Mr. Maybrick said, "Dick!," and then Dick said, "Oh. Al." He always said it just like that, as if he were expecting something good to happen, and Mr. Maybrick had happened instead. Mr. Maybrick ignored this and sipped his coffee while Dick punched up his response. "Can I do something for you, Al?"

"Yeah. You can put that Laurita filly in the allowance race on Thursday."

"You've got a condition book, then."

"Oh, sure. I want to know what races are being run. You trainers keep everything so dark—"

"Well, sure. Al, listen—"

"Dick, Frank Henderson thinks it's the perfect race for her. A little step up in class, but not too much competi—"

"I'll see."

"I want to do it. Henderson said—"

"Mr. Henderson—"

"Frank Henderson knows horses and racing, right? His filly won the Kentucky Oaks last year, right? He would have had that other horse in the sprint yesterday if it hadn't broken down. Listen to me, Dick. I shouldn't have to beg you." This was more or less a threat, and as he said it, not having actually intended to, Mr. Maybrick reflected upon how true it was. He was the owner. Dick Winterson was the trainer. The relationship was a simple one. Henderson was always telling him not to be intimidated by trainers.

"We'll see."

"You always say that. Look, I don't want to watch the Breeders' Cup on TV again next year. Henderson thinks this filly's got class."

"She does, but I want to go slow with her. We have to see how the filly—"

Mr. Maybrick hung up. He didn't slam down the phone—he no longer did that—he simply hung up. If Dick had known him as long as Mr. Maybrick had known himself, he would have realized what a good thing it was, simply hanging up. And here was another thing he could use with his wife. He could say that if he didn't have to pass all those turds in the morning he could start off calmer and his capacity for accepting frustration would last a little longer. It was scientific. When they didn't have the dog, he had gotten practically to the fourth phone call without offending anyone. Now he got maybe to the second. He took another sip of his coffee, and called his broker, then his partner, then his general manager, then his other partner, then his secretary, then his broker again, then his AA sponsor (who was still in bed). This guy's name was Harold W., and he was a proctologist as well as an alcoholic. Mr. Maybrick had chosen him because he was a man of infinite patience and because he knew everything there was to know about prostate glands.

"I want a drink," said Mr. Maybrick. "There's turds all over the house. I bet you can understand that one."

"Good morning, Al. What's really up? You haven't had a drink in two years."

"But I'm always on the verge. It's a real struggle with me."

"Say your serenity prayer."

"God—"

"God—"

They said the serenity prayer together.

"Look," said Al, "I got this pain in my groin—"

"No freebies. That's the rule. My partner will be happy to—"

"It's like water trickling out of a hose. I can't—"

"You need to be working on your fourth step."

"What's that one again?"

"Taking a fearless inventory of your character defects."

"Oh, yeah."

"Trying to get something for nothing is one of your character defects."

"I never pay retail."

"Then you need to work on your third step, Al."

"What's that one?"

"Turning your life over to your higher power."

Mr. Maybrick cleared his throat, as he always did when someone said those higher-power words. Those words always made an image of Ralph Peters come into his head, the guy who used to be head of the Mercantile Exchange in Chicago, and who foiled the Hunt brothers when they tried to corner the silver market back in '80. Peters was an Austrian guy. He had "higher power" written all over him, and he was the last guy Mr. Maybrick had ever feared. He would never turn his life over to Peters.

Harold went on, "Let's think a little more about the last day. What about rage? Have you been raging?"

"Well, sure. A guy in my posi—"

"Should be filled with gratitude. Your position is a gratitude position. Thank you, God, for every frustration, every bad deal, every monetary loss, every balk and obstacle and resistance."

Harold often teased him in this way. Mr. Maybrick felt better for it, because it made him think Harold W. liked him after all, and it reminded him, too, of when his old man had been in a good mood. Joshing him.

"Every non-cooperator, every son of a bitch, every idiot who gets in my way, every slow driver, every—"

"Okay."

"I've got to go to work."

"But I— There's wine in the liquor cabinet."

"Throw it out. I've got to go to work. The assholes are accumulating."

Mr. Maybrick laughed. Harold W. laughed, too. Harold W. wasn't a saint, by any means. He had been in AA for thirty-two years, at a meeting almost every day. Mr. Maybrick didn't know whether to respect that or have contempt for it, but he knew for a fact that Harold W. was a force to be reckoned with, and he thanked him politely, ragelessly, and hung up the phone.

Now Eileen trotted into the room. It was clear to Mr. Maybrick that the dog was intentionally ignoring him. She clicked over to her bowl and checked it, took a drink from the water dish, circumnavigated the cooking island, and then, casually, leapt onto the granite counter and trotted toward the sink. "Get down, Eileen," said Mr. Maybrick. It was as if he hadn't spoken. Eileen cocked her little tan head and peered into the garbage disposal, noting that the stopper was in place. Her little stump of a tail flicked a couple of times, and she seemed to squat down. She stretched her paw toward the stopper, but her legs were too short; she couldn't reach it. She surveyed the situation for a moment, then went behind the sink, picked up a pinecone that had been hidden there, and jumped down. Only now did she look at Mr. Maybrick. She dropped the pinecone at his slippered feet and backed up three steps, her snapping black gaze boring into his. "I don't want to do that, Eileen," he said. Her strategy was to take little steps backward and forward and then spin in a tight circle, gesturing at the pinecone with her nose. But she never made a sound.

"You're not a retriever, Eileen, you're a terrier. Go outside and kill something."

Indeed, Eileen was a terrier, and with terrier determination, she resolved that Mr. Maybrick would ultimately throw the pinecone. She continued dancing, every few seconds picking up the pinecone and dropping it again. She was getting cuter and cuter. That was her weapon. Mr. Maybrick considered her a very manipulative animal. He looked away from her and took another sip of his (third) cup of coffee. Now she barked once, and when he looked at her, she went up on her hind legs. She had thighs like a wrestler—she seemed to float. Mr. Maybrick had often thought that a horse as athletic as this worthless dog would get into the Kentucky Derby, then the Breeders' Cup, win him ten million dollars on the track, and earn him five million a year in the breeding shed for, say, twenty years. That was $110 million; it had happened to others. He had been racing and breeding horses for eleven years, and it had never happened to him. This was just the sort of thing that made you a little resentful, and rightfully so, whatever Harold W. had to say about gratitude. He closed his eyes when he felt himself sliding that way, beginning to count up the millions he had spent running horses and thinking about deserving. With his eyes closed, Al could hear her drop the pinecone rhythmically on the tile, chock chock chock chock, the bass, her little toenails clicking a tune around it. Didn't he deserve a really big horse? Didn't he? And then, while his eyes were still closed, dog and pinecone arrived suddenly in his lap, a hard, dense little weight but live, electric. With the shock, he nearly dropped his coffee cup, and as it was, spilled on the counter. "God damn it!" he shouted. Eileen jumped down and trotted away. "Hey! Come here, Eileen," he said. "Eileen!" Eileen sheared off into the living room, and he realized that he had forgotten to let her out. Mr. Maybrick put his arms up on the table and laid his head upon them.

2 / ROUGH STRIFE

THOUGH IT WASN'T customary for Farley Jones to find himself out
with the first set of horses at 5:00 a.m. or so, he didn't mind it today, for he
hadn't been sleeping well lately, and it was better to be up and about than lying
in bed wondering what was going on with everyone who was up and about.
Oliver, his assistant trainer, was home with the flu. They were working under
lights, and the horses, the best group in Farley's barn, were all galloping today
rather than working. And he was alone in the grandstand at Santa Anita, and
it was pleasantly quiet now that the hurly-burly of the Breeders' Cup was
over. The weather was good, too, for all the talk about the imminent arrival of
El Niño.

It wasn't until his horses were finished and trotting out, a good twenty
minutes of blessed solitude, that anyone joined him, and that was Buddy
Crawford, another trainer, with his assistant. They came abreast, like a sand-
storm, bringing turbulence in with them, and Farley felt his body gear up to
charge for the exit, then felt his mind resist that impulse. On the one hand, he
wasn't done looking at his horses, and on the other, there was something he
had to say to Buddy Crawford that he hadn't been looking forward to saying.
He had sworn he wouldn't seek an opportunity to say it or say it in front of any
other trainers, and that condition now applied, and he was stuck. He put his
hand on the railing to hold himself in Buddy's presence. And then the horse he
had been intending to discuss with Buddy trotted by below, grinding his bit
and pulling, his ears pinned and his back end bouncing. When he got a hundred yards away, he reared up, but the exercise boy was ready for him and
kicked him forward. Buddy leaned out and shouted, "Work five is all!" Then
he turned to his assistant, handed him a slip of paper, and said, "Take this to
the clockers' shed." The kid walked away. Farley's sense of turbulence increased
rather than diminished. "Hey, Buddy," he said.

"Hey, Farley. How's it going, old man?"

"Not bad."

"I hate working in the fucking dark. My old man worked the night shift, did you know that? He hated working in the dark, too, and sleeping in the day. But what the fuck, I don't sleep a wink anyway."

"I haven't been sleeping very well lately, either."

"This is a fucking lifelong thing with me. To tell you the truth, I don't know if I can't sleep because I worry all the time, or if I worry all the time because I can't sleep. I can't stand to be in the fucking bedroom, with the windows shut and with the carpeting and all. The cars going by on the street make me think of horses galloping, and then I got to get up and see what they're doing. It's a fucking mess."

"You know, I knew a guy who went to a sleep-disorder—"

"It's not a fucking sleep disorder. It's a horse disorder. It's a too-many-horses-in-the-barn disorder!" He laughed, but not mirthfully. Then he leaned over the railing and shouted to the riders of two horses who were trotting along together, "You two need to break from the gate. Don't let your filly pass the other one, Gaspar." Then, to Farley, "Fucking Gaspar. He rides like a fucking girl. If he lets that filly take hold and pass the other one, he'll have a runaway on his hands. Teach him a fucking lesson."

Now Buddy, who was wiry and little, was pacing, and Farley was glancing down the track, hoping and not hoping someone else would come along. He saw the last of his set exit the track down where the path came in.

Farley could see the horse in question heading toward them. He was a big bay horse with a distinctive white stripe on his face that ran between his eyes for a few inches, then veered off to the right and ended at the horse's nostril. He said, "How you doing with that colt?"

Buddy glanced at the animal.

"He's training pretty good. Inconsistent. He's got some speed. Dam's a Rahy mare. She had some speed, too."

"Wedding Ring."

"That's the one."

"She was steady as they come."

"Yeah, steady hot, Henry says. He had her in his barn before she went back to New York. This one, though, he's up, he's down. But he's got to learn his job and bull through it. That's the name of the game. Hasn't raced in three weeks. Vacation's over."

Once Farley had watched his former wife suggest to her sister that she wasn't giving her one-year-old daughter enough attention. The sister had been looking out the window, and, hearing this rather mildly stated reproach, had turned her head to look at Marlise, whose own two-year-old (with Farley) was babbling at her feet. What really happened was that the sister's head swung

around in surprise with a definite wrecking-ball look to it, and after screaming
at one another for ten minutes, causing both the children to cry, and startling
both the husbands out of two years of prospective longevity, the sisters didn't
speak until their children were six and five. And they lived in the same town,
and saw each other at nearly every family dinner. It was with this in mind that
Farley never offered any suggestions to other trainers about their horses. But
now he said, "Buddy, you should have that horse's stifles X-rayed. I had a filly
who moved like that in the hind end, and she—"

"He moves fine. He had an abscess. That's why he's been off. But the gravel
erupted two weeks ago."

"Maybe, but—"

"Watch this work."

The horse shot past them. You could see the exercise boy gritting his teeth,
the horse was pulling so hard. Buddy said, "That horse loves to run, and I'm
not going to stand in his way. In fact, I'm going to provide him with an opportunity to do what he loves to do."

"Buddy—" But in the end, he couldn't bring himself to say what he was
thinking, which was that the horse was going to break down.

"You know what?"

"What?"

"These horses are here to race and win. Their owners pay me seventy
bucks a day and all they fucking care about is racing and winning. But that's
not even it. The owners don't care as much about racing and winning as I do. If
the fucking horse falls over two steps after the finish line, he's done his job that
he was born into this world to do."

"I don't think—"

"What? A Thoroughbred is not a natural phenomenon. His mommy and
daddy didn't fall in love, get married, and decide to have a baby. None of these
horses would be here if they weren't meant to race and win. The breeder is their
God and the racetrack is their destiny and running is their work, and any other
way of looking at it is getting things mixed up, if you ask me. The last thing I
want to do is get things mixed up, because, as fucked as I am now, I'd be really
fucked then, because I wouldn't know what I was doing."

"Buddy—"

"Farley, we've been training together around this track for twenty-five
years or so, right?"

"Yeah."

"Well, here's what I've noticed about you. You're smart. They all say that
about you, Farley's smart. Sometimes he's too smart, but he's always smart. I

ain't smart, if you'll pardon my English. If I'm going to get winners, it isn't going to be by being smart, it's going to be by sticking to what I know. That's how smart I am, exactly. I'm smart enough to know how to get by without being smart."

"Anyone can learn—"

"Can they? You had that colt Rough Strife, remember him? You had him around here for a year and a half. He was dumb as a post, wasn't he? He's a legend. He fell down at the quarter pole in his first race, and every start after that, he shied at the quarter pole. He couldn't learn not to. Lots of them can, but he couldn't."

"Just get his stifles—"

"I don't want to know about it. He's ready to run. As long as he tells me he wants to run, I'm going to run him." Buddy leaned out the window and shouted, "Gaspar, you were okay this time, so I'm going to put you on another crazy one. I think you're learning something!" And he turned and marched out of the grandstand. In the ensuing lull, Farley realized that his own second set were discreetly milling about, awaiting instructions. He sighed.

BY WEDNESDAY, Farley was back to normal, sleepwise, and Oliver was back to normal, flu-wise, so Farley didn't get to the grandstand until dawn was breaking over Pasadena. There were two or three trainers standing about, and Farley joined in the joking. Henry, who was over seventy but under eighty-five, said, "You know, there were these two veterinary surgeons who shall remain nameless, but you know them, golfing up there at Pebble Beach, before the Japs bought the place. They were on the third hole, there, in the woods, and the guy from around here says to the guy from Kentucky, 'See that tree down there with that knothole about four feet from the ground?'

" 'Yeah,' says the other one.

" 'This is the kind of surgeon I am. There's an owl in that tree, and I'm going to take these surgical instruments I got in my golf bag, and I'm going to remove that owl's tonsils without waking him up.'

" 'Nah,' says the other surgeon.

"But the guy goes down there, leans into the knothole, and comes back ten minutes later. He's got these two tiny little pink things in his hand, and sure enough, they look like tonsils.

"So they each take another shot, and the surgeon from Kentucky says, 'Gimme those instruments. I'm such a good surgeon that I'm gonna go down there and remove that owl's balls without him waking up.' So he heads down to the tree, leans in, comes back ten minutes later. He's got two tiny red things in his hand, and he says, 'Sleeping like a baby.' So the California guy says, 'You win,' and they finish their round.

"Well, around dusk the owl wakes up, and he goes out flying around for a while, and he comes over to a friend's tree, and lands, and they're sitting there talking, and he says, 'You know, there's something funny going on over there on the third hole. Stay away from there is my advice. I woke up tonight, and I can't hoot worth a fuck or fuck worth a hoot.' "

Everyone laughed and, after a while, headed back to the barns, except Farley and Henry. Henry looked up at Farley. He said, "So—Buddy Crawford says you broke that horse of his down."

"I did hear that colt of his broke down Saturday, but all I did was—"

"Shouldn'ta done even that."

"Even what?"

"Even make a suggestion, or a comment, or whatever."

"The horse was moving just like a filly I had. I knew for sure—"

"Shoulda kept your mouth shut. Buddy says you jinxed it for him."

"Henry, that's ridi—"

"You may think so, Farley, and I may think so. I *may*. I'm not saying I do. But this is a racetrack, Farley. Jinxes, curses, luck, superstitions, evil eyes—this is where they *live*."

"Breakdowns have causes, like stress fractures and toegrabs and bad conditioning."

"They do. But you tangled yourself in this one."

"I was right, is all."

"That's an even worse mistake, to be right about another man's horse." Henry shook his head, then he said, "I know something's up with you, boy. You haven't had such a good year this year. Those come and go."

"I know that. That's not—"

"Listen to me, I'll tell you something. I've worked all over California, here and up north and at the fairs. You know I saw Phar Lap? Down at Agua Caliente. Right there is what I'm getting at. The things I've seen men do to horses made me believe in sin, original and every other kind. And when I die, and that isn't so far away now, I expect to be punished for the sins I looked upon but didn't stop. But what I'm telling you is, that's the wages of a life at the track. You don't say everything you know."

Farley knew that this was true. Henry shook his head, then turned and walked away.

3 / IF WISHES WERE HORSES

THE REASON Tiffany Morse left her purse on the bench in front of the clothes dryer in the Spankee Yankee Laundromat in Lowell, Massachusetts, was that she had to run out the door into the dank November cold to catch her niece Iona, and in the panic of that, she forgot where her purse was. Then she had to make Iona look at her and understand that she was not to ever ever ever go outside without Tiffany ever again, but of course, Iona was too young to understand that—she was only three. Fast, though. Anyway, when she came back to dryer number four ("John Adams"—all the dryers were named after famous Massachusetts politicians, right down to "Michael Dukakis," number sixteen), her purse was open and her money was gone. The Laundromat was empty, too. The worst thing was that she hadn't fed any quarters into the dryer yet, and her wet clothes were sitting inside in a lump with the door open. It actually would have been easier if the thief had stolen the clothes as well as the money, since now she had to cart all those wet things back to her apartment and try to corral Iona, too, but he hadn't. Tiffany could not say that she was having a good day. She certainly could not say that.

But Tiffany didn't really require good days anymore. She was always willing to settle for a good morning, or even a good hour. And she and Iona had had a good hour just that evening, before coming out to the Laundromat. What happened was, Tiffany picked Iona up at her mother's on her way home from work because she had agreed to take Iona for the night while her mother went to choir practice and then out with some of the other choir members, and her mother had been making pork stew, and when she got there, tired and hungry, her mother had been in a good mood, and had sat her down at the table and given her a big plateful. Iona had been a good girl, so there had been no ill-tempered references to Iona's father, Tiffany's brother, Roland, who was up to no good in Ohio somewhere, or maybe Texas. The stew had lots of potatoes and carrots in it, and nice chunks of pork. In the larger war that was Tiffany's relationship with her mother, they had made a truce. The next thing that happened was that, when Tiffany got home, she saw that the Christmas cactus in her window was starting to bloom. Between them, the stew and the flowers made her feel good enough to endure the Spankee Yankee, but now, in retrospect, she saw that they had been bad, or at least false omens, because if she hadn't had that good hour she would have stayed home watching TV, and would not have lost her money and had to hang all her wet clothes around the apartment. By the time she did that, and got Iona to bed on the couch (never an easy task), she was exhausted and even more blue than she'd been when she first discovered the money missing.

It was more than the money, it was what the theft meant—that you couldn't afford to be happy, because being happy made you do things that then ended in greater unhappiness than you had been feeling before you got happy. Everyone knew that that's the way it was with love and sex and men—the happier you were when you fell in love, the more crushed you would be when it didn't work out—but what was even more depressing was that that was the way it was with simple things like pork stew and flowers. The whole depressing idea made your life pretty impossible, especially since all the time you were telling your mom that (1) things were fine and (2) everything was going to be all right. Tiffany had always told herself and her mother that she wasn't going to end up where her mother had—always saying things like "Don't count on that," and "There's many a slip 'tween the cup and the lip" (an assertion that everyday experience showed to be patently untrue) and "If wishes were horses," a phrase of her mother's that made no sense at all.

Another thing her mom always said was "Good-looking ain't necessarily good-acting." She usually said this in reference to guys Tiffany had turned up here and there, and in reference to Iona's father and Tiffany's brother, Roland. But often Tiffany expected that she was saying it in reference to her, because everyone said, and Tiffany herself knew, that she was a knockout, a fox, a babe, you name it. She was so used to being a drop-dead gorgeous black woman no matter what she wore or how she did her makeup that she didn't even care anymore. Where had it gotten her, now that she was twenty-one with very little to show for it? Iona was drop-dead gorgeous, too, the way tiny things are especially gorgeous because you can't believe they are so small and perfect, but Tiffany never complimented her. Drop-dead gorgeous was just a thing, like sleet or snow or flowers, that happened. And you had to be drop-dead gorgeous to know what a trivial thing it was. Tiffany often wondered what she would exchange her looks for, if she could. Something more interesting to do than working as a checker at Wal-Mart would be one thing, but the fact was, she couldn't think of what that interesting thing to do would be. That was her problem, she thought. She knew perfectly well what others wanted her to do and what she didn't want to do, but when she tried to pull up from her depths something she herself wanted to do, the bucket came up empty. Once in a while she did some research. There were programs on TV that showed you what other people did. They worked in offices or police stations or bars. Lots of them worked in show business. But none of them really did anything except sit around and make jokes, which was what Tiffany herself did all day at Wal-Mart, and so all of them looked as idle as she felt herself to be. Or she bought a magazine, but all the women's magazines made it seem as though everyone was either working full-time on her appearance, which Tiffany could afford to disdain, or else making different recipes all day, which seemed nearly as boring. There was a channel on the TV called the Discovery Channel, which Tiffany sometimes monitored, but those shows didn't focus on what the people did, only on the results of what they did. She didn't ever see how they had made the move from, say, Lowell, Massachusetts, to the plains of the Serengeti. If those people were calling out to her, then they were calling across an abyss of space that she didn't see how anyone could cross. Especially now that she had no money at all, not even bus fare to get to work tomorrow. She turned off the TV and went into the living room to check on Iona. Here Iona was, already three, already having her own ideas about stuff she wanted to do that weren't the same as your ideas about stuff Iona was supposed to do. That sort of thing made you think about how fast time went. But, then, here she was, here her mother was, doing the same things year after year, having the same arguments, not getting anywhere. That sort of thing made you think just the opposite, that time went all too slowly. She covered Iona and picked up the girl's shoes, which she set on the corner of the table so she could find them easily in the morning.

After she had gotten into bed and turned out the light, she thought that all she had was the same prayer she had uttered before. She lay on her back and looked at the ceiling. She whispered, "Please make something happen here." Tiffany sighed. This was a prayer that always worked. Unfortunately, it didn't always work as she hoped. For example, she had prayed for a job, and gotten hired at Wal-Mart. She had prayed for a boyfriend, and attracted the deathless interest of Lindsay Wicks, her dampest, palest co-worker. She had prayed for a couch, and her mother had decided to buy a new one, passing the seventeen-year-old brown thing on to Tiffany, who was required to appear grateful. She continued, "This time, I mean it."

4 / A USEFUL ANIMAL

Not long before Thanksgiving, Joy Gorham, mare manager at Tompkins Ranch, The Breeding Operation, Fine Thoroughbreds, A Subsidiary of Tompkins Worldwide Racing—Only the Best, found a note in her box from Mr. Tompkins' secretary. It read, "Take care of this, honey," and was attached to a letter. The letter was neatly typed on a computer, but in a cursive, girlish font, on stationery scattered with pictures of horses. It read,

Dear Mr. Tompkins,

My Mom uses your almond throat cream. She likes it very much. Thank you. There is a horse here in a field by my school. I give him some carrots every day, and I bought a rubber curry and a body brush and a soft brush and a hoofpick out of my own allowance. I also groom him every day. He is a very nice horse. I call him Toto. But my Dad showed me how to write to the Thoroughbred Protective Association, and find out about a horse because I made out his tattoo on his upper lip. I found out that his real name is *Terza Rima, and that he came over to this country in 1985 to run races for you. He was bred in Germany and raced in France. He is a stakes winner. You owned him for five years and raced him at Hollywood Park, Del Mar, Gulfstream, and Saratoga. He won seven races out of fifty-two starts, and was on the board twenty-two times, then you sold him and now he is here.

The thing is, my Dad is an army officer, and now we are leaving this base to go to Washington, D.C. I can't take care of Toto any longer, and I think he will die, because he is very skinny—you can see his hip bones and his ribs and his neck is very thin. Also, all the other horses bite him, and because he is gray with black skin, the bites show. He has a very short tail. I think the other horses in the field are very mean to him. His owner has too many horses. He is a bad man, and last summer he forgot to fill the tanks for three days when it was hot. My Mom and I filled the tanks ourselves, with a hose from the school. He thinks the horses are eating the grass, but there isn't any grass. All the horses are very unhappy.

I think that since *Terza Rima won $300,000 dollars for you, you should take him to your farm and keep him there. My Dad says that that is what a decent person would do, but he doesn't think very many horse people are decent. You are in California. We are in Texas. That isn't very far. I will be leaving here on December 1st. I look forward to hearing from you.

Yours very truly,
Audrey Schmidt, aged eleven
512-969-5225

Joy turned the letter over, and saw on the back a drawing in crayon of a white horse and a little girl, blue sky, yellow sun, green grass. Then she went over to the file cabinet and looked up *Terza Rima. Gray gelding, by Luciano, out of Templeogue, by Prodomo, turf horse, imported at five by Tompkins Racing. Everything Audrey said was true. Tompkins Racing had raced him steadily through his nine-year-old season, then sold him off at a dispersal sale for seven thousand dollars. All in all, Terza Rima had been a profitable investment for a horse who couldn't reproduce, though, of course, on every sector of the Tompkins Ranch, reproduction was the short-term, long-term, and interim goal.

A week later, two men in Tompkins white coats, driving a Tompkins Horse Transport Van ("Air Ride Perfection, 48 States, Weekly Runs from Kentucky to California"), handed Bucky Lord a check for a thousand dollars, one dollar a pound, and loaded the sorriest-looking animal they agreed they had ever seen onto the van with three yearlings from Kentucky. On the way out of town, the driver called the SPCA and the state police, and reported Bucky Lord for cruelty to animals. Every time they stopped the van and checked the horses, the emaciated gray had eaten all his hay. That night, when they stopped and gave him, along with the yearlings, a large bran mash, he inhaled it as they watched and nickered for more. Toward morning they pulled into the ranch, put the yearlings into paddocks, and put the old gray into an isolation stall, until the vet could look at him. It was a big stall, maybe sixteen by sixteen, bedded two feet deep in straw, with windows in every direction. When the driver led the old gelding into the stall, the horse's eyes actually widened in surprise, he thought. The driver shook his head, and paused to scratch the old boy on that spot in front of the withers where horses can't scratch themselves. The horse's head swung around in wonder and he looked right at him.

Joy didn't think the horse should have to be her responsibility. It wasn't like she didn't already have enough to do. The weanlings had to be handled daily, and mares who were put under lights to bring them into season early had to be blanketed and taken in and out. Soon the breeding season would begin again.

Every day, she got to the farm at seven and stayed until at least seven. It wasn't until almost dusk that Joy got a look at the old gray gelding.

Well, it was quite a change from his win pictures that were still in the file. Accustomed as she was to well-cared-for animals, Joy found the gelding's condition startling, almost an optical illusion. He had the head, the neck, the tail, the legs, the body of a horse—but it was all stark and skeletal, especially the neck, which looked like it hadn't been very cresty to begin with. Joy entered the stall and walked around the animal, gazing at him from the side, the front, the other side, the back. He regarded her calmly, his dark eyes almost triangular in his white face, smudged around the edges where the black of his skin showed through the white of his coat.

His feet were a mess, cracked and uneven from bad shoeing or no shoeing, whichever would be worse. His skeletal structure stood out like a picture from a manual. His spine ran from his withers to his tail, bony and prominent. The saddest part was his haunches. The atrophied muscles fell away from the spine in hollows; the croup, that rounded, shining world of power in a fit horse, was an unsoftened rocky prominence in this guy. And floating on the white like islands were black jagged shapes where other horses had taken nips and tucks. The black was the animal's skin underneath the white hair, but it seemed to lift off the surface and made Joy close her eyes and shake her head. The gelding was a good seventeen hands, and weighed maybe nine hundred pounds, when his natural weight would have been something like twelve to thirteen hundred pounds.

She looked down. All that was left of the horse was his legs. They were long, etched, muscular, and clean. He was a textbook example of how the column of the leg must stack exactly true, how the big, flat knee must face front, how the fetlock joint must rest in the hammock of the suspensory ligament but never stretch it too far, how the tendons must be straight and tight and (she felt them) cool. He was equally right in his back end. His hocks were plumb below the point of the gluteus, his pasterns straightened by the slightly deep angle of the hock joint. From behind, the points ran down in a line, glute, hock, fetlock, with the tail centered between them, ticking back and forth. His legs were a picture of how a horse's body should meet the ground, a stable system of springs and pendula. No doubt he was sound, in spite of seventeen years, fifty-two starts, and God knew what else. Joy got a little interested in him. He stepped across the stall toward her, and after a moment, bumped her with his head. She saw that he was a little interested in her, too.

"Terza Rima," she said. "Toto. Well, you seem a little too beat up for the one and a little too grown up for the other. I think I will just call you Mr. T."

He nuzzled her hands with his whiskery nose.

The problem with Thanksgiving, now thankfully past and so why should she still be thinking about it, Joy thought that evening as she was eating her supper at the Tompkins Ranchhouse Restaurant, Succulent Perfection in Beef, was not that she hadn't been invited anywhere and had thus been forced to eat alone in her efficiency guesthouse, it was that, although she had been invited two places, she had chosen to eat alone at her efficiency guesthouse, and now she would have to tell her mother that, and her mother would start looking at this as a symptom. You could take your pick of symptoms—no friends was one, not enjoying the acquaintances she had was another. With symptoms you could not win. If your mother was determined to see your life choices as a set of symptoms—depression, isolation, horse-obsession, overwork, no love life— then it was very hard to convince her that what these really amounted to was a sense of calm and peace, lively interest in a fascinating animal species, plenty to keep you busy, and a choice not to repeat old mistakes. But it was true that she had not enjoyed her solitary Thanksgiving very much, and, she thought, perhaps a friend would be an interesting change, if the friend were a sort of quiet, peaceful, non-intrusive woman of about her own age, someone not un-like herself. There, she would say to her mother, I have perfectly adequate self-esteem—my ideal friend would be just like me.

She looked around the restaurant. None of the dozen women were sitting alone—all were sitting with men, most were sitting with children. That was her problem in a nutshell. She finished her meal and went home. Her home, she thought, was just about the size of a nutshell, and she had given up years before the idea of finding something larger or more convenient. It had nothing to do with pay or scarcity of places to live. It had to do with being content to nestle like a nut inside her nutshell. And she was content—time was when she, too, would have been sitting with a man, her old boyfriend Dean, and she would have been listening to him go on and on about some 100-percent un-natural animal-breeding project he was trying to get funding for, and she would have been smiling and nodding, and, taken all in all, a nutshell was preferable.

Mr. T., of course, had to be isolated for at least a week, because there was no telling what he might have picked up at Bucky Lord's equine establishment, but after that, Joy didn't know quite what to do with him. On the broodmare side of the farm, the pastures were filled with broodmares and weanlings. Broodmares tended to be very firm in the standard of behavior they required of a male horse, and Mr. T. hardly needed any more of that. On the stallion side of the farm, the stallion paddocks happened to be full—the year before, Mr. T. might have gone over there, but Mr. Tompkins had brought a four-year-old and a five-year-old back from the track to give them a try this year. The training center was clear across the ranch, and Joy didn't want to put the old horse in a pasture with young ones. In fact, the vet said he shouldn't be put in with anyone at all, but given a rest from equine society, then maybe introduced later to a single friend, another older gelding, if possible. So he stayed in the isolation barn, which had no paddocks, and every day Joy led him out for a half-hour to eat grass. Right away he started noticing her and nickering for her. It was flattering. She started bringing him carrots, even though she didn't believe in hand-feeding treats. But the animal was the opposite of pushy. He took the carrot out of her hand only when she offered it, and then gently. He didn't bump her or look in her pockets, or even play his lip over her hand. If she didn't offer, he didn't ask.

There was another letter from Audrey. It read,

Dear Miss Joy Gorham—
    Please write to the following address and tell me about Toto. We went to California to see my grandparents and I made my Dad take me three times to Hollywood Park, and I bet all the grays. We had one winning day and two losing days. I did hit the exacta on two long shots, 15–1 (Bimini Baby) and 18–1 (Gimme Ago), on five dollar bets, and I came home with $170. This is equal to a six lesson package at my stable. My Mom said that we could not go to the racetrack again until the spring, and that she will pay for the riding lessons if I would stop betting, but my Dad said that betting is really money management, and that is something that everyone should learn. I don't care about betting. I just care about the horses.
    I miss Toto. I know he was a good racehorse. Please give him a kiss for me, and say my name to him, so that he knows who the kiss is from. Now it turns out we are going to France after Christmas.

Yours Very Truly,
Audrey Schmidt,
14578 Eglantine Street
Pokerville, Maryland

Joy could not help imagining Audrey as herself, twenty-five or thirty years ago—a wiry, blonde little tomboy, standing on her pony's haunches while he grazed and trying to reach an apple hanging from a branch. When the pony walked away too quickly (as he always did), Joy would slide to the ground and jump up, hurt, unhurt, who cared? Whatever the pony did was fine by her, because he was her very own pony, and if you were a certain kind of little girl, a pony of your very own was the world's finest treasure, and no matter how many times over the years your mother said, "It was that awful pony that started all this. I mean, he wasn't even pretty or nice! I told your father—," he still remained in your mind as the ultimate good thing.

She photocopied Mr. T.'s best win photo—the Warren Beatty Handicap at Arlington Park in Chicago, by four lengths—and sent it off to Audrey with an Almond Perfection Skin Nurturing and Refinement Moisturizing Sample Pack (Every Tompkins Skin Blessing Product in Convenient Trial Sizes) and a Tompkins Perfection Prime Steak Sampler (Shipped Frozen for Your Delectation and Enjoyment).

DECEMBER

5 / ROSALIND

ONCE, WHEN Rosalind Maybrick was still Rosie Wilson from Appleton, Wisconsin, on a school trip to New York City, she had seen a sight that changed her life. What happened was, the teacher who was leading the trip gave Rosie and her friend Mary permission to stay behind at the hotel because their hair was still in rollers and the teacher, even though he was a man, had sense enough to know that sixteen-year-old girls were literally not capable of leaving their room with bad hair. So he had told them what bus to take to the Metropolitan Museum of Art, where they could meet the rest of the class in the Etruscan collection. Rosie and Mary had taken only a 10-percent advantage of this privilege—they were three minutes late leaving their room and took the second bus that went past rather than the first, just so they could feel themselves standing at a bus stop in Manhattan, New York, surrounded by people who were short, dark, and voluble rather than tall, blond, and silent. The fatal part was the bus they got on. They of course stood, because they had been taught to do so, out of respect to everyone else in the whole world—they were from the Midwest, and deference was their habit and training. On the bus was a very well-dressed woman with a two- or three-year-old boy in a stroller. She wore a dark, slim fur coat and leather gloves. The boy had on a wool coat and a wool hat. The stroller took up a lot of space. Both woman and boy sat calmly as the bus crossed town, and then the woman pulled the cord and stood up. That was when things began to go wrong. The stroller caught something and began to fold. The boy began to cry. The driver opened the door and shouted angrily, "You gonna get off, lady? I got traffic here."

The woman was magnificent. She adjusted her coat and her gloves before doing anything else. Then she righted the stroller. Then she picked up the boy. She adjusted her purse on her shoulder. Then she picked up the stroller. Then, very deliberately, holding up traffic all over Manhattan, she lowered herself and her things down the steps, pausing before stepping down onto the curb. As the bus pulled away, Rosie looked back and saw the woman serenely strap the boy, who was no longer crying, into the stroller, then hand him a banana from her purse, then begin her promenade down the sidewalk. It was a riveting sight. She said to Mary, "Did you see that?"

"What?" replied Mary.

"That woman."

"God, she was rude," said Mary.

And from that Rosalind knew that Mary would live the rest of her life in the Midwest, which she did.

Rosalind saw that, if you had enough self-possession, you could reconnoiter, plan ahead, take your time. It went beyond being careful. Being careful was something you did if you were in a rush. If you were self-possessed, you never had to be in a rush.

And so Rosalind had cultivated her self-possession at Smith College, at *Mademoiselle* magazine, working as an intern, at *Condé Nast Traveler,* working as an editor, and in Westchester County, as the wife of Alexander P. Maybrick and the stepmother of his three children, who didn't especially like her but admired her capacity for resisting their father. This was the self-possession Rosalind put into play every time she chose to take Eileen on a commercial airplane with her, whether Eileen was allowed to be there or not. Right now, for example, Rosalind knew that the gate personnel working behind the desk sensed that Eileen was in her carry-on. Her carry-on was trembling, so she pressed it against the desk with her knee and said, "May I just go on the plane, then?"

"We aren't quite ready to board, ma'am."

Eileen made a little noise in her throat, a gurgling noise. Rosalind cleared her own throat to cover it, and then carried Eileen over to a seat beside the door, where she sat down and arranged the hem of her fur coat over the top of the carry-on. She never zipped Eileen in entirely—not enough air for her— and so she had to be careful of that little head snaking inquisitively out of the opening, and those eager button eyes catching sight of something.

Al had gone on ahead the night before in the company jet, but Rosalind didn't care for Fort Lauderdale, and planned only to take in the race and return that evening. It was the seventh race, and so she would, of course, have plenty of time. She always had plenty of time.

Inside the bag, Eileen flopped over, but just then the door opened, and Rosalind stood up smoothly and went down the jetway, soon taking her seat, 2A, beside the window. She slid Eileen in her case under the seat in front of her and placed one of the airline's own blankets over the opening, only allowing Eileen to look out at her for a moment or two. Then she slipped Eileen a cookie and told her to be quiet and good, that she, Rosalind, was going to take a nap. The best thing about Eileen, Rosalind thought, was that she had a perfect command of the English language, and she listened to what you were saying (though, of course, she didn't always obey). Between New York and Fort Lauderdale, the two of them had a lovely nap, and woke up refreshed. Only at the very last minute, as they were leaving the plane, did Rosalind reveal to the flight attendants that Eileen had been with them all along.

But Rosalind woke up in a funny mood. It took her twenty minutes in the limo to define the shift, so unfamiliar to her was any sort of shift. But at last she put her finger on it. She wanted something, but she didn't know what it was. Wanting something, for an accomplished shopper like Rosalind, was certainly not a novel feeling. Marriage to Al meant that there were houses to be filled, parties to be prepared, a wardrobe to be cultivated. The division of labor in their marriage was specific—he earned all day every day and she spent all day every day, and they both knew that she worked as hard as he did and that spending was no more or less a privilege for her than earning was for him. The sexiest thing he had ever said to her was "Rosalind, I have no taste whatsoever." Desire was, for Rosalind, both a talent and a skill, and she knew her way all around it. Therefore, she expected the object of her desire to filter up from her unknown depths and reveal itself. Something Florida-ish, she thought, maybe as minor as a new swimming suit? Or a catamaran? A cruise? Some cracked crab? It felt like that at first, just a small thing—less than a desire, more like an appetite. She gave Eileen, who was sitting beside her on the seat of the limo, several more cookies.

The limo driver took her to the owners' entrance at Calder, where, as planned, Al was waiting for her. Al opened her door and handed her out. Eileen jumped out on her own, and leapt at Al's knees. Of course she didn't bark, but barks were rampant within her. That was why she was jumping and spinning. That was why she jumped onto the hood of the limo. Al picked her up. He said, "Hi, Eileen. Hi, honey. Good trip?"

Eileen licked him on the chin, and Rosalind gave him a peck on the other side.

"Fine," she said. And they walked through the owners' entrance to the track.

Rosalind never wondered whether she really loved Al, as some of her friends wondered whether they really loved their husbands (of course, some of her friends had given up wondering long ago, and knew that they didn't love their husbands). Al was not an appealing man. He had no manners and no charm, and life as a successful manufacturer and importer of heavy metal castings from distant, impoverished nation-like locations had allowed Al to let go of many of the sorts of personal habits that make a man's humanity endurable to his intimate companions. Most of Al's bodily functions were noisy, for example, and so were most of his mental functions. His children reported that during their youth he had been a remote workaholic drinker who stayed out of the way and didn't say much. As a result of therapy and AA, he now said everything that came into his mind, and was almost always soliciting someone's attention. Rosalind knew that others wondered how she could stand the man, but Rosalind could stand him fine, because he was utterly himself. There was no mystery to Al. If he was screaming at you that he wanted sex, God damn it, then that was what he really wanted, and he was screaming because he felt like screaming. He could also take no for an answer. Rosalind had discovered this early on. The first two or three times that he had screamed that he wanted some love and attention from her, she had been intimidated and given in, but the fourth time, maybe a year into their marriage, he had started in, and she had just said, calmly, "No, Al. I don't feel like it." And he had looked at her, startled, and said, "Oh, okay." A good firm "no," spoken with integrity and self-possession, calmed Al down and reassured him. And a deliberate "yes," as in "Yes, I would like to have sex with you, Al," made him happy and playful. You just had to be clear and let go of the rest. Appearances weren't everything. It would surprise her friends that she would say so, because she had a lot invested in making a good appearance herself, but she didn't have a thing invested in Al's making a good appearance. In fact, contrast between them made them an interesting couple.

They found their box. Rosalind set her bag down, and looked out over the track. Some horses were running. She said, "What race is this?"

"Fifth."

"Do you have any bets?"

"Nah. I put fifty on that number-eight horse, but I can't say I had any conviction about it. She's a half-sister to that filly we had last year, the Jade Hunter filly."

The bunch of horses came around the turn and the thing that usually happened happened—those in the lead dropped back, and a horse that hadn't looked like much came up and won. Rosalind didn't especially like racing, because all the races looked the same to her. They weren't decided by the horses or the jockeys or the trainers, they were decided by the finish line. She wondered if she wanted to place a bet and picked up the *Racing Form*. Then she put it down. As always, the *Racing Form*'s attempt to individualize every horse, with statistics on the one hand and remarks on the other, dried up the whole enterprise for her even more. What she really wanted to do was to pay attention to this little appetite she was having, and to follow it out. It gave her a funny feeling of being on the verge of something. She took Eileen in her lap, flipped her over, and began rubbing her belly. Eileen's little short legs flopped, and she let her head fall back. She was nothing if not solid—one hard muscle from nose to tail.

After the sixth race, which, as far as Rosalind could see, was an exact replay of the fifth race, they got up and went out to the saddling enclosure. The trainer, Dick Winterson, was already there with a couple of grooms and the filly. Al went in with them, but Rosalind, because she was carrying Eileen, decided to stay behind the rail with the bettors. Rosalind saw that Dick greeted Al almost flinchingly and then tried to make up for it by putting his hand on Al's shoulder and waxing enthusiastic about the filly's chances in the race. The filly did look good. She was grinding her teeth against the bit, so that the groom had to stand in front of her and hold both reins. While he held her, the groom talked to her in a nice voice—down the row, another groom, with the trainer standing right there, was giving his filly a jerk in the mouth and she was throwing her head in the air. Rosalind didn't approve of that at all. Now Laurita arched her neck and moved in to the groom, but he stood firmly, only reaching up to scratch her on the forehead. Dick placed her numbercloth on her back, 4, and the assistant trainer placed the saddle on top of it. The filly stood quietly while they tightened the girth and then pulled out her legs, first the left, then the right. After she was adjusted, the groom walked her out in the circle with the other fillies, and then the paddock judge—wasn't that what they called him?—said, "Gentlemen, lead out your horses!"

Now the jockeys came out of their room like a flock of tropical birds, and the horses moved out in order to the walking ring. Al and Dick were walking along together behind the horse, and Rosalind felt herself momentarily look at them as if she were a stranger, one of the bettors. They looked confident and enviable—relaxed and chatting while a sparkling, beautiful large creature radiated life right in front of them. They looked as though you could ask of them, how could they have so much of all the good things in the world that they could ignore this one? Their very relaxation in the presence of what excited everyone else set them apart and made them attractive. The jockeys were like the horses and the men both. They chatted, like the men, didn't look at the horses, like the men, but their bodies were alive and full of contained grace and spring, like the horses' bodies. They acted deferential to the trainers and the owners, but it was just the noblesse oblige that life accorded to money, that was all. The horses paused in their circle, and the trainers threw the jockeys into their saddles.

Back up in the box, Dick sat with them as the horses came out onto the track and began their slow trek around to the starting gate. The race was a mile and a sixteenth. The starting gate was down the track to their left, being set in place. Rosalind looked at it for a moment, then turned her head and looked at

Dick Winterson, who had been training their horses for some three years now. She was perfectly familiar with Dick. She saw him every month or so. They had spoken cordially time and time again, and she had hardly noticed him. Now he gazed intently at the line of horses moving out with the ponies, and he transformed before her very eyes. He wasn't paying a bit of attention to her, was thinking some sort of enigmatic horse-trainer's thoughts, God knew what those could be, but they would be something expert and focused and habitual—that thought gave her a little shiver. His eyes were brown, she noticed, and he didn't wear glasses, and he had a nice, rather beaky nose. Something she had truly never noticed before was that he had lovely lips, neatly cut but full and soft-looking. At this Rosalind looked away, but then she looked back. When she looked back, and this was the turning point, she knew that he was, underneath everything, sad about something, and she felt her little appetite of the morning suddenly burst through her body so that she had to sit back and pick Eileen up again and pet her. And she sneezed. She sneezed three times. Dick Winterson said, "Do you have a cold?"

"No, not that I know of."

In Rosalind's view, those were the first words they ever spoke to one another. This was the moment when, afterwards, it seemed to Rosalind that she had cast her spell. There seemed nothing voluntary about it. It was more as if her wish that she hardly knew yet was a wish went out of her and re-created the world. The first thing that happened was that the horses arrived at the starting gate and loaded in, one by one, with Laurita routinely doing her job, as all Dick's horses did, because they were well trained and well prepared. Then there was that pause, so short, of equine uniformity, as all eight animals stood in a row. Then the bell clanged and the gate opened. Right then, Rosalind felt, she created the race of a lifetime. Six of the horses got away well, and Laurita might have also, but the number-three horse stumbled as the gate opened, and half fell into her path. The filly did an amazing thing—she launched herself and her jockey over the head and neck of the stumbling horse in a graceful bascule, and took off after the others. Everyone in the stands gasped, for the action was taking place right in front of them. Dick gasped himself, then chuckled in relief, and said to Al, "Those Northern Babys can jump, all right! Little did you know when you sent that mare to him! Ha!" But then he fell silent, they all fell silent, as the filly ran down the field as if they were standing still. She overtook them one by one, her stride seeming to lengthen by the second. And she hadn't ever been a heroic filly. It was as if the jump over the other horse told her who she was, and now she was glorying in it. Halfway down the backstretch, she was in the lead by a neck. The other filly, a rangy gray, was the favorite, and had already won over half a million dollars to Laurita's $104,000. And the other filly was a fighter. She matched Laurita stride for stride. Even though she had created this race, Rosalind didn't herself understand it. It looked to her as though the gray, bigger, longer-legged, more experienced, more mature, more expensive, and better bred, would surely press her natural claims and take the race. They were head and head around the second turn and into the home-stretch. Laurita was on the outside, and the other filly had the rail. They looked pasted together. The rest of the field was nowhere, and the grandstand was roaring, every bettor, no matter whom he or she had bet upon, screaming in joy. Now the jockeys went to their whips. But it was no contest. Laurita found another gear so easily it seemed she hadn't even looked for it. She simply drew away from the bigger filly, opened up daylight, and crossed the finish line by herself. The jockey had stopped with his whip, had lost his whip. Now he stood up in his stirrups, transfigured, his mouth open, his whip hand in the air. Later, when they published the photo of him in the *Thoroughbred Times,* you almost couldn't look at it, since the wonderment of eleven thousand onlookers was concentrated in his visage. Dick said, "I never saw anything like that in my whole life."

Then they all got up and came together in the winner's circle, horse and jockey, trainer, groom, owner, owner's wife. A few weeks later, they got the win picture. Rosalind taped it up in her bathroom. She looked at it often, pondering the blank look on everyone's face. Every human face, that is. The filly looked bright and interested, as if she had just awakened from a long, sleepy dream.

Their group left the stands right after that. Even the jockey, who had a mount in the eighth race, left, not because he didn't want to ride the horse, but because he forgot what he was doing for about four hours.

They followed the filly under the stands, through the walking ring, back to the test barn. The whole way was paved by a sea of smiling faces and shouts of "Great job! Wow! What a filly!" Al said nothing, rendered speechless for the first time in Rosalind's experience. Dick said nothing, either. And, of course, Rosalind said nothing. She was a quiet sort of person. But her powers were in full flood. Every time she looked at Dick, he looked at her and she didn't turn her eyes away and neither did he. She fancied that he knew she had made this race for him, to relieve his sadness, and now his sadness was relieved. Al never saw them look at each other, either. That was another thing she did. The last thing in the world she wanted to do was hurt Al.

When the filly had been put in her stall, taken care of in every way possible, and then left alone to contemplate her greatness, Al said to Dick, "Dinner? Champagne? I'll treat everyone. You round 'em up and I'll get the limo. Rosalind, you pick the restaurant, and call for a private room." Al was really happy—that registered. In the limo, back at the hotel, he caroled about plans, the way he always did when he was happy. "Rozzy! That filly's got Breeders' Cup written all over her. You know how I feel about the Breeders' Cup. I am a breeder! All the breeders, that's their test, the Breeders' Cup. Seven races, what is that, seventy horses, the best Thoroughbreds, of all kinds, colts, fillies, sprinters, turf horses. There's nothing like it. I always said there's nothing like it anywhere in the world, didn't I? You know I did! This filly—" But she smiled and nodded and listened and said, "Maybe so, Al, maybe." Maybe. That was an interesting word. Maybeness was something rather unusual for her.

It wasn't hard getting a private room for twenty at the best restaurant in Boca Raton, then transporting the whole crew—grooms, hot walkers, assistants, the woman who did the books, Eileen, everyone—over there, no matter what languages they spoke or what they were wearing. Smiles and welcome followed them everywhere. They drank Perrier-Jouët and ate pesto risotto with scallops, then ate osso bucco and veal piccata, and then the limos took everyone away drunk, and Al's cellular rang, and it was his partner, saying that Al had to get the late plane back to the City, because there was some fuckup in Croatia, where they had a factory, and so Al himself left, and there they were, Rosalind and Dick, sitting alone, except for Eileen, across from each other at a table littered with the remains of a very very good party. Eileen sat in the chair next to Rosalind, directly across from Dick. Her ears were forward and she was looking at him expectantly, and it seemed to Rosalind that he and she, the humans, could at last do what both of them had been longing to do for hours, which was to stare straight into each other's faces without stopping or turning away or speaking or wondering who might see them. Already, Dick's face was as familiar to Rosalind as her own. And his familiar face had a strange look on it, a scowl-like look that was not a scowl but a look of intense feeling—his inner life emerging unprotected into the rosy candlelight of the room. She was far more careful of her own look. She tried to make it almost blank, almost a mask, so that he would have to come out farther, reveal himself more, just to get a rise out of her. You would think she did this all the time, but she didn't. In her eighteen years with Al, she had considered it beneath her dignity even to flirt with another man. And she didn't intend to flirt with Dick, either. If he came toward her, it would have to be on his own, without encouragement. The appetite that had detonated inside her that afternoon was not for fun or amusement. It was for something mysterious and testing. No man, she thought, should be lured to that through the false advertising of a smile or a toss of the head. She thought of Nefertiti, making herself look like that, and she waited. Eileen was thinking of something, too. She put her forefeet on the table and drank delicately from a goblet of mineral water.

"Ah," Dick said. "Rosalind. Thank you for the party. Everyone really had a terrific time."

"Did they? Good." Eileen sat back down.

"I mean it. This is not a world that most of them—"

"It was Al's idea. Al is a generous man, in his way. Sometimes that isn't an obvious way, I admit." Now she permitted herself a smile.

The next thing he said would show, she thought, that he had made a choice, and she didn't dare influence that choice in one way or another. She guessed he would say something like "Well, then," or "Late, for me," or "Where can I drop you?" Perhaps all of those remarks passed through his mind, unselected. At any rate, he said, "You have beautiful hair."

She nodded.

"And beautiful eyes."

She nodded.

"And beautiful lips."

"All original equipment," she said, "even the hair. No one in my family goes gray."

"Yours is . . ." He shook his head. "I don't know, sunny. Sandy. Palomino! Ha!" He smiled in a friendly way, but he had let the cry out, no mistake about it. Rosalind took a deep breath, and then Dick said, "Where are you staying?" Eileen began to pant.

"I think Al was at the Meridian. We've bought a condo recently, but I haven't finished furnishing it yet."

Then he said, "Let's go there."

Then she said, "Let's."

WHAT SHE COULD TELL when he was taking down her hair, and then unbuttoning her jacket and her blouse, was how many years he had spent with horses. His gestures were smooth and consistent, and once he had his hands on her body, he kept them there. But they weren't eager and hungry; they were quiet and reassuring, warm, dry, and knowledgeable, as if he could find out things about her by touching her, the way he would have to do with horses, the way, perhaps, he would do with Laurita tomorrow, running his hands down her legs looking for heat. His touch, in fact, belied the look on his face, which was disturbed and eager. His touch was almost idle. When he had his hand on her neck, she felt him probe a little knot there, press it and release it, the way her masseuse did, then move down to her shoulder, and do the same there. It was as if no degree of desire could interfere with his habit of taking care. They had been naked for ten minutes when she spoke for the first time. She said, "I bet the horses like you." Eileen, who had been lying curled on the bed, jumped down and went under the bedskirt.

"They seem to, actually."

"You have a nice touch."

"I get along well with dogs, too. Though Eileen hasn't really made up to me."

"And you don't get along with . . . ?"

"Owners, maybe."

"Al likes you."

He looked her right in the eye. "Oh, they like me all right. I don't like them."

Rosalind threw back her head and laughed.

"And I don't get along with my wife."

"Is that why you look sad?"

"No doubt. Do I look sad, then?"

"You do to me."

He sighed. "I've been afraid it would get out."

"You looked happy after the race. Well, not happy, but excited. Almost happy."

"I was almost happy. Closest I've been in a pretty long time. She's a bombshell, that filly." Here was where Rosalind fell in love, because Dick had a whole different smile for this filly when he thought of her, a whole separate category of secret delight that crossed his face and pierced Rosalind for some reason she didn't begin to understand. She had been looking for mystery, hadn't she? Well, here it was.

Even so, they could still stop, get dressed, turn back. Their friendly conversation and her laugh showed that. In the atmosphere of the room, there was some levity, some detachment, some pure friendliness that they could build upon to get out of this. Rosalind knew it. But instead she put her fingertips on his lips and ran them gently around, a multitude of her nerve endings tickling a multitude of his. And then she leaned forward, letting her hair fall on his shoulders, and kissed him.

Maybe he wasn't getting along with his wife, but it was obvious that he had gotten along with her fine at some point, or with someone else, because his knowledge about what to do with Rosalind was instinctive and expert. First, he took her face between his hands and very gently and attentively ran his thumbs over her eyebrows, the planes of her cheeks, down the line of her jaw, bringing them to a rest upon her lips, where, after just a moment, he put the tips of them into her mouth. She could feel him touching her tongue and the inside of her lips. Then he smoothed that moisture into her cheeks and chin, over and over, until she was groaning. Then he ran one hand lightly down her throat, reminding her what a long and vulnerable throat it was. Then the other hand. Then he looked at her and kissed her, first just soft kissing, then firmer kissing, then tongue kissing, then gently biting her lips, kissing, biting, kissing, then kissing her neck, then biting, then kissing. Except the bites weren't bites, so careful and considerate were they, as if he were inside her skin and knew exactly what would be exciting and what would be painful. He bit her shoulders, left, then right. Meanwhile, his hands had found her breasts. Al's hands always happened upon her breasts as if he had never felt breasts before, but Dick's hands knew breasts perfectly well, and hers, it seemed, in particular. Pretty soon, but not too soon, his lips found them, too. She closed her eyes, because she didn't want to look at anything but his face now. His face was the only familiar thing in the room, and if she couldn't look at it, then what was happening in her body was too terrifying. Her body was already arching and shaking, but she wasn't orgasming. She was just responding to the lightness of his touch like iron filings to a magnet.

Now his hands moved downward, to her waist. She had not known the waist was an especially erogenous zone, but as he squeezed her waist and ran his thumbs and hands over her belly, she felt her whole lower body turn to fire, and sparks shoot out of her toes. It was as if there were some spot there, near her navel, that was sensitive and he knew it, he knew just where it was and how to activate it. She opened her eyes now, and saw that his eyes were closed, and that, furthermore, she was participating unbeknownst to herself. She was rhythmically pinching his nipples, and he liked it. His hands fell away from her waist to her buttocks, and now he wasn't so gentle with her. He squeezed them hard, over and over, pinched them, too, but it didn't hurt. Always there was that quality in his touch of being unable to hurt living flesh. It was alluring, but, more than that, it was fascinating. While this was going on, she opened her eyes again, and he was looking at her. He looked happy and fond. The look made her moan, because she didn't feel that she deserved fondness from him. Suddenly, and very very lightly, he touched her labia so that she cried out, and as she was crying out, he penetrated her, kindly but firmly, threw back his head, and closed his own eyes, seeming to pull her over himself as easily as a glove.

He penetrated her to the core, didn't he? He knew just how to do that, the way a racehorse knew how to find the finish line: wherever he penetrated her to, that was the core, and she felt it. He eased gently back and forth a time or two, and it wasn't so comfortable just then, but right when she was going to say something, or ask something, she got a wonderful feeling of moisture flooding her, and his penis turning to silk inside of her. She said, "What was that?"

And he said, "Sometimes it takes a moment or two for the foreskin to slide back."

"You have a foreskin?"

"I do, indeed. I was born in Britain when my father was training horses there for some years."

"I'm sorry I didn't notice. I guess I was looking at your face."

He smiled.

But then there was no time for talking, only for probing more and more deeply into this feeling she was having all through her body of melting around him as he went farther inside of her, and just when she orgasmed, he covered her face with his warm hands and made her go where he was inside her and she disappeared.

About two, Rosalind got up and put on a robe, and went over to the window and sat down, looking out over the beach and the dark ocean. There were stars everywhere, even in spite of the lights below. She hunched forward in her chair and looked down, then looked out again, taking her thick hair in her hands, hair that was her lifelong friend. She twisted it into a tail and curled it around her hand, then took a pencil out of a container on the desk and pinned it up. At that moment, she was thinking nothing. You could have asked her to swear, and she would have sworn, under oath, that she was thinking nothing. That she was utterly at peace and blank, well fucked, Al would have said, had said from time to time, referring to himself as well as to her. She put her hand between her legs and smelled her fingers, smelling the both of them together, then wiped her hand on the robe.

What was it that did it? She thought about this long afterwards, obsessed about it, even. What was it that switched her so suddenly out of that blank, satisfied state? Perhaps it was the knowledge that the care he had taken of her was impersonal, nothing to do with her, only a quality of his that he brought to everything, something she responded to, but nothing she could claim. And she hadn't intended to claim anything, had she? This wasn't about claiming, it was about investigating. Nevertheless, whatever it was, whether something she thought or something she saw when she turned her head to glance at him on the bed, her blank satisfaction dissolved once and for all into pure longing. All her powers drained out of her then and there, as lost as if they had dissipated into the stars, and tears began to run down her cheeks. Eileen emerged from under the bedskirt and yawned, then stretched, first backward, then forward, with slow relish. Then she espied Rosalind at the window and crawled over to her, low crawl, pushing with her short back legs and swimming with her elbows. Her head was up and her eyes were bright, and she made a funny picture, but she didn't even begin to relieve Rosalind's sadness.

6 / ALL IRISH

IF THERE WAS A VARIETY of female that fit in on the backside, either here at Pimlico or anywhere else in the racing world, Deirdre Donohue didn't know what it would be, but she did know that it wasn't her variety. Over her long five years as a trainer of Thoroughbred racehorses, she had learned that she was (1) too loud, (2) too opinionated, (3) not pretty, (4) without charm, (5) badly dressed, (6) too unassociated with men to be reliably heterosexual, (7) too liberal in her political opinions, (8) too taciturn (which fit in with her loudness and opinionatedness because she only spoke up when she was really pissed off), and (9) lacking a sense of humor. When the men trainers were telling dirty jokes during morning works and she came up, they always fell silent. Being generally men of the old school, they would naturally fall silent if a woman came upon them telling dirty jokes anywhere, but they resented the fact that they couldn't tell dirty jokes on the backside of a racetrack of all places, and so they resented Deirdre, without differentiating between her femininity and her lack of a sense of humor.

Deirdre could not say that her switch from training jumpers to training racehorses had been a success, but in the end it was easier to put a jockey, which she had never been, up on a talented runner than it had been to put a rider up on a talented jumper that she herself might have ridden if she hadn't broken her back falling off over a six-foot oxer at Devon. That was eight years ago, when she was thirty-two. Now she was forty, with no husband, no children, no friends among her colleagues, twenty extra pounds that felt like they belonged to someone else, and a manner that even she didn't like. She had two things going for her: a splendid Irish accent and a string of steady winners. Her old friends on the jumper circuit were still her best friends, partly because she still had an eye for a good potential jumper who might make a match with a rider she knew. More than a few runners she had retired showed up in *The Chronicle of the Horse*, their necks arched and their knees neatly folded over impressive obstacles, but she never went to watch them, and the people she

41

knew at the track acted as if that world didn't even exist except below a certain fiscal horizon. And it didn't. The racetrack, even in Maryland, where the big money most assuredly was not, thought of itself as Hollywood or Big Oil, and of the jumper circuit as writing poetry or owning a family restaurant—a good enough way to while away a life, but nothing Important.

It was thinking these sorts of thoughts at the track that kept Deirdre Donohue silent and pissed off.

It was only with her bookkeeper, Helen, and her assistant trainer, George Donohue, an actual second cousin who hailed from five miles away from the Curragh itself, that Deirdre put on her other personality, which was the one the horses knew—attentive, thoughtful, kindly, thoughtful, generous, thoughtful, and thoughtful. It was Helen, who had been keeping Deirdre's books since she had her first jumper barn when she was twenty-four, who had once pointed out to Deirdre that she had this alternative personality, and she often urged her to trot it out in company, but Deirdre kept it under wraps. To Helen, she said, "The men around here wouldn't recognize it if they saw it," and Helen had to admit this was true.

It was George who had all the Irish charm and all the Irish looks and all the Irish capacity for a wee drop, but at twenty-four himself, he had only risen about fifteen degrees on his alcoholic trajectory, and had many useful years left in him before he had to be shipped back to the old sod. The other thing about him was that, even though Deirdre's owners' wives didn't know it, it was George who was gay. That was why he had been shipped over in the first place.

They were a pretty good close knot of a threesome, and as a result, Deirdre was in a better mood than she had been in years. Life with horses had taught her to accept, expect, and even to enjoy the temporary quality of all good things. She, George, and Helen were a good thing. At the moment, she was sitting with one of her owning couples. Deirdre never made the mistake that some trainers did, which was talking to the man and ignoring the woman. In the first place, she would never do that, and in the second place, most owners came as a couple, and whoever had first accrued the money didn't matter, and neither did whoever first got interested in horses. In most, though not all, cases, horses seemed eventually to suck them in equally. Now she was listening intently to the Hollisters and making faces. She knew that Helen, who kept glancing in the window, was trying to signal to her to stop making faces, but she couldn't help it. What the Hollisters were saying was pushing every button she had.

Daniel Hollister said, "He's a good trainer. I asked around."

"You asked around?" exclaimed Mary Lynn Hollister. "Why in the world would you ask around?"

"It's called research."

"It's called gossip, Skippy."

Deirdre was almost always able to suppress a bark of laughter when Mary Lynn called Daniel Hollister, who was an anti-trust lawyer and Washington power-broker of nearly stratospheric importance, "Skippy."

"He said the horse could have won. I mean, everyone always says that, but he came right up to me and said, 'That horse won, didn't he?,' like there was a rumor that the horse won." He stuck in a note of petulance. "Like everyone around expected the horse to win."

"Not me," said Deirdre.

"Well, then," said Skippy Hollister.

Quod erat demonstrandum. Deirdre had had an excellent Catholic education that had left her with a whole collection of Latin phrases that no one else but George understood. "Speed kills," said Deirdre.

"What does that mean?" said Skippy.

"It means that the horse wasn't ready," said Mary Lynn. "It means he would have maybe thrown himself out of whack with a race like that and had a big bounce or worse. Why don't you ever listen to anyone, Skippy?"

"I listened to a good trainer who thought the horse was ready."

"Skippy, when you go into discovery, do you take the advice of the opposing team about what you should pay attention to and what you shouldn't?"

"I don't consider Harry Jacobson to be on the opposing team. He's a disinterested outsider. *And* he has a good reputation."

"He's on the opposing team to Deirdre here, right?" She cast a look at Deirdre.

"I would say so, yes," said Deirdre, as always beginning reasonably, "He's trying to steal the fucking horse," and then ending offensively.

"Oh, please," said Skippy Hollister. "When I asked him if he could do better with the horse, he said he didn't think so, that Deirdre is one of the best trainers around, and whatever the horse has, Deirdre will eventually find it."

"Mother of God," said Deirdre.

"Skippy, I wonder that you are my life's companion. I wonder that I allowed that to happen." Then Mary Lynn said to Deirdre, "Honey, I would appreciate it if you wouldn't use vulgarities in my presence. Thank you." She smiled autocratically.

"Max Weber uses the guy. He's won and won and won."

"Skippy," said Mary Lynn. "Has he *profited*?"

"Well, I suppose. How could he not?"

"Well, he has not. Jolene Weber told me they've spent millions on yearlings and two-year-olds in training and broodmares. They've won millions, too, but not as many millions as they've spent!" When Skippy looked at his wife, Deirdre had the distinct impression that she was going to slap him upside the head a couple of times. You could call her abusive in her way, but Deirdre found it rather satisfying. Other than horses, Mary Lynn Hollister did an incredible amount of volunteer work. She was a classic dragon of benevolence, and with luck Deirdre herself would end up in some care institution that Mary Lynn Hollister oversaw.

"You, Skippy, have profited," said Mary Lynn. "Thanks to Deirdre, you are in the one percent that has profited."

"These are horses here," said Deirdre. "I don't like to run them out unless they are at a fu— that is, at a hundred percent. Sometimes you use races to prepare for races. We've talked about this before." She heard her voice rise irritably as she mentioned this last. Harry Jacobson's voice was ever and anon respectful with every owner or potential owner, and since every person in the world, through the striking of lightning or an Act of God, was a potential owner, Harry Jacobson was uniformly respectful *to* them, if not *about* them.

"I want to move the horse. Just that horse. Just to try it. We've profited, but we haven't won a big race." Now the note of petulance in Skippy Hollister's voice was distinct. Deirdre wondered if maybe Mary Lynn had taken the wrong tack, treating Skippy like a child. She said, "I certainly respect your wishes, Mr. Hollister. If you wish to move the horse, you may. My bookkeeper will work up your final bill."

"It's an experiment, that's all. The horse can come back here after a few weeks. Or something. I think a change would be good for the horse, maybe."

Deirdre just couldn't keep it up. She knew that, theoretically, she had a choice, and that making the right choice was in her long-term best interest, but she said, anyway, "I don't fucking think so."

"What?" said Skippy.

"I said . . . Well, you heard me."

Skippy looked offended and so did Mary Lynn, unfortunately. Just then, George breezed into the office without knocking.

"Lovely animal, that one," he said.

"Which one?" said Daniel Hollister, grumpily.

"Why, that Cozzene colt you've got there. I'm telling you, when I first saw that one, I thought he was a weedy thing."

"We were just talking about him—"

"For sure you were, Mr. Hollister. They're talking about this lad all over the track now, with that last race he ran."

"What do you mean?"

"Mother of God, man, he's a corker. But you know, these Americans, they don't understand these Caro-line horses. Now, you know Caro, he was Irish to the core, that laddie was. You ever seen a picture of him? He looked like an Irish hunter, and he's produced a few of them, too. Just the kindest young boyo in the world. Great sire, if you ask me. And he woulda been a great sire if some farmer had had him out in the back, the way they do in Ireland, you know. You finish your chores and get on the old man, and go out hunting for a bit, then you come home and let the lad chat up a few females, and pretty soon you've got a whole field of good hunters. Well. But he was something!"

"The colt was quite expensive," said Daniel Hollister, stiffly.

"But, then, an expensive colt isn't for someone who can't afford it, is he?" said George. "Especially an expensive colt who takes some patience, some, let's say, faith. Now, any of these boyos can be getting themselves a hot Storm Cat yearling and turning him around in a year, and then watching him break down after three or four races. But it takes a real horseman like yourself to develop a horse from a classic line like this Caro line."

"I don't think—"

"That's what we say in Ireland—you can tell a horseman by his willingness to wait. A horse is no machine, is what we say, but a living, breathing, opinionated beast. You got to wait for them, and then wait some more. Isn't it so, cousin?"

"Fucking right."

"Listen to her! No manners, and a good education could do nothing for her."

"Are you saying," said Mary Lynn, "that another, less patient trainer might break down this extremely expensive colt that we paid, let's see, $247,000 for?"

"Might well do that. You know what they say all over this track?"

"What?" said Mary Lynn.

"Well, you know, they'll bet on anything."

"I'm sure," said Skippy Hollister.

"They've got odds on whether you'll have the stomach to stay with the trainer you've got, or whether you'll lose your courage and jump."

"They do?"

Deirdre had her arms on the desk and her head down, she was so close to laughing out loud. She knew she looked, however, like she was stricken with dismay. That was fine.

George went on. "I put a bit of change down myself. You know, Mr. Hollister, I could lay out a tenner for you yourself on this side wager. You could make a bit of change, as only you know what you're going to be doing."

"What would I be doing with the horse? The horse is doing fine."

Mary Lynn allowed herself one little smile, then there was a long pause, and then Daniel Hollister said, "Well, I suppose we've got that all settled now, huh."

Deirdre lifted herself up and shook herself out. "I guess so. And thank you."

"There's a girl," said George. "I almost always have to remind her to say please and thank you. But she's a sight better than her dad. Cousin Devlin never says a word."

Mary Lynn now turned toward George and seemed to melt visibly, though only within the bounds of propriety. She said, "You're a wonderful addition to the barn, George, and you make everyone's lives around here much easier, if you don't mind my saying so."

"You may say whatever you please, ma'am, as long as insincere flattery of myself is a part of it." George gave her a dazzling smile and a full-bore Irish twinkle. And then he did the same with Skippy, and then they were out of there. George let them get a step down out of the door, then he gave Deirdre a pinch on the arm and whispered, "Now, Cousin, you've got to walk them out of the barn and see them off."

"I do?"

"You do."

When she got back to her office, George and Helen were having a regular laugh fest. Deirdre greeted it as usual: "What's so funny? Are there really odds about this?"

"Not a bit of it," said George. "But Helen put on the intercom, and I saw what was in the wind, so I came up with something."

"If that horse went to Harry Jacobson, I hate to think."

"*I* hate to think," said Helen. Deirdre knew that Helen was considering the welfare of her fiscal condition, not that of the Cozzene colt, for her book-keeper had only yesterday managed to trap her in the office long enough to have some serious financial discussion with her. Fortunately, the gist of that discussion had now become hazy in her mind. Nevertheless, the Hollisters were good owners—they paid their bills on time, bought and sold their horses as per Deirdre's instructions, and didn't insist on expensive jaunts to tracks that Deirdre considered beyond her depth, like Santa Anita and Gulfstream and Keeneland. It was well not to offend them, both virtuous and wise. As George often said to her, "You can't persuade owners to recognize your native charm if you are cursing at them all the time, Cousin."

Now he said, "Well, Cousin. He is a nice animal, and he's going to do well for you."

"I think so."

"I'll take care of Daniel Hollister myself," said George.

"Call him Skippy."

"You know, I bet he would respond to that."

The three of them grinned at one another, and Deirdre felt her luck holding. It was a nice feeling. *Ave atque vale.*

7 / JUST A ROBERTO

ROBERTO ACEVEDO was sixteen years old, but he told everyone at the track he was eighteen, because he wanted to get some rides before he did become eighteen and was too heavy to be a jockey. That's what happened to all the Acevedos—things looked great for a while, then one by one they hit real puberty, grew beards, topped five five, and couldn't get their weight down below 123 pounds. The only girl, Inez, had developed even faster, and had to quit riding just after her seventeenth birthday. But they all were riding fools. The tragic irony, said Farley Jones, was that every Acevedo, male and female, emerged from the Acevedo foundation mare with great hands. Seven kids, fourteen great hands. Roberto was the youngest, the last in a classic line. The older ones, old enough to have their own kids, that would be Maurilio and Juan, had both married teachers, and even though they themselves still worked as exercise riders at the track, they had steered their own kids into things like algebra and gourmet cooking.

It was a generally held view in southern California that allowing Roberto Acevedo to masquerade as eighteen when he was only sixteen was a win-win situation, and also a way of bidding farewell to a long and honorable history. If you included Huberto Acevedo, the sire, then the Acevedos' great hands went back to 1960, the first time Kelso was Horse of the Year, quite a racing tradition.

And so Roberto got up when the bell rang, signaling the end of third period (elementary physics—they were doing acoustical experiments with tubes), and left school for the track, knowing this was a unique day in his life, the day he would ride in his first race. It was the sixth race, post time three-twenty, a mile-long, twenty-five-thousand-dollar claiming race for male horses four years old and up who had not won a race in sixty days. He was riding a five-year-old gelding named Justa Bob, he had drawn the number-one position, and even though Roberto had exercised upward of three to five horses a day for the last three years of his life, he was a little nervous.

It didn't help that when he got into the jocks' room everyone was looking at him but no one was speaking to him. This, his brother Julio had told him, was the inevitable sign that a prank would be played upon him, either before or after the race. Jockeys were terrific pranksters, in general, and another Acevedo characteristic was that they all reacted to pranks by getting hot under the collar. This was as a red flag to a bull as far as the other jockeys were concerned. The only way you could get at an Acevedo was by pranking him (or her). Any sort of abuse during the race, any pushing, shoving, shouting, razzing, passed an Acevedo without even making a scratch in the Acevedo consciousness, just as the acoustical properties of tubes had no effect on Roberto's sense of either the world or himself. But a prank. Well, what would it be?

The first race went off while Roberto was cultivating his appreciation of the jocks' room and his pleasure at being there. You had to stay in the jocks' room until your race was run. You came in before the first race and you stayed until you were finished. If you had a horse in only the ninth race, well, you sat around for five hours maybe. There were plenty of amenities—hot tub, sauna, massage table, salad bar, regular TV, monitor for watching the races at both Santa Anita and up north, free copies of the *Daily Racing Form,* the day's program, the L.A. *Times, The Wall Street Journal* for those who called their stockbrokers while they were waiting for their races, the magazine of the jockeys' association, some Spanish-language newspapers and magazines, and a collection of books jocks had brought in and left behind—a couple of Bibles, for one thing, in both Spanish and English, and some novels. No one ever picked any of these up, even to throw them away, so it was a strange collection—Louis L'Amour, Danielle Steele, Frederick Forsyth, Guy Davenport, T. Something Boyle. There was also a copy of Shakespeare's *Winter's Tale,* from the library of Pomona College. You got all kinds at the track, that was for sure.

One thing Roberto had noticed was that time passed differently depending on where you were on the track. For example, if you were in the stands, time passed very slowly. The horses came onto the track, they took an ice age to get around to the gate, especially if it was a turf race and they had to go up the hill, then they took forever to get into the gate, and then even the race was too long. This was probably the reason that bettors tended to perceive every horse as slow. The horses weren't slow, but time itself was. You could speed this up if you went back and forth from the saddling enclosure to the racetrack. Then time passed evenly and deliberately, the horses, since you knew them a bit, went a little faster, and the afternoon itself felt like an excellent day's work, even though you weren't betting. On the backside, in the mornings, time passed quickly for a while. It seemed as though you were standing in one spot—right at the end of the row of stalls, and bing bing bing, the groom was bringing you one horse after another, chestnut, bay, gray, brown, and you got a leg up and off you went, and the intervals out on the track, galloping or working, were much shorter than that moment when the groom and the horse approached. The slowest moment in the universe happened if you stayed late in the morning, till eleven or eleven-thirty, which Roberto sometimes did in order to avoid going back to school, and walked around the barn and looked at the horses lying down in their stalls. They were utterly reposeful. Time stopped, dust hung in the air with the quiet, and the only sound was the rhythmical scratching of one of the grooms raking the shedrow.

The revelation was that, in the jocks' room, time accelerated at a uniform rate. You came in, had a few thoughts, picked a tomato out of the salad bar, found your locker, started putting on your gear, because you had plenty of time, but then you didn't have plenty of time after all, and they were calling the sixth race, and you had to get your helmet on your head in a hurry. Roberto had imagined this would be like walking through water, everything in slo-mo, but it was like being shot through space even though you were walking, not flying. Right then you were walking out the door and following your horse and trainer and owner out of the saddling enclosure and into the walking ring, and then you were standing there, but just for a moment, and then the paddock judge was saying "Riders, up!" and you barely knew what your horse looked like—an impression of brownness—and you were on his back, ha, let out some of the air you had been holding in for the last hour. There he was, right in front of you, and you did now know, from déjà vu, or dreams, what your horse looked like—a long shining dark neck in front of you, two unique ears, and the feel of his mouth, his personality, really, right there in your hands. Here was where time got normal for about twenty minutes. Under the stands, over to the pony girl and her no-nonsense palomino, then out onto the track, with the stands lowering above you and the milling crowd seeming about to tip over onto you. The only reliable thing was the horse, Justa Bob, many starts, many finishes, some wins, no accidents, right there between your legs, walking and then jogging and then cantering calmly along, saying as loudly as if you could hear it with your ears, "You're okay, kid. I've done this a million times."

Justa Bob didn't care when they put him into the gate, a high point of anxiety for everyone at the track who knew anything, from the owners and trainers in the stands to the jockeys and the pony men and the assistant starters and the starter. But Justa Bob sighed, strode in, stood still, shifted his weight backward, and leapt as soon as the bell clanged. From that moment on,

Roberto felt that time was in the control of Justa Bob, no one else. Justa Bob hated the rail, everyone did, so hesitated a moment and let some of the others spurt to the front. Now he ran steadily but rather slowly, counting time with stride after even stride. All Roberto did was feel his mouth for him, to let him know that he was there. Around the first turn, Justa Bob picked an intermediate route, maybe five horses back and two lanes off the rail. Halfway around, he switched leads to refresh himself, and dug in a bit, lengthening his stride to pick off the fifth horse, but still running easily. As he passed the fifth horse, he pinned his ears for a moment, making a comment, perhaps, that only the fifth horse could understand. Down the backstretch, Justa Bob was like a metronome, and gave Roberto plenty of leisure to notice the melee around him. The two horses right in front of him bumped, the outside jock's knee just kissing the inside horse's shoulder, but the inside horse felt it and swerved toward the rail. Justa Bob switched leads again and overtook the inside horse. The noise was incredible—hooves pounding, horses breathing like the roar of a high wind, jocks talking and calling—and the whole time Justa Bob held Roberto's hands with his mouth, steadily and calmly. Now they were on the second turn. Roberto found himself wondering whether Justa Bob would choose to go wide or slip through the hole between the number-three horse and the number-two horse, and then, when he realized it was supposed to be him making the decisions, maybe, Justa Bob chose the hole, and threaded that like a needle. The bay horse on the outside turned his head to bite, and his jockey gave him a jerk. The chestnut on the inside seemed to go backward. Still Justa Bob was counting steadily, one two three. There was only one horse in front of him now, but there was daylight between them. Roberto thought of going to his whip, but Justa Bob informed him in no uncertain terms that that would be unacceptable. He was a class or two above the company in this race, and to whip him would be insulting. So Roberto just continued to hold the animal's marvelous mouth in his great hands, letting his own body stretch and fold with the rhythm of the horse. In the homestretch, their own noise was swelled by the noise of the crowd. Now Justa Bob began to close on the leader, a chestnut with a long silky tail that gleamed in the early-afternoon sunshine. Roberto could feel his horse gauge the distance and put on more speed, but Roberto didn't quite know whether to trust the horse's judgment. The chestnut's jockey was really riding—going for the whip, yelling—and the red horse was responding. But this was Roberto's first race; he literally didn't know what to do, so he went with his instincts—just do the thing that feels the most delicious—which in this case was to let Justa Bob take care of it. Now the animal's brown nose was at the other jockey's knee, then at the other horse's shoulder, neck, and head. The wire was upon them, and just then Justa Bob stretched out his nose and stuck it in front of the chestnut's nose. Three strides after the wire, Justa Bob was already pulling himself up. He cantered out calmly, turned without being asked, and returned to his groom, who said, "Hey, fella. No extra effort, huh?" Behind them, the tote board was flashing "Photo Finish!" and so there was plenty of time to be taken. But Roberto had no doubts, and neither did the groom. He said to Roberto, with a laugh, "This guy likes to give the bettors heart attacks, that's for sure. He is such a character."

Roberto said, "That was so much fun! Does he always make the decisions?"

"Always does. He does it his way or he doesn't do it at all."

"I can't believe he doesn't win every race. He seems to know how."

The groom shrugged, and now gave Roberto the best lesson of his life as a jockey. He said, "Some jocks can listen and some can't."

Now the trainer, Farley Jones, came over and said, "Good ride, son. Send your agent around. I can put you on something else tomorrow; the regular jock has the flu."

"I don't have an agent."

"Get one, then. Your brother Julio. He can be your agent for now. How did the horse feel?"

"Like the boss. I'd like to ride him again."

Farley laughed. "I don't see why not."

Pretty soon, Justa Bob's number went up on the board right next to the "1" and they stepped into the winner's circle. It didn't look like the owners were there, but that didn't matter; everyone else made a big deal of Justa Bob, and he knew it. Roberto dismounted and took his tack over to the scales.

And then, as they came out of the winner's circle and turned to go under the grandstand, the guy came out and hung that red tag on Justa Bob's bridle that showed he had been claimed by another trainer. "Huh," said Farley Jones. That was all he said, but Roberto could tell that he was upset. The assistant trainer was angry. He said, "I know it was Buddy. It has to be Buddy. Fucking Buddy Crawford. He's claimed every horse we've put out there. He doesn't care, you know he drove Ernie Jenkins out of business by taking all his horses, and Boris—"

"He did," said Farley.

Roberto saw the groom's face fall. There was something about it, thought Roberto. Most races were claiming races, and horses were claimed at the racetrack every day: they entered the starting gate belonging to one owner and left it belonging to whoever put down the required amount of cash in the racing secretary's office. It was absolutely routine, and everyone played the game—daring another trainer to take a horse that might be on its last legs, or hoping you could get away with a win without losing the animal. You could put a horse in a claiming race a dozen times and never have him claimed, or you could risk it once and bid the horse farewell. You never knew. Everyone was used to it, but somehow they all four of them slowed their gait and drooped as they went under the grandstand, in spite of the win.

"He was never going to stay an allowance horse forever. He'll be six," said Farley. Allowance races, Roberto knew, were like the middle class—a realm of hardworking stability that stakes horses rose out of on their way to wealth and greatness and claimers fell out of on their way to oblivion. Farley went on, "You've got to run them in races they might win or you've got to retire them. But I hate to see him go. He could end up anywhere. You know, horses start out in France and end up in North Dakota or Hong Kong. That's always given me a funny feeling, to tell the truth." The trainer sounded calm, but Roberto thought he looked depressed. Roberto sighed with him, even though for him the only challenge was getting Buddy Crawford to let him ride the animal.

The assistant said, "Better to end up in North Dakota than Hong Kong."

"Why?" said Roberto, whose idea of North Dakota was very similar to his idea of the moon.

"Because horses can't be re-exported from Hong Kong after they've been exposed to some disease there, so when they're finished racing they're put down," said the assistant trainer. He still sounded angry.

"I doubt," said Farley, "that Justa Bob will end up in Hong Kong."

"Buddy Crawford is bad enough," said the assistant, and Roberto didn't get the feeling that Farley Jones disagreed with him.

It wasn't until he was almost to the jocks' room that Roberto realized how dirty he was. And he realized something else, too. The way time passed in a race was not like anything else in the world. That was why the jocks kept riding, year after year, accident after accident. They kept wanting to feel that again, the rhythm of it measured in your body by the horse's stride and the simultaneous chaos of it in front of your eyes, ready to eat you up. Surely there was nothing else like it on earth.

They were waiting for him at the door, and about six guys, it seemed like, jumped him, then poured ice water on him, then slapped him on the back and put some ice down his neck, and everyone was laughing and screaming, Roberto, too, because he had won his first race, and on his first mount, and that was something special. And then, he thought, that was over, too. So he went over to the wash bucket and picked up the sponge to wash his face. Even now he could still seem to feel the horse's mouth in his hands like a gentle heat, and so he wasn't surprised when he dipped his hands and the sponge into the bucket and they came up orange. He didn't realize this was more than a mani-

festation of his state of mind until the guys behind him started laughing again.
Then he snapped into the present and realized that someone had poured Beta-
dine into the water, and that, furthermore, he had also thoughtlessly splashed
it all over his face. But he was an unusual Acevedo in this, that under the influence of Justa Bob he produced Justa Smile.

8 / THE TIBETAN BOOK OF
THOROUGHBRED TRAINING

ONE THING Oliver Haskins, assistant trainer, liked about working for
Farley Jones, trainer, was the cooking. Farley's exercise riders, male and
female, were always trying out this and that. For example, today Jorge brought
in a pot of chicken soup. The way he got just the right tang in the broth was to
simmer the chickens with a couple of chili peppers, and then discard them.
The way he took away the sting was to use barley instead of rice. The soup was
delicious, and all the riders, grooms, and assorted hangers-on kept after it until
the pot was empty.

Oliver was on his second six months with Farley, and part of the reason it
was a good job was that Farley not only took a day off himself every week, he
gave Oliver one, gave the grooms one, gave the riders one, gave the hot walkers
and everyone else one day off per week. This was a revelation to Oliver, whose
last boss, Buddy Crawford, neither took nor gave days off. Farley, in fact, never
looked at a horse on his day off. When he took vacations, he went to places
horses did not frequent, like music festivals and art museums and plays. On
the bumper of his truck, Farley had an Amnesty International sticker. Oliver
had had to ask Farley what Amnesty International was, and Farley had been
able to tell him, so Oliver knew for sure that the sticker had not come with the
truck. The other weird thing about Farley was that when he walked through
the barn he looked like a visiting physics professor—he was tall and slender,
with glasses, a trimmed white beard, and short, graying hair. He wore khaki
Dockers and button-down shirts and his cellular phone hung at his waist like a
slide rule. Of course, he didn't talk like a physics professor—he talked about
icing and hosing and inflammation and walking and working and one-on-one
and a fifth and galloping out a half and allowances and handicaps and big
horses and fillies and the condition book and turf and dirt and breezes and one
turn and two turns and lanes and stretches and the garden spot and good

movers and bad movers just like everyone else, but he talked the language as if he had learned it as an adult rather than as a child.

And then there was "The Tibetan Book of Thoroughbred Training," which was a laminated sheet of paper tacked to Farley's office door. It read,

1. Do not pay attention or investigate; leave your mind in its own sphere
2. Do not see any fault anywhere
3. Do not take anything to heart
4. Do not hanker after signs of progress
5. Although this may be called inattention, do not fall prey to laziness
6. Be in a state of constant inspection

Although these instructions were never spoken of, and Oliver was only conscious of having read them three or four times, well, you looked at them every time you went into the office, so he had begun, bit by bit, to take them rather literally. For example, it was his job to make sure that the stalls and the shedrows were clean and raked, and he did find himself in a state of constant inspection. Or, when one of the grooms got drunk and missed work, he found himself not finding fault with that. The grooms, after all, didn't make much money, didn't speak much English, and lived in a perennial state of culture shock. After six months or so of exposure to "The Tibetan Book of Thoroughbred Training," Oliver didn't have the heart to find fault with them for giving in.

Sometimes Oliver had one instruction running through his mind and sometimes another. If a horse stepped on himself in a race and was out for several months, there would be non-hankering after signs of progress. If a horse got into a temper and bit or kicked, there would be not taking anything to heart. If a race was coming up, and a jockey chose another mount, there would be not paying attention or investigating—soon enough another jockey's agent would show up, and the horse would have a rider. It was soothing. Oliver knew, too, that it was soothing to everyone. He often saw owners or strangers who were waiting for Farley to get off the phone gazing at or reading "The Tibetan Book of Thoroughbred Training," and he often heard the exercise riders say things that indicated they were aware of being attentive, or non-reactive, or whatever, but the topics around the barn, apart from food, were the same as around every other barn—who was winning, who was losing, who was riding, who was doing something crazy, who was doing something illegal, who was doing something funny.

Another favorable thing about Farley was that he had a good sense of humor. He always referred to his ex-wife and the mother of his four grown children as "the foundation mare." Then he always smiled. His smile was big and merry, and made Oliver smile in return.

The trouble with working for Farley these days was he wasn't winning a damn thing. Oliver was trying to bring a state of non-hankering after signs of progress to this problem, but he wasn't having much luck. Oliver's parents were Southern Baptists and great hymn-singers. They were opposed to gambling, but generally in favor of animals, so they hadn't minded too much when he had taken up horse-training as a way of life—reprobates and backsliders had cropped up in every generation of their family pedigree, and in his generation, he was considered a rather benign example of the pattern, since he had to go to bed at eight-thirty every night, and did not drink, smoke, or do drugs. As the scion of great hymn-singers, though, Oliver had a tune for every occasion, and lately he found himself humming one he didn't like. The words went:

> When death has come and
> taken our loved ones
> It leaves a home so
> lonely and drear
> Then do we wonder
> why others prosper
> Livin' so wicked
> year after year.

The chorus was meant to be reassuring:

> Farther along, we'll
> know all about it
> Farther along, we'll
> understand why
> Cheer up, my brother,
> live in the sunshine
> We'll understand it
> all by and by.

Maybe, thought Oliver.

"Wicked" was a good word for Buddy Crawford, better than "maniac," "butcher," "madman," "jerk," or "shit," the words most frequently used to describe him by other trainers, grooms who could speak English, jockeys, and jockey agents. The list of things Oliver had hated doing for the man during the four months he worked for him started with docking the already meager pay of the grooms for infractions like not getting the shedrows raked by 6:00 a.m. and ran right though firing riders, telling the vet to pin-fire some poor animal's ankles, keeping toegrabs on all of the horses even after that study about toegrabs' increasing the chances of breakdown got all over the track, galloping horses who were sore, running early two-year-olds. Sometimes Oliver tried to distinguish what he himself had suffered at Buddy's hands (screaming abuse if he didn't fax the man at home about how things were at the barn before 5:30 a.m., screaming abuse if he didn't manage to fire a rider before the rider quit, screaming abuse if an owner made any sort of complaint at all) from what others suffered, but it was all tangled together in Buddy's wickedness. And Buddy had a philosophy of wickedness, too. It was about culling the herd. He would say, "You don't get a Cigar by babying every horse and coddling every jockey. You get a Cigar by getting rid of whoever doesn't want to win, horse or man, jockey or owner."

And yet Oliver had worked for Buddy for four whole months, and conscience hadn't made him quit, either. What had made him quit was that he had gotten so tired from his work schedule that he started sleeping with his hand on the alarm clock, to be sure he'd wake up by 2:00 a.m., in order to be at the track by 3:15. Then he'd started dreaming about not being able to get up, and waking up every hour to check the clock. He had been making good money, maybe the best money of any assistant trainer at the track, since his earnings depended in part on the winnings of Buddy's horses. Even so, in sheer exhaustion, he had faxed Buddy his notice, and Buddy had called him instantly to scream at him that he'd intended to fire him that day, and how dare he quit before he got fired. He'd been sure after he quit that no amount of money was worth that, and he still held to this opinion.

But every horse Buddy had was winning, and good races, too, so lately he'd had his picture in the *Daily Racing Form* three times, with little squibs about his training philosophy, his toughness, his daring vision. "Finally," he said, "everybody in my barn has got to perform and they know it. Second place is losing. The betting fans know that, and I know it."

Oliver didn't know how, but the horses seemed to know it, too.

A claiming race was a kind of bet. Not every horse in a race got claimed, even—or especially—when you wanted it to. You entered your horse and took your chances, but every horse Farley ran in a claiming race, Buddy was claiming and, it looked like to Oliver, running to death. As his girlfriend had pointed out to Oliver, should he quit horse-training, and she would quite like it if he did, he would know a lot about hostile takeovers from claiming horses and having them claimed. Once you put your horse in a claiming race, it was very much like taking your small family-owned company public and having it bought out from under you. Sometimes, of course, your small family-owned company was a dud, and seeing it go was a pleasure. But other times the hostile takeover was painful. All trainers and many owners played this game, and Oliver expected to, also, but lately it hadn't been fun at all.

The owner of a nice filly Buddy had claimed the day before was sitting in Farley's office with Farley, asking, Oliver figured, about when they could claim the filly back. Through the window, Oliver could see Farley kind of shaking his head—not emphatically, not "no," but sadly, just "I don't think it's a good idea." The owner had bred the horse and was attached to her. The owner had been reluctant to put the horse in a claiming race. The owner was calling Farley's judgment into question. That was something Oliver hated to see, because he knew that that was just the sort of thing that could build up around the track, especially up in the Turf Club, where the owners sat together and lamented their fates and told each other that, given how much money they were spending on the game, more of them, a majority of them, deserved to win. One of the distinctions between owners as a class and, say, grooms as a class was that, whereas grooms sometimes knew what they wanted and took it, owners always knew what they deserved. Assistant trainers, in Oliver's experience, were generally unsure on both counts.

Farley, as you could tell by "The Tibetan Book of Thoroughbred Training," didn't know a thing about deserving, and so he and the owner were probably not even talking the same language. Oliver tried not to appear to be spying, but he watched as the owner stood up and turned toward the door. He was a good-looking guy, but he didn't look happy. As he pulled the door open, he said, "I'm losing confidence in you, Farley, I've got to say—" But then he saw Oliver and fell silent, only adding, "Well, I'll call you."

"It's up to you, John," said Farley, congenially. But after the owner turned away, Oliver saw Farley's face fall, just for a moment.

"You gonna claim her back?"

"I don't think so. Let's say the quickest I can get her back is a month from now. She'll undoubtedly have run a time or two by then, and worked hard in between. No telling what kind of shape she'll be in. No one I know who's ever claimed a horse back from Buddy has been able to run it in the same class as when it got claimed away. Stress fractures, tendon inflammation, wind problems. Better to let her go."

"What are you going to do?"

Farley looked at him. They both knew that Oliver was referring to the larger issue. Farley held his gaze, then smoothed down his mustache and beard in a habitual reflective gesture, running his thumb and forefinger along the line of his jaw. He said, "Every trainer goes through cycles, Oliver. The horses are earning their feed."

"But what if the owners start stampeding?"

"I don't know. You know, owners always think of themselves as predators. But they've always seemed kind of spooky to me. I don't know."

"But—"

Farley rocked back on his heels and his eyes began to twinkle. He was getting fatherly. He said, "Oliver, it's okay not to know for now. Eventually we *will* know."

"Farther along," said Oliver.

"Farther along," said Farley. "Did you get any of that soup? That was great soup. I loved that soup."

Oliver nodded, and Farley walked away with his university-professor walk, a little stiff, a little remote, a little awkward. Everyone who had ever worked for Farley said the same thing—he was a great guy, but deep as a well and twice as dark.

9 / A MIRE

IN THE WEEK between Christmas and New Year's, it was time for Wow to go off to the training center near Fair Hill. The other four yearlings Krista Magnelli had at her breeding farm had gone already, in September and October, but the Maybricks' trainer, Dick Winterson, had thought Wow, a May colt, needed some time to mature, which was fine with Krista. The months she had him to herself had lulled her into thinking she could do this impossible thing—be twenty-six years old and have a baby and a breeding farm at the same time. Maia was almost five months old now—she had been born seven weeks after the end of the last breeding season, or August 4, as time was normally measured. She was an easy baby, who let Krista so take for granted that she would sleep soundly, eat well, and play happily that Krista had let the nanny her mother hired for her go early. It was a dream—nurse the baby, put the baby down, turn on the monitor, go out and work with the colt, listen to the baby wake up and chuckle to herself, go in and nurse the baby. All of her friends from college were unemployed or hardly employed (if you considered graduate school employment), and here Krista was, running the farm her grandfather had left her, standing a stallion, breeding and foaling out mares, weaning, training babies and sending them off to learn to be racehorses, book-keeping, sending out bills, doing taxes. This was her fourth year. Of course, she and Pete hadn't planned to have a baby in their fourth year—their fourteenth would have been more realistic, but mistakes had been made that, in their usual fashion, had turned out to be destiny, and Krista felt pretty self-confident most of the time.

She had polished the horse up quite a bit, and it made her think of herself as something of a horse-trainer. She taught him how to load in and out of all the trailers on the place, how to stand for clipping and the farrier, how to have a blanket flapped all over him, how to take a bit in his mouth, even how to longline around the place. He let you do anything with him, was never coltish or wild. And then, after you were done, you put him back out in the pasture and he showed you his secret, his giant, oiled ground-covering stride. Now it was time for him to go. Krista was proud of him, of the good appearance he was going to make at the training farm. Sam the vet was to come out and give the colt a going over before the van was to pick him up, all easy and organized.

Except that, when Krista went out to feed at 7:00 a.m., she saw that Wow was out and covered with wet mud from eyeballs to hocks, and that, in that luxuriant tail that she had combed through just the day before, there were now cockleburs and twigs. It wasn't as though Krista hadn't thought of this. The rain in the night had come without thunder or lightning, and upon half waking up to it, Krista hadn't even considered that the colt might be out: she had put him in herself.

She brought the animal in and surveyed him. He could conceivably be hosed off, though the weather was cold for that. If you had plenty of warm water, plenty of wool coolers, some help, and plenty of time you could always get a horse clean, even in the dead of winter. Krista had none of the above. And then she heard a noise on the baby monitor, the noise of Maia waking up and crying. She did not, in the next few minutes, hear the other noise she expected to hear, which was the sound of the door to the baby's room opening, and her husband, Pete, entering the room and picking the child up. After another minute, she threw the horse in a stall she had bedded the day before for a mare who hadn't arrived yet, and stomped into the house.

Pete played right into her hands. Between the kitchen, the bathroom, and the baby's bedroom, he handed her three marital red flags: there was a dirty plate with four cigarette butts stubbed out in a piece of a bagel on it; his clothes lay in a pile right in front of the toilet, where he had stepped out of them and left them: socks in boots, with jeans, boxers, shirt accordioned on top, baseball cap hanging from the handle of the toilet, toilet seat up; his own self, naked in bed with a day's growth of beard, sleeping through the lonely grief of his very own daughter, who was now sobbing and catching her breath in Krista's arms.

Krista thought luxuriously that it was all too much, and said, "I hate this. I am at the end of my rope. I've had it. Enough is enough. This is nowhere."

"What?" Pete opened his eyes.

"Oh my God," exclaimed Krista, and marched out, the baby on her hip.

Now, it was true, as her mother had often said, that a wife was allowed a certain number of temper tantrums, and in fact the occasional temper tantrum was invigorating to a marriage. The breakage of a valued object was not to be sneered at, either, since everyone had too many things anyway. "In a good long marriage," she had said once, "the wedding presents go one at a time, so that by the time you've been married fifty years there isn't a plate or a soup tureen or, God forbid, a Hummel shepherdess remaining as a burden for the children."

Krista sat down on the couch and lifted her sweater and turtleneck, then undid the latch of her nursing bra. She maintained a noble motherly calm all through the right breast and then the left breast, and she was selflessly happy to see Maia settle and take her deserved nourishment. Time was passing, of course. Someone could have offered to give the starving child a bottle, but he hadn't, and that was perfectly all right with the mother, who never forgot *her* responsibilities. When Maia was full and satisfied, Krista did herself up again, all the time talking sweetly to her child, and went back into the bedroom. Pete, she saw, had drifted off again. She allowed this to go unremarked upon, though hardly unnoticed, and sat down gently on the bed. She said, "Honey, do you think you could change her? You put Wow out last night and he's quite a mess and the van will be here in an hour, I think."

"Hey, baby," said Pete to Maia, as if nothing was wrong.

Krista marched out of the house, her footsteps as eloquent as they could be, and past the stallion barn, where the stallion her grandfather had left her three years before, along with this place, the very stallion who had gotten her into this fix, was innocently passing between his stall and his paddock. His chestnut coat was dirty, too, and he happened to have allowed himself a leisurely drop in the penis department. He hadn't bred a mare in five months, so he was beginning to think again upon his lifework. His penis hung, as white as a girl's leg, nearly to the ground. Krista exclaimed, once again, "Oh my God!" and the stallion pricked his ears and looked at her. Unfortunately, he didn't think to sheathe his member, and the sight of it annoyed her no end. "You!" she said. "Look at you!" The horse lowered his head and turned right around and went back into his stall. She called after him, "Keeping a stallion is too much for me! I need help here! What if I have to sell you? You're the best

horse my grandfather ever bred! Don't you dare go anywhere else! I am not acting hysterical!" And then it began to rain again and she sat down on a hay bale
and burst into tears.

It was after nine. She curled up on the hay bale and put her face in her
hands and who was going to comfort her or help her now? What if she drove
Pete away with her temper tantrums and he took his outside income with him?
Then she and Maia and Himself (her nickname for Lake of the Woods) would
have to move into a trailer park somewhere, and that was good enough for
them and it would be so embarrassing. She would have to sell the farm. She
could see the article in *The Blood-Horse,* because her grandfather had been famous, and Himself had won the Gotham and the Woodward and gone to
England and won the St. Leger and the Cambridgeshire, which made him not
quite the thing, fashion-wise, as a stallion, so he had to prove himself, especially since he didn't have a drop of Mr. Prospector or Northern Dancer blood
in him. It would be a very tragic story, and there would be a picture of her
holding Himself by the leadshank, with the baby on her hip, and the headline
would be something like "Young Mother, Breeder, Sacifices All for Unproven
Stallion." And then there would be all the stories about the farm and about
what a great horseman her grandfather had been and how she was trying to follow in his footsteps, but it was always hard for a woman in the racing world—

And so she didn't hear Sam's truck pull in, and, yes, he found her dripping
wet curled up on the hay bale, her face pressed into her hands. She exclaimed,
"I've got to sell the farm!"

"First you've got to sit up and go into the tackroom, because you are soak-
ing wet. And shivering."

"Am I?"

"Aren't you?"

She was.

The tackroom was cold, so Sam turned on the kerosene heater and found a
wool cooler and wrapped her in it. Then, very Sam-like, he took a clean towel
off the stack she kept there and wiped her face and hair. But she had to look it
straight in the face. "I've got to sell the farm. Pete is going to leave me, and I
would never take any money from him other than child support, and the farm
is the only thing I own besides Himself, and I can't sell Himself. I told him I
might this morning, but I can't."

"Did Pete say he was going to leave you?"

"Not yet, but I'm such a bitch that he would be a fool not to."

"When is he going to leave you?"

Krista thought for a minute. "After I go in the house and scream at him for
not getting up with the baby and for leaving Wow out last night, when I spent

all day yesterday getting him ready to go off to that place in Fair Hill where all the horses are sons and daughters of Seattle Slew and Nureyev!"

"Then we have time to go over this colt today, before the van gets here."

"Oh, God! He's so dirty! You aren't going to want to touch him!"

"Well, it's ten. Let's have a look."

Krista sighed and unwrapped herself, then took an old waxed coat off a hook and put it on. She followed Sam out into the barn. Now she was really depressed. There was nothing heroically tragic about a dirty horse, and that was a fact. She said, "He's over here. A mare hasn't arrived yet, which I suppose is a good thing."

Wow was gazing inquisitively over the stall door, and as they approached he knocked his knees gently against it and tossed his head. Krista picked up a the halter and leadrope she had thrown on the ground. Sam said, "I've got this friend out in California, and he was the expert witness for a trial this week."

"You're kidding."

"They got the plaintiff on the stand, and the opposing lawyer says to him, 'Is it true or not true that you told the highway patrolman after the accident that you felt fine?'

"And the guy says, 'Well, I was walking my horse down the side of the road—' And the lawyer says, 'Answer the question yes or no. Is it true that you told the officer that you felt fine?' And the guy says, 'Well, I was walking—' And the lawyer turns to the judge and says, 'Please tell the witness to answer the question,' and the judge says, 'Actually, I would like to hear what the witness has to say.' "

Krista had her hand on the latch.

"So the witness looked at the judge and said, 'Well, I was walking my horse down the side of the road, minding my own business, when this big semi-truck came barreling up the road and hit us broadside and knocked us over the edge. Well, I was lying there when the cruiser pulls up, and I hear him crash through the brush and clamber down there, and he says, "This horse looks bad," and he shoots him right there. So, when the guy comes over to me, he says, "How you feeling?," and I say—' "

"Fine!" Krista said, laughing, though her face was stiff with tears. "That's the worst one yet."

"Worst what?" said Sam. "It's a true story." But he smiled.

Krista opened the stall door and put the halter over Wow's head, then led him forth. Sam said, "Well, he doesn't look all that bad, Krista." And it was true, he didn't. He was dry and actually fairly clean, though sprinkled all over with wood shavings. Sam said, "He must have dried himself off rolling in the stall while you were otherwise engaged." They peeped over the stall door, and sure enough, the deep clean bedding Krista had put in for the mare was mounded up and pushed around, a little dirty but not too bad for the mare. She said, "That was smart of him."

And so they worked companionably together. Sam spent a few minutes checking the horse over, which wasn't hard, since he had no known problems, then he brushed him off while Krista picked the burrs out of his tail, then he wrapped his legs while she washed his face with a damp sponge and picked a few burrs out of his mane, too. When the van pulled in, the horse didn't look perfect, but he did look like a healthy winter horse—fit and furry, well brushed, and neatly wrapped in cottons and green Vetrap. He was only going about twenty miles down the road and two social classes up. He got on the van like an old pro, and only at the last minute did Krista run up the ramp and give him a hug. Then she turned to the van driver. She said to him, "Just remember one thing."

"What's that, ma'am?"

"This yearling is as closely related to Secretariat as any yearling in the world."

"That right?"

"That's right."

Maybe. But it sounded good, and it reflected Krista's perfect faith in Wow's future, which from now on she would only see from a distance. She kissed the colt on the cheek and turned quickly and walked down the ramp. In five minutes, with a great wheezing and squealing, the van was out on the road.

Since she had cried enough already, she only turned away from its disappearing tail with a sigh, and there was Sam, right behind her, smiling. The simplest thing to say after such a tantrum seemed to be "Thanks for helping me. Don't you have work to do?"

"Some shots here, some teeth there. Nothing urgent. Would you like to talk?"

Krista knew his beeper could go off at any moment—colic, choke, laceration, skull fracture, subluxation of the stifle joint, abortion, pierced cornea—so there wasn't much time. She said, "Yeah. Yeah, I would." She had been doing this for three years now, letting Sam's large, practical presence calm her. It was almost worth all the vet bills, just to have him come over.

They went back into the tackroom, which was now even a bit too warm, and fragrant with well-soaped and much-used leather. Krista sat on a trunk. Sam sat in the desk chair. Right there on the desk were the bills she was already ten days late sending out. Krista sighed and turned her gaze into Sam's face, just so she didn't have to be reminded of that, but everything reminded her. She said, "We can't last much longer here, Sam. If we get through this foaling

season— Well, I don't see how we are going to get through this foaling season."
But then she sighed. "Okay. Well, I guess we are going to get through this foaling season. But I know that everyone around here just looks at us and thinks,
Haven't they let that place go, don't the horses look dirty, surely she's neglect-
ing that child. I almost don't dare go out anymore. My grandfather had
this place spotless. It was like he knew how to solve every problem before he
got up in the morning and knew what the problems were. And he got up at
four a.m. I've tried that, but Pete doesn't want to go to bed at eight o'clock, so I
don't get up until six and then I'm ashamed at not getting things done until
midmorning—"

Sam opened his mouth.

"I know we have to hire someone, but we can't afford anyone. I mean,
some junior-high-school girl would come out here and clean stalls until she
dropped and be grateful for the opportunity to be worked to death, but I can't
do that."

Sam coughed. What was he, Krista thought, about fifty? Kind of paunchy,
but big-shouldered and quiet, the way men who spent their lives stemming the
tide of equine disaster often were.

"And you know what my mother said? She said, 'Don't do it, Krista, don't
move there. Sell the damned place and the damned horse and do something
more fun than horse-breeding, like working as a data processor at the Pentagon
in a stuffy little cubicle for fifty years at ten thousand dollars a year.' She was
sure when told her I was pregnant that the next thing out of my mouth was
going to be that I was selling the farm."

Sam smiled. Maybe, she thought, she should have married a much older
man. Her best friend from college had done that.

"And a guy from Texas did approach me right after they ran that article in
The Blood-Horse about me taking over the operation, and he offered me, well, a
lot of money, and I didn't take it, and I haven't dared to tell my mother about
that, but—"

"If you didn't take it, you didn't take it." His voice was very soothing, deep,
and certain.

"My grandfather made it all look very easy."

"Your grandfather never seemed to worry, I'll say that for him. It was very
reassuring to work for him when I was just starting out. Take a deep breath."

She took a deep breath, thinking that it was nice to be instructed once in a
while.

"You know, one time your grandfather had me out to help him with a
maiden stallion. I don't remember his breeding. Anyway, we were the only two
around, and I was just starting out, and your grandfather was very breezy

about the whole thing. You know, at the big studfarms, they've got six or seven hands helping with every breeding. But he always said that, if worse came to worst, you could just turn the two out together and they would do it by themselves, so why worry if there were only two of you? But he never stopped whistling, never got in a twist, never communicated any sense that there was anything wrong to the horses. That was the thing he knew. Whatever might seem to be going wrong, everything is a whole lot easier if the horses don't know about it."

"Yeah," said Krista. She sighed. Then she said, "Well, he looked okay when he left, didn't he?"

"He looked fine. How's Maia?"

Sam's beeper went off.

Krista said, "Perfect." She sighed.

"That's all you need, then, isn't it?"

"Yeah."

They came out of the tackroom, and Krista looked down the aisle of the barn, eleven clean and empty stalls on either side, awaiting the mares that would begin arriving in a few days. Sam said, "He's the last one?"

"Himself is all I have here for a couple of days. Someday, maybe we'll have our own mares."

"I'm sure you will, honey," he said. "Start slow."

She followed him to his truck. Himself was standing in the doorway to his stall in the downpour, his ears pricked in their direction, and she could see Pete through the kitchen window, Maia in his arms. "What do I do now?" she said. "There's nothing to do."

"Take a nap," he said.

BOOK TWO

1998

JANUARY

10 / WINNERS CURSE

OFTEN DEIRDRE could not decide what it was she liked least about training racehorses, there were so many candidates for the honor, but always when she was at the sales, she became freshly convinced that it was sales. The two-year-olds in training sales bothered her for obvious reasons—you had to wince at the sight of those babies flying around the track, their tender legs pounding the hard ground. And the yearling sales bothered her for other obvious reasons—all those even younger babies, fat and shiny, bearing too much weight on their tender joints, overfed, overgrown. You didn't even have to look at the X-rays of their knees to know they were already compromised. But going to sales, and guiding her owners toward some simulacrum of responsible selection, was an inescapable part of her job, especially if (as Helen had pointed out to her only three days ago, when she was complaining about this trip with what she considered to be remarkable eloquence) she expected to prosper in 1998. Actually, the main thing she didn't like about breeding sales, or at least this one, the first of the year, was that the weather was so damn cold. In September, at least it was warm and pleasant to visit all the barns and ask to see the horses. In November, at least inside the big golden amphitheater where the horses were led onto the stage and the bids were taken, there was some respite from the outer chill. In July, at least there was plenty of iced tea.

She had come to Keeneland with George and Skippy and Mary Lynn for the January Mixed Sale of breeding stock and horses in training. Skippy and Mary Lynn had about five hundred thousand dollars to spend, and they intended to buy more than five and fewer than ten mares in foal to particular stallions. Since Skippy was single-mindedly focused on the Kentucky Derby, the mares' own sires, Deirdre advised, should be classic ones—Secretariat, Caro, Hoist the Flag, Vaguely Noble, Stage Door Johnny, Northfields, Key to the Mint—while the mares should be in foal to young, unproven stallions whose stud fees were not as high as Deirdre thought they could be, and would be. And though, on the way to Keeneland, Skippy had seemed to have a perfect

69

understanding of the essential concept of buy low, sell high, as soon as they got here he seemed to have lost all conceptual reasoning whatsoever. He kept coming to Deirdre and showing her the catalogue copy of mares who were in foal to A.P. Indy, Storm Cat, Seattle Slew, and Nureyev, and in whose eyes Skippy saw grand destiny. Deirdre found herself scattering bad language around like sawdust, but she got no relief from it. She dutifully marched around the barns in the cold and stared at all these mares, but the only thing she could see in their eyes was a general desire to be away from this place and in a nice pasture somewhere with other mares they could boss around, or be bossed around by.

Deirdre was not sure where he was getting this attitude. Usually, between the three of them, she, Mary Lynn, and George could manipulate, cajole, or contain him. Now Deirdre showed him a trim little brown mare by Hoist the Flag out of the dam of the great Canadian sire Vice Regent. She was correct and healthy, but she was eighteen years old. She was in foal to Manila. Deirdre liked everything about her, including the fact that Manila was something of a bargain, given his steadiness and lack of fashionability. She and Skippy were discussing this mare (Mary Lynn was trying to keep warm somewhere else), and she almost had Skippy paying attention, when a large fellow whose picture Deirdre had seen in *The Blood-Horse* sauntered over for a look. Skippy, who had been turned toward Deirdre in a posture attentive enough not to require a smack on the knuckles from the nuns, had they been present, went suspiciously rigid. The man said, "You looking at this *mare?*"

Skippy, the Judas, said, "Deirdre here likes her."

"Huh," said the man, Snell, his name was, Max Snell, and that was all it took. A minute later, Skippy followed the guy as if on a string to the circle gathered around another mare, a six-year-old winner of one and a half million dollars, by Seattle Slew, in foal to Seeking the Gold. As if herself on a string, Deirdre followed Skippy. No doubt about it, this was a nice mare, gold-plated. She had a great look about her—full of self-confidence, with an intelligent eye and a pleasant demeanor. But there was no way Skippy could afford this mare. The trouble was that, after looking at this mare and the few others like her, Skippy would be dissatisfied with what he could afford, and no matter what they managed to buy, he would think he hadn't bought up to his potential.

"Now," said the wee fella, "this is a mare! Look at that shoulder! Look at those pasterns! Look at that engine! This is your foundation mare right here, Hollister. And she's in foal to a great stallion. That's what you've got to look at. Seeking the Gold is a great stallion."

Deirdre said, "You aren't needing a fucking foundation mare, sir. You're planning to breed a few racehorses, that's all. Remember?"

"Is this your trainer?" And then, "Huh," as if perfect respect were the most essential quality in a trainer, far outshining horse sense or intelligence or even masculinity. "You know, I tried to buy a mare once, and my trainer talked me out of it. She didn't have the record this mare has, either. I went along with him, because he said she was overpriced, though, frankly, nothing is really overpriced for a guy like me, you know what I mean?" He eyed them both, and, yes, they knew exactly what he meant. "Anyway, you know what that mare's name was?"

How could they, Deirdre thought, fucking possibly know what that mare's name was?

"Gana Facil. She was in foal with Cahill Road. My trainer thought she was overpriced, and I didn't have the sense to go with my own instincts. I *saw* something in that mare. In her eyes. Frankly, I see the same thing in this mare's eyes, clear as day."

Deirdre said, "She has a nice eye, for sure, sir. A lovely eye." Then, "Are you going to be bidding on this mare, sir?"

"Well—" Snell chuckled a mighty chuckle. Skippy stiffened again. Then the other man spotted someone else he knew, hailed him, and walked away, leaving Deirdre and Skippy with their common sense of displeasure. After a moment, Skippy said, "I'm tired of looking at horses. They're starting to all look the same to me. I want to go back to the hotel and take a nap. Where's George?"

George was doing the driving.

The trouble with even this small sale was that the strata were so clearly defined. Skippy, who was used to being plenty rich and plenty important, didn't quite know who he was here. He didn't have a tenth the money that Snell had, or 1 percent of the experience that some of these lifelong racing people had. Nor was he the best-dressed in the crowd, which was always a help to an owner in a difficult social situation. And he was a lawyer. That meant that he worked for a living. Many here did not. But, then again, he did have George, and George was so charming, so Irish, so handsome, and so glowing with vitality that people stood around when George and Skippy walked by, and said to themselves, as they would say if Skippy dumped Mary Lynn and took up with a movie star, who's that with *that guy*? And then, when Skippy got into the back seat of the car and George got into the driver's seat, they were impressed. Oh my, how George loved the social power of Irishmen in America. All you had to do was open your mouth and say something anyone back home could say, and they fell at your feet. Deirdre thought George was getting a little overconfident. But here he came. Skippy brightened significantly, Deirdre passed the lawyer off to her cousin, and they left her in peace to pursue her plan for Skippy's benefit. The saving grace was that there were plenty of horses to look at, and she loved looking at horses.

AT THE DINNER TABLE, Deirdre noticed that Skippy was unusually quiet, as if he had been taken into custody for his own good. Beside her, George said, "Mary Lynn, darlin', are you feeling a touch ill, then?"

"Oh my God," said Mary Lynn, and staggered from the table to the bathroom. Deirdre forgot to follow her until George kicked her under the table, and then she said "Ouch! What?" before she realized what she was required to do.

Just the other night, George had said to her, "Cousin, it is beyond my understanding why the Lard above has given you so few instincts. A nice magnetic-resonance image of your brain would make an interesting article, I'm sure."

So she followed her, okay? And there Mary Lynn was, throwing up into the toilet, and so Deirdre put her hand on the woman's hot forehead, okay? And when she was done, she helped her out of the bathroom, and said, "What can I do for you?" Okay?

"Take me back to the hotel. No, have George take me back to the hotel. And don't let Skippy buy either of those mares."

"Which mares?"

"The Seattle Slew mare's right knee turns out, and the Storm Cat mare is a Storm Cat mare."

"Oh, those mares are too rich for us, Mary Lynn. Don't worry."

Mary Lynn gave her a look.

"We've got a plan, right?"

"Dear," said Mary Lynn, "I will tell you the most annoying thing about Skippy. You know, neither of us came from anybody. We met in college, and we never had any money, but that didn't matter. However little money we never had, Skippy would fill our place with bargains. In the early days it was yard sales, and the bargains all cost a quarter or a half a dollar. Later, it was Kmart, then Target, then Macy's. He's gotten bargains at Tiffany's, Barney's, Giorgio of Beverly Hills. Ever heard of Maxfield Bleu? That's a store on Melrose in L.A., where they mark up the clothes a thousand percent and sneer at you, to boot. Skippy can come out of Maxfield Bleu thinking he got a bargain."

"You're saying he thinks anything he buys is a bargain."

"No matter what the cost. Oh, God."

They returned to the bathroom.

AFTER GEORGE RETURNED to the sales pavilion from the hotel, Deirdre tried to concoct a strategy with him. The first element was to sit as far away as possible from Snell. The second was to position Skippy between the two of them. The third was to handcuff his hands to his seat. The fourth was to tape his mouth shut. And the fifth was to enclose his head in a bag. Having concocted this strategy, they were laughing, which put Deirdre in a pleasanter mood, but didn't give her any confidence in her influence over Skippy.

Deirdre herself had chosen ten good mares, and thought she would be lucky to get five of them. Only two were being sold this evening. When Skippy came to sit between them (they managed to put into effect the first two elements of their strategy), he was clearly at large again. The first thing he said was "So I suppose Mary Lynn is down for the night. I just talked to her on my cellular, and she doesn't feel at all well." He spoke triumphantly, sat forward on the edge of his seat, and plumped his hands on his knees. "When do they begin?"

They began.

"Ah," said Skippy.

Into the ring walked a lovely chestnut mare, as matriarchal-looking as any mare Deirdre had ever seen. She looked in her catalogue. It was Red Shift, a famous mare, daughter of a famous mare, Red Beans, sister of three other famous mares, Red Scare, Red Square, and Infrared. These red mares were so famous that, no matter whom they were bred to, their offspring got names that alluded to them. Red Shift had begotten Night Shift, Shiftless, Moveitorloseit, and Day Shift, a two-year-old filly of the previous year who had run second at Saratoga in the Hopeful Stakes, against colts.

Deirdre and George exchanged a glance, just as, quite unexpectedly, Skippy's hand went up. Deirdre snatched it down again, but not before the auctioneer noticed his bid. Fortunately, the next bid was immediate. Deirdre and Skippy had a little struggle, and Skippy said, in a tight voice, "Two hundred thousand is a bargain for this mare! I know that much!"

"It's three hundred thousand now," said George.

"That's a bargain, too. Let go of me!"

"Keep your fucking hand down," said Deirdre, too loudly. People nearby looked at her.

"She's a great mare! She's the best mare here!"

Deirdre now did something that later she wondered at. She swung her right leg around and mounted Skippy's lap from her own seat, so that she was facing him and he could no longer see the ring. In his moment of nonplussed stillness, she put her face right against his and said, "Skippy, my darlin', you do not deserve to own this great mare! I do not deserve to train her offspring! Leave her alone!"

She dismounted.

Skippy said, "What the hell are you doing? What the hell does that mean?"

"I have principles!"

"What principles? The mare goes to the highest bidder, no matter who he is!"

"I'll not discuss it!"

And then the bidding was over, and the mare had gone for $936,000.

George offered Skippy a drink of water, which he took. Droplets of sweat pearled his hairline. He muttered to Deirdre, "I didn't realize how strong you are. You look so little."

"Darlin'," said Deirdre, "when you have jumped thirteen-hundred-pound Holsteiners over five-foot and six-foot triple combinations and then turned back to a five-foot narrow and then galloped as hard as you could to a twelve-foot water jump, a lawyer isn't much."

"Well, don't do that again."

"Bid on what we agreed upon!" insisted Deirdre.

"Please," suggested George.

"Please," said Deirdre.

"Okay," said Skippy. And he gave her a look.

Not long after, the Storm Cat mare, in foal to Theatrical (Ire.), bumped and jerked into the ring. She was grinding her teeth, switching her tail, and kicking out. "There's a Storm Cat for you," said George.

"They win," said Skippy. He named the name of Snell and said that he owned four Storm Cats, two at the track and two at the farm. But he didn't bid. The Storm Cat mare went for $564,000.

Now the Seattle Slew mare entered the ring, Belle Starr her name was. The catalogue said that she was due in February, and she looked it. In fact, Deirdre had seen this mare race. Her present calm look was in interesting contrast to her performance on the track—Deirdre remembered her in the Kentucky Oaks several years back, as tough and aggressive as a filly could be, going wide and fighting the jockey to run. Deirdre had thought at the time that she might have been on steroids, but now she was big in foal, a bit of evidence that her grit was more or less natural. That *would* be a mare to have, wouldn't it. Deirdre glanced over at Skippy. He was sitting on his hands like a good boy.

She looked at the mare again. The bidding began, but it was slow. At the third bid, they were only up to seventy-eight thousand. Another imponderable, why some were hot and others weren't. Deirdre looked at her catalogue. She had written down her estimated reserve—$350,000. There was silence. She said, "Bid."

"What?"

"Bid ninety."

He bid ninety.

Someone else bid a hundred and ten.

"Bid one twenty-five."

He bid one twenty-five.

Someone else bid one fifty, and a third person bid one seventy-five.

Deirdre sat back, saved. She sighed with relief, and then the mare turned her head and looked across all the people in the first three rows, directly at Deirdre. How was it, Deirdre thought, that all horses' eyes were brown and large and set in the same spot on the horses' heads, and yet all looked different? How was it that some looked inward and some looked at the horizon, and some looked right at you? She said, "Bid."

"It's up to two twenty-five."

"Bid."

"Two fifty!" called out Skippy.

"Good Lard," said George.

It got to three hundred.

"I am in love," said Deirdre.

"Whose money are we bidding?" said Skippy.

"Yours," said Deirdre. "Bid three twenty-five."

In a moment it was at four.

"Snell is bidding against you," said George.

"He is?" said Skippy.

"It's only money," said Deirdre. "You have plenty."

It got to five, Skippy's limit, and, dutifully, he put his hand down and sat on it.

It got to six.

The mare lifted her head, pivoted her ears at some sound. She was a bay. To Deirdre, who had seen thousands of horses in her day, she looked uniquely splendid. Deirdre said, "Bid seven, I'll go halves with you."

"What!" exclaimed George. "Love, you've not got that kind of money!"

"I'll find it. Bid!"

Skippy raised his card and said "Seven." That halted the bidding, and a minute later, they owned the mare.

George said, "Have you not heard of the winner's curse, Cousin?"

"What's that?" said Skippy. Deirdre had floored herself too thoroughly to speak.

"That's an economic principle of auctions. Whoever wins is cursed, because they've paid a premium for the fun of winning."

"God in heaven," said Deirdre, realizing she would have to do something she had seen others do and sworn she herself would never do. "I'm going to have to mortgage my house for a horse!" She put her head in her hands. Deirdre's house was her pride—she had bought it after selling her best jumper for a hundred thousand dollars, and when she handed over the check, she had vowed to herself that she would never own another horse. That was ten years ago, and the house had continued to express its difference from a horse by appreciating in value at a steady 12 percent a year. But with her eyes closed, she saw that mare's face, clear as day, and, knowing it was now hers, she felt a bona-fide surge of joy. And now the man with the clipboard came toward them, and Skippy lifted his hand and signed the paper.

11 / THE BARON

DICK WINTERSON was a successful trainer and a busy man. He had a string of million-dollar runners (well, some half- and some quarter-million-dollar runners—the pool of million-dollar runners, though deep, you might say, was also naturally rather small in circumference, and Baffert and Lukas had bought up most of the shoreline). But Dick wasn't afraid of them. Most of the time. Some years before, Dick hadn't been afraid of them any of the time. Or of Allan Jerkins or John Kimmel. Name any trainer you like, and that was a trainer that Dick Winterson hadn't been afraid of. As a rule, Dick liked other trainers. They had something in common, and he was, or had been, an outgoing sort of guy. Probably now, unless, like dogs, they could actually smell it, Wayne, Bob, Allan, and John didn't as yet know that Dick was afraid of them. He still joked around with them and the others when he saw them. He still stood next to them during morning training and talked horse idiosyncrasies with them. He still drank coffee and ate toast with them in the cafeteria. But after the workouts were over, when the others went into their offices and called owners or did paperwork, Dick went off to his therapist. He was a racing man, of course, and so he envisioned his fear and his therapy in a

match race, neck and neck, Sunday Silence and Easy Goer, Affirmed and Aly-
dar, all the great racing couples. Or, God forbid, Foolish Pleasure and Ruffian.
The problem was that, even after the second turn, he didn't know which horse
was his fear and which horse was his therapy. Sometimes he tried to gull his
therapist with the idea that Thoroughbred training had changed when the
quarterhorse guys got into it—they were a harsher, harder-bitten group—but
his therapist ignored these realities and said that winning and losing was the
source of his distress, not its solution, that quieter, more organic images would
be more helpful. Blossoming. Budding. Fruiting. Digging the soil, sprinkling
the fertilizer, gently mounding the dirt up around the stalk of the plant, etc. It
was dead certain that Wayne Lukas never visualized his life in terms of garden-
ing, Dick thought. He nodded when his therapist suggested this sort of thing
to him, but couldn't, or at least didn't, take it in. Meanwhile, his fear and his
therapy had turned into the stretch, and Dick had the distinct sense that in a
matter of moments, so to speak, the race would be over. And now he was having an affair with the wife of one of his owners. That didn't mean he was *more
afraid,* he told his therapist, only that he was *afraid more of the time.* His therapist told him that this distinction was meaningless, but Dick actually found it
rather comforting. It meant, somehow, that he wasn't entirely panicked.

His establishment, he knew, the exercise girls and the grooms and his two
assistants and his office manager and the feed man, were all operating on mo-
mentum at this point. He had set them going years before and they all knew
their jobs. They kept their heads, took care of the horses, and rolled along. He
was still winning races—his win percentage in the fall was 18 percent, as high
as it had ever been. But none of the wins, not even the big-stakes wins, where
he got his picture into the *New York Times* and the *Daily Racing Form,* proved
anything to him except that life was fluky. He could send a horse out a one-to-
five favorite, have the horse come roaring in by ten lengths of daylight, and still
not be convinced. Convinced of what? Dick didn't know. His brother, who
taught French in a high school in Queens, said he was having an existential crisis. Dick didn't really know what that was, but it sounded like a bad thing
to have at Gulfstream, where everything was lovely, and an even worse thing to
take back to Belmont Park with him. Belmont Park was big—a track of such
vastness that it gave you the willies to begin with. Belmont Park was like an
ever-expanding universe, a vacuum forming at your feet—Dick shook his
head, scattering the images.

What he had to do was decide whether to take Luciano back to New York
with him.

Luciano was his horse masseur, and the only balm to his troubled soul.
Every day, after his therapy (over the years he had won so much money that he

could afford daily therapy), he came back to the track and watched Luciano massage the horses. Luciano was only half Italian—he was actually tall and Irish-looking, with reddish hair and blue eyes. Though he was just over six feet tall, he could palm a basketball. When the horses heard his voice in the aisle, they pressed against their stall guards to get at him. They loved him far more than they loved their grooms, and though Luciano only did horses and never people, Dick felt entirely certain that Luciano would be able to resolve his condition better than his therapist, one session, full-body, just squeezing and pushing the fear out. But he didn't ask; he only watched Luciano do the horses and chatted with him.

Though they had never spoken of it, Dick knew that Luciano knew that Dick was in trouble. Luciano, therefore, offered a lot of well-meaning advice, which was sometimes of an Italian nature and sometimes of an Irish nature. Today, when Dick saw Luciano pass his office door (he was pretending to be scanning the condition book in a rational manner, but about two weeks before, he had started picking races by tosses of the coin; this had not affected his win percentage), he got up and came around his desk, then looked out the door. Luciano was ducking under the stall guard of a four-year-old named Rah Rah, who had won about half a million so far. Dick flipped his last coin, received from that the information that the filly Laurita should run in the Shirley Temple Handicap for fillies four years old and up, a hundred thousand dollars added, and he walked out into the aisle. He could see Rah Rah's head, haltered, his shank hanging over the stall guard, and he could hear Luciano mumbling. He strolled over and said "Hi."

"Hey, Dick," said Luciano. "How's it going?"

"Okay. Had a win and a place yesterday, out of two races. The owners were thrilled."

"Great," said Luciano.

Dick, his own hands in his pockets, watched as Luciano pressed his fingers into the colt's neck, making small circles, sometimes pausing to manipulate little knots, other times stroking, other times running his thumbs part of the length of the muscle. Rah Rah stood calmly. Dick stepped toward him, and touched the animal's nose, knowing what would come next, and it did. Rah Rah lifted his nose and began working on Dick, on his neck right where it came into his shoulders. With his mobile upper lip, he pushed and dug at the skin of Dick's neck inside his shirt collar, sometimes moving down his shoulder, sometimes moving up his neck and sometimes working on the line of Dick's jaw. Dick let him do this, although he knew he was in danger of being nipped—during mutual grooming, horses often nipped one another, and because of their manes and coats, they liked it. Unprotected, Dick liked it less, but he recognized it as a gesture of equine attachment, and no horse had ever drawn blood.

"Now, listen," said Luciano.

"I'm listening," said Dick.

"How does your wife fit in here?"

Dick flinched, but hid it. He said, "She doesn't."

"Where did you say she works, again?"

"She teaches vocal technique at a college in New York."

"Like singing?"

"Yes, singing. She hates the track. And she hates Florida."

"Is she a good singer? These owners might like to, you know, talk with a good singer like that."

"She's a good singer, but she sings songs that don't have any real melodies. You know, Charles Ives. Anton Webern. Alban Berg. Sometimes she sings some Schubert."

"I've heard of him," said Luciano.

"I've found that, if you listen to those Schubert songs about fifty times, they get pretty."

"But she doesn't like the track?"

"Never has. She's a little afflicted with agoraphobia. The track is no place for an agoraphobic."

"What's that?"

"The word means 'fear of the marketplace.' Fear of busy places."

"Oh. So she wouldn't like to sit up in the boxes and talk to the owners about concerts and things? Ballet? Opera? Owners like to seem to have class."

"Some owners do have class, Luciano."

"That lady who owns that filly who jumped the other horse."

Dick stepped to the right, and Rah Rah began on the left side of his neck. Luciano had, meanwhile, moved back to Rah Rah's withers. "Laurita."

"Yeah. Mrs. Maybrick."

"Yes. She does have class."

They were silent for a moment. Luciano had gotten to Rah Rah's back, and was really digging in. Rah Rah now forgot about Dick, and lowered his nose nearly to the floor, at the same time turning his head to the side and extending his upper lip. He gave a couple of grunts, huh huh.

"He likes it!" chortled Luciano.

"They all like it," said Dick.

"So maybe she would like to meet your wife?"

Dick stared at Luciano, wondering if some mindreading was going on, then opted to say, "But Louisa doesn't like the track."

"How did you meet her, then?"

"We were in a band. Sort of. We hung around the band, and sometimes we played with them. I played guitar and she sang."

Luciano ran his hands sweetly over Rah Rah's haunches, and then began the small circles in the large muscles there. Rah Rah leaned into the pressure. Luciano said, "You were a musician?"

"Musicianlike. I was pretending to my father that I wasn't going to train horses, but it didn't last."

"Well," said Luciano, "I can see that. Training horses is a full-time job, as far as I can see. You're out here before dawn, you stay all day, you go to the races, you put the horses to bed. If your wife never comes to the track, when do you see her?"

"My therapist and I have been talking about that."

"Probably a good idea," said Luciano. He shook out his hands and came around the horse, beginning at the neck on the right side. He had been working maybe twenty minutes. He charged fifty dollars a session. Each horse who was on a training-and-racing schedule got one session a week. Dick had absorbed the cost himself, effectively lowering his training fees by fifty dollars a week per horse. On the other hand, his winnings had risen, sometimes and sometimes not making up the lost fees. The difference, the vig, you might say, was the amount of time he didn't have to spend explaining to the owners how much the horses liked it, how it wasn't mumbo-jumbo, how his barn was happier as a result, how *he* was happier as a result of their being happier, of watching them, every day, be made happier. Living at the track was a hard life for a horse—no grass, no turnout, no buddies to nuzzle. Fortunately, Thoroughbreds were pure workhorses. No plowhorse ever concentrated on doing his (or her) job the way the average Thoroughbred liked to do, but it still gave Dick a pang, the way they lived. But what was a pang to him, these days? A pang was a moment, every moment was a pang.

Luciano said, "So you seem a little down."

"Do I?"

"Change always brings stress."

"Does it?"

"You just don't know where you're going to be in six months."

"In six months I'll be at Saratoga." Heaven, thought Dick. I hope I'm in the mood.

"You think so now, but, hey, in six months you could be dead." He shrugged a specifically Italian shrug.

"Thanks, Luciano."

"Who says that's bad?"

"True enough."

The masseur eased toward the withers and the horse stretched his head and then rested it on Dick's shoulder. Luciano continued in a philosophical vein. "See, every moment, you pretty much know where you are, who you are. That's life. Even if you make the mistake, which I try never to make, of examining your life, you still are more or less the same from moment to moment. That's reassuring. But then all those moments add up, and pretty soon you're somewhere, as someone, that you never expected to be and, even worse, that you could never have understood if you had ever known you would be that person. Understand what I mean?"

"I suppose that's the story of my marriage, actually. Hers, too."

"Whose?" said Luciano.

"My wife's," said Dick.

"Yeah," said Luciano. "Everyone's the same. I take comfort in that. Of course, horses are all different. Now, take my dad."

"Your dad?"

"My dad was a baron."

"He was?"

"Sure," said Luciano. "He knew everything about being a baron, too."

"What is there to know?"

"Well, if you are an Italian baron, there's wine, there's women of various kinds, there's food, there's property considerations, there's debt, there's relatives all over the place. He knew all that stuff. But the war came along. The war, my dad always said, was not run by barons for barons, and so barons did not fit the war and the war did not fit the barons."

Dick laughed.

"Well," said Luciano, perfectly serious, "that happens. My dad happened to be here in Florida at the time of the war, and he stayed here. Nothing he knew really applied here, I mean, all his information was wrong, because it was Italian information, but he didn't know that, and so he did what he was in the habit of doing, and by the end of the war, he had a restaurant here that served good wines, he had a wife, a mistress, a couple of nice pieces of property, and some debt, too. So the war ended, and he went back to Italy, thinking everything would just resume where it had left off, but of course Italy was much different. The thing was, my dad was much different, too. Now he knew all about being a baron in Florida, but not much about being a baron in Italy anymore. Here's what I think. I think the two of them, Italy and my dad, were exactly equal in their difference from what they had been, and if he had made up his mind to really be there, he and Italy would have converged again, but he didn't know that. He just thought he hated Italy now, but he hated Florida, too, and he wasn't much pleased with either his wife or his mistress. So there was his mistake. He thought the problem was in them, but there was no problem."

Dick was beginning to lose Luciano's train of thought.

"There is no problem. When I think there's a problem, I come over here, and I put my hands on the horses, and then I go have a little plate of gnocchi with some gorgonzola sauce, and there's no problem. If I keep thinking there's a problem, well, then, I have a little glass of wine."

Now he came to Rah Rah's back again, and the horse did the same thing as before—he stretched his head down, closed his eyes, and grunted, only this time his knees started to buckle. Luciano said, "Has he been back-sore?"

"A little frisky when someone first gets on him. Your dad must have stayed in Italy, if you grew up in Rome."

"He did, but he spent the whole time complaining and wishing he was in Florida, so when I got over here I was supposed to go to California, but I ended up right here!" He laughed.

It was true. Luciano, perhaps because he was half Italian, was much wiser and more comforting than his therapist. Dick said, "Say, Luciano, you want to go back to New York with me? Live up there for the summer season?"

"Hey, I don't know. I mean, I know it around here. I can't say. It's expensive up there. You know, I've lived here all my adult life. Sometimes I can't believe that."

"That's a reason to go, then."

"We'll see."

"I'll have work for you every day, as much as you want."

"Huh," said Luciano, leaving it up in the air. And Dick's assistant, Andy, appeared at his elbow. He said, "Is your cellular turned off? You have six messages from Al Maybrick about the Laurita filly."

Dick sighed, pulled out his cellular, and turned it on. It rang at once. "Hey hey hey," said Dick, his cheerful greeting. This was the way he greeted the man he had cuckolded now, much more enthusiastically than he had when his irritability with Al had been simple and pure.

"This is Al Maybrick, Dick. I've been trying to get a hold of you. I'm a b—"

"Hi, Al. Yes, I'm going to enter Laurita in the handicap. You coming down for it?"

"I don't know. It's a big jump in class for her—"

"I thought you were eager for that."

"I was, but when I talked about it in my group, they said my eagerness was because of my grandiosity, and that I should listen to you more carefully because you are the expert, and not so subject to fantasies and all that."

Dick's heart sank at the thought of the two of them trying to come up with a rational plan together. On the other hand, the coin toss had been decisive. Dick said, "Well, okay, Al. I have thought about it, and I think she's ready. So let's do it."

"We'll be there," said Al.

"You and—?" That was good, that pretend ignorance.

"Rozzy and I. She's not much for racing. I've explained everything to her until I'm blue in the face, but she just gets that look, you know."

Did he know? "What look?"

"Oh, I don't know. Never mind. I'll be there, anyway."

"Great!" said Dick, so utterly, cheesily, frighteningly craven.

12 / WAL-MART

BONE BONES, whose baptismal name was Chester Johnson, after his maternal grandfather, surely did need some Pepto-Bismol, probably because he was finding himself in Lowell, Massachusetts. Bone had noticed about himself that his body was like a map of the United States, and the only place that didn't give him a pain somewhere was his old hometown of Boonville, Missouri. In San Francisco, a town that most of the other members of the entourage didn't mind, he always had pains in his feet. In New York City, he got headaches that ran around his temples. In Phoenix, his left knee always just killed him. But New England and the Pacific Northwest were the worst—all internal afflictions, stomach pains, liver pangs, sore throats. Anyway, he was out of Pepto-Bismol, so he persuaded Dolly, Ho Ho Ice Chill's other regular security provider, to stop at the Wal-Mart they were passing so he could go in and get some.

"No shirts," said Dolly.

"What?" said Bone.

"You're a sucker for Wal-Mart style. And no flip-flops. Your feet are too big for those things, and they're ugly, to boot."

Bone's stomach hurt so much that he agreed to these restrictions just so that Dolly would quit driving around the parking lot and let him out at the doorway. By the time he was in the pharmacy area, he could barely see, and he realized that he had to go to the bathroom, but he was in so much pain that he couldn't figure out where it was. He stopped and put his hand out, and leaned against some merchandise. Right then, maybe the most beautiful babe he had ever seen came around the end of the aisle and stopped in front of him. She was tall and she moved like long grass bending in the breeze, then standing up again. Her lips parted and her eyes widened, and her cornrows shivered and she said, "You okay?"

Her name tag said: "My name is Tiffany. May I help you?"

Bone said, "Where's the can?"

Tiffany said, "Turn around, then walk straight along. It's right over there."

He came out painfree and utterly revived, ready to buy a shirt, he thought, except that he had been forbidden. All members of the entourage were required to buy their clothes in Los Angeles. He went back to the pharmacy aisle, picked up two large bottles of Pepto-Bismol, and carried them to the checkout. The checker was bending down, doing something under the counter, so he didn't notice her until she stood up and smiled at him, and then he saw that he hadn't been wrong at all. Here was this Tiffany person again, and even when he wasn't in pain, her beauty was a balm to his soul, as his grandfather often called things that were especially good, like catfish from the Missouri River by Boonville, breaded in cornmeal, fried in butter, and served with hot sauce and steamed greens. Although he had never actually done this before (he had heard that they did this sort of thing in other groups, though), Bone said in a very cool voice, the way you would have to, "Ho Ho Ice Chill sent me in here to find you, sweetheart. Can you take the afternoon off?" This was made up. Ho Ho was taking a nap.

Tiffany rang up the sale, $10.67, and counted $39.33 into his hand. He saw that she wore no makeup, and her fingernails were unpainted and short. She was absolutely and in every way the real thing. She tore his sales slip and put it into the bag with his Pepto, then she handed him the package and said, "Thank you for shopping at Wal-Mart." Bone felt more than a little embarrassed, but also a little relieved.

And then, when he had turned and was two or three steps toward the door, she said, "Yes," so he had to go on with it. Right there, she laid down her little Wal-Mart vest on the checkout counter, and said, "Just let me get my handbag. I'll meet you at the front door." When he got to the front door, Dolly was way across the parking lot and Bone couldn't even warn him to keep a straight face or something. She came up behind him; Dolly pulled up in front. Bone said, "Hey," and opened the glass door.

When he piled her into the Suburban, Dolly gave her the once-over, and turned to him and said, easy as you please, "Well, for once you came out of Wal-Mart with something worth bringing home." Bone nodded like he was totally in charge, but actually he had no idea how this had happened or what was going on.

13 / JUSTA GOOD-BYE, JUSTA HELLO

ROBERTO ACEVEDO wasn't taking physics anymore. His father and, reluctantly, his mother had let him postpone his last year and a half of high school to keep riding while he was hot, and he was hot. With a double bug that allowed him seven pounds, he was riding at 107 pounds, about the same as some of the women jockeys, but he was strong, and they could put him on anything, it seemed. He had the hands, he had the hands, he had the hands. Everyone around the track knew he had the Acevedo hands the way Mozart had the Mozart ear: everything the other Acevedos had, and something extra. Roberto was superstitious, though. He suspected that the Acevedo hands were really Justa Bob hands, and he persuaded Buddy Crawford to let him ride Justa Bob in every race the horse ran in. It was a case of getting tuned up. Every few weeks, he would sense that he wasn't quite with it, and he would take a lesson from the Master, come away utterly relaxed and self-confident, and take what he learned to the younger and less experienced horses. Justa Bob's system was simple, and he never elaborated on it. It was, take a firm but gentle hold, pay attention, and go with the rhythm. Sometimes he showed Roberto how to find an opening, sometimes he showed Roberto how to go wide, and sometimes he showed Roberto how to not be stupid, because sometimes he indicated that, even though he and Roberto could see the opening, he wasn't quite the horse to get out of it, should he get into it. This was a good lesson for an inexperienced jockey—to learn to pay attention to how much horse he had—and Justa Bob always knew exactly how much horse he was. In four starts, they had a win, a second (by a nose), a fourth (by a nose), and a tenth out of twelve. In this race, Justa Bob had indicated from the beginning that he didn't care for the size of the field. Justa Bob now had thirty-two starts under his belt. He was six years old.

Roberto was standing there with Buddy when the guy came out and hung the red tag on Justa Bob's nose. Buddy was philosophical, or, you might say, indifferent.

Though Roberto was intimidated by Buddy (who wasn't?), he hazarded, "I hope the new owner lets me ride him. He was an education to ride."

"My bet is, he's going to Golden Gate or Bay Meadows."

"Oh."

"A good claimer here is an allowance horse up there." He walked away. He didn't ever have much to say to Roberto.

Roberto knew he shouldn't be sad about this. But he was glad he happened to be crossing the parking lot when the horse left two days later.

When they pulled him out of the stall, his legs all wrapped and ready to go, it was like seeing your old girlfriend on the street. He was, after all, Justa Bob, a brown gelding with no particular distinguishing features—no star or snip or white foot. He was lanky, with a rather big head, long ears, and a good eye. They led the other horses that were going north up the ramp; several of them were real eye-catchers. Justa Bob was just himself, and no one paid much attention to him other than Roberto, who could see his general air of perfect self-possession and confidence. What really made Roberto sniffle a bit was that he should know the horse so well, know him as well as he knew any of his brothers or his sister, and have to see him walk out of his life forever, know him not in a way that he could talk about, but in his body somehow. They lifted the ramp, the driver got up into the cab, and the semi engine roared to life. Roberto found himself standing beside the groom who rubbed the horse for Buddy, who had come up to watch without Roberto realizing it. They spoke in Spanish. The groom said, "Well, you know what I'll miss about that horse?"

"No."

"He's a real character, you know."

"Yeah."

"Every day, he shits in his water bucket. Every day, I clean it out, and I yell and scream about it. Every day, when I get to his stall, he's standing there, staring at his water bucket, like he's saying, How did all this shit get in here! I think he's joking with me!" The groom laughed. "He's the only horse I got with a sense of humor!"

Roberto laughed. Down at the end of the road, he could see the big Cargill van go past Security and head out to the road, then turn left and rumble away.

THE WINDOWS WERE OPEN, and Justa Bob, one of the last horses on, could see out of them. Fact was, he hadn't been away from the track, either Santa Anita or Hollywood Park, in almost three years, half of his life. The van rumbled down Century Avenue, past Jack in the Box and McDonald's, past pawnshops and homeless people, and a man in pink cowboy boots who looked up at the van and thought about horses he had known in Utah as a boy before the war. If Justa Bob and his companions had been expensive stakes horses heading east, the van would have headed toward the Ontario airport, but it turned north onto the 405 and Justa Bob and his new friends caught just a glimpse of the view from the freeway—the mountains and the cars and the buildings beside the road. They had a chance to contemplate the size of the L.A. basin and the size of the world, and its seething intensity. The van driver, who made this run every two or three days, had long since ceased contemplating the meaning of it all, whether as a manifestation of late-capitalist corruption of natural values by the industrialized commodification of time and distance, or as a manifestation of the human urge to build and then destroy, or as a manifestation of ever-thrusting, goal-oriented maleness pushing toward the blissful unchanging ocean just over the mountains. He sometimes thought how weird it was to be carrying a load of horses and he hoped to God, for he was a churchgoing man, that he never had an accident, because there could be no accident quite as spectacular as one in which a load of horses was involved. And as soon as he thought of that, he made himself not think of it.

After a while, they turned north onto the 5, and that was that for five hours or so. Perhaps the sight of the almond groves of the Central Valley was pleasing for them, or perhaps they didn't notice, or perhaps they dozed, or perhaps they spent their time (surely some of them did) focusing on how much they disliked the horses beside them, who kicked and pinned their ears unsociably. The ride, at any rate, was smooth, and there were no sudden frightening noises. Sometimes the semi stopped, and one of the men opened the door and checked on them. It was better to move than to stand still. Although they had to brace themselves against the movement, it was soothing. Most of the time, it was quiet in the van, and Justa Bob himself was in a state of grace as much as he was in the State of California. He knew exactly who he was, exactly where he was, no memories, no anticipations. Just as Roberto had noticed about him, he was a smart horse heading down the road toward wisdom. Reaching the goal was inevitable. All he had to do to get there was stand quietly, his weight equally distributed on that most stable of structures, all four legs.

WHEN THE HORSES got off the van in the early twilight, at Golden Gate Fields, Fred Linklater, their new trainer, and Jose Quiver, their new groom, thought they looked pretty good. Like all southern-California horses, they looked accustomed to the best of care and the best of accommodations. As a group, they were shiny and sleek, their white markings glistening, their manes pulled, and their tails flowing and tangle-free. They were claimers who had

lived among stakes horses, and, like the worst houses in the best neighbor-
hoods, they had benefited from the association. In fact, Fred always imagined
the horses from southern California getting off the van, walking between the
shedrows, and glancing around in dismay. Things were damp here. You could
smell and hear the bay. The barns were old. The stalls were a little cramped,
and the straw didn't look as deep. Accommodations for horses and grooms
were crowded. The horses knew, as the trainers knew, as the grooms themselves
knew, that there were mothers and babies and children and men and even old
people living in horseless stalls. But of course no one said a thing about it.
Everyone was poorer here. There would be no Missing Link (thirty-five dollars
per bag), no brown sugar in the feed, no little packets of vitamins. There
would be less massage and chiropractic; there would be more bute and less
Tagamet. There would be fewer pain-relieving injections of hyaluronic acid to
the hock joints and ankle joints. Everyone would be expected to do the best
they could for as long as they could. Most important, there would be no return
to Santa Anita or Hollywood Park or Del Mar. Those days were gone forever,
at least for these horses.

Justa Bob unloaded with his usual equanimity, looked around with his
usual alertness. Jose liked him right away. Both Jose and Fred noticed that he
was a little off in the right front, which seemed like it was always the case when
you claimed a horse. Jose took him to his stall, led him in, turned him around,
removed his halter. He didn't really have time to spend with the horse—others
had to be unloaded, too—but he paused to pat the horse on the neck and to
speak to him in Spanish, *Caro caballo, muy bueno, sí señor.* You will be good
here, no? Win Jose some races, no? Then Jose bent down and blew gently into
the nose that Justa Bob always won by (this, like all of his other quirks, they
would learn on their own and wonder about). Justa Bob flicked his ears. Then
he went over and sniffed his hay (slightly different-smelling from the hay he
was used to, but he would eat it eventually); then he went over and scoped out
his water bucket. He didn't take a drink. In the morning, Jose would remember that moment when Justa Bob stood staring at his water bucket and Jose
didn't know why. In the morning, Jose would know why.

14 / SAVED

SINCE FARLEY'S HORSES were in Barn 26 and Buddy Crawford's filled up Barn 88, Oliver didn't run into Buddy very often except on the track. Buddy was too nervous to eat, or so it seemed. No one had ever seen him eat anything. He drank coffee and Dr Pepper, cases of which he kept with the supplements in the feed room. Thus it was that Oliver was much surprised and, he had to admit, disquieted when he was coming out of a stall where he had been looking at a new three-year-old filly from France only to see, or, rather, to feel, Buddy blow toward him down the shedrow like a damp gust presaging a storm. The odd thing was, he had no one with him. Normally, he strode around like a member of the royal family—he carried nothing, not money, not cellular phone, not even, maybe, a handkerchief. One assistant trainer on the right side and another on the left were supposed to answer to such requests as "Where's the God-damned phone?" and "How do you get this God-damned thing to work? Dial the fucking number."

Nevertheless, here he came, the thing itself, an unaccommodated man. Oliver stepped back into the stall, but saw when he did that he didn't need to. Buddy's eyes were focused on the closed door to Farley's office, where the laminated "Tibetan Book of Thoroughbred Training" gleamed in a ray of noontime sunlight. Farley's blinds were open. Oliver could see him inside, leaning over his briefcase, putting things in it.

Now Oliver watched Buddy's back hunch as he arrowed down the shedrow. After a moment, he saw Farley look up and out the window. A look of surprise crossed his face, instantly replaced by the look of not paying attention or investigating. He closed his briefcase. Buddy flung open the door and closed it behind him. Talk about not investigating. Normally, Oliver liked to linger for a few minutes at noon, sauntering between the barns, glancing in at the horses, washed, dried, wrapped, and bedded, like brooches in velvet boxes, onyx, pearl, amber, garnet, but not today. Rather than linger outside the office, trying to divine what was going on, he sprinted for the cafeteria. Whatever was going on, there would be news of it there.

Four tables were more or less full. Oliver took his coffee and sat at each for a moment. At the first table he learned that Harry Isenman had kicked out the beautiful English exercise girl he had been living with for the last six weeks because he hadn't won a race since she moved in. This, he thought, couldn't have anything to do with Buddy, because he looked at women even less than he ate. At the second table, one of the old-time trainers was telling the story of how Native Dancer got bred—there was the first part of the story, about how Native Dancer's sire, Polynesian, was suffering some sort of apparently terminal lethargy until he got into a bees' nest and was stung all over the head into a stakes-winning career. And then the second part of the story, that the great mare Geisha wouldn't load into the trailer, so, rather than fighting with her, they just walked her across the road to Polynesian and eleven months later came up with, perhaps, depending on your preferences, the horse of the century. Then there was the usual discussion of luck, on the one hand, and who the horse of the century was and why, on the other. At the third table, there was the tiniest lead—Buddy and another trainer who trained for the same owner had gone up to the farm in Santa Ynez over the previous weekend to look at the yearlings. At the fourth table, there was a larger lead. Somebody had been in the racing office that morning, very early, that time when only Buddy was around, and had seen Buddy scratch all his entries for the weekend. During Oliver's tenure with Buddy, he had been sent over to scratch a horse only one time. Usually, Buddy said, "Aw, let the damn jockey scratch him if he doesn't like the way he's going." But that was the end of it. And, to tell the truth, no one was that interested. That was how you could tell that Buddy hadn't many friends around. Everyone in the cafeteria was much more interested in Harry Isenman's love life than in anything about Buddy Crawford.

When he got back to Farley's office, Farley was sitting there in his chair, gazing up at the ceiling and tapping a pencil on the edge of his desk. Seeing Oliver brought him to. He stood up and picked up his briefcase, glancing at his watch. He said, "Still have time for a nap, if I leave now."

"What was that all about? Did he accuse you of jinxing him again?"

"Nope."

"He didn't have anyone with him."

"Nope."

"Well?"

"Walk me to my car."

They walked through the quiet, sunlit repose of the backside at noon, the day's work done, racing not yet begun. The horses who weren't sleeping deep in their fresh beds of straw were dozing over their hay.

It wasn't until they were out in the open that Farley said, "Well, he said I didn't jinx him after all, that that horse broke down because, uh, Jesus required it."

Owing to his upbringing, Oliver was not unfamiliar with this line of reasoning. He said, "To open his eyes?"

"That seems to be the case. Horse didn't die. That seems to be part of his reasoning. Jesus required injury but not death, that's a sign of God's mercy, and the horse is recovering beautifully, for which Buddy is grateful."

"Grateful? Anyway, Buddy's had two other horses break down since that one."

"Yes, but no one gave him the warning on those. I gave him the warning on that one in the fall, which is another sign of Jesus' mercy, and so those others count as a kind of emphasis. I called him to account, and he paid no heed. That's how he said it. He came over to thank me for calling him to account, and to ask my forgiveness for his heedlessness. He also said he would stop claiming all my horses."

"What did you say?"

"I said that every trainer here has horses on his conscience, myself included."

Oliver wondered.

Farley responded without being asked. "About seven years ago, I had a gelding who was blind in the right eye. I ran him maybe six times, but I always scratched him if he drew an inside position, because he got nervous when horses came up on his blind side, and he was good enough to run the long way around and make some money. The owner loved him. Anyway, one time he drew the number-two spot. I was all ready to scratch him, but he was so fit and ready to run that I didn't. I didn't decide not to, I just let it slide. Every race I'd run him in, he'd broken in front, so I told the jockey to try and get a good jump, and if he didn't, just let the horse drop back and go around. Plan A and plan B. Well, what happened was, the gate opened, and the number-three horse got bumped by the number-four horse and knocked right into this horse and put him over the rail. Broke his neck. I knew if he could've seen them he was quick enough to get out of the way, or if I'd scratched him he wouldn't've been there in the first place. Jockey broke his shoulder and was out for two months. And then, because they didn't have any money coming in, the jockey's wife didn't take one of the kids to the doctor, and she got pneumonia." He glanced at Oliver. "She recovered, though, for which I was more thankful than I can say."

"You can't—"

"Blame myself? I don't blame myself for the accident. Accidents happen all the time. But what happened was, I let myself go ahead and see what might happen. It was a funny feeling, like the feeling of any other sort of temptation. I regret toying around with that feeling."

"You can't take responsibility for every little feeling."

"You have to, though. You can't but you have to, anyway. You are not able, but you are obliged to."

This idea made Oliver feel suddenly exhausted. He sighed. Farley glanced at him and grinned his marvelous grin and said, "Don't worry. You already do."

"I do?"

"You do." They walked a few more steps. "Anyway, Buddy said that, when he was at the farm this weekend, Jesus presented to him, one by one, all the cripples he's made, two-year-olds, three-year-olds, four-year-olds, and up, hobbling around in paddocks, big knees, big hocks, you name it. He said they were lit as if by halos. That guy he trains for, you know, he's got thousands of acres up there. He lets 'em come back to the farm and hang around when they're done at the track, so I guess there was quite a selection."

"Well, so what," said Oliver, anger shooting like a rocket out of his exhaustion. "It's fine for him to be saved. What about them? That's what I never understood about my folks' church back home. They always seemed to be extending the hand of welcome to the returning sinner, but the effects of his sins were still right there for everyone to see, this black eye and that broken arm and these kids going without food and all that. I finally just thought that the sinner was more interesting to everyone than the consequences of the sins, so what happened was, they all gathered around him, or her, for that matter, and to hell with the rest of it. Somebody being saved was the easy part. Cleaning up the mess was the hard part."

Farley didn't respond. They went through the parking-lot gate, and came to Farley's car. He unlocked it, opened the door, and threw in his briefcase. Finally, he said, "I'll tell you what I think. I think it's not our job to forgive him. We're not the ones whom he's injured in any real way, or at least, we're not at the top of the list. But I guess I'm just going to see what happens. That's always the best part, anyway, seeing what happens."

This was the strangest thing about Farley, Oliver thought, this way he had of seeming to stand back, ready and alert, waiting to see what happened. It was consistent. It didn't interfere with his willingness to help or even to take charge, but it was cold, wasn't it? Right next to his liking for you was this other thing, his interest in what might happen to you.

Farley slammed his door and Oliver backed away from the car. He had a few more things to do before he headed home himself. Farley waved, and drove out the gate.

When he came back to the parking lot, an hour later, there, of course, was Buddy Crawford. He had the trunk of his Lexus open and was bending over, peering inside. Once again, he was alone. Oliver scurried to his car with his head down, but it was no use. He had his key out and was poking it into the lock when he heard the fatal footstep and felt the fatal hand on his shoulder. "Son," said Buddy.

Buddy was a good deal shorter than Oliver. When Oliver looked down at him, Buddy took his hand down. Oliver said, "Hey, Buddy. How are you doing?"

"Well, son, that's a wonderful question, and I'm happy to answer it, because I'm doing better than I've ever done in my life."

In order to preempt the confession, Oliver smiled and said, "I was just talking to Farley."

"Well, it's fucking good news, isn't it?"

"Yes, I guess it is, Buddy."

"You want to hear how it happened?"

"I'm kind of late, actually—"

"Son, you're never too late for the Lord."

"I suppose not." In the end, Oliver still did not have the fortitude to stand up to Buddy. While Buddy was relating the details of his conversion, which had something to do with his cousin's wife and a high-school basketball game and a fellow he met from England who had racehorses, in France, but also raised sheep for Muslim sects that still performed ritual sacrifices, Oliver found himself unable to pay attention or follow the line of the story. Instead, he stood looking into Buddy's face and remembering what it was like to work for him. Incidents that had been hazy in his mind now replayed themselves in crisp detail. He had been working there for about a week, it must have been, when Buddy had called him a shithead for the first time. He had said it in a normal tone of voice, instead of "Hey, Oliver, look at this colt's fucking knee," he had said, "Hey, shithead, look at this colt's fucking knee." Oliver had thought he'd said the wrong name, like Skinner or Lincoln or something, but then he'd caught the eye of the groom, who had nodded. Hey, shithead. Some two or three weeks after that was when Buddy instituted his 3:00 a.m. policy—Oliver was to get to the barn by 3:00, not by 4:00, as he had been doing, and fax Buddy by 4:00 about the condition of the horses. Checking the legs of a hundred horses in an hour was impossible, so of course he didn't ever get the fax in before 4:30, and this led to perennial complaints. "I'm *waiting* for you. You fucking think I want to sit up and *wait* for you?" But he hadn't reacted at the time. The abuse was like a heavy rain or a cascade of something. Some people actually professed to like Buddy—he was earthy, honest, lively, sometimes funny, and always, always, always, what you saw was what you got. Lots of people considered this a virtue. It was supposed to elicit its complementary virtue—being able to take it. While he was working there, Oliver had accepted that this was part of the learning curve at the racetrack—being able to take it was a general quality that would stand him in good stead. When he quit, he had felt some shame at not being able to take it.

Now he felt the anger that he hadn't felt then, or since. It was the conversion that did it, Buddy's beaming face, his evident joy. And it was joy. Buddy always won and often won big. He had sent horses to every major stakes in America and won quite a few of them. What you would see in his face then was not this same thing, triumph or vindication or whatever. Now, as Buddy wound up his story, his expression was totally un-self-conscious. His smile passed through his features as through a veil, revealing his inner self as truly, Oliver suddenly realized, as all the abuse had also revealed his inner self. It was true with Buddy that what you saw was what you got, and you could see something else now, something entirely new that had not been there before. It was what his mother and aunts would call a God-given miracle, and Oliver, who was well trained to recognize such things, recognized it.

That didn't mean he accepted it. What was that parable, the one that showed God's perfect grace? The guy went out and hired workers for his vineyard, and paid those who worked an hour the same as those who worked all day. Those who had worked all day got annoyed at that, but the master had no sympathy. Not only did he hold them to the letter of their contracts, he set the latecomers ahead of them, and corrected the complainers. How many times had Oliver heard this parable in his life? Maybe a hundred. How many times had he nodded and understood it? Maybe a hundred. But, looking into Buddy's beaming face, he found himself wondering about justice and deserving and a hundred horses here and at Hollywood Park who could barely walk but were made to run every five days, week after week, month after month.

He saw that Buddy expected him to say something.

He said, "Gotta go, Buddy. Congratulations. I really mean it."

He got in his car and drove off.

FEBRUARY

15 / PASSION

ONE THING Rosalind Maybrick realized about hopeless affairs, now that she had committed herself to one, was that they were certainly enlightening. She knew more about herself, Al, Dick, Louisa, life, love, and horses than she had ever known before, and probably more than it was healthy to know. Of course she should have settled for knowing about fine collectibles. Al's children would have joked for the rest of her life about how shallow and empty she was, and she would have gone to her grave and disappeared without leaving a trace, even for herself, but that opportunity was past now. She seemed to herself to leave traces everywhere, streaks of light when her hands moved through the air, afterimages when she turned her head, phosphorescent footprints wherever she walked, an aura of herself upon the air when she moved from place to place. These latest lovemakings she and Dick were having shone with a terrible light that pressed against her eyelids no matter how tightly she shut them. When he asked her why there were tears in her eyes she couldn't tell the truth—that the light was blinding her. She could only say something about how dry her eyes had been lately. He, of course, thought she was crying—he said that: Why was she crying? What was wrong?

Oh, she was a seer now, a fortune-teller, a prophetess, and a witch. Had not every second-sighted woman since Medea been hopelessly in love with a man who could not see the light all around them? Who had his mind on something else—for example, the sea; for example, the mountain; for example, the finish line? Hopelessness was something every seer paid in order to see, and not voluntarily, either. No one in her right mind would want to see any of this at all. Most nights in New York she saw Al. Here he was, getting up from the dinner table, glancing over at the empty liquor cabinet, feeling his pockets for the cigarettes he hadn't smoked in ten years. Here he was, scratching his ass. Here he was, pushing his hair back. Here he was, hitching up his pants. Here he was, glancing at her. He had been a prepossessing man once, years before she knew him, but years of success had imprinted him. He had forgotten how to watch out for the eyes of others, and if he saw someone looking at him, you could see the thought "Fuck 'em" cross his face. Of course, he didn't treat her in that way. He was always kind to her. But you couldn't think, "Fuck 'em," about almost everyone and not have a "Fuck 'em" way of being. But if it were only that, or purely that, Rosalind would have left Al long ago. Superimposed over his present self, though, was another and another. There was the guy who was sorry for who he was, who knew he offended others and drove them away, and did whatever he could to stop doing whatever it was that he was doing that he didn't understand that he was doing that drove people away, and in that also drove people away. This was the man Rosalind was committed to, the one she had vowed not to be driven away from. This was the man she caught looking at her from time to time, such deep longing and bewilderment in his eyes that she knew it was coming up from way beneath marriage, way beneath love, way beneath manhood or fatherhood. She could see that look as she had never seen it before she became a seer, and it struck her to stone. Superimposed over that man was still another, a sixty-four-year-old mortal truly in need of a miracle, whose inner contradictions had finally hardened so completely that they brought him to an impasse. Aggressiveness had gotten Al out of Schenectady, New York, a life like his father's as a bricklayer. Flouting authority had made him inventive and innovative in his approach to business. Eagerness to get things done had brought him not only money but tolerant children, houses, winning horses, lovely surroundings at every turn. His vast energy had allowed, and even demanded, hard work, and he had enjoyed the effort of it, and the bragging rights, too. Time was when these qualities of Al's just appeared on Rosalind's radar screen as random thoughts she had about him. Now, though, she saw the whole package, saw that it was a package, and it made her hopeless for him and for herself. She could not leave him, and he could not change. Where was love in there? Rosalind didn't know, because, now that she had had her face pressed into love for eight weeks, she knew even less about what love was than she had before, when she'd been in the habit of sitting around with her women friends and discussing everyone's affairs.

Rosalind could see herself as clearly as she could see Al. Love had broken her into parts. There was the psychotherapeutic part, all about her father and mother and sisters. Her mother attentive and perfect, her father taciturn, the two of them fighting (frequently? infrequently?). There was the social-class part, all about moving from middle-class Appleton to upper-class Manhattan. She knew she was a newcomer, and even if those around her didn't expect her to act with perfect propriety, and, in fact, saw the perfect propriety as Appletonian, and the perfect propriety that she took refuge in was the very thing that prevented her from having any relief, giving that up was too great a cost for getting relief, rather like being disemboweled, she thought. There was the temperament part. Stubborn she was, stubborn she had been, stubborn she had been labeled. These qualities were said to be inbred. There was the feminine part. She knew Dick didn't love her as much as she loved him, if he loved her at all. Any woman in such an undignified situation had only her dignity to protect her. Then there was the part about being an arrogant fool, which she had been when she thought that day on the plane that there was some little thing she needed, and then she had reached out and taken it, and it had been more than she could handle, and so she had made her bed, and now it was just that she had to lie in it. Then there was the part about being vulnerable for the first time in her life. The fact was, she was rather a nicer person these days than she had ever been. People smiled at her in a genuine way. She herself was warmer. She got touched more often, addressed with endearments more often, complimented more often on things other than clothes. She got thanked and thanked others more sincerely. Several of her friends told her she had unbent; a couple of the ruder ones told her they liked her more and that others liked her more, too. Then there was the part about the great sex. The sex was great. She was transported, Dick was full of compliments. She recognized compliments as compensation for lack of love, and their recent increase in number as a way for Dick to try to persuade himself that there was something in this for him after all, but Al wasn't much of a complimenter, so the compliments were delicious to her.

Well, she saw Dick, too, dissected and labeled. His job terrified him. Once in a while, when they spent a night together, he was as likely to wake up with a nightmare as not—horses breaking down, horses trapped in the starting gate, horses on top of jockeys and the jockeys screaming underneath the bulk, incapable of being found. Once he woke up in the morning, a real morning, the morning of his day off, so after sunrise, and told her that he dreamt that every horse in the barn had been X-rayed and found to have four broken legs, even though they were all standing peacefully in their stalls. The track officials had come around and insisted they be euthanized on the spot, and he had awakened just as he had agreed to do this. He had awakened with a cry, and said to her, "Now I'm sure they all have stress fractures." He felt isolated from his wife, and unable to help her. He had no friends that Rosalind would recognize as friends, except her. And he talked to her only, it seemed, under duress, when he couldn't hold it in any longer. He was some twenty years younger than Al, and so he didn't seem so locked against himself, but he did seem impossible to save. She had discovered the limit of her powers with him—at most she could distract him from a little anxiety from time to time. At the worst, her presence gave him anxiety, and she became who neither of them could bear for her to become, a source of discomfort for him and a reason to get away.

What she learned about love was that it was impossible. What she learned about life was that it took more strength to survive the more you knew. What she learned about horses was that anything could happen, even after you cared. Before she had cared, she found this rather interesting. Now she found it frightening, and there was no remedy for it.

All of these thoughts crossed her mind in an instant when Dick entered her with a groan and she felt the usual surprise of his foreskin slipping back and all inside her turning to warm taffy. All of these thoughts intervened between his groan and her cry a moment later. Then all of these thoughts let her go, and she lost herself once again in the blackness of this illness, this love, this torment, this presence, this terror, this detonation. Oh my God, she said, Oh my God. Oh, my God.

Eileen came out from under the bed and stood alert, staring at Rosalind and vibrating her little stump of a tail back and forth. The cries on the bed increased, an awkward harmony to Eileen's ears. And then they stopped. Eileen turned and went over to the radiator and lifted her leg. She was a female. On the other hand, she was a female Jack Russell. So she lifted her leg.

Dick did what he often did when he was pretty sure Rosalind had fallen asleep. He turned his head and quietly looked at her. Maybe the thing was that she was the first blonde he had ever slept with. She had beautiful hair, thick, streaked honey and champagne, straight. Usually she wore it up. When it dropped, which always seemed like something that it did of itself rather than something she or he did to it, it fell down her back in a thick curtain. Her skin was of the same smoothness and paleness as her hair, and her eyes were pure blue. She generally wore pale colors, too, tawny buffs and beiges and taupes, down to her lace underwear. She did not show wear and tear of any sort. Had he not known how old she was (five years older than he was), he would never have been able to guess. Over the last weeks, perhaps because of this all-over blondeness and smoothness, he had found her an extremely restful person to be with. Everything she did, every gesture she made was measured, not, he thought, as a result of cerebration, but as a natural physical deliberateness. Even her smile was slow, even her sexual response was slow. Her sexual response had fascinated him in its contrast to Louisa's. All their life together, it had seemed that Louisa needed holding back. Making love to her was an act of splendid self-restraint—their charm was "not yet; not yet, not yet." Making it last until neither could bear it any longer was the challenge and the game. Making love to Rosalind was quite different. More often than not, he never knew exactly when the lovemaking started, where it was going, whether either one of them was aroused or not. Arousal slipped in unannounced and took them by surprise, or, rather, took him by surprise. Nothing seemed to take Rosalind by surprise. At first he had wondered when this slowness would turn into work, but it never had. Making love to Rosalind was like a long contemplation of something, as restful as she was. He had not thought this affair would last as long as it had, given the pummeling he got from his conscience, but he had been unable to give up this contemplation, though what he told himself was that she would get tired of him sooner or later, since he didn't give her much time or attention and the only thing he seemed able to do was complain about his job. And he had stopped going to his therapist.

Lately he often wondered whether he was getting through to Rosalind at all. Her natural calm seemed to have enlarged, and he figured that this was a sign she was getting bored with him. Perhaps, he sometimes thought, that would be a relief, though the things it would be a relief from, like secrecy and lies, he had fully incorporated into his daily routine. Certainly it would be a relief from the betrayal of Louisa, though, on the one hand, he had accustomed himself to betraying her, and on the other, the betrayal would still have taken place even after it ceased until some unknown date and mode of confession and penance, to which he did not look forward. He and Rosalind had never had an argument or even a conflict. Dick did not know what this meant, since it was a first in his life. Was the source of this her innate composure? Was it the sign of true love or the sign of true indifference? Was it the result of the infrequency of their meetings? Was it because he wanted to please her or she him? Life with Louisa and with horses had taught him that it was in conflict that you saw into the other. Without conflict, he felt he was seeing only a surface. At one point in the fall, he had been sitting with another owner and his wife, and Al and Rosalind had come up in conversation. The husband said, "I always think wheels within wheels when I see those two."

"Hardly one wheel," said the wife dismissively. "That woman has the least to say of anyone I ever met. All she is is good manners."

Dick found himself smarting on Rosalind's behalf remembering this remark, though he hadn't paid much attention at the time, but also wondering if what he saw in her was only something he himself made up. These were all issues he could discuss with his therapist, if he got up the guts to go back to him.

She opened her eyes. He rose up onto his elbow, eased the hair out of her face with his right hand, and said, "How are you?"

"Lovely, thanks." Only then did she turn to look at him. She regarded him for a moment, and he saw that she was beautiful, but there was something about her face that did not invite you to respond to her as a beauty. He thought, I am not man enough for this. Maybe that was why Rosalind was married to Al. Al was such an insensitive lout that he wouldn't be able to see Rosalind for what she was.

Al. Of course, Dick had feelings about Al, too, and they were not a credit to himself. Once he had seen Al as just another owner—a pushy know-it-all, like most owners, who had to be prevented from getting a copy of the condition book, but basically human. Now he saw Al as a brutish schlemiel who never did anything right. The way he stood offended Dick. The way he spoke offended Dick. The way he walked offended Dick. Even the way he always paid his bills on time offended Dick. And Dick gloried in being offended on Rosalind's behalf. In this, Dick felt his only kinship with Eileen. Dick knew enough to know that it was his own offense against Al that was offending him, but he let it wash over him anyway, raising his hackles. He said, "When do you have to go?"

"I have a while. Are you running anything tomorrow?"

"Two. One in the second and one in the sixth."

"I have to fly back to New York tomorrow. I have a dinner party to give Saturday night."

"Then I won't see you for a while."

"When is one of our horses running again?"

"There's a good race for Laurita a week from Saturday."

"We'll see, then."

It was these sorts of simple exchanges that Dick found so pleasant. Their voices were relaxed and accepting. The certainty of the future was a comfort. Horses might die between now and then, but this space would be here to return to, Rosalind would be radiating assurance, this room, like the other rooms in the condo she and Al had bought in Florida, would remain cool, bare, and cleanly Japanese in style.

Now Dick closed his eyes. He felt her put her hand on this shoulder and begin to stroke him there, from the shoulder along the side of his neck, up into his hair and down, around to his trapezius muscles, then down his biceps, back up his neck to his cheek, along his chin, down his throat, her whole palm slipping over him. He fell asleep.

Eileen jumped on the bed, walked up to the pillow, snaked her little nose under the covers, and squirreled down next to his belly, her rough coat against the hair on his chest.

After stroking Dick to sleep, Rosalind put her hand over her own face for a moment, then got up. She went into the bathroom and did her hair, then went into the closet and chose a wheat-colored linen dress, sand-colored shoes, and a coral necklace. She put off leaving the bathroom for as long as possible, because she was afraid of her last look at his face. Almost two weeks without seeing him was a vacuum that could well suck her right out of herself. But that was what she always thought, and somehow the time had passed before. She changed her shoes, to a darker color, then stepped across the bedroom and sat down on the bed. His eyes opened. They were hazel, almost green. She touched his lips with her thumb, then, as he watched, touched her thumb to her own lips. She said, because she dared not say anything more, "Thank you, darling." He nodded sleepily, and said, "I thought you had a while."

"I have to stop a couple of places on my way to dinner."

"Oh." She noted the disappointment in his voice. "Rosalind—"

But he paused. She hated that, when he paused. She knew he had something important to say to her. Part of the reason she was leaving was to avoid that, because she was so sure it would be that this couldn't go on. She put her hand to his lips to shush him, and he shushed. She held his glance for a minute or two. That was enough to fix his face in her mind. She nodded slightly then, telling herself to go, and she stood up. Next to his chest, Eileen roused, pressed herself against his skin, and then emerged. The last thing he heard Rosalind say was "Come on, Eileen. Come on, sweetie." The door closed behind her. Dick licked his lips and said what he hadn't had the courage to say in her presence, "I love you."

Out in the hall, waiting for the elevator with Eileen sitting at her feet, Rosalind remembered something she had been meaning to tell him, that she had come up with a name for that two-year-old. What it was, was a label for her love for him, Dick, though she would have been too reserved to tell him that part. It was "Limitless." Then she closed her eyes and wondered if she would have to do something dramatic and messy in the end.

16 / EPIC STEAM

WHEN HIS CELLULAR RANG and Dagoberto Gomez answered it, standing on the trainers' stand at Gulfstream and enjoying the sight of the palm trees swaying in the infield, it was Gordon Lane, the owner of Epic Steam, calling. He was a considerate man—he always called at 7:30 a.m. Eastern Standard Time, no matter what time it was where he was. Dagoberto had met him in person only once, about two and a half years ago, at the Keeneland September sale. The person Dagoberto usually dealt with concerning the man's yearling purchases was a bloodstock agent from England, Sir Michael Ordway. Dagoberto, as an exile from Castro's Cuba and a resident of Queens, felt that he had earned a dispensation in regard to sorting out the relative social positions of Mr. Gordon Lane and Sir Michael Ordway, toady extraordinaire. Once, his wife showed him a picture, in *Vanity Fair*, of Mrs. Gordon Lane, a princess of some sort, but Dagoberto had never seen her or the two daughters, also princesses. However, when contemplating the sirs and the princesses, Dagoberto sometimes felt the smallest ghost of a shadow of a momentary mote of sympathy with that shit of the twentieth century, Fidel Castro, and wondered if his chosen career of training racehorses wasn't just the littlest bit corrupt after all. He said, "Good morning, Mr. Lane. How are you this morning?"

Crackling from China, the purring silken Middle Eastern and Irish voice of Gordon Lane said, "Dagoberto, son, I hear this Epic Steam horse got his gate card."

"Yes, sir, he did. He's a tough, smart horse, I think."

"Good lad. What are your plans, son?" Although Mr. Gordon Lane always called Dagoberto "son," Dagoberto was probably some ten years older than the man. But, then, Gordon Lane, even on one meeting, exuded that air of mysterious and ancient corruption that necessarily came from a life of habitual secrecy.

Dagoberto looked across the track, where Epic Steam was working four furlongs with an A.P. Indy colt, and said, "He should be ready to run when he actually turns two, sir. That's in about two weeks. He's a monster."

"How much did we pay for him, Dagoberto?"

"Four hundred twenty-five thousand, sir."

"Worth that?"

"He's a forward animal, sir, but he's hard to handle. A bit treacherous."

"How does he like to run?"

"The boy has a hard time rating him, sir. But we don't know quite yet how he likes to run. I put my strongest boy on him." Sure enough, at the turn, Dagoberto could see Epic Steam pull away from the A.P. Indy colt, though the boy had been given strict instructions to keep even with the other colt. Then Epic Steam moved precipitously to the left, in front of the other colt, causing him to pull up all of a sudden and throw his head. Dagoberto frowned. You didn't like to see one colt hand a distressing moment to another colt like that. And then the boy, who had been instructed to gallop them out easily, was standing in his stirrups and raring back, and Epic Steam had his head down, trying to pull his rider out of the saddle. Other horses on the track scattered out of his way. This was the work of a moment. It was also the work of a moment that Dagoberto said to Mr. Gordon Lane, "Sir?"

"Yes, son."

"My, uh, instinct right now is to sell him."

"Barretts' two-year-olds-in-training sale?"

"Yes, sir."

"You're the boss, Dagoberto. Call Sir Michael, would you?"

"Yes, sir."

They hung up.

Dagoberto couldn't quite believe that he had just gotten rid of his most promising runner and maturest two-year-old. Ten minutes ago he had been watching the horse and planning his first race, thinking idly about the animal's whole two-year-old season, which seemed to lay upon a table before him, six or seven wins, plums to be picked one by one out of a bowl and put into a basket he was carrying. The horse was as classy and talented and healthy as any horse Dagoberto had ever seen.

Epic Steam came around in front of him and he called down from the trainers' stand, "What was that, Jonas?"

"He nearly pulled my arms out of the sockets."

Jonas, who rode in tank tops here in Florida because of the heat, had the biggest shoulders on the track. The muscles fanned down from his neck over his back, and his shoulders and biceps bulged like grapefruits in a sack. But the muscles in the horse's neck and shoulders were smoother and stronger. And he was not a horse who seemed to feel pain.

Dagoberto put his cellular back in his pocket. The A.P. Indy colt and his rider trotted below them. Dagoberto called out, "I saw that. Your colt okay?"

"He din like it, boss. I tell you, he ain no pussy, this boy, but that black one makes him nervous. When we was standin' in the gate, this boy, he wan to push himself over away from that one, and he watchin' him the whole time."

"We won't train them together again, then."

Epic Steam was a hot walker's nightmare. While he was being bathed, he tried to bite at the streams of water running down his chest. He pawed and struck out with his hooves, he jumped around. You had to run the chain of the shank under his lip, over his gum, and hold it tight, and you also had to have your elbow at the ready to pop him in the face if he tried to bite you. Only Rosalba was strong enough and calm enough and tall enough to handle him. As for Epic Steam, he respected Rosalba just a little bit, because once in a while, when he was pursuing his own agenda with special fervor, she would grab his ear and twist it hard until he had to put his head down. She was tricky about it. She didn't do it very often, and always when he wasn't expecting it. Her hand shot out quick as a snake and grabbed it. It was for this reason that he wasn't really headshy, and so no one, least of all Dagoberto, realized that he was being treated in this way. As for Rosalba, she thought the horse needed more of the same. When a horse came to the track, it was already bigger and often faster than you were, but it didn't know that yet. You had about a month to get in there and confirm the horse's opinion of your power and his weakness. This Epic Steam was a very good example. He didn't give Rosalba one bit of trouble. He had a healthy fear of her, even though he didn't like her. But there was too much talk about that kind of stuff in Rosalba's opinion anyway. The world didn't run on liking and disliking. It ran on everybody knowing who was the boss. With Epic Steam, she was the boss. It was as simple as that.

But Epic Steam did not live in a world of liking. Since no one had ever liked him, he didn't know what liking was. He was rarely, perhaps never, stroked. His groom, the one who would normally stroke him, talk to him, and give him carrots, was afraid of him. He kept Epic Steam's stall scrupulously clean, wrapped him with care in his night bandages, and did everything by the book. Lots of the time, if he was going to have his back to the horse for more than a moment, he got Rosalba to hold the animal for him. But in the end, he felt guilty about how he treated Epic Steam, and so he stayed away from him even more, hardly even looked at him or said anything to him in the course of the day. From the way the horse looked, that was fine with him. He never offered himself to you the way most horses did, and he was studdish, to boot, which was an annoyance on its way to being a problem. He whinnied at fillies all day and pounded around his stall if a filly in heat passed by. Most colts got used to coeducation if quarters weren't too close and a trainer took some precautions, but Epic Steam did not. When Dagoberto told everyone the colt was leaving in a few weeks for California, there was prospective relief at the end of all the noise.

Rosalba was personally of the opinion that they ought to geld the animal and get it over with.

Epic Steam's groom was of the personal opinion that they ought to geld the animal and get it over with.

Jonas was of the personal opinion that the horse was already so strong in the neck and shoulders that if they didn't geld him he would become unridable.

Dagoberto thought he might have suggested to the world-traveling and unreachable owner that the horse be gelded, but now he was going to be sold. A horse with his breeding and talent would get tens of thousands, maybe hundreds of thousands less at a sale as a gelding than as a colt.

Well, everyone thought, they only had to put up with him for a while longer. That was a relief.

It could not be said that Epic Steam, standing in his stall, neatly wrapped for the night, spotlessly clean, and strikingly beautiful, had all that many intentions. Yes, he was a monumental hassle from the moment the groom got to him first thing in the morning until everyone was happy to dispense with him for another twenty-two hours. But he didn't exactly mean to be a jerk. That was the way he knew how to express himself. In fact, now that he was at the track, he was happier than he had been ever in his short life. Without knowing what a track was, he had known when he set foot on it that he was right where he should be. He loved to run. He expressed his love of running by rearing, bucking, bolting, veering to the left or right whenever his rider tried to rate him. He thought maybe if he got rid of the rider he would be able to run in his own way and for his own purposes. It was clear to him that the purpose of running, as of everything else in life, was to make contact with fillies. Fillies gave off a loud and clear signal that they were waiting for him and that the other colts on the track were very much in the way. It was his job as a colt to get those other colts out of the way, even though plenty of them were older and more experienced and tried to demonstrate to him that they were in charge. Mornings out on the track were, for Epic Steam, a gauntlet of challenges by older colts. Almost all of the older colts and the fillies, too, knew plenty that Epic Steam did not know—they had been in races, knew about running, strategizing, winning, knew about being cared for, liking others, and being liked. They lived in a social world of humans and horses. Epic Steam, in this context, was a primitive and a brute. He was not truly crazy, as his sire was, but the rumors drawing a genetic connection between the two of them were in every mouth. Epic Steam was getting famous around the track already, and he hadn't even run in a race. As he stood munching hay in his stall, was he nursing his grievances and getting ready to make trouble? Everyone thought so.

He was doomed to get bigger than life, doomed to be discussed and exaggerated about, doomed to live up to his fate, or so it seemed.

17 / SCHOOL'S IN

THE TRAINING FACILITIES at Tompkins Ranch California Headquarters—Central Valley Complex, Worldwide Racing and Breeding, The Finest Thoroughbreds, which were located five miles down the highway, past the resort and the restaurant and across the road from the almond and apricot orchards, did not allude, in their architecture, to England, Ireland, France, or

Kentucky; that is, the buildings were not elegant, or mossy, or old-looking. They could have done that—the Tompkinses could import and pay for anything, even the sort of drippy, misty moisture you needed for mildew and eternal damp—but the architect they'd hired in the thirties had done his last work at a grocery-store/movie-house/department-store complex in Hollywood, and saw everything in terms of the Baghdad/Mecca/Culver City axis, so the training facility had tiles, fountains, and flowers; domes and pendentives distributed along the length of the roof of the barn; a minaret growing out of the hay-storage facility. The windows of the large-equipment shed were domed and pointed and outlined with mosaic pictures of small boys in turbans. The horses in training were groomed and saddled in a garden courtyard before being led to the training track under an arch that sported a faded mural of Bedouins galloping their Arabian mounts across the sands. It was here that Froney's Sis was transported, along with four of the other forty-two two-year-olds still belonging to the ranch, when she was brought back into training after two months out in pasture, on the first of February.

She was put in a stall. Froney's Sis had been in a stall the last time she was here, but she was otherwise accustomed to a large, sunny, irrigated pasture with only some tin-roofed sheds for shade. She was accustomed, as well, to the constant physical companionship of other fillies, who bumped her, nudged her, groomed her neck and withers, bit her, kicked her, and in general told her every minute of the day and night what she was supposed to be doing. In her new accommodations, she could see one filly on one side, one filly on the other, and several colts and fillies across the way, but the most she could do to touch them was to stick her upper lip through the bars between them. Her relationships, which had been endlessly palpable, had suddenly gotten abstract. And so Froney's Sis paced her stall. Her groom noticed it the first night and the second night and the third night, after all the other fillies and colts had begun to settle. Back and forth, back and forth, from one front corner to the other, turn right, turn left. The other youngsters ate up their hay with contemplative gusto, but Froney's Sis left much of her hay and most of her grain. By day four, she had lost, Jack Perkins estimated, fifty pounds. "She's still a worrier," he said.

Nor were her daily lessons going well. The horses came out in a group. The first day, all he did was lead them around the Moorish complex, showing them the hydrangeas and the bougainvillea and the roses, the fountains and the gravel paths. They were led around the large-equipment storage shed and allowed to snort at the John Deeres inside. They were led out to the training track. When they snorted and reared and backed away, their handlers followed them with soothing words. The older horses, called "ponies," there for reassurance, looked on without interest. Each session on the first day took about an hour. Froney's Sis's first session took two hours and tried everyone's patience, including that of the pony, an old paint horse who began to pin his ears at her approach. Finally, though, she managed to make trembling progress from fountain to garden to shed to training track to garden to fountain. At the end she was so covered in sweat that she had to be bathed, which, fortunately, she was too tired to mind.

The next day, when the other youngsters were progressing to a pleasant stroll around the perimeter of the training track, Froney's Sis had to repeat her lesson of the day before with another, more gracious pony. At the end of that day, the trainer had consigned her, in his mind, to the slow-learners group. Orphans were sometimes like that. He could count on one hand the orphans he'd had that made racehorses. Somehow, they just seemed to have less sense than other horses.

Still, though the filly's progress was slow, for seven days or so, it was steady. She was not an ill-disposed filly. She seemed to like her groom. She stood for bathing, picked her feet up nicely. She never pinned her ears or got irritated. She was just nervous, or confused, or both. New experiences seemed to do her in. On day eight, the groom brought her out, stood her next to the pony, and placed a light racing saddle on her back. Then he went around to the left, pulled the girth underneath her chest, and buckled it on the first hole. She stood still. The groom looked at his assistant, who looked back at him, then tightened the girth one more hole. The filly stood still. The groom smiled. The third hole was the charm. The worst thing that could happen would be for the saddle to slip around the filly's barrel and get under her legs. At the third hole, it would be tight enough not to do that. He gently pulled up the girth, and got one buckle into the third hole. The filly stood still, and the groom thought he was home free. He began tightening the other buckle. Normal procedure, normal reactions. Everyone felt hopeful.

The filly fell down as if she had been cold-cocked.

The pony jumped back two steps.

The groom's assistant ran for the trainer.

The four of them, groom, trainer, groom's assistant, pony, stood around the filly in a circle, regarding her. The groom's assistant thought she was dead. The groom thought she was a pain in the ass. The trainer thought she was too complicated for a man whose heart was no longer really in his work, now that he had taken up golf as a sideline avocation and had a two-sixteen tee time on the resort course. The pony could not remember ever making such a big deal of anything as this filly made of everything.

The groom's assistant said, "You want me to throw water on her or something?"

"We can wait her out."

The pony gave an eloquent grunt.

She came to, bucking.

The groom kept firm hold of her and followed her backward, sideways, forward, sideways again, backward again. She bucked as if born to do it, twisting her head from side to side, kicking forward and backward, rearing, humping her back. The three other yearlings and their handlers had scattered at the first buck, and now watched her from the barn entrances, as did the trainer. The groom, he thought, was handling her nicely. He was a young Mexican boy, about twenty-five. He was utterly impassive, as if the bucking were not even taking place. That was just the sort of attitude the trainer liked to see in a horseman. Horses, especially young horses, were exquisite receivers of emotional signals. A good horseman had to have feet of lead, hands of silk, and the temperament of a sandbag, in the trainer's opinion. He didn't even like to see the handler talk soothingly to a horse in a state. If you talked soothingly to a horse in a state, then the horse concluded that his state was justified.

At last, the filly came down on all four trembling legs and stayed there. She was still in a funny posture, shrunk in on herself as if she could make a space between her skin and the saddle, but she was standing still, maybe too tired to move. The groom stepped toward her and stood by her head. After a moment, he began stroking her around the eyes. She was covered with sweat. The groom looked at the trainer, who nodded and made a gesture that he should lead her forward, which he did. She took a step or two, stopped, humped her back, then took another step and another step and another step. After about ten steps, she relaxed her back, shivered once, and then walked forward more agreeably. As soon as she had done so for maybe a minute, the trainer held up his hand, the groom stopped the filly, and between the three of them, with the pony standing right there, quickly ungirthed and removed the offending slip of leather. The groom took the filly off and gave her a bath.

IT WAS WELL AFTER DARK the same day, and Joy Gorham was driving Elizabeth Zada to the ranch. Elizabeth Zada was the largest woman Joy had ever known—six feet tall, anyway, and 175 pounds for sure. It was reassuring for Joy to be in Elizabeth's orbit, because of her Paul Bunyan quality. Large objects, Joy thought, like renegade space stations, could fall from the sky, and Elizabeth would deflect them without stanching her conversational flow. Elizabeth's conversational flow was prodigious. Elizabeth was sixty years old. Right now she was discoursing about her sexuality.

"You see, when you have an orgasm, it's an outward flow of energy. Just dissipated, gone. You can't afford that. I realized years ago, even before I began my studies of this, that after a certain age, which turns out to be twenty-four, actually, you dissipate that energy and you have less. You have to keep that energy within yourself, so that it builds up."

Joy, who was driving her truck, shifted on her seat cushion, thinking of a pressure cooker, its little gauge rattling and knocking.

"And then it goes out through your head."

"Pardon me?"

"Well, it goes out through your head. The top of your head. You see, there's an energy space there, where spiritual energy shoots upward toward the Godhead. Personally, I always think of a baby's fontanel. You want that fontanel back. It closes over in the first year as the baby separates from the Godhead, but later on, through meditation, you open it. But that's my own thought. There's nothing about that in any of the teachings that I've read. All this other stuff, though, it's well attested."

Joy, a trained scientist, knew better than to ask by whom.

"At any rate, here you have this sexual energy in your lower self. You contain it, move it upward through your spine—there's a pathway there, you know, a narrow channel—then it blossoms in your head, you might say, and then, whoosh, out it goes. Lovely feeling, I must say." She cleared her throat. "My goodness, I haven't been around a horse in so long. Five years anyway. But thank you."

How it happened that she and Elizabeth Zada were driving to the ranch after dark was that Joy had been at her dentist's office having a filling replaced, and the hygienist had brought this loud woman into the room and had said to Joy, "Elizabeth here is looking to read some horses' minds. No kidding. I saw that you work out at the ranch." And before she knew it, Elizabeth had overwhelmed her reserve and taken her out to dinner, and started talking and kept talking, and here they were.

Joy said, "I feel like I haven't been around anything else. When I think of the people, they seem like they're on TV or something, even Mr. Tompkins, especially Mr. Tompkins, but when I think of the horses, they seem like they're all in the room. The thing about horses is, they're always right there with you." Joy made the last turn to the back entrance of the farm. It was nearly eight. She said, "There's about a mile to go."

"Men are *not* responsible for your orgasm. That's a trap we fall into, especially in marriage. I know I did. For years I complained to Nathan Zada that his technique was off. You know, touch me higher, touch me lower, be more tender, be more masterful, be someone else, for God's sake! Who am I, the princess Elizabeth, to be stuck with you, Nathan Zada, a mere furrier? Poor Nathan, may he rest in peace."

"Is your husband dead?"

"Oh, my goodness, no. He left me for a florist. They live in Arizona now."

"Oh."

"I meant, may he rest in peace after he dies in that burning car crash on the highway." Elizabeth laughed a big laugh, and they pulled through the back gate of the farm and turned toward the stallion area, where Mr. T. now resided. One of the stallions had been sold, and so Mr. T. got an eyeful every day, an eyeful of mares walking by, to the breeding shed, an eyeful of stallions capering and prancing and showing off. Even though he was a gelding, he did a little capering and showing off himself. Joy wasn't sure it was the best place for him, but the paddock he lived in had good, expensively irrigated grass all year round, and he had improved his condition in only a few weeks. He still needed about a hundred pounds, but he was a different horse from the one he had been in Texas. Everyone who saw him thought he was one of the stallions—proximity fooled them—but to Joy he was the absolute model of that most useful of equines, a gelding. The difference was in his neck. Testosterone always thickened a stallion's neck, made it heavy and cresty. Mr. T.'s neck was refined, so that when he was too thin he looked ewe-necked. But when she put him together, or when of himself he trotted around his paddock with his ears up and his neck arched, it made just the right curve, tapering upward out of his shoulders, tucking delicately into his throatlatch. He was light and athletic, the sort of pure working organism that only a horse without reproductive urges could be.

Joy parked the truck and she could see him, a white blur in the darkness. He lifted his head from the grass and walked over to the gate, ears pricked. The other paddocks were empty, because the stallions got put in for the night. As soon as she got out of the truck, he greeted her and she heard the gate creak as he pressed his weight against it. He drew her toward him, that's what it always felt like, whether out of friendship or beauty or something more basic. She loved the old guy. She bragged about him until the others she worked with rolled their eyes at her, but look at him, she thought. She had investigated his pedigree, for example, and discovered that he was inbred to St. Simon, the greatest horse of the nineteenth century, about whom the book she read claimed, "Having no faults, he passed none on." When she looked at the painting of St. Simon, there was Mr. T., his head black instead of white, staring back at her. Joy was as proud of that classic head as if it were her own. She was proud of his tendons, too. They had tried a pasture buddy, a pony from the track who was laid up, but on the second day, he had bitten Mr. T. below the hock. When the vet ultrasounded Mr. T.'s tendon, she said, "How many starts did you say this guy had?"

"Fifty-two."

"Amazing," said the vet. "What does he do now?"

"A little hacking out so far."

The vet shook her head. "Normally, I don't see tendons like this on a race-horse after they're about three years old." She might as well have said, "Your child is a genius and we know that the DNA comes directly from you."

"This," said Joy to Elizabeth, who had been talking the whole time Joy was contemplating Mr. T., but whom Joy had not heard, "is the horse I was telling you about. You could start here."

"What's his name?"

"Mr. T."

"Hmmm," said Elizabeth.

This is what Joy had brought Elizabeth out to the farm for, and late, too, in the dark, after all the others were gone. Elizabeth had explained to Joy at dinner that her ability to communicate with animals was tied to her awakened sexuality, and both had come on late in life, after menopause, but, after hearing the words "animal communicator," Joy had lost the thread of the argument, as she lost the thread of arguments about sexuality. Elizabeth was not to be denied, however, and here they were.

"Now," said Elizabeth, "I'm more accustomed to communicating with predators, whose thought patterns and sensory patterns are more or less similar to ours. But there are so few of them. I thought I would try horses because it's a larger sample population."

Mr. T. stood between them, thoroughly alert. First he looked at Joy, then he looked at Elizabeth. Actually, thought Joy, if I believed in this, I would think that he looks ready to talk. She patted him on the neck, but he moved away from her hand. "Hmmm," said Elizabeth. "Let's go inside. Can we do that?"

Joy opened the gate and followed Elizabeth into the enclosure. Mr. T. placed himself between them. After a moment, he bumped Elizabeth on the chest. Joy thought that was interesting, because normally he wasn't a very physical horse and he liked his personal space. Then he bumped Joy on the chest. Elizabeth said, "He's streaming."

"What's that?"

"It's a flow of images. I don't really understand what they mean, because I don't know anything about horses, frankly."

She squatted down, her hand on the fence for balance. Mr. T. lowered his head toward her. Joy said, "Does he want anything?"

"He wants something large and red. Like a brick, a big brick."

"That would be a mineral lick. He has one of those."

"Well, maybe he wants another one."

"Is he cold? Does he want a blanket? The other horses get to go in at night."

"No, he likes it. The cold is refreshing."

"How does he say that?"

"He streams me an image of rolling in the mud and jumping up and kicking his heels up."

"He does like to roll."

"I don't think he's cold."

"Who does he like? Does he like any of the other horses?"

"He likes you."

Joy flushed. It was amazing how this thrilled her, especially since she knew that he liked her already, from his attachment behaviors.

"Is there another gray horse around, one he can see?"

"There's a gray stallion, two paddocks over. He's only a four-year-old. He came off the track in December."

"Is he injured?"

"He bowed a tendon. They're going to breed him a little bit, then try sending him back to the races in the fall."

"Right front?"

"Yes."

"Mr. T. says this is a very fine animal in his opinion. He has a big heart."

"Like he's loving, or like he literally has a large heart?"

"I don't know, it's the image of a large hot thing inside the horse's chest."

"He is a wonderfully bred horse. He's got Mahmoud and Blue Larkspur and War Admiral on his bottom side."

"I don't know what that means."

"It means he probably has an extra-large heart for a horse."

"Mr. T. likes him. The others he can take or leave. He doesn't like one very dark-colored horse with a bright-white stripe on his face from about the eye to about halfway down the nose."

"That's Halo Highlights. He bit off his groom's finger two years ago. But he isn't that bad."

"Mr. T. says he would like to be."

"How does he say that?"

"I just see a dark horse making his head shake and doing something with his ears. Mr. T. says that he is sneaky and he wants you to stay away from the horse."

"I do."

"Mr. T. knows that if something happened to you he would go to a place."

"What place?"

"I see a flat, hot arena or something like that, with lots of horses packed together and no shade. A man with a whip keeps coming in the gate."

"Bucky Lord."

"Who?"

"Mr. T.'s former owner. He starved them."

"He also beat them, Mr. T. says."

Joy, who had intended to remain skeptical, believed every word, even though she had been to fortune-tellers before, and knew that they gave you what you wanted right away so you would lower your defenses. She said, "Does he have any aches and pains?"

Elizabeth was silent for a moment, then said, "No."

"Does he want anything?"

"He wants to open the paddock gate and go out and walk around the farm and look at everything."

"I've seen him working at his gate latch, actually." Joy was beginning to feel that it was too much, that the inside of the horse's mind was overwhelming her, even making her faint. Elizabeth spoke contemplatively. She said, "Now, remember, I haven't done horses at all, so I don't know how sensitive I am to them, but Mr. T. seems very cerebral. He looks around and watches things. He feels anxious a lot of the time, because he fears what might happen. He gave me an image of a mare walking toward the breeding shed. He said that her mind was blank, as if she were in shock. It made him afraid."

"A mare reared up and fell down last week, and then the stallion bit her. It was quite a to-do."

"Could be the same one."

Joy was sure it was.

"What time is it?" said Elizabeth. "I'm exhausted."

"It's about nine."

As they drove home, Joy could not stop feeling that a veil had been lifted between herself and the horses, and a not very thick veil, at that. It gave her a chill, and yet it seemed so simple and obvious. Why not? Why not, indeed?

NOW A VERY IMPORTANT stallion came in from Kentucky. He was fourteen years old. He had won the Preakness and the Jockey Club Gold Cup and the Santa Anita Handicap. He had produced several good stakes winners over the years and had plenty of excuses for not producing more. Within a week of the news that he was moving to California, his book was full—eighty mares at five thousand dollars a pop. Mr. Tompkins told Joy by e-mail (Mr. Tompkins loved to e-mail her from across the office and then sit there with his dusty cowboy boots up on the desk and watch her read it, a bona-fide miracle of modern technology) that Jack, over at the training complex, would be expecting Mr. T. He could pony in the morning and she could ride him in the afternoon. She turned in her seat to nod, and he said, "No! No! E-mail me!" So she e-mailed him that she would trailer the horse down there that afternoon. "Great! Thank you!" he e-mailed back to her.

And that was how Mr. T. became Froney's Sis's regular pony, and the filly's training began to move along at a faster pace once Mr. T.'s participation became routine. For one thing, everything that a man could in good or bad conscience do to a horse was old hat to him. Saddling, bridling, longlining, sacking out with a bag on a pole, the weight of an arm across her back, the weight of an arm and a shoulder, the weight of a chest, the weight of a rider. The filly trembled. Braced her legs. Passed through panic and came out on the other side, where Mr. T. was standing calmly, one hind leg cocked in relaxation.

They taught her to pony, to walk along beside him, led by his rider, and discovered that Mr. T. was strict about ponying. He didn't like her head to get past his shoulder, but he didn't like her to lag behind, either. When she misbehaved, he pinned his ears and wrinkled his mouth at her and kept going. She elected to go along. And he was big where she was small. It seemed to Jack that she took some sort of reassurance in the gelding's grand proximity. Jack saw the whole thing as a typical male-female relationship—the gelding had wide-ranging interests and concerns, the filly only had eyes for the gelding; his accommodation of her was rather impersonal, an expression of his natural character, but she took every attention personally, and, frankly, she blossomed. She was still immature, compared with the others, but toward the first of March, she was beginning to function as a racehorse.

Joy came every day after her own work was done, lugging her dressage saddle. All the horses were put away by this time, and Jack let her work the old horse in the infield of the exercise track. Once in a while he watched her. He'd seen dressage before. He didn't think much of it, at least for Thoroughbreds.

One day, he made himself some work and lingered until Joy brought the old horse back into the courtyard. That leisurely chock-chock on the gravel was a sound Jack especially liked, the rhythmical accompaniment of his entire adult life, and he fancied that he could hear a good mover as well as see one—four solid, distinct, even beats in which the horse sounded his relaxation and self-confidence. Mr. T. came chock-chock-chock-chock across the gravel, Joy stopped him and pulled off his saddle, and Jack said, "You should gallop him around the track every week or so, as long as he's over here."

"Good Lord, Jack, he's eighteen years old. He's just coming back from starvation."

"Do him good. That dressage business is stiffening him up."

"Dressage supples them. It makes them lengthen their topline and come under."

"How many starts did you say he had?"

"Fifty-two."

"You gallop him. Slowly, to start. He'll like it, and it'll get all those fluids moving around in his body, clean him out."

Joy smiled a little private smile. This idea sounded very much like something her grandmother would have said. But she said, "I can't, anyway. I sold my jumping saddle. Galloping is awkward in a dressage saddle."

"Use an exercise saddle."

They looked across the courtyard at the pieces of nothing that were holding stirrups together on the saddle racks. Joy shook her head. "If you think he needs to gallop, okay, but someone else can do it."

"You've never done it?"

Joy shook her head. Jack caught her gaze, and in his face she saw, even though the thought was not actually in his head, a judgment, "What kind of horseman are you?"

She said, "You show me, then."

"I will. That old guy's a good one to learn on. He's big and steady and experienced and he doesn't want to fall down. You'll have fun."

Joy glanced at Mr. T., standing beside her, grinding his teeth, acting for all the world as if he hadn't heard a word of this conversation.

The next afternoon, Jack himself hoisted her up onto the little slip of leather that had been girthed over Mr. T.'s back. She put her feet in the stirrups to about her big toe. Her knees were in her throat, along with her heart. The groom led Mr. T. into a walk, and Joy felt like she was swaying from side to side on a moving fence rail. For maybe the first time in twenty years, she grabbed mane. A ripple of fear ran up out of her chest and into the back of her neck, but then some pictures of jockeys came into her mind. When she folded herself up as they would, she felt more secure. The groom led her across the grass and onto the training track. Jack was standing at the rail already, a big grin on his face. He said, "Just nestle in there, stay over his center of gravity, and let him balance you. If you're right in the center, and make yourself small enough, the faster he goes, the more secure you'll feel. It's the gyroscope effect."

Mr. T. was clearly intrigued by this new development. He flicked his ears back and forth and took big, happy strides. She saw that several of the grooms and exercise boys were now drawn up along the rail. She hoped it was only to see the old horse perform, not to see the old girl bite the dust. Of his own accord, Mr. T. lifted himself into a big trot, launching her with every stride into a high post. She fitted her hands around the wide rubber reins, and took stronger hold. The horse tucked his chin, not objecting, but taking stronger hold of her. It made her feel like the back of her head was connected to his jaw by a wire that both held her in place and vibrated with information. She trotted once around the track and came up to Jack again. He said, "Now, this guy isn't much in condition, but you can't weigh more than ninety pounds. Pick up a little canter here, canter slowly to halfway around, then chirp him into a gallop. When you come around to me again, bridge your reins, put your hands up on his neck, curl up, and let him do what he wants to do. He'll probably change leads and really take hold. Don't lose your reins when he does that, and don't fight him. He's going to use you a little bit to keep his balance. He has to do that to compensate for your weight on his back. When he starts to tire and seems to give you something, just bring him down."

Yeah, thought Joy, we'll see. She loosened her grip a bit and he moved up into a canter. Her plan, as opposed to Jack's, was just to canter pleasantly around the track and try this galloping thing another time. But the canter was sweet—she didn't rock with it; it seemed to rock beneath her, floating her along like a flea on the horse's neck. Coming around the turn, she most assuredly did not chirp, but he moved smoothly into second gear anyway, and after two or three strides, she thought she could feel the quick four beats of the gallop beneath her. She said, "Hey!" The horse seemed to elongate and get lower somehow. Her eyes were tearing and her ears seemed filled with blank sound. She said, "Whoa!" But he did not whoa. Old and ill-conditioned as he was, he moved forward smoothly and there was no holding him. She got back to Jack significantly faster than she had gotten away from him. As she passed him, noting his grin that looked like a smear, she bridged the reins. Immediately, Mr. T. braced himself against her hands and arms and shoulders, so that she had to press her fists into his neck. If she hadn't been right with him, he would have bounded out from under her. But she was right with him. He seemed to fill her with power as he sped up, power that ran from her toes and her hands to the center of her body and gathered there, giving her the strength and the balance to be still. He was running as fast as any runaway she had ever ridden, but she got no sense that he didn't know what he was doing—exactly the opposite, in fact. He knew where every foot was, because he put it there. Her hearing and sight were useless now—her eyes were entirely blurred and all she could hear was her own voice, making a sound that wasn't speech and wasn't moaning. They went some distance. She could not have said how far. He seemed to surge with each stride, so that she gave up the idea of checking or holding him, and then the surging dropped off, and then her body knew that he had spent himself and was ready to come back to the trot. When they had done so, she realized that she was trembling all over as if she had lifted a huge weight and exhausted herself. By the time they were walking, she was ready to fall off.

"How'd ya like it?" called Jack.

"I don't know," she called back. "I need a nap!"

His laugh rang out.

Mr. T. did not need a nap. No one who fulfills a long-standing passion to be once again a long-legged colt, flowing with movement and energy, needs a nap, at least not until the next day, when the aches and pains set in, and you can barely hobble around your own personal Arabian-fantasy domain and even the precious-as-emeralds-and-rubies irrigated grass doesn't look quite as good as a quiet doze in the shade.

MARCH

18 / TWO-YEAR-OLDS
IN TRAINING

I F BUDDY CRAWFORD had thought regular life at the track was a life of stress and pressure, and he had (Who else had the sleep problems he did, he would like to know? Who else had the bowel problems, for that matter? Pressure twenty-four hours a day and seven days a week, that had been his life for thirty years and he wasn't complaining, though maybe it didn't suit him. He often thought that being a professor at a college or something like that would have suited him better—he had this cousin who read books all day and took some notes and he lived a good life though he wasn't physically fit. Kind of fat. Really fat, actually. But maybe that was a decent trade-off. Sometimes over the years he had thought about that in a sort of wishful way, when the pressure really got bad, but of course it was too late for that), then let's talk about the new life.

Talk about pressure. Running two-year-olds was pressure, always had been. If you adhered to his culling theory, then the two-year-olds were the base of the pyramid. A whole lot of them came in, then a whole lot of them went their way, and what you were left with was the three-year-olds who had survived being two-year-olds. The kind of pressure he was under now, though, pressure supplied by Jesus himself, was a new kind of pressure. The thing about Jesus was that he laid down the rules, but you had to figure out how to abide by them yourself. Or, as Buddy's father used to tell him, "I just say 'em, I don't explain 'em." Jesus did not allow you to run a two-year-old whose growth plates hadn't closed. Jesus didn't allow you to run an unfit horse. Jesus didn't allow any toegrabs or turndowns. Jesus didn't allow you even to think about buzzing the horse's neck with a hot electrical device to remind him that he hadn't arrived at the finish line yet. What Jesus liked, Buddy quickly discovered, was a fair race—no gimmicks, no drugs, no subtle interference on the part of jockeys. No trying to evade the rules. And the thing about Jesus, as everyone who had ever been to Sunday school knew, was that, unlike track officials, he couldn't be fooled. Jesus saw every minute of every race as if his eyes were a million video cameras, shooting from every angle.

Add that to running maidens and see what you get. Buddy's horse Elijah was making his first start, and he wasn't the only one in the race. Out of seven horses, three had never been in a race before, and one had only run once. The jockeys were terrified. Buddy's own jockey, experienced as he was (every limb broken twice, skull fracture, broken nose, punctured spleen, cracked ribs), whitened as Buddy told him something he would never have told a jockey in the old days, that the horse lugged to the right and was a little clumsy. "We'll give him a chance," Buddy said. "Everyone deserves a chance." The jockey looked at him, "Why?" expressed clearly in his eyes.

They loaded. You could thank Jesus for that. While they were loaded, you couldn't see them very well, and you could thank Jesus for that. Then the bell rang and the gate opened, and the chaos began. Three jumped right out, two were a stride behind, one was a stride behind that one, and the last lonely fellow let the others get a hundred yards away before his jockey managed to whip him into the race. Then he stopped dead. Buddy shifted his gaze to the field, through his binoculars. Elijah was in front of one other colt, who had that startled look of a horse getting dirt in his face for the first time. Right as Buddy was noticing that, Elijah took off, first to the right and then to the left. If the last horse had been within twenty lengths, he would have gotten cut off, but that one had thrown in the towel and was barely cantering. Only the first horse wasn't weaving. Behind him, Elijah was now caught in a traffic jam that looked very much like four scared children clinging together for solace. They crossed the finish line in a photo, and one by one straggled and stumbled down to a trot. No one hurt. Thank Jesus for that. Elijah on the board for a little bit of money. Thank Jesus for that. And Buddy Crawford saw that he was out of the starting gate, too, on his new life within his old life. His hands were shaking. He hadn't won, thank Jesus for that, because one of the things he had to get used to was being a loser. Jesus himself had said that, as hard as it was for a camel to get through the eye of a needle, it was even harder for a trainer with a 25-percent win ratio to get into heaven.

And then, about two weeks before the Barretts' two-year-olds-in-training sale, Buddy got a call from an old acquaintance of his, Sir Michael Ordway. Sir Michael's plummy accent always used to get Buddy's goat, but now he was in such a state of confusion that its very familiarity was reassuring, and he couldn't quite believe how pleased he was to hear from the horse agent. Sir Michael was most pleased to be speaking to Buddy, too, and this gave Buddy the sense that perhaps you could even say that they were friends. Maybe they'd always been friends, and Buddy simply hadn't noticed? Anyway, Sir Michael got right down to business. "Buddy, lad," he said. "Remember that mare Pure Money? She produced Pure Profit and that filly that went to Argentina, Pacifier?"

Buddy remembered all three of them quite well, as who did not? But Sir Michael was fussy in his way of talking, like all Brits.

"You know she's got a two-year-old by Land of Magic. You remember him?"

Land of Magic had beaten Buddy's big horse, Magnesium, three times that year. It had been a mini-version of one of those famous rivalries. It had burned Buddy up, to be frank.

"He's hip number ten at the Barretts' sale."

"What did they pay for him as a yearling?"

"Four hundred twenty-five thousand."

"How's he training?"

"Superbly."

"Who's training him?"

"Dagoberto Gomez."

"I bet I saw that colt at Keeneland. Nice colt."

"He's a speed horse. A California sort of horse."

"You think?"

"He belongs to me now, and I have a potential owner in mind."

Buddy's interest perked up. Sir Michael hadn't included him in one of his scams for a couple of years. "Does he own any horses at the moment?"

"A computer-software company, a cellular-phone company, several hotels in Canada, a minor-league baseball team, and the wife has several clothing companies with factories in China, but horses, no."

"Age?" said Buddy.

"Forty-eight."

"You the seller's agent?"

"Indeed."

"Who's the buyer's agent?"

"Dermot Callaghan." One of Sir Michael's very oldest cronies.

"Where does the guy live?"

"La Jolla. San Jose. Lake Tahoe. I believe he has a house on Kauai. You understand." Yes, Buddy understood. The golden apples were waiting. The golden-apple tree only needed a good shaking.

"Wife?"

"Hates all animals until they've been skinned, tanned, and made into garments, furniture, and bed coverlets. Third wife. A bit of a young thing, don't you know. But they're thinking of going into horse racing in a big way. My wife met them at a party. They allowed as how they do everything in a big way. A point of pride for them. She told them I knew several reliable West Coast trainers." Michael's wife, Lady Ordway, went to a lot of parties. Although she was a lady, she never minded talking to anyone with scads and scads of discretionary income.

"Well, I'm here," said Buddy.

"Very good," said Sir Michael.

Buddy set down the phone and looked straight ahead, at the wall, remembering his conscience for the first time since hearing Sir Michael's voice. No writing appeared there, though, nor did any qualms appear in his conscience. Jesus was keeping his mouth shut on this one.

Sure enough, the next morning, while Buddy was reading the faxes from Golden Gate about how his horses worked that morning, the phone rang, and a loud voice introduced itself as Jason Clark Kingston. You couldn't pick up a paper in California without seeing the name of Jason Clark Kingston, and the picture, too. He was a heavy, dough-faced sort of fellow. Whining about regulatory agencies was his stock-in-trade, publicity-wise. "Mr. Kingston!" said Buddy. "It's an honor to be speaking with you."

"I hear you're a good horse-trainer."

"I do have a lot of horses in training and a lot of experience."

"Are you any good?"

"My win per—"

"Are you any good?"

Once again, Buddy consulted the wall in front of him and his heart within. Quiet as a summer day.

"I like to win, Mr. Kingston, and I don't do anything I don't like."

"You ever won the Kentucky Derby?"

"No, but I've won the Preakness and I've won two Breeders' Cup races—a sprint and a mile. You know, Breeders' Cup day is the pre-eminent horse-racing day. Not so specialized as, say, the Triple Crown. And the Classic is worth at least four million dollars this year. And I've won every major race in California, some of them more than once."

"All these guys say you're great."

"Which guys are those, sir?"

"Let's see. I wrote it down. Sir Michael. Callaghan, the Irishman. This guy in Kentucky, Beaufort Hall. Barry Kennedy. Guy in New York, Moishe Kellerman. And this other guy, Martin Norman."

"That's a strong list, sir." A strong list of Sir Michael's dearest pals. With himself, that would be seven, but for a phone reference most of them would be getting 1 percent at the most. That was how it had worked in the past. "Are you a horse-lover, sir?"

"I could be."

"You have some experience with horses, I trust?"

"No, I don't. That's why I need reliable advice. You know, I'll tell you something right up front. I don't know shit about horses, but I want to go into racing in a big way."

"Why is that, sir? Racing is dying, you know. You might be better off investing in some other sport." Buddy knew that Jesus knew he was being very truthful.

"Thank you for your candor, Crawford. I'll respond in kind. I had a dream, a recurrent dream. I had it three times. A horse galloped onto my front lawn here and whinnied up at me, and I went down and it came to me and put its head next to mine. I woke up happy as I've ever been. You know what?"

"What, sir?"

"Well, I made my money in software design for cellular-phone systems, and my first idea about that came to me in just the same way. The same dream, three times. I was born in Skokie, Illinois, and now I am worth seven hundred million dollars, so I pay attention to dreams."

"Thank you for telling me that story, sir. Did you mention that to Sir Michael?"

"He was quite interested in that story, and told me he'd had a similar experience."

"No doubt," said Buddy, no doubt that Sir Michael's desire for a growing intimacy with seven hundred million dollars was a profound one. "Why don't you come out to the track and I'll show you around. We'll look at a few horses and have lunch." Jesus surely had no problem with a man being friendly and helpful.

In fact, Jason Clark Kingston and his wife, Andrea Melanie Kingston, came out to the track four days in a row. Kingston himself was a big, awkward guy with enormous feet, maybe size fifteen or sixteen, even though he himself couldn't have been more than six two. The wife was indeed young. Buddy felt a little sorry for them until they opened their mouths. They had been married for three years. The first year they had bought several houses and had them done up. One was a tear-down of some five thousand square feet that was now a Spanish Colonial of some twenty-three thousand square feet. The second year of their marriage, they had collected enough art to fill all the houses. Europeans were in one house, American primitives were in another house, Oriental things were in a third house, and the fourth house was twentieth-century eclectic. "It looks like junk to me," said Andrea Melanie, "lots of spiky things all over most of it, but we don't go to that house much anyway. It's for when people ask us to host fund-raisers and so we let these organizations use it, and give cocktail parties and dinner parties there, and get a lot of donations."

Buddy said—delicately, he thought—"There must be a tax deduction in there."

"Oh, sure," said Jason. "And whenever there's some sort of Republican shindig in our neck of the woods, they do, you know, five-thousand-dollar-a-plate dinners there. It's a good deal all around."

"I'm sure it is," said Buddy.

"Last year, we got into a bunch of things. Jason bought some antique cars, and I bought some Italian furniture. Museum-quality, it was. We bought an island in the Caribbean. Jason tried to buy the Cleveland Indians? You know them?"

"Yes," said Buddy.

"He was going to move them to La Jolla. Everyone thought it was a joke. I'll tell you something, and I tell you this just because you're so nice. When you get to a certain level, you can't get rid of it fast enough, and it's hard to get rid of. I never thought I would say that, but it's true. I wake up nights about it."

"In what sense?" said Buddy.

"You can disperse it," said Jason irritably, "in the way you want, or you can let the government disperse it for you. If you don't do the one, you will be forced to do the other. Gets my goat, I'll tell you."

"I'm a Republican myself."

After four days with the Kingstons, Buddy got a day off. He called Sir Michael. Sir Michael said, "You met them, then?"

"Yup."

"You listened to their hopes and dreams?"

"I did."

"You think their needs can be satisfied?"

"Absolutely."

"The horse is getting to the sale three days before. Your interest in the horse will run you $125,000."

"Fine."

"You can pay me after the sale." The trick was simple. The four co-conspirators would reimburse Sir Michael the half-million he had perhaps paid for the horse, then split the difference between the half-million and whatever Kingston ended up paying. If that were two million, say, Buddy would make $375,000 on his $125,000 "fee."

"Sounds good."

"There will be two underbidders. One of them is Farouk."

"Got ya. Say," said Buddy, confidingly, "do you get the sense with some people that they are really and truly asking for it?"

Sir Michael cleared his throat. "You know, laddie," he said, "here's something I've often thought about my compatriots as opposed to yours. Perhaps it's because we all went to school together and have known one another since God was young, but there's one thing an Englishman never forgets."

"What's that, Sir Michael?"

"That everyone he is acquainted with is asking for it in one way or another."

That was the last he heard from Sir Michael. He would not, of course, appear at the sale. Now that the little scheme was in place and his part in it was set in stone, Buddy expected to hear from his conscience, or from Jesus. A sign would have been a good thing—a flaming bush, waters parting, a horse speaking in tongues. Even just a sense of guilt, since Buddy knew the technical word for their little plan was "fraud." But there was silence. Here his conscience had been goading and nagging and prodding him for weeks, had been raucous around all sorts of things since Jesus grabbed him by the scruff of the neck— how long ago was it, six weeks, six lifetimes? nothing like personal transformation to slow down the passage of time—and yet all was clear and smooth now. Perhaps Jesus didn't care about money? Perhaps Jesus didn't care about Jason and Andrea Melanie? Perhaps Jesus was like the SEC, which, Buddy knew, had declined to regulate the Thoroughbred industry on the grounds that those investing at the high end had more money than the government with which to buy legal counsel? At any rate, Jesus was deep undercover, and so, when the horse arrived, Buddy went out to Pomona to see it in a state of pure disinterest.

The sales agency in which Sir Michael had yet another crony was one of the flashiest, and so they had a big setup in a good spot, near the front, with a thirty-two-inch TV/VCR right there for watching the tapes of the two-year-olds' works. Each horse had a sign, painted with green-and-gold lettering, giving the animal's date of birth and breeding. Buddy peeped in at a few. Two-year-olds in training were always beautifully prepped, and looked as though they were ready to run this very afternoon if only they could bum a ride to the track. The works, of a furlong, took place in the morning, and the numbers were posted. The horse, Epic Steam his name was, had already done his, a lightning 10.3 seconds. People would be talking about that. He went up to Marv, the manager of the agency, and said, "Hey. What's news?"

"Hey, Buddy."

"Got anything nice?"

"Got everything nice, Buddy, you know that. Hell, last year we had Darling Corey. You saw what she did."

"We all saw what she did."

"Nice filly. I thought so at the time. So—how they hanging?"

"Better than ever," said Buddy. Out of the corner of his eye, he saw the girls open the stall door for hip number ten. It took the colt a moment to come out, a long moment, but then, when he came out, he just kept on coming. It wasn't only Buddy who was staring. Everyone around turned to look. He was big and shining and all but black and, well, mysterious. He looked like a Cadillac with a Mafia don inside. They brought him out into the courtyard and stood him up. Every single person standing around stepped back, whether they were in the way or not.

"You ever see Land of Magic?" said Marv.

"Saw a hell of a lot too much of him, if you'll remember."

"You remember the way he looked, out over your head, as if you weren't even there? Like he was catching the eye of the person in the last row of seats in the stands? Look at this colt. He's got the same look."

"Land of Magic was a son of a bitch and still is, I hear."

"Ah, this colt's not bad to work with. You just keep your eyes open like with any two-year-old. He's a mite touchy about that left ear, but that's all."

The colt whinnied all of a sudden and arched his neck. Buddy saw that another horse had been taken out of its stall down the shedrow. Marv said, "A tad studdish."

Buddy could easily interpret all of these remarks. The horse was an ornery son of a crazy sire and the only sensible way to handle him was to geld him.

Best not to show too much of an interest. "What else have you got?"

"Nice Deputy Minister. Dam's out of Mount Livermore. Nice Twining out of a Nureyev mare. First crop. Looks good, you ask me. Couple of Salt Lakes. They're hot this year."

And so on and so forth. Buddy spent the afternoon looking at tapes, looking at two-year-olds. Buying half a dozen for his various owners would be no trouble at all.

Hip number ten would come up the first night, so Buddy made sure that the Kingstons' chauffeur-driven Lexus 470 picked him up in plenty of time. When they stopped at the Ritz-Carlton in Pasadena to pick up the Kingstons, Andrea Melanie was quite bubbly about the car. She said, "Don't you like it? We just got it today. We didn't have any sport-utility vehicles, can you believe it? Sometimes you just overlook some things, and then you are so surprised when you realize it. I thought maybe there was a Suburban or something like that at one of the houses, but I called around, and no! I just laughed. Anyway, we saw that there were a lot of sport-utility vehicles at the racetrack, and I said to Jason, Well, if we're going to do it, we have to look like we're going to do it, so we bought this right off the floor. We hardly ever buy any car right off the floor, but this one happened to be fully loaded, so why not? You can always take it back later and have stuff added if you want."

Buddy looked around the interior of the Lexus. "Fully loaded" was a nice phrase, and Buddy himself had always been ineluctably drawn to any upscale vehicle that was fully loaded, but now he suspected that Jesus would soon require him to drive something like a Dodge Caravan. He said, "What would you add?," just to hear them say it, whatever it was.

Jason said, heavily, "Every car in our fleet has a cellular computer-modem link and a laptop computer available to the passenger seat and both rear seats."

"A minibar," said Andrea Melanie, "with a refrigerator."

"Ceiling-mounted mini-TV," said Jason.

"Jason has his shows," said Andrea Melanie fondly.

"A burl-and-brass box—"

Andrea Melanie leaned over and whispered in Buddy's ear, "For sexual equipment, you know. Isn't that silly?" She laughed and cast Jason a coquettish glance. Then she whispered to Buddy, "We like a lot of spontaneity."

"You know," he said, "I came out to look at this horse yesterday, and I think you'll like the spontaneous quality that he has. Everyone notices it about him."

"Oh!" exclaimed Andrea Melanie. "I hope we get him. I love him already!"

Buddy always thought it was interesting that when you took a new owner to an auction they seemed to think that dropping a vast sum of money on a horse was a privilege. He said, "Well, Mrs. Kingston, this is a good way to get into the game. The horse is trained and ready to run. You don't have to wait the way you do with a yearling, and you don't run the risks that you do with breeding." This was entirely true, thank you, Jesus.

"You make up your mind and there you are," said Jason. "I like that. You know what I say? I say, always act on impulse, because your impulse is always right. My business is full of guys who used to act on impulse and now they don't. They used to be interesting and fun and now they aren't. They used to run their own companies, and now some guy from Coca-Cola does it for them. That's death, if you ask me." He sighed. His wife looked at him sympathetically.

The auction went like clockwork in one sense. Buddy came in and showed the Kingstons his reserved seats. He introduced them to a few benign and trustworthy souls—no other trainers, for sure, but a vet he knew, a couple of breeders, a couple of consignors, a guy who wrote for *The Blood-Horse*. Then they went out to the paddock area and stood among the other patrons looking at the horses waiting to come in. The buyers and their agents stood about in their usual groups. The Brits and the Irish had on their Barbour jackets and their wool caps. The few Aussies had on their big hats. Cowboy hats and boots abounded—this was southern California, after all, and anyway, on the first night of the sale, all the top trainers who'd started out in quarterhorses were much in evidence. Buddy had on a suit. According to Jesus, a nice charcoal-gray suit was the most appropriate attire in any circumstances, and one of the side benefits of finding Jesus had been the resolution of a lifetime of sartorial indecision. While they were standing there, Callaghan came up to them, and Andrea Melanie said, "Oh! Dermot! there you are! This is Buddy."

"Ach, Buddy," said Callaghan.

"Hey, baby," said Buddy. "We've done some business over the years, haven't we, old man?" All of it dirty, too.

"Business, indeed." Dermot grinned cheerfully. There were people in the world who, walking down the street, might see a hundred-dollar bill lying on the curb. Rather than bend down and pick it up, these men would bet a saw-buck on whether the next guy along would pick it up, or the guy after that, or the guy after that. And if they won the twenty and lost the hundred, they would consider themselves well repaid. Dermot Callaghan was one of those. Buddy knew for sure he was coming at this deal in some cockeyed way that might well lose him his quarter interest, but that wasn't Buddy's problem.

"Thanks for taking us to that restaurant last night, Dermot. We just didn't know where to go." She turned to Buddy. "And he took us to the garden at this library around here?"

"The Huntington Library," said Callaghan.

"What did you say he made his money in?" said Jason.

"Railroads," said Callaghan.

"And his name was Huntington?"

"Just like the library," said Callaghan.

Buddy strolled away, just for a moment.

The horse was brought out as the first couple of two-year-olds were going under the gavel. His handlers led him around the paddock area, but kept him slightly apart. Buddy let Callaghan point him out to the Kingstons. They were suitably impressed, because he was suitably impressive. You didn't have to be a horseman to see that he was bigger, blacker, and more full of himself than any horse in the paddock. Buddy and Callaghan let the couple's round eyes fill to the brim with the animal, and then they led them into the amphitheater. As they took their seats, Buddy saw Farouk taking his seat over in another section. Melanie said, "This is like a theater in the round, with that little stage down there. I was an acting major in college, you know."

Soon enough, the sales board flashed the colt's hip number and they led him in. He came in easily enough, four or five steps, then he stopped dead, lifted his head and his tail, and stared at the assembled bidders. The lights in the room lit up his blackness in brilliant circles that slid over his shoulders and back and haunches. His nostrils flared and he whinnied a challenge. "My goodness," said Andrea Melanie.

At the signal from the auctioneer, Farouk started the bidding at three hundred thousand. Andrea Melanie sat up in her chair and craned her neck. The other underbidder, whom Buddy didn't recognize, came in at three fifty, and Callaghan raised his hand for four. Someone else came in, then someone else. They dropped out at a million. Farouk and the other underbidder and Callaghan pushed it up to two million. Buddy stole a glance at Jason, who was sitting next to Callaghan. He looked calm and interested, but neither daunted nor nervous. Every time another bidder spoke, Andrea Melanie, next to Buddy, said, "Oh my God!" At three million, Farouk glanced in their direction. This was the most sensitive moment. Farouk had pushed the bidding as high as he thought he could. Probably Sir Michael had estimated what he thought the Kingstons would pay, and this was about it. Now it was up to Buddy and Callaghan to bail Farouk out, bail all of them out. If you had a couple, Buddy knew, this was where you had to try and understand the marriage. It was no coincidence that one of them had the man and one of them had the woman. But Buddy wasn't sure that they had divvied up their responsibilities properly. Callaghan was a hand with the women, and Buddy most assuredly was not. Buddy heard Callaghan say to Jason, "Well, what do you think?"

Jason didn't say anything.

Buddy looked at him. He looked like he was having second thoughts. At this point, he always wondered if there wasn't some way that they could work a scam that was more guaranteed, but of course there wasn't. There had to be a gamble, didn't there? Every racing man preferred good odds to a sure thing.

Andrea Melanie was looking at Jason now. She looked like she was wondering whether to push him.

When you thought about it, Jason Kingston did seem to be the sort of guy not all that susceptible to pressure.

Jason Kingston looked at his wife, then he looked at Buddy. Since Buddy did not at this point have a guilty conscience, he didn't think that was showing in his face, but perhaps, he thought, a lifetime of dishonesty was showing in his face. Was Jason Kingston astute enough to see it there?

The auctioneer said, "I have three million. Dermot?"

Buddy didn't dare look at Farouk.

He saw Dermot give the auctioneer a little cock of the eyebrow, asking for a moment more.

Jason Kingston withdrew his gaze from Buddy's face, and made no sign. Buddy licked his lips and whispered to Andrea Melanie, "I think this horse can win the Kentucky Derby." And that was true, too. As true as the sun in the sky. So why did it feel like a lie?

She turned instantly to Jason and said, "Please, honey?"

Jason poked Callaghan, and nodded.

Callaghan raised his finger.

The auctioneer said, "Three million one hundred thousand?"

Callaghan and Jason nodded simultaneously.

Now Buddy looked at Farouk. He shook his head, feigning disappointment.

The auctioneer said, "Sold to Dermot Callaghan for three million one hundred thousand."

Andrea Melanie let out a scream, "Oh, God, I want more!"

And so they got more. By the end of the auction, the Kingstons had spent ten million dollars on two-year-olds, and Buddy had to find stalls for six more horses. He had to find room in his bank account for the $375,000, give or take a commission or two, that Sir Michael had sent his way. He had to make room in his future for a return favor (Jesus probably knew what that would be already, some sort of test, which maybe was the long-term point of all of this to begin with), and he had to make room in his already busy day for the endless stroking of Andrea Melanie Kingston, which he saw, now that he had the return on his investment, could turn into a significant penance. That Jesus was a trickster, never more so than when he was keeping quiet and waiting for you to make up your own mind.

By the time Epic Steam had been in Buddy's barn for only three days, whinnying and stampeding around his stall, staring at all the fillies, and in every way creating a ruckus, Buddy was ready to geld the animal. But you didn't go to an owner and tell them that a three-million-dollar two-year-old who hadn't run his first race yet and had the breeding of a king needed his golden treasures, truly a set of family jewels, removed just for the sake of some grooms and exercise boys who made three hundred dollars a week. And you didn't go to Jesus and tell him that, just because you maybe hadn't passed the last test, you weren't going to pass the next one, either. At least, not right away.

19 / THE KENTUCKY DERBY (I)

T HE THING Tiffany enjoyed most about her relationship with Ho Ho
Ice Chill was visiting Ho Ho's family in Connecticut. Ho Ho's father was a
handsome sixty-two-year-old former defensive back on the New York Giants
named Lawrence Morton, who lunched with Kiwanis Clubs, played golf with
the other real-estate agents in his town, gave little talks on positive motivation,
and always had a smile on his face. But the smile on Lawrence's face wasn't
nearly as big as the smile on the face of his second wife, Marie, who was a
Frenchwoman from the actual nation of France. They had a ten-year-old
daughter named Alienor who had already developed and put into place her
personal style. Alienor idolized Paloma Picasso, and always wore the same outfit every day—black jeans and a dazzling white T-shirt, with little black French
sneakers and a necklace of tiny jet beads. She told Tiffany that she didn't see
why she should ever have to vary this outfit for the rest of her life. Marie told
Tiffany with a shrug that this was a very French attitude. Knowing what a
French attitude was gave Tiffany a terrific thrill. The reason Marie always had a
smile on her face was that she adored Lawrence, and why shouldn't she? Everyone adored Lawrence. Lawrence's sense of peace was like a depth of clear water.
"Well," said Marie over some tea and cookies in the Mortons' sunny kitchen,
"it took me a year to get Lawrence to fall in love with me, and I was very beautiful then. But I knew that if Lawrence ever really looked at me, and fixed it in
his mind to take care of me, then that would be forever. Ah! Ah!" She smiled
and closed her eyes, just at the thought of Lawrence.

Ho Ho Ice Chill was Lawrence's only rap-singer offspring. Ho Ho's sister
Ivy was a tax lawyer, his sister Helen was in real estate with Lawrence, and
his brother, Norman, was a marketing executive at Microsoft, out in Seattle.
Sometimes, when Ho Ho needed a little advice, he got on the Internet and got
Norman's marketing group to brainstorm a promotional campaign or some-
thing like that. As a result, Ho Ho's record company was being eyed as a possi-

ble takeover target by Microsoft. But, Ho Ho explained, so was everything else. The children's mother was a community activist in Oakland, California.

Sometimes, when Tiffany remembered how she had bolted out of Wal-Mart with Bone Bones, she imagined she had known that this was where she was going, but, of course, that was impossible. What was really true was that she had been bored enough to try anything, and she had set aside her usual distaste for trading on her looks and lucked out.

Tiffany liked every word that she heard at the Mortons' house—France, tapenade, Paloma Picasso, Microsoft, please, thank you, honey, sweetheart, chéri, Earl Grey, orchid, garlic, closing, investment, nude (as in a painting), terrace, riding lawn-mower, maman, s'il vous plaît, ce soir, assiette, coq au vin, daube, glace. Ho Ho, for his part, had a focused interest in all the words Tiffany knew but hated to use, which referred to drugs, sex, violence, being tough, and making a name for oneself in spite of worlds of hardship. Ho Ho, it had to be said, liked Tiffany, but he idolized Roland, Tiffany's brother, whom he had never met. Yes, Roland had been in prison. Yes, Roland had a friend who was murdered. No, Roland had never killed anyone. Yes, Roland was a great and hypnotic talker. Yes, Roland was a bad man or a lost soul, or both. Yes, Tiffany hoped that, brother or not, she would never see Roland again.

Ho Ho had been a rap star for about two years. Tiffany had heard of him. He wasn't as big as some, was bigger than others. Like the rest of the family, he was dynamite at marketing. He had a real instinct for knowing what people wanted just before they wanted it. He also had his father's height and build, which made him look more threatening than he really was. He had an entourage. He had girlfriends. He had videos and advisers and hangers-on. What he didn't have, and where would he get it, Tiffany thought, was a sense of himself as a killer. Instinctively, Ho Ho knew that he wasn't going to jail, the way that instinctively Roland had known when he was ten that he *was* going to jail. Ho Ho thought that his career might last another year and then he would market something else. But to get that other year, he thought, he had to have some new material, and that was what Tiffany was for, telling him everything she could remember about Roland, which he then wrote verbatim into songs. Although she and Ho Ho did a good imitation of being hot for one another, they weren't, and they both agreed on this. She didn't like sex much and Ho Ho was in love with one of his comparative-literature professors from his only year in college, whose Ph.D. dissertation he kept next to her picture by his bed. Tiffany liked the title of her dissertation, "Getting from Here to There: The Visionary Travels of Matsuo Basho." Even so, when Ho Ho talked about the woman and what she did all day, Tiffany didn't think that was what she, Tiffany, would like to do. Nor, when all was said and done, did she want to linger much longer at the lovely house in Connecticut, even though she preferred that to traveling to musical engagements, and most of the entourage liked it so much there, they were ready to move right in. After it was clear that he didn't expect her to devote herself to satisfying his passions, she often said to Ho Ho, "Well, baby, what do you think I should do?"

School. Office work. Modeling. School again. A restaurant career. Retailing. Property management. School. Actually, thought Tiffany, the surroundings were nicer but the problems were much the same in Connecticut as elsewhere. And the weather was depressing her. There were daffodils out, but it was chilly and damp. It looked like you could go outside, but you couldn't. Marie offered to teach her to cook, but though Tiffany enjoyed those dishes and very much appreciated their names, she did not want to make any of them for herself or others.

It was Ivy who, when they were sitting around the dinner table one Sunday, eating one of Marie's cassoulets (another wonderful word, Tiffany thought), said that Ho Ho ought to buy a racehorse. Lawrence shook his head. He said, "That used to be a good tax write-off, ten years ago, but now you've got to pay attention to it."

"What's a tax write-off?" said Tiffany.

Ivy looked at her kindly. "It's when you're making too much money and you need something that you're losing money on to offset what you're making."

"Well," said Ho Ho. "I like horses."

"I've never seen a live horse," said Tiffany. "Only on TV." Everyone was careful to use standard English around Lawrence, even the rougher members of Ho Ho's entourage.

Everyone at the table looked at her.

Marie said, "Mon Dieu! Chérie, you have never seen a horse? My father back in France, he used to rescue the horses. Once we had thirty horses in our yard, and the newspaper came and took a picture and wrote a piece, and all of the horses went away to homes."

"I want to win the Kentucky Derby," said Ho Ho. "I want to be the first black man and rap singer to own a Derby winner."

"There was a great black jockey, you know," said Lawrence. "Won the highest percentage of races of any jockey ever. His name was Isaac Murphy."

"What's the Kentucky Derby?" said Tiffany. She was sort of joking. But it was always interesting to see where Ho Ho went with her queries.

"Ho Ho," said Ivy with a laugh, "buy this girl a horse. She needs to be educated."

Ho Ho turned around in his chair. The chair creaked under his weight. He was one of those big black men who looked fearsome alone on the street. Part of the reason he had an entourage, Tiffany knew, was to reassure white people—no group of black men could dress so outrageously, cop such an attitude, and be so numerous without corporate sponsorship. To not be intimidated by him, you had to get close enough to see his eyes, dark, twinkly, and good, the eyes of a man who could and would still sing the lullaby his mother had sung to him twenty years before. He said to her, "You want a horse, baby?"

Tiffany nodded.

"What kind of horse you want?"

"*Do* you want," said Marie, correctively.

"What kind of horse *do* you want, baby?"

"The kind of horse that wins the Kentucky Derby," said Tiffany.

"Well, we'll do that, then," said Ho Ho. "Who've we got from Kentucky?"

"Lamar is from Kentucky," said Helen.

"We'll call him tomorrow," said Ho Ho.

Though she had never seen a horse in the flesh, he came easily, fluidly into Tiffany's mind, some kind of red color, like a penny, and shining. Tiffany saw that Marie was smiling at her. She said, "What was it like, having all those horses around?"

"It was a great deal of work. Some of them were very thin and sick. We fed them and brushed them and petted them. They were most grateful."

"They were?"

"You know, a horse is a very affectionate beast," said Marie.

Tiffany turned to Ho Ho. She said, "How about after supper, um, dinner?"

Everyone laughed indulgently. That was the way they laughed in the Mortons' household, always indulgently.

20 / WRECK

IT WAS FUCKING COLD. Even though the stands faced into the setting sun, there was no warmth, and the forty-degree breeze felt like a freezing torrent. In twenty-two years in America, this was the thing Deirdre hadn't yet adjusted to—the weather: ninety-four degrees and 90-percent humidity in the summer, bitter cold in the winter, and not much in between. The twelve horses in the race, all of whom had looked chilled in the paddock, were now trotting around to the backside, where the gate stood like an ice tray in the pale sunlight. George was betting. The horse Deirdre was running was named Mighty Again, but in fact he would never be mighty again. Three weeks before, Deirdre had had him gelded in a bid to focus his attention. The owners, two guys in cold cuts, were down on the rail. They had been bettors for years, had only just gotten to be owners. They still preferred it down on the rail and they always wore their lucky clothes when they were running a horse. Their lucky clothes were a motley collection of items from all fashion eras, including the one's father's lucky oxfords from the 1940s, when the father in question had hit a 125-to-1 shot at Oaklawn. Deirdre couldn't decide if these owners had style or had no style, but she liked them. They were Irish way back, Mahoney and Byrne. But that wasn't why she liked them. There were whole populations of Irishmen that Deirdre didn't like.

One of these was not George, who came up the steps and sat down. He said, "Good Lard, Cousin, it's colder than the devil's navel up here!"

"Don't be picturesque with me, young man."

"You're smilin', Cousin."

"I don't know why."

"Once in a while you can't help yourself. Try as you might—"

"Try as I might."

Deirdre put her glasses to her eyes to watch the loading. Uneventful but lengthy. Twelve horses was too many. Always too many, but especially too many at this time of the day. She sighed.

"Did ya see the filly, then? Ah, you're smilin' again, so ya must have."

"I saw her." Deirdre had flown all the way to Lexington to have a look at the newborn foal, born perfectly on the first of March.

"And the goddess?"

"And the goddess."

"Lovely pair. She's going to make a first-class racehorse, that filly." Deirdre had brought back pictures.

"Bite your tongue, George!"

"You're not smilin'."

"Bite your fucking tongue! I will not have you refer to the future of this filly in any terms whatsoever, bad or good!"

George looked at her, then nodded. "I apologize, Cousin." His handsome face was serious. He meant it. The bell clanged, and they remembered to watch the race.

The twelve horses came out in a good line, no one lagging, no one bolting. Deirdre had her glasses trained on Mighty Again, and saw that he was running fairly well, settling. It took about a month for the testosterone to clear a new gelding's system, but the horse's attitude showed definite improvement, as it had in training. Now the field was bunched along the backstretch the way twelve claimers would be—no strategy, no system, just trying to do the best they could.

If only it hadn't been the front-runner, the number-five horse, who had gone to the rail right away and pulled ahead. It was a piece of special bad luck that it was the front-runner, because, when he stumbled and flipped, landing on his side crosswise, he landed in the path of every horse behind him, and over the next ten seconds four of them went down, one by one, like dominoes. Jockeys went down, too. Two horses managed to check and go around, one of which lost his jockey, and six pulled to the outside of the track fairly smoothly. Perhaps they ran home. Deirdre could not have said. George was on his feet, screaming. So was she. So was everyone. As soon as the last horse went around, the ambulance that followed the race was there, and Deirdre could see the vet's car and the horse ambulance come onto the track. Deirdre strained her eyes and her glasses to see Mighty Again; he was a bay. One bay had gotten up. Someone grabbed him, and when Deirdre focused on him, she saw that his hoof was dangling. That didn't make much difference to him, though. He wouldn't be able to feel it for fifteen minutes or so. Deirdre caught his look in her glasses. It was a look of astonishment, and it wrung her heart. Four horses in one accident! God in heaven! Now two were on their feet, but Mighty Again was still down. She said to George, "Let's go."

They ran down from the boxes, through the betting arcade, down the steps, and out the gate to her car. She hated not being able to see anything, but she knew what was out there anyway. Death lay before them. It was only a matter of how many and who. She muttered, "Hail Mary, Mother of God, pray for us sinners, us horse-trainers, who have brought these poor beasts to this pass. Make their suffering short and show them your mercy. Amen. Why didn't I wait? Why did I bring this horse to Philadelphia?"

She pulled next to one of the barns, jumped out of the car with George, went under the backstretch rail, and stood up. Briefly she took his hand. Then they went over to Mighty Again, who lay on his side, his eye rimmed with white, from fear, and his lips slightly parted. He looked normal, but he hadn't gotten up, which was unusual for a horse. Horses hated to be down. Dominic, the jockey, was kneeling beside the horse's head, his own face covered in dirt and blood. Ronald, Mighty Again's groom, who had run across the infield, was squatting on his haunches, just shaking his head from side to side. Deirdre said, "Dom? Are you hurt?"

"Rib is all. Broke rib or something."

"Dear, get into the ambulance."

"They all went down together. How did they? We were up and then we went down. I don't get it. Just tell me."

She took his hands and turned him away from the horse. "The lead horse flipped, darlin'. Now you've got to get into the ambulance."

"I'm okay."

"Maybe. We'll take care of the creature." She touched her hand to his face. "Get into the ambulance, love. I don't want any of your inner parts bleedin'. You're a good boy."

He got into the ambulance.

Mighty Again was still breathing, but his breaths were noisy and labored. His eye was now closed. He had never been one of her favorite horses, trouble from the beginning, and not very smart, but he had a pretty head. She knelt beside him and smoothed his mane along his neck, saying, "There now, sweetheart. You'll be fine in a moment." Ronald, who had complained about the horse, too, had tears on his cheeks. He wasn't saying anything. The vet came up, the head vet here, whom she only knew by sight. He knelt down beside her and said, "We've got to roll him over."

"This is bad."

"It doesn't look good that he's not getting up."

"What happened?"

"My guess is, the front-runner blew his aorta. His gums are white as paper. His jock got stepped on, but he can move everything. Another jock's out cold. None killed. We might have lucked out."

Mighty Again's bulk was warm and huge. Never was a horse so huge as when you had to get him up. Once, at a show, a jumper belonging to another trainer had collapsed in the trailer, his legs underneath him. The only way to get him up was to whip him and encourage him until he made up his mind to get up; in that tiny space, there could be no lifting. But Mighty Again, stretched out in the middle of the expanse of sandy racetrack, they lifted. They wrapped slings around the knees and hocks, then, with some people pulling from behind, and some pushing from in front, they got his legs in the air, up and over. He groaned a deep hollow groan. As soon as he was over, he stuck out a foreleg and stood up. It was clear what the problem was—the left shoulder, the one that had been underneath before they rolled him over, was smashed, and he had a long gash along his rib cage, which was dented, as well. He stood on three legs. His left foreleg dangled. Deirdre looked at the vet. She said, "He's a goner."

"He's a goner."

"God in heaven forgive me for this sin."

"Deirdre, it was an accident."

But she shook her head.

Ronald led Mighty Again over to the horse ambulance, a matter of four steps or so, and the horse paused, then got himself in. Deirdre said, "George, go get the owners and bring 'em to the barn if they want to come. We'll wait to euthanize the horse until we've talked to them." There the two horses were, in the horse ambulance, a broken shoulder and a broken leg. They would be dead by the start of the next race, Deirdre suspected. She shook her head. The front-runner was already so dead that he no longer looked like a horse. The fourth horse was lying there, too. She glanced at the vet. He said, "Broken neck." Deirdre groaned, feeling herself surrounded. She said, "Is this what it feels like on a battlefield?"

"I think so," said the vet.

She looked across the field at the grandstand, at all the eyes and bodies straining to see and know what she saw around her and knew. It was too much. The physical enormity of death was too much for her—too much blood, too much bone, too many rasping breaths, too much sweat and stink too suddenly. She had seen several deaths, human and equine, over the years. She had almost died herself, for that matter, when she got pneumonia after breaking her back. How many times did you have to come back to it before you could stand it? It seemed like her ability to do so was growing weaker rather than stronger.

Behind her, George said in a low voice, "Nel mezzo del cammin' di nostra via."

She looked at him and replied in English, "I have lost the path, George." Her cousin's blue eyes were as beautiful as they could be, but there was no salvation in them. They walked together behind the horse ambulance as it made its funereal way down the track.

21 / A DAY AT THE RACES

FIRST THEY STOPPED by the liquor store his dad owned, and Jesse got a candy bar out of the cabinet while his dad opened the register and took out a handful of money. He didn't even count it, but just shoved it in his pocket. After they got in the car, Jesse surreptitiously looked down at his father's socks. They matched, plain gray. They also matched his pants. That was a relief. They traveled in silence for a while, and Jesse stared out the window.

He rather liked the drive out to Santa Anita. It was long and sunny. Along about the time they were passing under Highway 5, his dad piped up: "Ah, Jesse! Look at that tree, there. That's a beautiful tree. You know, that tree's been sitting by the side of this road for fifty years, I'll bet, and I never noticed it before. You go through life, and you travel the same road over and over, and all of a sudden you notice something. That's a gift. That tree tells me something. That tree tells me we're going to have a good day. Don'tcha think?"

"I hope so, Pop."

"I got my lucky socks on. You got your lucky socks on?"

"We hit that daily double that time when I had these socks on."

"Your mom wash 'em since?"

"Well, yeah."

They pondered this together, then Leo said, "Well, maybe that doesn't matter."

"Dad, I've worn them a lot of times since. We hit that daily double last summer."

"But not to the track?"

"Not to the track."

"This is the first time you've worn them to the track since then?"

"Yeah."

"Okay, then."

Jesse let out his breath.

Leo began to sing. Then they pulled off the highway and drove into the parking lot—on a lucky day they always parked in preferred parking, so they wouldn't have to walk so far. That was five dollars. That was a part of your overhead, which you wanted to keep as low as possible. They parked, got out of the car, and locked it. There were two things his father never looked at at Santa Anita—the shopping mall next door and any Mercedes Benz automobiles that might be parked between him and the gate. It was okay if Jesse looked at them; in fact, it was better if Jesse spied them and reported them. Today there weren't many, and Leo managed to keep his head down. He counted the money, too: $278.32, with the $.87 Jesse had in his pocket. They had to combine their money. That was lucky, too.

They were almost to the gate, and no Mercedes, when disaster struck. "Ah, fuck," said Leo, softly and seriously. Jesse knew he shouldn't, but he did it anyway. He said, "What's the matter, Pop?"

"I looked at a fucking nun."

"What?"

"I can't believe I looked at a fucking nun. There she was, and I looked at her!"

Looking at a nun was the worst thing you could do, Jesse knew. Now they might as well go home. He looked around, though. Nothing. He proffered, "I don't see any, Pop."

"Over there." Leo gestured toward the west without daring to look. Still Jesse saw no nuns, not even any women. But Jesse knew better than to argue. After a moment, he said, "Do you want to go home, then?"

Leo stopped walking and turned to Jesse. He had a very serious look on his face, and he put a hand on each of Jesse's shoulders. Jesse lifted his face and looked his father right in the eye, as he had been told to do many times. "Jesse," Leo said. "Jesse, son. On the one hand, we've got the, uh, you know." Yes, the nun. "And on the other, we've got the socks, two pairs, the tree, no Mercedes, no shopping mall, and almost three hundred bucks. I'll tell you what. Here's the *Racing Form.*" He pulled it out of his pocket and opened it to the first race. "Read those starters." Leo threw back his head and closed his eyes, listening.

Jesse read, "Lonesome Jones, Howdy Babe, Hickey's Prince, Gottalotta-yotta, Prigogine, Sandtrap, Baby Max, and Holy Mackerel."

Leo remained silent, mulling, for a long moment, and then said, "Don't you have a friend named Max?"

"No," said Jesse. "No Maxes."

Leo threw up his arms. "Okay, then! Let's go! That may just turn the trick. Let's go look at some horses, boy!"

They passed through the gate, where the woman smiled and said, "Hi, Leo! Have a good day, now," then went through the betting hall and out again, onto the tiled apron that sloped down to the homestretch, the finish line, and the winner's circle. It was a sunny, clear day, a good March day, and the arc of the mountains was dark green against the blue sky. Since it was Wednesday, there weren't many people in the stands yet, and so Leo staked out his spot—he had his *Racing Form,* covered with the notations he'd made after dinner the night before, his seat cushion, which he always brought but never sat on, his binoculars, his thermos of coffee, and his extra pens for making more notations on the *Racing Form* if he had to. He was smiling. He ruffled Jesse's hair and said, "Well! Got here! Good deal! Really, this is the best place in the world, don't you think? Hard work, harder than standing around the liquor store, but better, in the end." Leo took a deep breath and threw his shoulders back, looked around his personal domain, and then said, "Okay, boy! Better get to work, there's money to be made."

In the first race, a thirty-thousand-dollar claiming race of seven furlongs, for three-year-olds and up, they boxed Lonesome Jones and Sandtrap in the exacta. Sandtrap was the favorite, but Leo thought he was coming down from his peak form. Lonesome Jones, however, had had a bad trip in his last race, his first start after a six-week layoff. He'd been bumped in the backstretch and gone wide on the turn as a result, but still come in third by only a head. His speed ratings in his previous starts had been at or close to the top for the horses in this race, and Leo thought, as a three-year-old, the animal could still manage a jump. Best of all, he was a good bet—the morning line of ten-to-one had dropped, but not very far, only to eight-to-one. Sandtrap was clearly the class of the field. Even coming off his best form, he was a contender, and the bettors were backing him heavily. Leo also boxed the two horses with a horse he liked in the second race, See Me Now, for the daily double. After placing his bets, he was very calm, and stood with Jesse in the grandstand to watch the horses make their way to the gate, which was positioned in the chute, as far away from the grandstand as possible. The announcer, whose pronunciation was clarion-crisp, said, "The horses are approaching the starting gate. The horses have reached the starting gate. We have Lonesome Jones in. Now Howdy Babe," and on down the line, to Holy Mackerel. There was a pause, then a clang, and the gates were open and the horses were away. Leo's binoculars were pressed to his head, and he was deadly silent. Jesse could see only the colors of the jockeys' silks, but he knew that Lonesome Jones was in purple, and that purple was trailing by open lengths. The favorite was one of two horses in yellow. One of the two was in the lead. "All right!" breathed Leo, as the purple horse began to pass the others. And the announcer said, "And we have the number-one horse, Lonesome Jones, now passing Howdy Babe and Prigogine. Still on the lead is Sandtrap, the favorite." Leo began to get more agitated as the horses came around the turn, bouncing up and down on his toes. Jesse could see them clearly now, from the front, their heads down, their feet up, the tiny rounds of their toes reaching up and forward, echoing the tiny rounds of their flared nostrils. Then they came into the homestretch, and the angle was different. They were horses now, pulled out like rubber bands from their noses to their tails, with the jockeys on top, also pulled out, hands, arms, heads, backs, and then the curl into their legs. Some of the jockeys' colored arms were rising and falling, another stretched-out thing, a shoulder, an elbow, an arm, a hand, a whip. Behind Jesse was a lot of yelling, and beside him, too, from his father, because there came Lonesome Jones on the rail, finding a hole and slipping through it, eating up the track. By contrast, the red horse fell back, the green horse fell back, the blue and the black-and-tan horses fell back. Leo's hand was on his head, and suddenly pressed down as the horses crossed the finish line. In a moment, the tote board flashed "Photo Finish," and they had to wait. But Leo was sure. "They did it! They did it! I knew it! Perfect pick! One and six. That's always been a great pick for me, because I dated this girl when I was sixteen, her name was Peggy Sue! It really was, and that song was such a great hit that my statistical average with one and six over the years has been way out of the normal range! Now, you've got to have the information to back it up—only losers just bet patterns—"

The results flashed, and the winner was the number-seven horse, Baby Max, by a head. Lonesome Jones and Sandtrap were second and third.

"God damn!" said Leo.

That meant that all bets were off, the exacta, the daily double. Sixty dollars, Jesse thought, gone already. He said, "Hey, Pop, let's go home."

Leo was staring at Baby Max, who was being led into the winner's circle, but he shook himself and looked down at Jesse and smiled. "Nah, nah. We're here. We've just got to work a little harder. Here, here's ten bucks for something to eat. Go away and leave me alone for a while, I got to concentrate and you're a little distracting. It isn't your fault. I just have to get into a zone, you know. That's a good boy."

Jesse took the ten and followed Baby Max and his associates as they walked under the stands and out into the open air. The jockey and the trainer were smiling, but professionally so. This was only the first race of many today for the jockey. Jesse liked looking at him. He was, in fact, about Jesse's height, but he walked like a man, and a very self-confident one, at that. When he looked up at the trainer to tell him about the race, he didn't seem to be looking up, but to be looking down. Jesse liked looking at jockeys, and always tried to do so. They had different stomachs and backs from anyone at the track, strong, straight, supple, powerful. Something in their stomachs, as far as Jesse could see, was the thing that made them able to hold those horses. Leo didn't pay much attention to jockeys, and had advised Jesse not to. "A winner never bets the jockey," he said, but Jesse always thought that if he could get what the jockey had in his stomach into his own stomach other things would go away— butterflies, gas pains, that feeling that all his insides were dropping.

Out in the open air, he saw that the horses for the second race were leaving the saddling enclosure to go to the paddock.

Leo didn't like watching the horses get saddled, or the paddock parade. He said it was too confusing, and that you ended up betting hunches when you should be betting form, numbers, past performances. Watching the horses in the saddling enclosure was like tempting yourself to fall in love at first sight, and if you couldn't control yourself, then you had to control your circumstances, which Leo did by staying inside the track. Jesse liked the preliminaries the best, though. It allowed him to think that horse racing wasn't really about betting, but about looking at the animals. The coolest thing about them was that they were all different. For example, in the second race, for maiden two-year-old fillies, there were six entries idling with their connections. Of all the fillies, only one was calm. She was a chestnut, number two. She stood quietly with her head up and her ears pricked while her trainer smoothed the number-cloth over her back.

"That's Buddy Crawford, that trainer," said a woman standing next to Jesse. "He's won a lot of races. They say he's kind of a crook."

Jesse liked the horse, though. He looked at the program. Her name was "Residual." Jesse leaned on the barrier to get a better look at the filly. The people around the filly put the saddle on her, then did the girths. They petted her a lot, and Jesse could see why. She was very shiny, but even apart from that, something about her made you want to pet her. He wanted to pet her himself. Around her, all of the other fillies were doing something—twisting their necks or jumping around. One stood there rigid with tension, lifting one foreleg and curling it under herself, then putting it down and lifting the other. The only thing Residual did was rub the side of her nose gently on the sleeve of her groom one time, as if, Jesse thought, she was reassuring him. Now the number-one filly headed out, and Residual followed her. Behind them, the last four fillies made a ruckus, but Residual only looked at the fans lining the rail of the walking ring, and when she came to the spot where she was supposed to receive her jockey, she stopped and stood. Jesse took one last look, and ran under the grandstand. Leo was sitting on the concrete steps, still studying his form. Jesse went up to him. As Residual walked onto the track, he exclaimed, "Look at number two, Dad! You've got to bet on her."

"I never bet maiden two-year-old fillies," said Leo. "That's like playing the lottery."

Jesse looked up at the tote. He said, "Her odds are six to one. That's good odds."

"Those are good odds, yes. But I have standards, Jesse."

Jesse said, "It's Pincay, Dad."

"Even so." He put his hand on Jesse's shoulder and looked him in the eye, then said in a very serious voice, "Jesse, son, these little girls don't know a thing about racing. The gate is going to open, and they are going to be wondering what to do next. Anything can happen—"

"But that's good, Dad."

"Well, that is good in a larger sense, in a, let's say, universal sense, in the sense that if you spend your life drawing a weekly paycheck, and that's what you know you're going to get every Friday for the rest of your life, unless the boss decides to give you a two-percent raise one of these years, and you know the wife is going to spend so much for food and so much for rent and everything, well, some people like to live like that, and some don't. So, in that sense, the idea that anything can happen is a liberating idea. But in this sense, in this race, the things that can happen aren't good in that way—"

"I've got ten dollars at home. I would give it to you if you would bet that on her now."

"Jesse, the thing is, I want you to benefit from my experience. Now, my dad, he would bet on any race, but I've—" Then he stopped. Then he said, "Well, you've got to learn sooner or later. Okay. How do you want to bet your ten dollars?"

The horses were jogging. Residual continued to ease along. Pincay, the strongest jockey, the oldest jockey, the most amazing jockey, sat calmly atop her. Three times, he reached down and stroked her neck, slowly, not as if reassuring her, but just as if he enjoyed it. Jesse said, "Two across the board. Two more to win, and two more to place. The odds are at eight to one, now, Dad. I think she's way undervalued."

"Okay, son. If you can use the word 'undervalued' and know what it means, I suppose you're ready to make up your own mind."

The lines at the betting windows were short, so they got back out to the rail in time to see the horses begin to jog and then canter past the stands on their way to the gate in the chute. The number-five filly was nearly climbing her pony, she was so ready to lose it at the noise and turmoil of the fans in the stands. None of the others liked it, either—even Residual looked—but soon enough they had all been led away from the noise, little suspecting that they would have to run back into it before long. Jesse held his tickets in his hand. He knew the fillies had to go through this—a time or two and they would be like the horses in the first race, ready, and even eager for this pandemonium— those in the first race that didn't prance at least perked up. But these fillies skittered and jumped and the pony riders held them close. They disappeared after the turn, and only by putting his hand up and squinting could Jesse see the gate at the front of the chute. After a bit, the first horse and pony approached it. That filly shied and backed. The pony went with her for a step, then stood until the filly came back up to it. A man standing next to them said to his friend, "All them jocks is prayin' right now."

The friend nodded.

"You know," the man went on, "there's culling takes place in everything, but horse racin's the only thing where they cull the ones that ain't gonna cut it right in front of ya."

"Football."

"Now, there's a difference right there. You let a kid come to practice month after month and then warm the bench all season, and pretty soon he gets the idea that he's no good, and he goes off. But horses, they don't get to warm no bench. They got to try it all equal with each other. They're more equal in these maiden races than they'll ever be again."

"Yup," said the friend.

"Culls 'em. Breaks 'em down."

"Yup," said the friend. "Who ya got?"

"Well, I got a pick three that's still got a breath of life in it. I did a five-five-five this time."

"Hell, that's a crazy bet. I know a guy who did this thing for a year. He played the horses that he liked best across the board, and also the longest shot in the race. He did it for a year, and even though he ended up with a lot of favorites, those eighty- or a-hundred-to-one shots came in just often enough to put him in the black for the year. I always thought it was a good system."

"Why don't you use it, then?"

"Ah, it was his system. I got one of my own."

"Don't we all."

"Jesse," said Leo. He had the binoculars to his eyes. Jesse said, "Are they in?" Leo, for the first time ever, handed him the glasses.

The bell clanged and the gates opened. Residual, of course, was in the second hole. The thing was, when the gates opened in a normal race, a line of horses leapt forth. A good start was a nice thing to see, everyone doing the same thing for a moment, then, boom, everyone different. But this was a bad start. Residual leapt forth, but the filly in the number-one slot stood for a moment, and the filly in the number-four spot jumped out, then stopped dead in her tracks. The outside filly crossed to the rail, not as if her jockey was taking her there, but as if she was out of control. And the number-three filly reared up and dumped her jockey. Jesse took the glasses down from his eyes and looked up at Leo, who was shaking his head. But there was no time for that. Now the field organized itself tentatively. Residual and the number-six horse were in front, but right behind them was the riderless filly, her reins dangling. The number-one filly was out now, but fighting her jockey. She and the other two had at least four lengths of daylight between them and the first group. Jesse focused the glasses on Residual. As she disappeared behind the stuff in the infield that hid everything from the gaze of the fans, she looked awkwardly boxed in. The filly with the jockey seemed to be pressing against her where she was on the rail, and the riderless filly was right on her heels. But she floated, that's what Jesse thought, she floated.

He set the glasses on the beginning of the turn and waited. When they came into his view, things had changed. Now all six horses were strung out along the rail, nose to tail. The number-six filly, whose jockey had a white cap, was first, the riderless filly was second, Residual was third, the number-one filly was fourth, the number-four filly, the one that had stopped dead, was fifth, and galloping along behind was number five. They came around the turn in just this order, as if they were a merry-go-round. Jesse heard Leo say "Shit!" with a certain amount of surprise in his voice, more than he normally cared to allow. As they entered the stretch, Jesse could see some of the jockeys begin to do stuff. The leading jockey glanced back, and then went to his whip; the last two pulled to the outside. The horse behind Residual simply ran out of steam, and disappeared from Jesse's view. Pincay did nothing for a moment, then he simply moved his hands up the filly's neck and seemed to lift himself off her. How he could do this, Jesse could not say, but, then, Leo always said that Pincay could do anything. Residual continued to float. She floated around the riderless filly, who, as they came under the stands, threw her head in fear at the noise everyone was making. She floated away from the fillies behind her, and she floated right up to the lead filly, seemed to encompass her and then to overtake her. They crossed the finish line. "Photo" once again flashed on the tote. Jesse handed the glasses to Leo, and Leo said, "Well, maiden fillies is maiden fillies, is what my dad used to say. There's never been a man in the world who could see into the heart of a maiden filly."

"Residual was perfect, Dad."

"She ran a pretty good race, son. She kept out of trouble, but I don't think she won."

"Nothing bothered her, Dad. All that stuff was all right with her. She didn't even notice it."

"Son, from the perspective of the bettor, perfect is a win. The other stuff is just nice."

The results came up. Residual had not won. But she had come in second. Jesse pulled his tickets from his pocket. He still had two place bets and one show bet. He looked at the tote and added them up. Then he said, "I still get thirty-five dollars, Dad, plus my original ten. That's forty-five dollars. That's good investing."

Leo ruffled his hair and said, "Yes, it is, son."

Jesse noticed that, when the grooms went out to retrieve their horses, Residual came up to her groom and nosed him on the arm. After Pincay took off his saddle but before he turned to walk away, he gave the filly a long stroke and she gave him a look. Pincay laughed. Jesse heard him say to the groom, "Nice girl, this one." Then Buddy Crawford was there, and he and Pincay talked. Pincay was nodding and smiling. Buddy Crawford was shaking his head. Then Pincay laughed, one of those laughs you saw sometimes, where you realized that the person laughing just knew everything was fine, and he was right. Your dad could say this, and your mom could say that, and the trainer could be mad about some little thing, and maybe not everything went your way, but if you saw how there could be floating in spite of all that, then everything was fine anyway.

Leo, who had gone to cash the tickets, came back with the money and put it in Jesse's hand. Jesse looked at it. Leo was smiling, but it seemed strange to him. He wondered if he would ever know the same things that other people knew, ever look at something as simple as money and know anything simple about it. Even the numbers in the corners seemed mysterious. His dad was always telling him things, always pointing out what it was that going to the track taught you about, like life and the president and how you should be and stuff. What the track taught you was very detailed, and there was a lot to remember, and his dad knew all about it. But his dad hadn't seen how the filly floated. Maybe no one else had seen that, either, maybe only he and Pincay had noticed that. Pincay had noticed it, Jesse knew from the pat he gave her when he got off. She was a nice girl, that filly.

His dad was bouncing up and down on the balls of his feet with his hands in his pockets. It was the third race. He and his dad always got to this point at about the third race, where Leo had to go off by himself and do his thinking alone. Without being told, Jesse went to one of the benches by the walking ring and sat down. He pulled out the comic book that he had in his back pocket.

Then the fourth race.

Then the fifth race. Even if you won one, Jesse thought, a day at the races was a long day.

Then the sixth race. When they came out for the sixth race, Jesse realized that he must have dropped off to sleep, because a black lady with a big sunhat on was poking him. He sat up and said, "Oh, I'm sorry," thinking that he had maybe fallen over on her, but she was saying, "Honey, look at this. I got these two in this race. Here's Easy Pieces, he's that big chestnut, he's by Sea Hero, you know who that was, and here's Boraboola. He's a Pleasant Colony." Jesse gazed at the giant animal, nearly black, with one white sock. "Now, which one do you like? Here's my thinking. This race is a mile and a sixteenth on the turf. This Boraboola horse is a distance horse, maybe. He's got the breeding and the bone, and he's been pretty lightly raced, like they're saving him. Those Pleasant Colony horses tend to develop late. Now, Sea Hero was a great racehorse, but he hasn't proved himself as a sire, so you don't really know how to judge his get, you know. But this chestnut, now, to my mind, he's built."

Jesse said, "What's his form?"

"Honey, I don't look at the form, I look at the horse."

"Me, too," said Jesse.

"I don't know," said the lady. "I just don't know."

"I like the black horse."

"Well, he's not black, but almost. They say no Thoroughbreds are black, but I've seen one or two, you ask me."

"He's the one I like. He's very proud of himself today."

"Okay, then."

The lady got up and walked off toward the betting windows, and Jesse thought about going to watch the race, but he really didn't want to, because he might run into his father, and that might be too much. If his father wanted him, he would find him. He felt the money in his pocket, and remembered he was hungry.

They ran the race while he was eating his burger and onion rings. He saw it on the monitor. Boraboola won by a length. The chestnut was third. Jesse felt a very private sense of pleasure descend upon him, from wherever it came from. He hadn't bet, of course, no nine-year-old could bet alone, but he had picked a winner. He knew he would think about that tonight in bed, then tomorrow, when he got up and went to school. It would be a good thing to think about over and over.

Lots of people, of course, left during the ninth race, just to miss the rush hour, or to get away, or because they were tired, but for Leo, leaving before the end of the day was not a possibility. Leo always promoted hard work and doing a good job. But the ninth race could be a killer, Jesse knew. The eighth race was the feature—it always had a name, good money was attached, and the best horses and trainers competed. The ninth race was what Leo called the dogfood run, lots of old geldings or mares who'd seen better days, nothing that could go to the breeding shed, and probably too unsound to be sold off, so their trainers and owners were extracting the last drops of their investment before sending the animals away.

"Where?" Jesse asked once.

"Where do you think, son?"

Jesse knew. And Jesse knew cattle went there, hogs went there, sheep went there, chickens and turkeys went there. Why not horses? But if he tried to imagine, let's say, Residual or Boraboola or Easy Pieces going there, it made him anxious again.

The reason the ninth race might be a killer was that, if his dad had had a winning day, and had parlayed all his bets, then he could lose it all in a matter of moments. If he'd had a losing day, then he might keep betting to get the money back. Theoretically, he could win it all in a matter of moments, too, but that was less likely. And the horses, being unsound, old, unpredictable, were harder to bet, and his dad would be tired, too. Jesse decided to find Leo, though. The fact was, he missed him, and his desire to know how he was doing suddenly outweighed his fear of knowing the same thing. He came out in front of the stands and saw Leo right away, stock-still, binoculars to his face, staring at the line of horses approaching the starting gate, which was out at the chute. This was a six-furlong race, quick, at least. It was impossible to tell from a distance whether Leo was winning or losing, he was so still. When Jesse went up to him, just as the horses left the gate, Leo dropped his hand on his head to keep him quiet. The race had a small field, only five. A man standing nearby said, "Look at these plugs. This is gonna take till midnight. That number-four horse looks like she has to remember how to move her feet."

The five mares and fillies came around the turn. Leo's hand pressed Jesse a little harder. When the horses crossed the finish line, the number-two horse first, the hand lifted, and after a moment, Leo said the magic words, "All right!" Jesse looked up at him. He was smiling. Leo had had a winning day. He said, "Just had a little bet on that sweetie-mare, but let's cash it anyway. Goosey Lucy. What a name! I love how they name these Thoroughbreds. That's a poem in itself. You know, sometimes you read down the program, and it's a song, or a poem, or something like that. Goosey Lucy. Well, sweetie, you made me a winner today."

Goosey Lucy had gone off at four-to-one, so Leo walked away from the window with twenty-two dollars, which he arranged carefully in his wallet with the rest of the money. Dollars weren't falling out of his pockets the way they did once in a while, when Leo hit a big exotic bet, but there was a thick wad in the wallet that would make for a nice evening.

On the way home, with the sun setting over the 210 and all of Los Angeles displayed before them, Leo sang his usual hymn. Jesse liked to hear it. "There's no place like the racetrack, son. Everyone of every sort is there. No one is excluded at the racetrack. Blacks, Jews, Hispanics, Chinese. Koreans love the racetrack. Kids play there. People picnic there. Families break bread together at the racetrack. Rich, poor, and everything in between. It doesn't matter what you do in your life, son, the richest man you will ever see will be someone you saw at the track, walking along, holding his tickets just like you. And probably the poorest man you ever see will be at the track, too, because there's always somebody, every day, who managed to wipe out all his assets at the betting windows. A beggar on the street with a sawbuck in his hat is richer than that man. Now, that's just the socio-economic aspect, which I appreciate, but which is just an aspect. These jocks are great athletes. Now, some say they're crooked, but I don't say that, I just say they're great athletes. If you blew up a jock's body to the size of a basketball player's, the jock would be stronger, more muscled, more coordinated, more you name it. Jock just is. They've done studies. So you get to see that. But the other thing is, and the thing I love the most is, every single horse race is something that can't be understood. Eight or nine times a day, day after day, men and horses go out and line up and start running, and the next thing you know, you are in mystery-land. Which horse has a hairline fracture, which horse sees something funny, which horse is feeling especially good, which jock pushes which other jock. It's a mystery that can't be plumbed by the form, by the theories, by any known science, and it happens every day, for me to look at. And, then, it's a story, too. Every horse, every jock, every owner, every trainer, every bettor, every race. A football game is one story, one day a week. That's boring. A day at the races is thousands of stories, with grass around, trees around, a breeze, some mountains in the background. You know, in the summer, we'll go to a real horse heaven. We'll get out to Del Mar."

22 / JUSTA NECK

March 15. Race 2 (Golden Gate Fields): Rah Rah Mother of Twins Club. Approximate Post Time: 1:15. Seven furlongs. Purse $12,000. For male horses Four Years Old and Upward, 117 lbs. Non-winners of two races at six furlongs or over since January 1 allowed three pounds, of such a race since February 1, five pounds. Claiming price: $10,000. If for $8,000, 2 lbs.

In Massachusetts, there was a white gelding still running at fifteen. He had almost two hundred starts now. Among the dark Thoroughbreds he ran with, he looked like Hi Ho Silver streaking down the track. He always went off as the second or third favorite, just from sentimental bets. At every track in America, there were horses standing in stalls with more than a hundred starts beside their names in the *Form*. Two shedrows over from Justa Bob's stall was a ten-year-old mare who'd run 125 times. She had the end stall and she stood there all afternoon, her chest pressed against her stall door, all her attention focused in the direction of the track. When she heard the sound of the bell and the gate opening, she whinnied. Every three weeks or so, they took her out and ran her in a turf race. As often as not, she won or placed. She hadn't been away from the track in eight years.

Justa Bob, six, had thirty-nine starts. Rest day, walk day, jog day, gallop day, work day, race day. He knew all there was to know about each one. Today was a race day. The grate across his stall was closed to prevent interference with his state of mind and state of body. Other horses went out to work and he ate hay. His hay was taken away, then his water bucket. Some horses got nervous or irritable on race day, but Justa Bob just dozed a little more than usual. He knew what to expect, and his only job was to receive it. He expected to be cleaned with extra care, and he was. He expected to have his back legs wrapped and taped, and they were. He expected to be led out and down the shedrow, and he was. He expected to walk around the saddling enclosure, to enter one of the slots, to be bridled and saddled and patted, and to have his feet picked out, and he was. He expected to be led out into the cool sunshine with one horse in front of him and one behind, and he was. He expected to feel the weight of the jockey on his back, and he did. Like an experienced cardplayer who can pick up a deck of fifty-one cards and know that one is missing, Justa Bob could gauge how much weight was on his back, how hard it would be. This formed another of his expectations. He expected the pony who led him around to the gate to be a little irritable, and he was. And so it was that, with all of his expectations fulfilled, Justa Bob was just as relaxed as a horse could be. He took a quiet moment in the gate, then leapt forward when the doors clanged open.

Once he and all the other horses were out of the gate, Justa Bob had enough experience to know that he could expect certain things. Over the years, he had been bitten, bumped, whipped by another horse's jockey, fallen against. Though he had stayed on his feet, horses behind and beside him had gone down. This race didn't look to be any different. There were horses on either side of him, which was preferable to being on the rail. A few of them pulled ahead of him. He steadied himself just a bit for this, then settled into a rhythmic stride. Unbeknownst to all humans, because no studies had been done in this area, though one was planned at UC, Davis, Justa Bob could count to three. That is, he could recognize that there were more than two horses in front of him, but fewer than many, which was defined by his brain as four or more. Thus, there were three. Three was a good number. He galloped and galloped, working at his job, a job he enjoyed. Pretty soon, the third horse tired and dropped back, and Justa Bob decided that the second horse didn't look very fit, either—his haunches were wobbling just a bit. Justa Bob overtook him, drawing on some of the energy he always saved by being perfectly relaxed. Now there was a single horse in front of him, and Justa Bob recognized his type, the front-running type. They came out of the turn, Justa Bob on the rail and pulling forward. The first horse rolled his eye and pinned his ears at Justa Bob, but Justa Bob recognized this as a bluff. The other horse's jockey went for the whip, on the left side, and the horse shifted a bit away from Justa Bob. But the shock of the whip caused the other horse to tense just enough for Justa Bob to stretch out and overtake him. Now Justa Bob felt that familiar surge of power that came from the noise all around him, the expectation that the race would soon be over, and the way the jockey on his back was working him. Everything was normal. In front of him the track was empty. The horse at his side seemed to drop away.

But, of course, expectations are made to be challenged, even equine expectations, and Justa Bob wasn't the only being at the track who was taken aback when the horse he had just passed reached over, grabbed Justa Bob's jockey by his pants and the flesh of his thigh and pulled him right out of the saddle. It was hard to say, in fact, who was more surprised, the other horse's jockey, who had an eyewitness seat, or Justa Bob, who, as a horse, had almost 360-degree vision, and could see it all perfectly. Justa Bob's jockey was himself pretty surprised at the realization that only a few yards before the finish line he was going to drop between eight pounding legs, with another sixteen not far behind. He did not really want the horse who was biting him to let go, or his pants to rip. The moment, the duration of a stride, perhaps, lasted eternally, but in the end, the horse spit him out and there he was, suspended, his arms around Justa Bob's neck, and Justa Bob weaving and shifting in an effort to come under him and straighten him up. It was the other jockey who saved the day, by taking his whip and slashing his own horse on the side of the face, to move him suddenly to the outside of the track. When the space opened up, Justa Bob's jockey dropped off his neck and balled himself up on the track, and two or three seconds later, Justa Bob crossed the finish line riderless. The noise was tremendous. Justa Bob slowed, stopped and turned, then trotted back to meet his groom, who was running to catch him.

After that, all through the steward's inquiry, Justa Bob stood on the track with his groom patting him and the jockey limping around and patting him and the trainer patting him and he let the race be in his mind. Was there something to be afraid of? Was there something to avoid? It was hard to decide. All in all, however, Justa Bob decided, nothing like this had ever happened to him before, and so it was just a fluke. Nevertheless, the whole incident did reconfirm his settled opinion that the best winning margin was just a bob. The wait was a long one. He stretched out, dropped his penis, urinated, and relaxed into a doze. The groom laughed and said to the trainer, "Who is this guy?"

The trainer laughed and said, "Justa Bob."

The inquiry took forever. The book said one thing—that a horse must have a rider to win the race—but the heart said another. Far above Justa Bob, the officials discussed and watched the video and discussed and watched the video. Finally, they went by the book, placing the aggressor last and Justa Bob second to last. But it was invigorating all the same, just to see such a thing happen. Justa Bob's trainer thought it was the best loss he had ever sustained.

23 / ALL-NIGHTER

THE MOMENT the phone rang, Krista opened her eyes and looked at the red digits of the clock. It was 1:37. She picked up the cellular phone. She heard her own voice say, "This is Donut. I am foaling. Get up." Krista sat up and reached for her jeans. Behind her, on the other side of the bed, Pete rolled over. He murmured, "Need me?"

"I shouldn't."

"I'll come."

"It's all right. Maia might wake up." She leaned forward and pulled on her socks. She would have liked to think that she was wide awake and perfectly alert, but when she stood up, she staggered and had to catch herself, so, as she went through the kitchen and passed the refrigerator, she grabbed a Diet Coke. This was the sixth foal of the season. She had eight more to go. So far, nothing she had dreaded had come to pass. This foaling part had been the part that everyone, including Sam the vet, said that she shouldn't do without qualified help, but a foaling manager was expensive and fourteen or sixteen mares foaling over the course of five months wasn't enough to warrant the expense. Instead she had invested in a device—there was a little sensor Sam sewed into the mare's labia, just outside the vaginal opening. When the waters came, the sensor transmitted a signal to a receiver, which called her up. Everyone who had tried it said it was infallible—many fewer false alarms than with a belt thing she had seen that went off when the mare lay down. And so she had missed only three nights' sleep, really, since one of the mares had foaled in the afternoon and one had foaled at nine in the evening. Each of the three previous seasons she had slept in the barn and tried to keep an eye on whatever mare was waxing or streaming milk, but this method was actually more restful than her months nursing Maia in the night, mercifully now over.

She pulled on a jacket against the late-March chill and went out to the barn. She had expected this call, since the mare's bag was full and she had been a little agitated earlier in the evening. The stars were brilliant. She felt terrific. She slipped the cellular in her pocket and thought of the twenty-six colts and fillies she had foaled out over the last three years. It seemed like a lot, like a treasure, like a testament to her devotion and competence. And they were all good-looking—that was the influence of Himself.

The mare was down on her side in the deep, clean straw, her wrapped tail stretched out behind her, the familiar sight of her contractions that convulsed her enormous belly reassuringly strong. She was an older mare, not a race-horse, but a hunter mare from the neighborhood who had won a lot of blue ribbons and then been retired. This was her first foal. Krista lifted the heavy black tail aside.

There it was, disaster in the making. The foal had already begun to emerge, but instead of two tiny hooves, offset, and one tiny nose nestled on top of the cannon bones, there was only one tiny hoof. This is called a dystocia, she thought, then she pulled out her cellular and called Pete in the house. He was awake when he answered. She said, "I need you."

"I just started giving Maia her bottle. I can be out there in, like, fifteen minutes."

"I need someone right now. Sam is forty minutes from here."

"Call Margaret Lerner. She said you could."

Krista sat back on her heels. The mare gave another contraction, and the malpositioned foal moved slightly, coming more into view. On the one hand, Margaret Lerner was the world's most helpful person, as well as a veteran with mares and foals. On the other hand, Krista avoided Margaret Lerner on every possible occasion, which was difficult to do since the woman lived right across the road. Pete said, "Krista?"

She said, "Okay." She pushed the "end" button and then dialed Margaret's number. Margaret was awake, too. When Krista described the position of the foal, Margaret said, "Oh, Lord, I'll be there in a minute." And she was. And Krista was glad to hear the sound of her truck wheels on gravel and to see her face as she came into the stall. Margaret exclaimed, "Get her up!"

"I've tried. She's not responsive."

Margaret knelt beside the mare's shoulder and said, "Rise and shine, Mama." She poked her, then gave her a push. Krista shook the leadrope that she had snapped onto the mare's halter and the mare opened her eyes wide, looking at her. Margaret said again, "Got to get up, sweetie," and gave her a resolute, unsympathetic slap on the neck. Finally, the mare rolled onto her sternum and bent a foreleg, but then a contraction took her and she stopped.

"Now!" said Margaret. She pushed on the mare, and Krista pulled her to her feet. Then Margaret went behind the mare, moved the tail aside with one hand, and put her large palm into the vaginal opening. She said, "Lean against her shoulder and neck with your shoulder and neck." Krista did so. Margaret, watching the contractions, suddenly gave a tremendous shove just as a contraction eased. "Okay," she said. "I did it."

"You pushed the foal back in?"

"Yup. Now we've got to walk her."

The mare was reluctant at first, wishing to go down again, but with Margaret poking her from behind and Krista pulling her from the front, she took two steps, then two more, then three more. Finally, she was walking steadily around the stall. She was still having contractions, but her belly now extended downward, and Krista could see the shape of the foal dropping backward into that great space. Margaret pulled an obstetrical glove from the pocket of her jacket and said, "Stop a sec." Then she reached in. Krista could see her arm and shoulder move as she felt delicately for the stuck limb. Finally, she said, "Got it. Just bent at the knee. This we can do, I think. We'll just give it a little turn, here. The bones are hard, but the joints are loose, aren't they, Mama? Turn the knee a little to the outside, then find the foot. Ah. Got it. Then hold it and ease it out. Man, I wish I could get two hands in there. Oh, good boy. I can feel the fetlock and the tendon. No problem that I can feel, just turned wrong at the last moment. Little fellow wanted to gallop out of his mama, didn't he?"

"I'm so glad you're here," said Krista.

"I've seen worse," said Margaret.

Krista was sure that she had. She started the mare walking forward again, and Margaret said, "Say, did you hear about those two horses in that barn by the river last week?"

Krista shook her head.

"Well, the guy who owned them knew that the road might wash out in that big storm, so he fed 'em extra, and then he went home. He came back two days later, you know, after the big storm, and he didn't have an easy time getting in there, either. One of them drowned in his stall. Water got in there, and I guess the horse lost his footing and fell in the water. The mud level was as high as the door—"

Krista closed her eyes and swallowed hard.

"And the other one had a broken leg from struggling. Had to shoot 'im right there on the spot. The leg was dangling. Two horses. What a fluke, huh?"

"That's a terribly sad story."

Margaret shook her head. "I think so, too. But why didn't the guy trailer them out of there?"

"Maybe he didn't have a trailer, or the road was already washed out or something."

"Then there was this other guy—"

"Don't tell me."

"No, this is a good one. This has a happy ending."

Krista doubted it, knowing Margaret, but she nodded.

"Guy comes home from the track late. Goes down to visit his horses in his barn, and he's looking them over, you know. It's a shedrow barn, and of the four horses, two are looking out their back windows with their ears up. The other two aren't doing anything, just eating hay, you know. So, anyway, the guy goes out of the stall and up to the house to take a shower, and while he's in the shower he hears a big noise, and then comes out in his robe. Well, get this, this giant oak has fallen into the shedrow! Not five minutes after he walked out of the stall, the very place he was standing was crushed to nothing by this tree!"

"I thought you said this story had a happy ending."

"No! The horses were fine. Even the one standing in that stall jumped out of the way and pressed himself against the wall. He was a little scared, that's all. Most of the tree hit the tackroom. Five minutes! Those two horses who were looking out the window, though, they knew something. They felt the ground move, you ask me."

"Or they heard the tree creaking, maybe."

"I've been to that guy's barn. Biggest tree."

"She wants to go down again," said Krista. The mare had begun to brace herself and paw. When they stopped pushing her forward, her knees buckled. Krista stood back. The mare gave a large grunt and stretched out on her side.

Margaret said, "Remember that mare of Bob Roberts' who went up to New Bolton Center, and when she came back she just looked fine. They had her in one of the paddocks out behind their place, it wasn't breeding season or anything, I think she was barren, and anyway, pretty soon the mare next to her had raging diarrhea—"

"You know, Margaret," said Krista, "I don't think I know anyone who has more stories to tell than you do. It's amazing."

"I do kind of collect them. Anyway, this mare who'd gone up to New Bolton, she was shedding salmonella, they said, and the other mare—"

"But I have a hard time with them sometimes."

"They had to euthanize her after about four days, and when they autopsied her—"

"This one, for example, really bothers me."

"She had salmonella abscesses everywhere. It was amazing she lived that long. This bothers you, huh?"

"It does."

"Here's what I think—"

Krista crawled around to the hind end of the mare and lifted her tail. What she saw was reassuring—the two little feet, properly offset, and the little nose. Another contraction pushed the head out up to the ears, and then another contraction pushed the rest of the head out. Krista gave a large sigh of relief. One, or at the most two more contractions, and the foal would be out. With her little finger, she cleared the baby's nostrils. Margaret said, "She's given up for some reason. Come on, Mama. Give the little fellow a push."

But the mare seemed uninterested, perhaps exhausted. "Lazy girl," said Margaret. "Come on, mare, push that baby out." Still nothing. Krista and Margaret exchanged a glance, and Krista felt the panic that she had been deflecting hit her full-force. You could tell by the size of the foal's head and feet that he was a big one, and needed something extra from the mare. But Donut was lost in space somewhere, as gone as if this weren't even happening to her.

"You can never tell what a maiden is going to do," said Margaret. "Who is this, that mare from Black Oak? She was a nice jumper. One time—" But then she said, "Okay, baby, old Margaret's going to drag you out of there."

She sat down in the straw, facing the mare's tail, and put a booted foot on each of her buttocks. Then she reached into her and grabbed the slippery foal around the cannon bones above the fetlocks. Then she bent her knees, bent her back, bent her head almost into the nose of the baby, and suddenly gave a huge heave and grunt. The foal moved forward about three inches. Margaret said, "Let me try to get a better hold here." She wiped her hands on her jacket, then grabbed the horse's legs again. This time she cocked her body so that she could exaggerate the torsion on the foal's shoulders, forcing them to come out one at a time instead of together. She gave another heave and another grunt, and suddenly her knees straightened and the foal shot out of the mare into Margaret's arms and lap. They sat still for a moment, then Krista laughed. Margaret gently smoothed the amnion away from the foal's face. The baby snorted and took a deep breath, and Krista said, "Oh, wow."

"Big boy," said Margaret.

"No," said Krista. "Big girl."

"You know," said Margaret, "your grandfather always chose the ones he was going to keep and the ones he was going to sell within a few hours of birth. It depended on how they faced life."

The mare was out of it, so they wiped the filly down where she lay. She was dark, but she had a fan-shaped white star between her eyes and a snip of white between her nostrils, as well as one white foot, the left hind.

Margaret said, "This mare better wake up and look at her baby. Maidens are so unpredictable."

The filly, though, was wide awake and looking around. Two or three times, she turned her gaze to Krista's face and regarded her for a few seconds. She also turned to look at the bulk of the mare, who at last lifted her head to look at the filly. Now was the moment for a maiden, Krista knew. Some maidens were so amazed by what had happened to them that they couldn't take it in, couldn't relate to the foal, couldn't give way to their hormonal drive to nurture. But Donut nickered—not loudly, but firmly. The filly looked at her and nickered back. Krista had the eerie sense that the foal knew more than the mare did. After another moment, Donut understood, got to her feet, stepped through the straw, put her head down to the filly and nosed her, then started licking her face. The filly turned her face up to her mother, and the mare ran her tongue here and there with increasing conviction and pleasure. Margaret and Krista stood up and moved away, not without patting the mare on the neck.

"Okay, then," said Margaret.

"Seems to be," said Krista. "Thank you." The mare would go down once more and birthe the placenta, but that was almost never a problem.

"You want me to come over tomorrow and help you check the placenta? You're going to have Sam over in a day or two to check for uterine damage, aren't you?"

"Yes, sure," said Krista. "Look at her. She's a lovely filly." And then the filly unfolded herself and rose to her feet.

APRIL

24 / OUT OF ADJUSTMENT

WHAT DICK WINTERSON did when he found out on the morning of the race that his wife, Louisa, planned to come out was not anything. He did not discourage her and he did not call Rosalind to warn her. He was already full of dread at the prospect of sitting between Al and Rosalind with the damned dog staring at him and letting him know in every possible way that should she learn to talk she would tell Al everything first crack out of the box. Dick was so full of dread that there was no amplification possible, only a kind of wrong-end-of-the-telescope experience where all of these people seemed to be coming at him in tiny vehicles from very great distances. He was standing at the pass gate, smiling. He could hear the announcer, Tom Durkin, calling the fifth race. Laurita was running in the seventh race, the Rokeby Stakes, a Grade Two race for three-year-old fillies, a mile and an eighth on the grass. Al, Rosalind, and Eileen emerged from the Mercedes. It was driven away. They whirred toward him as if on wheels. They were very small, bright, and sharply defined. He greeted them. He said, "Do you mind if we wait here just a few more moments? My wife, Louisa, wanted to see the race, too."

"Lovely," said Rosalind instantly, smiling.

"Yeah?" said Al. "She a racing fan?"

"Not really, no. I don't think she's been out to Aqueduct in years. Once in a while she goes up to Saratoga in the summer. We used to rent a house there that we liked very much, but now I understand it's been sold. I don't quite know what I'm going to do this summer. That house—"

"How's the filly?" said Al, knowing bullshit when he heard it. But he didn't wait for Dick to answer. "You know, that filly might go in the Breeders' Cup. I've been thinking about it. If we start thinking about it now, then we might be ready when the time comes."

"Well—" said Dick, but here came Louisa in their Camry, as tiny and bright as the other three. Dick was so dazzled that all of what Al was saying rose on the bright air around him, unheard and disregarded. Louisa pulled up to the valet-parking attendant and sat quietly for a moment, then another moment. "What's the problem?" said Al. "That her?"

"Yes," said Rosalind.

The door opened, and Dick started toward his wife. She sat there for another moment, the attendant standing over her and looking down expectantly. Then she got out of the car with a sudden jerk and dropped her purse. The attendant picked it up. By this time, Dick was right there, handing the attendant a five-dollar bill. His hand went out from him into another world, the tiny distant world of the parking attendant. "Hi!" he said cheerily. Louisa gave him the look.

She had offered to come to the race. She didn't know he was sleeping with Rosalind Maybrick. Now that he had betrayed her, he saw her through a thornier and thornier tangle of words that could not be said, and his love for her filled him more and more, as if the conduit between them, once short and wide and capable of carrying off many acre-feet of love, was now long, narrow, and partly blocked. What could not get from him to her flooded him over and over.

The look was a glance of anguish and remorse, arising from the fact that she was having an agoraphobia attack and had come to the racetrack anyway. The racetrack was an agoraphobic's worst nightmare—crowded, vast, noisy. Dealing with Louisa when she was having an attack was very much like dealing with a spooky horse. You had to exude self-confidence—her heightened sense of alertness always took its cue from him, or from other companions. This was something she could not control, an electricity or pheromone thing, below the level of consciousness. Dick instantly, and without touching her, organized himself inwardly to simply be with her in utter calmness. He imagined himself as a containment building, three-sided, warm, small, no windows. She could enter if she wanted to, if she noticed. She had to enter, though, of her own accord. Nor could you pull a horse into a trailer without tempting him to rear up and hit his head. Horses had died that way.

He introduced Louisa to Al and Rosalind. Rosalind said, "How nice to see you."

Al said, "We going up to the box? Let me get a *Form*. Dick, I tell you, I'm not kidding about this Breeders' Cup thing. She's a good filly, and let me tell you, I've been in this business long enough. What, eleven years? How much money have I spent on this? Rosalind, how much money have I spent on these damn horses?"

"I don't know, darling."

"Well, plenty. The Breeders' Cup is at Churchill this year. We've got to—" And then all his words vaporized again. Dick could see his yap yapping, but couldn't hear a thing. He said, "Better not to count on anything, Al—" Yap yap yap. Now he was barking unintelligibly himself.

But he was watching Louisa. Later he decided that this thing that happened was what broke his heart. The first thing was that Louisa cleared her throat. Then she put her palm over her mouth, bent her head back, and closed her eyes, only for a second. Then she ran her hand down her neck, pausing at the base of her throat, continuing until she was pressing on her chest over her heart, as if to still it. All of this took only a second or two, and perhaps she wasn't aware of him looking at her. At any rate, after that, she took a deep breath and smiled at him, her husband, and said, "Let's go, then." There it was, her whole history of not being able to go where he spent his life, in a large, chaotic space where nothing at all could be predicted or even planned, and where he had been perfectly comfortable for many years. How could it be that they had so thoroughly gone their separate ways that they could barely enter each other's world now? Did he enter hers any more often than she entered his? Perhaps it was years since he had been to the college where she taught, and he hadn't been to many recitals, either—he found the music she preferred grating and hard to listen to. At home, on their familiar turf, in their living room, kitchen, bedroom, study, dining room, all rooms that she could live in with utter familiarity and apparent normalcy, he was just as she was, apparently normal and apparently happily married. But, he realized, he hadn't been even as willing to go as far with her as she was to come, again, to Aqueduct. If someone was trapped in a small room, fearful of going out and fearful of staying in, then it was himself, not her. It was a small room that Rosalind Maybrick entered and left at will, as free, Dick thought, as anyone could ever be.

"I'm ready," said Louisa.

"Good," said Rosalind, her voice resonating like a bell. And he followed Louisa as she performed the rituals that allowed her to move, longing to take her elbow, but not daring. You never touch an agoraphobic in the middle of an attack.

THEY CAME TO the saddling enclosure. Rosalind looked down at Eileen and told her to sit. Eileen sat right down, boom, the way she always did, as if showing off. The groom and the assistant trainer already had the filly in her slot, though the horses for the sixth race were only just going out. Dick said brightly, "Here she is. You see, Al, she's got quite a bloom on her." Rosalind knew what that meant now—that the horse was training hard but in excellent health, well oxygenated and happy, 100 percent, as racing men said. Rosalind picked up Eileen and the four of them entered the saddling enclosure and went over to the filly. The two men then drew off. Rosalind could hear Al's persistant whine: "It's April. We've got to put her in some of these fancy races. I'm telling you rumble rumble rumble drone drone drone Breeders' Cup—"

Though she was younger than Rosalind by five years or so, the wife was one of those women for whom time had passed, and not kindly. Her face was a little puffy and her hair a little contrasty, brunette and gray. Of course, Rosalind knew, she was an artist, a singer, and appearance was of secondary importance to her. Rosalind respected that. Today, though, she radiated something that Rosalind couldn't quite figure out. Pain of some sort. Well, if Rosalind herself didn't radiate pain, it was only because her containment facility was in perfect order, on a regular maintenance schedule serviced by Elizabeth Arden, Bliss, Isaac Mizrahi, Jil Sander, and Giorgio Armani.

The thing about the wife, that is, Louisa, was that Dick had been married to her for twenty years, with her longer than that. Rosalind had delicately extracted from him the information that he was not a habitual adulterer, that, though not 100 percent faithful over the years, he had learned whatever it was he knew about love and sex through marriage, not outside of it. Rosalind, herself not previously an adulterer at all, was perhaps not as much a connoisseur of the erotic as she was of Persian carpets, American Chippendale furniture, nineteenth-century American painting, or Chinese porcelain, to name four things she had more experience with than sex and had formerly liked more than sex. But she had plenty of experience in being a satisfied customer, and with Dick, she was most assuredly a satisfied customer. At least for a moment. In that moment just after they were finished making love, she was satisfied to the eyeballs, but then, when he turned away from her, to drink something or to go to the bathroom, or to blow his nose or whatever, the satisfaction always began to dissipate, and continued to do so, so that, by the time he left to go wherever it was that he had to go, usually to the track, or she left to go wherever she was pretending she had to go, she was lost and aching again, though she dared not let him know.

Now the filly was saddled and they followed the groom, the horse, Dick, and Al out to the walking ring. The jockey had appeared and was walking along between the two men, cocky as could be, chatting them up. Rosalind could hear herself talking to Louisa—You just decided to come out suddenly, you don't come out very often, then, racing isn't my cup of tea, either, really—but she wasn't actually looking at her until they came into the stands above the paddock and she heard Louisa inhale sharply and cry out. In front of her, Dick stiffened like he'd been shot, and Rosalind felt herself emerge from her shell of self-involvement and take notice. She said, "Are you all right?" She put Eileen down again.

A terribly anguished look passed over Louisa's face and she took Rosalind's hand. She said, "Just hold my hand until they open the gate and let the horses out." Rosalind made up a reassuring smile, and they stood there while the horses moved out onto the track and began walking around to the gate. Eileen on her leash trotted right behind them, her head about ankle high in the crowd, but nevertheless, as always, undaunted. Louisa let go Rosalind's hand when they mounted to their box, and then Dick paused long enough for the two of them to catch up to him, still talking to Al. Al, of course, was still babbling about his rights and privileges as a racehorse owner. Rosalind passed Louisa to Dick and he gave her a little smile, grateful, unlike any other smile they had shared. Rosalind expected to see him put his arm around his wife and draw her against him, but he didn't. He let her pass in front of him, then he followed her up the steps and over to the box. She sat down and seemed to coil up, her hands in her lap and her feet under the seat. Dick sat on one side of her, and Rosalind on the other, with Eileen in her lap. Eileen got up, put her forefeet on the railing, and pricked her ears as if ready for the race. Al sat on the other side of Dick. He said, "About time this filly got back out here. It's been two months since her last race."

Dick said, "She's ready today. And, Al, if you want to go to the Breeders' Cup, you've got to let her save something for later." He sounded enthusiastic, but as the horses approached the gate, Rosalind knew from conversations they'd had that he was worried. He hated the starting gate. One thing for sure, since the onset of her illness, which was how she thought of their affair, she had learned a good deal more about horse racing than she had ever known before. Too much, probably. Anyway, now she knew enough to worry, whereas in her former life she had skimmed in blissful ignorance above the whole socially unredeemed enterprise.

Dick put his glasses to his eyes, as did Al, and Laurita went into the gate second. She was in the seventh position from the post, a good position in this race. The last horse to go in resisted, and Dick coughed, a sign of distress. Did Al recognize this? Did Louisa recognize this? Perhaps only Rosalind knew enough about what was going on with Dick to recognize that cough. Then the horses were in, the bell rang, and they were out again, streaming over the green grass in a bunch. Rosalind, who had no binoculars, couldn't make out which one was Laurita, but that was okay. She let Al and Dick take care of winning. She herself only took care of safety. She closed her eyes, gripped Eileen around the shoulders, and exerted her powers. Her hearing was good. She could hear eight horses, sixty-four legs, everyone safe and sound. This was a newish thing for her, knowing that the horses were safe by the separate and even beats that all of their hooves made in the track surface. She might have been astonished by it, but she had seen *Rain Man,* and she knew that the power to make order out of chaos was a fairly common one among the mentally unusual, which she now was. She could hear the horses round the second turn. If you closed your eyes, a race seemed to go much faster than it did if you watched it, which she considered a blessing.

And then Louisa rose out of her seat like a missile through the still surface of the ocean and ran. And Dick rose out of his seat and went after her as if on a string. And Eileen gave a single bark. Al said, "What's up with them? The race isn't even over."

Rosalind remembered to turn her eyes to the homestretch, where, sure enough, Laurita was flattening out to hold off the bid of another filly, who had attained her shoulder but could attain nothing more and, at the wire, dropped back to Laurita's hip. They jumped up, cheering, and Rosalind exclaimed, "That filly works hard for you, Al."

"—Breeders' Cup. But where did those two go? I can't go into the winner's circle alone."

"Al, I think there's something wrong."

"What's wrong? How could anything be wrong? We just won a big stakes."

"Adrenaline doesn't cure everything, Al."

"What does that mean?"

But then he was gone himself, leaving her to make a more dignified progress to the track. A few moments later, she saw him out there. He shook the groom's hand, then the jockey's hand. Then he gave the filly a clumsy hug. She made her deliberate way to the filly. Dick was nowhere to be seen, which was rather awkward, though no more awkward than other social situations Rosalind had dealt with in the past. What she hated was that she had not prepared herself for his absence, which she had to do in order to accommodate herself to it. Whatever was happening to Louisa, she thought, could be no more agonizing than what was happening to her (her self vanishing into darkness, irretrievable, deadly), she was just more in the habit of closing down the containment facility to prevent a total meltdown. But the alarms were ringing so loudly while they were standing for the picture that she thought surely every ear in the stands could hear them. And Al said, "What's the matter with you? What's the matter with everyone? I don't get it."

LOUISA MALONE-WINTERSON was perfectly capable of understanding what was happening to her—it had been happening for ten years now, and she had had plenty of therapy. She was even perfectly capable of deploring it, excusing it, and forgiving it, but she was not capable of stopping it. She had always imagined a full-blown agoraphobia attack as the experience of knocking at an address she thought she knew, expecting the door to open, and a friend to smile at her and invite her into the house, but instead finding herself sucked into a wind tunnel, slick, featureless, buffetting, with only a slender thread of knowledge to hold on to—progress through the wind tunnel was inevitable, the attack would end, the door at the other side would open when she got there. This thread of knowledge was more comforting when she was not having an attack, but she had learned to hang on to it even when she was. It was also probable, she knew, that she would not get hurt, though falling down, running into the path of a moving vehicle, and even running into a wall were remote possibilities. Ah, well, there was a room in her mind that was separate from this, from which she observed her behavior through a small, protected window.

She ran through the betting hall and out onto the concourse in front of the track. She found herself where the ramp swooped up to the subway stop, not a good place to be—in fact, the very worst place to be, because the roof of the concourse seemed to run toward her or away from her, as if she were in the center of a funnel, and the grandstand loomed behind her, too tall for her to dare to look at. Now Dick was with her, toppling toward her, and he grabbed her, even though she recoiled. He grabbed her by the elbow and began pulling her back inside, through the pass gate and the vestibule, and into the hallway below the escalators, and from the small safe little room in her mind, she ordered herself not to fight him, but to go along with him. He had always taken her somewhere safe before, and so she ought to have had faith in him, but the reluctance to be touched was so powerful that it came into her mind to bite him or kick him, a horsey thing to do, he liked horses so much. He said, "Darling, close your eyes. Close your eyes." He took her over to the wall behind the escalators.

She had done this in the past, long before, and she tried to remember how to do it. But her eyelids were pasted open in horror and fear. She had no control over them. Finally, he did what he had to do, which was to put his hand in front of her eyes and block out everything she was seeing. Then he sat down on the bench against the wall and pulled her down with him, still keeping his arm around her and his hand over her eyes. It was brutal and made her want to run away. But that was the thing about agoraphobia. In the middle of an attack, there was no going and no staying. The impossibility of either course of action put her into a dilemma that could not be solved in this physical universe, so she started screaming. She knew she was screaming; it was pretty obvious, and it echoed around the glassed-in space, but she couldn't stop. And then Dick said, "Louisa, you will damage your voice. Please don't do that to yourself, darling."

"Let go of me."

He let go of her. Immediately, the urge to run lifted off. His hand was no longer over her eyes, and so she put her own hands over her eyes. A bit after that, she was able to take a deep breath. Then she realized what had been happening, and the relief of finding the door at the end of the wind tunnel turned into humiliation and remorse, so she burst into tears. He did not put his arms around her. She had trained him not to. But he sat beside her on the bench while she cried.

NORMALLY AL LEFT the track after any race his horse ran in. He wasn't all that interested in the horses belonging to the other men he knew. One group of men to be in, his AA group, was enough for him. But this time, he was so confused that he just followed the groom and the horse. Frankly, he didn't quite know what to do. Dick and his wife had disappeared in a very mysterious way, and then Rosalind had said that she couldn't take it anymore and gotten into their limo with the damned dog. When he had tried to get in with her, she said, "Later, Al, if you don't mind." Well, actually, he did mind, but perhaps, if she couldn't take it anymore, it was better not to give it to her anymore. Of course, this was not unexpected. Even though she had never said that before, that she couldn't take it anymore, he knew that people had been wondering for years how she could take it with him. In his AA group, they even said it to his face—how can your wife take it with you?

So, after the filly pissed the way she had to following the race, to show that no one had dosed her with any illegal substances, he followed her back to her stall. This guy, Luciano, was there waiting for her. He told Al he was the horse masseur. Now, this was immediately interesting to Al, and he forgot for the moment that his wife couldn't take him anymore. He said, "What am I paying you? You massage the horse?"

"Dick pays me fifty dollars a session, and yes."

"I pay my own guy that."

"Is that all?"

"Well, I got a couple of massages up at the spa last summer for ninety. Not a bad gig, to tell the truth. That's what I think. Though after my guy does me he is in a sweat."

"Has trouble releasing you, huh?"

"I guess."

Luciano had begun on the horse, but now he cast a professional eye over Al, then said, "Looks to me like you need some chiropractic. Massage can only do so much. If you're out of adjustment, you walk around and just get back into the same way of going. Muscles do hold the bones, yes, but the bones pull on the muscles. I think of it as a dialectical process, myself. Thesis—your spine is out of alignment. Antithesis—your muscles are working against your spine. Synthesis—kablooie. Fuck, that hurts!" Al and Luciano laughed together, and Al leaned against the doorway of the filly's stall. The filly looked at him for a moment, the way she had before the race. Then she stretched out her head and closed her eyes. Al said, "She likes that, huh?"

"Don't you, when you get it done?"

"I don't know. I guess. I must like it if I get it done regularly."

Luciano was an easy sort of guy, Al thought, not like most of the guys he spent his time with, so he made himself even more comfortable. He said, "The time this filly won that race in Florida, there was this big celebration. I paid a pile for that party. And that wasn't a big race like this one."

"I was there. Excellent champagnes. Thank you."

"Yeah, well. My wife does all of that. You know—" But he stopped.

"What?"

"I don't understand what's going on here. Dick and his wife ran off, then Rosalind ran off, and here I am. The barn's empty. It's a big-stakes race, and it's like nobody cares."

Luciano stopped massaging, his hands still on the horse, and thought of telling Al that Dick and Rosalind were having an affair, but then Al went on, "I guess I'm kind of a grumpy guy, and I bitched about that bill after I got it, but that doesn't mean I don't like to celebrate. You know"—he eyed Luciano for symptoms of envy, and, seeing none, went on—"I've got so much money from my business that the win doesn't count for much, so that isn't in itself a celebration. And the filly probably is just as happy to be getting worked over as anything else. I just want to get to the Breeders' Cup, that's all. I nominate all my foals. Costs me five hundred dollars apiece. That's not pocket change when you think about it, but I've never—"

"You sound lonely."

"Who, me?"

"Well, yeah."

"Lonely?"

"I would say so."

"Huh. Maybe I should call my sponsor in that case." But he didn't want to do that. Al hated calling Harold, because Harold would just tell him some practical steps he could take that would involve submission to something or other. "Say," he said, "Dick and his wife ran out of there. I couldn't figure that out. He didn't see the end of the race. She let off a little cry, like she got hurt or something."

"She has a mental condition. He told me what it was. It's a fear thing."

"Then Rosalind—" Al's face fell. Soon enough he was going to have to deal with the fact that she couldn't take it anymore. And she had been so good at taking it, a real champ. He sighed. There was silence punctuated only by the low grunting of the filly as Luciano released the tight spots in her haunches one by one. "But you know, I deserve a run in the Breeders' Cup. The filly's a good filly. *She* deserves a run in the Breeders' Cup. You know I've been in this game for eleven years? All the time I'm reading about guys who started running horses three or four years ago, and already they've got a Derby winner or something. You know what? I don't care about the Derby. That's how I'm different. I do care about the Breeders' Cup, though—" After all was said and done, he was beginning to feel a little angry.

Luciano glanced at Al, then at the filly, then at Al again. Finally, he said, "You like gnocchi? A little glass of wine? This is my last horse of the day."

Al, who hadn't actually had a relationship with another man undefined by obligations and one-upmanship on both sides in maybe forty-five years, if ever, at last shut up about the Breeders' Cup. After a moment of silence that even he appreciated, he said, "Well, okay. Yeah."

25 / PITTER PAT

TIFFANY WAS SITTING with her new trainer. Tiffany had been to the races three times—twice to Aqueduct, and also to Belmont to visit the trainer's barn. She liked Belmont better. It was the closest thing she had ever seen to never-ending beauty, she thought. Lawrence had used his contacts to find Ho Ho a trainer named Dagoberto Gomez. Dagoberto was all business. His barn was spic and span, his grooms were all Cuban, he kept his owners in line with a blazingly firm gaze. There were several things owners were absolutely not allowed to do: raise their hands above waist level, feed the horses anything except carrots supplied by Dagoberto, in the presence of the groom, wear inappropriate clothing or footgear, bring children into the barn, have a condition book and make suggestions about upcoming races, talk to any other trainers or owners who were with any other trainers. On the other hand, an owner was allowed to ask Dagoberto any question in the world, about horses, about cuisine, about music, about politics, about literature, about God, and Dagoberto would immediately give that owner a considered and articulate answer. Yes, said Lawrence, Dagoberto was a control freak as only a Cuban could be, but a year with Dagoberto would teach Ho Ho and Tiffany something that they might not otherwise learn.

Tiffany was wearing what Dagoberto had told her to wear, a respectable black pants suit and black Gucci loafers. He did not like his owners' female connections to wear anything filmy, ruffly, or pastel-colored, nor did he like them to wear jeans. The track was a class society, said Dagoberto, and everyone there, horses and people, had to exhibit class. The whole entourage gave over their L.A. rap-singer clothes and put on their sport jackets and button-down shirts. They grumbled that it was like going to school. Yes, Tiffany thought. Yes. The others had begged off going to the track today—even Ho Ho, who really was going to own the horse should they get one, thought it was kind of boring. They all liked fifteen-minute quarters, for example, not sporting events that ended a minute and a half after they had begun. But Tiffany couldn't wait to come. She had made a tape off the radio of a guy calling the Kentucky Derby. Quite often she played it. All the words he used and the excitement in his voice made her happy. She had a whole new list of words that she sang voicelessly to herself: furlong, off the pace, sire, dam, yearling, gaskin, withers, hock, router, cannon bone, garden spot, long shot, favorite, girth, blinkers, colt, fetlock, and, of course, filly. That was the loveliest word of all, she thought, filly, a word of great natural sweetness. She had noticed that Dagoberto always said that word a bit affectionately, hard-hearted and hard-headed self-made man that he was.

Dagoberto liked Tiffany. He sat with her in his box as the horses went out onto the track, and he questioned her about them. "Number one, missy. What do you like about that filly?"

"She's got a pretty head."

"Yes, she does."

"She takes big steps."

"How do you mean?"

"Well, it looks like the back feet go in front of where the front feet step."

"Now number two."

"She's got a very rounded butt. And she shines."

"What don't you like about her?"

Tiffany contemplated. The horse moved into a trot, was brought back down. "There's something wrong with her back legs. They're too straight or something."

"Number three."

"She looks scared. Her head is up. She's all sweaty."

"Number four."

"She's very pretty all over. She's littler than the rest, well, not littler, but more delicate. She reminds me of a ballet dancer. I saw a ballet on the TV a couple of times."

"Number five now."

"She looks sad."

"I think so, too. Number six."

"She's boring-looking. Pretty enough but not really pretty. She looks like she wants to work at Wal-Mart for the rest of her life. She wouldn't be my friend."

"Number seven."

"She looks mean or something. I don't like her at all."

"Number eight."

"She looks like a baby, but I like her brightness."

"Her brightness?"

"The others look like they, uh, dated too many guys in the neighborhood and think they know everything, but she's still interested."

Now for the big question. "Which one do you want?"

"Which one of these?"

"Ho Ho said to claim one for you now you've got your owner's license, so I put in a claim. Which one do you want?"

Tiffany rattled her *Racing Form,* but Dagoberto put his hand on it before she could open it. "No, chiquita, you look, cara mia. Tell me from looking."

Now they were cantering. Tiffany scanned the field, choosing. She threw out the boring one, the mean one, the one with straight hind legs, the scared one, the sad one. After a moment, she threw out the ballerina. Now it was between one and eight, big steps and brightness, big steps and brightness. Tiffany licked her lips. She said, "You always got to make a choice, huh? Because the bright one can't be the one with the big steps."

"Not at this level. At this level you have to make a choice. But making choices is good."

The fillies loaded into the gate. Tiffany said, "Number eight. I like number eight." The gate clanged open.

"Bueno," said Dagoberto. "That's the one I chose for you, because she hasn't learned yet to lose. She is not the fastest or the best built or the best bred, but she is the easiest for me to teach, so I have claimed her."

Tiffany looked at the program. "Tellmeenow."

"That is her name."

"Tellmeenow."

They watched the race. Number one faded in the stretch. The mean one ran second to the ballerina. Tellmeenow went wide on the turn, then came on to take third from the bored one.

"She didn't win," said Tiffany.

"This is her third start," said Dagoberto. "She still hasn't learned to run. But she wanted to beat the fourth horse, and she did. Let's go look at our new baby."

Tiffany's heart started to pound as they stood up and went out of the box. She followed him down the steps until they were overlooking the winner's circle. They watched briefly as the winning filly and her connections celebrated, then she followed Dagoberto away from the grandstand. While she wasn't noticing, she saw, someone had hung a red tag on Tellmeenow's bridle. That was for her. That was her red tag. Tiffany walked behind the horse without expressing her excitement, and saw the two white hind feet—her feet now—and the shining, fluid tail—her tail now—and the square shape of the "haunches" (another great word)—her haunches now. For now, that back end was enough to enjoy, to possess, that and the ringing on the concrete of the filly's shoes—Tiffany's shoes now. Dagoberto was nodding and muttering, "Sound. Pretty good mover." Tiffany didn't hear it all. The filly's dark coat gleamed in the late-afternoon sunlight. Dapple. That was another word. The filly turned her head to the left, then to the right. She walked along. She was tired, Tiffany thought. Now they walked along a wide path toward the building with a fence around it. On the fence was a sign that said "test barn." They walked into it, and Tiffany saw one of Dagoberto's grooms step up to the filly with a halter. Now the groom who had been leading her took off her bridle—he brought the piece that went behind her ears over her head and waited a moment. The filly paused, then opened her mouth and let the metal piece, the bit, go. Then the halter was on. Dagoberto was saying to Tiffany, "Okay, now. Want to pet her?" Tiffany reached out the tips of her fingers and ran them down the filly's neck, then she stepped closer and touched her lightly over her splendid large eyes. "That's right," said Dagoberto. "That's right. Don't stand right in front of her. She's got a blind spot there. Stand to the side. There you go." Tiffany put her hand down, cupped upward, and the filly put her nose into it and snuffled, tickling Tiffany's palm with her whiskers. Her breath was warm and soft. Tiffany, who knew all about beauty, thought she was certainly the most beautiful creature she had ever seen, and at least twice as lovely now as she had been as someone else's horse. "You're moaning," said Dagoberto.

"I bet I am," said Tiffany. "I bet I just am."

Now the filly turned her head and deliberately set it on Tiffany's shoulder, and suddenly blew through her nostrils. Tiffany turned her own head and the two of them, filly and girl, gazed into each other's eyes for a long moment. The groom caught Dagoberto's eye and smiled cheerfully, then shook his head. Dagoberto shook his own head and smiled. What could you do? Sometimes, in spite of yourself and everything you knew about appearances' being deceiving, even though you were ages old and had been in the horse business all your life and had seen every deceptive appearance fall away to reveal the plain and sometimes ugly reality within, even though you had a wife and kids who had kids of their own and you knew in your very bones that beauty was the most fleeting thing of all, appearances ravished you anyway, and gave you the strange sensation of a finger running up your spine and tickling the back of your neck until you thought that, if you weren't in public every day, surrounded by cynical and hard-bitten men, you might tremble at it.

26 / ANIMAL FARM

ALWAYS AT THE END of April, southern-California racing moved from Santa Anita to Hollywood Park. Although Oliver was still in a non-hankering-after-signs-of-progress mode, he did allow himself to pray for mercy. He felt good, moment by moment, but when he looked up, there were still no winners. There were, to be sure, winning horses in the barn: Redhead (half-sister to the great fillies Red Shift, Red Scare, and Infrared, all daughters of the great race and broodmare Red Beans, and granddaughters of the great runner Red God), who had won two million dollars and all kinds of big races, went out for the Santa Anita Derby in perfect condition, five-to-one, perfect odds for the best horse in the field of males, was running down the backstretch in apparently good form, only to have her jockey pull her up. "I thought she stepped on herself," said the jockey, and though on the videotape there was no sign of a misstep, the jockey was resolute in his conviction that the mare had grabbed herself and that the only safe thing to do was pull her up. Farley agreed with the jockey, though all over the track bettors were consulting their favorite hitmen to see how much it would cost to have the jockey eternally retired.

And then there was A Likely Prospect. A Likely Prospect was a two-year-old by Mr. Prospector himself, out of a Secretariat mare, as well bred as an earthly horse could be. He was ready to run, training perfectly—knew how to break from the gate, knew how to run in company, knew how to move off the rail and onto it. He was getting ready for his first race, galloping on the track. The exercise rider had just finished the gallop and was trotting the horse out when another two-year-old threw his rider and came barreling blindly into A Likely Prospect, knocking him out cold, in fact, so that when the exercise rider jumped up she was screaming, "He's dead! He's dead!" And then the horse lifted his head, and then Farley got there from the grandstand, with Oliver right behind him. The horse scrambled to his feet, but he was hopping lame, and turned out to have broken a sesamoid bone. They didn't have to euthanize the horse. He would live to, perhaps, reproduce his own sire's stud career. But he was out of the barn.

There were others. The whole meet at Santa Anita had been full of fluky accidents and incidents. It didn't help Oliver that Farley's way of assimilating them was to relate stories, of which he had an endless supply, of even flukier accidents—a Horatio Luro story about Hialeah, where the horse won the race, broke through the rail into the infield, and drowned in the infield pond; the story of a training accident where the horse had just worked and was pulled up to catch his breath facing the rail, when two other horses ran by and the inside rein of the outside horse broke, the horse veered off, into the standing horse, and the irresistible force killed the immovable object. And then there was the worst one Farley had seen himself—a good horse was doing a fast work on the rail, and as he came around the turn he collided head-on with a loose horse taking the rail in the opposite direction. Both horses were killed. Whereas Farley seemed to gain some sort of it-could-be-worse peace from telling these stories, they only made Oliver feel more anxious, as if accidents and deaths were littering the track and he had to pick his way around them every day.

But, of course, the most dispiriting thing was Buddy Crawford's success. His win percentage was around 30, and Oliver could see, every day out on the training track, all of his horses, from claimers to stakes winners, training like monsters. He had stopped claiming Farley's horses, but it was small enough consolation.

Farley's problem, in Oliver's view, was that, instead of figuring out a way to reverse his decline, he was paying too much attention to the pig.

The pig had arrived in February, a gift from a farmer down in San Diego as thanks for allowing him to take away for free the hay and grain that had been left over the summer before. The pig was about a month old, and weighed maybe twenty pounds. Farley thought it was cute—it was a black-and-white pig, which Farley said was a Poland-China pig—and put it in a wire-mesh pen out in the yard. Then a filly came in who was a nervous wreck. She paced her stall, bit at her stall guard, kicked out when other horses passed. Farley put the pig in with her. The filly calmed down at once, instantly interested in the pig, sniffing the pig, nuzzling the pig, rolling the pig over with her nose, herding the pig here and there. At first the pig was afraid of the filly, and the barn was filled with high-pitched squealing, which made the other horses nervous. But at afternoon feeding time, the pig discovered that he could troll for feed under the filly's feed bucket, and so he shut up. About three days later, the pig discovered horse manure, and made this the principal item of his diet. Both the filly's groom and Farley found this a matter of much satisfaction, the groom because he no longer had to clean the stall, since a large quantity of horse manure was now recycled through the pig into a much smaller quantity of pig manure, concentrated and easy to dispose of. This, said Farley, was the Hong Kong principle—in Hong Kong, where Farley had been to the track a number of times, provisions went in vast quantities into the big expensive restaurants early in the evening, were passed, in smaller but still-considerable quantities out the back door somewhat later, and into the kitchens of lesser restaurants, and on down the line, until much smaller quantities ended up, five hours and five cycles later, in the food stalls by the water. Farley stood around and watched the pig sometimes for twenty minutes on end.

And then there was a crisis. Farley ran a two-year-old in an allowance race that the colt wasn't quite ready for. He got a little washy in the walking ring. After the jockey had mounted, Farley said to Oliver, "He's going to scratch the horse. I know it." Then, after they went up to the stands to watch the race, Farley said only one thing more. He said, "You know, that was my conscience talking. This horse shouldn't be running." The horse ran fifth, not a bad race, but the owners were disappointed. Back in the barn, Farley said only, "I will never do that again," and then he didn't run a horse for a week. No one in the barn could figure out what was going on. The horses were working and galloping but every one entered in a race was scratched. The chorus of whining from the gallery of owners swelled to a roar, and all Farley did was observe the pig. The pig was now a sight larger than it had been, and was following the filly around, right between her back legs, hoping to catch, and succeeding at catching, much of the manure as it dropped. The stall was immaculate, though the pig's head was dirty. Manure would land on it, and he would shake it off and wolf it down. Even the grooms, always prepared to take a more basic view of survival than others, were a degree more disgusted by this than Farley was. That was something you could say about Farley—nothing unusual disgusted or bored him.

On Friday, Farley told Oliver to scratch the one horse they had running and took the plane to San Francisco to go to a play about a Chinese man in the twenties with three wives, who decides to convert to Christianity so that he can have a marriage based on love and companionship. One of the wives, Farley told Oliver the next morning, kills herself with an overdose of opium, and another dies mysteriously, and the man is left with the only wife he never liked in the first place. "What do you think?" asked Farley. "Should he have converted or not?" Oliver had no idea why they were having this conversation. "I don't know," said Farley. "I think the play was saying that personal happiness is not the point."

Oliver very much felt that Farley's own thoughts should not travel too far in this direction. And then Farley told him to scratch the only horse they had running that day, too. Buddy Crawford won the second race, the third race, and the ninth race, with a horse he had claimed from Farley when he was still claiming Farley's horses. The weather was lovely, the trees were swaying, the horses were beautiful, the afternoon was passing into twilight, but Oliver all at once felt that nothing could make him understand the game ever again. Every face he looked into was a blank wall, telling him nothing about who he was, where he was, or what he was doing.

It was no help that his girlfriend was out of town with some other travel agents, making an inspection tour of all the sites in the British Isles that seemed to have been built by space aliens. They were putting together a big seventeen-day tour that also included shopping at Harrods and Fortnum and Mason and going to a musical in London as a two-day commercial respite from the vast and mysterious. By the time he had gotten some swordfish tacos with pico de gallo and some rice and beans and brought them back to his apartment, eaten them, and set his alarm for three so he could get back out to the track by five, his dad's hardware store back in North Carolina was looking pretty good to him. Washers, bolts, screws, ax handles, hammers, tool belts, circular-saw blades, nails, eyebolts, lock sets, sanders, slot-head screwdrivers, routers, ripsaws. There was a lot to be said for the orderly and calm contemplation and then selection of objects that could not move of their own accord, that had no agendas of their own, that stayed where you put them. In that world, being well organized would actually have a terminal effect—you would put something away, or hang it up, and come back an hour later, or a year later, and find it right there, essentially unchanged. With a horse, you never found anything unchanged. The best you could hope for was minimal change along a predictable path. At three o'clock, without having slept, he hit the alarm before it went off, and got dressed and went back to the track.

He was always the first one there, and only in June and early July did he arrive after sunrise. Wasn't it depressing somehow that he hadn't missed a sunrise in five or six years? Was he really a morning person? He didn't know. Horses were morning people. All the horses were wide awake. He went down the rows of stalls, stripping off wraps and feeling legs, noting which animals had a little heat, which were iron cold, knee to foot, front and back. That was a pleasure, he had to say, feeling the legs of a horse who had galloped or worked the day before and thinking of a wrought-iron post—hard and cold and incapable of pain. In Farley's barn, more were cold than hot. In Buddy's barn, yes, more were hot than cold. Some days, every one was hot. He reminded himself that there were twinges of conscience that he had suffered every day of the four months he had worked for Buddy that he suffered no longer. But, on the other hand, he also couldn't remember them very well, and he was beginning to remember the money and the winning very well.

Farley came in when they were exercising the second set. The only thing he said after asking how all the horses were was "Scratch Duplicate Deputy in the third."

"But he's ready," said Oliver. "He's fit. He's sound."

"It's not the right race for him."

"Why? I think—"

Farley shook his head, always agreeable, always poised. "Scratch him."

Oliver turned on his heel without saying anything, and headed for the racing office.

In the racing office, he was disloyal. Two or three people were in there when he scratched the horse, and he let them hear him, then, when they looked at him, he rolled his eyes and shrugged. Then he said, "The horse is ready. I don't know." He acted like he knew what he was doing and Farley didn't. And then, every step back to the barn, he regretted it.

Farley was in his office with the blinds drawn, on the phone. When the third set was ready to go out, Farley came out and gave them their instructions, then followed them out to the track. It wasn't a pleasant day, windy and chilly. Just as they entered the grandstand to watch, Farley's cellular rang. Farley answered it, and Oliver listened in on the conversation. Farley's side went: "Hey, Bob. . . . You're a lawyer? . . . Yes, Ms. Hornsby. . . . Yes, I know that Mr. Huxley is the CEO of Soma Features. . . . I don't train any horses for Mr. Huxley." There was a pause. Oliver knew all about Bob Huxley. He had fabulously bred horses, but he was exacting, to say the least. Farley said, "Yes, I am. And with pleasure." When he put away the cellular, Oliver said, mildly, "What was the pleasure?"

"Refusing to train any Huxley horses."

"He has good horses!"

Farley looked at him, amused. He said, "Well, after he stopped threatening me, he put his lawyer on, and she threatened to sue me three times in that call alone."

"She doesn't mean it. That's just the way they talk to each other in Hollywood."

Farley shrugged. Oliver knew that, if he opened his mouth right now, the end result of it would be sorting hardware back in Carthage for the rest of his life.

After all the sets were finished, Oliver had to go into the office. Farley was reading some papers. He made some marks, took off his glasses, said, "How's that pig? I love that pig."

Oliver didn't say anything.

"Say, you know, Oliver, you know what I've been thinking about?"

"What?" He knew he sounded angry.

"Well, this happened a couple of years ago, just after the foundation mare and I broke up the studfarm and went our separate ways."

Farley never talked about his divorce, so Oliver sat up and listened.

"About nine months or so after I moved out, I got up one morning, and the first thing I thought was 'Why am I not getting laid?' "

Oliver was twenty-eight, and this was a familiar thought to him.

"Now, I had been in therapy for two years at that point."

"You had been?" Nobody at the track ever admitted to going to therapy.

"Sure. And going to a support group two or three times a week."

"You did?"

"Well, of course. This is California, isn't it? Anyway, I had several women friends whom I liked, one or two of whom I liked a lot, actually. I knew the answer to my question perfectly well. There were lots of answers, both specific and general. One of the women had another boyfriend. One was recovering from an abusive relationship. One was sexually active and I didn't want to get into that STD tangle. And I had been working hard to understand my sexual history, which hadn't been pretty."

"It hadn't? Too much or too little?"

Farley guffawed, but didn't answer. Instead he said, "I knew why I wasn't getting laid, but I thought, 'Because no one wants to sleep with you, no one loves you, you aren't desirable, everyone else is getting laid. This one has a boyfriend, this one has lots of boyfriends, this one will soon have a boyfriend, and *you aren't him.*' "

Oliver coughed. Actually, he wasn't angry anymore. Farley was too weird. You couldn't be angry at him for long.

"Even the people in my support group were getting laid. They weren't supposed to be, and they would sit around during meetings and share their anguish about how ambivalent they were about getting laid, and how getting laid made them feel exploited or exploitive or lost or punished, but deep down, they all seemed relieved that they were getting laid and I wasn't. I was the example, the bottom, the thing to be detested above all. No amount of moral superiority could persuade me that day that they didn't see me in that way."

"Wow."

"My therapist was getting laid. Everyone at the track was getting laid. My ex-wife, Marlise, seemed to be getting laid, because she was eating out a lot, and that was foreplay for her, as I well knew."

Oliver cleared his throat.

"I wanted above all to understand some things about myself and to stop making the same mistakes I'd been making all my life. I didn't want my past to dictate my future. I wanted a space there, a space of sitting out, a space between the past and the future where I might learn something. Those were the things I wanted with all my heart and soul."

Oliver felt his face redden. The only hearts and souls you felt comfortable talking about at the track were horses' hearts and souls.

"I was strongly drawn to one of these women, so strongly drawn that, in my eagerness to learn something, I told her the absolute truth—I dared not sleep with her—and she believed me, because I was being utterly honest and open and sincere. But it didn't matter all of a sudden what was smart or wise or true or real or sacred. I didn't think I could take another step without getting laid, or kissed, even, without knowing that some woman, preferably that woman, felt desire for me, Farley, this particular man."

"What did you do?"

Farley leaned forward, his face very sober, and Oliver couldn't turn his gaze away. He said, "I got up and got dressed to come to the track. I got in my car, and about ten minutes after I got onto the freeway, thinking all the time about this woman, I wrecked my car. There was a stray tire in the middle of the right lane, and I was so preoccupied that even though every car in front of me was going around it I hit it, deflected off it, went into a bridge abutment, and totaled the thing. I liked that car, too."

"Shit, Farley."

"It was shit, Oliver. But it was a good lesson."

"Not to—"

"Not to think that I knew what I was doing."

"Are you talking about winning? If you're talking about winning, I don't understand. All I know is, I want to win."

"I like to win, too."

"In any athletic thing, you've got to want to win more than anything!"

"I think in this it's the horse who has to want to win more than anything. The humans have a little leeway."

"Do we? I don't know what's going on!"

"Nor do I."

"What lessons are we learning here?"

"I don't know yet."

"Why are we doing this if we aren't winning?"

"I don't know."

"After all this time you don't know?"

"I know less and less."

"But you don't sound upset by that."

"I'm not at this very moment."

"Why not?"

"If I were capable of knowing what is going on, there wouldn't be all that much going on."

Oliver sat back in his chair and looked out the window, wondering if it was time to change jobs again. The thing was, at the racetrack, if you weren't winning, you were supposed to engage in irrational behavior until you started winning again. Cursing, anger, little good-luck rituals, at least courting some owners. He said, "What happened to that woman?"

"She got married. She has a baby now. She was a lot younger than I was."

"What did you get out of waiting?"

"Well, she named the baby 'Farley.' "

Oliver couldn't see how that was much of a consolation, but Farley was smiling to himself, one of his beatific Farley smiles.

Oliver got up and went out of the office, no longer angry but only wondering if his confusion was terminal. As he passed the stall where the filly and the pig were keeping each other company, he saw that the filly was calmly eating her alfalfa and the pig was standing behind her. Just as Oliver glanced at them, the pig rose up on his hind legs and bit the filly on the left hock. She lifted her tail, dropped a load; the pig came down on his forelegs and went to work.

MAY

27 / TROISIÈME COURS

AUDREY SCHMIDT could not help thinking that, if it had been her father who had taken her on this outing, it would have been warm, with the sun shining. It seemed to her that every time over the years that her father had taken her on a special outing, and all of their outings were special, because they were planned for well in advance to accommodate his duties in the Army, it had been sunny. Her father, she would have said, though not aloud, came with a supply of sunshine. This was not sunny. It was so foggy that you could not see the château and you could barely see the railing on the other side of the course. Audrey and her mother stood quietly, Audrey's shoulder against her mother's arm. They did not complain.

Audrey held her *mutuel* strip in her hand. It was filmy and silver, the sort of thing you could easily drop or lose in your pocket. Her mother didn't like to bet, but she was willing to give Audrey anything now, and so she had put a hundred francs down on a filly that Audrey liked, a horse named Zania, by Linamix out of a Darshaan mare. Audrey didn't know as much as she would have liked about French horses, but her default option was always to bet the grays. Linamix's offpring were gray. The horse was trained by a woman named Christiane Head, who was the most famous woman trainer in France. Audrey and her mother had watched Madame Head saddling the horse before the race. She had that way of doing things that Audrey liked in a woman—calm, steady, flowing. Audrey had stared at her for as long as she could.

Audrey had been anticipating this outing for so long and in such detail and it was so different from what she had imagined that it seemed like a different outing entirely, so different that it gave her a sense of being not inside her own self but inside the self of another eleven-year-old girl who was doing with her mother what Audrey herself was doing with her father. She almost thought that she could look to her left or to her right and see the real Audrey Schmidt with the real Richard Schmidt, standing in the spring sunshine comparing notes on how the horses looked and what they might do.

But the real Richard Schmidt was really dead—Audrey made herself say that word, "dead," to force herself to believe it. He had gone off to work fourteen days minus one day ago, just as usual, and then, in the middle of the day, his commanding officer had shown up and told Audrey's mother that her husband had suffered a massive heart attack at his desk and had not even lived to get to the hospital. Of course, everyone in the military was fully trained in CPR, but Audrey's father had probably died before his head hit his desk. They had been in France exactly a month. Audrey had had to give up her riding lessons and her hopes of owning a horse in order to move here, and this outing was to have been a consolation prize.

How this death could have happened was not readily understood. Colonel Richard Schmidt had been patted and prodded and tested and adjusted and investigated as to his physical fitness every six months since he entered West Point. Colonel Richard Schmidt ran three miles every Monday, Wednesday, and Friday, and five miles every Tuesday, Thursday, and Saturday. He lifted weights on Sunday. His hair was brown, his skin was ruddy, and no one could remember a day of illness. The chaplain kept telling Audrey's mother, Florence, in Audrey's hearing, that sometimes it is simply time to go. Florence nodded, as did Audrey. Its being time to go was a simple concept, in theory, if you didn't ask why. After the chaplain left, Florence would stop nodding and start shaking her head. For now, Audrey saw that her mother was so amazed by what had happened to her father, and to them, that these were just about her only responses, nodding for a while, then shaking her head for a while, then nodding for a while. Florence had tried to sit down with Audrey and make something of it all, but had had no luck with that. Finally, after two tries, she said, "Audrey, I've got to ask you to wait for me. My mind is moving very slowly. I can't seem to speed it up. But things will be all right."

At any rate, the sunny two-day outing in the beautiful spring weather that Audrey and her father were supposed to be having here had turned out to be a foggy two-day outing of penetrating cold and loneliness. Not even visiting the horse museum the day before had lifted her spirits. Because of the weather, Audrey and her mother were two of only perhaps twenty-five people at the equestrian demonstration. The riders came out on two Lusitano horses, two grays. They trotted around very elegantly, then had the horses do some tricks, like bowing and sitting and lying down. When the horses finished and went back inside the stable, they were dripping, not with sweat, but with cold mist. Audrey felt sorry for them, having to leave their warm stalls and go outside. The exhibits in the museum were nice enough, mostly pictures. The stable was like a castle, not like any stable Audrey had ever been to at home. It was so elaborate and well built that the horses seemed like house dogs or house cats, not outdoor creatures at all.

After the horse museum, they had gone out to eat at a restaurant, and tried out local specialties that were heavy with cream, butter, and ham. Then they had gone back to the hotel and tried to read for the rest of the evening. There were no friends around. The fog was thick and scary for her mother to drive in. When they turned out the light at nine o'clock, Audrey heard her mother start to cry and knew that she herself dared not cry, because if everyone in any one room cried then the sadness was too much to bear, and might finish them off. In the morning, Audrey woke up early and lay in bed pretending to be asleep. The hours passed very slowly, until at last she heard her mother roll over and sit up. Then her mother said, in a tone of amazed conviction, "I guess we'll go back to Maryland. I certainly don't want to go back to Texas." Audrey didn't reply. Then there was the relief of getting up.

Audrey's own mind wasn't moving all that quickly, either. What she was trying to do, the project she had set herself, was to hear her father's voice in her head. So far, she had had no luck. This was the way, above all ways, that she knew he had vanished and was truly gone. All her life he had been busy and often absent, but always she had been able to hear his voice in her head, telling her to make her bed, to help her mother, to think happy thoughts, to act responsibly, to think of him while he was gone. From her earliest childhood, he had said to her, "If you miss me, just think of me, and I am with you." She didn't know how she could know he had said this to her without being able to hear him saying it, but she could, and since she couldn't hear him saying it, she couldn't feel that he was with her. It made her afraid.

The fog lifted a bit and the horses went to the start. There was something very unserious about this sort of racing, Audrey thought. The tractors and machinery and crowds and buildings and loudspeaker and litter of betting slips that she was used to in America were absent, especially today. Racing in America could be grim, but it was never lonely. In France, it looked like, it was probably never grim—the turf was too green for that—but today it was very lonely. Audrey's mother said, "Now what?"

Audrey didn't know what to answer, since she herself didn't know now what, either. So she pressed her shoulder against her mother's arm a little harder, and then her mother moved her arm and put it around Audrey. That reminded Audrey how small the two of them were. At least back in Paris the whole U.S. Army was trying to make up to them for her father's death.

The fog lifted a bit more. Now you could see the equestrian museum, a thicker gray through the veil of the fog. The turf seemed to radiate its own green light, and the gate opened and the horses swarmed out of it silently, their hooves muffled by weather and turf. Even though she had a bet, it was hard for Audrey to get excited. And then, in the space of a few seconds, the fog dropped over the horses and removed them from this world. There was a silence in the crowd as the horses vanished, and then much conversation in French. Could anyone see them? Where were they? Would they stop the race? Audrey's mother looked at her as if she would know the answer to this question, but Audrey shrugged. She knew she should worry about the horses—could they see anything? Might not someone be hurt? But the horses had vanished; what was there to worry about?

People started milling about and shouting in French, and the horses did not reappear. Audrey looked at her watch, but you could tell nothing from that—she hadn't checked her watch when the horses disappeared. And then the fog fell upon them, and Audrey's mother, too, vanished. Of course she was there—Audrey could feel her arm around her shoulders—but she could not see her mother at all—could not see her drawn face, her paleness, her grief, her confusion. Well, it was something of a relief, to stand there utterly alone and utterly surrounded. For the first time in two weeks, she felt a moment of rest. She took a deep breath through her nose and let it out her mouth. She rubbed her *mutuel* slip between her thumb and forefinger. And then the breeze came up and blew that fog backward, toward the grandstand, and there were the horses, right in front of them, galloping, racing, rolling, surging over the turf as hard as they could go, as if their eyes were foglights. They were all so wet that they were all dark-colored. You couldn't tell who was who. And then, just before they crossed the finish line in a bunch, the fog enveloped them again. The photo was blank, gray. A few hooves appeared at the bottom, but no noses, no numbers, no jockeys.

"Well," said Florence. "That was the strangest thing I ever saw."

"Me, too," said Audrey.

"I wish your father were here to see that!"

"Me, too," said Audrey.

They sighed.

But, oddly, Audrey felt a little better. Something interesting had happened. By contrast, in the last two weeks, everything had been new but at the same time darkly tedious.

"Would you like something to eat, sweetheart?" said Florence.

Audrey nodded. Florence took her hand. After a few steps, Audrey said, "Dad *could* be with us, couldn't he? He doesn't seem to be, but he *could* be."

Florence looked at her, then said, "Yes. Yes, he could be. Lots of people in the world would say that he is. But, you know, it's not something that I'd made up my mind about."

"Let's say that he is and see what happens."

"Yes," said Florence, "let's do just exactly that."

28 / HUNTER-JUMPER

As soon as Deirdre turned down Cold Spring Road and was driving between the white board fences that defined the contours of the land on either side of the gravel, her heart started to pound, and it kept pounding, faster and faster, as she drove into the parking lot beside the barn, pulled into a spot, turned off the ignition, and looked through the windshield. She had expected a reaction of some sort, for she had not been to her old barn in six years, since finally selling it off to Ellen. She had not consciously stayed away, she thought. Every type of horse business, she thought, was life-consuming. There were people at the track who never went anywhere else at all. That she sometimes took in a concert, she thought, or a good meal made her a degree less single-minded than many. But still.

Of course there were changes—Ellen had put up an indoor arena, which Deirdre had wished to do but been unable to afford. The barn had been repainted. Accent trim formerly green against the white walls was now black. The pastures had been divided, so that more horses could be turned out in less space. Deirdre found reassuring these little shoots of disapproval already cropping up around her chest-thumping anxiety. Disapproval of the way others ran their businesses and treated their horses was the meat and drink of the hunter-jumper business and still pleasantly nourishing after all these years. She opened her door and got out. The number of cars in the parking lot told her that plenty was going on, but it wasn't until she rounded the end of the long center-aisle barn that she witnessed it.

At least ten people were riding, six in the main arena and four in the jumping arena. Two others were cooling out their horses on the grass. Three instructors, of which Ellen was one, were standing, staring at their charges in attitudes of dismay, real or mock. As Deirdre came onto the scene, she heard

Ellen exclaim, "Lorelei! You are riding a horse, not a motorcycle! If you lean into the turn and don't balance him up, he will stumble!"

Lorelei, on a little bay, nodded. Deirdre went up to the rail of the arena and leaned on it. Without glancing at her, Ellen called out, "May I help you?"

"Well, then, I don't know, Miss. Have you a harse I might ride, then?" Deirdre put on the real Irish.

"Deirdre! You came! I'd lost hope!"

"A bit late, but better that than early."

"Do you really want to ride?"

"That was just a bit of a joke."

Well, she was very affectionate, coming over to the fence and giving Deirdre an uninvited hug and a kiss on both cheeks, not so bad, in its way, for it calmed her inner turmoil. She managed a grunt, just to reflect Ellen's grin, and said, "When you called, I thought I'd better come over and see whether you've broken down that lovely filly I sent you in the winter."

"Hot as a pistol! Can't break her down if we can't ride her!"

"You know the statistic about sixteen percent of any and every group of humans being jerks? Well, sixteen percent of all horses are useless as bent nails, and that filly is one of them, but you would have her!"

"I would have her, and you would sell her! How's George?"

"The curtain goes up on George's play every single day and he does himself a star turn. It's getting a bit boring the way they all light up when they see that boy. You're lighting up yourself, and you know better."

"No one knows better with George."

"He's just an Irish boy, no different from all the rest of 'em."

"Ha. Well, he's a lost cause, I know that, so we'd better go look at the horses."

They came into the dark, wide aisle. Dust rose on every golden sunbeam that fell from the clerestory windows. At the sound of Ellen's voice, a horse head popped over every stall guard, eyes alert and ears pricked. Right there at the front would be the Jackal, Ellen's Grand Prix horse; Deirdre recognized the white diamond inside his left nostril. Deirdre had broken him as a two-year-old some twelve years before, when Ellen was just starting out with jumping and Deirdre would ride anything over anything at any speed in any type of class. She stepped up to the Jackal and cupped her hand under his chin. Smooth and whisker-free. She said, "Now, how do you expect the poor beast to find the grass if you shave him clean like this?"

Ellen laughed. "I've never seen him have a speck of trouble with that."

"Then how do you expect him to sense the fairies and the ghosts all around?"

"Look at this one, Deirdre. I got him from Mike Huber in Texas. He had him up to Intermediate, but his rider couldn't hold him cross-country even in a double-twisted wire snaffle, but he's a great jumper. I've just got him in a full-cheek and he goes fine. He's jumped six feet. I want to make him a Puissance horse."

"Listen to you now, dearie. Who's that girl who used to cry out, 'Oh, Deirdre! Don't put 'em up! Are they three feet? Don't put 'em up!' " She was smiling again.

"Here's the filly."

Clean as a whistle and fat, the filly Deirdre had sold Ellen in the winter came out of the stall as out of a silk glove, on her toes, her ears pricked and her nostrils wide. She swept around them in the wide aisle, her tail flowing. Ellen said, "I put her out in the indoor and she goes over and looks in the mirror. This way, that way, posing. She'll spend forty-five minutes at it, sometimes. I just love watching her."

"You're not riding her?"

"She needs a little more time to calm down from life at the track."

"Ah, what a princess she was! Dainty about her food and dainty about her footing and dainty about her company. Tsk! What a useless beast! Best shoot her. And don't be tempted to breed her."

"You said that."

"She's not got the temperament nor the pedigree."

"I know, but she's—"

"Darlin', you're a lover of horses. You have no standards. You love the lame, the halt, the bad-tempered, and the blind most of all. But if you're going to breed them, they have to have some generally accepted usefulness. We've discussed this before."

"I know, but—"

"Promise me you won't breed this filly, at least until she shows she can take up a life work and do well at it."

"I promise."

"All right, then."

"She's so pretty—"

"Marilyn Monroe was pretty, too, darlin', but she was not intended to be anyone's mother."

"Okay."

They went out and watched the lessons again, and finally Ellen got to the point. She used that voice of concern that Deirdre found so maddening. "George told Martin about the wreck. Martin told Hope, and Hope told me."

"Ah, well." When they used that voice of concern with you, your own voice had to be especially cool and ironic.

"Have you talked to anyone about it?"

"In what sense?"

"In any sense."

"I told the owners the horse would be euthanized."

"That's it?"

"What's there to say? The jockey broke a rib and was out a week is all."

"You need to talk to someone."

"Perhaps you mean therapeutically?"

"Perhaps I do. Perhaps I mean as a friend."

"What is there to say?"

"How did you feel?"

"You want me to get down to the nubbin right now?"

Ellen looked at her soberly, and said, "Yes, I do."

"I can't do that."

"Why not?"

"Ah, well, you can't lead me there that way, either."

"You don't look good."

"I never look good, darlin'. I always look cross and misanthropic, because I always am, and the sun has turned my once fair complexion to leather, and my back hurts so that I am the despair of my chiropractor."

"But normally you just look angry and determined. Now you look—"

"Well, do tell, dearie."

"You look hopeless."

"Perhaps, were I to cover the gray, then—"

"Tell me what it was like."

"You don't want to know."

"I want to know."

"I don't want to tell."

"I want you to tell."

Deirdre sighed. She was being worn down.

Ellen said, "I'm going to make us a cup of tea."

"I think I'll be going."

"No, you're not. You're going to have a cup of tea with me."

And so they did, in the lovely tackroom with the border around the baseboard of hunters and hounds galloping over some Irish landscape of the mind, and oak cabinets full of trophies and ribbons. Ellen scattered the corgis and Deirdre sat down. Ellen handed her a cup of tea. Deirdre said, resolutely, "It will not do me good to tell."

"Why not?"

"Because I don't want to give it life or power."

"I can tell by looking at you that it has life and power. And Martin said—"

"Ha!"

"—you told five of your owners to move their horses."

"Cheap horses."

"A trainer does not live by stakes horses alone."

"Cheap horses are more likely to break down."

"How are you going to support yourself?"

"I hear this every day. Clearly, I am not going to support myself, or that's what my bookkeeper says."

Ellen looked at her cup, then said, "How do you feel about that?"

"That's why you called me! You've talked to George, and now the future of my livelihood is the topic of general conversation!" She was beginning to feel irritated.

"Not just that, not primarily that!"

"Does George think I need some therapeutic conversation?"

"He thinks you need to go to church, frankly, and talk to the priest." Then she said, "How angry are you? I can't tell."

Deirdre set down her cup a bit emphatically, but said, "I don't know."

"Deirdre, I was the one who went with you to the hospital when you broke your back, and sat outside the recovery room and waited for them to tell me whether you would walk again."

"Yes, you were, and I did thank you for it."

"Not graciously."

"I will be gracious in my next life."

"I don't care if you are gracious or not. I love you even though I hardly ever see you. You gave me a life, this life, and I give thanks every day for it."

Deirdre thought that was the most amazing thing of all. She said, "To whom?"

"To whoever is listening when I say the words. Anyway, I don't just love you out of gratitude. I love you, who you are. I miss you."

Deirdre looked at the other woman. What did it mean, that Ellen would say she loved her? George loved her, but he had to, being employed by her and of her breed. She and George loved each other the way the right hand loves the left hand. So it took her by surprise that Ellen would say these words that no one else in the world ever ever said to her. Just say them. In the course of conversation. To cover her surprise, she said, "I will tell you the one thing I wonder about."

"What's that?"

"Well, the horses were bunched. It was a big field, and there were several stragglers, but eight of them were bunched right together, and the lead horse was the one who went down, flat out, across the track. He dropped the next three like bowling pins, but the next four got around him, and were fine. You know, when they have one of those multicar pile-ups on I-95, fifty or a hundred cars smash up before you know it. I wake up thinking about it."

"How do you mean?"

"What did it look like to them? How did they see it?"

"Or what did it feel like to them?"

"What?"

"Well, maybe they saw something. We don't know how they see, really. But maybe they also felt something, some disturbance in the field."

"What's that?"

"Well, like a magnetic field, or an energy field, or a gravitational field. A rock in a stream."

"And the horses were water that flowed around it."

"Fish that swam around it. They aren't like us. They don't have to know that they know, they just have to know it."

After a moment, Deirdre said, "Remember that jumper I had for a while, Tinker?"

"Big paint horse?"

"Well, he was the most irritable thing. Bucked on every turn, reared up in the in-gate. Ah, he was a nerve-racking ride, that one. But I did take him to the Penn National that year, and I'll never forget there was a triple combination three strides out of a corner right after a big square oxer. Horse had to stretch, then turn, then huddle himself up. Well, I heard his toe hit the oxer, just a little tick, and it distracted me into the turn, and I cocked my head, and then there was the triple combination. For a second there, I'd forgotten all about it. Well, that Tinker exploded through that combination all on his own. Boom, no stride, boom, one stride, boom, and out. He just did it."

"They do it all time. All the time they just let us buy on credit. That's how I know they like it."

"Like what?"

"Like what they do. What they do that we ask of them."

"Do they? That's what I really wake up wondering. Am I flogging these poor beasts to their early destruction, sinner that I am? They weren't built to run so far, so fast. They weren't built to live in a barn, without touching one another. They certainly weren't built to jump over fences, be weaned at six months, be ridden, eat grain and hay, wear blankets. Och!"

"No, they weren't built for that, but the building accommodates it, and the soul inside the building likes it. Deirdre, they like to have something to think about. They like to have problems to solve. If we don't give them some, they'll find some. I had that Appy gelding, remember him, that little guy, almost a pony. He used to let himself out of his stall, then let all the mares out and herd them down the aisle and around the barn in a parade, as if to show all the other geldings that he was the boss."

"Ah, well." It could not be said that she felt better, Deirdre thought, but it could also not be said that she felt worse. It could be said that she felt Ellen's friendship, a taxing but pleasurable feeling that she had felt many times in the past. Well, she was an inward-turned sort of person. Why that was didn't bear investigating. It was an Irish thing, no doubt, pursuing her around the world in the way of Irish things. She sighed.

"I bet you could ride again."

"God in heaven, girl!"

"I bet you could."

"I bet I could poke myself in the eye with a sharp stick, too, but that doesn't mean I want to do it!"

Ellen laughed, then said, "Well, you never change, dear. You just make me laugh."

"I'm leaving now." Deirdre stood up. "Don't breed that filly and we'll stay friends."

Ellen stood up, too, and they wandered out of the lovely tackroom. The aisle was full of horses and ponies standing on crossties and little girls attending them. Every one of them had that look of a girl infatuated with horses, the happy, fated look of a passenger setting sail on the *Titanic*.

At Deirdre's car, Ellen opened the door for her and said, "We'll stay friends."

"Ah, well, I'll think about it," said Deirdre. But it was true. Ellen was one of those steady ones you couldn't shake.

29 / HIDDEN AGENDAS

AFTER RESIDUAL broke her maiden in her second race, defeating a Seattle Slew filly, a Gone West filly, a Storm Cat filly, and an In Excess (Ire.) filly by ten lengths wire to wire, all of her connections, past and present, were in full agreement about her final destination: Churchill Downs, Breeders' Cup Juvenile Fillies, November 7, 1998.

Well, yes. Breeders' Cup. Buddy had a hundred horses in training at any one time, and a certain proportion of those were going to be looking at the Breeders' Cup, at least from a distance. Jesus, though, who had revealed himself to be a tricky fellow, had put this Breeders' Cup flea in everyone's ear. He heard it fifty times a day, from everyone who had anything to do with that filly, and there was the trick, because normally people were so superstitious at the racetrack that they never said anything about plans or hopes. That's what the newspaper people were for, raising hopes so that they could be dashed at the last minute. When they asked you about your plans, and you told them that this was horses and you couldn't count on anything, they always wrote about your modesty, as if the single most important lesson of a life at the track was not that you couldn't count on anything, as if this was news and they, the newspaper people, had never learned a damn thing. Well, yes, these tricks Jesus had up his sleeve did make Buddy irritable. But, of course, then he was required to find even more patience to counteract, or at least cover up, his own irritability. But at least he could soothe himself with the knowledge that he had learned something, and what he had learned was that, the smoother things went, the more careful you had to be. When you were in the shit, you had only one choice, which was to get out of the shit. When you were in clover, you had choices every minute, and for a man like him, a man who had acted on impulse every day of his life up until the last few months, choices were always dangerous.

One night, when he was praying his usual prayer, he suddenly got up from his knees and sat down on the bed. He looked out the window, up toward the full moon, in whose region he imagined Jesus to be, and he said, "Okay. Here's the deal. I thought I was saved. That was what was advertised. I would accept you as my personal savior, and there we were. And, you know, I felt it, too. I felt saved and everything. I was happy. But I find out all the time that I've got to keep getting saved. Am I saved? Am I not saved? What do I do now? Did I do the wrong thing? Should I be remorseful, or just go on and try to do better? Are you talking to me? Are you not talking to me? Am I good? Am I a sinner? Still a sinner? You know what? I'm tired! I'm only fifty-eight years old! My father's eighty-six, and he's still alive, and his father died at ninety-three! That's thirty years of this! I'm exhausted at the thought! I can't do it!" And he did something only a loser would do, he burst into tears.

About a moment later, of course, his wife came into the room. Buddy loved his wife, probably. She was a nice person, like his mother had been, but not very interesting. She had been a good mother to all those ungrateful children they had who never stopped expressing their opinions about everything, as his own mother had been. He had stopped having sex with his wife a long time ago, and didn't have sex with anyone else, either. What with all those horses in training, and his anxieties, and the fax machine starting to spit out reports at four o'clock in the morning, what time was there for sex? His wife went over to the closet and opened the door. She didn't let on that she knew he was in the room. She kicked off her shoes and then bent down and set them on the shoe rack. She unzipped her dress down the back, took it off, and hung it up. She slipped off her hose. They had been married thirty-two years. She looked it. After she had put on her robe, she said, "What's wrong, then?"

Buddy, who realized that he had stopped crying in the course of watching her, said, "Oh, nothing."

"Buddy, you're crying. I've never seen you cry in all these years. What are you crying about?" She didn't sound all that sympathetic.

"Well, I don't think I'm saved, after all, to be frank."

"Why not?"

"Because things just get harder and harder, not easier. Do you feel saved?"

"I don't know. I like going to the church. The people there seem to take an interest."

"In what?"

"In me."

"Oh." Buddy himself felt an immediate lack of interest in this idea, and looked out the window again.

She said, "Why did that make you cry?" Her voice was softer now, and she put her hand on his leg.

"Well, you know something? When the Lord came into me, it was such a good feeling, I thought, Well, I can do anything because of this feeling, but then there was all this stuff to do and to think about, and I don't remember the feeling all that well."

His wife was smiling at him. She said, "Doesn't that remind you of something?"

"Yeah, the first time I ever had a horse win a stakes."

"Anything else?"

"That's the deal here. Everything is a test."

"I'm sorry. I didn't mean to make it a test. It's just that what you said reminds me of marriage."

"It does?"

"Yes."

"I never thought of that."

She looked at him, first coolly, then warmly, then, well, she looked like she was about to laugh. At last she said, "Buddy, sometimes I wonder if you've ever experienced our marriage at all!"

"Of course I have! We've got this house, don't we? We got four grown-up kids and we go on vacations."

"We haven't been on a vacation for a long time."

"You come to the track."

"I haven't been to the track in a long time, either."

"We go to church together every Sunday, and I've been to a couple of those get-togethers they have there, too."

"Yes, honey, but that doesn't mean you've experienced being married to me."

"Who else would I experience being married to?"

"That's my point. I don't think you've experienced being married."

"We've been married for years. What else would I have experienced?"

"Some idea about being married that doesn't have anything to do with me."

"Is there something you want?"

"You mean, is there something I want from you that would show me that you've experienced being married to me?"

Buddy found this sentence confusing, so he said, "Yeah."

"No."

"What, then?"

"I want something from you that would show *you* that you've experienced being married to me."

Buddy felt very confused now. It was like she was throwing words at him in long strings, and just as they got to him, she twisted the strings so that they changed meaning. The best thing to do was maybe to just throw the whole thing back in her lap. He said, "Well, what makes you think you've experienced being married to me?"

"I don't know that I have. I mean, I've experienced having you in the house. It's like living with a loud motor running all the time. Up, down, into this room and that room, eating supper, jumping from the table, cursing all the time, yelling over the telephone about things, laughing, making deals all the time. You take up a lot of space and make a lot of noise." She looked at him, and he must have had some look on his face, because she smiled a bit and said, "You know, you're very lively, Buddy, and you are always exactly who you are. Everything about you shows on your face."

Buddy thought of his anger and his dishonesty and his cruelty and his carelessness with animals and people, and he said, "I know."

But she said, "I still love your energy. Life doesn't seem to have diminished you the way it has me. You are like a rubber ball that can't be held underwater for more than a second."

"I am?"

"Sure. It doesn't matter what happens, you always go back for more. Most of the time you don't even seem to notice what's happened. You don't seem to take anything to heart."

"I don't?"

"You're very reliable."

"I am?"

"Sure. The motor never stops running, never seems to need a repair or a tune-up. Don't you realize how unusual that is?"

"No."

"Well, Buddy, I know you're not very introspective. That's why being saved is so hard for you. But I think you're doing a good job."

"You do?"

"Yeah, I do." She kissed him on the forehead, the way his mother might have. It was a little disconcerting. You married someone and then ignored her for thirty-some years and then it turned out she had all these opinions about you, and she kissed you like your mother did, and that was okay, in fact it was fine. He sighed. But he still felt disconcerted, so he said, "You think I can get this filly to the Breeders' Cup?"

"Why not?" she said.

"There are two or three of them. That horse Epic Steam, too. This could be my best year. I could be like Baffert or Lukas," said Buddy.

"Ah, honey—" she said, but he interrupted her, as always. He said, "Why would I, though? That's what I don't understand."

As for Residual, early the next morning, attached by a tie to the eyebolt in her stall, being groomed and tacked up, she was one of those beings in whom all good things combine. The front end of her pedigree was good but not fashionably great. However, back past the five generations provided through the Equine Line by Bloodstock Services, and purely coincidentally, she was inbred many times to St. Simon, many times to Stockwell, many times to the great nineteenth-century mare Pocahontas. Added to that, Baba Yaya had been a lovely broodmare—attentive and experienced, kindly and firm, high up in the hierarchy of the mare herd. And everything all of Residual's connections thought about her was true. Her owner spent money freely—on supplements, vitamins, massage, all the good things. Leon, whom Buddy tended to call "the idiot assistant trainer," paid special attention to her, making sure her legs were stone cold every day, watching every step she took, checking her in her stall many times, giving her carrots and apples. She got to like him—whatever *his* program, her program was to make him her very own human, and she did. So shining red and silky, so kind and large of eye, who could resist her? She was made for love, the way she laid her chin upon his shoulder and looked into his eye. And she did mesh perfectly with her exercise rider, Deedee, with the woman's easygoing femininity, her light weight, and her soft voice. She gave herself to her exercise rider, and was a pleasure to ride. The jockey enjoyed her, too. What the filly had learned from racing was a simple thing—every time she had drawn upon herself for the extra something that it took to flow through an opening and get in the clear, St. Simon, Stockwell, and Pocahontas had supplied what she needed; anatomically, it was a higher volume of oxygenated blood passing from her large heart into the rest of her body, preventing the buildup of lactic acid in her muscles—but she felt this ease as a larger ease, as the kindness and interest that she sent out returning to her from every direction. Everyone saw it. What they said to each other was that she was easy on herself, but what they meant was that she was easy on everyone. And so, when her groom led her out of her stall, everyone around her stepped forward with a smile.

Which did not mean that she had any plans whatsoever to go to the Breeders' Cup.

30 / JUSTA QUARTER CRACK

IN REVIEWING HIS LIFE after he developed a painful quarter crack in his right front hoof wall, Justa Bob could find no precedents for either the place he now found himself or the people he found himself with. There was indeed a fence, though it was low and mostly made of vertical slats. The space it ran around was small and contained no grass. Rather, there was a house that people of all sizes went into and out of, there was another small house, containing chickens, and there were several unusual objects that the smaller denizens of the house ran to every day and climbed about on. Justa Bob's corner of this compound contained his buckets of water and feed and his mound of hay. It was divided from the rest by only some slender boards. He remained inside it more out of courtesy than anything else. Every day, though, a very small old human who appeared to be female came to him four times, fed and watered him. Twice a day, she snapped a shank onto his halter and led him carefully around the compound, scattering the children and chickens if she had to. All of this was quite different from the racetrack and from the studfarm where he was born and the training center where he received his education. Other than this woman, there were two men who attended to his foot. They touched it, looked at it, nodded at it, smiled at it, talked to it, put something into it that was rather soothing for a moment. Justa Bob did not have the sense that they recognized him except insofar as he was attached to his foot.

As odd as it was, Justa Bob had no complaints about this place. The feed was sweet and wholesome, the hay was rich, the water was quite nice, no off tastes, and the old woman always treated him kindly and tactfully. She adhered to a strict schedule, and in gratitude for that, he held off manuring in his water bucket. When the children ran under his feet, as they sometimes did, he stood still, though occasionally he aimed a stray kick at one of those damned chickens.

Lin Jay "the Pisser" Hwang was eager to get the gelding Justa Bob back to Golden Gate, but there was no reason to pay a fifty-dollar-a-day fee to his trainer just to have the horse stand in the stall. You never knew with a quarter crack. It could grow down and disappear, it could linger for as long as the horse lived. There were various techniques, old and new, for treating it, but it was slow, rather like growing out a damaged fingernail or a bad haircut. Even so, you had a chance. The Pisser, who had an affinity for making odds, since he had started out as a math-genius Red Guard handicapper just off the boat from China back in 1983, often tried to specify the odds on a quarter crack or a bowed tendon or a condylar fracture or an ankle chip, but too many horses had defied the odds one way or another. The odds, he finally realized, had to be reserved for a reasonably sized statistical population, say the eight or ten horses in one race. One horse could not help defying the odds.

This horse, Justa Bob, or, as his mother called the animal in Chinese, "The Iron Plum," had "odds-defier" written all over him. He didn't look like much, just a brown horse, but after forty-two starts, eight wins, six seconds, four thirds, and a handful of fourths, he seemed unchanged by his experiences— that is, unchangeable by experience. "Good horse" was what his mother said, in her usual oracular fashion. The Pisser was himself fifty-five, so that made his mother near eighty. She knew a good horse when she saw one, and since she herself was unchangeable by experience, she recognized a kinship with the animal. She hadn't liked one of the Pisser's claimers this well in years. That was why she took care of the Iron Plum herself. The Pisser was reasonably sure that she was slipping some herbs into his feed. That was okay, too. In fact, everything his mother did was okay with the Pisser.

The Pisser was much changed by experience, even though he had always, since his school days in a small city in Hupei Province, been known as the

Pisser. At first he had gained this name because in schoolboy pissing contests he had been able to go twice as long as the other boys. After that, it was just a name. When he got to America, he found out that a "pisser" seemed to be something especially strong or interesting or unpleasant. That was what he aspired to be, and so he translated his name and kept it. Americans were shocked and put off by it, just a little. That was fine with the Pisser. The way he had gotten to the racetrack, Golden Gate Fields and Bay Meadows, was that, when he couldn't find a job in his field, which was teaching algebra, and, as a result of his experiences in the Cultural Revolution, when he had spent several years planting paddy in Guangzhou Province, he had chosen not to repeat his experiences with menial work, but to try gambling. As a mathematician, he preferred variables to pure chance, and so he had ended up at the racetrack rather than playing the numbers or visiting poker rooms. He probably hadn't actually lifted his eyes from the *Form* to look at a horse for the first year or more, but when he did, he liked what he saw. Another thing that he saw was that if you owned and claimed horses you could play both ends, sort of like raising crops and playing the commodities market at the same time, so he always had a couple of horses with a couple of trainers. He was always out in the a.m., watching works, and he went to just about every race. His wife was resigned to all of this, even though she would have preferred to live among other Chinese people in the middle of San Francisco rather than out in Pleasanton with the whites, where they could keep a horse who happened to be on the DL. She herself had a job she liked, selling designer dresses at Saks. Her customers, whom she called "clients," often spent more for a dress than the Pisser spent for a horse.

The Pisser's mother had lived a life that the Pisser had witnessed much of but still could not imagine. Waves of history and death had passed over her as rhythmically as surf. The thing about her that the Pisser found the most intriguing was that she had named herself, because her own parents, peasant farmers in Fukien Province, had not valued their seventh daughter enough to do so. His mother's name, in English, meant Round Pebble, a name unlike that of any Chinese female he had ever heard of. It was possible that she had never seen a horse before the Pisser brought home his first project. Certainly on that occasion she had walked and walked around the animal, a nice filly named Ladidah who won three races for him before being claimed away. Anyway, maybe his mother was four feet six, maybe not. Maybe she liked him, maybe not, maybe she liked his wife, maybe not, maybe she liked his children and grandchildren who came around, maybe not. His mother seemed to have no desires, no wishes, no hopes, no fears, no illnesses, no complaints; in fact, she seemed to be just what she called herself, a round pebble.

THE THING the Iron Plum found most intriguing about the Round Pebble was her fragrance. He often put his nose up to her face and snuffled her in. She let him. After her face, he would sometimes work his way down her shoulder, or over her back, or down her chest, or into her hair. She let him. Her hand never came up to touch him or pet him, she never looked at him or spoke to him, but she was available for investigation, and the Iron Plum investigated. She was endlessly fascinating to him. If he wanted to lick the front of her dress, as he did a couple of times, or lick her hands, or even nip her on the cheek, she made no reaction, not even a contained startled reaction of the sort any observant horse could sense. The Iron Plum recognized that the Round Pebble was absolute stillness, a space there in the clutter of the house and the chicken house and the garden and the tools and equipment and vehicles and trailers and noise and chatter and wishes and frustrations and dreams and dissatisfactions. Such a space was unique in his experience, so he snuffled and nosed and probed and pushed her gently with his head and dropped his manure in one spot in the corner of the pen, where it was easy for her to pick it up. Track grooms, perhaps, did not think this sort of choice could be a part of a horse's repertoire, but, then, there was no track groom like the Round Pebble. When she led him around on his scheduled program, he watched her and smelled her. It was a complete change of pace.

It was the Pisser's mother who held in check the natural sense of superiority that a dialectical education had given him. He often caught himself looking around at the Americans he knew and saw and marveling at their foolishness, loudness, carelessness. Even their largeness seemed, sometimes, to be somehow their own fault, as if they didn't know the proper moment to stop doing anything, including to stop growing. And his fellow workers, the bettors at the chosen scene of his operations, seemed even less controlled, if possible, than most. They were always whooping, shouting, lamenting. If they hit a long shot, they thought it was meaningful in terms of their personal glory. If they lost a big race, they screamed as if the jockey, or even the horse, had designed the loss just for them. Even his best American friends, the ones who had shock-proof systems, who never looked once at a horse, who took into account all sorts of extraneous factors, like where the turf rail was placed, and the direction and speed of the wind, even these Americans were tempted regularly by the notion of personal salvation—that the numbers were going to look *right at them* and take mercy upon them. At such times, the Pisser felt himself fill, molecule by molecule, with contempt, and then he drove home, and looked at his family and his house and his life, and he felt the contempt he had for others surge back over himself a thousandfold. It was then that he looked at his mother, creeping along in front of the horse, the horse staring at her, his ears pricked, his nose just inches from her neck, and he was so mystified by this sight that he decided that he knew nothing after all, and he decamped from the high ground of his contempt, and went in the house and had a glass of water, and felt better.

ON THE DAY when the Iron Plum was to go back to Golden Gate Fields and resume training, the Pisser got up earlier even than usual, way before dawn. The Iron Plum was still asleep in his pen, flat out on his side, his ankles relaxed, his toes almost pointed, his ribs rising in single heaves, his ears flopped. The Pisser had already hitched the trailer to his old truck and set out the horse's wraps by the time the animal sighed and rolled up onto his breast-bone, then put a lazy foot out and levered himself to his feet. The Pisser per-formed his tasks in orderly quiet, and soon enough the horse was on the trailer, his nose in his hay net, and the trailer ramp was latched up. One last check of the hitch and the lights and the Pisser was ready to go. He picked his cup of coffee up off the railing of the Iron Plum's pen, and went around and got in the truck. When he opened the door, the overhead light revealed the small figure of his mother in the passenger's seat. The Pisser contained his astonishment— the Round Pebble had never gone to the track with him before—let out the parking brake, and drove out into the street. He could feel all of his expecta-tions for the day, and they had been utterly routine, slip away. He smiled.

The fact was, when you had your mother settled in one spot, and she did the same things all day, day after day, you didn't have to think about her much, but when you got her out on the road, driving through the neighborhood and then onto the highway, and you could see that she was looking out the win-dow, everything, from the truck cab itself to the highway on-ramp to the pass-ing semi-trucks, looked big, fast, and amazing. Sometimes the Pisser himself was reminded, especially by his dreams, that he had passed through several universes to get to this moment. It was intimidating in retrospect, especially if one dream held objects or persons from different universes. The Pisser some-times thought of the old topology problem, the four-color problem, which stated that only four shapes in a two-dimensional space could actually touch each other, and that therefore a mapmaker needed only five colors to make his map. Only in a nightmare, then, could teachers from his childhood, his fa-ther's death during the Great Leap Forward, a beating he got just after leaving his university and going into the countryside during the Cultural Revolution, the first man he had ever met who had gone to America and come back (a math colleague at the school where he taught), and his wife in a black suit and high heels, standing in front of a row of dresses, seem to squirm together like snakes, all touching in an impossible way. He had to wake himself up and remember all the steps he had taken in between, every step working out the manageable and credible distance between individual universes. And there was time, too. In dreams, time and distance collapsed, but in life, time and distance were one and the same; walking and waiting, having to make your slow and deliberate way, prevented the special terror of having to be in two or three universes at once.

How much stranger things must be for his mother, sitting there, a cipher, a curl against the door (he checked to be sure it was locked), her hand on the dashboard, her eyes on the road, her feet barely touching the floor under the seat. She wore loose, khaki-green-colored pants, a white shirt with buttons, and a pair of child's sneakers; her hair, gray, coarse, and thick, made a ball at the nape of her neck. She could not read. She had never been taught to read Chinese, of course, and reading English had been out of the question at her age. He wasn't really sure how many children she had borne. He and his wife had figured out seven, but there could have been more. Formerly, the Round Pebble had had a fair amount to say, mostly instructions and admonitions, not much about herself or her life, though. But now for years she had said very little. There was an American expression that no American children seemed to abide by, that children should be seen and not heard. That was his mother, in her second childhood—doing this, doing that, busy all day long, always in evidence, but never more than a word or two, and those always in English.

FOR HER PART, the Round Pebble knew perfectly well that Hwang Lin, her son, continued to think of her as his mother, even though she herself had grown out of motherhood years ago. It was like all those other things about her that she had once thought were her, but had left behind—her parents' daughter, her brothers' sister, a wife to the man her parents had sold her to, a wife to the man she had chosen on her own after the first one was killed in Hunan Province by some thieves, it was said. A mother a mother a mother a mother, over and over, a woman who swept, a woman who cooked, a woman who carried nightsoil, a woman who minded other women's children, a woman who changed beds in a hospital and washed the bloody sheets by hand, a woman who planted gardens and killed chickens and bled hogs out and carried water and waited to be told what else she was to do, a woman. All of these things she had shed like husks, one after another. Now she called herself nothing but the

Round Pebble. Work found itself done after she had passed through it, but she no longer felt herself work any more than she felt herself breathe. Soon enough, she would shed the final husk. Sometimes she wondered what she might find out then, but wondering was something she also did little of anymore, since it made no difference of any kind what you wondered about, what you wished for, or even what you got. At this point, what the Round Pebble knew was that just about everything there was was larger than she was. Even her great-grandchildren were larger than she was, for the most part. But it wasn't as if this hadn't always been true. Her mother, her father, her brothers and sisters, her husbands, her sons and their wives, wars, revolutions, famines, epidemics, the sum of money her parents had sold her for, the work she was put to, the orders she was given, now these horses. You name it. But her feelings about that had changed, too. Largeness had once been frightening to her; now it was not. Now that she wondered nothing, wished for nothing, and cared nothing about what she got, the largeness of everything outside of her carried her along smoothly, the steady deep current of a broad river passing through a spacious valley under a generous sky. She was only a small pebble after all; she required no violent force of nature to lift her to her destination. She sighed as she looked around. The sun rose before her in the windshield of the truck, and she shaded her eyes. When they came to a stoplight, the Iron Plum stamped a bit, and she could feel the truck beneath her shiver with the vibrations. Hwang Lin looked around, but the Round Pebble knew it was only the horse making his music.

The Pisser was glad to get to the track, where everything was familiar business. For sheer activity, you couldn't beat the backside of a racetrack at seven in the morning. Horses looked over the doors of their stalls. Other horses cooled out on their walkers. Others were being mounted and ridden out to the track. Still others, steaming in the sunlight, were being sponged and scraped. No horse was ugly on the backside. All lifted their heads, turned their bodies, swished their tails, pricked their ears, tossed their manes in an endless series of graceful gestures. The Pisser had seen lots of horses in his day, of all breeds and ages. Horses in general, he felt, were good. But Thoroughbreds in general, he felt, were more than good. Beauty flowed through their bodies like a steady ocean breeze, sometimes seeming, if he was in the mood, to pass from one to another in an exchange of energy that netted them all together, and all their humans with them, their genetic tie become nearly visible to the naked eye as the body electric, a single body electric repeated everywhere you turned your head. Those were good days. But driving with his mother had filled him with longing, made him think how little he could do for her. If she wanted something, he would surely give it to her, but it didn't do a bit of good to ask. There was never anything she wanted. He had come along too late to give her anything, and it made him, just now, feel useless. He drove the trailer carefully to Barn C, where his trainer was already mounted to go out with his third set. That was okay, though. The Pisser knew what to do, and the stall was bedded deep in yellow straw. The horse's hay net was hanging by the door.

The horses left for their exercise, and the Pisser got out of his truck. He closed the door carefully and went around to the trailer. He opened the side doors and untied the gelding, then went around to the back and let down the ramp. The Iron Plum stood calmly until the Pisser said, "Okay, fella." Then the Iron Plum stepped carefully backward, his hooves feeling for the ramp. The Pisser reached for the leadshank, but there was his mother, before him, her hand scooping it delicately from his. The horse looked around.

HERE HE WAS AGAIN, Justa Bob, justa racehorse. Justa Bob flared his nostrils and snorted in the familiar smells, yes. Pivoted his ears like satellite dishes, yes. Turned his head this way and that to focus his big eyes on the scene he was born to see, yes. His skin shivered over his muscles as if flies were landing on him, but it wasn't only the excitement. He hadn't seen another horse in a long time, and now he was among them, signals flying everywhere. He whinnied a single loud greeting, and other whinnies answered him immediately, Hello, hello, hello, I'm here, I'm here, too, hello, a ripple of whinnies spreading from Barn C out over the backside, until, far away, they had nothing to do with Justa Bob at all, only to do with Hello, I am here, where are you, I'm here, too.

WHILE HIS MOTHER held the horse, the Pisser squatted beneath him and unwrapped his legs, throwing the wraps off to the side. Then he ran his hands down where the wraps had been. Cool and tight. The quarter crack had grown out nicely, ready for a patch, and the coronary band was smooth and whole. He was a stable system, this Justa Bob horse. Not the fastest thing in the world, or the prettiest, but his architecture was damn good. The foundation sat square under the rest of him, and the rest of him moved squarely upon the foundation. He was indeed a plum, and he was indeed made of iron. The Pisser said, "Okay, Ma. Let's walk him around a little, then put him in his stall."

He did not take the horse away from her, as he was tempted to do. It wasn't so easy to walk around here on the backside of Golden Gate. Conditions were crowded, and the footing was uneven. All he needed at this point was to see his child-mother stumble and fall underneath the horse, even for the horse to step on her. As little as she looked at home, she looked even littler here, smaller than the smallest jockey. And the horse was clearly excited to be back, arching his neck, picking up his feet. So the Pisser turned away and busied himself with cleaning out and closing up the trailer so as not to interfere, so as not to let her see that he had tears in his eyes. His mother was passing through his life. The speed of her passage was accelerating. He had nothing to give her, no going-away present. All he could do was watch her for a moment, watch her with that horse, who, for all the distractions around him, still followed the Round Pebble attentively, his nose inches behind her neck, his ears pricked, his steps careful. Oddest thing he ever saw.

THE ROUND PEBBLE led the Iron Plum into his stall and turned him around so that he was facing outward. She reached up and undid the buckle of his halter and slipped it off his head. Meanwhile, the Pisser adjusted the animal's blanket. The groom would come around about noon and wrap the horse's legs for the night. Light training would begin tomorrow. If they were lucky, the horse would run again in six or eight weeks. Whatever, thought the Pisser. His mother preceded him out of the stall, and after he did the latch, he paused to give the horse a piece of carrot that he had in his pocket. His mother did not look back. It was impossible to tell if she felt affection for the horse. She headed down the shedrow. The horse looked after her, his ears as far forward as a horse's ears could be. And then he started in again, whinnying and whinnying. He beat his knees against the stall door, turned and plunged and whinnied and turned and plunged. The Round Pebble did not look back. The horse's distress grew. The Round Pebble opened the door of the truck and got in, then shut the door. The Iron Plum watched, whinnied again. The Pisser had never seen anything like it. He shook his head, then he closed the top half of Justa Bob's stall door and latched it, then he himself walked to the truck. Sometimes you just had to leave a horse in the dark in his stall to figure it out and get over it.

JUNE

31 / A BAD FILLY

FARLEY WAS STANDING in the grandstand, staring out at the training track, watching Arturo attempt to pony Froney's Sis. The plan had been to trot twice around the six-furlong track, then gallop once, then bring her back and cool her out. She had ponied the day before and the day before that and the day before that. Before that, one of the hot walkers had walked her all over the backside, the way he liked to do with all of them when they first came in. She had seemed ready to be ponied, but she had gotten less ready as she went along. Now she didn't seem able to learn anything, and every day was worse. She bucked and reared and kicked out, no matter how tightly Arturo held her to the pony. Every horse that came near her frightened her. When she got back to the barn, she would be pouring with sweat and quivering.

Arturo was getting annoyed.

The pony was getting annoyed.

Farley was getting interested. One of Neil Drysdale's two-year-olds came up on the filly's right, not close at all, and the filly twisted her head around to see him, then reared up and pulled away, like a kid at the movies who insists on looking at the monster and then screams bloody murder. Arturo urged the pony, hoping to pull the filly forward, out of her panic and into the idea of running, but the filly dug in her back heels and threw her head up.

Oh, she was a bad filly.

Farley called out, "Just walk her, Arturo. She's panicking." He saw Arturo nod, and they came down to the walk and moved over way to the outside.

She was a bad filly and a filly of obscure breeding, a common glass bead on the Tompkins string of pearls. At best she would run in allowance company and make Mr. Tompkins a few tens of thousands of dollars that would directly to the IRS. More likely, if she even made it to the races, she would make it as a claimer.

Given her mental problems, she would be time-consuming and costly to train.

Her dam had died, so even the motive of improving her dam's produce record was out. There was no percentage in wasting his time on this one.

But she was interesting.

Arturo and the pony and the filly left the track and headed back to the barn.

Farley regarded them, stroking his beard, as he followed them. "Hey," he said to Ron Ellis. "Hey," he said to Mel Stute. "Hey, hey," he said to Neil Drysdale. "Hey, man," he said to Bobby Frankel. But he didn't see any of them, winners all. He was warming to something he always found it interesting to warm to, which was a lost cause, a futile attempt, a Zen koan—how do you train a useless animal to perform a useless function?

He was smiling.

When he got back to the barn, Arturo said, "I don want to pony this filly anymore. She making me mad, boss. I don like to be mad aroun the horses."

"We'll think of something else, Arturo."

AT 6:00 A.M., Joy drove her old Ford Ranger into the foaling complex to see if anything had happened in the night. It was the beginning of June; 176 foals had been born and only a few were still circling the farm, as it were, waiting to come in for a landing.

She walked down the barn aisle. It was bright day now, time to let out the mares whose foals were old enough and strong enough to frisk about in a space larger than a stall.

Jose helped her lead out the mares; Jorge walked along with the foals, one arm around their rumps underneath their tiny twitching tails, the other arm around their chests.

When they were done with that, she saw a van in the courtyard bringing a mare to be foaled out and then bred to a Tompkins stallion. Zora, one of the broodmare handlers, was at the top of the ramp. She said, "You better come look."

The mare in the van was standing with her legs spread apart and her head down. She was covered with sweat and hugely in foal. She was groaning. Zora waved her papers in the air. She said, "She's due in a week. She seems exhausted. I can't believe they shipped her this late, and in this weather."

"Where did she come from?"

The driver said, "I picked her up in Temecula." Then he said, "I had to stop to sleep, you know."

"When did she get on the van?"

"About three yesterday afternoon."

"Did you check on her at all on the way here?"

"Well, the other driver's out sick?"

"We've got to get her off the van," said Zora, "and into a foaling stall. I called the vet."

Joy went to the mare's head and pinched a fold of skin at the base of her neck, where it met the shoulder. The fold stayed pinched. Joy said, "She's very dehydrated." She lifted the mare's upper lip and pressed her finger against the mare's gum. It seemed to take forever for the blood to come back into the white circle her finger left. Joy said, "And she might be shocking."

The driver said, "I guess I slept a little too long. I had this long trip the other night, from—"

"Well," said Joy, as she led the mare off the van, "the owner shouldn't have waited this long to ship her, and you shouldn't have fallen asleep, and it just all came together, so let's get her walking here and give her some fluids."

Zora went into the barn and came out with a light fly sheet, and Joy led the mare to a bucket of water. The mare took only a sip. Joy said, "Oh, Mommy. I am so sorry." Inside that van, alone for fifteen hours, the mare might have wanted to pace, and had become distressed because she was tied. She might have wanted to roll, sensing perhaps that the foal was malpositioned. Joy handed the leadrope to Zora and took the papers. The mare was by Hoist the Flag, a great broodmare sire, and was in foal to Avenue of Flags, an expensive California sire. There was no reason for the owner to have been careless, but he had been.

NOW IT WAS almost noon. Everyone had left. The grooms had gone to eat. Dunya, Farley's bookkeeper, had gone out for her daily run. All phones were silent. All the owners were busy elsewhere in the world making money hand over fist. Farley had noted down the results of the day's training and put his paperwork in his briefcase. Only FitzGerald, the acupuncturist, was around—down at the end of the aisle, working on the High Brite colt. All up and down the aisles, horses were eating, dozing, sleeping. Even the pig, in the last stall at the end of the shedrow, was sleeping. Farley closed his office door and walked down to Froney's Sis. She was facing the back corner of the stall. He said, "Hey, girl. Turn around and look at me." She ignored him. He lowered his voice and clucked to her. She cocked one ear backward. He said, "Come on, girlie. Things aren't so bad out here. You'll like it if you try it." He shook her hay net and she turned her head. But she turned it away again. He pulled a carrot out of his pocket and snapped it in two. At the sound, the filly turned around, stepped over to him, took a piece of the carrot between her lips. Then she did the hoped-for thing. She looked for another, ears up, neck arched. He put another piece between her lips and stroked her cheek, then her chin. When she had finished the carrot, he took the halter with its attached shank off the hook beside the stall and slipped it over her head, then he folded back the stall guard and led the filly out. "Come on, sweetie," he said, "let's just go for a walk."

THE DISTRESSED MARE was now standing in a stall. She had gotten banamine to relieve her pain and lower her temperature (which had been about 103), and mineral oil down her nostril into her belly to prevent any possible colic. Now she was getting intravenous fluids. At this very moment, Joy was watching her urinate, a good sign, though the urine was still a little dark. Most important, she looked more comfortable and relaxed. Joy had groomed her a bit, so she was clean and dry, no longer caked with sweat. Maybe, Joy sometimes thought, that was the most important thing, just the attention, just the conversation and the stroking. You always underestimated, didn't you, how it hurt a horse to feel lonely and isolated.

The foal, the vet said, was fine—strong heartbeat and big, it looked like.

A horse didn't like to be by herself year after year, with only her stuff around, thinking her isolated thoughts. A horse didn't like to have only one friend. A horse didn't like never to be touched—nibbled over the withers and nipped on the cheek. A horse didn't like to go for months without entwining her neck around the neck of a friend. A horse didn't like to graze alone day after day, with no one to switch the flies off her chest for her. A horse didn't like to stand off in the corner of the pasture by herself, looking at the others and wishing to be with them but afraid of it. That sort of behavior made a horse think too much, ponder every decision too carefully.

Now Joy was sweating. The sun was well up over the Central Valley and her eyes were beginning to hurt. Probably it was going to be so hot today that it would be inhumane to ride Mr. T., her greatest joy. She went into the office to find her sunglasses.

The flyer in Joy's box read, "Tompkins Equine Employees! Sign up now! Last trip of the spring! Mr. Tompkins will take ten equine employees to Hollywood Park on June 7 for a day at the Races! First Come First Served! Several Tompkins Worldwide Racing horses are entered to run!"

Joy looked across the office at Hortense, Mr. Tompkins' personal secretary, then out the window to see if there was any evidence of the man himself. Nowhere in sight. She said, "Hortense. Do we have to wear the white jackets?"

"He said chambray shirts. It's a little too hot for the white jackets. That's what I told him."

"Thank you."

"You going?"

"Well, I never have."

"Oh, it's fun, honey. That DC-3 is something else. Right out of the Second World War. I love to go. Let me sign you up. You look like you could use a break, sweetie."

"I think I could, Hortense. How many have signed up?"

"Only two, plus you. And it's day after tomorrow. He's going to be disappointed. But I tell him nobody likes to be trooped around like a bunch of school kids. He doesn't listen."

"Do you think I could take a friend?"

"I don't see why not. He always likes a crowd."

MAYBE, THOUGHT FARLEY, if he started every day with a nap in the parking lot, every day would turn out like this one. What happened was, he stopped at a deli on Century Boulevard about five and got himself a bagel with lox cream cheese and a cup of coffee. Then he set them on the dashboard of his Yukon and drove into the trainers' parking lot. It was still cool out, and not very bright, and just after he parked his car, he was overtaken by the most soothing knowledge that, instead of opening the door of the truck and getting out, he was going to put the seat back and fall asleep, and then he did. When he woke up, maybe ten or fifteen minutes later, the sunshine had come through the windshield and warmed his bagel and his coffee was cool enough to drink, and so he sat there, biting and chewing and sipping, and he knew he was going to have a good day.

He had two in—one in this race, and one in the ninth. This race was his very own race—he had persuaded the racing secretary to write this race for his French filly, and even though the racing secretary had written it for horses of both sexes, this filly was strong and fit. Farley thought, in the barn, that she could take on any turf horse at the track, and when he got her out there and saw the others, he knew it. She had a pleasant manner, but she was self-possessed and self-confident. She was also big and built in that French way—legs like posts, lean body, low-set neck, big ears. Her owners had made their money, together, in cable TV, selling home food-dryers and herbal supplements. The filly had a whole agenda of herbal supplements that she was given every day, along with regular chiropractic, massage, and acupuncture. "We would never treat our animals less well than we treat ourselves," said the wife, Alise. Farley had been given to understand that, though Alise and Vincent had only one racehorse, they also had five cats, four dogs, a goat, two ferrets, a chicken, three guinea hens, and a donkey. Should he be reincarnated yet again, Farley thought, he would like to come back as any animal belonging to Alise and Vincent.

Now the filly had been saddled, had Chris McCarron on her, and was jogging around to the starting gate. Farley was enjoying the comforting presence of Alise and Vincent, who were sitting beside him in his box, holding hands and talking quietly to one another. They always spoke quietly. They never asked questions, but they were always interested to hear what he had to say. They had excellent manners, like the filly. Perfect owners. Farley yawned. He almost never yawned before a race. He was almost always a little tense. But there was something entirely reassuring about that French filly and her owners. He felt better today about his career and his life than he had in months. In the light of this good day, he saw how bad he had been feeling.

Now a group came into the next box, Joe Zimmer's box. Farley smiled, because it was a Tompkins group, probably from the ranch. Kyle Tompkins had horses with trainers all over the track, all over the country, all over the world. The group from the ranch were all wearing chambray shirts with "Tompkins Ranch Means Perfect Beef" in a circle around the head of a Hereford steer. Only one of them, an extremely tall, large woman with a loud voice, had escaped the uniform. She sat nearest to Farley, just on the other side of the railing. There was still a long way to go to the starting gate—the horses were only beginning the backstretch. The sun was warm. Overhead, round-bodied jets were arriving from Europe. Farley closed his eyes.

"Which one is ours?" said the loud voice.

"The chestnut with the blaze. The jockey is in all white with a silver 'T' on his back."

Silence.

"No. Can't see it," said the loud voice. "That chestnut is ouchy in his back, just behind the saddle."

"I don't think Mr. Zimmer would run an unsound horse."

"He's not unsound yet. Just ouchy enough not to want to really put out."

"Who do you think?"

Silence.

"That brown one in the pink shirt with the green dots."

"She's a filly. The rest are colts. I don't know."

Silence.

"Well, she's feeling good from top to toe."

Yes, thought Farley, and opened his eyes. The other woman, not the big one, but quite a little one, was looking right at him. When he opened his eyes, she smiled. He said, "You're talking about my horse."

"The filly?"

"Yes. She just came over from France about a month ago."

"What's her breeding?"

"Blushing Groom." The horses went through an opening in the inside rail of the dirt track and up the hill to where the gate was positioned on the grass.

"Mmmm," said the little one, still not looking away from him. He knew he was smiling. She was smiling, too. He said, "No white coats."

"We threatened to strike if we had to wear the white coats off the ranch, so he compromised with these. Tomorrow we have shirts that read 'Perfect Skin Can Be Yours' across the back. He flew us down in the DC-3. On the tail, it reads 'Tompkins Fleet Perfection.' " They laughed.

"I train a few for Kyle Tompkins."

"They're in the gate," said Alise. Farley tore his eyes away from the little one. She was very pretty, he thought, in that half-sundried, sparkly, horsey way. She had blue eyes. The gate opened right in front of them, and the filly took off. She ran as if alone, two or three lengths ahead of the other horses. Farley put his binoculars to his eyes and focused on the jockey's face. Chris looked relaxed and happy. His lips were moving.

It was the most boring race Farley had ever witnessed. The filly ran well ahead all the way around, and then took off after the second turn, and eked out another three lengths. Her ears were pricked the whole way. When she crossed the finish line, Alise said, "How marvelous! What a lovely day we are having. Thank you so much, Farley." And Vincent said, "Good job, I must say!" There was no screaming. The Tompkins horse had come in third.

Well, the thing was, they had to go down to the track and the winner's circle. They had to make much of the filly, who was hardly sweating. They had to do this and that and that and this, and when Farley got back up to his box, the Tompkins crew was gone. Before the fifth race, he called Joe Zimmer's cellular and Joe answered. He said, "Hey, baby. This is Farley Jones. You know that Tompkins bunch?"

"Yeah."

"What was the name of the little one? The little blonde one."

"I don't know, Farley. I didn't catch it. Was she cute?"

And then Farley was embarrassed, and so he mumbled something, hung up, and put the whole incident out of his mind. Do not investigate or pay attention. Do not take anything to heart.

Sometimes these precepts were harder to follow than other times.

TWO DAYS LATER, in the office, Joy took Mr. Tompkins' copy of the *Thoroughbred Times* out of his box and leafed through it. She put it back. She took out the new *Blood-Horse* and leafed through that, but it was no use. There were no pictures of Farley Jones in either of them, and after she had looked for five minutes, she was so embarrassed at herself that she shoved the magazine back in the box and scurried out of the office the moment she heard Hortense returning from the rest room.

AS FOR FARLEY, it was a shock, was it not, to return to what had become his normal state of mind. He knew for sure that very day, that very moment when Joy was looking for his picture, that he was just enduring. The one day in months when he hadn't had to keep his spirits up had shown him just how hard he was working every other day to do so. Today. Tomorrow. Telephone calls–horses–death. The connection jumped into his mind instantly, and even though he laughed at it at once, so silly, too silly ever to actually say, it stayed right there, a Black Hole the size of a pinprick right in the center of his brain.

32 / BELMONT

DICK WAS ALONE in his box, binoculars in his hand, waiting to want to watch Laurita make her way around the track to the starting gate, which was a furlong down the track. Her morning line had dropped from two-to-one to eight-to-five. She was the favorite, with Exotic Wood, who had shipped in from California, the second favorite at two-to-one. A year older and several lifetimes meaner, the California mare would be hard to beat, and Dick was a little intimidated by her and her connections. Or he would have been, if he'd had the mental space anymore for anything other than reliving his time, now finished, with Rosalind Maybrick.

Although the Bird of Paradise was a big race, and Laurita's picture had gotten into the *Form,* Rosalind and Al were not in New York but in Europe somewhere. Al was sorting out the production of large metal objects that could only be lifted by heavy equipment, and Rosalind was sorting out the consumption of small porcelain objects that could only be lifted with the utmost care. Hungary. That's where they were. Al had told him that. They were supposed to call him tonight and find out about the race.

In fact, it was good to be alone. He sat quietly. Sometimes he thought about Rosalind, or, rather, he re-experienced, as if it were actually happening, the feeling of her fingers on his shoulder and neck, over his cheek and chin, back down his neck to his shoulder again. That's where she had him, not in the lovemaking or the gazing or the other accoutrements of an Affair, but in that liquid touch. Right there, the very thing at the nexus of his marriage, touching, and the nexus of his life with the horses, touching, right there he found the source of his deepest longing for Rosalind.

On the other hand, there was Louisa's cousin, who had just come to visit and to talk to him about Louisa. Louisa, in the opinion of the cousin, was holding, but barely. He was worried about her. They had spent two days wandering around the track, the cousin in dress shoes, discussing Louisa with much intensity. Dick had not confessed his affair, but the cousin had commented that he seemed a little on edge.

It was nice to watch a race. In a race, anything could happen. Laurita was behaving herself very nicely. She was one of those horses who could have had any sort of life and done well in it.

The cousin was a therapist, which had reminded him that he could go back to his own therapist, which, guiltily, he had not. The cousin had started out as a comedian many years ago (he was now over fifty), moved into psychotherapy, and now counseled only the dying. He called himself a death therapist. In Dick's estimation, the man, though kind and well meaning, and certainly fond of Louisa, was obsessed with his own death.

As nice as Laurita was, though, this Exotic Wood mare made her look like an amateur. She strode out, glanced around, put the pony in his place. She had "boss mare" written all over her.

Another way Rosalind had liked to touch him was just to stroke his stomach and chest, lightly, idly, first down, then up, then around in an inward-turning spiral, then back around, in an outward-turning spiral. They would be talking about horses or something and he would barely be noticing. So how was it that right now he could feel the hair under his clothes flatten this way and then that way? He almost looked down his shirt to see what was going on in there.

The cousin's father had, indeed, suffered an unusual fate, but Dick wasn't sure what meaning there was in it, or if it had any meaning at all. At one point, he had given up his day job, insurance underwriting, to take up his first love, playing the trumpet in a big band. All during the death therapist's early life, the father was away much of the time on musical engagements. The band went by bus.

Now the horses got to the starting gate and entered as quietly as debutantes lining up to receive admirers. After they were all in, there was an unusually long pause, during which Dick imagined all these experienced fillies and mares discussing their male trainers and jockeys in the frankest terms. And then the bell rang and the gate opened.

Sometimes, not even erotically, Rosalind's fingers wandered over his testicles and down the insides of his thighs. Dick stifled a little gasp at the memory.

The young ladies were running well, in a bunch, the way they might on the range somewhere.

One icy night in New Hampshire, the band bus got into a terrible accident, and several of the band members were badly injured or killed.

The speedball, an A.P. Indy filly named Ann Page, put daylight between herself and Exotic Wood. Laurita was fourth or fifth, deep in the pack.

Other times, she would just run her finger up his spine and tickle the back of his neck.

One of the band members who died instantly was the death therapist's father. He was impaled on his trumpet. When the death therapist said these words, "impaled on his trumpet," Dick had laughed so hard he nearly fell down. Fortunately, the death therapist had been doing therapy for so long he took nothing at all personally, so he waited calmly for Dick to pull himself together.

Exotic Wood began her move on the turn. Ann Page dropped like a rock. Laurita, who should have been making her move, made no move.

Once, he had been lying on his stomach, half asleep, and he had felt her cool palms and cooler fingers encircle his heels. When he glanced over his shoulder at her face, he saw that she was pondering his feet, it looked like. Looking at her face made his feet get warm.

Laurita still didn't fire, but another filly, an Irish Kenmare filly, did, and moved up to duel it out with Exotic Wood.

It was 2:00 a.m. on a bus in New Hampshire. Wouldn't the trumpet have been in its case, under the seat? Did he have it in his lap? In his mouth? Was he playing at it? Looking at it? How could it be that, at the very moment when the trumpet was poised as a weapon, the bus crashed?

Exotic Wood flattened her ears to her head and bared her teeth. The other filly was intimidated, which sometimes happened in races for females, and lost her concentration. Exotic Wood crossed the finish line first, by a length. Laurita was fifth. Dick got up and went down to talk to the jockey, but it was clear enough what had happened, or, rather, clear enough that something had happened that was fairly mundane.

What did it mean, to do something you loved, something as normally safe as playing the trumpet in a big band, and be killed by it? Where had the wrong choice been made? By whom? Jockeys made life-or-death choices every day, but musicians? As a rule, jockeys' children did not go on to become death therapists. They often went on to become jockeys.

He knew it was true that his longing for Rosalind had intensified after she broke off their relations. What had happened was, she had met him for dinner at Forty-four's, on, of course, Forty-fourth Street, while Al was off somewhere and Louisa was teaching late, and over the crayfish risotto she had said, "This is too much for me," which was quite a surprise, because the whole thing was too much for him, but he'd thought it was not quite enough for her, and so he had said, without meaning to, "Yes," and had not said what he meant to (or sort of meant to), which was "Don't," and Rosalind had turned her head, and he had felt exactly as much relief as sadness, and when she turned her head back to him, she had read that in his face. They finished their meal and split the check, and he had had the sense not to ask if this meant he was no longer their horse-trainer, and she had never touched him again.

This jockey, the son of a jockey, said that she hadn't liked the footing. A little deep from rain the day before. The filly never really took hold. Dick nodded. Perfectly understandable.

How did the cousin's own dilemma reflect on his ability to advise Dick about Louisa? Was there a thread here, tying together the trumpet and the cousin and Louisa and Rosalind and the personality of Exotic Wood and all of these solitary moments and thoughts and his utter inability to accept the end of that touching? At the hub of all of this, Dick felt perplexed and overwhelmed. Meanings seemed to press themselves upon him, but what meanings? Wasn't the lesson of racing that there was no meaning, no pattern, nothing except chaos daily engaged with? Dick thanked the jockey, patted the filly, and sent her back to the barn with the groom to be massaged and made much of. Then he went out to valet parking and asked for his car. When the guy brought it, she wasn't in it, even though it was commonly said that anything could happen at the racetrack. But Dick was also willing to admit that, during the affair, if Rosalind had unexpectedly appeared, he was as likely to have flinched from her as embraced her, or, rather, first he would have flinched, then he would have embraced, or vice versa. Only now, with embracing out of the question, did he want to be doing it all the time.

33 / MATCH RACE

WHEN BUDDY GOT into his Lexus at three in the morning to head for Hollywood Park, he was already in a cold sweat. The press had him on the hot seat every single day now, it seemed like. He was getting as famous as Baffert or Lukas, and even though, let's say, five years ago Buddy would have licked his chops at the whole experience, now he woke up in a panic every time he managed to get to sleep in the first place, which wasn't more than every three or four nights. The publicity was all good so far, but any publicity presented Jesus with the perfect opportunity to trick you. Buddy thought this way about everything now. Each morning he got up and prepared himself to negotiate the day's landmines—avoid them, defuse them, fall into bed eighteen hours from now exhausted from the effort, and lie awake worrying about the day to come.

You would have thought he only had two horses in his stable, Residual the angel filly and Epic Steam the devil colt. They were neck and neck. After breaking her maiden at the beginning of May, the filly had won an allowance and a stakes, in the clear by six to ten lengths and run a close second in another stakes. Now Buddy had her pointed at the Valley Girl Stakes, a week away. The very next day, Epic Steam was running in his fifth race, the Albert Brooks Handicap. After breaking his maiden, also in May, he had bitten his groom in the chest, knocked him down, and pawed him, then won his own allowance, then won the Hollywood Producers' Stakes and the Century Boulevard Handicap. His running style was different from the filly's: he was a stalker, and liked to have the pace set for him. On his way through the pack, he had to be restrained by the jockey from biting the other colts, and there was always a moment when the jockey had to make a fuss to get him in front. The choice was to run or fight. So far, with considerable terror on the part of his regular jockey, Rinaldo Ortega, who had always liked to think he could get any horse to go somewhere, the horse had chosen to run. The filly had won $148,000. The colt had won $214,000. Should they both win, the filly's earnings would rise to over three hundred thousand, and the colt's to nearly four hundred thousand. The filly's owner, an elderly woman with pots of old California money, considered Buddy a natural-born, bona-fide saint for discovering this filly as a twenty-three-thousand-dollar yearling at Keeneland and "bringing her into my life. She is an angelic presence. I am so lucky," she said to every reporter who called her, interviewed her, glanced in her direction. To Jason Clark Kingston, Buddy's sainthood was still an open question, but as Epic Steam closed in on half a million dollars in winnings, Jason was thriving on his new status as a sportsman. He had a firm grasp on the fact that the animal's real fiscal potential was as a stallion rather than as a racehorse. He would therefore have disapproved of Buddy's current hormonal program for the horse, which included a nice progesterone implant in his neck, underneath his mane, where no one would ever feel it, because no one ever petted the animal. There was nothing illegal about using progesterone in a filly. Trainers did it all the time. It put the gal out of season for the season. But using progesterone in a colt to mitigate his aggressiveness was so unheard of around the track that Buddy knew the animal would never be tested for it.

Buddy liked to think that putting Epic Steam on progesterone was an inspiration from Jesus himself, a demonstration, through Buddy, of Jesus' charitable nature. The horse was a menace, and the groom's misadventure had been a specific sign that it was time to do something. Unfortunately, the obvious thing, or at least the obvious mode of doing it, cutting the horse, could not be done, precisely because it was too obvious. The horse had a set of testicles like a pair of grapefruits, and Jason Clark Kingston would recognize their absence. The man himself was a sex maniac, Buddy thought, and Epic Steam's overt sexual characteristics were the other thing besides the money that recommended him to his owner. There couldn't be much else—the sort of mooing affection that Residual's owner showed for her, and that the filly seemed to reciprocate, with nickers and nuzzlings and long warm looks, wasn't in the cards for a horse that you could hardly approach without a weapon in hand. Jason liked those testicles, and the one time Buddy had done the right thing and urged the owner to have them removed, using the usual excuse, that they seemed to be "bothering" the horse, Jason had said, "Well, if they're bothering him, then he won't like having them touched after he works. Let's try that." And so Buddy had been obliged to walk up to the horse and grab his testicles right in front of Jason, and he had done so; the horse, for once, had stood like a gatepost. No pain, no gain, at least for those who had to deal with the animal moment by moment. Jason's problem, as far as Buddy was concerned, was that, even though he knew nothing about horses, he was interested and he was smart. He always knew what was two and he always could get from two to four to eight to sixteen with no trouble at all. Jason came out to the track all the time.

Press-wise, it didn't help Buddy that Jason courted news coverage, so the news that he was a successful racehorse-owner was a Godsend for everyone in every section of the paper. The owner of Residual, too, frequented the news-papers, though in the society pages rather than the business pages, and as a mover and shaker of humanitarian causes—she could move the earth (get any number of people to a fund-raiser) and shake the money tree (every fund-raiser she put on broke a record of some sort). All of this was seen by the reporters themselves as a dream-come-true for Buddy, who was portrayed as a hard-working middleweight horse-trainer who had never really made it big. Rather than run down the list of the races he had won over all the years while he was mistakenly thinking he was successful and important, he listened to Jesus and kept this mouth shut and his lips stretched into a charming smile.

A lot of press coverage, though, meant different things to different people, and to Buddy it meant that not only was there the remote chance that someone would get wind of Epic Steam's implant (was it working? was it not working? Buddy changed his mind every day), there were other remote chances, too.

There was the remote chance that the fact that the truck owned by Curtis Doheny, D.V.M., was parked outside his barn every single day would be no-ticed by someone and commented upon. Curtis Doheny was a crooked vet. Many years before, when Buddy was mostly running claimers, Curtis and Buddy had worked closely together on several projects, as Curtis liked to say, and very few of their associates had been on a need-to-know basis with regard to these projects. Certainly not any jockeys, exercise riders, other vets, other trainers, owners, racing officials, or officials of the Jockey Club. Curtis' course in life had taken him through several detoxification programs, and even his dearest friends, like Buddy, had lost confidence in Curtis' ability to keep his mouth shut. Curtis' strategy of late had been to engage in a form of advertis-ing. Whenever a trainer was known to be hot, with several good horses run-ning and winning, he would park his clearly marked truck outside that barn, whether or not he happened to be working on any projects with that trainer at the time. The intent, Buddy thought, was to imply to other trainers, specifi-cally the younger and more ignorant ones, that the hot streak was owing to "the old Curtis magic," as Curtis had been wont to call it. Curtis' truck had been parked outside of Buddy's barn for ten days. All he needed was for one of those reporters who actually knew something—for example, Curtis Doheny's reputation—to ask him about Curtis. Then to ask Curtis about him. Curtis, like all track characters, had a deep well of stories that he liked to dip into, and no sense about whom they might hurt. For example, he could tell those Marcaine stories, where you would block a joint so the horse would feel no pain. Usually, he would come back alive, but not always. Or there would be the Sublimase stories. Sublimase was a synthetic thing like morphine, kind of. It had seemed like a good idea at the time, though part of the good idea was never to tell the jockey that the drug had been administered, either before or after the breakdown. And how many horses had Curtis nerved for him over the years? You cut the nerve above the knee, and the horse didn't feel his tendon or his suspensory ligament ever again. Trainers had been doing that for generations, maybe. At any rate, Buddy didn't think his mentor, Simon Dawkins, who had come from England by way of Australia as a young man early in the century and had known all the tricks, could have run a training stable without nerving 10 percent of the horses he had.

There was the remote chance that one of these reporters would turn up for the first set of the morning, which Buddy liked to have out there just as the sun was rising over Century Boulevard. Should such a reporter be astute enough and have night vision, he might see that the lovely Residual was not quite the girl she had been at the beginning of the season. It would have to be a very astute reporter, because no one—that is, except Buddy—could quite put his or her finger on how the summer campaign was affecting the filly. She still ran easily, with her ears pricked. Her loss had been quickly and honestly attributable to a virus and a fever spiked for many witnesses, some of them unimpeachable. Yes, his vet said, if the filly were 100 percent, she might not have gotten that virus, but a virus was a virus. The press understood a virus. Baffert's horses got viruses. Skip Away got a virus. Even Buddy, not known as a man of science, could explain to a reporter that hundreds of horses gathered in one spot during warm weather after a wet winter presented a virus with a field day. But with almost a hundred horses in his barn, Buddy also had several vets. He had always had several vets, even in the old days, when most trainers used one vet for everything. Vets differed in their opinions. For example, one of his vets thought the filly was feeling the pressure of the campaign. She had begun to eat less even though she was training hard. That vet put her on some Tagamet every day just to make sure. After a week she began to clean up again. Another of his vets was more philosophical. Of course she was feeling the pressure— that was just something you helped her deal with. First, you gave her progesterone to remove the added stress of going into season every three weeks, then, you know, steroids often had a wonderful effect on a filly, especially if she began to run with colts. Steroids were in common usage, not illegal, though they often made fillies hard to deal with. In fact, Buddy couldn't see much of an effect upon Residual. She retained maybe 98 percent of her former personality. Did she run a little harder? Was she a little more competitive? Hard to tell—as a front-runner with speed, she didn't have to be all that competitive.

In fact, he had fallen, was falling deeper, into what his dad, always a man who called a spade a spade, called "the insurance trap." The first step into the insurance trap was thinking that something might go wrong rather than letting something go wrong. The next step was buying something that might or might not prevent the thing that might go wrong from going wrong. Then you began to look for signs that what you had bought was working, and then you lost your sense of what was really happening, so you bought more stuff, and pretty soon, there you were. You didn't know which end was up, so, in your confusion, or, as his dad would have said, because your head was already up your ass, you pushed it farther in because at least it was a cozy spot. The two horses confused him, because the only thing he really knew about both of them was that they were extreme—he was an extreme son of a bitch and she was an extreme sweetheart. Now every time each of them acted more like a normal horse—he saw a person pass his stall without lunging at the stall guard, ears pinned and teeth bared, or she switched her tail—Buddy was tempted to think his insurance was working, and therefore to try something more, just to wedge his head higher up into that warm, tight spot. Why this was he wasn't quite sure. Neither owner needed more money, and they knew that, unlike some owners. Even he, Buddy, didn't have the old craving for funds that he had felt for so long. Picking the pocket of Jason Clark Kingston had had an air of superfluity about it, not to mention bad conscience. Both horses could end the season right here and have done more than well. There were trainers all over the world for whom five races was enough for any two-year-old.

But how good were they? In the old days, it was an accepted thing—race 'em race 'em race 'em. Eventually, as with Lexington, Stymie, John Henry, Kelso, Phar Lap, Citation, Count Fleet, you realized what you were seeing was something that you would remember all of your life. But what did Jesus think of that? What did that tempt you to? To the contemplation of greatness? Into the cruelty and exploitation that Buddy had engaged in so routinely in the past, for money and fame and just because that's all he knew how to do?

The fact was, he had not known Jesus long enough to know how he thought about these issues. Buddy's preacher had pointed out to him that Jesus kicked the money changers out of the Temple, but it wasn't clear to Buddy that that referred even to gambling. The Bible was not a definitive guide on a number of subjects, and so you found yourself getting into that insurance trap there, too, leafing here, trying this passage there, opening in the middle of that chapter over there, and learning that, for example, "many are called but few are chosen." Well, racing racing racing surely did separate the few that were chosen from the many that were called. Or that the Angel said unto her, I bring you tidings of great joy that shall be to all men. That didn't seem to apply to horse racing in any way, no matter how you sliced it. And once you were buying insurance, secret insurance, there was no one to ask, because no one besides you knew all the facts.

It was no relief at all to get to the track. When he pulled into his spot in the parking lot, people were already looking at him. He waved and smiled in the time-honored presidential, I-am-not-a-crook manner and strode with all deliberate speed toward the barn. Even though it was barely light outside, and not light at all inside, his aisles were suspiciously abuzz. The feed man was standing at one end of Epic Steam's aisle, shaking his head at several men Buddy recognized as journalists. He was shaking his head because Buddy had instructed him that when in doubt he should pretend not to know English. The guy from the San Diego paper was trying Spanish, but the feed man, from Tijuana, was pretending not to know that, either. Buddy walked past the four men, who turned to pounce on him, with another of those practiced waves. "How are you boys this morning," he said, not as a question. At the far end of the aisle, beyond Epic Steam's stall, stood Georgette, his office manager. She was pretending she couldn't speak at all. Everyone else was standing across from the two-year-old colt's metal door. It was a long walk, as walks made in ignorance always are. Halfway there, Leon, his assistant trainer, came up to him, his manner studied and casual, waved at the reporters, and said in a low voice, "I tried to call you at home, boss, but you'd already left."

"How did these reporters know I was working these horses right now?"

Leon shrugged, then said, sheepishly, "The thing is, Buddy, you always work your hot horses first thing. People know that—"

"What else is wrong?"

But there they were. There it was. Oscar, Epic Steam's groom, held it up for him to look at. It was a stiff gray cat. He said, "Foun it in straw, boss."

"He found it in the straw," said Leon.

"Horse keel it," said Oscar.

"The horse killed the cat," said Leon.

"He hit it gainst wall," said Oscar.

"He picked it up by the neck and threw it against the wall," said Leon.

"Foun it in straw."

"Yes," said Leon. "He found it in the straw when he was picking out this morning." They both looked at him. They all looked at him.

Buddy spoke smoothly and carefully: "I don't think the horse killed the cat."

As if in answer, Epic Steam caught his eye, pinned his black ears, and lunged at the stall guard.

Buddy said, "I think the cat must have picked up some rat poison somewhere, and wandered over here to die."

The cat's neck was broken and his head was turned sharply to one side.

Buddy said, "No doubt, he curled up in the straw."

The cat's skin was abraded where the horse had pawed the fresh corpse.

"And the horse, showing typical two-year-old curiosity, pawed him a little bit."

Epic Steam snorted and gave forth a mighty challenge.

"He's all boy, but it's mostly playful."

"Right, boss," said Leon.

"Right, boss," said Oscar.

"Oscar," said Buddy. "You get rid of the fucking cat."

Oscar nodded.

"But, first, tack this guy up and let's get the first set out there."

He walked back to the reporters. He said, "Oh, a cat died in the horse's stall. Looks like poison. No one wanted to touch it, you know. Superstition. All that. Bad sign."

"Think it's a bad sign for next week?"

Buddy laughed cheerfully. "Depends on the work."

The reporters laughed cheerfully, too. He herded them back toward his office. One of them said, "Horse ever taken down game before?"

Everyone laughed again. Buddy said nothing in reply.

Fifteen minutes later, when the first set was lined up to be mounted, they had Epic Steam, as always, right up front, the stud chain firmly set across his gum. As always, they did their little ballet. Buddy stepped up to him; twenty yards away, at the end of the row of stalls, a groom led a filly across the aisle; Epic Steam stopped grinding and jumping just for a moment and stood there, ears pricked; Buddy bent down and felt his legs firmly and quickly; as he stood up, Leon stepped forward and threw the exercise rider on top, and then the horse moved out. No matter what, the exercise rider was instructed to keep him going forward. A horse going forward was less able to rear, buck, crowhop, bolt, spin, you name it. Less able, not unable. But it worked. His predatory urges possibly assuaged by the death of the cat, Epic Steam moved off almost normally, and the reporters were glad to look at Residual.

And just as they all had backed away from the colt, they all stepped closer to the filly. Two of them reached out to pet her, possibly not even realizing it. Buddy didn't stop them. Better that their brains were fogged by sentiment.

Yes, she seemed to come to your hand, as if affectionateness expanded her. She pricked her ears, arched her neck, flared her nostrils, sniffed the hand of the *Form* reporter, then turned her head and looked deeply into his eyes.

Buddy bent down beside her and felt her legs. Cold today, cold enough for anyone to feel. Last week he had felt just a degree of heat in her left ankle. He had chosen to start her on Legend, not to X-ray. The heat was gone now. She stood squarely but alertly, as if on tiptoes. He threw the rider up and the filly moved out immediately, eager to get to work. As she walked down the aisle, every head, horse and human, chicken and goat, cat and Jack Russell terrier, turned to look at her. Walking behind her with the reporters, Buddy said, "She's shaped up into a nice filly. But there are nice fillies every year."

He glanced at the reporters; they were staring after the filly's scintillating red haunches, white ankles. This was a view Buddy liked of a horse, the shimmering tail like a waterfall, the sharply defined hocks, and below, the graceful lift of perfect pastern angles shading the hollow, silvery heels. Looking at a horse from behind like this told you all about running, all about how a thousand-pound body could seem airborne. People didn't think Buddy was much of an esthete when it came to horses, and it was true that he didn't swell up at the sight of a pretty head or a graceful neck or a kind eye, but, walking behind a horse like this, he could stare at those miracle ankles for quite a while.

The instructions were that three of the horses in this set were to do a timed work—three-eighths for the fillies, a half-mile for the colt. The colt was to jog the wrong way around the track out ahead of the fillies to the eighth pole, then turn, gallop to the half-mile pole, and then break off to work a half-mile. Residual and a rabbit filly by Glitterman would backtrack to the wire, then turn and gallop to the three-eighths pole, and get timed from there. They would be done with their work by the time Epic Steam, who always worked alone, was ready to go. The other horses in the set were only galloping. As they walked out to the trainers' stand, Leon in the front, then Buddy, then the reporters in a semicircle around him, Buddy found himself unable even to hear their questions, or to hear his answers, though he was making some. Jesus, he thought, would have to take care of this. He supposed he would find out what Jesus had said in the next day's papers.

Epic Steam disappeared behind the tote board on the far side of the track. The fillies were still on the turn, the rabbit on the rail and Residual on the inside. Already, of course, Epic Steam had quite a reputation, and Buddy didn't have to see him demonstrate it by whinnying, squealing, rearing, and champing at the bit. Everyone else would keep their distance. They always did.

Buddy trained his glasses on the fillies. He could see them easing to the pole, and then they were off. The lights over the track had begun to pale as the sky lightened. The Glitterman filly was a brown, so the two were easily distinguishable, even at this distance. The fillies ran neck and neck for about a furlong, as per instructions, and then Residual began to pull away. What a Ferrari she was. At two furlongs, the Glitterman filly seemed to hit a wall, though that was only an illusion. Buddy's clock said she was running as well as ever, though perhaps her heart was breaking. That was something else you sometimes had to do on the way to the Breeders' Cup, pick a rabbit and break her heart over and over, every five days, just to keep the big horse thinking well of herself. Residual was to do three-eighths, but not a bullet work. Just something to keep her tuned. She came around the turn toward the box, running easily, ears pricked, happy. The girl, Deedee, sat still on her, coiled like a cat, the wave of the horse's stride passing through the girl's body. One of the reporters said, "They remind me of water. That girl ever tried to be a jockey?"

"Too long in the leg," said Buddy. That was what he said. Later, he remembered that perfectly.

The Glitterman filly was trotting now. Buddy noticed that. And other horses were scattered around the track. The sun was coming up pretty good. All seemed in order. And then one of the reporters said, "Look at that," and there was Epic Steam, just to their left. What he had been doing Buddy didn't know, because he was watching the fillies. Epic Steam must have been watching the fillies, too, or at least watching Residual, because first he was squealing, then he was bolting right after her, and his rider was yanking and pulling on his mouth, trying to twist his head around. But the horse had a neck of granite and a mouth of steel. He bore down on the filly, those muscular shafts they called legs stretching and folding, stretching and folding. The filly, who was coming down to a jog, flicked her ears, and Deedee, Buddy could see this, tensed and turned her head. It must have been a frightening sight, the sight of that giant dark beast heading down the track at them, for only Jesus knew what purpose. The filly flicked her ears again, backward, forward. It was hard to know his intention. Normally, a stallion wouldn't dare approach a mare incautiously, but that would be a stallion who knew something. You never knew what Epic Steam knew. As he ran at the filly, she took off. They were right below the trainers' stand. Buddy could see Deedee's white face. But she took hold, steadied the filly, and crouched against her neck. The girl and the filly had decided to run for it. Around him, the reporters noticed the same thing. They shut up and hunched forward. In a moment, the big dark horse was on the filly's heels, his own rider standing in the stirrups and leaning back against the reins. They ran like that into the turn, the filly on the rail, the colt right against her, her ears pricked, his pinned. Every horse in their way scattered to the outside. The colt was fighting the bit. Buddy knew he wanted to bite her. Some stallions were like that. He'd seen it in the breeding shed, a stallion attacking and biting the mare, knocking her down. And he was so much bigger than she was—he probably outweighed her by two hundred pounds—he had muscles upon muscles. But, coming out of the turn, she did it—she floated away from him as easily as she had distanced the sprinting filly, effortless, joyous even, happy to whip him. Soon she was two lengths in front of him, and they stayed that way, the colt straining to catch the filly, the filly easy and smooth. Twenty strides? That many? And then the colt's fatigue brought him inside the circle of the rider's strength, and the rider managed to turn his head to the outside, and pull him up. As soon as they were out of danger, the filly and her rider floated to a trot like a big jet plane coming in for a perfect landing.

"Wow," said one of the reporters.

"Shit," said Buddy.

"Yeah," said another of the reporters, "that can't be good for your plans, huh, Buddy?"

"Filly looked good," said the guy from *The Blood-Horse*.

"That filly—" said the guy from the *Thoroughbred Times*. And then they all looked at each other. What their faces said was: You saw it, didn't you? You saw what I saw? Yes, yes. If they never race again, still we saw something.

"Just think if the rider hadn't been fighting him the whole way," said another guy.

"Geld him," said the guy from *The Blood-Horse*. "Geld him and you'll win the Kentucky Derby."

"But that filly!"

It went on. Buddy watched the filly through his glasses, trotting, trotting, walking. She looked done in now. What had she run altogether, a mile? That was a lot of ground for a two-year-old. Her head was down; even from this distance he could see she was blowing as hard as she could. He turned his glasses to the colt. He was still pumped with adrenaline. Still fighting, still wound up, but in spite of that, Buddy saw that he had two tired horses, two very tired horses, who probably should be scratched from their respective races.

What a relief that was.

And it was a relief, after all these months of patience, to have a temper tantrum back at the barn, after the reporters left. "Boss!" exclaimed Duane, Epic Steam's exercise rider. "I couldn't hold him! We got over there too fast, and then he was rearing up and spinning and pulling me around. There was guys all over back there. I just thought, Maybe he can run some of this energy off!"

"Boss," said Leon, the assistant trainer, gravely, "I have no idea how these reporters found out about this work. Really. No idea. But I will look into it, I promise that."

"Boss," said Deedee, the exercise rider, softly, "I was just scared shitless. But I knew she could outrun him. I didn't know what else to do."

The tantrum, the excitement, the morning, the hundred horses to train, the day's races, the day itself ebbed away, and the next thing Buddy knew, he was sitting on his bed four or five days later, taking off his shoes. It was just dark, and the green light on the fax machine glowed, as did the red digits on his alarm clock. Really, you had to admire the way Jesus answered those prayers, even the ones you didn't know you had made. The press, for example, was gone. No calls, no approaches, no stories about his career that made it seem strange to him. And Epic Steam was gone, too. On the day of the race he was supposed to run in but had been scratched from, Sir Michael Ordway had called him and told him he had just happened to see Jason Clark Kingston at a party in Los Angeles, and he had just happened to ask him how the horse was doing, and Jason had just happened to tell him that the horse was an uncontrollable filly-rapist of whom Andrea Melanie was deathly afraid, and Sir Michael had just happened to have spoken that day to a man in New York who was interested in a promising runner and had some money to spend, and blah blah blah, and so they had made a deal, Jason Clark Kingston holding out for $1.2 million, which, since the new owner had recently sold his chain of toy stores for four billion dollars, seemed like nothing to him. Epic Steam, well and truly tranquilized, had been put on a plane back to New York, and everyone in California, except, of course, Jason Clark Kingston, had profited from his sojourn there.

The filly's elderly owner, adept at looking on the bright side of things, was concerned that the filly had tied up a little upon returning from the barn, and then colicked a little the following evening and had a little filling in her right front ankle. "Oh, the poor thing," she lamented. "I talked to the vet myself, Buddy, and I know you hate that, but I felt that I had to really just get his unvarnished opinion, and I am sending her back to the farm. She's done enough and more than enough for such a baby. Poor thing. I'm sure she was frightened to death."

And so the filly had gotten on the van just that morning, and was right now, probably, getting to know the good life near Santa Ynez. And then the filly's owner had said, "But let's do go to Saratoga for the sale this year. That filly has just given me something to look forward to every day. Thank you, Buddy, you are a genius, darling."

And so Buddy set his shoes beside the bed, closed his eyes, and gave thanks, real thanks, heart-opening thanks, that the tests were over for the time being, and Jesus was giving him a break, a rest, five weeks until the yearling sales, to marshal his forces and catch his breath.

JULY

34 / ONTOLOGY

I T A L W A Y S P E R P L E X E D Joy that the first Tompkins, Jacob his name had been, had established his ranch right here. From almost any point of view, "right here" had nothing to offer, and didn't even have any "right-hereness" about it, since the landscape stretched away for miles in every direction as flat and dry and featureless as any landscape Joy had ever seen. Anyway, even without humidity, it was too hot to think, ride, talk, touch horses, or lift your eyes from your feet. The Tompkins Ranch Hotel and Resort (Destination Perfection) had three swimming pools and was designed to remind the weary resort-hopper of a combination of Tahiti and Jamaica right here in the middle of nowhere. It was considered highly imperfect for the ranch personnel to insert their dusty Central Valley selves into the Caribbean–South Pacifican roadside fantasy, no matter how hot it might become.

Nevertheless, Joy did not hesitate when the phone rang in the office and Elizabeth Zada invited her to join herself and her new lover, Plato Theodorakis, at the resort, where Plato had taken a suite for three days. Elizabeth and Plato had been seeing each other for some undefined period of time, at least undefined to Joy, and Joy had not met him yet. He turned out to be thirty-two years old and remarkably short and hairy, not Joy's type at all, but clearly Elizabeth's type. And she, post-menopausal and loud, seemed to be his type, too. Ah, well, thought Joy, surveying the spectacle of their relationship, you really never never never knew.

Plato was an assistant professor at Berkeley. His field was future theory. In her own way, Elizabeth was also working on future theory, because she was writing three books simultaneously, the journal of her personal spiritual journey, the description of her system, and her spiritual guide to household tasks. Plato specialized in the future of buying and selling. This included everything from the future of money to the future of natural resources to the future of mercantile relationships. Plato, who had been born on Crete, had returned to graduate school after making a not-inconsiderable sum trading currency in

Chicago, but, as he told Joy, at heart he was a theorist. He was also a big spender, but, as a theorist of spending, he kept careful records, and deducted everything he spent from his taxes. He had seven years to produce a book, and a profit. Plato and Elizabeth had met when she called him to ask about house-hold management in that land of the future, China. They liked each other's voices so much that each other's appearance had hardly made a dent in their mutual attraction. "You know," confided Elizabeth to Joy when Plato went for a dip, "I never liked a hairy man before, but if you already like him, then the way the water runs off him like rivulets through long grass is more endearing than anything else." Joy supposed so.

The three-pool complex, embraced by the luxurious arms of the resort, was blocked from the rest of the ranch by several rolling hills that Mr. Tompkins had installed as a part of the concept. You lay on your chaise longue under a series of pergolas and umbrellas that shaded you from the relentless Central Valley sunshine, and everywhere you turned, you saw the trickle and plash of waterfalls and streams connecting the pools to the golf course to the veil of palms and pines imported from Hawaii that hid the view of the hundred-thousand-head cattle feedlot beyond. Cabanas and guesthouses hung with irrigated bougainvillea and jasmine and surrounded by royal palms disgorged guests into the compound, where they were confronted at every turn by tables laden with food, mostly chilled fruits and pastel-colored drinks. Beef (Tompkins Perfection Blue Ribbon) appeared only as a subtle accent on these tables, most often dressed in exotic spices and herbs. The pervasive cowboy ambience of the rest of the ranch was noticeably absent here. After they had gazed at Plato swimming and diving for a while, he rejoined them. He said, "You know, once I saw a production of *Romeo and Juliet* set in Scandinavia. There were runes all over the stage, and Romeo and Mercutio and Tybalt all wore helmets with horns. Everyone else wore fur hats. There was something of a Russian accent, too, in the boots. That's what this place reminds me of. Things yoked together that might never otherwise meet. But that's the future. That's why I like it here."

"You ought to meet Mr. Tompkins," said Joy. "Diversifying is his life."

"Does he have a company theoretician?"

"I don't know. But everyone wears white coats. You've got to be willing to do that."

"What is it you do here again?"

"I work with the racehorses. The breeding stock, really. In the spring, I work with the broodmares; in the summer and fall, I work with the weanlings. Then the breeding season comes around again."

"You live here?"

"Well, in Waterone. I lived on the ranch for a while a long time ago. I rent a little guesthouse in Waterone."

"People in Waterone have guests?"

"I don't think so. I've rented this guesthouse for years."

Plato looked away from her with evident lack of interest in her staid and rusticated occupation, but when his eyes fell upon Elizabeth, who was wearing a black-and-silver swimming suit and a silver sarong, he smiled with evident pleasure. She smiled back at him. Joy felt a sudden pang of loneliness. Although she had not wanted a friend, and Elizabeth had not been the friend she had wanted, and she often thought of her friendship with Elizabeth as something good for her as well as a defense against several things generally deemed undesirable, like the concern of others and lots of brooding and overwork. Since the onset of this affair, she had seen Elizabeth less and she missed her. Of course, she had thought of Elizabeth's age as her protection against that trial of adolescence, your best friend getting a boyfriend and you not getting one. But, in fact, Elizabeth had been warning her that something like this could happen at any time, because her sexuality was a work-in-progress. One good thing about watching them was that they were too wrapped up in one another to notice, and another good thing about it was that it really made you believe that two souls could find one another, love one another, and desire one another whether either one, or, in this case, neither one, conformed in any way to accepted standards of pulchritude. As if to confirm Joy's observation, as she was watching, Elizabeth reached over and began to tickle the pelt over Plato's breastbone, and he then took her other hand with evident ardor. Their gestures were idle. Really, they were looking at one another more than anything else. Perhaps, Joy thought, she, with her envy, jealousy, and loneliness, felt their touch more than they did. She wanted to look away, because it was unpleasant to think of how long it was since she had last been in love, but she wanted to look, because it was pleasant to think that love existed, and close at hand.

Elizabeth said to Joy, "How's Mr. T.?"

"Ask him that."

Elizabeth looked at her and laughed, then said, "Okay." A moment later, she said, "His automatic waterer isn't working, and he's thirsty."

Joy sat up in alarm. "Really? In this heat?"

"What's going on," said Plato, "who's Mr. T.?," as Joy jumped up and went over to the phone on the towel stand.

When she had come back from putting a call in to the stallion manager, asking him to investigate Mr. T.'s waterer, Plato was sitting forward, looking at Elizabeth with particular glee. He was saying, "He told you that another horse had some disease that radiographs didn't pick up, and when it was scanned another way, they saw it?"

"Oh," said Joy. "That navicular horse. The barrel horse from the western side. Yes. Though it isn't a disease. It's a syndrome where a little bone in the horse's hooves starts to deteriorate."

"He saw it as flashing lights," said Elizabeth.

Joy hadn't realized how routine these conversations had become for her and Elizabeth, but Plato's disbelief and amazement made her feel weird, as if she had wandered into craziness without knowing it.

Elizabeth said, "But I can scan them myself. We went to the track once and I scanned every horse in the race and picked out the only one who really was healthy from top to toe. She won, too."

Joy hazarded, "Didn't you think that trainer had a pleasant face?"

Plato ignored her. "Did you have a bet on her?"

Elizabeth said, "No. Forgot to bet."

"You went to the races and forgot to bet?" Plato's amazement at this burned up all previous amazement. "You know, when I was in Cambridge that year, I went to the race meets every weekend. Betting in England is the purest form of market speculation there is. The parimutuel is a philosophical abomination in my opinion, a form of socialism. You know, in England, the owners have pedigrees, the horses have pedigrees, the trainers have pedigrees, the punters have pedigrees, the bookies have pedigrees, the jockeys have pedigrees. You could put them all in a database and sort through them the way they do with horse pedigrees, and you could plot their relative rates of success and failure, their historic relationships, and the relationship of nature to nurture. I mean, the human-genome project would be nothing to a study like this."

"You always think big, darling," said Elizabeth.

"Mr. T. has English bloodlines," said Joy.

"So what have you asked him that's interesting?"

"Oh, let's see. What he thinks of the other horses. How he's feeling."

"Everything immediate."

"Well, yes," said Joy. "Horses are very immediate in their thinking. Be here now, you know."

"How do you know?"

Joy smiled, then looked at Elizabeth, who was looking at her.

"Well, that's just the way they are. Physical," said Elizabeth.

"How do you know?"

"Doesn't this discussion sound crazy to you?" said Joy. "I have a scientific background, and I always think—"

"Look around you," said Plato. "What is crazy?"

Joy looked. It was true. A Rastaman and a blonde woman in a white coat, wearing Rollerblades and carrying a tray of pineapples cut to look like the

World Trade Center, were chatting idly beside the pool. When they skated and glided their separate ways, she saw behind them two sets of identical twins, one male and one female, all dressed alike, pulling identical bags to the second tee. Plato continued, "Let's go over there. Where do they keep the racehorses?"

"We don't have to go over there. The channel is clear as a bell."

"The channel?"

"Well, it's not a channel, really. I call it a pervasion."

"A what?" said Joy.

"A temporary ubiquity caused by paying attention. I've had to coin my own terms. Pervasion. Ubiquity. Alertion. We asked him that earlier question, so he is in a state of alertion."

"Why don't you just say he's alert?"

"Because he isn't conscious of it. He's not noticing anything but he's available. He could even be sleeping. When we go over there, he's attentive to us, but that's just physical. My favorite word is 'unitive.' When he's really in a state of alertion and I am really in a state of pervasion and ubiquity is all around us and in us, then I say that we are unitive."

"Darling, you're a genius," said Plato. Elizabeth smiled with what looked to Joy like the knowledge that, whether or not she was a genius, she was certainly well loved.

"What do you want to ask him?" said Joy to Plato.

Just then, the phone on the towel stand rang, the towel manager picked it up, spoke, and then gestured to Joy. When she came back she was gratified to report that, yes, the automatic waterer, which had been jammed, was now unjammed.

The unflappable Plato Theodorakis, man of the future, looked at her, thoroughly flapped. Elizabeth laughed. Joy said, "This sort of thing happens all the time with that horse."

Plato sat back and closed his eyes for a moment, then sat forward. He said, "What does he make of it all?"

"What all?"

"Don't specify. See what he says. Just ask him, what does he make of it all?"

Elizabeth beamed at Plato, then closed her eyes. After a moment, she said, "Of what all, he says."

"*It* all. Let him identify it."

Elizabeth closed her eyes again, then opened them and said, "Manure."

"What?"

"He says, he makes manure of it all. Hay, feed, grass, which he would like there to be more of, many many times a day."

"I told you they prefer the immediate," said Joy.

"I think he's joking," said Elizabeth, without opening her eyes.

"Okay," said Plato. "Let's see. Ask him what he is."

"He's a horse," said Joy and Elizabeth simultaneously.

"But what does he think that is? How does he define it? You know, subject peoples are always turning out to reserve some name for themselves that redefines their identity in opposition to the general name for them. The Lakota don't like to be called 'Sioux.' That kind of thing."

"He doesn't object to being called a horse."

Plato shook his head. "I mean—"

"He says it's better than being called a dog."

"Called a dog or being a dog?"

"Either one."

Plato sighed. "He's toy— Uh, I'm being toyed with."

"Maybe," said Elizabeth. "I can't tell."

"I wish we could see the look on his face," said Joy. "I'm getting pretty good at reading his expressions."

"Are you teasing me?" Plato said to Elizabeth.

She opened her eyes and smiled enigmatically.

"Theoreticians are always being teased, you know, because they take things seriously."

"I might be teasing you."

The two of them dissolved into smiles at the very thought of this.

Joy said, "Ask him what, of all the things he knows, he knows the best."

They looked at her, then Elizabeth closed her eyes again. There was a long pause, then she said, "I get a picture of the ground."

"He knows footing," said Joy.

"This is interesting," said Elizabeth. "I get a stream of pictures. At first I couldn't figure out what they were, but now I see that, even though they look like water flowing or streaming, what they really are is land flowing or streaming—turf, dirt, hills, dips, flat areas, but there're also close-ups of the ground, green plants and grasses and leaves and other vegetation."

"Grazing," said Joy.

"It's all flowing toward him, like a river."

"Or he's moving across it."

"But it isn't only visual," said Elizabeth. "It gives me another feeling, a feeling in my body, an undulating surface that my body is conforming to."

"Why not?" said Joy. "Think about it. They keep all four feet on the ground at all times, and have their noses to the ground most of the time, too." She knew she sounded blasé, but really what Elizabeth was saying gave her the oddest, most exciting sensation, the heretofore still and steady earth moving toward and enveloping her. "Think what it feels like to go thirty miles an hour with your nose first. Talk about alertion!" She laughed.

"What else does he know?" said Plato.

"He knows Joy," said Elizabeth.

"What kind of joy?" said Plato.

"Our Joy. Joy right here. But he gives me an interesting picture of her. It's like a fish-eye-camera picture. She's in the center, large and dressed in white, and she's surrounded by other horses and people, smaller and dimmer. I think this is a picture of love."

"Ask him," said Plato, "if he knows what love is."

There was a moment of silence. Joy's heart was pounding.

"He says of course he does."

"Horses are very affiliative animals," said Joy, but actually she could hardly speak.

"Well, what is it?" said Plato.

Elizabeth was silent for a long time, with her eyes closed and a perplexed look on her face, but finally she said, "Well, I guess the best way to describe what he's showing me is to say love is pervasion." Then she said, "But he says that it's particularly pervasive when Joy is around."

Ah, Joy thought. I am such a fool. I have walked step by step away from strict functional definitions, scientific methods, biology, physiology, chemistry, biomechanics, and order and here I am in a new world where I don't know how to exist or who I am, and it's not like any future I ever imagined.

Plato said, "I wish we could get some social theory out of this horse. Some economics. Some, I don't know, some Gemeinschaft und Gesellschaft. No more Weltanschauung."

"Maybe later," said Elizabeth. "He's tired, and he doesn't really understand what you're getting at anyway."

Joy leaned back in her chaise longue and looked at the pergola above her. Yes, she thought, she could hold all these things in her mind at the same time—the ground undulating toward her, the horse's love surrounding her like a beautiful glass globe, her own sight of Mr. T.'s graceful lines and intelligent face at just that moment when he would notice and turn toward her, and if she held these things suspended together in her mind, they worked as a spell against drudgery and loneliness, glare and fatigue, envy, even, of Elizabeth and Plato kissing right beside her. She sighed happily. On the green hillside across from her, sprays of irrigation water rose on the bright air, as expensive and glittering as diamonds.

35 / TWO PUNCH

Y OU KNOW," said Louisa, "how many things you want for years and years, and then you get them, and it's just the same old thing, no different? Almost everything, really. But I spent all of those years asking for a Tuesday-Thursday teaching schedule, and finally I got it for the summer, and it's just the way I thought it was going to be."

"How's that?" said Dick.

"Heaven on earth," said Louisa, smiling across the table at him. It was eight-thirty on a Monday morning, and in front of him he had a fried egg, two pieces of raisin-brioche French toast, a patty of sausage, and a glass of cranberry juice. The same thing was in front of her. They were eating breakfast. Together. With the sun well up in the sky. Even more amazing, they had a plan for the day, to drive upstate and have a late lunch in Woodstock. Perhaps, when they got home, they would go to a movie. It was just like a date. It was maybe the first time in several years that they hadn't gone out together either in order for one of them to demonstrate that he or she *was* interested in the other one's life, or else to fulfill some necessary function having to do with the basic human needs of eating, sleeping, clothing, or habitation. Louisa's agoraphobia had been quiet for a couple of months now. Dick thought this outing was probably both a celebration of that and a test of it. He was therefore rather ambivalent about it.

About that and everything else. He was running a horse these days, a two-year-old that the owners had bought at a training sale in the spring. "What shall we name her?" they had said, perhaps idly. "Ambivalence," he said, a joke. But it was an appropriate name, given that her sire was Two Punch, so that was how they had registered her. Sometimes she ran, sometimes she didn't. Well, of course, most of them were like that, but because her name was Ambivalence, she *had* to be like that. It was a good name, but of course he was ambivalent about it.

The deal was, he had lost his sense of how best to train this horse, and she was contaminating the rest of them. With a two-year-old, you brought along the body, but you also had to bring along the mind. It took a long time for some of them to figure it out. Frequent works and steady racing focused them and showed them what to do, especially fillies. But frequent works and steady racing were hard on them. And Ambivalence had an ambivalent pedigree. Stage Door Johnny was in there, but so was Storm Bird. Her dosage was heavy on the sprinting side, light in the middle, and heavy on the staying side, unusual for an American horse. Was she a sprinter? Was she a stayer? Of course, he was ambivalent about dosage, too. The result was that he would decide to train her one way—work every five days, rain or shine—and then he would decide to work her another way—long slow gallops, works only when she seemed to need sharpening up. The result was, either he had no idea who she was, or she had no idea who she was. One or the other.

"Dick?" said Louisa.

"Sweetie." But the fact that she had broken in on his reverie brought up a very sudden and sharp annoyance.

"Are you with me here?"

"Kind of." That she sensed his annoyance (he could tell this by the tone of her voice) annoyed him even further. Maybe, he thought, the very fact that you did not expect a fight today of all days ensured that there would be one.

"Can you be really with me? Because, if you can't, I don't see why we bother."

"Bother with what?"

She cleared her throat, leaving him to guess, or, rather, to know. Bother with each other was what she was getting at, though she allowed him to think she was just talking about their plans for the day.

"I'm sorry, sweetie," he said, a good try. But now her face was clouded. Their day would not be perfect. He realized as he thought this that that was what he had been planning—a perfect day as a springboard into a new and less ambivalent life together. If you could have a day, or even an hour, or even a moment of pure love for your spouse, he suspected, that would be enough to fix everything, but the moments kept getting away from him, tainted by ambivalence and inattention. Of course, he suddenly realized, ambivalence *was* inattention masquerading as indecision. Ah, it was a tangle. The cloud in Louisa's face gave way to something harder—conviction, it looked like—and, sure enough, she pushed away her plate. She said, "Do you ever think about anything besides horses?"

"Of course, I—" But the residue of his now largely dissipated annoyance was still there, and she could hear it, and that was enough.

"Really?" Her chin jutted forth. "Don't say 'of course.' Think first."

Because he thought about Rosalind Maybrick most of the time, he said, "Horses are on my mind much of the time, but—"

"But?"

"But I often dream about other things."

"Like what?"

"Being naked in a restaurant. Not having done my homework."

"With enjoyment?"

"What?"

"Do you dream about being naked in a restaurant with enjoyment?" She sounded angry.

Which brought his annoyance back as resentment. "Yes. I do enjoy it. I am not embarrassed at all and women are getting up from their tables and coming over to me and looking at me with intense desire."

She sat back suddenly in her chair and stared at him. Of course he had never had a dream like this in his life. This was a lie designed to hurt her feelings.

She said, "I thought this was going to be a nice day."

"I did, too."

"Then why do you want to wreck it?"

He almost said one thing, something about how he didn't want to wreck it, but then he said, "Because a nice day would be fake for us."

"What?"

"I can't stand a nice day. That's exactly the thing I can't stand the most, a nice day. We have to have either a perfect day or a disastrous day."

"Why?"

"Because, if we don't have something black or white together soon, we won't know why in the world we *are* together."

"I love you." But the look of conviction had passed, too. Now her face had a look of fear.

"Do you?"

"Yes. Don't you love me?"

"I don't know, Louisa. I don't know what love is anymore. If I ever did." He saw that he had embarked upon honesty at last. He sighed.

"Don't say that."

"Why not?"

"Because it makes me feel dizzy."

"Dizzy like you're having an attack?"

"I don't know. No. Dizzy like I've lost track of everything. Dick, we've been together for twenty-five years."

"I know that."

"Do you love me anymore?"

"I don't know what love is. I don't. I don't know what anything is. I walk around and look at all these guys at the track who know what everything is, even if they're wrong and they never win and they break horses down every week and they can't pay their bills, but they know it all. They just know it all, and they're willing to tell you all the stuff they know every minute of the day, but I can't say that I know a God-damned thing." She wasn't listening. If he couldn't tell her that he loved her, then she couldn't listen. It was as simple as that. So he tried honesty again: "I had an affair."

"Who with?"

"Rosalind Maybrick."

"Were you having it when I came out to watch that race?"

"Yes."

"I thought so. Did you love her?"

"Yes."

"Did she love you?"

"I don't know."

"I like that, that you know what love is with her, and you know that you love her, but you don't with me."

"I was ambivalent about her, too."

"I hate that."

"What?"

"Just get the fuck out."

"Out of?"

"Out of this apartment. This is my apartment. This is my furniture. These are my dishes and my napkins and my chairs and my—"

Her face was blazing. He saw that she was being as bad as she could be, to say "my, my, my." She had been kind and generous all their life together. She closed her eyes and thought of another way to be bad. She said, "You have no sense of rhythm. When you were playing with the band, your tempo was always uneven." She smiled nastily. "Everyone talked about it behind your back."

It almost made him know he loved her, that these were the worst punishments she could think of. He sighed again and stood up from the table. He thought he would go pack, but he would do it slowly, in a way that would goad her and cause their marriage to devolve as far as possible in one day. That, he thought, was their only hope. He turned away from the table and headed for the bedroom. Behind him, she burst into noisy tears. He found that incredibly irritating, but recognized that this was an excellent start, about which he wasn't in the least ambivalent.

36 / LONG SHOT

FLORENCE SCHMIDT'S therapist, paid for by her husband's death benefits from the Army, was Marguerite, a sympathetic and lovely woman who was always perfectly groomed and beautifully dressed, but who didn't have that air of impermeability that most of that sort of woman had in Florence's estimation. Marguerite did not push Florence, because, as she said from time to time, she was waiting for Florence to push herself, and, as the fact that she had raised seven children showed, she was a woman of endless patience. Since Army death benefits were endless, too, they could wait all this lifetime and into the next, said the lovely therapist with a smile. There was no hurry. Florence told her friends that she went for the therapy, but really she went for the beauty tips. These tips had nothing to with attracting another man, everything to do with trying to discover her own identity; that's why, Florence thought, she didn't scrutinize women on the street, only Marguerite. While they would be sitting, sometimes talking, sometimes quiet, Florence would note what her therapist was wearing and how she had done her hair and what her natural physical advantages were and how she was making the most of them. For example, the woman had dark-brown eyes, but she was a blonde, an unusual combination. After several weeks of therapy, Florence deduced that she dyed her hair, and went home and looked in the mirror. It was true that her dark hair streaked with gray was too contrasty, and so she went to a beauty salon and the therapist there, Martine her name was, gave her a color weave. If she had expected Marguerite to comment, she would have been disappointed, but she didn't expect that. She knew Marguerite wanted her to announce her color weave and solicit comment, but she wasn't ready to. For a while, the color weave looked to Florence like an optical illusion, and then she got used to it. The next thing she observed in Marguerite was that her stockings were certainly not L'eggs. So she went to the lingerie store and did a little survey. The ones that looked like Marguerite's were silk, and cost fifteen dollars a pair. She bought two pair, and allowed Natalie, the sales consultant, to slip into a bag two pair of cream-colored thong underpants and a pair of peach-colored silk pajama bottoms. After that, she spent about four weeks, and four hundred dollars of military allocations, observing Marguerite's shoes. Marguerite wore different shoes every day; that would be four different examples of European leathercraft at, on average, $175 a pop. The next time Florence went to Macy's, she walked into the shoe department *as* Marguerite and allowed Denise to sell her one pair of black Arche flats, zippers up the back, and one pair of tan, woven slingbacks. The next time she went for an appointment, she wore the tan shoes with the stockings and the underwear. Marguerite hazarded the comment that Florence seemed to be more self-actualized than usual. But even so, the waiting went on. Florence was a follower. Had always been a follower. She knew perfectly well that she couldn't have bought those things without Marguerite, Martine, Natalie, and Denise.

The next day, she went with Audrey to Los Angeles, to visit Richard's parents for the first time since his death. She knew she would miss Marguerite, but, on the other hand, the rapidity with which Marguerite was forcing change upon her was exhausting, and she needed a break. She also didn't know why she was being required to change, since it was entirely possible, and even desirable, for her to go along looking exactly the way Richard knew her for the rest of her life, alone with Audrey, supported by the taxpayers, and her mind blank with overwhelming grief.

On the plane, sitting next to Audrey, who was perusing the *Thoroughbred Times,* Florence added up what she had spent on her appearance so far, none of which was covered separately from her living expenses. The answer was six hundred dollars, about five hundred dollars more than she could afford to spend on shoes, underwear, and hairdressing. She sat back and looked out the window, wondering if she was trying to improve her appearance, or simply to have one. Next to her, Audrey said, "Do you think Grandpa will take me to Del Mar? They're running five stakes races Saturday." Speaking of appearance, Florence thought, Audrey was no longer a slender little girl with a narrow face and lank, dark hair. Her shoulders were broadening, her hair was thickening, and her chin was beginning to square up, as if the first step in instituting her life plan was coming to look more like Richard.

"If you want to go, I'll take you, Audrey," said Florence. It wasn't that Florence gave Audrey whatever she wanted. It was that Audrey, like Richard, had a mission, and Florence did not. Taken all in all, Florence thought Audrey's mission was fine enough.

What Richard's father did, though he had to work that day in his clothing store, was to give Audrey a hundred dollars to bet, and so, once they made the long drive to the track, Florence found herself following Audrey back and forth from the paddock to the betting windows to the stands, watching the intensity with which Audrey made her choices. Of course, it was Florence who had to place the bets. Audrey coached her. She said, "Now, you go up, and you say, 'First race, ten dollars on number five to win,' and then you give him the money and take your ticket. Don't forget to check your ticket before you leave the window." Florence didn't mind what most mothers would call Audrey's imperious tone.

Horse number five in the first race was dark and the jockey was wearing red and white diamonds on his shirt. That was all Florence noticed, but Audrey was informative. She said, "This filly's by Rainbow Quest out of a Gone West mare. I don't know. She looks good, but the jockey I've never heard of. He's got a double bug." She looked up and scrutinized the boy again. In fact, she glared at him, Florence thought, as if reading his mind. And then, oddly, he looked straight at her, and smiled. Without taking her eyes off him, Audrey said, "That's his apprentice weight allowance. But okay. He's okay. Let's go place the bet."

The horse came in at eight-to-one. Florence barely had time to get her ninety dollars back before they were headed for the paddock again. The weather was pleasant and Del Mar a garden of colorful flowers. This was, Florence thought, very similar to, in fact almost indistinguishable from, a vacation. Had she not known better, she would have said she was having a good time. Audrey said, "Put the ninety dollars we won in one pocket and the ninety left from what Grandpa gave us in the other." Florence did so. Audrey took up her post again, and made her pick. She chose a red horse with a jockey in purple on its back, but then, when the jockeys were going out of the paddock to the track, that apprentice jockey, who was on another dark one and wearing green, smiled at Audrey and waved, and when she went in to bet, she told Florence to put fifty on that one, and only ten on the other one. "But it has to be fifty out of our winnings from the last race. The ten has to be out of Grandpa's."

"What's the difference, Audrey? Money is—"

"Please, Mom?"

When they got back their three hundred dollars on the green horse, Florence wadded it up and put it into her pocket without question.

For the third race, Audrey's pick was the favorite, who was going off at only three-to-two, a bad bet, but Audrey wanted to put ten of Grandpa's money on him anyway. But the young jockey, whose name they had discovered was Roberto Acevedo, looked for her again. She stood right where the paddock gave onto the path under the stands. As he went by, this Roberto leaned down quickly and touched Audrey on the top of the head. Audrey didn't have time to react right then, but afterwards she pushed Florence ahead of her as they ran to the betting window. They put a hundred out of the right pocket on Roberto's horse. He came in at twelve-to-one. Florence could hardly breathe when she picked up the thirteen hundred dollars after the race. They had won $1,580. Audrey looked Florence firmly in the eye. She truly was Richard all over now, with the look he'd had the day he told her they were going to France. She said, "We're going to bet a thousand dollars, Mom."

But Roberto wasn't in the fourth race, and all Audrey did was bet ten of Grandpa's money on a gray filly who came in fifth.

When they were standing by the railing before the sixth race, Roberto came out of the jockeys' room, stopped, looked around, saw Audrey, and came straight for her. He was cute—Hispanic-looking, Florence noticed, and young. He was about Audrey's height, about Florence's own height, five three—when had Audrey gotten that tall? He walked right up to Audrey, put his hands on her cheeks, and kissed her full on the lips. Florence was startled, but Audrey was not. When Roberto turned and ran over to his mount, laughter and murmurs following him as he went, Audrey turned and raced for the betting windows. Florence ran after her. They put down their thousand dollars.

The horse came in at three-to-one. They had now won $4,580. Florence said, "Audrey, I want to go home. We've got a lot of money, and it scares me to carry it around."

"One more," said Audrey, in Richard's commander voice. Florence licked her lips. Mostly, she wondered what Roberto would do to follow up that kiss. She said, "That was quite a kiss, Audrey. You don't even know him."

"He's a jockey."

"So what?"

"I'm a rider, too."

"So what?"

"So everything's okay about that. It's not about kissing, Mom. If it were about kissing, it would be disgusting. You know that."

Well, Florence had to laugh, just out of gratitude that Audrey wasn't so grown up after all.

So they stayed around for the eighth race. The horses came out. The owners and trainers came out. The jockeys came out. Roberto looked around for Audrey, who was already staring at him, waiting for his gaze. When they saw each other, it was a long moment, and after he mounted, Audrey stood there for a while, indecisive. "Well?" said Florence. The odds on the horse were five-to-one. They could bet two thousand, keep two thousand. Florence was excited at the prospect, already counting the fourteen thousand dollars they were destined to go home with. The horses paraded out of the paddock. Roberto gave Audrey a kind smile as he went by. "Well?" said Florence.

"No bets. He's lost it."

"What?"

"I don't like the horse. Roberto's lost it. Bad race. Too many horses, and they're all old. Let's go home."

"Don't you even want to see it?"

"No. Let's go."

"How do you know he's lost it?"

"I don't know."

"Does he know he's lost it, or just you?"

"He's wondering, but I know. That's why I didn't really look at him. I don't want him to go into the race knowing he's lost it. He might get hurt or something."

"Audrey, I don't understand this."

"Well, jeez, Mom. I don't under*stand* it, either. But it's true."

"Don't say 'jeez' to me like that. It's rude."

"Sorry."

This, Florence thought as they looked for her father-in-law's car in the parking lot, was something she understood, rudeness between a twelve-year-old daughter and her middle-aged mother. And it was sort of a relief, to tell the truth. In her right pocket, the wad of cash bulged like a lightbulb. They got into the car and bore their winnings northward.

AUGUST

37 / YEARLINGS FOR SALE

YOU HAD TO KNOW the hell of Keeneland in July to recognize the heaven of Saratoga in August. Even if it got hot, which wasn't very often, thought Buddy, the trees were so large and shady that you were inspired with thoughts of earlier, pre-air-conditioning times, and were led to believe that you could not only endure but thrive on the heat, become one of those nineteenth-century men, like Colonel Bradley, who raced Man O' War, men who had fewer conveniences but more energy, less education but more intelligence, and shorter lives but longer days than poor late-twentieth-century sinners like himself. Saratoga was the one place he'd been to lately that didn't make Buddy Crawford wish he were dead.

Buddy distinguished this wish from a desire to commit suicide, which he had none of, because he was not a depressed sort of guy and never had been. He was an angry sort of guy, and always had been, and Jesus fully understood that, and, you might say, even sympathized with that, because hadn't he himself gotten mad at that tree, whatever it was, that didn't fruit out or something when he ordered it to? Buddy wasn't much of a reading man, either, and even though he'd gotten himself one of those Bibles that were written in regular English, he tended to fall asleep over the stories unless he skimmed them, but the fact was, if you read really fast, your eyes picked up the main points and then Jesus came into you and told you what was important about the rest. The difference between wishing you were dead and wanting to commit suicide was that wanting to commit suicide was a kind of sad-sack impulse characteristic of losers, and wishing you were dead was just a choice, like oatmeal for breakfast instead of a cup of coffee and a cigarette. Especially now that Buddy knew that his eternal reward was waiting for him, wishing he were dead seemed more like, say, wishing to move to Hawaii or something.

If he were dead, Buddy thought, he wouldn't go on mulling over this dilemma he had. Yes, he had gotten rid of both Epic Steam and Residual, but it had made no difference. He was still winning, winning, winning. The Hollywood meet: 103 runners, thirty-four winners, twenty second, twenty-six third, a not quite 30-percent win average, there in the *Form* for every loser at the track to see. And so far at Del Mar, only two weeks, things were going about the same. However, Jesus, it was well attested, liked a loser, especially a *good* loser. That was his dilemma. He could not seem to become a loser, but the meek blah blah blah. It was perfectly clear. Still, it was a toss-up, when you woke up in the night and told yourself that Jesus would like you better with a 4-percent win average, whether that was enough to compensate for how much you wouldn't like yourself. But the reason he didn't wish he were dead in Saratoga was that it wasn't polite to do so, and so nobody did. Also, his owners were traipsing after him in a herd, waiting for him to designate his chosen future winners. The fact was that every racing man who had ever been to Saratoga had made a fervent wish never to die, so that he could return to Saratoga year after year until the oceans dried up and Thoroughbreds became extinct.

The yearlings looked good this year, Buddy thought, at least they maybe sort of looked good, but he found himself having odd feelings. For example, they'd stand up a yearling and he'd bend down in the time-honored way and check to see if the animal's legs were straight and correct. Yes, he'd think, or no. Yes or no. A man like him, a trainer for decades, knew correct. Not only did he know correct, he was known for knowing correct, otherwise why did he have a herd of owners? But then something about one of the legs would throw him off and he'd start to doubt his own expertise. Did the knee turn in? Was the leg a little bent? Yes? Or no? Was the fact that the white sock seemed to vibrate in front of his eyes throwing off his judgment, and then was the white sock really vibrating? If the white sock was vibrating, what did that mean? It was like back in California and you woke up and you thought sure the bed had been shaking, but now it wasn't. Was it an earthquake? Was it a heavy truck on the highway, a dog under the bed, a dream, his heart beating its way to a heart attack, an intruder trying to wake him up, a horse in his barn miles away keeling over and shaking the ground, Jesus asking for his attention? In that moment just when you woke up, you didn't know. Any of these things was possible. So yes or no? And then so what? Horses with straight legs often ran like fat women, and horses with corkscrew legs often ran like cheetahs. And, given his dilemma, which ones did he want, winners or losers? And by the time all these thoughts had gone through his head, he couldn't remember whether the animal's legs had looked straight to him in the first place, and he was squatting there staring like an idiot, so he stood up and went on to the next, and the whole thing was a blur, sort of like his life had become since the day he'd accepted Jesus and thrown out the drugs and the buzzers and the toegrabs and the steep turndowns.

So he stood up and went to the next horse, closely followed by the click of Andrea Melanie Kingston's high heels and the flap flap of Jason Clark Kingston's big feet. They thought nothing of nearly treading on the counters of his shoes in their eagerness to buy buy buy. This was a big chestnut colt, and here was Farley Jones, all by himself, exhibiting his usual coolness, stroking his beard, keeping himself to himself. Farley squatted down, then stood up, and said in tones of perfect lack of self-doubt, to himself, it seemed, "Good feet. Straight in front. Good hocks."

Buddy noted the hip number, and when Farley moved off, he turned to his owners' gallery and said to Jason Clark Kingston, "That one might fit your program."

Taken all in all, and knowing that he would wish he were dead again as soon as he got back to southern California, Buddy hoped the Saratoga sale lasted an eternity. You could do it—horses getting shipped in, horses getting shipped out, money getting shipped in, money getting shipped out, but the trainers and agents and owners just wandering around day after breezy day in a fog of yearlings until Jesus came and put everyone out of their misery.

IT WAS ALWAYS TRUE, Farley thought, that avoidance bred approach. For example, he had been avoiding Buddy Crawford all day, and all day Buddy Crawford had been right there. Back in southern California he didn't see Buddy Crawford for weeks, but here in Saratoga he couldn't turn around without seeing Buddy looking at him, flanked by a regiment of owners who were also looking at him. And in Buddy's eyes Farley thought he saw, could it be, longing. Farley tried not to feel uncomfortable about either the owners or the longing, but pure naked longing, unleavened by irritability, anger, spleen, resentment, aggression, and the other invigorating hot-headed emotions, was clearly a painful feeling for Buddy, and posed a social challenge for Farley, probably, he thought, because he felt a touch of that longing himself. He had come to the sale without a single owner in tow, and he didn't really have a purpose here, except the usual Saratoga purpose, which was to enjoy oneself. And so he had attempted that very thing—he had strolled around downtown, strolled around the sale, strolled around the grandstand and watched some races, taken his rental car up into the Adirondacks a bit, driven over to Tanglewood and taken in some Mozart, even though none of the other trainers knew this, gotten out of his car and taken a little hike. And though he was originally from the East, New Jersey, the humidity had surprised and wilted him. No, he wasn't having a good time. Yes, he was out of place—he should be in Del Mar. The regret he felt about this mistake swelled with his every attempt to relax.

The owner he didn't have in tow, hocking him, nagging him, worrying about money, having bright ideas, showing off, having to be restrained and guided, followed him around, a black, owner-shaped hole, much like a shadow, and blindingly visible to every trainer who did have an owner in tow. The fact was, it was an owner who made you what you were as a trainer. Without the owner's greed, impetuousness, ignorance, and *money*, you, the trainer, had no need for experience, skepticism, or wisdom. Without an owner you were just a guy.

Farley had thought he was making it. All around southern California he had been walking, talking, and acting just as if he knew what life was all about—virtue being its own reward, taking the bad with the good, letting go, rolling with the punches. He probably counseled Oliver in these precepts every single day. But as he idled around the sale, pretending to look at the yearlings but not really seeing them, he knew that, in the end, you really did have to have that egomaniacal owner right at your elbow, yammering in your ear about his needs, in order to know yourself by contrast.

But just as he didn't have a horse to bring for Saratoga racing, he didn't have an owner to bring for Saratoga buying. His owners these days were as cheap as his horses. The ones who had some class personally, like the herbal-supplement people, happened to be fiscally cautious, and others, who were more eager, just happened not to have any money. He looked at the yearlings anyway, but as the hours wore on, Farley felt his spirits dip lower and lower. It didn't help that some of his past owners, two or three that he had found especially child- or even toddlerlike during former associations, were here, howling on the arms of Buddy Crawford and others, beating out the old refrain, Kentucky Derby, Triple Crown, Breeders' Cup, I want I want I want.

Cellular phones were ringing everywhere, but his was not. Who am I? thought Farley. Where am I? What am I doing here?

And then he fainted dead away.

When he came to, Buddy Crawford had his hand on Farley's forehead, and when Farley looked at him, he said, "Jesus Christ, what the fuck, you bastard, you okay?"

It was reassuring, in a way.

Buddy was immediately replaced by an attractive smooth-faced boy of about thirteen who identified himself as a cardiologist with one of those hyphenated hospitals in New York City. Behind him loomed the face of Ralph Halliberton, a trainer at Belmont and Aqueduct whose picture Farley had seen in *The Blood-Horse*. Ralph said to the boy, "Did he have a heart attack, doc?," and the boy said something that sounded unaccountably like one of those Mozart flute solos he had heard three nights before, and that was that, he closed his eyes. The only thing he could make out was the voice of Buddy

Crawford, rattattattatting above the din, who the fuck what the fuck why the fuck how the fuck when the fuck.

Time passed. Farley sat up. Someone brought him a chair. He took a few deep breaths and a sniff or two, rubbed his face with his hands. The first things that came back to him were odors—the ever-familiar odors of horses and hay, of men sweating. After that, sounds—people talking, hooves clopping, whinnies and snorts. Smells and sounds, the evidence of life resuming. Farley put his hand behind his neck and gave his head a twist, first one way, then the other, then he smoothed down his beard and heaved a deep sigh. At last, what he was seeing took on significance. The face of the boy cardiologist rose before him like a moon, and the mouth said, "Well, I don't think you had a heart attack. But let me take a little history."

He answered the usual questions. His age and gender were against him, his weight and life-style were for him. His cholesterol was low, his family background was unsuspicious. Still, you never knew. Farley nodded. Buddy's head bobbed behind that of the doctor, his eyes still full of longing. Farley shook his head and closed his own eyes. Then he said to the boy doctor, "Can I get up? I think I would like to go back to my hotel."

"I don't see why not." Then, almost shamefacedly, "I've got some more horses to look at myself."

"You're an owner?"

"Well, yeah. I've got one or two. No Derby prospects, though. At least, not yet." He grinned.

Farley sighed, then said, "Did you save my life?"

"No. Your life wasn't in danger."

"Well, I'm grateful to you anyway, so I'm going to tell you something I've never told anyone before about the horse business."

"What's that?"

Farley opened his mouth. The boy cardiologist looked at him expectantly, sweetly.

"I'm sorry," said Farley. "I can't remember."

He got up from his chair and headed for the parking lot, where he almost bumped into a woman who was standing like a statue at the end of the shedrow. Smoothly blonde, pale of complexion, of no discernible age, dressed in shades of ecru and beige, in sunlit contrast to the dark green of the wooden barn, she caught him as he stumbled toward her. She seemed to set him back on his feet with no effort, though he was tall and she wasn't. Her grip was solid, deceptively strong, and reassuring. He continued to feel it, on his elbow and his chest, after she had removed her hands. He said, "Thanks! I'm so sorry. I just—"

Rosalind gave one of her slow smiles and said, in a serene, vibrant voice, "It's all right, dear."

ROSALIND WAS WAITING FOR AL. They did everything together now. She heard and saw everything Al Maybrick did, hour after hour, day after day, night after night. They were never apart; Eileen trotted at Al's heels as if pasted there. Here he came now, from the men's room. He looked a little florid today, but that was okay, an improvement. He had looked nearly apoplectic the day before. "I don't know," he said when he came up to her. "There's something going on. You got any of that Immodium stuff?"

Rosalind opened her bag and handed him a packet of tablets. Eileen, right behind Al, cocked her head upward and snapped Rosalind a glance, then flopped down on her belly, all four legs stretched out. Rosalind said, "That A.P. Indy colt we saw in the catalogue should be right in this barn."

"Huh," said Al.

They turned together. Rosalind put her hand through Al's arm and they walked like that down the barn, their progress counted out by the passing stall doors. Eileen trotted behind them, whirring along as if on skates. "What's that hip number?" said Al.

"A hundred and four," said Rosalind.

"Say," said Al, "I heard a story about Nureyev. Seems this guy in Texas got himself a zebra from somewhere, some kind of special zebra, and he had his heart set on breeding her to Nureyev."

"Oh, Al," said Rosalind.

"This guy swore to God. Anyway, Nureyev breeds at night, you know, so, when the Texan offered them a million bucks' stud fee, they were tempted. He's not all that fertile anymore, they say."

Step step step. It was interesting to Rosalind to place herself inside Al's personal space. It felt like being inside his body, especially since he himself focused so intently on his body. He had pills, tablets, lotions, ointments, lozenges, drops. Rosalind carried all of them in her purse, along with his crushable hat. She might have thought this would be unpleasant, but it wasn't. Al was so focused on his body that she could look past it perfectly well. Perhaps he had personal qualities still. Others reacted to him as if he did, but Rosalind didn't experience them any longer. Perhaps she experienced nothing in the normal sense anymore. No past, no future. Perhaps if she should experience things in the normal sense, she would be afraid of what was happening. But she wasn't. She was curious. She was fascinated.

"So the studfarm agreed to accept the zebra, and they brought her there after midnight, and they took her in. Well, Nureyev pawed and squealed and, you know, showed a bit of an interest, but he seemed a little scared of her, so they let it go. Next night, they brought her in, brought him in, same thing. So the stallion manager went up to the horse, most expensive horse in the Bluegrass, they say, maybe in the world, and he tried to calm him. Took him over to the zebra and let him sniff her and all. She was receptive. But, still, he wouldn't mount, and they didn't want to get a lot of guys out there, you can understand that, with the Jockey Club and all, so they let it go another night."

Step step step. The barns at Saratoga seemed very long this year. Eternal. That was okay, too. Every experience of endlessness gave you time to review all that flux you had given up. Most dramatically, you had given up the flux of presence and absence. Where was Dick? Was he here yet? Was that his step? No? How soon? Now? What was he doing if he wasn't here? Was he late? How late was he? Here he came. Here he was. Did he look the same? What was he going to do now? What did that mean? Was it what she wanted him to do? How could she know what she really wanted him to do? In the room. In her arms. In her. And then not in her. And then not in her arms. And then not in the room. And then not in the vicinity. And then, it felt like, not in existence, as if love itself had died away. Try as she might to tell herself that he was only a man, working, earning a living, conditioning horses, and subject to his own perplexities and anxieties, whenever he left there was an utter goneness about it that emptied her out for a day or two, until, bit by bit, she put herself back together, retrieved from some distant region of her mind an intention, then a plan. Would she see him tomorrow, the next day, next week, in two weeks? But, after all, plans were the worst. They drained you of every bit of present life, until all you were was a containment building, and the ghost of yourself was lost on the vapors of the future, waiting to exist. Enough of that. Better to give up all personal qualities, all hopes, all plans, all dreams. Better to exist in a permanent startle, moments lighting up like sparks and flashing out, goodbye, good-bye, good-bye.

"The next night, they brought the zebra mare into Nureyev's breeding shed again. She was winking and all that. Couldn't have been more ready. The vet palpated her and she had a follicle the size of a kumquat. Perfect. But, still, Nureyev couldn't, or wouldn't, do it. So the stallion manager takes Nureyev aside and he whispers in his ear, 'This is a million bucks, boy. It's the end of the season. This is eight mares you don't have to do. One time, no guarantee. That's in the contract. No guarantee season.' So Nureyev does that stallion thing, where they wrinkle up their nose, and he nods his head up and down. She's ready. He knows it."

Step step step. And on the surface, apart from the empty center of her that she felt but didn't understand, purchases, dinner parties, horse races, clothing and hairdresser's appointments, Al's body, Dick not around to run into for some reason, everything okay, everything far away.

"But then he looks at the stallion manager, Nureyev does, and he leans closer, and he says to the guy, 'What I don't understand is, if she's so ready, why doesn't she take off her pajamas?' Here's the stall number," said Al. "This must be the horse."

Rosalind remembered to laugh.

IT WAS LATE. The bay filly out of Belle Starr was waiting to enter the pavilion and step up on the golden stage where her value, in tens or hundreds of thousands, even in millions, would register on the display above her head as the bids flew around the amphitheater. For now she was known as hip number twenty-six. She moved deliberately, but with a swinging, ample stride. Her head turned easily from side to side as she took everything in. The filly's handler paused with her outside the sales pavilion. She stood quietly, her leadshank loose. Her handler gave her a couple of pats, then ran his hand down her neck. She was so clean for this sale that her coat was almost too fine for his callused palm to feel, but he nevertheless appreciated, as he had in the past, the wide expanse of a healthy horse's smooth silkiness. Really, when you thought about it, no dog's ear, no woman's belly, no child's cheek, no cat's electric back offered such an inexhaustible field for a man's palm. A moment later, the handler walked her in and stood her on the little stage. A hand went up, and then another. When the auctioneer called out, the filly's ears swiveled.

Al was sitting next to Rosalind. He rather liked this filly, and he thought of bidding. He glanced at Rosalind for a sign, any sign, that she liked the filly, too. Rosalind's consumer instincts were infallible. But in fact Al got no sign of anything, even that Rosalind was there. He knew that if he poked her and asked her for something she would hand it over with a smile; that was why he asked her all the time for so many things. But when she wasn't handing something over, the lights were out and the family wasn't at home, that Al could see. He sighed and glanced around the pavilion. He thought for a moment about one time they'd had together, seven or eight years before. They'd been driving up in the Catskills by themselves. They'd been way back in the hills and had gotten a flat tire. No cellular then. As the man, Al had gotten out and started changing the tire. But Al was all thumbs with this stuff. His dad had told him that he'd better make something of himself, because if he was going to have to handle tools he wasn't going to get far. So he was fiddling with the tire and the tools in the trunk and all, and cursing and getting mad, and Rosalind floated out of the car in her cream-colored suit and said, "Go sit down, honey." The fact was, she was from Appleton, Wisconsin. It wasn't like he didn't think she could change a tire. But the tools kind of jumped into her hands, the tire kind of jumped onto the axle. Could he have seen that on film? Al didn't know. Maybe she was just handy. But she changed that tire in about ten minutes, never got a dot on her suit or her shoes, wiped off her hands on a Kleenex, and off they went. When the lights were out and family wasn't home it was the exact opposite of the sense that tire had given him, of everything being safe and basically okay, in spite of his mistakes and tantrums. Someone else bought the filly, and Al sat quietly.

ONE SECTION OVER and a few seats back, Farley watched the filly leave the sales pavilion and turned to looked at that blond head again, as well as the grizzled, balding head beside it. They were a strange pair, the cool, ageless blonde and the fidgety attention-seeker. Somebody's owners, but with the self-confidence or the knowledge to come to the sale by themselves. Farley sighed. If he had had that heart attack he thought he was having today, someone, or, better still, a whole line of people, would be telling him what to do next. Having not had that heart attack, he still had to figure it out himself.

BEHIND HIM, but with his eye right on him most of the time, sat Buddy Crawford. His owners had bought everything he had advised them to buy, and every time Farley Jones nodded, shook his head, or even twitched, Buddy doubted himself. His reaction was to buy even more. Right next to him sat Andrea Melanie, her hands twitching. She said, "Oh, Buddy, listen to this. When I went off to college, you know, to Bennington, my mom took me right down to Gump's and she said to the salesladies, 'Bring everything out, all the fives and sixes,' and you know what, we bought everything that looked the least bit decent. That was the most fun I ever had in my whole life next to this."

"Well," said Buddy, truthful as always, "horse racing is for fun. You've got to think of it that way."

"Oh, Buddy," said Andrea Melanie, "I do so admire you. You always call a spade a spade. No wonder everyone says you're a saint."

Wouldn't it be nice, thought Buddy, to be sitting there so quiet and self-possessed, like Farley Jones? When he went back to southern California and to wishing he were dead, that would be the reason.

WHEN THE HANDLER led the filly out of the pavilion, he looked up into the late dusk under the giant trees. A fragrant breeze billowed gently around horses and humans, fragmenting words, whinnies, and smells, dispersing human intentions with the rattle and brush of leaves and branches. Here, then, was the heaven of Saratoga—all budgets and business plans, all ambitions and self-serving dreams broken up and cooled under the ancient trees by the yet more ancient wind, "I want" turning to "Ah, feel that!," "I've got to have" turning to "What an evening!," discontent with the past, fear of the future turning into a long, satisfied sigh already a hundred years old, but still fresh, still an astonishing surprise.

38 / A DUD

TWO WEEKS after the sale, Al found himself going back up to Saratoga alone to watch this dud that they had named Limitless, for some reason, make his third start. Al didn't have a lot of interest in the horses anymore—they hadn't bought a thing at the sale—but he didn't have anything better to do, so he was walking past Grand Central and it was kind of fun getting off the train and taking a cab to the grandstand entrance and not having the valet parking. Saratoga did always make you feel good in some way.

Laurita wasn't scheduled to run, as far as Al knew, but, then, he had not been in close contact with Dick Winterson for ten days, since he had discovered that Rosalind had had a thing with him. The extent of the thing he hadn't gotten into. Love, sex, one night, one week, when it began, when it ended, what it meant to them, whatever. There were things that happened around you that you were wise to know one thing about but not everything about, which is what he had tried to tell some of the Republican congressmen he knew about this Clinton thing. What he had said to D'Amato himself when he last saw him was: If people like me lose interest in the guy's dick before you do, then you're the one who looks like a schmuck, not him. And then he put his hand on Al's shoulder and he looked him in the eye, and he said, "Al, I am losing interest in the guy's dick. I just am. Take that as a sign and pay attention," and Al had said he would, but there was no sign of it. Still, the whole Clinton thing made you feel slightly different about anything you yourself might have done over the years, and even about anything your wife might have done with your horse-trainer, and why him, he'd like to know. It kind of took you out of that

I'm-gonna-kill-her frame of mind and put you into a these-things-happen-all-the-time frame of mind (which was more or less your own frame of mind when you were doing over the years what you had done over the years).

So he picked up his program and his *Form* and saw that the horse was in the third race, a maiden special weight, eighteen thousand dollars, all of which Dick had told his secretary the day before but he had forgotten, not having planned to come up here. And Dick wasn't expecting him, either. And Dick maybe did not know that he, Al, knew about the thing he had had with Rosalind. There was a little thrill in that, wasn't there?

The horse's form was bad. In his first race, in a field of eight, he had run seventh by fourteen lengths. The line on him was "Showed no commitment." In his second race, in a field of nine, he had run seventh again. The line was "Went wide on turn." But all you had to do was look at his fractions and see that he had never gotten into either race. Dick hadn't figured the horse out yet. That was clear from the *Form*. Suppose he talked to Dick about the horse. But between them, the horse, the trainer, the wife, and he himself, the owner, had gotten into one of those swampy interpersonal areas that Al especially didn't like, where no one knew what to do, everyone was sorry, and no one was saying much. And what they were saying was all a cover-up. In his former life as a two-fisted drinker, Al would have produced some of what his sponsor called "bottle wisdom"—"Shit or get off the pot," "What the fuck is going on here?," maybe "Who the hell do you think you're dealing with?" Now he was required to be more patient, and, to be perfectly frank, there was a lot about patience that felt just like not caring much at all. But that was a state you could take a little rest in, not a state you could live in. It was too boring, and, most of the time, he hated being bored most of all.

He saw that the horse had drawn the number-four spot, the race was five furlongs, and the handicapper said of him, "No breeding, no form, no chance. Two good works do not make a racehorse." Usually when the handicappers got dismissive of his horses like that, Al had a little reflex of defensiveness, especially with a homebred, but sometimes when some guy got down on you, you had to just say, Yeah, you're right, and leave it at that.

So he went up to his box. The horses hadn't come out for the first race—he was way early. No one he knew, none of the other owners, seemed to be around, either, so he just sat down and stretched out his legs. The shade was cool, so he closed his eyes and tried to enjoy it. Actually, riding the train had put him in kind of a funny mood. It was nice that no one on the train knew who he was, or cared. It was nice to buy your ticket and say thank you and not have the ticket agent treat you like anything special. It was nice to go up to the counter at the station and wait in line for a bagel and have the guy say, "What about you, buddy? You want something, or are you just taking up space?" It was nice to have the conductor take your ticket without looking into your face, and stick the stub in the back of your seat. It was even nice to sit right up next to your seatmate, a black guy carrying a cake on his lap, and wonder where the guy was going. It was nice not to have to be Alexander P. Maybrick all the time, or Al M., or even just "honey." It was nice to be unnamed.

Sometimes these days, Al woke up in a panic. That was maybe the only result of his knowledge that Rosalind had had a thing with the horse-trainer. All he knew about the thing was that there had been a thing and now there wasn't a thing any longer, because the way he knew about the thing was that he was rummaging under the bed for his watch a couple of nights after they got back from the sale, and he had come upon a note from the horse-trainer dated only a couple of months ago saying, "I don't know what I am doing now and I didn't know what I was doing then, but I did love you and probably still do. I'm sorry." It was not actually addressed to Rosalind, but it certainly wasn't addressed to Al, so, if you had four and took away two, you had to get two. All he had thought at the time, oddly enough, was, So that's her problem. Two days later, though, he had awakened in a panic. He had been snuggled up to Rosalind, with the damned dog's hairy body between them, and he had lain there, just putting his arm around her a little more tightly. The thing was, when he had his eyes closed, it seemed like she was all the way across the room, even though when he opened his eyes he saw that she was an inch in front of his nose. Then he realized that it didn't matter where she was. He had always relied upon her to keep him safe, but now he saw who she was, a territory unexplored and unknown. She could not keep him safe. It wasn't a matter of willingness. Shoulda, coulda, woulda, they were all the same. That was why he didn't care much about the thing with the horse-trainer. The mistake had been his own, in more ways than one. If there was no safety in Rosalind, there was even less safety in his money and investments and assets and sponsor and colleagues—of course he ran down the whole list, that only took a second. He had felt his panic intensify. And then he had gotten up and gone to work and his meeting and tried not to think about the thing she'd had with the horse-trainer. But the panic had happened since, twice.

How did you balance these two experiences? On the one hand, surrounded by your stuff and your name, snuggled up against your wife, who had chosen not to leave you, and you felt a panic; on the other hand, alone on the train, alone in the stands at Saratoga, and okay, really, just a guy. If the other owners weren't around, you didn't even have to be an owner and all that implied, you could be just a guy.

The horses for the first race came out and Al hadn't even placed a bet. But he was glad to see them. This what they called introspection was taxing. At his AA meeting, there were women, and even guys, who engaged in this sort of thing all the time. Normally, Al felt a good deal of contempt for them, but now he saw that they maybe deserved a little more respect.

EVEN THOUGH Al had all these plans about going out to the saddling paddock and all that normal stuff, when the second race came around, he just kept sitting there, as if the horse in the race belonged to someone else. He didn't even get up to place a bet. Some other owners came in that he slightly knew, and all he did was wave to them. Woulda coulda shoulda, none of it mattered. He just sat there. The horses came out, jogged and cantered around to the gate, wherever it was placed, the bell clanged, the gate opened, the horses ran around the track, the track cleared, and then it happened again. How strange, Al thought.

Now the horses came out for the third race. His horse, bay and otherwise not distinctively marked, paraded to the post with only a number to identify him. Al's silks looked good on the jockey, but so did everyone's. When you looked at it objectively, it was all the silks together that made the picture, the bright kaleidoscope that the horses made of the jockeys as they wove themselves a race. It wasn't much of a race, just five-eighths of a mile. Al sat forward and looked around, as much to shift his position as anything else, and then he saw that guy, Luciano, the horse masseur, coming toward him. That was a strange thing he had done, go out to dinner with the guy at some inexpensive Italian place in the City. Of course, now that he thought of it, Luciano would have known about the affair. No doubt, that was why he had taken him out to dinner. The very moment he was remembering this, Al saw that Luciano was looking at him and waving. And then here he came. Al turned his head away, hoping that the guy would pass on by, but he stopped and said, "Hey! Mr. Maybrick! You know, Dick doesn't even know you're here."

"I'm not."

"Yeah, I won't tell him. Well—"

Al relented. "Well, so sit down."

"Yeah?"

"Yeah. Sit down. But don't talk to me about the horse."

"Okay."

The horse and his gray pony went around to the starting gate.

Luciano stretched out his long legs and put them up on the seat next to him. "So," he said, "how about this Clinton thing? Talk about a scandal! I watch it every day. My feeling is, what's Hillary got to say about it? No one dares to ask her."

"Maybe she doesn't know what to say."

"Oh, she knows what to say."

"What?" Al looked at Luciano, genuinely curious.

"Ay yay yay, what the fuck are you doing?"

And then they put their heads back and laughed big laughs. The horses were almost to the starting gate. Al had lost track of which one Limitless was.

Luciano went on. "Did you see that movie they had, about John Travolta as him?"

"No. I don't go to the movies much."

"Why not? I think the movies are great. Some weeks I go to a movie every night."

"Are there that many good movies?"

"Nah, but I don't care about good. Good is for risotto, great is for gnocchi, you know? Something that takes real genius. Movies just come and go, like everything else. I laughed all through that movie. If Hillary were really Emma Thompson, then we would all be better off; you know, she had the same problem."

"Who?"

"Emma Thompson. With that guy."

"What guy?"

"Kenneth Branagh. He was running around on her. Now he's playing Woody Allen, I hear, in a Woody Allen movie about a guy who's always running around on his girlfriends. I heard that from one of Dick's owners, who has a production company in the city. Movie people love the racetrack, you know."

"I heard that. Say, do you think that adultery is universal?"

Luciano looked at him, which confirmed for Al that he'd known all along about the thing Rosalind had had with the horse-trainer. But somehow it wasn't mortifying, the way you'd think it would be. There was something comforting in it. Luciano sucked his teeth meditatively, then said, "It's one or the other. You know, in Italy it's universal. But over here? Well, if you do it, it's universal, and if you don't, it doesn't exist. I've got this girlfriend."

"What does she do?"

"She rides for another trainer. We came up from Florida together. I'll tell you what happened with her, want to hear?"

"Sure."

"Well, myself, I always ran around on my other girlfriends. I thought that, as an Italian, that was the least I could do, you know. I mean, I didn't *think* that, but I really did, the way, if you're a man, you tend to think with your dick and your past and who your father was, rather than with your brain. Anyway, when the two of us got together, the sex was really good some of the time, and not so good some of the time, so I was thinking about finding myself another girlfriend, because, you know, I've decided I'll never get married. But then, one night, we were out at the movies. We weren't living together at the time, so I had to get home so I could get up and come out to the track—her, too. Anyway, we were talking about this and that, about the movie and about each other and about our relationship, which I'm telling you is something I hate to talk about in the normal course of events, but, anyway, we were at her house, and I was about to leave, and I went to kiss her good night there in the kitchen, with all the window shades up and everything, and the first kiss, she just turned to jelly and I got hard as a rock, and big, too, like my dick was climbing to my navel, if you'll pardon my saying so, but it's part of the story. Anyway, we kissed for a few minutes, but I had to get home, so we didn't go into the bedroom or anything, and after that, I thought, What a lost opportunity for a great fuck, you know?"

"Yeah," said Al. The horses were approaching the starting gate, and Al saw on the TV with which the management had kindly supplied his box that the first of them went in.

"But I'm really glad we didn't fuck that night, because I learned something that I've never forgotten. We got ready for each other like that, by talking and being together, not by doing anything. You always think, Well, I've got to work this gal up to something, by touching her in this spot or that spot or kissing her for so long, or like this, or something, and sometimes, you think, I've got to work myself up to that somehow, too, and if she doesn't touch me here or rub me there, we aren't going to make it. But that night, we already were right together. And since then, I've noticed that every time—when we're there mentally, we're there physically. If we aren't there mentally, we aren't going to get ourselves there physically, no matter what we do. Better just go out for some tortellini or a movie. So now we learned that, and I don't run around anymore. That's what happened to me. Best fuck I ever didn't have."

The gate opened and the horses broke. The race lasted about a minute. When the horses crossed the finish line, Limitless was fifth, having beaten four horses, about six lengths behind the winner.

Al said, "Go on."

Luciano said, "You want to know what I think? Here's what I think. You grow up running away from the girls you know, trying to find some girl that you don't know enough to make her into whatever you want, but you keep getting to know her, because that's what girls want. You're making it all the time, and every time you make it, it feels like less and less. Then, if you're lucky, you make it with someone you want to get to know, and then you never want to make it with someone you don't really know again."

"What do you know about her?"

"I don't know. I can't say. Everything I know about her is what I know about her." Al looked at him. Luciano was smiling happily at all the things he knew about this girl, whoever she was. Al said, "That's what they want, women. They want to talk all the time before having sex."

"Oh, yeah. I don't mean that kind of talk, you know, so-and-so hurt my feelings and I've had such a bad day and, honey, what's wrong with me. That's not the kind of talk that gets you there. She knows that. It's more like: Here is what I saw, here is what I felt, here is what I did, isn't that interesting, how about you, honey? That kind of talk."

Al could recognize the difference. He said, "My wife hardly talks at all."

"Well," said Luciano. "Ask her what she saw today, what she felt today, and what she did today. Maybe she'll tell you."

The horses had disappeared and the track was empty. Luciano leaned forward as if he were about to get up and go. Al felt a pang. He said, "So now talk about the horse."

"Oh, the horse! My God!"

"What do you mean?"

"Dick doesn't know what the fuck to do with that horse. The horse doesn't know what the fuck to do with himself. He weaves, he paws, he presses against his stall guard with his chest, he grabs your clothes when you walk by. My advice is, send him back to the training farm. He's not ready for track life."

"Have you said that to Dick?"

"Yeah, but I'm not the owner. You say it to Dick. You're the owner."

"I am the owner, that's right."

Luciano stood up. "Well, nice to talk to you, Mr. Maybrick."

Al left with everyone else after the race. He hadn't placed a bet and he hadn't talked to anyone other than Luciano, and he was ready to go back to the City. That's what he was thinking about, but when he put his foot down on the escalator that took you under the red-and-white awning and down into the courtyard, he knew he was going to see Dick Winterson, and sure enough, a minute or two later, out by the walking ring, he did see him, and the horse-trainer saw Al, too. And because he had come out and watched the race and hadn't said anything to his trainer, the trainer now knew that he, Al, knew that the trainer had had an affair with his wife. And that they had a dud of a horse between them, too.

Nevertheless, Al went up to the guy, and that was an education, too, because once you knew a guy had slept with your wife, one time or many times, who knew, who wanted to know, then you looked at him differently from before. You saw that he was a nice-looking guy, of a certain type. Younger than you by twenty years, maybe, his hair still dark and thick on his head, his belly still contained, his shoulders still where shoulders ought to be. You saw that the guy wasn't young, of course, but there was a subtle shift that he hadn't made. His body was still his friend, rather than some big dog farting and shitting and pissing all over the house, barking, whining, gobbling his food, yanking at the leash, itching, aching, all of it. He was kind of pretty, too, not like any movie star, but pretty for a regular man. You could see how there was a contrast between the two of you. Al had never been pretty. He hadn't even been cute as a baby. The best thing anyone had ever said about his looks was "dynamic."

So Al went up to him and they shook hands, and the guy said, "I missed you before the race. I didn't know you were coming up, Al."

"I wasn't going to, but I got the notion. The horse is a dud. Not like that Laurita filly."

"She's a good filly. She's a little tired, is all. That happens in August."

"As long as it doesn't happen in November." He almost said "Breeders' Cup," but he didn't have the heart. It could be that the two of them had talked about him, that he had seemed like a fool to them about this Breeders' Cup thing, for example.

"You know, Al, I don't think the horse is a dud. I just think I haven't found the key to him yet. He's got energy to burn, but he doesn't know how to direct it."

Here was where the guy was daring him to find another trainer, Al thought. He said, "Keep talking."

"Well, he's very sensitive. Now, most horses who are very sensitive get mad or get scared when you cross a certain line with them. This guy doesn't get mad; he doesn't have an angry bone in his body. And he doesn't get scared, either. He gets perplexed. I would almost rather he got mad, you know, because you can direct that. But it's like I've got to figure out a way to make things clear to him. He's a little immature."

"Send him back to the training farm. They liked him, as I remember."

"They did like him. But I'd like to solve this riddle myself."

"What's the point of that?" Well, yes, he said that a little aggressively.

The guy gave him a glance and said, "Well—"

Then the old Al interrupted him. He said, "If you don't know what to do in your gut, then you can't figure it out."

"Yes, but—"

"Now, listen. I've got all these businesses, right?"

"Well, of course—"

"I'll tell you when I buy them. I buy them when the guys who are running them start trying lots of new things all at once. When they do that, that means they're forgetting how to make things work. The business hasn't fallen apart, and the guys are pretty excited about all the new things they're trying, because they don't know that trying lots of new things is the first desperate step."

"I'm not trying new things—"

Al lowered his voice and softened it, too. He said, "Dick, you're a good trainer, and I don't want to move the horse to another trainer. If you like him, I'll believe that he's got some talent—"

"I think he's the sort of horse who can get a distance—"

"Fine. Let's say he doesn't like two-year-old racing and needs to wait it out at the training farm."

"Al—"

"Dick." You could see it in his face, the struggle. Instead of saying anything, Al just stood there and watched it. Clear as day, the guy's face said, "Don't I get to have this one little thing? Not even this? This unimportant attempt?" Then the guy sighed and shook his head. The answer was no. He said, "Okay, Al. You're the boss. I'll send him back to the farm and tell them to turn him out for a few months."

"Tell them to let the horse do whatever he wants."

"Yeah."

"No, I mean that. Tell them to figure out what the horse wants to do, and let him do it. They charge as much as a boarding school in Switzerland, so they can treat the horse the same way those boarding schools treat the kids."

Dick smiled. He had a pretty smile, too. Rosalind would like that. She was drawn to pretty things.

"I hear you, Al." They shook hands again. Then Dick said, "Thanks for coming up." And damn if he didn't look like he meant it, so Al said, "Yeah. I'm glad I did." And that was that. Everybody knew all the same stuff now, Al was sure of it. When all was said and done, there was something to be said for that.

39 / NO HORSES, FOR ONCE

MARY LYNN AND SKIPPY lived in an architectural statement in Potomac, not, actually, very far in terms of distance from Deirdre and George's venue, but too far to travel, Deirdre thought, without holding the invitation to the birthday party in your hand like a visa, ready for presentation at every checkpoint. George didn't feel this, and he laughed when she used that word, "checkpoint," as in "Do ya think this stoplight is the checkpoint, then?"

On the way over in the car, George kept going on about the possibility of making contact with real or potential owners of racehorses who were looking for a way to redistribute some income. "They're Democrats," said Deirdre.

"A difficulty, but not a fatal one. Democrats own racehorses."

"Cheap ones. They feel too guilty to spend several hundred thousand dollars on a horse."

"Not Skippy. I'm telling you, Cousin. They're into animal welfare. You can work that around—"

"You are going on and on about this, George. You know my views."

George's chiseled lips went together in a line, denoting a rare state for him, actual vexation. Deirdre was momentarily intimidated, and looked out the window. He said, "I feel I am going to have to take you in hand, Cousin."

"Try it," said Deirdre.

"You are hiding your light under a bushel. There are horses you could do something with that could, pardon me for mentioning it, earn us a living. Earning a living by giving a poor beast a job is not a sin. Now, you see, this time last year you had a barn full of happy workers, but you weren't satisfied with that, and although I have vowed never to delve into our common past in an effort to discover why you would find self-destruction appealing, darlin', I am mighty tempted. The word 'perversity' comes into my mind."

There was the wreck, of course. Deirdre knew that this was in both their minds, but since they no longer drew the same conclusions from it, it had become an unmentionable. It was like they had come to an intersection together and then disagreed about which road to take. They had taken her road, but as they got farther down it, the discord got more serious. This was much like marriage, and one of the reasons she had avoided that condition. Also like marriage was that she knew what it would cost if she barked back, so, rather than turning toward him, she looked straight ahead and said, "Thank you for expressing your views," and thirty seconds later he drove the car between the gateposts of Skippy and Mary Lynn's architectural statement. Once inside, they sprang apart and headed for opposite ends of the house, which made Deirdre feel lonely as well as enraged.

The architectural statement had several graduated degrees of inside and outside, with large plants and randomly set single walls confusing the issue. It wasn't until she was a hundred feet away from the refreshment table that she was truly in the open, and not far beyond that, the landscape, or the garden-scape, began to contract again as it met what looked like the boundaries of the property. Elegant, indeed, and Deirdre had no objection to it per se, above and beyond her bottom-line objection to life in general. Och, she was a bitter woman, George was always telling her, and the marvelous mare and the won-drous filly that had been got from the marvelous mare this year were no longer enough to lighten her existence. The mare's last foal, also a filly, had been sold at Saratoga this year for two hundred thousand dollars as a yearling, which was a good omen for next year. The sales were where conventional horsemen's wis-dom (it's never too soon to sell a horse, for he could commit suicide the next day) and capitalism (the workers cannot afford to buy what they produce) intersected. Mere money, and a considerable amount of it, could very well flow into her account a year from now. But the wondrous filly would be trained by someone else, someone in southern California. "Cousin, you cannot be pleased," George had said, and of course he was right.

She drifted into a copse of trees, went around a hedge, and was just about to admire some fruit trees espaliered against one of those random walls when she saw that she had found her hostess, but that the hostess was in the arms of someone not Skippy, someone not even of Skippy's ethnic and racial classifica-tion. Mary Lynn did not see her, since her eyes had rolled well back in her head and she was pressed very tightly against her partner. Deirdre turned on her heel and fled.

It was only when she had several of the random walls between herself and the kissing pair that she felt safe, but within moments, of course, Skippy, heretofore invisible, turned up right at her elbow. He said, "You're here! I saw George. I was looking for you. Did you have trouble finding the place? It's al-most finished. It's going to be in *Architectural Digest*. You have to meet the ar-chitect. Are we running anything in the next two weeks? I have to go to Seattle for business all the time. Have you ever thought of shipping a horse or two out there? I have this big case out there this coming year. We could—"

"Hello, Skippy."

"Have you seen the—"

What she was doing was herding him gently back toward the house. She didn't think she was doing this for his sake. Possibly she was doing it for Mary Lynn's sake, so that the woman could pass all the way through whatever ecstasy she was engaged in and into a more satisfied and contented frame of mind. Or, perhaps, she was doing it for herself, avoiding the occasion of discomfort. They arrived at the table. Skippy had been burbling for a number of minutes at this point, though Deirdre had lost track of his train of thought, and even of his subject matter. When he paused for her to reply, she said, "Have you had any of the refreshments, then?"

"Not yet, I—"

"Well, come on. It's a fine feast. I had to drag myself away from it." And so she led him around the big table, filling a plate for him. And also keeping her eye out to the west, for a glimpse of Mary Lynn, though, the way the architect had set this place up, it looked like you had good cover everywhere. You could basically get from any spot on the property to any spot in the house without drawing fire.

She was not alone with Skippy for more than half a minute before the opinion-makers had surrounded them.

"He's been doing this for years. I told Stephanopoulos—"

"Stephanopoulos? *I* told Carville. I told him more than once. He never did listen to Stephanopoulos."

"He never did listen to Carville. *I* said to Jordan, time after time—"

"Jordan! Come on! The only one he ever listened to was Web—"

"Not for a moment, Jake. Not for a moment. He had a way of seeming to listen—I always thought he seemed to listen to me. I can't tell you the number of times I had him in a corner in the Oval Office—"

"How could you have him in a corner in the Oval Office—"

"I used to want to shake him—"

Skippy perked right up. Deirdre patted him on the shoulder and eased herself out of the group, not forgetting one more smoked-salmon mousse on endive leaf with baby shrimp perched on the curlicue.

As she passed into the living room, which was decorated in cheerful blue-and-white chinoiserie with ornate yellow satin accents, she stopped to admire George in her anger. George did not look at her. He was standing in a group of his own, mostly women. She could hear laughter chiming over him, a waterfall of delight.

She turned to look at the stack of presents. It was depressingly large. Deirdre felt sure that Mary Lynn would not welcome so many new items into her already (a glance around) well-packed domicile. But, then, Deirdre took a dim view of gifts, as a rule. She sighed and turned away, only to find herself standing face to face with himself, the man Mary Lynn had been kissing in the garden. He was a good-looking black man in a lovely gray suit and very fashionable glasses, small and oval. He smiled at her, though it did not seem with recognition. She smiled back, noticing her own sudden amazement that Mary Lynn, a woman who would have in Ireland been called plain as a bun, had been kissing such a man. She said, "Looking at the pile of gifts, then?"

"Always a marvel."

"How so?"

"Well, think of it this way. This is one woman. She already owns, maybe, ten thousand objects, depending upon how you categorize them. Here are another hundred, hundred and fifty, and most of them have more than one part. And Daniel, he has more objects than she does, so in this house alone there are twenty to thirty thousand objects. Now, there are two hundred and fifty million people in this country. Let's say that each one has only three thousand objects, on average. Still, that's houseroom for seven hundred fifty billion objects. That's seven hundred fifty billion things that were made and distributed and sold."

"Makes you never want to shop again."

"I already never want to shop again. How about you?"

"I shop only for horses, and then only so I may thank the Lord when I haven't bought any."

"What kind of horses?"

"Racehorses."

"You must be—"

"I'm their trainer."

"You should meet—"

And then she came through the door into the room, and put her arm through the man's arm. He said, "This is just the very one I was mentioning. But I'm sorry, I didn't catch your name?"

The most beautiful woman she had ever seen smiled at her and Deirdre said, "It's Deirdre. Deirdre Donohue." Then she held out her hand, almost graciously, and said, "You have horses? Are you a friend of Mary Lynn's?"

"No. I just came along with Norman. I kind of date his brother. Norman's with Microsoft. Skippy and Norman are working on that case together. I'm Tiffany Morse."

To cover her rapidly evaporating savoir faire, Deirdre said to Norman, "So which present is yours?"

Norman pointed out an elaborately wrapped cubical box.

"What's in it?"

"Software." He grinned mischievously, and Deirdre found herself saying, "So how is it that you were kissing the birthday girl in the garden a bit ago?"

"Oh, Norman," said Tiffany, wearily.

But Norman didn't miss a beat. His smile didn't dim or harden, but grew truly, Deirdre thought, happy. "Ah, well," he said. "I do believe that Mary Lynn is my girl."

"Oh, Norman," said Tiffany again. And she shook her head. Then she turned to Deirdre and said, "Every single person at this party is talking about Clinton." Then Tiffany put her hand on Deirdre's elbow in a very natural manner, and turned her away from the presents. She said, "Let's go outside and talk horses." Deirdre glanced at Norman. Tiffany said, "We don't need Norman. All he wants to talk about is Mary Lynn. I came along just to have a look at her, really. Good-bye, Norman. Go eat something so I can gossip about you."

Norman dutifully turned around and went out into the dining room.

"He had her eyes rolling back in her head. I do believe they were breathing quite heavily."

Tiffany glanced at the ceiling, then said, "Myself, I don't understand Norman and Ho Ho at all. Or, actually, anyone in their family. They are not like anyone I ever grew up with."

"Ho Ho?"

"Norman's brother. He's a rap singer, and sort of like my boyfriend, except he has this CD that's bombing, and so he's going to quit the music business and go to cooking school. His hobby is making sausages now."

"He's going from rap singing to making sausages?"

"And he gave me the horses the other day. His accountant told him he probably won't need the tax write-off any longer if he goes into the restaurant business. Probably not the entourage, either, so they're all looking for something else to do."

"Is Norman serious about Mary Lynn?"

"He loves her commanding manner. What is she, forty-five? He's only thirty-two."

"She does have a commanding manner indeed."

"He had this girlfriend in Seattle who was an officer on an aircraft carrier. She was just the same way, his stepmother told me. I never knew her. I've just known Ho Ho for about eight months."

By now they were sitting on a sofa. Deirdre could think of nothing to say, so it was easy to ask the one question she had perhaps asked more than any other over the years. "How many horses do you have?" Tiffany's presence more or less put her right out of her fucking mind.

"Two running. I just got a yearling at Saratoga. Red Ransom."

Deirdre sighed.

"I wish I were a trainer," said Tiffany. "I go out to the track every day."

"Och, that's not a promising wish, darlin'."

Tiffany said, "I know what you're going to say. My trainer says it all the time. Do I know how long it took him to get where he is, into the middle class? Do I know how many times there wasn't enough money in his business account to pay for hay, or to make his mortgage payment, or to pay his kids' school fees? Do I know how many owners stiffed him over the years, how many horses popped a splint before a big race or threw a shoe during the race or bumped the jockey over the rail coming out of the gate? Some just die— pulmonary embolism or something more mysterious. Now they're running, now they're dead. Do I know how hard it is to find grooms who can groom, exercise guys who can ride, owners who can shut up and listen, horses who can relax? When I used to tell him all about it, he would yell at me in English. Now he yells at me in Spanish. He thinks I should stick with Norman's family. They love me. But I don't want to go to school. All of them go to school like it's heaven. You know, when Ho Ho decided to get out of the music business, he still had enough money, even after the horses and the entourage, to just open a restaurant, and a good one, and to hire a great chef, and everything. But in his family, the thing is, you never *buy* it. You *learn* it. There isn't even any discussion about it. When you can't think what to do next, you *enroll*." She sighed.

"You didn't like school, then. Me neither. Those nuns had me in such a box. The baby Jesus on one side, the Virgin Mary on the other, maths goadin' me from behind and Shakespeare screamin' at me from the front."

"I love the way you talk."

"Do ya now. Well, in America, you can say anything you please in an Irish accent, and they love it. My cousin George can babble one inanity after another, and they cluster about him, nodding like peonies."

"You want to hear how I talk?"

"I do."

"Girl! What you know about this party—" and then there was something eloquent and completely incomprehensible to Deirdre. Tiffany went on, "Ho Ho loves me to talk like that, or he did. He would write it all down. I never saw a horse before I was with Ho Ho. But now that's all I think about." Deirdre felt herself smiling and smiling, but she covered up in the habitual way, saying, "What class are they running?"

"Well, I told Dagoberto that, even though Ho Ho was taking care of things and at that point those kinds of expenses were nothing to him, the horse had to support itself, so he got me some good claimers, and we do that, trading around and mostly trading up. But, you know, two horses aren't enough for me to think about. I want to think about twenty horses or thirty horses. I don't want to go out there and just watch my horses work. Now I go out there every day, and Dagoberto has other owners to see and other things he has to do, and he thinks I know enough already. Dagoberto has kept my stable in the black since day one, but I'm bored with that now."

"Well, training isn't boring. But horses are tragic beasts, especially good horses, especially good Thoroughbreds. I used to ride jumpers, ya know. You can have a good jumper of any breed or no breed. Lots of warmbloods are good jumpers. Jumping isn't all that hard on them, contrary to appearances. They can get around the jumps before they know they're working, if they're not afraid. But racing, now, there's always a moment in a race when a horse has to decide to press on. A Thoroughbred is likelier than not to press on. That's what we ask of them. But, I ask myself, at what cost? We rely on them not to consider the cost, but to press on anyway. That's heart, you know. They have great hearts. But it's their downfall, that they don't feel the cost until they've paid it. Every day, especially when I have a horse running, I wake up and I say to myself, Can I ask this horse, this day, to pay that cost if he has to? I don't know what I would do for a living if I didn't do this thing, but—" She sensed someone behind her and turned around. Tiffany turned around, too. It was George. He smiled at Tiffany but not at her. She said, "Och. I thought you were occupied, Cousin."

Tiffany regarded him, and Deirdre took the opportunity to regard her. Talk about beauty. Nor was it merely how she was shaped, or her pretty mannerisms or her delicious style (she had on an amethyst linen sundress and a necklace of gold suns with jolly faces etched into them; perfect cornrows sculpted the shape of her head, then fell to her shoulders with a tinkle of gold glass beads). It was that beauty was a continuous flow within the boundaries so delicately defined by her skin. You could almost follow it with your eyes, eddying here, surging there, as she said to George, "Do you train horses, too?"

"With Deirdre. Have you some horses, then?"

"I have two. Three, with the yearling."

George caught Deirdre's eye, then said, "And a Democrat, then?"

"Not exactly. I've never voted."

George came over and sat down. "No doubt she's been going on about the horror of it all."

"I want to do it," said Deirdre. "My horses have won ninety-four thousand dollars since April."

"Where are they?" said George.

"They're stabled at Belmont. They run there and at Aqueduct and Saratoga."

"If you brought them to Maryland, you could step them up in class—" suggested George.

Deirdre put her heel on George's toes and ground it in hard, until in spite of himself he yelped, then she said, "If your horses are making money on that circuit, you don't want to be moving them to Maryland, believe me."

George made a noise in his throat, very Irish, a combination of disgust and resignation. Deirdre tossed her head and continued to Tiffany, "Keep your horses in New York, dear. That's where the money is, and the good footing, too." There, she had done it again, sent away the very thing that she most wanted for herself. She glanced at George, who was looking annoyed again. "But if *you* come to me, I'll teach you some things. We'll see how far we get." Then she turned to George. "You go away, George, you can take me to task later." He heaved himself out of the depth of the sofa and went off, but not without cuffing her on the head. She knew that cuff. It was more affectionate than angry by now. She smiled to herself. It was not at all pleasant to be on the outs with George. Meanwhile, here was Tiffany. She said, "Now. You tell me whether your friend Norman is going to break up this fine establishment, because the best part of my livelihood depends upon Mary Lynn and Skippy, and I can't do without either one of them, and if she moves to Seattle, well, they call it racing out there, but—"

"She's already told him no."

"But her eyes were rolling back in her head."

"That's why she told him no."

"Marriage kills passion?"

"Lots of people think so."

"They do, don't they?"

"It's almost a rule."

Deirdre nodded, having never been married, and having never, she supposed, felt passion. Tiffany turned her head away, and looked across the room, so that Deirdre could see her profile. What she saw was that moment you saw rarely enough in a child, not often in an adult, the inner warmth of true happiness infusing the features quietly, one by one. Then Tiffany turned to her—the girl couldn't have been more than twenty or so, half Deirdre's age—and said,

"Thank you, Deirdre, I'll be there in a week," and kissed her on the cheek. Later, when she was driving home with George, she said about meeting Tiffany, "That was fucking well almost worth venturing into Washington society and having to listen to them talk about Clinton all afternoon," but she actually didn't feel nearly so ironic about it as that. What she felt was simple, and certainly ephemeral, certainly fleeting, certainly momentary, and certainly fickle joy, groundless and feeble-minded and gormless. All George said was, "Ah, Cousin, you take everything to heart." She saw that he was no longer angry at all, but resigned. That was perhaps not the best of omens, but it was all the more convenient for pursuing her contrary way.

40 / EASTWARD HO

JUSTA BOB LEFT Golden Gate Fields in a shipment of horses headed for Arapaho Park, in Colorado. He was claimed away from the Pisser by Lily Dodd (aged twenty-three), whose father and grandfather were trainers before her; she had a second and a third with him out of three starts. He was then claimed away from Lily by Hakon Borgulfsson, an Icelander, the only trainer in America of Icelandic parentage, who had a six-horse trailer and liked to combine racing claimers with supporting his daughter Thora's career singing opera. She was rehearsing *Judith and Holofernes* in Denver, which Hakon considered a difficult and depressing piece of work, but not nearly as bad as *Wozzeck*, which she had been in last year, in male costume, in Houston, while Hakon ran some horses at Sam Houston. He tried to get her out to the track as often as possible just to give her some relief. Justa Bob had several infirmities. He had a tiny chip in his left knee, and both his ankles were beginning to get a touch of arthritis. He had a stress fracture in his pelvis. The dry weather in Colorado could do him a world of good.

Colorado was an education, especially for a Cal-bred, like Justa Bob. You couldn't say, and Justa Bob didn't say, that Hakon wasn't a horseman, but, for all his good intentions, Hakon wasn't a horseman. Hakon was a reader, an esthete, a charitable human being who never failed to give something to a homeless person. Hakon could whip up a nutritious meal in a half-hour over a Coleman stove, something he often had to do when he was trying to save money for books by living at the track, and he always had some to share. Hakon had kept that Dodge truck of his going for fifteen years and three hundred thousand miles, but horses were a divine mystery to him, and no amount of reading, discussing, consulting, observing, and receiving tips from well-meaning friends could shed any light upon that mystery. He gave Justa Bob so much bute over the course of their time together that the horse's stomach was beginning to know it. He fed only a little alfalfa hay, because he couldn't afford anything more, so Justa Bob hadn't had much to do all day. He fed bran mashes that were too hot, water that tasted poor, soy oil rather than corn oil. He wrapped all his own horses, because he couldn't afford a groom, and he wrapped them unevenly, so that too much pressure on one part of the leg alternated with too little on another. He almost never called the vet, because he had his own theories about how horses got better and because he usually didn't quite understand what the vet was telling him. Living with Hakon, for his horses, was an exercise in gratuitous survival, and other horsemen Hakon knew always cited, in his regard, the old racetrack adage "Lucky is better than good." Hakon was lucky. He almost never worked a horse fast enough for its accumulated minor damage to result in a breakdown, but when his horses got claimed and went off to other trainers, who were not so lucky, the more normal sort of work sometimes did break them down. Hakon considered himself a natural-born genius, his very unconventionality a testament to his talents.

After an eventful month, in which Justa Bob loafed around the track during training hours and then loafed to a win and a third in two starts, Hakon Borgulfsson, Justa Bob, and Thora parted company—Hakon back to the Bay Area, driving his empty six-horse trailer, with some money in his pocket to claim a couple more horses, and maybe take them to Arizona for the winter; Thora on a plane to St. Louis, where she was to sing all the parts of all the female leads in a compressed version of the *Ring* cycle; and Justa Bob to Chicago, where his new owner, William Vance, had a stable at Sportsman's Park.

William had twenty-seven horses in training, all of them jointly owned with an assortment of friends and relatives. When Justa Bob arrived at the track on Cicero Avenue in the midst of a heat wave, he had already gotten fairly dehydrated. Nor was William there to greet him, since William's son Alphonse was being honored for work he had done in a state-sponsored summer program at the local high school. When the groom put Justa Bob in his stall, deeply bedded but with an unusual-smelling straw, and well provided with hay but timothy rather than alfalfa, Justa Bob turned away from all of these unfamiliar sensory experiences and manured in his water bucket as a gesture of despair. He was tired from the long van ride. He was thirsty, but now that he had manured in his water bucket, he no longer cared to drink from it. He looked around. Everything was unfamiliar. He closed his eyes.

The groom checked the horses one last time and then decided to leave early. William didn't like for the horses to be left alone, but he was due to arrive himself in less than an hour, so the groom thought it was all right to leave. Justa Bob wasn't the only horse who seemed lethargic. A few were sweating in their stalls, even though they had fans blowing right on them. The groom, unfamiliar with Justa Bob, of course, didn't realize that he was a horse who rarely failed to take an interest in his surroundings.

And then, leaving his son's high school, William Vance's car blew a rod, and was rendered undrivable. William thought everything would be fine, though. He had no one running that afternoon, as if anyone would be running with this heat index; his groom, Homer, was on the job; probably those new horses hadn't arrived yet; and, all in all, he wasn't worried about a thing, and he was very proud of his son, who had a scholarship to Wesleyan University in Middletown, Connecticut, and a nice girlfriend who was going to Connecticut College for Women, and he decided to go home and take a nap and get to the track later in his own girlfriend's car, but she was at work until four. He took the bus to her apartment to wait for her, which was why, when his buddy Romero saw that Justa Bob was groaning and looking at his flanks, indicating colic, he couldn't reach William at home.

And then the power browned out, and Romero got busy with other things.

Inside Justa Bob, his large intestine was beginning to increase the frequency of its peristaltic contractions, which gave him a little pain. He began to pace around his stall, stopping every few minutes to paw through his straw. Sometimes he stretched out his head and neck and opened his mouth. The pain increased. He took a look at his flanks, but there was nothing visible on the outside that gave any evidence of what was going on on the inside. He pawed some more, then lay down. For a while he curled his legs and hooves under him, trying to relax. But he found that he had to look with increasing fixed intensity at the bland expanse of his side. It was such a mystery, this pain. Finally, about an hour and a half into his ordeal, he stretched out on his side, and then rolled over, a time-honored way of expressing and sometimes relieving belly pain—what you did was roll back and forth, back and forth. However, Justa Bob was unfamiliar with the dimensions of his new stall, and after he had rolled over, he discovered that he was cast against the wall and couldn't get back onto his other side. He had been cast before. His natural inclination, which had saved him innumerable times in his life, was to wait. There are horses who wait and there are horses who can't wait. Those who can't wait get into more trouble. Justa Bob was a waiter, but when he rolled over and got cast, something else happened, which was that his large intestine flipped over 180 degrees. A bit of the hay from the van that he was still digesting stopped moving and began to compact. It hurt very much more even than before, but Justa Bob kept trying to wait.

"Almost dead" is a relative judgment. Justa Bob's heart was still fine and his brain was functioning, but purely in terms of time, Justa Bob was much closer to death by five in the afternoon than he had been at noon. At noon he had been in one country, the country of good health, and death had been in another country, and the two countries had shared nothing, but in the course of the afternoon, colic had made a bridge between them. Justa Bob was beginning to go into shock. His eyes were half closed. He was groaning. Once in a while, purely involuntarily, he hit his feet against the concrete blocks of the stall, and scraped his own legs with his own hooves. Horses stalled nearby watched him and whinnied from time to time. They all noticed when William Vance finally showed up about five. William would have noticed their higher level of anxiety—it wasn't all that subtle—but he was still groggy from his nap and lethargic from the ordeal of driving through the streets of Chicago in a car without air conditioning in this heat.

He made his way toward what he thought was still an empty stall in a leisurely manner.

William Vance was a middle-aged black man from central Missouri. His first memory was of a mule his father owned named Hyacinth, and his subsequent memories were all of the saddlebred horses his father trained, or retrained, at his little place near Sedalia. His father had begun as a farrier, then added working with sour or broken-down animals and getting them back into the show ring. William had seen his first Thoroughbred when he was nineteen, when he and some friends of his father's had gone down to Kentucky to a big saddlebred show and sale. One Thoroughbred was enough for William. He'd found a farm to work at as a groom in Kentucky right that day, and stayed behind when his father and the other men had taken their horses home. His father had told him he would never make a living as a black racehorse-trainer, because white men wouldn't bring their horses to him, so he had made a living as a black trainer for black owners. He had an interest in most of the horses he trained, so when they won he made some purse money. He paid his bills, he did not live at the track, his son didn't have to work during high school, except when he didn't get A's on his homework, in which case he had to clean stalls, something he preferred studying to. William's win percentage hovered at around 15 percent. He enjoyed himself.

He neared Justa Bob's stall and heard a groan. The moment he saw that the horse was cast and only semi-conscious was one of the worst moments of his life.

Choosing whether to spend five thousand dollars on colic surgery for a horse was a decision you had to make beforehand. You had to weigh the animal's value, both commercial and sentimental, and the potential effects upon his performance. You had to decide whether the animal was a pet, an agricultural asset, or an athlete. You had to know your regular income and expenditures. You had to understand the worth of your nest egg and know your priorities with regard to drawing upon it. William Vance had duly made a distinction among the horses in his barn, which were worth the surgery and which weren't, but he had no way of deciding into which category to place Justa Bob. He didn't know the horse personally, and had very little idea of how he ran or what his potential was. He had never done more than run his hands down the animal's legs and feel his feet, right after the race in which he claimed him. He didn't even know if he was a good-tempered or bad-tempered animal, though he knew that as a gelding he had no future in the breeding shed. And so, for a short moment that seemed very long, he felt every single impulse as a temptation to sin.

There was the temptation to sin against his bank account, and just call the vet and do what was necessary, even though that very day he had been wondering where the extra money that his son's life in Middletown, Connecticut, would require might come from.

There was the temptation to sin against manhood, just to turn away and pretend this wasn't happening. As he was recognizing this temptation, the power browned out again, which reinforced this impulse; he could go right home and turn on the air conditioning and take off his trousers and—

There was the temptation to sin against compassion, to know what was happening, to recognize it, to be present for it, and to watch it happen. As he was recognizing this temptation, the power went on again.

But, in fact, his body was more decisive than his head. Even as he was considering his options, he was calling out for help. Romero came running down the aisle, and they went into the stall and grabbed the horse's tail and pulled his haunches away from the wall. While Justa Bob was getting himself up after that, William was calling the vet on Romero's cellular, and the vet was only one barn over, and was answering him, and was on his way. And so the decision had been made, because, once a vet and a trainer got together and started relieving pain and distress, it got to be very hard to stop yourself from going on with it, until the animal was standing and the vet bill was more than you could afford.

It was after Justa Bob had gotten to his feet, though unsteadily, that William realized he was going to carry this out to the end, and that the money would come from somewhere. Why this should come as a surprise to him was what should have come as a surprise to him. He always said, "Well, the money will come from somewhere, I guess." He stroked the horse on his sweaty neck and head. The horse's body seemed to creak—that's what the groans sounded like.

And so that was how Justa Bob happened to get on a trailer to make the nightmare trek through the snarled traffic to Naperville. At one time there had been a surgery at the track, but no more. It was Naperville or bust, literally, in terms of Justa Bob's colon. William Vance had the sensation all the way out there that all the cars in Chicago had moved aside to make straight the highway for our Bob. Perhaps that was a sign that the compassionate choice was the right one, but all the time he was driving, William had more misgivings than he could shake a stick at. The surgery was only the beginning. If the horse died, it would be the end, too, but still five thousand dollars, and that might be the better outcome, because the aftercare would cost plenty, and then the horse would be out at the farm, burning hay and oats for three months at least until he could come back to the track and go back into training, as a six-year-old, don't forget, and sometimes they never come back from colic surgery able to perform. But the only times in his life that William had ever hoped for a horse to die were when the horse was so injured that such an outcome was inevitable and better sooner than later. Right here was the difference between Hakon Borgulfsson and William Vance, even though Hakon was educated, benign, and kindly, and William was irascible and sometimes hard to get along with— Hakon thought that horse injuries and death came to you out of nowhere, the workings of blind fate, and William knew that usually death, and often injuries, too, were choices you made for the animal. Death had been a choice he could never make, even as a wish.

At the clinic, the choice was taken from him as soon as the horse came off the trailer into the possession of the vets, the anesthesiologist, and the assistant. "Come on, fella," they said. "Easy, now. Keep walking. Here we go." They took him into the ultrasound room and ultrasounded his belly. William watched this, not knowing what to hope for. The vet knew, however, and there it was, the simple twist in the large intestine, nothing as ugly and life-threatening as it would be in the more delicate small intestine. Then they walked him into the operating room, gave him Rompen and ketamine to collapse him, and eased him down. Then the straps on the rails came over, and they padded and strapped his cannon bones, and the straps tightened as he was winched up and swung over to the table. Then they lowered him onto his back, put rails and cushions around him, and a large tube down his windpipe. William left, and so he didn't see Justa Bob lying there, his open unseeing eyes flicking left and right as he drifted deeper and deeper into unconsciousness, his legs in the air as if he were a dog sleeping on its back, flexed, his long black tail draping softly to the ground.

As William drove home, he apprehended from his short experience of Justa Bob in distress the same thing about the animal that all of his owners had discovered, that he was patient, well disposed, and sensible, that he knew some things and could be taught more, that, though he wasn't pretty or hugely athletic, he was worthy. William sighed the way he always did. The money would come from somewhere, the way it always did. By the time he dropped the horse trailer and the truck at the track, and checked one last time on the other horses in his string, it was nearly eleven o'clock and he was tired. He drove his girlfriend's car to her house, and when he let himself in with the key, he saw that the lights were out and she had gone to bed. He slipped off his shoes and went softly into the bedroom. Her musical voice murmured, half sleepy, "Hi, babe. I missed you. Everything okay?"

So he took off his clothes and slipped in beside her, and she turned and put her arms around him, and he said, "Yeah, things are okay. Weather's a bitch."

"Thanks for coming back. I thought maybe you'd—" and then she was asleep.

At the clinic, saving Justa Bob was fairly routine. They made a six-inch incision through the fascia of the midline. The gas-filled large intestine seemed to bubble out of the incision, and they cut that open. A miasma from the sour, fermenting feed rose around them, not the sweet, healthy smell of manure, but a darker, more threatening odor. Then they cleaned the colon and washed it gently, always touching it as little as possible, knowing that, everywhere they touched it, it could be damaged and later adhere to the walls of the abdominal cavity. When it was clean, they sewed it up and allowed it to fall back into the spacious cavity that it had so recently filled up. Then they stitched the two sides of the abdominal wall firmly together, overlapped them just a bit. If the horse was ever to run again, intestinal-wall fortitude was the key. Then they stapled the shaved skin back together. It was a simple procedure, really, though neither easy nor quick. While they were at it, since the horse was totally relaxed, they cleaned his dangling penis, which Hakon had never bothered to do. Justa Bob was then moved again, swung over to a stall, where he was laid upon his side and where his eyes began to flick back and forth again, showing that he was waking up. As soon as he was mostly awake, the instinct to stand at all costs took over, and up he got, full of painkillers and soon attached by the neck to bags of fluids. His legs were treated and wrapped where he had abraded them. He was petted and made much of.

41 / FAIRY GODGELDING

W HEN HE GOT BACK to the West Coast from Saratoga, it was late, after eight, and after nine by the time Farley stopped by the shedrow at Santa Anita just to make sure all the horses were alive and standing. And they were. One two three four five, all the way up to forty-two. It was reassuring, all those haunches in the air. It was thus, perhaps, all the more unexpected when he went into the office and opened the refrigerator for a bottle of water and saw the pig's head in there, black and white, much bigger in the context of the refrigerator than it had been in the context of the filly's stall. And even though Farley did recognize the pig's face, he found himself, a moment later, running down the shedrow to the filly's stall, just to make sure, and indeed, the filly was eating her hay all by herself, no pig. By now it was nine-thirty, and Farley was going to find Julio, the night man, or call Oliver, but he knew they were sleeping, and anyway, what would they tell him that he couldn't surmise? The pig was big now. Farley had been half wondering what to do with it. The Guatemalan grooms, probably, had done the obvious thing. No doubt there were a couple hundred pounds of succulent pork scattered around the backside, in this refrigerator or that one. It was reasonable. It was rational. It was the only thing to do.

As soon as Oliver saw him in his office the next morning, he walked in, saying, "We are in deep shit about that pig."

"I'm sure—"

"I tried to call you, but you'd already left the hotel, and then I tried your cellular." Accusingly, "I left you a voice mail."

Farley didn't confess that he had decided to spend one day without checking his voice mail. He said, "As soon as I opened the refrigerator, I figured—"

"They chased it. That thing was running all around the shedrow and they were chasing it with knives."

"Who?"

"Mario and Heberto and two of Logan's grooms, too. He fired his. Horses were going nuts with the squealing." Farley stifled a smile, but not quickly enough. Oliver said, sharply, "The track officials are up in arms. You went too far with that pig. You let that pig go on too long."

"I did," said Farley. "Did anyone get hurt?"

Oliver shook his head. Then he said, "Well, except the pig." Right then there was the whoosh of air brakes, and Oliver leaned back and looked out the window of the office. "And by the way," he said, "Tompkins is sending down another horse."

"How old?"

"Not a racehorse. You'll see. He called while you were gone and asked about that filly of his and I told him she couldn't settle. He's got a theory about her." And then he got up and exited. Farley wondered if he planned to quit.

Farley went out and saw the big Tompkins van. The driver had gotten out and was letting down the ramp. Then a woman he recognized at once got out of the cab and came toward him, smiling. That smiling face.

No doubt about it, Joy Gorham was a pretty girl. A little on the diminutive side, a little unkempt, a little androgynous in that horsey way. Her hands were surprisingly big and strong-looking, and Farley knew from watching her that she was built of muscle, the sort of muscle a ninety-pounder needed to get cooperation out of a twelve-hundred-pound horse. But even while Farley noticed all these things, he set them aside. The important thing was that he had seen that face only once before, and yet he remembered it perfectly. That had been a good day, a relaxed day, a day without fear or anxiety. Looking at Joy's face made the feeling of that day flow back into him, in spite of the pig. Oh, lucky me, he thought.

Here he is, thought Joy, the man with the kindest eyes she had ever seen. Oh, lucky me, she thought. She handed him an e-mail Mr. Tompkins had sent her, watched her read, then had her print out. Mr. T. paused at the top of the ramp, alert. Joy went over and received the leadrope from the driver. Mr. T. descended. He looked about, first at the barns, then at the few horses walking by. She led him down the ramp. Farley went over and gave him a pat on the neck. Then he nudged Farley in the chest with his nose. Of course Mr. T., once dark gray with a diamond-shaped star and a white sock, now white with no distinguishing marks, remembered every human he had ever known. That's what a horse was obliged to do as a relic of his ancestors' lives as prey animals. Some humans, like Bucky Lord, were painful to think about, but Farley, his old trainer, was a pleasure to remember. He concurred with Joy's view that kindness radiated off the man, heat or light, or simply promise and reassurance. Did now, always had.

Farley read, " 'Jack Perkins said the filly trained pretty well with this guy, so I sent him down. Try him out.' " Farley's hand moved to the horse's neck, up his neck to his ear, and Mr. T. dropped his head to enjoy the caress. Joy said, "He's an old stakes horse that ended up back at the ranch. I ride him, and the filly did well with him."

"What's his name?"

"Mr. T."

But she didn't mention his registered name, which Farley would have recognized; the last time she read through his race record, she hadn't noticed the names of the trainers.

Mr. T., a horse of excellent manners and great reserve, didn't press his attentions upon Farley. Feats of memory didn't surprise or impress him, anyway, nor did coincidences. He was a horse. He had no expectations about what was normal. His whole life was a demonstration that anything at all could happen at any time. You could go anywhere, do anything, have anything be asked of you, from running and jumping in paradise at one end to starving in Texas at the other. He sighed a large horse sigh, though. Some of Jim Logan's horses walked by, followed by Logan himself. He shouted, "Hey, baby!" And then he snorted like a pig. Farley saw that it was going to be like that all day.

He said to Joy, "What are you doing for breakfast?"

Joy said, "Waiting for you to ask."

"We can go to the cafeteria, but there's going to be a lot of pig noises. I became a legend yesterday."

THE NEXT DAY, Orlando rode Mr. T. out to the training track, and Arturo, her regular rider, rode Froney's Sis. The two horses greeted each other subtly, or perhaps they did not greet each other at all, but the large steady presence of the old gelding did seem to relax the filly and make her less susceptible to the influence of the other horses on the track. She jogged nicely in his shadow, straight and smooth. Farley and Joy leaned companionably on the white plastic railing. They had eaten breakfast. They had eaten lunch. They had gone to the races. They had eaten dinner. They had heard the story of the pig from every possible point of view, and in every form, tragedy, comedy, satire, lament, outrage, joke. She had stood with him beside the remains of the pool where the pig was bled out. She had looked at the head in the refrigerator. He had driven her to her hotel at night and picked her up in the morning. Now they were talking the easiest talk—horse talk.

He said, "He's a nice mover."

"He won some stakes in Europe."

"How many starts did he have?"

"Fifty-two."

"Huh. Where did he run?"

"Around here. Lots of places."

"I wonder who trained him?"

"I don't remember. I can ask Hortense when I get home."

"When do you have to go back?"

"Oh, tomorrow, I guess. Do you think I could—"

"What?"

"Do you think I could ride him around the backside tomorrow one last time? I've been riding him every day all year." She didn't say what she was thinking, that there wasn't much for her at the ranch with Mr. T. gone.

She was looking down, then looking intently at the two horses. How many times had Farley seen that look over the years, the gaze of someone looking at a beloved equine, a mixture of softness and rue, wonder and reserve and pleasure? Love animated her features, a love that he perfectly understood himself. What was it, fourteen hours they had spent together? Plenty of time when you thought about it. Farley said, "Say. Joy. Why don't you not go back? I've got work you can do. It's August. I've got horses here and at Del Mar, and it's been a little bit of a stretch this year. And your broodmares don't start showing up till December, really. You could—"

"It's a critical time for the weanlings, though. . . ." Joy thought of herself trudging alone from hot, dusty pasture to hot, dusty pasture. She looked at him. She already didn't know what he looked like anymore. She turned her gaze and looked at Mr. T. and Froney's Sis, at all the other horses and riders. At the trainers leaning on the rail, at the grandstand and the liveliness and the lush landscape. How much did it take to trade in the Central Valley for Pasadena and Del Mar, at least for a while? She licked her lips. Yes, she thought. "Yes" was a hard word for her to say. "No" was much easier. She was a "no" sort of girl all the way—no roommates, no friends besides Elizabeth, no boyfriend, no parties, nothing unusual supposed to happen at any time. She didn't think she could get herself all the way up to a yes, so she said, "Okay."

He grinned, which reminded her of what a good sport he had been all day the day before about the pig.

She said, "Are they ever going to let you live down that pig?"

"And sacrifice a story like that? Nope, I'm eternally attached to that pig now. I'll be lucky if they don't start calling me Piggy." But he smiled.

A moment later, he said, "Ever ridden a racehorse?"

"Only Mr. T."

"Well, you're built for it."

In the years since his divorce, he had dated plenty, and had, in spite of the story he'd told Oliver that time, eventually gotten laid, too. During these years, he was interested to note, he had grown increasingly indifferent to what a woman looked like or could do. Every woman these days looked great and could do something. Women in their thirties and forties and fifties at the end of the millennium were doers without peer. They lawyered, they mothered, they doctored, they cooked, they show-jumped, they organized their closets, they developed real estate, they openly discussed sex, politics, money, gender roles, and his own idiosyncrasies. Going among women these days was a succession of splendors, Farley sometimes thought, and he counted himself lucky to be having this opportunity after so many years of marriage. Even Marlise had become a butterfly of doing—her real talent, she told him, lay in target-shooting with some sort of special pistol. It turned out she could shoot in time to the beating of her heart. She went to competitions all over the state where she ran up hills and threw herself behind barriers and shot into targets shaped like the silhouettes of men and antlered prey.

In the admittedly few hours they had spent together in the last day, Joy had talked about horses and Mr. Tompkins and this woman Elizabeth and sometimes about what she had done at a university in the Midwest before taking the job at the ranch. She was kind and competent with animals. But unlike most of the women he knew, she didn't seem to aspire to anything, or to have an agenda of wants or needs; she didn't ask him about horses who might be leaving the track or talk about horses she wished to have. She rode this old gelding. In their fourteen hours together, she hadn't talked about owning anything.

He remembered, as a very little boy, maybe three or four, lying on a blanket in his backyard where he had been told to take his nap, watching his mother hang sheets on the line. His mother would have been about twenty-seven then, blonde and graceful. The sun, as he remembered, was behind her, and would cast her dark outline on each white sheet as she pinned it up—her upraised arms and elbows, her hips and waist. Below the sheet, she would rise on her toes each time she attached a clothespin. It was like watching a shadow play. As he lay there sleepily watching, he saw her pass along the line of sheets, setting poles between the sheets to prop up the lines, sometimes as a shadow, sometimes as his mother, and the brevity of the moments between the sheets, when she was there, glancing at him, her real self, made them startling and filled him with love. There she was, and then, a few seconds later, there she was, and then there she was again. Something about that moment reminded him of Joy—something in her was momentarily visible from time to time that was not looks or doing or wanting or intending or even having done anything.

It was something else that was perhaps visible only to him, and perhaps not even there. He couldn't tell yet, but that's why he was suddenly so interested, he thought.

He turned after a moment and watched the two horses again. The filly really did seem quite relaxed. The gelding, though, was tossing his head and pulling. Farley shouted to Orlando, "Send him in a little gallop!" He nodded, and then they were off—about three strides of canter before the old horse took hold, changed leads, and shot away from the filly. "Uh-oh," said Farley. "That was a mistake."

Orlando was a strong rider, and immediately steadied his bridged reins on the old horse's neck. A horse not under human control was presumed to be out of control altogether, but it was clear to Joy as she watched the white gelding lengthen his stride that he was under his own control. He was resisting Orlando, but actually he wasn't paying much attention to him. He was watching the other horses. His ears were pricked. He was neither upset nor frightened. He was simply going very fast.

"Beautiful big stride," said Farley.

"I've felt that," replied Joy, "but I've never seen it."

"Look how open his shoulder joint is. His forelegs are long, and he can really stretch them. And even though he must be ouchy somewhere at his age, he's very even and efficient. There we go." The horse came back to the trot. Farley said, "Well, I don't think there's going to be a problem working the two together, unless she can't keep up with him. Boy, I would really like to know who trained him. How old did you say he is?"

"Eighteen."

"Huh."

Froney's Sis had bucked once and tossed her head when the gelding galloped away from her, but now she trotted calmly up to him, and the two riders brought their horses down to a walk and moved way to the outside of the track.

Only then did Joy realize what she had agreed to do. Staying here? Leaving her little cocoon? Finding a new place to live? Moving or discarding all that stuff? Changing her routine? She glanced at Farley, who was saying to another trainer, "Yeah, the head is in my refrigerator, but Heberto swears he's got some recipe for it." The scariest thing was all her stuff. Her little house was stacked and jammed with piles of horse equipment, clothing, books. She herself could barely function there—when she ate she had to clear a space on the table, when she slept she had to clear a place on the bed, only the bathtub was empty—the stuff would never come out of there—

The other trainer left and Farley turned to her again. He said, "You know, here's an idea. Stay through the Oak Tree meet. Maybe the filly will learn enough in three months so that Mr. T. can go home at the end of the meet, and by that time you can decide if you like this life. One thing's for sure, there's nothing like it. My office manager can help you find a room—" And so he went on, a kindly lullaby. Joy nodded and nodded, and by the time they had followed the horses back to the barn, she knew what her duties would be and what her pay would be and what she would learn. She managed another "Okay."

"Did I ask you Mr. T.'s registered name?" That she had said "okay" delighted Farley more than he dared show, if not to her, then to himself, so he pursued this neutral topic.

"Oh. No. Let me see. Terza Rima." Joy coughed. Second thoughts had shot up all around her, a palisade. She looked at her feet.

"You're kidding."

"No. That's what it was. When he came in he was so ratty-looking, I thought it was a little preten—" It took her just a moment to recognize the true amazement in his voice. She looked him in the face.

Perhaps it was the first time they had made distinct and prolonged eye contact. It had its customary effect.

Farley was laughing in amazement. "I trained that horse myself for about a year! He was such a beauty! They had a picture of him in the paddock at Hollywood on the back cover of some publicity brochure for years!"

"Really?"

Later, that's what Farley marveled at, not the death of the pig, or even the arrival of Joy and the way those events woke him up, but the unlooked-for return of the old gelding, whose stride he now recognized perfectly, who was strangely unchanged for all the damage that age and miles had wrought upon him. And then, the next morning, the head of the pig was gone from the refrigerator, and Farley didn't ask a single thing about it.

SEPTEMBER

42 / A DREAM

WHEN DICK WINTERSON got back to Belmont Park from Saratoga in September, he realized that maybe he should have spoken to Dagoberto Gomez about this Epic Steam colt before shipping him out from California, but, then, what difference would it have made anyway? The animal could run, he was bred to the max, he was a monster of equine beauty, he might win the Derby, the Preakness, the Belmont, the Travers, the Withers, the Ascot Gold Cup, the St. Leger, the Grand Prix de l'Arc de Triomphe, the Breeders' Cup Classic, the Dubai World Cup, any, all. So he had bolted at Hollywood Park. A bolter was a bolter. There were bolters all over the world. And a little studdish, that was obvious. But he was a Land of Magic colt. Land of Magic colts littered the landscape. You got tough with them, they backed down most of the time. As he looked at the horse in his stall, ears pinned, lips wrinkled, the color of mink, shining like stainless steel, hooves counting out a tattoo in the straw, he found himself thinking that he had been training horses for, what, twenty-five, thirty years? If he played this out right, it could be the culmination. Maybe a little bit of a challenge was what he needed to get him out of the doldrums. So, after all, it was a good thing he hadn't spoken to Dagoberto. Dagoberto would have warned him off, started him thinking about why not rather than how. The only way forward into the future was how. Why, why not, those were questions he couldn't answer anyway, better to leave off trying.

And anyway, what experienced horseman had he ever known, in racing, jumping, dressage, cutting, you name it, who looked at a horse at the beginning and said, "Won't even try"? Out west there were guys in the rodeo who climbed on different bucking horses over and over, and hoped to hell the new horse would give them a jolt no horse had ever given them before. You could almost understand that if you didn't think about it very much. "I can do it" was something a horse brought out in a guy, something Epic Steam brought out in Dick Winterson. So what if he couldn't do it with his wife, couldn't do it

283

with his mistress, couldn't do it with himself. At least he could do it with a horse, whatever it was. The day after he got home, he had the vet tranq the animal and give him a going-over. When nothing turned up, he sent him out for a jog. It was about two months since the now famous bolting incident, reported in both *The Blood-Horse* and the *Thoroughbred Times*. What Dick took away from the article, other than the fact that the exercise riders had botched things, was that the filly was a speedball, but that the colt had nearly caught her even though he was fighting his rider the whole way. That showed, Dick thought, that there was something real inside the horse that you could get at if you had a little imagination.

But the animal was no fun, no fun at all. Biting, pawing, and trying to strike, arching his neck and whinnying at any and all females. The first step was to set him up with his tough guys—Wayne, his cowboy groom, former rodeo clown, former polo-player, former stud groom in Kentucky, who'd already had a finger bitten off by a horse because he'd been just a hair too slow. He wasn't too slow any longer. Dick meant to have him walk the horse when he was hot, too, since he didn't really trust any of the regular hot walkers to stay out of trouble. Then there was Frankie, an exercise rider who sometimes worked for him, who was of normal human size, about five eleven, 165, and lifted weights to boot. He rode big bad horses all over the track, and the owner paid extra. Then there were the mares. Dick had four older mares running this year, two five-year-olds, a big four-year-old, and a six-year-old. They were tough girls, on progesterone so they never went into season. They had a serious interest in manners on the part of any male in their vicinity. Dick thought he would just try stabling Epic Steam among the mares, and see if they could communicate their standards of behavior to the youngster.

The real danger, of course, was chaos on the track. You could solve that by working either before or after most of the other horses, which meant before dawn or after 10:00 a.m. Since there was a meet at Belmont right now, it was hard to find a spot, but he chose to try late rather than early, in the heat rather than before it. There were always the possibilities of taxing the guy, tempting exhaustion. Often they behaved better when they got more exercise. The catch in this one was that they got fitter and fitter and needed more and more, and you risked working them to death, but this colt had no apparent flaws that a lot of work would uncover.

When he had seen enough, he went to Wayne and told him to move the mares, then went back to his office, where he fell into a reverie about legends. The colt was already a legend, or at least a figure. In the space of about a minute, Dick had concocted a wonderful fantasy, in which he himself was the star, and the colt the co-star. The Stations of the Cross were all the big three-year-old races, and heaven was himself, talking to a reporter fifteen months from now, self-effacingly discounting his own legendary horsemanship, I knew he had something, I saw it there, blah blah blah. There was a knock on the door, and the vet came in. He put something on the desk. Dick said, "What's that?"

"Progesterone implant. It's for cattle."

"Yeah?"

"Yeah. I took it out of that colt's neck. It was lodged up under the mane."

"I never heard of that before."

"Some guys have tried it. Quarterhorse guys showing stallions sometimes use it to cool a stallion's jets. The racing authorities would never look for progesterone in a colt's urine, so it never tests. It could test."

"So, now that you've got it out, does that mean he's going to be worse?"

"I don't know. There's no evidence that progesterone has any effect on testosterone-related behavior. Might. Might also screw him up in the breeding shed. Don't know. I'm going to make my futile plea."

"Cut him."

"Cut him."

"The owner has one-point-two million into him."

"He's talented."

"On the other hand, he could break down tomorrow. One-point-two million down the drain, no future as a stallion, probably no future as a riding horse. If you cut him and he couldn't race, you'd probably have to put him down. What if they had cut Mr. Prospector? He hardly raced, and he's made more money in the breeding shed than any horse in history."

"The American Thoroughbred would be sounder, straighter, and less inbred if Mr. Prospector had been cut. That's my opinion, not a scientific finding. Cut him."

"I want to try a few things first. We've had bad actors before. We've handled them."

"Yes, you have, and no accidents or injuries, and you're lucky you've got Wayne and Frankie, because horses pay attention to them. So I'll say the other thing I came to say."

"What?"

"Good luck. His heart beats about twice a minute. It must be the size of a Volkswagen. Think you can ride the tiger?"

"Don't know."

And he didn't. After the vet left, he looked at the implant, about the size and shape of a thick, headless nail, lying on his desk. There was an idea, wasn't there? How about two?

Late in the morning, Frankie took the horse out for a jog around the main track, the vast main track. Dick watched his every step, which wasn't easy, because he curvetted and pranced and bucked and reared and squealed. He was a good bucker. Athletic horses generally were. Frankie came back laughing. That was Frankie for you. Dick sent them around again, just to start on the exhaustion idea. When they came back this time, Dick called out, "How much do I have to pay you to ride this guy all day?"

"Who's the owner?"

"He just sold Toys Galore for seventeen trillion dollars to the Chinese."

"I think an annual wage of a hundred thousand dollars would cover it."

"You got it, baby."

The horse put his nose on his knees and bucked. Frankie hauled his head up and laughed, then he said, "My girlfriend, she rides event horses. She got on a guy like this in Ireland, and when he bolted, she let him run right into a tree. He never bolted again. Now she rides him in a twisted-wire snaffle."

"I'll think about bitting options."

"She's got this old English book about the sorts of bits and things they used back in the old days. You could have something made."

"You could get some sense and stop riding these kinds of horses."

"I got expenses, man."

They laughed again, and Dick went back to his office.

THE NEXT DAY, the horse was a tad quieter, and so Dick actually saw his way of going. It was rhythmic but not fluid, which was surprising, given the stories about his speed. But they were still jogging. He had a big walk, and that was usually more telling in a Thoroughbred than the trot. Once again, Frankie came back laughing. That was something, anyway. The horse was fit and ready to run. The Belmont Futurity was coming up—nominations hadn't closed yet, and the owner would certainly like the idea of turning his investment around as quickly as possible. Again, it took maybe a second for Dick to do the thing he was usually well guarded against—construct that fantasy walk into the winner's circle, followed by that fantasy slide down those greased skids to the Derby, the Preakness, the Belmont Stakes, blah blah blah.

There were, of course, other horses in the barn. Before Epic Steam, Dick had been favoring a few, calculating as coolly as possible what races to put them in, how to profit from their individual abilities. He no longer tossed the coin, anyway. In that, he was back to normal. And he was known as a good race-picker—fully versed in the adage "A trainer keeps the best company he can find and a horse keeps the worst." The handicapper's job was to prevent your good horse from stealing money from horses of lesser talents. Your job was to outwit the handicapper. Dick was good at that, and he had a barnful of profitable horses whose winnings made it up to sensible owners that they weren't getting their names and pictures in the papers for big races. But Epic Steam threatened to blast all of that away. It seemed like you could put him in any race and he had a chance. It *seemed* like that. That would be an illusion. Dick recognized it as an illusion. But that didn't mean he didn't believe it.

On the third day, Dick thought the horse could stand a gallop, and maybe the rider could control a gallop. A very long trot the day before had tired the horse, so, when they were tacking him up and walking him out to the track, he looked for all intents and purposes to be within the normal range of bad behavior for a two-year-old. Frankie was happy going out. Wayne said, "I think I've got this guy figured out. He's not all that bad. Touchy around the left ear. You know Rosalba Somebody, she walks hots for Gomez?"

"No."

"She twists their ears sometimes. I've seen her do it."

"No telling what this guy has been through."

"That's for sure, boss."

But they made a happy group, walking out to train, everyone thinking that this was easier than they had expected after all, and taking personal credit for that.

And the horse galloped very nicely. Went off straight, behaved himself, showed off a beautiful big stride, galloped about twice the usual distance, and came back to the trot quietly. Of course, that was where he stumbled. That was where he went to his knees and then got himself back up, and trotted off uneven, and instead of coming right when whatever it was that happened sorted itself out, the horse stayed uneven, so mildly uneven that you almost couldn't see it, and Dick didn't want to see it, and he told himself that he didn't know the horse's way of going at all well, and maybe this was just him—there were sound horses that looked awkward all over the place. But Epic Steam was, of all things, not awkward. He was uneven. He was lame.

And Dick, who hadn't seen the horse four days ago, felt his heart breaking inside his chest.

There was always this little space, after you saw something wrong with a horse and before the vet examined the animal, when you made up your mind not to cross bridges, borrow trouble, look on the dark side. When you hummed along with a sense of hope. But it was no use. Your heart, which knew the truth, had already broken. When the vet sat down in your office to give you the bad news, he wasn't lowering the boom, he was picking up a piece of your heart and offering it to you—this is what's wrong. It's specific.

What was wrong with Epic Steam was a chip in the fetlock joint of the right foreleg. Almost undetectable on the X-ray. Almost not there. But there. Then the vet answered all the futile questions. Why?

"Maybe the run-off I heard about. But he's been shipped since then. Could have had it before, too. Sometimes it chips and then breaks off later."

How long?

"Oh, four months should be plenty of time. Thirty days in a stall, then ninety days at the farm. Back into training beginning of January, say. I think there's all kinds of hope for this. But you've got to give it time."

Full recovery?

"If you give him the time."

They looked at each other. Bad news had been passed across this desk so many times, Dick didn't think that the vet really understood that this was unusually bad, somehow. The vet said, "Listen. You remember the story of John Henry?"

"Yeah."

"He was a dud and a bastard. They thought he was worthless and gelded him and turned him out. Then they picked a sucker and passed him off for twenty-some thousand bucks."

"Greatest last-laugh story in racing, but—"

"He came back mentally able to run, and he ran for six years."

"He was a great horse. No breeding, but—"

"They cut him and turned him out. I can cut him while he's standing there eating his dinner. He came back a different horse."

"Can't do it. Have to tell the owner."

"Tell the owner. He's never had a horse before. Tell him what he should know and what he should do."

"The horse was behaving pretty well."

"You're not listening and you're not seeing."

"I don't want to do it."

"Why not?"

"He's not John Henry. You can't extrapolate from one horse to another, though people always try to. Every flip of the coin is new, the odds are the same no matter how many times it's come up heads. Your evidence isn't evidence, it's just a way of saying the same thing all over again. The horse can be handled. We've had three days with him before this happened. He was starting to be handled."

"You are starting to be very stubborn."

"Am I?"

The vet shook his head as he went out.

Well, maybe he was starting to be very stubborn, but maybe he just had a vision. You didn't know ahead of time whether something was a fantasy, a plan, or a vision. But you didn't limit your options up front just because you didn't know.

He picked up the phone. The owner didn't have a farm himself, of course. Epic Steam was his only horse. The man picked up on the second ring. "Hi, this is Herman Newman." Dick said, "Hi, Mr. Newman. This is Dick Winterson out at the racetrack."

"Hey, Dick! We all set for tomorrow? Sir Michael's coming along. He didn't want to, but I said—"

"Well, Mr. Newman, the horse isn't quite right. I've just had the vet in here—"

"I thought the horse was vetted in California. Sir Michael told me he had the best vet in the state look at him."

"I know he did, sir. But when the horse galloped the first time, he stumbled to his knees, and when he got up, he didn't come right after a bit, so I got my vet to examine him. He's got a tiny little chip in his right front fetlock joint. That's the joint below the knee. It's like your knuckle joint. It would be hard for Sir Michael's friend to see it if the horse hadn't alerted him by traveling in some unusual way. It's very subtle."

"He's got a broken leg? Have we got to put the horse to sleep?" The man sounded completely floored.

"It's not like *Black Beauty,* sir. The horse can hardly feel it. It's a tiny piece of bone that's broken off the joint. The horse's life is not in danger from this."

"They sold me an unsound horse?"

The evidence was inconclusive. He said, "The horse is unsound now. You bought him six weeks ago. He hadn't galloped or stressed himself after he ran off that time, and so you might say there could have been an undetected condition. Or he could have done it today, when he fell to his knees. The horse is a handful, sir. He's big and strong and full of energy. He could have done it in his stall one night."

"So now what?"

"The horse needs to go to a lay-up farm for about three, four months. They'll put him in a stall for a month, then a paddock."

"He can come back in November?"

"More like end of December."

"What about the Derby? That's the first Saturday in May."

"Well—" But Dick couldn't say it, either to Newman or to himself. So he said, "Iffy, but not out of the question. Depends on how he heals, how he trains. Time would be short."

"But I don't understand how it's all so black and white."

"Sir?"

"Yeah?"

"You know, about July of every year, all the trainers start wondering if they've got a two-year-old that can get to the Derby. Lukas has fifty. Baffert has a hundred. That's lots of horses just between the two of them. And then there are the rest of us. Among us, we've got maybe a hundred real prospects. Sounds like a lot. But only twelve or fourteen or seventeen of those ever even get to the post, and only one wins. There's an expression you're going to hear a lot, and use yourself. It's 'That's horses.' Guys who come into this game from other types of business don't really know that the asset can crash any minute of any day. If you don't like that part, then you should consider your lesson well learned, and, actually, cheap at the price."

"He's a good horse? I mean, relatively speaking?"

"One of the best I've ever seen. But he's a handful. I'll be frank with you. He's a heartbreaker. If all you lose with him is money, then you'll be lucky."

"What do you mean by that?"

"He's unpredictable. Added to the natural unpredictability of horses in general, he's got more. He can give you the moon. He's run several quite impressive races in California. But he doesn't behave consistently."

"Is he crazy?"

Dick didn't answer for a long time. He thought of the last three days, of every time he had stood in front of the horse's stall, of what Wayne said and what Frankie said and what the vet said, and then he said, "No. I would say for a horse that crazy means tormented in some way. He's just got lots and lots of energy and a very large agenda."

"What should I do?"

Now was the moment to say, Cut him. But Dick didn't say it. He didn't even think it. He said, "Lay him up, bring him back, see what happens. Do you consider yourself lucky?"

A little abashed. "Well, as a matter of fact, yeah."

"Well, there's a saying in racing, better lucky than good."

"Okay, then."

"Okay, then."

AND DICK HAD A HORSE running in the fifth race, one of those older mares whose second job would have been to assert mare power over Epic Steam. It would have been nice to know if it might have worked. As he saddled her for her race, he admired her. She was a tough little gray mare, with some forty starts under her belt. She ran consistently in decent allowance company and had won about two hundred thousand dollars in three years of racing. When she stopped making a profit, her owner, who didn't breed, planned to do with her what he did with all his mares (he only owned fillies and mares), sell her for a pot of money to the Japanese. Some owners were both lucky and good, and smart to boot. But it made Dick sad to look at her. There was no excitement in her. She was everything you wanted a racehorse to be, if you were sane—sound, determined, female, competent, profitable, consistent. Five years ago he would have been happy to have a barnful of horses like her. But he didn't know how to get back to that, how to give up this longing he had that Epic Steam had perfectly assuaged for three days, that now was back, doubled and redoubled, so that everything he had looked like nothing to him. He threw the jockey up. There were just the three of them, jockey, groom, and trainer. The mare went uncelebrated by her owner, the way everyone who went to work and did a good job day after day went uncelebrated. He watched her go out onto the track. It was a lovely day, almost autumnal. He went and placed his bet, fifty dollars on his mare to win, at four-to-one odds (second favorite), then went up in the stands. The huge track and the spread of land around it did what it always did to him, soothed, reassured, and terrified him, all at the same time.

As he watched the mare jog around to the post, Dick thought about all the good old days there were to miss in horse racing. You could miss the eighties, when, okay, the horses had been good enough but not great, but there was champagne in the office at 10:00 a.m. The owners not only had money (owners always did), they gloried in spending it. Or you could miss the seventies, a decade, the last decade, of great racehorses, or you could miss the sixties, the fifties, the forties, the thirties, Kelso, Nashua, Citation, Seabiscuit, all the times that you weren't around for and didn't remember, but that weren't at all like right now.

43 / EXCUSED ABSENCES

NOW THAT HE had a man teacher, Jesse dreaded the conferences he used to not mind. For first, second, third, and fourth grades, Leo had come in with him, smiled sweetly at his teachers, made a joke or two about being a little nervous himself, don't even mention Jesse, he, Leo, hadn't done all that well in school, and he was here to tell you the end of *that* story, but for all he said, the teachers, white-haired, brown-haired, blond-haired, smiled and were charmed, and everything went well enough. They overlooked his excused absences (five to ten per semester) even after Leo admitted that they were so that he could get Jesse out to the track. Mr. Snowdon wasn't so impressed with that idea. In fact, he wasn't impressed at all. Mr. Snowdon, it was said, had six or nine children of his own (the kids in the fifth grade didn't actually know how many). Jesse recognized that, as a father, Mr. Snowdon had a different take on Leo from the one a person not a father might. As it happened, today was not a full school day: some sort of teachers' meeting somewhere in the afternoon, so leaving a bit early was not that big a deal—all they had remaining before lunch was art and recess. Even so, when Jesse told him the day before that he would be leaving early with his dad, Mr. Snowdon had called Leo and asked to have a word with him, which Jesse did not consider a very good idea.

Another thing that made Jesse dread the special conference was that Mr. Snowdon's favorite thing to talk about was taking responsibility. Everything they did in class turned out to have something or other to do with taking responsibility. For example, one morning on the playground this kid Kevin went up to this girl Nicole, who was wearing sweatpants, and he grabbed her sweatpants by the pockets, and he pulled them down around her ankles. She lost her balance and fell down, skinning her knee and her hand. She cried a great deal. She didn't come back from the school nurse's office until after science, which was almost lunchtime. Since Jesse sat in the first row, he heard everything that Mr. Snowdon said to Kevin, and, he thought, took it to heart more than Kevin himself did.

Jesse would have thought that the incident was about being mean to Nicole, and causing her to hurt herself, but Mr. Snowdon told Kevin it was about taking responsibility. He didn't ask a single time whether Kevin would have liked someone to pull his pants down, nor did he say anything about treating girls differently from boys. What he said, his very words were "Well, here you are, Kevin. You're standing in front of me, and I have to decide how to handle this situation and what to tell your parents and what sort of punishment you should get for this. What do you think is the worst thing about that, Kevin?"

"I don't know," said Kevin.

"Well, say anything."

"Uh, are you going to send me to the principal's office?"

"I could."

"I don't want to go there."

"You don't get to say whether you're going to go there or not, do you?"

"No."

"Who gets to say?"

"You, Mr. Snowdon."

"That means I have the responsibility here."

"Yeah."

"Who gave me that responsibility?"

"The principal?"

"Nope."

"The school?"

"Nope."

"I don't know," said Kevin.

"You did."

"I did?"

"Yes. When you stopped taking responsibility for what you were doing, you gave it away. Now you don't get to decide anything. Now I have to decide, then the principal, then your dad or mom."

"Are you going to send me to the principal's office, then?"

"I don't know right now, but I'm the one who gets to decide. Do you understand that?"

"I guess."

Maybe, maybe not, thought Jesse. It wasn't hard to get into a circular sort of argument with Kevin. Jesse, however, understood perfectly. If you took responsibility all the time, then you got to pretty much decide what you were going to do. If you forgot and did something like pulling down a girl's pants, then someone else got to say what was going to happen to you, and it was clear in this case that Kevin would be at the mercy of at least four adults—Mr. Snowdon, Mr. Larson (the principal), Kevin's own dad, and Nicole's dad, too. It was like some kind of math problem. One person gave away something and then four persons got it. This was a lesson Jesse thought of as the time for the conference approached.

The other kids went out for recess, and Leo entered, car keys jingling in his hand. Maybe the hardest thing was just watching the two of them together. Leo was tall and handsome, with that face that Jesse had looked into so often that revealed everything Leo was thinking as if by flickering lights. Mr. Snowdon you wouldn't look at twice on the street. He smiled and held out his hand to Leo, and Leo took it briskly, saying, "Well, it's good to see you, too. Maybe. You would know, I guess?" He laughed. Jesse got up from his desk and walked forward. Mr. Snowdon motioned him to a seat at the front table.

As a preliminary, perhaps, Mr. Snowdon began to explain to Leo what the class was doing. Leo said, "Uh-huh. Uh-huh. Oh, yeah. That's good." He was nodding agreeably.

"We are deep into fractions—"

Leo said, "Oh, I know all about fractions." Jesse closed his eyes.

"Oh, really," said Mr. Snowdon. "Well, the fractions these children—"

"For example, a twenty-two-second fraction in a five-and-a-half- or six-furlong race, you know, a sprint, is fairly common. But in a longer race, you want the later fractions to be the faster ones. Yesterday, in the seventh race, you know, the feature, which was a mile and a sixteenth on the turf, the winner ran the last fraction in twenty-two and a half. My own prediction, based on the animal's past performances, is that he has a shot."

"A shot?" said Mr. Snowdon.

"A shot at the Breeders' Cup Classic, though, to tell you the truth, all of these three-year-olds come up suddenly these days. It's not like when I was a kid, and you watched a great horse develop over the course of a year or more."

"The fractions we've been working on—"

"It's not the same thing, I know that. But, you know, there's never been a time that Jesse here didn't know his halves, his quarters, his eighths, and his sixteenths. In first grade he knew that the San Juan Capistrano is a mile and three-quarters, which is fourteen furlongs. Not a single other kid in his grade knew that."

When Jesse opened his eyes, he saw that Mr. Snowdon was sitting back in his chair in amazement. "I'm sorry. Fractions aren't really the reason I asked you to come in—"

"Oh. Well, sure. What's this?" He pointed to an essay of Jesse's that had been pinned to the bulletin board.

Mr. Snowdon smiled. "Jesse wrote a very nice piece about a book we read aloud in class called *Where the Red Fern Grows*. I read this book aloud to the children—"

"Some of them can't read in fifth grade?"

"I believe that reading to the children even after they can read on their own is an important way of sharing literature with them."

As Mr. Snowdon said this, Leo went over and read through Jesse's essay. When he was finished, he said, "I wouldn't have thought a book about a kid who wants to have some hunting dogs who tree helpless animals so that they can be killed for no apparent reason would be relevant to the kids' lives here in L.A. You know, you might consider a field trip to Hollywood Park toward the end of the year. You can't find a place that's more relevant to these kids' lives. For example, they would have to go through Inglewood. There's a history lesson for you. Did you know that, during the riots a couple of years ago, they couldn't bring the planes into LAX along the regular flight path, because they were afraid of people shooting at the planes? And, then, all sorts of people show up there, from all over the world. You hear Korean, Spanish, Chinese, English, Russian, you name it, every language. And a trip to the backside is the real experience, close up, of how this country works. Do you know how this country works, Mr. Snowdon?"

"Well, of course, I—"

"If you'll pardon me for saying so, *Where the Red Fern Grows* is not how this country works." He turned to Jesse. "How does this country work, son?"

Jesse said, "Um, there are stakes horses, allowance horses, and claimers. And then there are speed horses and routers. Mostly it's in the pedigree, but sometimes the horse just has heart, and so he does better than his pedigree says he's going to do."

"For example—" encouraged Leo.

"For example, Holy Bull," said Jesse. "He was by Great Above."

"Holy Bull was a horse with heart," said Leo with a sigh. "Go on."

"It's, uh, easier to go down in class than to go up," said Jesse. "You don't get to be a stakes horse all your life." This was one of Leo's favorite truisms.

"What about betting?" encouraged Leo.

"It's all betting," said Jesse.

"Now," said Leo, turning informatively to Mr. Snowdon, "that's the truest thing there is. When these kids come in here in the fall, you handicap them right up front. They've been handicapped every year since kindergarten, and by now their form is pretty well established. And you can't help looking at their form, and placing your bets accordingly. You split them up into groups and you teach the one group, the stakes horses, something different than you teach the claimers. The kids all know who's a claimer and who's the big horse. What are you, Jesse?"

"I'm an allowance horse, Dad."

"But you want to move up in class, don't you, son?"

"Yes, sir." Jesse didn't dare look at Mr. Snowdon.

"A good teacher," said Leo, "doesn't pay a lot of attention to past performances, or to form itself."

"Well," said Mr. Snowdon, "predictors are of course not one hundred percent—"

"Predictors. Now there's a word. Personally, I have more faith than you can have in predictors." He leaned forward, ready to tell Mr. Snowdon something important. Jesse looked out the window. Leo said, "There are signs. There are always signs."

"Signs of what?"

"Whether or not you are going to have a winning day."

"I thought you owned a liquor store, Mr. Harris?"

"I do. That's a going concern. But a man has to have passions, too. Do you have a passion, Mr. Snowdon?"

"I, uh, do some woodworking. I wouldn't call it a passion. Perhaps we should get back to Jesse. Jesse in general shows a great sense of responsibility. I admire that very much in him. Well, Jesse is a fine boy."

"Never gets into trouble, huh? Well, I'm glad to hear that." Leo laughed cheerfully.

"I mentioned when I called you that I felt that Jesse's excused absences to the track were not in his best interests. I have to say I do not feel a child should be taken out of school to attend sporting events of any kind."

Leo sniffed. "But it's clear to me that Jesse here, though he's my boy, and I say so, is wise beyond his years. You tell me which of these other kids has a system? Jesse has a system." He leaned forward and said to Mr. Snowdon in a low voice, "It's the dad's responsibility to bequeath his son a system, maybe his only responsibility. I take my responsibility very seriously."

Now there was silence in the room. Jesse could tell that his father had been too much for Mr. Snowdon, because Mr. Snowdon was starting to put together his papers as if it were time for the conference to be over, and it had only been about ten minutes. But it was as though there was nothing more to say, that saying things had ceased to be worth the effort. Jesse felt a collapsing in the stomach, as if Mr. Snowdon were giving up on him. He looked at the man, and saw that he was smiling at him, Jesse, and realized that Mr. Snowdon wasn't giving up on him, but perhaps on Leo. That, in fact, was not unusual. Then the teacher put his hand on Jesse's head and said, "You have a fine boy, Mr. Harris. I admire him." He sounded sad, as if he were saying good-bye, although the school year was just beginning. But Leo didn't seem to notice that. He stood up, or, rather, bounced up on his sneakers, and said, "Well, thanks for everything, those words. He is a fine boy. Nobody knows that better than I do, unless it's his mom." He laughed. "And thanks for giving us this ten-thirty time. Opening day of the meet today. I love Santa Anita. There's always a little dry spell in southern California between the end of Del Mar and the opening of the Oak Tree meet. Simulcasting is all very well in its way, but a day out at the track, well, that's an education and a pleasure. You ready, boy? I don't want to miss the daily double."

They strode out of the room, out of the school. Got into the car. When they were settled and had buckled their seat belts, Leo said, "Got your lucky socks on?"

Jesse nodded. Leo said, "I can't hear a nod."

"I've got them on, Dad."

"Good boy. Now, let's see. We need some signs."

Jesse looked over at Leo, who was driving, leaning forward, glancing around, smiling, eager, the way he always looked when they were headed out to the track, as if he didn't remember that chances were he would be disappointed and angry at the end of the day. But how could he not know? Jesse was only eleven, and he knew. His mom never went to the track, and she knew. Jesse was used to thinking of his father as smart. No one talked like his father, no one impressed upon him all those differences in class and talent and pedigree the way his father did, and yet here was a simple thing, the simplest thing in the world, that his father didn't know. Jesse looked out the window. They were approaching the 110.

School would be over for everyone by now, so there was nothing to miss, but Jesse thought that he missed it anyway. What if Mr. Snowdon had forbidden Leo, had simply said, "No, Mr. Harris, I won't let him go. I can't let him go." A showdown, like a movie. But as soon as he thought of it, Jesse knew it was impossible. Leo could do whatever he wanted to with him, and even a man teacher couldn't stop him. Mr. Snowdon was someone else's father. You could think of it this way, Jesse thought as they went up the ramp: there had been one chance out of however many to be Leo's son, and nine chances to be Mr. Snowdon's son, and he had beat the odds, in a manner of speaking. The car accelerated, and Jesse's body was pressed against the back of the seat.

OCTOBER

44 / AN UNEXPECTED TWIST

AFTERWARDS, Krista didn't know what made her go out to the barn. It was cold and damp for October, and she and Pete were about to go to bed. At nine, when she'd checked the horses, everything had been fine. Now it was eleven, and Pete wanted to watch one last thing on CNN, but Krista was tired of listening to the TV. Maia was sleeping peacefully—she checked her on the way out. She had no inkling, no inkling at all—how could that be? The old mare, Wayward, was rolling back and forth in the corner of the pasture, colicking badly. She dialed Sam's emergency exchange on her cell phone as she ran back into the house, and when she told Pete, he was on his feet in a second, heading out the door and putting on his coat. But they couldn't leave the baby, could they? She ran back into the house and looked at Maia, then she ran out again, but as soon as she ran out again, she wanted to run back in again.

The old mare was a sight to behold, on her back like a dog, snaking her head in the wet grass, her legs folded above her, slowly twisting and rolling from one side to the other. She was making a sound deep within herself, a groan like the creaking of her whole body that went on and on. Her belly, which didn't seem that large when she was standing, spread out over her as she rolled, and Krista found herself paralyzed by the thought of the foal inside, shifting back and forth like that. Several months before, Sam had ultrasounded all the mares and Krista had stared at the ghostly little horses within, their threadlike legs wafting in the amniotic fluid, their upside-down heads and necks waving and floating. It was much stranger than the pictures of Maia had been. She seemed at home in the watery bath, rounded and curled like a fish, but foals did not—their legs were too long, made for running, not swimming. Krista approached the mare from the head and bent down over her, speaking softly. "Hey, Mama! Got a bellyache? Can you get up, sweetheart?"

The mare noticed them. That was a good sign—when they were really far gone they noticed nothing, or at least that's what the emergency-vet-care book said about colic. The mare was willing to get up, though. She rolled onto her chest, her legs folded, and let Pete snap on the halter. Then he patted her on the neck, and she got up with a different sort of grunt, not so much a groan. Krista answered the cell phone. Sam was in the neighborhood, on his way, and said not to make the mare walk. Then Krista went back in the house to check on Maia. The mare stood quietly enough next to Pete, with her head down. Pete scratched her ears. Krista came out again, stood for a few minutes, then said, "Maybe I should bring her out here. The baby monitor doesn't really work this far."

"She's asleep, right?"

"Yeah."

"She's been sleeping through the night for four months—"

Krista opened her mouth to say something, something irritable, but here came Sam, saving everything, even that, once again. Getting out of his truck, he was already pulling on his vinyl sleeve that went all the way up to his shoulder and greasing it with lubricant. He didn't have to reach far up the mare's anus. He said, "Uterine torsion, twisted to the right, clockwise."

"What's that?" said Pete.

"Well, the whole uterus—foal inside, of course—has flipped over. I can feel the left broad ligament on top and the right broad ligament underneath."

"Oh my God," said Krista. "I'm wondering if I should get Maia—"

"Well," said Sam, "I need both of you. There's a lot we can do, but four or five would be better than three."

"She's fine," said Pete.

"Okay," said Krista, but she felt doubtful. A baby's loudest screams, it always seemed to her, came when the mother wasn't there to hear them.

Sam said, "Got a board, like a two-by-twelve, about twelve feet long?"

Krista ran and got one, from the stack of boards they kept for fixing fence, and dragged it over. It was dark, and she stumbled several times, but didn't fall. Sam was giving the mare some shots. He said, "That should take a moment or two." He sounded rather calm, actually. Krista couldn't tell if this was because a uterine torsion wasn't all that serious, or because he was just Sam the vet, professionally serene in every crisis. Then he stood by the mare's shoulder and gently bent her head toward him. The mare's legs began to buckle at the knees. He pulled her head a little more toward himself, then pushed her shoulder away. The front went down first, then the back end. She sank onto her sternum, then eased over onto her right side. Her eyes were half open, and Sam lubricated them with something, then tucked a towel around them. The mare's legs extended. She was now laid out flat. Sam took the board and placed it like a seesaw, with her belly as the fulcrum, one end resting on the grass and the other sticking past her spine about a foot and a half. Then he said to Krista, "Sit on that, honey."

"What?"

"Sit there on the board, right on the mare, about halfway between the spine and the midline. Pete and I are going to roll the old girl over, and your weight is going to keep the baby in place."

Krista and Pete exchanged a glance.

"I wish we had one other person," said Sam, "to handle her head."

"It's midnight," said Krista. "Margaret Lerner might be up, but she—"

Sam stared at her for a moment, then said, "I think I can do it. Get me some more towels." Krista, who was reluctant to sit on the mare's belly to begin with, ran for them. Too soon, she was back. He built up a little stack of them under Wayward's head, lifting her nose in the direction she would be going. He said, "Don't make any noise. We don't want her to wake up."

"Now?" said Krista.

"Now," said Sam.

Krista and Pete exchanged another glance, but she sat down on the board. She could feel the mare's belly give underneath her weight. Then Pete and Sam each went to a set of legs, Sam in front, where he could monitor the head, Pete behind. They began slowly to lift. Krista sat still, trying not to think of the pressure of her weight on the foal inside. They paused and Sam did something with the head, then they resumed lifting the mare's feet and knees. Krista sat. They lifted. Krista sat. They lifted, heaving, groaning, breathing hard. The mare showed no distress, breathed, in and out, softly. She was on her back. The two men skittered sideways, grunting, Sam stepping carefully over her head and neck, and then they lowered the legs, bit by bit. "Jeez," said Pete. Sam switched the stack of towels to the other side just before the mare's hooves came down on the damp grass, and she was facing the other direction. Sam and Pete paused to catch their breath. "Jeez," said Pete, again, panting. "Heavy load." Krista stood up.

"Four or five hundred pounds apiece," said Sam, who was also panting. They stared at each other, catching their breath. Then Sam got his rubber sleeve on again, and knelt down behind the mare and inserted his arm. He was shaking his head as he pulled it out. He said, "Still twisted. Let's try again."

They lifted off the board, and, with Krista holding the head, they rolled the mare back over.

The second time was easier. Everyone knew what to do, and did it. Whereas the first time it had seemed to Krista that she was sitting on the board for hours on end, the second time went quickly, possibly because she dreaded what Sam would say when he palpated the mare again. He said what she dreaded, "Nope." Then, "Once more."

They did it once more. Now the time was scudding by to Krista, because she knew what the end would be—something horrible, like death.

When Krista stood up this time, she closed her eyes and waited for that to come up.

Instead, Sam said, "She's waking up. That's good. We're going to try one more thing." He cleared his throat and put his hands in his pockets, waiting. Pete said, "Maybe one of us should check on the baby."

Krista nearly jumped out of her skin. She had forgotten about Maia, another thing to be ashamed of. What if— She ran for the house, where the baby slept on, quiet, revealing nothing. Krista bent down in the dim light of the nightlight and checked her cheeks for drying tears. Nothing.

By the time she got outside again, the mare was lifting her head. Krista removed the towel from around her eyes, and saw that she was wide awake now. Then the old girl got up, with a grunt, and braced herself, all four legs spread a little wide. She shook herself. She seemed perfectly alive. Krista couldn't help imagining what that would be like, having your uterus and baby simply turn 180 degrees to the right. She had never heard of its happening in a woman, though. Thank God for that.

She said, "Does this, uh, happen more with older mares or anything?"

"Oh, I don't know. The problem with horses and big dogs is that everything is pretty loose in there. Gets to rolling around."

Pete said, "I thought maybe I missed some signs at feeding time."

"She was probably totally fine at feeding time. You know, some things in life, you see them coming. Other things pop out of nowhere. A hole opens up right where you're standing, and something unexpected is present." He shook his head, and said, "Let's lead this mare over into the light, here, and then rig up something, some kind of light source. I want to be really able to see what I'm doing."

It took about ten minutes to find a couple of utility lights. By that time, the mare was fully awake and looking around for some hay, still full enough of painkillers not to worry about the potential inner catastrophe. But Krista was worried. She was worried that this easy moment right now would be the last easy one for a long time, that she would look back at this very moment and remember it so clearly as the peak she might never climb again, if the mare died, and the foal died, and there were bodies to get rid of and grief and regret and another chance to say, "Well, that's horses." She imagined the foal as a corpse, known and recognized only for a moment. Himself was a chestnut; the mare was a bay. All those Nearco–Nasrullah–Bold Ruler–

line horses were bay or brown, so the foal would be one or the other, no doubt. But maybe Himself would have thrown a bit of color, a little star or a blaze, a white sock or two. You never knew. Krista imagined herself looking at the baby—so little at this stage, maybe the size of a large rabbit, lying there in a little dark bundle, a white marking standing out on his forehead like a moon.

"Okay," said Sam. "You've got a set of stocks in the stallion barn, right?"

"Yeah."

"Let's go."

They went. The only horse in there now was Himself, and when they turned on the lights, he blinked. When they led the mare in he came fully alert and began to give deep, impassioned snorts. Pete closed the top door to his stall, but they could see his nose over it, trying to get a whiff or a look or something. "Stand her in the stocks there, then rig these two lights up so that they shine right on her hip." He went out to his truck and returned in a clean white coverall and surgical gloves. He had four syringes in his hand and a mask around his neck. The mare entered the stocks with perfect willingness, clop clop, and now she stood there, looking over toward Himself. Now Sam looked at Krista and said, "Krista, do you want to call the owner and tell him I'm about to do a three-thousand-dollar operation on her?"

"I should. Can the foal be saved otherwise? Or the mare?"

"Nope."

Krista closed her eyes. If he balks, she thought, we'll pay somehow. She felt a profound rush of financial vertigo. Then she said, "Do it."

"You're on, sweetie. Don't worry."

He gave the mare the injections, two in the neck and two in the spinal column. He said, "Ever heard of an epidural?"

"Yes."

"Well, she just had something like that. I want her wide awake and standing up, but not feeling anything. Now watch her spine."

Krista watched. After a few moments, it got a curve in it, almost a wave, toward the right. "See that?" said Sam. "All the nerves are blocked on this left side, but not on the right. That's what causes that effect. It's not permanent and it doesn't hurt. Ready?"

"For what?"

"For something you may never see again."

"I'm ready."

Sam took his clippers out of his pocket and shaved the mare's side, from the hip forward, then scrubbed it three times with three different scrubbing sponges. Then he stepped back, looked for a moment, and stepped forward.

Now he produced a scalpel and, in one fairly quick motion, cut a vertical incision into the mare's side, maybe eight or ten inches long, exerting some effort to get through the grid of muscles as well as the skin. The incision opened up, but didn't gape. Not much blood came out. Krista stared. Inside, revealed by the lights, was the buff-colored mass of the uterus, swollen and glistening. "There we are," said Sam. "Take a look." Krista took a look, and Pete came around and took a look, too. Actually, Krista expected to see more, maybe the outline of a hoof or a nose. Still, it was intimidating to think that only one membrane, like the membrane of a balloon, separated the foal from the world.

Now Sam had his long rubber sleeves on again, on both his arms this time. Once again, he said "Ready?" But it seemed as though he was saying this to himself more than to her. He faced front, bent down against the horizontal bar of the stocks, and reached the nearest arm into the incision, carefully but firmly. With his other hand, he grabbed the bar of the stocks and balanced himself. He muttered, "Got it."

"Got what?"

"The, uh—" He was concentrating. Now he leaned against the side of the mare, and his shoulder seemed to Krista to press in an alarming way into the incision. "The, uh, the horn of the uterus. Okay, baby, easy does it." There was a pause. Krista could see the cords of his neck stand out, and what had not looked like a lot of blood before looked like quite a lot as it spread around his collar and over his white front. He bit his lip. He said, "There's the ligament. Oh, ouch, baby. No wonder that hurts, Mama. Good girl, stand still." The mare seemed utterly indifferent to what was happening to her. She didn't even look around. Pete was stroking her neck on the other side, crooning into her ear, but Krista could only watch Sam. Now Sam said, "Okay, I've got something."

"What?" said Krista.

"Oh, I've got some part of the foal. Haunch, maybe. That's what I like to get."

The mare began to shift from side to side slightly, in a rhythm, and Krista realized that Sam was rocking her, rocking her uterus back and forth, the way you rock a car back and forth that has gotten stuck on ice. She said, "Omigod." But quickly, so as not to break his concentration. Now she couldn't watch the mare's flank, so she watched Sam's face instead. His eyes were wide and lips were pursed with the effort of exerting strength and kindness at the same time. The mare rocked. Sam's arm moved back and forth. Sam rocked. Krista wanted to moan, it was taking so long. She glanced at Pete, but he had leaned his head against the mare's, and the two of them seemed to be in a humming trance, with Pete mumbling, "You're all right, honey. You're all right, baby. Good girl, good girl, good girl."

Sam crooned, "Come on, my love, come on, my darling," his voice pressed out with the effort, but gentle, too.

Suddenly, the vet pulled one harder stroke. Then his face relaxed into a smile, and he stood up, withdrawing himself from the incision. "There we go," he said. "Up and over."

"You're kidding," said Krista.

"Nope. She's fine. The ligaments are good, no tears that I can feel, and the uterine wall seems to be intact, and the foal is moving around in there normally, though we'll ultrasound him tomorrow or the next day just to be sure. Whew!" He stretched his arms above his head and rolled his shoulders, then closed his eyes and twisted his head and neck from side to side. "The hardest thing about this is trying to move that weight with your arm extended. Between the foal and the fluids and all, it must be fifty pounds. If you could just get in there with both arms. But you can't do that. Well, hot dog. Good one. Better sew this mama up. What time is it?"

"After two," said Pete, yawning. Then he handed Krista the leadrope. "I'll check on Maia."

She said, "You should go to bed."

He nodded. He had work in the morning, and anyway, it was better for one of them to be in the house. She wondered if she would remember to get a better baby-monitor in the morning, or whether everything else would come up and overwhelm that thought, until the next time she was going to wish she had it. Sam was now taking neat little stitches. The mare seemed unconcerned still. Sam said, "I haven't seen one of these since vet school."

"Of course it would be here. Does it have to be a straw that breaks the camel's back, or can it just be your usual truckload of large boulders?"

"Big established farms have emergencies, too, Krista."

He didn't sound unkind. In fact, he sounded deeply kind, but embarrassment seared her anyway, and she refrained from further whining. It was three-thirty by the time he drove away.

A half-hour later, she checked on Maia and finally got to bed. Actually, she thought, if you watched your baby sleeping through the night moment by moment instead of obliviously sleeping though the night yourself, it was all that much more amazing. Already, she could hardly remember what she had seen. What Sam had done seemed so unbelievable that her memory denied it, turned off the lights that lit up the scenes one by one, so that the normal darkness of an October evening enclosed it, shrank around it, finally covered it over. Pete was snoring, a comforting sound in its way. She closed her eyes.

In the morning, she was so tired. Maia looked like she was crawling around underwater. There was no way Krista could make it to naptime, she thought, three long hours away if she was lucky, so she gave in about 10:00 a.m. and called her mother, who came over. All her mother said before mercifully taking the baby with her to Nordstrom was "Your grandfather loved Sam. I'll say that." And then, thank God, she didn't start in, but just said, "Well, I'm glad everything worked out, honey. I really am. Oh, look at my darling sweetheart. Maybe if some of that first crop get to the track before the New Year—"

"Some are. No one's winning yet."

"Oh, well. I'm sure they will." And then, for the first time ever, as Krista was buckling the carseat into her mother's van, "You know, honey, if you need a bit of a loan, look at that babyface, my goodness—"

And Krista didn't get defensive. She just said, "I'll let you know." And then, "Say, see if they have a better baby-monitor, one with a longer range."

And her mother just nodded.

45 / JUST THE MIDWEST

IT WAS NOT up to Justa Bob to analyze how and why he had come to this farm by this pond with these horses and mules and been, you might think, forgotten. In the first place, Justa Bob had only a hazy sense of time. The multitude of sharp pictures that constituted his memory were not sequential in the human sense. They were more like an account upon which current experiences drew. He had plenty of access to them, but he didn't mull them over; rather, he sometimes had occasion to re-experience something remembered in conjunction with something taking place in the present. At the moment of the re-experiencing, he could not quite tell the difference between what was happening in the present and what it reminded him of, but he always got to where he could in a few seconds or minutes. That would be called learning—he could learn the difference between the past and the present. What set Justa Bob apart from horses of lesser intelligence was that he was ready, and even eager, to learn that difference.

He had now been in this pasture with these horses and these mules, being taken care of by this old man, for a long enough time so that he knew how he stood. It wasn't high, and it wasn't low. On the one hand, several of the other animals were irritable and even, you might say, dictatorial. On the other hand, there was plenty of grass, and you could stand in the pond, which cooled his ankles. Justa Bob stood in the pond during part of every day, and dozed for a long time.

The fun, for Justa Bob, did not come from the old man, but from three other, small humans who were never around when the old man was, and often around when the old man wasn't. For example, Justa Bob would watch the old man's white truck leave the place, and then, pretty soon after that, the jockey-like humans would show up, and while the old man was gone, they would run after the horses and mules in the pasture, pet them, give them carrots and apples, climb on them, fall off of them, kick them, yell at them, wrestle among themselves, run around, swim in the pond, and then, at the first sight of the white truck, run away.

He got more treats after the small humans realized that they could climb on him and not be bucked off. Justa Bob wasn't a bucker. He had been a hard-working forward-looking racehorse for so long that it never occurred to him to object to a rider. They got on him in a very unjockeylike way, two at a time, pulled on his mane, yelled, stood up, rolled around, urged him into the pond, slapped, patted, and hugged him, then gave him carrots and sugar and apples. They called him "Sammy." After a while, they would start shouting his name—"Sammy! Sammy! Sammy!"—as soon as they came over the crown of the hill, and Justa Bob would trot or canter out to meet them. He could always feel them, when they were riding him, sliding this way and that, so he would slow to a walk or a halt while they secured themselves or fell off, and he could see them under his feet and under his belly and behind him. Their noise and activity didn't irritate him the way it did some of the other equines, because he was used to noise and activity, and found life in the pasture rather boring by contrast to life at the racetrack.

All in all, Justa Bob was having a lovely vacation.

And so he was not happy to see the face and figure of William Vance standing at the gate one morning. He had a perfect memory of William Vance, though he had not thought of him once since coming to this place. Along with his memory of William Vance came plenty of pain and discomfort, which Justa Bob did not feel as a thing that was happening, but as a thing that could happen in the presence of William Vance. And so, rather than going up to the gate as the other animals were doing (the old man was carrying buckets of feed), Justa Bob turned and trotted the other way, over the brow of the hill and down to the trees on one side of the pond, where he secluded himself in the shade. Sure enough, after a while, here they came, halter and leadrope in hand, carrying a bucket of feed. Justa Bob was hungry for that sweet taste, but he recognized this trick and ducked out from his current spot. Because he was an enterprising horse, it didn't take long for him to understand the possibilities of the pond, and so he waded into it, up to his knees and hocks, though the weather had gotten a little chilly for this sort of activity lately. It was not that he had the foresight to understand the reluctance of the men to go into the pond, it was that, once he was in the pond, he could see the men stop at its verge and stand there. He was in, they were not; that was enough. He swiveled his ears. He could hear them talking.

"God damn," said William. "What now?"

"That guy loves this pond. He stands in here a couple hours every day."

"I ain't got all day. I want to get back to Chicago tonight."

"It's only about two feet deep. Go on in and get him. But we could also go get some breakfast ourselves. My bet is, he'll come out and go up and eat with the others. I ain't seen ya in, what, three or four months?"

And then the men turned and walked away, over the crest of the hill and out of sight. Justa Bob felt the urge, a primal urge, to see where they were going and what they were doing. That was the way it was with humans—when they turned their backs on you, you found yourself following them. Dogs were the same. Dogs ran into the pasture, you ran away; the dogs veered off in that easily distractible doglike way, and you trotted after them. But Justa Bob did not follow the men. The sense he had of William Vance, that wherever he was pain could be or would be, was too strong. And the chilly pond was soothing. Sometime later, the other equines appeared over the hill and came toward him, seeking a post-breakfast doze. Once they had situated themselves, Justa Bob felt even less motivation to leave the pond.

At some point, the humans appeared again. Justa Bob had moved, the water had sloshed around him, but it was still again. William Vance said, "Well, shit. You got any boots?"

They turned and went back over the hill.

While they were gone, the rest of the herd moved off to another part of the pasture, where there might be fewer flies. The trees were turning and the weather was cooling, but the flies were still everywhere. As a Cal-bred, Justa Bob found these swarms of flies unprecedented. He contemplated following the others, because, to tell the truth, the flies were getting annoying. There were at least three kinds: Big horseflies that got into his ears and under his mane and latched on. These you had to actively bite off of yourself, or shake off. Then there were smaller ones that bit and flew, bit and flew. Their bites were sharper and more annoying. You could switch your tail all day against those and still not get anywhere until night fell or you got inside somewhere. Other little flies flew around over the surface of the water. They didn't bite, but they got into his belly hair and tickled, crawling around sensitive areas up between his back legs, where the hair was sparse. Sometimes during midday, all of the pastured equines found the flies too much to bear, and they ran around until they were worked up and sweaty trying to get away from them.

The men came over the hill again, leadropes, carrots, bucket, smiles on their faces. The man he was suspicious of began to wade into the water. Justa Bob stood quietly. The man spoke to him kindly. He said, "Hey, baby. How ya doin'? I've missed you. Don't you want to go back to the track, baby? Look at you. A horse with forty-some starts, a real racehorse, a tough guy, Justa Bob, a horse with a plan. You don't want to waste your life hanging out in a field with a bunch of mules. You're too good for that, baby." He was almost there. On the one hand, Justa Bob liked his voice. On the other hand, his belly began to twitch uncomfortably. Without really understanding why he was doing so, Justa Bob backed a step or two, then turned and walked farther into the pond, which disturbed the insect life that had colonized him. His skin quivered all over and his ears twitched. The man's voice stayed the same. He said, "Now, don't do that, baby. Don't walk off like that. These aren't waders, they're just boots. I don't want to get my feet wet. And this water is cold. You like this? That what you like? My daddy says you stand here all the time. I bet you've done yourself a world of good. That's what I bet. Come on, sweetie. Come to this guy. We're going to have fun together. I make friends with all my runners, yes, I do." His voice was so low that Justa Bob had to turn his ears in that direction to hear it. And there was another thing about him, he was a slow-moving, easy sort of person. Justa Bob, like most horses, had a good sense of that. There were jittery humans. No matter what they did, it was kind of scary, and you sometimes wanted to give them a monitory kick, both to wake them up and to get them out of your vicinity. There were peaceful humans, and whatever they did, even if they smacked you a good one, it wasn't scary at all, but just what you deserved. Those humans, well, it was nice to be near them. Then there were all the others, not consistently identifiable. You just kept alert and did what the situation required with them. But even these reflections didn't halt Justa Bob's progress deeper into the pond. Pretty soon, he was belly deep, deeper than he had ever been. The bottom of the pond sucked his hooves right down into it, which was rather a pleasant feeling, and the surface of the water lapped coolly where the bugs had formerly been. Now the bugs were crawling over his flanks and haunches.

William Vance stood where he had stopped, his hands down at his sides. Justa Bob could see him with his right eye but not his left. With his left eye, he could see the other equines some distance away. A few of them were grazing, but most of them were looking at this human. William waited for a moment, then turned partly away from Justa Bob and looked in the other direction. Justa Bob felt that primal urge again, the urge that made him want to approach and see what the human was doing. His feet were stuck in the mud enough for him to resist the urge. Now there was a long moment. Having very little sense of time, Justa Bob could not have said how long this moment was, even relatively. Things happened during this moment. Flies bit him and he bit them. He switched his tail rhythmically, back and forth. He took a drink of water. He manured into the pond. The other horses moved off. But William Vance stayed still. He did not move his hands or arms or legs or head. He did not bring his gaze back to Justa Bob. He said nothing. He breathed, that was all. Justa Bob could hear that, see that, and sense that, one breath after another. And while the human was breathing, Justa Bob felt the possibility of pain and discomfort move further away. He learned—the pain and discomfort were not taking place now. The human had no pain and discomfort with him at this time, but, rather, he had with him quiet, gentleness, peace, carrots, sweet feed. Feelings and scents that mingled pleasantly together, that made a promise. It wasn't a long-term promise, for Justa Bob had no way of understanding a long-term promise, but it was a short-term promise that grew increasingly attractive. The man laughed. The sound itself was pleasant, and it drew on several memories that Justa Bob had of humans. Laughter meant good things—more treats, more pats, a general cheerful feeling. Then the man turned away and stepped out of the water. Justa Bob right then didn't see why he shouldn't just follow. And so he did. The man kept walking. Justa Bob kept following. Out of the pond. Up the hill through the grass. Over the hill. Across the flat piece. To the gate. The man turned. Justa Bob stopped, stepped forward a few more steps, and then touched the man on his front with his nose. He understood then that this was a man you could be right next to without feeling a disturbance. The man put the halter around his head, buckled it, gave him a carrot chunk by chunk, spoke to him, opened the gate. Justa Bob felt no pain, and so the possibility of pain receded even further, and he allowed himself to forget about it.

William Vance, who only dimly understood this process, was patient nevertheless. Like Justa Bob, he had a sense. He could stand inside the personal space of a horse and know what was there—intelligence, a good disposition, ready forgiveness, curiosity, pleasure in work. All of these he sensed in Justa Bob to an unusual degree. That didn't make him any more certain that he would earn back what the horse had cost him, but it did fill him with gladness that he had spent the money. Later, when they had finished their journey from

Missouri to Chicago, he put him in a good stall, between a couple of nice geld-ings whose owners always had carrots and liked to make much of their ani-mals. And even though he tried not to, he took a special interest in him, stopping to talk to him a little more than the others, giving him a carrot him-self from time to time. The adventure that was always the same and always fresh, finding out about a new horse, began again. Made William Vance feel a little happier all over.

46 / A MAIDEN

INSIDE HER STALL, behind the metal-mesh stall guard, Froney's Sis stared at the assembled group with interest and pleasure. The warning sign posted both on the stall guard and on the wall beside the stall indicated that the filly could not be approached, at least by strangers—she was racing today. Joy always thought those signs were like "No Trespassing" signs. They regis-tered the trainer's intent, but didn't do anything actually to protect the horse from interference. Her support network did that, and here they all were, Joy herself, Farley, Oliver, the groom, the exercise rider, Elizabeth, Plato, Mr. Tompkins, who had been in L.A. on other business, and, of course, Mr. T. This was the filly's third start, a maiden special weight for two-year-old fillies, six-teen thousand dollars. In the *Form,* next to the filly's record, the handicapper had written, "Why do they keep racing this filly?" They had agreed that he had just overlooked her last start—she had run fifth, beating two other fillies.

But it didn't matter what anyone said, or that the morning line on her was thirty to one. Every day, there was some horse who had a morning line of thirty to one.

"Okay," said Farley, looking at his watch. "Time to get her out there." Oliver unlatched the stall guard, and the groom went in, speaking softly. Mr. T. stood calmly in his assigned spot. Elizabeth was looking at him. Farley said to Mr. Tompkins, "This filly is easily frightened, so we give her a very strict ritual, so that she always knows what's going to happen next. For example, Umberto, the groom, never approaches her without speaking to her, always halters her in the same way, always tacks her up in a certain order. When she goes out to train with Mr. T. here, they always go at the same time of day, and in the same order—him in front of the line, her just behind him. They always take the same path to get where they want to go."

"Sounds like you're indulging her, to me," said Mr. Tompkins.

"I am," said Farley, "but it's worked. It's the only thing that's worked."

"Her head fills up with fog," said Elizabeth, helpfully.

"What?" said Mr. Tompkins. "Who are you?" Joy noticed that Mr. Tompkins was actually taller than Elizabeth, and broader, too. She hadn't thought of anyone as bigger than Elizabeth.

"We've met before, in the summer, but perhaps you don't remember that occasion. I am an animal communicator. I've communicated with her. If she gets outside boundaries that she understands, her head fills up with fog."

Mr. Tompkins looked at Elizabeth, his face a blank, for about three steps (they were going out of the barn now), then he said, "You're a horse psychic?"

"Yes, I suppose."

"Who's going to win this race?"

"I don't know. I'm not a seer or a prophet. I'm just an animal communicator."

"I've had racehorses for forty years," said Mr. Tompkins. "I've never—"

"She's an unusual filly," said Farley.

"Oh," said Mr. Tompkins, his face perking up.

"Not unusually talented," said Farley.

Mr. Tompkins' face fell.

"Just unusual."

"Then why train her?"

"Because it's interesting," said Farley. Joy smiled at him. The timbre of his voice was often enough for her. He didn't have to be talking to her or attending to her in any way, but his voice vibrated right through her, setting up a harmonic effect. In her last relationship, with Dean, back at the university, nothing had ever been quite enough, either for him or from him, but this was much different. There was no waiting or wishing for the next thing, only being grateful right then, as she was right now just to hear him talk to Mr. Tompkins.

"Who are you?" said Mr. Tompkins to Plato.

"I am a futurologist."

"Is the horse going to win the race?"

"Futurology is not equipped to track either a small sample or an immediate event."

"What is it equipped to track?"

"The course of your family's fortunes over the next fifty years, or maybe a hundred, depending on the model and the precision of your tracking requirements."

"Do you work at the track, too? You sound like one of those guys with a betting system and no money."

"I am an assistant professor at Berkeley."

Farley had dropped behind the two men and now took Joy's hand. Soon enough after that, he took his hand out of hers and slipped his arm around her shoulders. As they walked along, she found herself getting closer and closer to him, as if, contrary to the very thing she had just been thinking, there was no getting enough. This sort of behavior was a shameless, daring thing to do at the racetrack, where gossip and teasing were the rule and sentiment was dangerous to feel and dangerous to show, but they did it anyway—open, endless, glorious affection.

"Have you investigated the course of my family's fortunes over the next fifty years?" said Mr. Tompkins.

"I used the public data in an experiment I did for a paper, yes. There were other families, too. Rockefeller. Milken. McCaw."

"How'd we do?"

"Fine, but there were unknown personal factors."

"Such as?"

"Whether your children from your first marriage are planning to contest the ownership of family property with your children from your second marriage. That sort of thing drains resources very quickly, and they are usually unrecoverable."

"Why would they?"

"They often do. In the majority of cases where the worth of the assets is over a hundred million dollars, it's almost a given."

"How can I stop them?"

"That was not an element of my model."

"Why didn't you call me and warn me about this?"

"The experiment wasn't about you, Mr. Tompkins. It was about the model. I wanted to see how it worked and what it said. You were just data."

"Oh," said Mr. Tompkins.

"It was my dissertation."

"Got you," said Mr. Tompkins.

Farley said, "This filly looks good. When she came off the farm she was little and weedy, but look at her. She's blossomed with the work. That's a good sign." Joy's ear was so close to his chest that she thought she felt the resonance of his words rather than heard them.

Mr. Tompkins gazed at Mr. T., then said, "So this guy's had a happy ending."

"Yes, sir," said Joy.

"Must like it back at the track," said Mr. Tompkins.

"He has an effective betting system, but no money of his own," said Elizabeth.

"Does he think this filly is going to win this race?" Joy noticed that when Mr. Tompkins looked at Elizabeth he seemed a little intimidated.

Elizabeth glanced at Mr. T., who was strolling along. They were almost to the place where he had to turn back. He wasn't allowed to cast an eye over the horses in the saddling enclosure like the other bettors. Joy gave a little cough, but Mr. Tompkins really was regarding Elizabeth with fascination. Finally, she said, "He says you never can tell. He's streaming me a picture of a straight green place with rails on each side and big white buildings."

"Longchamp," said Farley and Mr. Tompkins simultaneously.

"He's galloping behind another horse and overtaking him, and then a dog runs out of the stands, and, let's see, it seems to scare the other horse, who bumps Mr. T., and so they go off to the side, kind of, and then another horse comes from the far left and beats them."

"That's possible," said Mr. Tompkins. "The French take their dogs everywhere. But what about this race?"

"He has to stay here," said Elizabeth, "but usually I go look at the horses, and then we discuss them, and then I make my bets."

"You're kidding," said Mr. Tompkins.

"I'm in the black for the year," said Elizabeth. "Way in the black. Plato and I went to sex school in Hawaii on my winnings of the spring."

"Sex school?"

"You know, Tantric yoga. Penetrating your chakras with rosebuds and turning them clockwise and counterclockwise? That sort of thing. It was very informative."

"Fun, too," said Plato.

"Thank you, Mr. T.," said Elizabeth. Mr. T. paused, halted, turned back. As he walked away from the filly, she turned her head and gave a plaintive whinny.

They kept her walking. "She's not as afraid as she was," said Joy. "She used to rear and spin when he left."

Elizabeth looked in her handbag, pulled out a tissue, blew her nose. "We're trying to get her to reinterpret her world."

"What does he say about my children and my wife?" said Mr. Tompkins.

Elizabeth paused. Then she said, "He wants to know how many mares are in your band, and whether your children are weaned or not."

"Really?"

"No. He has nothing to say about your estate-planning problems."

They entered the saddling enclosure as a group. Joy felt herself separate from Farley as they had to to do their business. The groom walked the filly around the slots exactly twice before walking her into her slot, number five. There were six other fillies in the race. Froney's Sis stood with her head up and her ears pricked, staring tensely around her at the other runners. The support network closed in on her, and the groom began unwrapping her legs. Oliver put the numbercloth over her back. No one said anything except the groom, who murmured continuously. Farley set the saddle on the filly's back, counted to three, reached under for the girth, which Oliver handed him. Joy stood at her head, stroking her ears and forehead lightly with her fingertips. She seemed to feel Farley's every movement through the filly's body. When he was done, he stood back and the groom led her out again, and he came back over to Joy and took her hand. What if, Joy thought, this contact were to end? What if that? After a bit, the jockeys began to come out of the jockey room. Roberto Acevedo, the jockey they always used, approached them with a smile. Farley introduced him to Mr. Tompkins.

In the walking ring, they surrounded the filly again while Farley threw Roberto up into the saddle. Mr. Tompkins took Elizabeth's elbow and said, "What's the word?"

"Well," said Elizabeth, "he says they're a mixed bunch. He's seen all of them train at one time or another, though the number-six filly he's only seen once, but she's long-legged and awkward, the kind who has some growing to do. He doesn't think much of her."

"She's five-to-two."

"I never pay attention to human handicappers. This one he considers a turf horse, not suited to the conditions of the race. He doesn't give her much chance."

"My head is spinning."

"Maybe I should just give you his bets. Our filly to win, number two to place, and number seven to show. I'm going to bet a three-way box myself. Fifty bucks."

The whole group of them followed the filly out of the walking ring and under the stands, and then Elizabeth and Mr. Tompkins peeled off to go to the betting windows.

The tote board had Froney's Sis's odds at sixty-to-one, but by the time they were sitting down, they had dropped to forty-to-one. Joy said, "What's he doing?" Actually, conversation between them seemed superfluous to Joy.

Farley laughed. "You know, if I ever saw Tompkins bet twenty dollars on a horse, I don't know when it was. But look at the money bet on her. It went from twenty-three hundred to seventy-five hundred. I didn't know Elizabeth was such a persuasive person."

Out on the track, the filly was jogging calmly with her pony, not looking around, not jerking her head, not even flicking her ears. She had grayed out pretty well over the summer, and built up muscle, too. Plato said, "Elizabeth is the most persuasive person I ever met. I hope she's persuading Mr. Tompkins to give me a job."

"You've got a job," Joy pointed out. "At Berkeley. Isn't that good?"

"I prefer the Tompkins life-style to the Berkeley life-style. Don't forget, I was a commodities trader in Chicago. I feel that a change is coming over me again."

Farley said, "You know, I feel a change is coming over me, too. I'm beginning to have a notion of an idea of a thought of a hope for this filly. She looks happy. There she goes, right into the gate."

"You know," said Plato, "horse racing is the perfect sport of capitalism. In every race, one horse wins, and then everyone discusses it—was it luck, or ability, or strategy, or breeding? And then there's another race, and another horse wins, probably a horse who lost last time. In the microcosm, the structure is very strict, but in the macrocosm, the structure is very forgiving."

Elizabeth and Mr. Tompkins joined them right then, as the gate opened and the seven maidens headed down the track. It was a lovely race, at least from their point of view. The gray filly broke smoothly, right alongside the big chestnut, and the two of them moved to the rail, the chestnut on the outside, Froney's Sis on the inside. The chestnut was a reliable, straight runner, and Roberto was able to use her as protection for his filly. Froney's Sis, used to the same sort of protection and steadiness and size from Mr. T., seemed to match the other filly stride for stride, and when the chestnut tried to pull ahead, she could not. In the meantime, the front runner dropped back, and, coming around the turn, four of them found themselves in a bunch. Farley said, "Fractions aren't bad, either. Maybe this filly can run."

As they came into the stretch, Joy saw Roberto ask the filly to make a decision. The other fillies had choices to make, too, about whether they were too tired. And the big filly was. She dropped back. The lead filly was, too. She dropped back. Now Froney's Sis was running just half a length behind the favorite, a bay filly by Deputy Minister who had class flowing over and around her like the jet stream—Mabee was her owner, Baffert was her trainer, Stevens was her rider. This was only her second start, and she had run third in her first start. She owned this race. Except that, for some equine reason to be investigated later, Froney's Sis dropped and stretched and at the wire was ahead by a neck.

The tote flashed "photo," but that was for third and fourth place. Right there, right in front of them, the filly's number, five, went up easy as you please.

Farley said to Mr. Tompkins, "How much did you bet?" He gave Joy a squeeze.

Mr. Tompkins, never daunted by mere sums of money, said, "Oh. Five thousand. That was what I had in my pocket, and Elizabeth said I should just reach into my pocket and bet what I came up with. I forgot I had that, but I—"

Plato said, "You won two hundred thousand dollars."

"Yes, I did."

"I won fifteen thousand dollars myself," said Elizabeth, "since I hit the trifecta."

Plato said, "You know, Mr. Tompkins, I was wondering how you feel about the question of the concentration of income and assets in the hands of a very small percentage of the population."

"Well," said Mr. Tompkins, "I'll tell you. The more I spend, the more I earn. I don't know why this is."

"Karma," said Elizabeth. "Dharma, too."

"What do you mean?"

"Well, it is your dharmic purpose in life to be swimming in dough. Maybe in your last life you starved to death or something, and so you chose the Tompkins family to be born into so you could get a square meal. Something like that. Are you tired of all this money?"

"Well, yeah. My kids talk about it too much, that's what I'm tired of."

"Could I," said Plato, "could I interrupt, sir, to ask you for a job?"

"Doing what?"

"Future management. Orienteering. Mapping the unknown dimension of time. Theory and application both. I could be your house intellectual in a very new field."

"What sort of salary do you want?"

"Two hundred grand would be nice in the first year."

Mr. Tompkins cleared his throat. The filly was trotting back toward the winner's circle, evidently pleased with herself. Mr. Tompkins watched her for a moment as Umberto went up to her and took hold of her bridle. He said, "All right. I don't understand half of what you're saying, but if you can do this one thing, you got the job. Go to the big payout window with this ticket. They know me, and they'd take half of it away from me right there, but they don't know you. Get the money and bring it back. Whatever you get you can have as your first year's salary. You can take care of the taxes on your own. I have to go to the can after this photo."

They got up and went down to the winner's circle, all of them. Just as the photographer was taking the picture, Elizabeth said, "Well, back to Hawaii in March for the intermediate-level course."

Farley smiled down at Joy and stroked her cheek. She decided for the umpteenth time not to wonder what she had done to deserve all of this.

NOVEMBER

47 / BREEDERS' CUP

A L WAS DRINKING COFFEE and reading the *New York Times*. His knee hurt, his head hurt, his shoulder hurt, his back hurt, his big toe hurt, and one of his molars hurt. He wondered if it was too early to wake up Rosalind and complain to her. Last night they'd had a word or two about the Breeders' Cup, this year at Churchill Downs, not so very far away, and they could have stayed at that bed and breakfast in Versailles, what was the name of it, but where was Laurita? Where was his trainer? Where, for that matter, was his helpmeet? Yes, she was in bed, but where was she with regard to this, his dearest wish? Al drank the last of his cup and poured himself another one, then reached for a doughnut. He had already been out this morning, on his own, in the Mercedes, and while out, he had bought doughnuts, the very worst possible thing for his heart, arteries, stomach, colon, you name it. He looked at the doughnut, number four, and the doughnut looked good—orange frosting and black sprinkles. A doughnut like that was almost as good as a drink. He looked in the box. He had also chosen a blue doughnut and a pink doughnut. They were there, waiting for him. Regression to childish appetites, he understood from his AA group, was often the recourse for those who did not get their way. Maybe so, but the doughnut (Al took a big bite) was fantastic.

On this particular morning, the morning of the biggest day of the year in horse racing, Al would have liked it to be duly noted by his trainer and his wife that he was a saint. He had let this thing go by that they had had together. He had said nothing about it but had been *understanding* and *forbearing*. He had made a real effort to overlook the injury done to himself, Alexander P. Maybrick. He had opened his eyes, which was what his first wife was always telling him to do—open your eyes, Al, wake up and smell the coffee—and seen that Rosalind was at least as unhappy as he was, and, okay, Dick, too, with that weird wife of his, no wonder someone like Rosalind would appeal to him. He had brought the whole thing up in his AA meeting several times, had been counseled to be grateful and do nothing, and he had been grateful—sincerely grateful that Rosalind hadn't left him when she very well could have and even, it was implied by a few, should have; she would not be widely blamed for doing so, but probably consoled and admired for putting up with him for so long—and he had done nothing. But not only was there no acknowledgment of his sainthood on the part of either Rosalind or the horse-trainer, there wasn't even much sympathy for the fact that he once again did not have a horse running in the Breeders' Cup. Laurita's excellent spring and summer had been followed by a lackluster fall—two starts, no wins, and then a condylar fracture, and there you had it. What got his goat was their tone. They were impatient with his disappointment. Al thought, and he was sure even his AA group would agree with him, that, given the events of the last year, they could cut him a little slack, be a little sympathetic. A major betrayal didn't have to be accompanied by a minor one. Injury didn't have to be accompanied by insult. Al felt himself steam up in a way that not even the doughnuts could ameliorate.

He thought he would go down to the City and watch the races at some anonymous OTB shop. He thought he would leave without telling Rosalind, but he wondered if she would even know he was gone.

AT THE FARM in Maryland where Limitless was still cultivating his own concept of himself, it had been rainy and chill all week, so the horses were kept in at night. The fields were muddy, there was no grass to speak of; it was better in every way for the horses to be eating nutritious first-cutting hay. The barns were airy and convenient, the training facilities perfectly thought out, the staff intelligent and experienced. Night after night, Limitless tore up his stall furnishings. He sat on his automatic waterer until they removed it altogether and put in a bucket, but he managed to get that off the wall, too, along with the corner feeder. He tore that down three times, so they started feeding him out of a rubber feed tub, but you could see him with that—as soon as he'd taken a bite or two, he'd pick it up in his teeth and flip it over. He made a lot of noise. The stableman whose apartment was in that barn woke up two or three times a night at the kicking and pounding. The morning of the Breeders' Cup, they got up to find that he had taken down the entire wall between his stall and the one next door. The two horses were uninjured, but had switched places. It almost gave the stableman a heart attack when he saw the two faces looking at him over the wrong doors. The wall rebuilt, Limitless pawed at the straw, the clay floor, the decomposed granite beneath it, as if tunneling to freedom. Breeders' Cup day, they let him out. Yes, the footing was treacherous, and, no, there wasn't anywhere good to put him, only a big drylot without any protection from the weather at all. He ran and ran, mane flying, tail in the air, stopping, turning, kicking up his heels. As a rule, you don't like to see a horse run like that—anything could happen—but Limitless had made his point. The farm manager and owner agreed that he could live out for the winter.

IT WAS RAINY and chill on the backside at Pimlico, too, where Tiffany was bedding the stall of Hopefully, a four-year-old gelding who was out galloping and would be back in twenty minutes or so. She had dragged the bale of straw into the stall, and now took out her knife and cut the baling twine. The straw, golden and clean smelling, popped apart. Tiffany put away her knife and picked up her fork and began poking the flakes of straw and tossing them. Deirdre liked the straw to be deep all around, and mounded up against the walls in a big cozy nest. Tiffany wasn't thinking about the Breeders' Cup, or about anything else. She was just poking and tossing and hearing the comforting rustle of the dry stalks, feeling the now familiar wooden handle of the fork in her hands, bending and stretching and lifting. Bedding stalls was almost as pleasant as rubbing the horses. First you attached the horse by his halter to a tether in his stall, then you took the black rubber currycomb and made small circles all over his body from his ears to his tail, but never on his legs. Then you brushed him down with a stiff brush, this time including his legs. Then you brushed him down with a soft brush. That was when you did his face, down the nose, around the ears, under the jaw. Usually they turned their heads toward you for that, even the ones who didn't like currying and brushing. Then you stood on his left side, facing the back, and picked up his feet and cleaned them out with a metal hook called a hoofpick. Then you combed his mane and forelock and picked the tangles out of his tail. And then you woke up and noticed that fifteen minutes or twenty minutes had passed and not only did you feel kind of warm and buzzed inside, the horse looked shiny and neat. It was just the way Tiffany had thought it would be at Dagoberto's when she was begging Dagoberto to let her get closer to the horses. As close to the horses as possible was exactly where she wanted to be, close enough to touch them and pet them and hear their jaws masticating hay and their bellies gurgling and the air moving in and out of their nostrils. And the Breeders' Cup had nothing to do with it.

ROSALIND GOT OUT OF BED, sat down at her desk, read over entries for all the races at Churchill, then took out a sheet of stationery, and quickly wrote down seven names: Silverbulletday, Answer Lively, Reraise, Da Hoss, Escena, Buck's Boy, and Awesome Again. Then she sealed them into an envelope and signed her name across the back of it. She slipped it into a drawer in her desk and locked the drawer. Eileen, who had been under the covers, jumped off the bed, stretched, and went out into the hallway. Rosalind barely noticed. She was thinking that she knew horses now. What it felt like was that somehow all those years of being around Al and Dick and the trainers they had before, all those years of going to the races and going to the backside and listening to them all talk, had not been wasted, but had been waiting for a slot in her brain. Making that space for Dick, painful as it was, had made that other space, too.

It was clear from the shadow of an argument that she and Al had had the night before that Al was on to her. That, in itself, was an embarrassing dilemma, and Rosalind felt exposed. Feeling exposed led to several other unpleasant feelings—shame, grief, ambivalence, fear. All of these feelings had their ignoble side. In the case of the fear, the ignoble side was just about the only side it had. Fear was most certainly always about not getting away with something, that's what it looked like to her now.

She got up from her desk and went into her walk-in closet, where, in accordance with her usual habit, she assayed her pale, elegant, expensive wardrobe and decided what to wear. Except today these clothes had a distinct fleeting quality about them, as if they were not hers, as if even choosing, buying, appreciating, and wearing them, having them mold themselves to her body, had not quite established her possession of them. It gave her a moment of vertigo, and she leaned against the door.

ROBERTO ACEVEDO was in the hospital with three broken ribs from a training accident at Hollywood Park just the day before. The colt jerked away from him, tossed his head, and fell over the inside rail. It was a freak accident, and Roberto's first real injury. The horse got right up, unhurt. Roberto was five three and a quarter now, seventeen years old, 115 pounds, hungry hungry hungry. He didn't have long, so he planned to be out of his hospital bed by that evening and back on a horse Monday. Normally, with training and race riding, he averaged eight horses a day. As a concession to his injuries, he planned to cut back to six. For inspiration on this score, he read Dick Francis novels. He had one right there in the hospital with him, mostly about landscape painting, but a little bit about horses, too. He had read so many of them by now that he knew perfectly well what he was going to do after he hit five four, 120 pounds. He planned to go to England and become the first Mexican steeplechase jockey to win the Cheltenham Gold Cup.

<hr>

HAVING DECIDED on an activity for the day, and a strategy of demonstrating his dissatisfaction by leaving without telling anyone, Al got up from the breakfast counter and took his coffee cup to the sink, where he turned the water on low and ran some into the cup. Eileen entered the kitchen and leapt silently onto the breakfast counter, making it on the first try.

AUDREY, WHO HAD just had her thirteenth birthday, got up before dawn. She had the special editions of the *Thoroughbred Times, The Blood-Horse,* and the *New York Times.* She had also culled from the Internet every article about the Breeders' Cup and printed them out. The first thing she noticed was that that jockey, Roberto Acevedo, was not riding any of the California horses, which was a bit disappointing. However, she favored Da Hoss in the Mile, Silverbulletday in the Juvenile Fillies, Escena in the Distaff, Buck's Boy in the Turf, and Skip Away in the Classic, but it would be foolish, she thought, to bet against entry one in the Classic, three excellent horses running as one betting interest. And there was considerable doubt in her mind about whether Skip Away could handle the footing at Churchill. He'd had trouble there before. Her mother wasn't even awake yet, but Audrey was dressed, lying on her bed, weighing her bets.

In the pre-dawn dark, she could sometimes hear her father's voice in her head, as she had often heard it when he was alive. He'd always gotten up between four and five, made himself coffee, gotten ready to go for a run, hummed or talked to himself, checked on her, given her a kiss, straightened her covers over her. He knew nothing of the house they lived in now, nothing of her school or the stable where she took riding lessons, or her new friends. But a year ago they had talked about Skip Away, the wonderful gray, all morning before he went to work, and then he had called her from the office and they had watched the race together. When he came home, he had a surprise for her, the forty-six dollars he had won on the race in the office betting pool. Now, besides herself and her mother, of course, Skip Away was about the only thing unchanged between last year and this. Audrey sat up and looked at the horse's picture again, then lay down and closed her eyes.

AL TURNED from the sink just in time to see Eileen remove the pink doughnut from the open box and, head high, trot across the counter and leap to the floor. The most maddening thing was that she would trot in that off-hand way, her insolent comma of a tail pointing in the air, and his only intention, at first, was to make the little bitch run for her life.

JUSTA BOB WAS eating his morning hay. He had galloped four furlongs and trotted out four furlongs and was pleasantly fatigued.

ELIZABETH AND PLATO had taken advantage of his regular 4:00 a.m. erection. After they made love and he turned over to go back to sleep, she got up, energized, and went into his new kitchen (he no longer lived in Berkeley, but in a nice condo in Fresno) and had her favorite breakfast—white-corn tortilla chips with parmesan-jalapeño-artichoke dip and a bowl of matzo-ball soup. Today she planned to begin her chapter on non-reactive child-rearing. While she was eating, she realized that the first line would be "As soon as your child can talk, you may teach him to say to you, when you are angry, 'Mommy, what are you afraid of?' " After she wrote that down, she went out in her robe and picked up the paper in the driveway. She turned at once to the sports section. Coverage was pretty minimal, but that was okay, she had made her picks. Mr. T. had no access to information about many of the horses in the Breeders' Cup—no way to judge between Skip Away, whom he didn't know, and horses he had seen. And he himself had never raced at Churchill Downs, so he had no comment to make on the footing. The problem with a betting system devised by a horse, Elizabeth reflected, was that it was very immediate—there weren't many patterns you could extrapolate as general principles. But Mr. T. wasn't big on general principles as a rule—it was only because he was a gelding that you managed to get any larger perspective at all.

FOR ROSALIND, the first question was not what was Eileen doing and why was Al yelling, but how had a pink doughnut gotten into the house? That was the very thing that was going through her mind when Al put his hands on her shoulders and came very close to shaking her but did not. Instead, he took his hands down off her shoulders without hardly gripping her. Contact had been made for, at the most, half a second. She knew that even while their gazes locked and they stood there at the door of the bedroom, staring at one another. But she had felt his strength, anyway, the difference between her weight and his, the difference between her size and his, the difference between her gender and his, all of that information passing as if digitized between them. She made herself look away, down the long hallway toward the kitchen, the richness of the floors and the Persians, the wintry light falling through the windows, the dark uprights of the doorposts and the window frames, everything solid and stationary and quiet. She recognized that the moment to be afraid was already over, and she took a deep breath.

AUDREY'S NEW riding instructor, Ellen, picked her up in the Cherokee. With her were some people Audrey didn't know, and Audrey kept her mouth shut, a little disappointed. But as they drove, the horse talk rolled and splashed and bubbled around her, and she had her money and her picks, and when she talked about them, the Irish one, Deirdre, who turned out to be a horse-trainer at Pimlico, thought they were good ones. The other one, Tiffany, owned some horses in New York and was working for Deirdre and was really pretty, too. Of course she could almost sense her father in the car with them as they drove to the simulcast, and when she mentioned this, that her father took her to Pimlico four times, Deirdre gave her a little squeeze around the shoulders, and she realized that they all had talked about her before coming, and they all knew that her father was dead, and at first that bothered her, but then it was almost comforting.

THE ONLY THING Sir Michael Ordway liked about parties anymore was the remote possibility that *she* would turn up. He used to be interested in the rest of *them,* but the beauty died, and one by one he got jaded, the way you do. *She* was the last, most piquant pleasure. He looked for her at every gathering, his expectation feeding on the very knowledge that *she* couldn't possibly show up, until he got himself into a bit of a fever about the whole thing. It was just like the only thing he liked about life anymore—which mogul, at any moment, could he sell a horse to? It was so easy, selling racehorses to moguls. He'd sold horses to software, hardware, stocks and bonds, of course they were naturals, lingerie, cosmetics, toys, golf-course developments, commercial rentals, American trailer parks, rock and roll, rap, hip-hop, and Bach (a cheap horse, a hard sell, a challenge met). He'd sold a horse to every enterprise except maybe French Deconstructionism, and that was just because the Deconstructionist had had a heart attack before he sent the check. Every sucker (American word, he liked it) got what he paid for—four legs and a fantasy. He watched the door. *She* was in Scotland, last he heard. He wondered who *she* favored in the American race. He sipped from his glass of wine. He talked, as always. Sometimes he checked in on his talking with his actual brain. It was a good party, moguls abounding. And then there *she* was. *She* had not come in by the door, but perhaps through the roof, from the Empyrean. *She* was there, across the room. *She* was carrying her handbag. *She* was smiling. *She* was there. "Sir Michael," *she* said. "Your Majesty," he replied. "Are you well?" *she* said. "Very well," he replied. "You know," he said. "Yes," *she* replied. "I know a lovely colt by Land of Magic that might be available. Remember him?" he asked. "I do," *she* said.

WHAT HAPPENED WAS, Buddy said to his wife one day that on Breeders' Cup day he wanted to be as far away from the whole deal as he could possibly be, and so, two days ago, they arrived here, on the Big Island of Hawaii, about three arduous miles back into a jungle canyon at the northern end of the island. Buddy, a man without inner resources, had been asleep more or less since they arrived. The suites were treehouses and, of course, had no television or newspapers. Before they left Pasadena, she had removed all copies of horse magazines from his suitcase. They had also brought their own food, which was converting itself to mold before her very eyes. As she sat gazing at him and listening to the waterfall outside, scenting the mildew that rose from their sheets, Buddy's wife was not quite sure that this was the place she should have chosen, but tomorrow, after the dangerous day was over, they would be moving to the Mauna Lani, a real resort, where she would no longer have to ponder her own lack of inner resources, where she could buy some magazines, go shopping, call the children, and get away from Buddy, who must have been better company thirty years ago, but maybe not.

AL PUT HIS HANDS behind his back, though he knew they were no longer a danger to him, and he held Rosalind's gaze as long as she held his. When she turned away, he looked down. He knew she knew that all his force, whatever that was, had risen up against her, a thing he had thought impossible, and he knew that she knew that it had now converted, every last molecule, from anger to shame. He said, "I need some shoes," and he stepped past her into the bedroom, and then into his closet.

"WELL, LET'S SEE," said Sam the vet. He was at Home Depot, in the plumbing department. The young man, say twenty-five, that he was talking to looked rather new on the job, willing but nervous. Sam sniffed and rubbed his cheek with his hand in that old-Vermonter way. "Yes," said the young man.

"How about a nice four-inch PVC connector, about twelve inches long, you know, for a septic connection." Sam could see these out of the corner of his eye, and sure enough, the young man went over to the bin and pulled one out. "Oh, that's good," said Sam. "That one-and-a-half-inch joint there. Isn't that it? Why don't you measure that?"

The young man got out his tape measure and measured the diameter of the offshoot. He said, "That's right, sir. One and a half inches."

"Good. Here we go." Sam pulled a length of vinyl sleeve out of the pocket of his coat and fitted it over the end of the pipe, folded it back, slipped it through, folded the other end back over the other end of the pipe. He said, "How does that look?" He held it up to the young man, who looked through it. "Fine, sir," he said.

"Good," said Sam. "Now, let's see, we need a reducer for this part"—he pointed to the end of the offshoot—"and a screw-in valve. See, we have to be able to take the valve off and fill the outside of the sleeve with warm water, and then put the valve back on, and then, if it's too tight, we have to be able to let off some of the pressure."

"The pressure?"

"The pressure on the penis."

"Oh." The young man looked at him without moving, so Sam began looking through bins. He said, "You know, a valve like a valve for a bicycle tire."

"Oh. Yes. Well, let's see." He turned his head, but Sam, who knew where they were because he'd done this before, walked over to a bin and picked one up. "Oh, yeah," he said. He handed the young man the length of pipe, saying, "You hold this." Then he began screwing the reducer and the valve into the offshoot. "There we go," he said. "Now, you see, if you need to, you can just let a little bit of the water out, and it doesn't hurt. All we need now is a nice tight cover for the end, so that none of the collection drips out."

"The collection?"

"Right. But we want it soft, so that he can bump against it without hurting himself."

"Who?"

Sam turned away with a smile, pretending not to hear this question. He found a cap for the pipe, and said, "Maybe I'll just pad this. Got any foam rubber?"

"That would be in building supplies, sir."

Sam took the PVC pipe out of the young man's hands. "Well, thank you very much. I think the other things I need are probably in building supplies." He turned away, slowly. Sometimes they didn't ask.

But this fellow said, "Who's going to bump against the end?" And then, "What is it?"

"What, this?" Now Sam was smiling.

The kid nodded.

"It's an artificial vagina for a miniature horse."

"A what?"

Sam made an effort to be loud and clear. "An ar-ti-fi-cial va-gi-na. Looks great. Thanks for your help."

"Thank you for coming in, sir."

The fact was, it wasn't really the breeding season yet, but, Sam thought as he walked to his truck a few minutes later, nothing wrong with being prepared.

AFTER AL WENT OUT, getting into the Mercedes on his own and driving off to God knew where, Rosalind thought she should have said something. What she had done, turned and left the room, gone into the living room and then out into the dormant garden, was just the sort of thing that she would do. She had never been quick of wit, or quick to speak. She had always thought that giving people time to regain their composure was the absolutely best course in any crisis. And, then again, she hadn't really been in the wrong for several decades, and so even apologizing, truly apologizing, was unfamiliar to her. It was only while she was out in the garden, after Al drove off, that she realized that an apology was appropriate. The trouble was that even in the garden, by herself, with Al miles away, it was hard to form the words. "I'm sorry" wasn't so hard, but identifying what she was sorry for was. In fact, she was mostly sorry that she had made herself so unhappy, that things hadn't worked out, that nothing had come of so much inner turmoil. Her betrayal of Al seemed rather a distant and manageable side-effect to the central drama, so to look him in the eye and apologize seemed rather insincere, an effect of fear rather than love. And she suddenly wished for someone to talk to about this, if only to register that at least she was being honest with herself, and recognizing her motives for what they were.

RESIDUAL, BACK AT WORK, put in a lightning three furlongs for Leon and Deedee. They agreed afterwards that they had this filly figured out. With Deedee sitting right there, Leon called the owner and told her how marvelously the filly was doing, how healthy and happy she looked, how Buddy was on vacation. The owner was *very* friendly, thanked Leon for keeping her in the picture, and said in a whispery voice, "In some ways, dear, I wish you were her trainer. Buddy is a genius, of course, but you're the one she likes." Leon pretended to ignore this, and said only, "I know Buddy is a little lax about communicating, Mrs. Warren, but he means well. He just has so many horses and owners."

After Leon hung up, he and Deedee smiled happily at one another for several minutes. Buddy seemed to play into their hands in every way these days. Even the close call they'd thought they had in the summer, when Leon tipped off that guy from the *Racing Form* and he told all those other guys and they showed up *that day*, turned out okay. Buddy blew his stack, but then he was so glad to get rid of Epic Steam he forgot about it. Leon said, "Next year, it could be us in the Breeders' Cup, you know."

Deedee took Leon's hand tenderly in both of hers and told him she was pregnant.

HERMAN NEWMAN was sitting in front of the television, watching the Breeders' Cup show and trying to learn something. There were all different kinds of races. The Classic had a purse, he read, of five million dollars and change. That was three million to the winner. That was something, Herman Newman thought. That was certainly something. Just then, the phone rang, and Sir Michael, out of the blue, asked him if he would like to sell Epic Steam to the Queen of England. Herman looked around for his wife, but she had gone out into the kitchen. What he wanted her to do was to take the phone and hear for herself what Sir Michael had to say, because he thought she would never believe this in a million years, but he just said he would think about it. That's what he always said. He liked to work his way through the pros and cons on everything. After he hung up the phone, he sat at his desk, remembering his grandfather telling him how, one day when he was walking down the street in St. Petersburg in 1910, he saw his apartment explode in front of his very eyes. That night he hid out with his friend V. I. Lenin. As the horses on TV paraded to the post for the sprint, Herman wondered if this episode of family lore should have any bearing upon his decision whether or not to sell his horse to the Queen of England.

AL HADN'T ACTUALLY tried to find a parking space in Manhattan for several years. Driving around in the Mercedes, Third Avenue to Park, Fifty-fifth Street to Fifty-eighth, around and around, he couldn't shake the notion that someone else could be, *should be,* finding this parking space for him. He resented that he had to find it himself and kept thinking that all he had to do was tell someone to find him a parking place, his partner, his accountant, his driver, his other partner, his secretary, Rosalind, and a parking space would be found. There were, of course, parking garages. There was a parking garage at his office building at Thirty-fourth Street and Sixth Avenue that he could go into for free, but he had standards. If he wanted a parking space in the Fifties, he wanted a parking space in the Fifties. Al realized that he was devolving. It was like watching something expensive, one of those Chinese vases Rosalind had put in their living room, fall off the shelf. You brushed past it and continued on your way, only to turn around and see it tip, tip more, launch itself into mid-air. That's where he was, in mid-air, moments away from the inevitable fragmentation.

FARLEY WAS OUT on the track with the last set, and Joy was fussing around Mr. T.'s and the filly's stalls. The TV was on in the office, and they were doing the intro to the Juvenile Fillies. She went into the office from time to time to see if the post parade had begun. It still amazed her that there were horses and people she had seen around this very track getting ready for that race, a race Farley himself had gotten ready for four years before, when the race was run also at Churchill Downs and he had had a good daughter of Kenmare named Kennett Square, who had run sixth.

Joy was not exactly an exercise rider and not exactly an assistant trainer. She didn't exactly work for Farley and she didn't exactly work for Mr. Tompkins, but she was happy in her job. She took care of Mr. T., of course, but she also took care of some other special cases. For example, after Joy pointed out to Farley that high-level dressage horses and fit open jumpers often got taken out twice a day rather than once, he set her to ponying two of the three-year-olds around the training track in the afternoon. He also used her riding skills. Horses who were out of balance and unsure of themselves got a little dressage work to develop their back muscles. So, including Mr. T., she was riding three or four horses a day, taking another one or two for hand walks. She talked to owners and their wives, she answered the phone, she went to sales with him, did some minor vet care. Just a week ago, on the first of the month, she had given up her own apartment and moved her things into his condo. She'd hardly noticed the change, except that there was more unnecessary stuff underfoot. Six months ago, when she wondered what love was, Joy didn't realize that it would turn out to be easy and peaceful and friendly and interesting.

Now the horses in the third set began to come back from the track. Joy ducked into the office and saw that the post parade was on. There was Silverbulletday, Mr. T.'s favorite in the Juvenile Fillies, but she herself favored Excellent Meeting. She didn't have to see Farley come into the office, or hear him speak; as he entered, the office filled up with his gravity and she moved into his orbit automatically. He took her hand and said, "I've always liked Silverbullet-day." He was, she thought, where love was concentrated, where that thing, normally vaporous and thin and unstable, collected and solidified, and what small wandering object like herself would not be drawn right to it?

AFTER THE TURF RACE, Herman Newman decided not to sell his horse.

AT THE TRAINING FARM, it was dark when the head stableman came out of his house after watching the Classic. He was thinking that he wouldn't have picked the winner but he would have bet the entry. He stretched and yawned. He could hear the thud of galloping hooves in the distance, as he had all day. He shook his head, uneasy.

AFTER NOT FINDING a parking place and returning home, then sitting in the garage in the Mercedes for some undefined length of time, Al went in-side. Only a few lights were on, and Rosalind was not to be seen. Al didn't really look for her, though he noticed that the box of doughnuts was gone, which was probably just as well. He closed himself in his home office and got on the phone with Aeroflot. He made a reservation to go to Moscow. It was time, he thought, to build a large factory for the manufacture of some heavy item not as yet determined but certain to be a lot of trouble for everyone.

JUST BEFORE GETTING into bed, Rosalind opened the envelope she had sealed first thing in the morning and read over her picks. She was seven for seven. If she had bet that pick six they had, she would have won more than thirty-four thousand dollars. She sat quietly for a moment, her hand idly scratching Eileen's belly, and wondered about this disjuncture. How could she know nothing and everything at the same time? It felt impossible and yet para-doxical enough to be true. At this very moment, she knew nothing about what was to happen next, and yet it felt like something was already inside her, al-ready completed, and the force field of ignorance between herself and it was very weak, only just strong enough to resist her. Actually, she supposed, every-thing you thought was about to happen was already finished. Sometimes you could remember it and most of the time you couldn't. Maybe it was that idea that was allowing her right now to feel a measure of calm.

48 / EILEEN TAKES NOTE

I T M A Y H A V E B E E N that Eileen, as a Jack Russell terrier, had her own agenda of desirable activities. It may have been that this agenda, in several of its particulars, did not exactly suit Alexander P. Maybrick, Eileen's main rival, these days, for the attentions of Rosalind Maybrick, and it may have been that Alexander P. Maybrick's opinion mattered not in the slightest to Eileen. Or, rather, Eileen did not *care* what Alexander P. Maybrick did and did not like, but, at sixteen pounds, she sometimes had to concede defeat. Alexander P. Maybrick was not all that hesitant to put Eileen outside and leave her there. Nor did Alexander P. Maybrick understand the nuances of meaning intended by the various locations of the fecal markers that Eileen left for him. There was a language there. Any Jack Russell—any dog, even—could have easily read that language, but Alexander P. Maybrick chose not to. Fine. And he had to bear the consequences. But, as with any miscommunication, the consequences redounded to both parties. Eileen kept trying to make her point, Alexander P. Maybrick kept trying to make his, and the result was that Eileen was occasionally swatted, and more often than that had to perform a ritual submission, all form and no substance, but inconvenient nevertheless. More seriously, when Rosalind happened to be out, and happened not to have taken Eileen with her, Alexander P. Maybrick happened to put Eileen in her kennel, sometimes for considerable periods of time.

For a dog whose ancestors were grasped by their tails and dropped into fox burrows, sometimes collapsing fox burrows deep underground, time in a kennel was no hardship, and was even a respite from having to maintain control over household events all day and all night, but it was the principle of *being* kenneled that offended Eileen, which was why, after some particular enormities of this sort (where was Rosalind, anyway?), she took the opportunity presented by Alexander P. Maybrick's open closet door, and went in and defecated and urinated upon some of his shoes. The ones most strongly carrying his scent were to be preferred, for a statement was required, and, as a Jack Russell terrier, Eileen never shrank from making a statement. Eileen finished with the shoes and went out of the closet. But then she bethought herself and went back in. The corner of Alexander P. Maybrick's bathrobe was dangling on the floor. Eileen took the opportunity to continue her statement, and give it one last little flourish. Then she left the bedroom and went into the kitchen, where, as luck would have it, the door to the outside had been left slightly ajar. She pushed it open and went out.

The day was only beginning, and Eileen was full of energy. The first thing she did was to make her daily attempt to solve the conundrum of the mole. There was a burrow at the back of the yard with four entrances. A mole, Eileen knew, went in and out of this burrow all day long, all night long. He had four ways in, four ways out. When he moved around inside that burrow, as he often did, Eileen could hear him mocking her, but she couldn't figure out how to foil him. Birds on branches, she often could and had come down upon and killed. Rats, mice—no problem. But that mole. With regard to the mole, Eileen felt her lack of another Jack Russell companion and teammate very keenly. The mole problem would not admit of a solution by a single Jack Russell. It was all very well to scrape dirt into the entrances or to try to dig up the whole burrow, but both courses had proved futile. All she could do in the end was to attend to and appreciate the scratchings and scrapings of the mole within and hope that something would happen that would afford her an opportunity. Which was just what she was doing when the longest of the black vehicles rolled around the driveway and disgorged the beloved Rosalind right before her eyes. Eileen ran up to her screaming, and Rosalind laughed, bent down, and picked her up.

"Oh, my darling little one!" she exclaimed. "How are you? Were you good while I was in Singapore? I'm so sorry I couldn't take you! And I was gone a whole two weeks!" She held Eileen against her chest and nuzzled her face, then stroked her ears. This was wonderful treatment, and convinced Eileen that she was the preferred one after all. In the end, of course, it was the uncertainty that hurt. Had she been sure once and for all either way, up or down, she might not have been forced to act against Al as she did, but when he was up she had to put him down, and when he was down she had to make sure he knew it.

Rosalind carried Eileen into the house. She spoke to that woman, Delilah, who was always around, but whom Eileen considered unworthy of her attention, mostly because she knew that Delilah considered her—Eileen!—unworthy of attention. That woman, Delilah, said, "Mr. Maybrick has gone to Moscow for three weeks, ma'am, on sudden business."

"Oh. Yes. Well," said Rosalind. Then she carried Eileen into the bedroom and set her on the bed. Eileen jumped down immediately. Rosalind sat down on the bed. She said, "No, Eileen, come here, sweetheart." Eileen did so. Rosalind picked her up again and fondled her face and ears again. Eileen licked Rosalind on the chin, then struggled politely, just to show Rosalind that, though she was extremely happy to see her, the day was advancing and there was much to be done. But Rosalind didn't let go. She kicked off her shoes and lay back on the bed, with Eileen in the crook of her arm, so that Eileen's back leg was cocked under the weight of Rosalind's body. Eileen struggled again, this time more assertively, and finally she broke away and jumped off the bed. As it happened, just then a squirrel ran by outside the French doors, and so Eileen had to race to the door and bark vigorously and put her feet up on the glass and then, when the squirrel paused and sat up a few feet from her and made those squirrel faces that they were always making if they dared, Eileen had to leap into the air against the door an uncountable number of times (Eileen could count to five, so she probably leapt six or seven times). By now she was yodeling at the top of her lungs, because you never knew how clearly those outside could hear you if you were inside. This was also a signal to Rosalind to do the right thing and let her out, but Rosalind only lay on the bed quietly and said in a low voice, "It's all right, Eileen. Settle down." Eileen, of course, settled down, because that low voice was suspicious and worrisome, so she gave up on the squirrel and jumped back up onto the bed and licked Rosalind on the face. Rosalind didn't respond, so Eileen licked her right in the mouth, which, in her experience, always stirred them up pretty good, but Rosalind only pushed Eileen's head away, and gently, too. No spitting, no gagging.

Now Eileen rocked back on her haunches and regarded Rosalind. Rosalind wasn't sleeping, or getting ready to sleep. Her eyes were open and her body was not relaxed, and the breaths she was taking were not even, relaxed sleep breaths, the sort that meant that Eileen could crawl under the covers and press up against Rosalind's warm belly, something she had missed over the last few weeks. The fact was, Eileen did not know what was going on. She regarded Rosalind for another moment or two, then she felt the urge to bark at her, but she could not, so she spun a few circles. All that happened was that Rosalind's hand went up and came down on Eileen's back. A minute or two later, that unworthy human came shuffling in and said, "You all right, Mrs. Maybrick? Can I get you anything?"

Rosalind sat up suddenly, and Eileen jumped off the bed. The Unworthy One said, "Hush, you mutt!" but Eileen kept barking full-bore until she heard Rosalind say, "I'm just tired. It's okay, Delilah. I'm okay." She stood up.

The Unworthy One said, "I'll bring you a cup of tea, Mrs. Maybrick."

"Thank you, Delilah."

Eileen went out of the room and into the kitchen for a drink of water. She sat alertly at the feet of the Unworthy One while the woman made the tea, and listened to the woman mutter, "She didn't know that he was going away, you can count on that, my friend. Absolutely! Things are going on around here, my friend, just ask Delilah. I've seen it. Just ask me!" Then she followed the woman back to the bedroom. Rosalind was now wearing different clothes, and boots. She said, much more perkily, Eileen thought, "Well, I can't sleep. Delilah, would you have John bring the Mercedes around in ten minutes? I'll drive it myself."

"Yes, ma'am."

"Thank you."

And then, in no time, they were enthroned there in the Mercedes, with Rosalind driving and Eileen lying on her back beside her, having her belly scratched up and down, down and up, with the sky passing above them through the windshield. Start, stop, this way, that way. This, Eileen thought, was a whole lot better than the kennel, and if Rosalind planned to do this forever and ever without end, Eileen was for it.

After a long time, Eileen woke up from a doze to catch sight of Rosalind handing something out the open window, and to hear her say, "Thank you, Harvey," and then they turned and stopped, and Rosalind looked down at her and said, "Here we are." Eileen knew perfectly well where they were. The diverse and delicious perfumes of the place were unmistakable. They were at the racetrack.

Rosalind opened her door and Eileen was out there. Rosalind paused to put on her coat, and Eileen got pretty far away from her before she realized that she had lost her head, and paused to wait. No, she ran back. Running was better than waiting. And leaping in the air was better than running. She heard Rosalind laugh, ha ha ha, so she leapt in the air again.

But they went to the usual place after all. Eileen had been all over the backside of the racetrack. In her experience, there wasn't a more interesting place in the world than the backside of a racetrack. Racetrack vermin were fat and had self-confidence. They tended to preen themselves and to not take Eileen quite as seriously as she knew she deserved to be taken. Also, in Eileen's experience, just being a Jack Russell terrier was a bonus at the racetrack. You never got petted and made much of and admired quite so much anywhere in the world as you did at the racetrack if you were a Jack Russell terrier. All in all, it was a heavenly place for Eileen, but the good stuff was not where they usually went. Dick Dick Dick, which was what Eileen called the guy, because that's what Rosalind had called him when she and Eileen were first with him, kept no animals except horses, not even cats.

Rosalind opened the door to Dick Dick Dick's office, and he looked up and said, "Oh, hi!"

Rosalind said, "I just got back from Singapore."

"Really! How was it?"

"It was fine. I'm opening a gallery now. It was Al's idea. I've been working on it since the summer, really."

"Where is it?"

"Madison and Seventy-fourth."

"Hmm."

"Good location."

"I'm sure it will do great."

"Art is the only thing I like anymore."

Eileen noticed that the door was ajar and went out. She stopped and surveyed the premises. There were several delicious fragrances that mingled on the air, and she did not want to decide too quickly which one to follow up. Yes, it was true that when she was with Dick Dick Dick, Rosalind gave Eileen more free time. But "more" was relative. The backside of the track was a big place, and only if she were to have days at a time would she be able to explore it to her heart's content. And now she heard, "Eileen, come!" So she turned and went back into the little room, just in time to hear Dick Dick Dick say, "Yes, I'm living out in Queens now, not far from the track. It's just temporary."

"I can't believe you told her. It was over."

"She was asking for it."

"Oh, Dick."

"I don't mean that the way it sounds. I mean it literally. She was asking for me to go one way or another instead of everlastingly refusing to make up my mind, and I did. Telling her about you was the only thing that could have broken the deadlock."

In Eileen's opinion, Dick Dick Dick still had that manner so irritating to a Jack Russell terrier of not knowing quite what to do. Eileen always knew what to do, and knew it with utter conviction, even if it was the wrong thing to do. The door was still ajar, and Rosalind was staring fixedly at Dick Dick Dick, so Eileen went out again, and this time she raced full-tilt down the shedrow so as to be out of range when Rosalind came to her senses and called her again.

Ah ah ah ah! What joy! Horses' heads popped out over their stall guards as she passed. Horses, Eileen knew, were generally contemptuous of dogs. Horses in general, Eileen had noticed, held a very high opinion of themselves, and looked only to each other for approval and instruction. Jack Russells were like that, too, not like other dogs, who seemed to be willing to take humans as real top dogs instead of "as if" top dogs, which is what Eileen did. Perhaps this shared humoring of humans was why horses and Jack Russell terriers admired one another. Eileen veered off to the right, came out of the barn, leapt onto the manure pile, and rolled around on it in ecstasy, then took a little digging practice, and after a few moments' effort, nosed her way into the hole she had made and rubbed around in its warm, pungent dimness. Then she backed out of the manure pile, fully enrobed in its delicousness, and ran up to the top to survey the area. Crows had landed not far off that needed barking at and chasing, and so she ran down the side of the pile and gave them exactly what they required. They flew away. Another in a long line of victories against crows, who were forever trying to settle to earth, it looked like, and forever having to be launched. Then she turned to head back to the manure pile, and she ran into the booted legs of someone, who picked her up. She looked into the person's face (she was so pungent herself now that she had to consult visual signals to understand if she knew this person, and she did). "I found you," said the person, a woman. "Come on. They're looking for you."

And so they dragged her back to the domain of Dick Dick Dick, and then what did they do but put her in a sink and give her a bath and wrap her up in a towel and rub her down, laughing all the time, and then they handed her back to Rosalind, who was with Dick Dick Dick looking at one of the horses, who was standing in a line with some other horses. Eileen struggled in Rosalind's arms, and she heard Rosalind say, "Just a minute," and then what should happen but Rosalind reached into her pocket and pulled out a leash and snapped it on Eileen with no ceremony at all.

She sat down at Rosalind's and Dick Dick Dick's feet and surveyed the hooves of the animal in front of her. They were big. One was white. All four of them seemed firmly set upon the ground, but that could change at any moment, Eileen knew. Horses had a sparkle about them, especially about their feet, that was not bigness, since people did not have this sparkle about them, nor did very big dogs. When the sparkle changed, Eileen moved. It was a convenient way to avoid trouble. Dick Dick Dick bent down now and put his hand on the horse's leg, smoothing it downward, pausing here, going on, pausing here, going on. Then he did the same to the other leg. Then he stood up and threw one of the women on top of the horse. Then he said to Rosalind, "You should watch a few gallop, since you're here." They turned and followed the horses down the aisle. Eileen trotted between them.

Babble babble babble. The amount of babble streaming through the air between two humans at any given moment was a source of constant annoyance to Eileen. Sitting, babbling, standing, babbling, walking along, babbling, lying in bed, babbling, eating, the most sacred time of the day, babbling. And then they were offended by the purposeful sound of real barking. Yes, the leash always put her in a bad, dim mood. Rosalind dragged her forward. Eileen did not like to be dragged forward. She left the Dumpster behind, followed them across some grass, and then they were on that platform with some other men. Rosalind and Eileen were the only females. Eileen went over to a post in the corner, at the end of her leash, and lifted her leg on it. Rosalind exclaimed, "Oh, Eileen! Not here!"

But what was done was done, a principle Eileen lived by.

"I'm bringing the horse back from the training farm next week," said Dick Dick Dick. "They say he's matured a lot. Did Al tell you? Look at this one, though." But, of course, Eileen had no interest in craning her tiny little neck and straining her bright little button eyes in order to catch a glimpse of a galloping horse hundreds of yards away whose purpose in life was a mystery to her to begin with. She understood about them that they did not kill vermin, did not even aspire to kill vermin, but would rather have vermin killed on their behalf, so that was that about horses. The booted feet of the men on this platform were another story, though. As an idle, leash-bound activity, she deciphered where all of them had been recently. Dick Dick Dick said, "Here, take the glasses and have a look at him."

There was a pause. Eileen noted that one of the men had dropped bacon grease on the toe of his boot and she licked it off for him.

Babble babble babble.

They turned to leave the platform and there was more dragging, since Eileen hadn't quite made up her mind to follow them. But Rosalind didn't seem to notice. This was the maddening thing about Dick Dick Dick, always had been. He rendered Rosalind blind and deaf to Eileen's pressing concerns.

Then they went back to Dick Dick Dick's office. Dick went in first. Rosalind went in second. Eileen scuttled in right on Rosalind's heels, just as Rosalind firmly closed the door. Here in this office, Eileen felt dimmer than ever, so dim she could barely stand up, so she jumped into Rosalind's lap and curled up with her eyes half closed. She could still see him, though, across the room, staring. And then Rosalind said, "I feel lost. It's been six months. I still feel lost. I feel more lost."

"Rosalind, I am lost. I live in a place I don't recognize when I get up in the morning."

"I'm sorry I hurt you."

"Did you? How did you hurt me? Starting things? Continuing things? Breaking it off?"

It was so dark in here, Eileen thought, that the only thing that would save her would be a cat walking arrogantly through the room. She whimpered. Rosalind's hand fell heavily on her head, but it wasn't soothing. In fact, it rather hurt.

"I thought if I came here I might find something that would, I don't know, remind me of something good."

"But—"

"But it reminded me that even then it wasn't good. I had forgotten that. I had to do it and I loved you to distraction, but it was so painful for me."

"Why do you think you had to do it?"

This, Eileen thought, cannot go on. She sat up, jumped down, and began to spin right in front of Dick Dick Dick, but spinning did nothing, so she barked at him, yap yap yap, yap yap yap. She went over to the desk, where she stiffened her legs and her tail and barked herself into a frenzy. Dick Dick Dick was looking down at her in shock, and both the humans were so surprised that they gave her a certain amount of leeway before Rosalind jerked on her leash and said, "Eileen!"

Ha! It was clear that the woman didn't mean it. Eileen swelled. The next phase of barking lifted her right off her feet; she hopped around with it. "Eileen! Eileen!" Jerk. Jerk. Yapyapyapyapyapyapyap. And then he smacked her with his giant hand. She felt herself rise into the air, sail across the room, and hit something. She and it fell with a crash to the top of the bookcase, and then over the edge of that and to the floor. "Oh my God," said Rosalind. "What are you doing?"

Eileen lay stunned on her back. The barking had stopped. The crashing had stopped. There was complete silence in the room. Dick Dick Dick jumped out of his chair and came across to her, knelt down where she lay, and put his hands underneath her. Eileen looked over at Rosalind, who seemed to have turned to stone. Dick Dick Dick was all different now, something Eileen did not approve of, but of course, since Rosalind was out of commission, any port in a storm. She licked his hand. He carried her over to his desk and laid her upon it, with one hand nestled against her, then he dialed a number on his phone, and said, "Hey, Larry. This is Dick Winterson. Where are you? Can you come over and do a bit of small-animal doctoring? It's an emergency, yeah. Thanks. We're in my office."

Now the pain began to come. Back, head, leg, but, actually, nothing special. She had known worse a couple of times. Still, she lay there quietly, staring at Rosalind, who only came to life when there was a knock on the door. Dick yelled "Yeah!" and another man came in. He had the smell. Eileen rolled over and stood up. Rosalind stood up, too, and came over, and stroked Eileen's ears while the examination went on. The vet said to Rosalind, "It hasn't been as long as it looks. I have Jack Russells myself, and I do all my own vet care. Was she kicked by a horse? I had one launched one time. As soon as she landed, she came back at the horse, ready to kill him. She's okay. Just keep her quiet for a day. She might be a little stiff tomorrow."

"Thanks," said Dick.

"Anytime, baby," said the vet. He went out.

"We'd better go," said Rosalind. "I see I shouldn't have come. I'm tireder from my trip than I thought."

"Rosalind, I'm so sorry."

"I think we've found the bottom of each other, somehow. I thought we would avoid that, but—"

Rosalind took Eileen in her arms, and Eileen snuggled up to her soft chest and closed her eyes. She heard Rosalind open the door, and they went out. Usually when people went away from one another, there was more babbling, but not this time.

Ha, thought Eileen. She whimpered once as they walked down the shedrow, and again as they got into the car. Really, she felt fine. When Rosalind put her down on the seat, Eileen jumped into the footwell to investigate what at first looked like an old French fry. But it was just a bit of mud. She jumped back up on the seat and looked out the window. A human walked by, wearing a hat, smelling bad, and barkable by any standard, but Eileen had learned her lesson. She kept her mouth shut. So did Rosalind.

DECEMBER

49 / LOVE

T HEY HAD BEEN LAUGHING. Their faces were still open and happy
from it, and, Farley thought, that's why, even though he should be heading for the walking ring, he had come up to the stands, anyway. Bernard
Baruch's owners were serious men, brothers. They named all their horses
after financiers. One of their big winners had been a horse named Lorenzo
de Medici. They said they did it as a joke, but they were unfunny men, unplay-
ful, unjolly, unfull of delight. He needed a dose of Joy just to get through the
race with these two. And they were big bettors, too. Big bettors who had no
sense of carelessness were a bit dangerous. But they had good horses, of which
Ba nard Baruch and his stablemate, Ivan Boesky, were the first Farley had been
asked to train. Ivan Boesky was a filly. The brothers thought that was a good
joke, too.

He sat down next to Joy and she turned to him and his arm went around
her shoulders as if there were a groove there, and her arm went around his
waist, and in the months they had known one another they had not had a single argument, which made him sigh with delight. He said, "I've got about two
minutes. I thought you might be having too much fun up here."

She turned her face to him for a kiss, and he kissed it, then greeted the
others. Plato was already going.

"The model I like to use," he was saying, "is a model of the weather. One
of the things physicists have discovered over the last few years is that there are
some systems they have analyzed, some systems they can expect to analyze,
and some systems they will never analyze. The weather is one of those. Horse
racing is another. The future is a third." He preened himself, Farley thought,
thinking that analysis of the future was his department.

"The key," said Plato, "is what I call the cascade effect. Systems that can be
analyzed are ones that are basically stable. They keep going along as they
began, and they continue that way until some outside force destabilizes them

for a moment. A bad marriage is just like that. The force it takes to destabilize it gets greater and greater. He drinks more, she takes more lovers, they fight more, he threatens her, but the marriage only gets worse and worse anyway. They get a divorce, and the marriage achieves new levels of badness as the partners hold even their separation against one another. That's stability for you. Northern Ireland, the Balkans. Those are stable systems." Farley laughed, thinking of his marriage. There hadn't been drinking and adultery, but there had been conflict, misunderstanding, and thinking that you knew just what was going on with the other person when you didn't know at all.

Elizabeth ran her hand up Plato's hairy arm. Farley tightened his arm around Joy's shoulders. Elizabeth said, "I shouldn't have bet the number-four horse."

"Why not?" said Joy.

"Mr. T. doesn't like him."

"How come?" said Plato and Joy simultaneously.

"He saw him work earlier in the week. He thinks they worked him too fast and he's got nothing left for this race."

"Are you communicating right now?" said Joy.

"I consulted him as I was leaving the betting window."

"How did you identify him to Mr. T.?" asked Plato.

"Color, age, white markings, sex."

"This still seems imprecise to me," said Plato.

"No betting system is perfect," said Elizabeth.

Farley could not say he was convinced that the old horse was communicating anything. He could only say that Elizabeth had a remarkable record at the windows. He could also say that, more often than not, he agreed with the animal's general analysis.

"Why did you bet the horse in the first place, then?" said Plato.

"I would have to say of Mr. T. that, although we are in communication, we are not always in agreement." Everyone laughed. Elizabeth said, "Go on, honey."

"You can analyze an unstable system, too, if you know the source of the instability. Let's take the settlement of Europeans on the North American continent, something most people call American history. Everything about the system is unstable—migration, affluence, the three branches of government, the market economy, voting behavior, the relationship of the government to the media, the ethnic mix of the population, patterns of sexual behavior, family life. Micro and macro, it's cosmically unstable. Peace follows turmoil, turmoil follows peace, now I've got a job, now I don't."

"What are the sources of the instability?" said Joy.

"There's only one," said Plato. "That's why it's analyzable."

"What is it, then?" said Joy.

"The conviction that there is something unknown that is different from all the things that are known. Sometimes that gives rise to curosity, sometimes it gives rise to fear, but it's all the same conviction. In a stable system, everyone agrees that everything is known. In a stably peaceful system like France, they all agree that what is known is good, and a lot of the national energy goes toward self-congratulation. In a stably conflicted system, like Northern Ireland, they all agree that what is known is tragic and bitter, and a lot of national energy goes toward self-destruction, but when there is widespread belief that many things are unknown, then there is no agreement, only waves of hope and fear, and both are destabilizing."

"Hope," said Joy, "is the American dream."

"Dreams," said Plato, "are illogical delusions resulting from the random discharges of electricity in the sleeping brain. They cannot be made sense of nor truly shared."

"What I love about you," said Elizabeth, "is your perfect lack of sentimentality."

The horses entered the starting gate. The gate opened, and they were off.

Plato said, "It's not true that anything can happen at the racetrack, only that many things can happen at the racetrack. But every one thing that happens has a small chance of having a measurable outcome. Every measurable outcome enters into a geometric rather than an arithmetic relationship to everything else that is happening. How many horses are in this race, ten? And ten jockeys? And right now they are all bunched into the first turn. If we think of the ten horses and the ten jockeys as twenty universes, or twenty galaxies, or twenty stars, we can see why racing is so dangerous. Universes, galaxies, and stars are separated by vast distances. Any little process that takes place in one is isolated and insulated from the others by space. As those horses close up on each other while moving at speed, any little process that takes place in any of the twenty universes—"

"Like a stress fracture," said Joy.

"—has a greater and greater chance of affecting one other universe, or several. It might only take a single fiber, or a single electrical impulse, or a single chemical miscommunication."

"They're spreading out now," said Elizabeth. "Mr. T. was right. He said that gray horse could come from off the pace."

"How did he know that?" said Joy.

"He said that horses that like to come from off the pace hate to work and love to race. He's never seen this guy put in an honest work." Nor had Farley.

Farley said, "I didn't realize he was paying so much attention to the other horses in the morning."

"What else is there for him to do?" said Elizabeth. "Besides, if there was ever a horse with a theory, he's the one."

The horses crossed the finish line. The number-three horse had left his race on the training track. The number-six horse had come from off the pace and run second by a nose

"We got any tickets to cash?" asked Plato.

"No," said Elizabeth.

"Nothing bad happened," said Joy. "You really had my heart pounding there for a minute. All I could think of was that one of those horses would stumble. Thank God."

"That's what I think," said Elizabeth. "That's what I think every day. Worlds are in collision. Thank God that most of the time they just pass through one another."

It was six weeks since Joy had moved into his condo, almost five months since the day she arrived with Mr. T. She gave every evidence of loving him as simply and truly as he loved her, and he liked to think of this thing they had as an example by contrast to his marriage—where there had been obligations, now there were gifts. Where there had been disagreements, now there was co-incidence of outlook and desire. Where there had been ongoing negotiation, here there was peaceful silence. It was powerfully satisfying to him. The thing that wouldn't die, though, was his goading feeling that he had not secured her, that she was temporary, losable, fleeting. Most of the time he put this down to the years he had spent at the track, watching horses come and go, watching talent come and go, watching soundness come and go. He had thought, in the spring, that he was resigned to that at last, wise at last, philo-sophical at last, but here was Joy, and his hard-won equanimity about his career had spawned his old anxiety with a new face.

He said to Joy, "You coming to make nice with the brothers?"

"Would you like me to?"

"They like you. You might serve as a reminder that a twenty-percent re-turn on your investment is not the only thing there is to life. Hug me, kiss me, hold my hand, make them envious."

And so he got what he wanted, her presence, the sensation of her body against his, the feeling of her hand deep in his hand.

Bernard Baruch was there in his slot, an excellent example of what money could buy in terms of horseflesh. By Gulch out of a stakes-winning Nureyev mare, he was big, classy-looking, calm, smart, correct, and interested. If he didn't break his maiden today, he would soon. The brothers were standing by the rail, besuited, waiting for him with congenial smiles on their faces. And, yes, when they shook hands with Joy, each of them took her little hand in both of theirs, lucky them.

"Looks good," said the older brother.

"Very fit," said the younger brother.

"Nice horse," said Farley.

"This should be fun," said Joy.

Now the jockeys came out. The brothers' silks were a yellow color, maybe the closest Farley had ever seen to real gold, and they were beautiful, and Desormeaux looked striking in them. Joy took Farley's hand as they stood in the open paddock, but he noted how comfortably she conversed with the brothers, how she brought them out of their seriousness a bit. At one point, she got on her tiptoes and whispered in the older one's ear. The two of them laughed. Farley held her back a moment after he threw the jockey on the horse, and she said, "I told him we had a source in the barn who thought Bernie would win the race."

"Did you tell him it was a horse?"

"You've got to break them into that slowly."

Everyone loved her, Farley thought, with a prick of jealousy. It was only that she had lived so secluded a life that made her think she was a solitary sort.

After Bernard Baruch won the race, and they took the picture, and the horse peed in the jar, Farley met him back in the barn to assess his condition. He felt his legs and looked them over, along with his feet. No scratches or cuts. The horse seemed sound, and happy, too, though of course he would be stiff in the morning. The adrenaline from the race always took a while to break down, so the horse was still, literally, feeling no pain. But as thoroughly as Farley went over him, feeling his back and his feet, running his hands over his whole body, he could find nothing suspicious. Now the only question was a mental one—did the horse like it? Well, given that he ran first most of the way around, out of harm's way and under a very kind ride from Desormeaux, it was unlikely that he had conceived of any bogeys. It was running itself that the horse had to decide about, not chaos, not dirt in his face, not bumping and jostling, not slippery going or, perhaps the hardest thing, who he was compared with the others. For today, anyway, he knew who he was compared with the others, and who he was was who he wanted to be.

Just because he was concentrating on the colt, speaking in a low voice to the groom and the feed man, that didn't mean that he wasn't noticing Joy out of the corner of his eye, down the shedrow, leaning over Mr. T.'s stall guard and talking to him. He saw the horse put his white head against her chest and press against her a bit, to which she responded by pressing back. Her hands went to his ears, and stroked them gently. Farley could feel that touch, had felt that touch. It almost made him wish he had furry ears himself. A horse's ears, he had noticed over the years, were eminently strokable, if the horse liked it. Your hands just fit around them, and they slipped through your palms like silk. It was old horsemen's wisdom that you never stood directly in front of a horse's head, because that was where he couldn't see you, and that head, should it shoot outward, was quite a powerful blunt object. But he had always thought that, even though a horse couldn't see you there, that was the place he could most strongly feel you, and if he trusted you, he would enjoy your presence there, your hands on his ears, your cheek against his forehead, which was where Joy's now lay. The horse's head was nearly in her lap. If a horse could not feel love as we know it, he thought, what was that he was witnessing? Maybe the horse didn't carry it away with him, and brood over it, and wonder about it, and reflect upon the changes it had made in his life, but look at that—he certainly felt it, came out to meet it, reached for it, relaxed into it, could not get enough of it.

There were horses who had died for love, Farley knew. It wasn't a common story, but it was a story you heard from time to time. Swale had died mysteriously, just a little bit after being separated from his groom. You could think that he had died of grief; some people did. Males and females did express affection differently; Farley sometimes thought it was the colts and the geldings who had a harder time handling their attachments. Fillies were often quite affectionate; mares at the studfarm lived in a world of connection, a hormone haze of sisterhood and motherhood. If you want to know how to be a good mother, he had once said to the foundation mare, upon the occasion of a memorable and not easily forgiven dispute, go out to the farm and stand among the mares and their foals and try to *get* it. A bad mother was nervous but neglectful. A good mother was attentive and calm. It was as simple as that, he had said. What a twenty-year-old broodmare didn't know about love and power wasn't worth knowing. Stallions and colts were different. They lived alone and didn't even approach the mares most of the time, even in the wild. Geldings, unlike stallions, tended to have friends and passionate attachments. They took that sexual energy and sublimated it, and the interesting thing was that people had done that to them, and then the horses had made something new and not natural out of their condition. Geldings had a culture among themselves, didn't they, and it was a culture based on affection, love, passion, whatever you wanted to call it. Geldings were the proof that love was not an instinct but a choice, a learned behavior, something you developed a capacity for over the years.

Farley stood back from the colt, and said to the groom, "Okay, Rafael. He looks good so far. Wrap him and put him to bed. He's a winner now. Make sure he thinks he's living in the penthouse."

"Yah, boss," said Rafael, smiling. And then, when they had turned and headed down the aisle, of course the groom kissed the horse on the neck. You couldn't help it.

Joy came up behind him and put her arms around his middle. He felt her lay her head on his back, and he pressed against her. What if? he thought, a way that he hadn't allowed himself to think in years. "What if" was an infinitely branching road through a dark wood that eventually brought you to paralysis and despair. "What if the horse wins the Derby" was as dangerous as "What if the horse falls and breaks his neck." Years of bad marital stability were supposed to have made him permanently averse to the temptations of "what if." But here it was again, one of those repeatedly unlearned lessons. He turned around and enveloped her in his arms, as much out of fear as out of love.

BOOK THREE

1999

JANUARY

50 / WHO THEY ARE

JANUARY 1. Today they are three years old. Of the 55,431 mares bred in 1995, some forty-four thousand managed to conceive, and then, in 1996, 32,217 foals were born. Of those, 11,056 got to the races as two-year-olds. One two-year-old or another won each of the 4,639 two-year-old races. In three short years, some have died, many have failed, many have cost a lot of money that will never be recouped. Thirty-two thousand foals mean thirty-two thousand stories, because a Thoroughbred horse never goes unnoticed or undiscussed. And most of the stories are the stuff of drama. To the man whose beautiful and expensive two-month-old foal (stud fee already paid and unrecoverable) was bitten in the nose by a poisonous snake six times and found dead in the pasture, the year has had a tragic cast, even though his four other foals live and frolic and prosper. To the woman who sent her barren mare to the studfarm in January for an early breeding, and got a call that the mare was carrying a seven-month-old fetus, the year has had a cast of serendipitous comedy—after all the attention, all the ultrasound, all the watching, the mare had kept her secret anyway. And, of course, the filly is a beauty, dark and substantial, with a shining moon-shaped white marking between her eyes. To the owners and fans of Silver Charm and Skip Away and Real Quiet and Silverbulletday and Da Hoss, the year has had an epic quality, because every win is against the odds and the odds of winning any race are fifty-five thousand to one no matter what the handicappers say.

Three-year-old dressage horses are mostly still untrained, three-year-old jumpers have yet to see a jump, three-year-old driving horses have yet to see a cart. Three-year-old cow horses, bucking horses, pleasure horses have most of their education and all of their careers ahead of them. But three-year-old Thoroughbreds run in the Kentucky Derby, the Preakness, and the Belmont Stakes. Three-year-old racehorses are peaking, preparing to fulfill their owners' wildest dreams, preparing to get legendary if they can.

William Vance has some three-year-olds in the barn, a couple potential

351

stakes winners, though none of them lives in the same universe as the Kentucky Derby. He does, however, have Justa Bob, now seven. To William Vance, in the midst of the strangest thing that has ever happened to him, life is a romance. Here is this plain brown horse, about sixteen hands and not much to look at. His back is a little swayed, his neck is a little ewed. His right forefoot turns a different direction from his right knee. He's a little cow-hocked and a little blocky in the head. His lower lip tends to dangle. His ears are a tad muley. But since coming back to the track, first at Hawthorne and now here in Louisiana, he has won four times in four starts. After the second race, William took him out of claiming company altogether. Now he is winning allowance races, and always, of course, by a nose. The gallop is an asymmetrical gait, a series of rhythmical leaps. A horse's head nods both from side to side and up and down as he springs over the ground. When his nose is down, it is also farther forward. To some degree, speed and the will to win minimize the nodding—the anatomy of the gallop is not 100 percent of destiny. In spite of Cartesian skeptics, a racehorse may himself understand how to put his nose out in front of the nose of another racehorse, and may desire to do so. William Vance does not have to address this philosophical issue, but he does have to say something, because people want to talk about it, and so he always says, "I don't know. I don't know," not wanting to test his luck.

Then the horse wins a fifth time, and a guy from the *Times-Picayune* comes around and wants him to say something interesting, so he says, "I've been training horses for twenty-six years, and I've made a living at it. I generally have about fifteen or twenty horses in this barn, so I've seen a few over the years, but I've never seen one like Justa Bob."

He gets the sense that that's not interesting enough, so he leans down and shows the guy the scar along the midline of the horse's belly, where he had colic surgery.

"We had a huge hot spell right after I claimed the horse out in Colorado," says William, "one of those welcome-to-Chicago hundred-and-twenty-degree-heat-index weeks, and when I got to the barn late that night, the horse was in bad shape. The surgery ended up costing me sixty-eight hundred dollars, and putting the horse out of commission for three and a half months. And you can't count on seeing a return on that kind of money from a six-year-old claimer."

The newspaper guy nods and smiles. William isn't quite sure how much he knows about horses.

"The vet told me his performance level might never be the same after the surgery as it was before. And he wasn't a stakes winner before. I just thought, well, a good deed is a good deed."

Then he says, "You can't run this horse if you got a weak heart. Or he'll kill you."

The guy laughs at that and writes it down. He says, "How much have you won, then?"

"About sixty thousand." William coughs at this, and hurries past the number—even around the track, where all these numbers are common knowledge, William, as a Midwesterner, considers it slightly ill-mannered to talk specific sums. He says, "The thing is, I've got owners now who wouldn't have thought of me six months ago."

Is that the best thing? wonders the reporter.

"Nah, nah," says William, laughing. "He's an exciting horse to watch. You always wonder, will he misjudge that last inch? He never does."

Later, when the article appears (after Justa Bob has won six but before he wins seven and eight), William thinks he did okay with the interview, but what he really likes is what follows:

"Bettors around New Orleans love it. They love to bet on Justa Bob and they love to bet against him. Mary Hardesty, a track regular who always bets on Justa Bob, says, 'He's a sure thing who doesn't look like a sure thing. You get tempted to bet more and more on him, and then, right there at the wire, you think, "Oh my God, I've lost it all." But then that nostril is right out there.'

"Hanging on the wall of William Vance's office are six photofinish win pictures. Horsemen think that might be some kind of record. And William hasn't been averse to betting on his own horse. 'Let's just say,' he says, 'I've set aside some money toward my son's medical-school tuition.' Does he have an explanation for the horse's performance? 'You know, when he was down at my dad's in Missouri for all those months, he stood every day in a spring-fed pond. That'll cure what ails you.'

"But that's not why he's smiling. He says, 'This is a nice horse. He's easy to get along with and a pleasure around the barn. I always wonder,' adds Vance, 'whether he has a sense of humor.' "

William takes the article to Kinko's himself and has it laminated to a piece of particle board right above Justa Bob's seventh win picture. After that, when people want to talk about the whole deal, he gives that to them to read.

51 / ANONYMOUS

IT WAS INTERESTING to Rosalind to note that in all of her travels, even in all of her china-buying, she had somehow never been to Ireland, where she found herself in the new year. Everyone either came from Ireland or went there, especially everyone in the horse world. Al, in fact, had been to the Curragh, and Coolmore Stud, and the yearling sales several times, but Rosalind had never had occasion to come until now, when she was supposed to be looking at paintings but could not because the painter, having missed his flight from Ankara, would not be back at least until tomorrow and maybe the next day, by which time Rosalind herself would be in Spain on her way to Delhi. And so she was in Dublin, with a free day. Since Irishness pervaded the world, and it seemed that most people spent at least part of their education and a bit of each day having feelings about things going on in Ireland—much more so, say, than things going on in France—it was all the more surprising to Rosalind that she had no friends here and was herself unknown to anyone, so she didn't have a soul to call, and as wealthy and well connected as she was everywhere else, here in Ireland she was a nobody.

How her heart soared at the thought.

No light blinked on the telephone in her hotel room.

No faxes or messages were waiting for her, since she had spoken to the artist himself upon her arrival the day before.

No one knew that today, this very day, she was turning fifty years old. No one had arranged a birthday party for her. She had no self-preservation or self-consolation appointments at any salons or spas. None of her friends had made lunch reservations at Cité Grill or Lutèce for the sake of common lamentation at the passage of time.

Instead, January 3, 1999, was an utter unknown for her. Even Al might not call, since he was in Siberia looking into building some sort of steel-rolling mill. The worldwide cellular-telephone system only intermittently connected with Siberia, and Rosalind had told him not to worry about it. They had hardly seen each other at all since the Breeders' Cup.

As she came down the wide, beautifully burnished dark oak staircase into the lobby of the hotel and turned left to go into the dining room for breakfast, Rosalind looked at her watch. In fact, it was only just after 1:00 a.m. in Appleton, her natal city. She was still unborn, though the labor that had resulted in her was well progressed.

The hotel dining room was a pleasant combination of seedy and beautiful, a place where nothing was new but everything was well taken care of. She sat down at her brilliantly white and sparkling table, former seven-pound, two-ounce female baby with only the lightest down of hair on her head. Fifty years on. Hard to believe.

Just then, one of those handsome, blue-eyed men appeared with a basket of something warm, and set it on the table. He said, "There you are, then, dear. It's nice currant scones this morning, and the butter's right there. Coffee or tea this morning?"

"Tea, please," said Rosalind, lifting the napkin on the basket. Five or six square buns were tumbled in their nest. She picked one up. Both its flat bottom and its domed top were deep, crispy golden. The butter that they had been brushed with came off on her fingertips, which she licked. Then she bit off a corner of the scone. It was warm and savory. The buttery shell of the crust, the heavy, soft, crumbly interior. It was just sweet enough to remind you that the marmalade on the table beside the pale, creamy butter would go perfectly if you could pause long enough to smooth it on. Rosalind closed her eyes. The fragrance was delicious, too—biscuity and fruity and buttery. Her grandmother had been a great baker of biscuits—big tins of biscuits coming out of the oven every morning for her grandfather and her father's brothers who worked the farm, who were just coming in the door from the first milking as Rosalind came down the back stairs from the sleeping porch. She would have been, what, five, maybe six, and it would have been summer, because that's when they went out to the farm. Her father's brothers were big men, three of them, heavy in the belly and the shoulders, all waiting to get married in those days, and so bulking large around the farm. As they came back to her, she saw all of their rounded, heavy accoutrements, too—black Buicks, black-and-white cows, tractors, bales of hay, everything big and dangerous, everything that she was supposed to stay away from and be careful of. The farm was supposed to be fun—that's how her mother and father presented their annual trips to herself and her sisters—but the fields were full of cowpies, the blackberries had thorns, the pond was slimy, they weren't allowed to climb the trees,

and her grandfather was short-tempered with all of his sons, who, she realized
now, should have been long gone by that time. She bit into the scone again,
and felt a stab of anxiety at how they would all come in, tromping, stepping
out of their boots, already arguing among themselves by breakfast. They ate
heartily and with a lot of banging of silverware and glassware, with yelling and
growling. None of it was ever directed at her or her sisters, of course. They
were treated like special company, delicate and easily damaged, but among
themselves, anything went—table-pounding was routine. She and her sisters
would look at each other under their bangs and lose their appetites, and so
they would be required to sit there all the longer, until they finished what they
had taken onto their plates—no waste was the rule around the farm. Eventually, after the men went back out to work, they would choke it down. Rosalind
bit off another piece of the scone.

She opened her eyes, and her tea was in front of her, and in addition to
that, a woman was sitting at the table with her, a slender young woman of
about thirty with dark hair, in a black suit with a white, high collar. She was
smiling. She said, "Hullo, do you mind if I sit? There's absolutely not another
spot in the place, and I have to wait for this woman I'm interviewing. She's a
great poet, and very particular and all that, and her publicist told me I mustn't
be late on any account, and so I'm twenty minutes early, can you believe that?
But all the tables are taken, and the maître d' won't let me wait inside the
restaurant at all, so I told him I was with you, because you looked so lovely
here, like a beach in the Caribbean, if you know what I mean."

Rosalind laughed aloud, and said, "That's the nicest compliment I've had
in years."

"Ah, so you're American, then. I thought so. You were enjoying your scone
quite a bit."

"Was I? Would you like one?"

"Oh, yes. With a bit of this marmalade, it would be divine."

"I was remembering my grandfather's farm. My grandmother made what
we call biscuits. They're very like scones. But it wasn't a happy memory. Sort of
frightening, really."

"And so you hate breakfast? That's what happens. You find yourself hating
something simple, like breakfast, and then you pay thousands of pounds to
have it traced to how your parents once leapt across the table at one another
with their forks raised. That's what happened to me, except that it didn't."

"What didn't?"

"That fork incident. No one, none of my brothers and sisters, none of the
aunts or uncles, ever remembered my parents trying to gouge each other with

forks, and really, that sort of thing isn't in them. So, after talking about this fork-gouging incident with my psychoanalyst for weeks, I found out it didn't happen, so she said, 'Well, let's pretend that it did.' So we did that. I must say there was great weeping and gnashing of teeth that day! And then she said, 'Now let's remember that it didn't, and so you can eat breakfast anytime you want,' and so I said good-bye to that fork-gouging thing, and I must say that was a relief to everyone in the family. Yes, the thousands of pounds to the psychoanalyst happened, but not the forks. But, you know, after that, we saw that you could entertain any thought as a memory, and then get rid of it, and it worked perfectly well. I thought it was quite a breakthrough myself, not being attached to any idea that these things you remembered had ever actually happened. Lovely. And all of that stuff that really happened, well, you could get rid of it, too, because you can't remember, so it's just a story."

Rosalind laughed.

The young woman said, "I do believe that I've had the only successful psychoanalysis in the history of the world. Ah. There she is!"

Across the room, a woman with great upswept gray-blond hair whooshed into the restaurant. She was wearing a purple garment and in every way taking advantage of her artistic status. Rosalind said, "I met her at a party once. Have a good interview."

"She'll say anything, you know. That's the brilliant benefit of interviewing her. You turn her on, write it down, give it a little continuity, and you're finished. Thank you for the scone."

"Thank you for the tip." But the young woman had already turned her attention to the poet, and Rosalind was alone again. She finished her tea and ate another scone. Really, that was enough. It left her feeling light and eager for the day. The day. Her fiftieth birthday! She looked at her watch. Still not born yet. But soon.

Maybe it was these thoughts that prevented her from understanding a word the concierge said when she asked him about taxis. When he was done talking, and smiling at her again, as helpful as could be, she realized that she had not been listening at all. He might as well not have been talking. She was sufficiently embarrassed that she said, "Thank you. That's very helpful." And she went out of the hotel. There was a park across the street and whizzing traffic passing right in front of her, so she turned right and began walking down the street, an unknown street in an unknown country on a sunny day in some direction she hadn't bothered to ascertain. She felt happier than she had in years.

She came to the light and crossed, for the traffic seemed actually to stop.

In any case, she had no sense of danger. Quite the contrary. There was a right-ness about every step she took. She turned again and crossed again, and came into a busy walking street paved with bricks. It was lined with all sorts of shops. Ah.

Shoppers, especially wealthy woman shoppers, got very little respect, but it was clear to Rosalind that shopping made the world go round. She and Al, for example, appeared to be at distant ends of a particular continuum. He erected factories for the manufacture of giant heavy metal objects. He employed strong sweaty men, and went to places like Eastern Europe and Siberia, be-cause those were the last bastions of strong sweaty manhood. The only giant heavy metal object Rosalind ever touched was her Mercedes. Carryable and beautiful things made up her world, and knowing where they were meant to be situated and getting them there was her art. But, in fact, usually she had lost interest in the object itself as soon as she bought it. What others thought was the product, beautiful rooms, was only the by-product. The product was the flow itself. She paused and looked down the street before her, knowing that at the end of a couple of blocks she would have modified in a significant way the flow of objects around the world. What was now resting, in windows and on counters, would soon take flight, borne, like all objects, upon the current of money. The current of money had a little vortex right in her house with Al, right in their bank account. So much came in and so much went out that their bank account generated a little Gulf Stream, a warming current of consump-tion that eddied around the world. Nor was she a purely economic woman, however. Doing her bit for capitalism was only serendipitous. The real payoff, for her, was rediscovering, every moment of every shopping experience, what a good appreciator she was. That was her real privilege. Of course, you could certainly appreciate uniformly manufactured large heavy metal objects. They were useful and often gracefully formed. But a born appreciator needed variety and singularity to really develop her talents.

Rosalind crossed the street again and perused a window full of finely made wooden boxes and cabinets. Next to that window was a window full of Belleek china and Waterford crystal. She saw that there were three styles that she hadn't seen before; a set of water goblets, opaque, with a clear feathery design, was the most charming. Next to them were shoes. Shoes were interesting, hav-ing both a functional side and an artistic side, and both sides being linked to price only in a slippery, undefined way. She went back to the box shop and entered.

For Rosalind, mercantile relationships were always happy ones, and the more expensive the shop, the happier she and the proprietors were to see one another, because as soon as she walked in the door they knew she was the person they had been waiting for. In this shop, for example, three people were standing behind the counter. They looked up, they saw Rosalind, they smiled, and the man came out from behind the glass case. He, Rosalind thought, would be the manager, or even the owner. His smile was not even mercenary. He was truly happy to see her; that's how she knew what a great shopper she was. She said, "You have some lovely things in here."

"Thank you, darlin'," he said.

"Are they handmade?"

He grasped her left arm above the elbow, the friendliest of gestures, and said, "Watch the carpet here, luv, it's a little uneven. Here we go." He had gotten her into a little nook toward the back of the shop, a nook full of chests. They rose in front of her, tall, narrow, silky amber-colored, knobbed in what looked like garnet-colored stones. He said, "Now, look at these, dear. Padraig Mahoney makes these out in Galway. He makes one a year. I've got four here, that's four years' work. This is 1993. This is 1994. This is 1996. And this is 1997. I sold 1995 last year and 1992 three years ago, and I've made arrangements to get 1998 here, but I haven't got it yet."

"They are quite interesting."

"Aren't they, though? Absolutely useless, of course." He grasped a little knob between his forefinger and his thumb, and pulled out a drawer. "Now, what would you put in that? It's too shallow."

"It's not for putting into," said Rosalind, "it's for looking at." And indeed it was, because the bottom of the drawer contained a whole inlaid scene in various shades of wood. Up in the left-hand corner was a wolf, and down in the right-hand corner was a man. Crossing a hill between them, in various attitudes of excitement, was a pack of wolfhounds. The "drawing" of the animals was astounding, not only in detail but in line. Each hound, or part of a hound (some were partly hidden behind others), was distinct and full of energy and movement. "May I touch it?" said Rosalind.

"Thank you for asking. Yes, you must."

But there were no edges. The inlay had been sanded and smoothed.

She stepped back. The outside of the chest was simple until you looked at it and saw that the boards had been split and bookmatched, so that the deep golden grain of the wood formed a helical pattern up the side of the chest, and then a sunburst pattern over the top, but it was subtle.

"I'll tell you this, if you don't mind," said the proprietor. "Padraig Mahoney never makes a mistake. You see how smooth these corners are, all the corners? The average cabinetmaker gives himself a bit of decoration here and there so he can make a mistake, but this lad Mahoney, he does every bit with antique planes he's restored, and he never makes a mistake."

"They don't look stark, though," said Rosalind.

"Ah, well, he has a sensuous eye, doesn't he?"

Rosalind turned her head and looked at the proprietor, who was looking at the chest with manifest pleasure. She said, "Yes, he does."

"Yes indeed," said the man. The shop bell rang, and the man glanced around. Someone had come in, so he said, "I'll leave you to admire this piece, then. Take your time."

And she did. Beginning at the top, she opened every drawer. There were twenty of them, twenty episodes of the story that included the man and the dogs and the wolf, and also a woman combing her hair, and a pair of horses trotting between the shafts of a carriage. The marvel was not that this Padraig Mahoney took a year to make one of these, but that he took only a year to make one. Even so, she felt her spirits sink as she closed the bottom drawer. It was marveling that did it, in the end. Of course she was not, she thought, an artist of shopping, or a first-class appreciator; it was all too evident that she was not an artist of anything. She got down on her knees then and bent down and twisted her head to see underneath the chest. Sure enough, there was yet another scene, this one a portrait of a man with an aquiline nose and heavy eyebrows. Above her, the proprietor, who had returned, said, "Ah. There you go. That's the artist. He puts that on the underside of every piece. I had one customer—he bought the chest from 1975, I believe—he called me a year ago and said that he'd only just discovered the picture. And they're all different, too. You could stand them all up, from all these years, and see Padraig mature and age."

"I'm amazed at this."

"He does that to us all. Let me help you up, dear. Yes. It's no use comparing ourselves to Padraig Mahoney. Or to any of them. I grew up comparing myself to Laurence Olivier. My goodness, I wanted to be an actor like that. An *English* actor, mind you, though we have some fine Irish players, but being an Irish player wasn't good enough for me. I'm happier now, as a useful sort of man who opens the shop and does the books and closes for the night."

"Has he made any with a racing theme?"

"Ah, yes—1994. He lost a bit of money at the Curragh, and tried to recoup it over at Cheltenham. You know, when they run the Gold Cup, they take enough away from the Irish punters to finance English racing all the year round." He opened a drawer, then another one. No narrative, this time, but a myriad of racehorses, running, jumping, falling, jumping, rearing, bucking, running, jumping, chestnuts, blacks, grays, bays, browns, all rendered in glorious detail. Rosalind said, "How much?"

"I'll not tease you, they don't come cheap."

"How much?"

"Fifty thousand pounds for the racing one, fifty-five for the other one."

And here was where everyone became happy, because it did seem cheap to Rosalind, both because of how much money she had and because of the care and inspiration that had gone into what she was buying. She said, "I'll take the racing one, for my husband. He's a racing man."

"Wonderful. Mr. Mahoney will be pleased, indeed, as he rarely has a sale. He will come to Dublin himself to oversee packing and shipment, and if it arrives with the least damage, which has never happened, he will fly to your home and repair it himself."

"Thank you. I feel truly as though I've never seen or bought anything like this."

"You haven't, darlin'." And it was true. And Al, who came as close to having everything as anyone in the world, most assuredly did not have one of these. There couldn't be a more perfect culmination of her work, Rosalind thought, than to give Al something on her own birthday that he did not have and could not have found and didn't know existed and that wasn't in the least useful to him.

Sometime later, she found herself out of the shop, standing in the street again. There were urchins and people playing music and general happy chaos. The weather actually wasn't bad for the time of year. There was even a bit of sun. She continued walking and looking into windows, but then she thought, having had a peak shopping experience, she might as well knock off for the rest of the day. No china, no item of clothing, no painting, no musical instrument, nothing was going to beat this.

And so Rosalind proceeded down the street, looking into the shop windows still, but doing as others did it, and she herself once did it, separated, as if by glass, as if by no money. After a while she crossed. After a while she turned, walked down another, less busy street, turned again. What a sunny day it was. Everyone she passed commented on it. First sunny day all winter. She looked at her watch. She was born now. Her own birth, of course, was the only one she had ever experienced. Perhaps, she thought, that was an odd thing. Especially odd here in Ireland, of course.

If there had been a time when Rosalind wanted children, she couldn't remember it. When she married Al, who was forty-five to her thirty, part of her relief had been that of course there would be no children; Al, as he said then, needed some God-damned rest. Melissa would have been thirteen or fourteen, Al Junior a senior in high school, and Georgina a senior at Wellesley. Now, of course, it struck her as odd that this choice on her part had gone unexamined, had not even seemed like a choice. There were so many things in her life like that, weren't there? How she put up her hair. What she put on in the morning. Whom she had lunch with. Even where she lived. After moving into Al's house all those years ago, she had redecorated it from top to bottom, but it had never occurred to her that they could live somewhere else. Maybe Al had even asked her if she wanted to build another place, but maybe she hadn't even heard the question. Maybe the only things she had ever chosen were purchases after all. She looked up. She was coming to some large, official-looking buildings. She had no idea what they were for—some sort of government offices, perhaps. She paused and stared at them, not because she wanted to know what they were, but because she wanted to know why she had never chosen whether to have children or not.

The image of her mother came into her mind. How many years had she spent listening to her friends complain about their mothers? Forty? And she had never joined in. Rosalind's mother was someone you could not complain about, try as you might. She was calm, affectionate, stoic without being long-suffering. She had never spoken to Rosalind or either of her sisters in an unreasonable voice. She had a beautiful smile. It was a smile that a daughter could not get tired of. Rosalind supposed that she had been quite enamored of her mother. Her sisters had been, too. No disagreement there. But even so, her mother had always said, "Children are such a responsibility." And she had taken her responsibility toward them very seriously, doing homework with them, sewing their clothes, making sure that they had the most nutritious possible meals, talking to them seriously about boys and dating and sex, showing them how to clean their rooms, how to do laundry properly (she had a special thing about leaving clothes in the dryer after it stopped—no matter what she was doing, she would leap up and run down into the basement to take out the clothes and hang them or fold them), how to make a white sauce and a pie crust. She had overseen their piano practicing and gone to every school function. It was clear from every moment of Rosalind's childhood that motherhood left no time for anything else, and was not an enterprise to be entered upon with a light heart, though, of course, Rosalind's mother didn't have a naturally light heart, either. Ah, well. Sometimes Rosalind didn't miss her. Sometimes her sisters didn't miss her. They had confided that to one another once, in Antigua.

She thought she could almost feel a bit of resentment rising up within. And then a man who was passing said to her, "Here's the bus you want."

There were buses right in front of her. She hadn't noticed them, and didn't want one.

"This is the one that will take you. You go to the end of the line, and get off right there. It's only about a twenty-minute ride."

"Are you talking to me?" said Rosalind. The man was very handsome, about forty, she thought, in a soft blue sweater.

"Better get on, luv," he said. "He's ready to leave."

And so she did. He waved to her as the bus pulled away from the curb. She waved back, and mouthed, "Thank you."

She settled back into the seat, prepared to take on her resentment of her mother, but then she couldn't find it. Her mother was her mother. It was as if she had left her resentment standing at the bus stop. She laughed. Was it as easy as that? Did you leave your emotions behind you, holograms of yourself dotting the landscape? It seemed as though you could, in Ireland.

The bus went away, crossed a river—that would be the Liffey—then sped onward. It was about half full. Once in a while it stopped, but no one got off or on. Somehow, the fact that it was an Irish bus explained this, and so Rosalind stopped wondering about it. The scenes they passed were flat, not picturesque in particular. At the end of the line, they came to a large, surprisingly green space for this time of year. When the bus stopped, she said to the driver, "Where are we now?"

"This is Phoenix Park, dear. The bus leaves here for the city center every twenty minutes until six this evening, then every forty minutes thereafter." And she got off. She looked at her watch. It was almost noon. Maybe it had been a decade or two since she had spent an afternoon in a park. In the first place, she was a culture girl, not a nature girl, and in the second place, walking in the park was for people who had nothing else to do and no money to do it with. In the third place, it was the third of January, which was, perhaps, why the place was deserted. And so she walked in the park.

What exactly her mood was, she could not say. Normally, she would be feeling a certain impatience, a certain fear of boredom at the prospect of an afternoon alone with trees and grass. She was fifty years old now. For the last thirty years, with a machinelike implacability, she had planned her days, her weeks, her years. She traveled with guidebooks and systems. When she came away from the new place, she had an excellent overview of historic sites, fine-art and decorative-arts museums, better shopping, restaurants, and musical venues. When she came back to these places later, she always knew what she had missed and wanted to see this time. Her friends called her all the time and asked her what they should see and where they should eat in any given spot, and she always had a brilliant suggestion. In retrospect, it was as if she had been mapping the world. But what for? Perhaps, she was willing to admit, it was because she didn't have anything better to do.

Here in this park, with no one around, it was easy to think of all the things that there were to do in the world. She was standing in this still, empty center, and spiraling around her in a great galaxy of activity were five, six billion people, all of them busy except her, and she would be busy again soon. In one of the outer arms of the galaxy was Al, who was walking with some men around a site. Everyone was talking excitedly in English and Russian about building a road, bringing in water, carrying off wastes. It was a vast undertaking, made all the more exciting by the prevailing local conditions, which were worse than primitive—the original, primitive potential of the site had been destroyed. Rebuilding was next to impossible, and so the challenge was even more exhilarating. In another arm was Dick, now just getting to the track, just beginning to sort through the daily requirements of fifty horses, ten exercise riders, eighteen grooms, twenty owners, five hot walkers, the feed man, the vets, the bookkeeper, all the others. It was a vast undertaking, made all the more exciting by the unknowability of the horses and the myriad opinions clinging to every one of them. Her friends in New York would still be sleeping, but they were busy, too, dreaming one dream after another. How many children were there in the world? And so how many mothers and fathers and grandmothers and aunts and uncles and child-minders were wiping faces, offering food, pushing little arms through little sleeves, tying shoes, talking about, reading aloud to, reprimanding, kissing, tucking in, looking for, playing pattycake with, lamenting over, cleaning up after, walking beside, throwing into the air, explaining something to, ignoring the cries of, beating, hugging, expecting, missing, touching the face of, holding the hand of one child or another? How many were hoeing, planting, cultivating, pruning, harvesting something or another? How many were cooking? How many were eating? How many were defecating? How many were picking up their tools, putting down their tools, turning on the television, turning off the television, placing telephone calls, playing a musical instrument, dancing? How many were talking? Arguing? Making love? Picking up weapons? How many were whispering a secret to someone else? How many were answering the telephone calls that others had just placed? How many were waiting for something? How many were standing in line, driving cars, riding buses, hailing taxicabs, climbing onto trains, walking down jetways, taking off? How many were walking down a lane in the country? Mucking out after cows or pigs, walking dogs? How many were planning to buy? How many were planning to sell? How many were worrying about money? How many were placing one stone upon another? How many were felling trees? How many were reading quietly? How many were looking at paintings? How many were logging on to the Internet? How many were floating on a lake, a river, the ocean? How many were making their way through heavy jungle, up steep mountain slopes, over ice fields, down Broadway, down Rodeo Drive, along the Champs-Élysées, through Tiananmen Square, through the Piazza San Marco? How many were looking at the moon? How many were looking at the sun? How many were contemplating death, marriage, love? Billions and billions, of course.

But even though she was doing none of these things, even though she was just standing there, Rosalind was not unhappy. It was a relief to be freed of those activities for a moment, to stand here and feel a space open up right here, in Phoenix Park, a circle around her in which there was nothing at all. She took a deep breath. It went through her, top to bottom. She took another. The same thing happened. It was like a sigh. Dick had told her once that he loved to hear a horse sigh. The sound of a horse sighing was the sound of a horse giving up his fear. She took another breath. It seemed possible to walk around the park, and so she did.

Of course there had been someone. For twenty-seven years she had been careful not to make too big a deal of this someone, Henry Dixon. She saw his name from time to time still. He had spent his life rebuilding lofts in SoHo. She didn't know anything else about his life, whether he had children or wives, for example. He would be almost sixty now, because he had been thirty-two to her twenty-three when they were seeing each other. She hadn't had the experience to comprehend Henry when they were together, but later, with all the builders and remodelers she worked with, she saw that he had a methodical quality the rest of them shared that was reassuring, a way of moving easily back and forth between the larger project and its details. But, of course, once she was knowing builders, then she was hiring them. She could have hired Henry, had she wanted a loft in SoHo, and paid him anytime with a check. She had thought that evil thought from time to time, hadn't she?

And why was that? Henry had treated her with perfect kindness. He was cordial, almost formal; he thanked her, he greeted her, he inquired about her day, he apologized. He was no less mannerly at the end of their affair than he had been at the beginning, and she had resented that, as if he was holding her at arm's length. He was handsome and well formed. He touched her. He held her hand, rubbed his thumb over hers, put his arm around her waist, her shoulders, kept her against him. He seemed always to be appreciating her with his hands, no matter what else they were doing. Affection untainted by resentment. How often did you find that? She had never found it since.

Such a thing was more unique than lots of money, in her experience, but she hadn't known that then. She'd thought the affection belonged to her desirableness, not to his sweetness. Affectionateness was something she would be grateful for now. And he was a good lover. He taught her how to make love to him, and she had thought, for a while, that that was something as well that she possessed by herself, rather than something they possessed together. And then she'd discovered it wasn't, and then she had forgotten about it. It wasn't un-common, among the women she knew, to regret the poor man you'd missed out on, to wonder, privately, if the habit of big money had a bad effect, since so many of their husbands seemed unhappy themselves, or made others unhappy. Rosalind's mother and father would have said that big money did have a bad effect, but, then, so did everything else. Experience itself had a bad effect, and the only thing you could do in the face of it was to keep quiet and endure.

Looking back at Henry Dixon, all she could say was that it seemed like he had had a larger capacity for love than she had, that she had measured his ca-pacity by her own, that she had failed to decide, and they had gone their sepa-rate ways, and what she turned out to have chosen was not a life based on love but a life based on something else, let's say knowing what she wanted, which required knowing what there was to want, which required casting a cool eye over everything, judging workmanship and value, being skeptical and hard to fool. But, then, she had a been a fool about Dick Winterson, hadn't she?

She sat down on a bench and crossed her legs. Looking out over a large lawn dotted with trees, she remembered something about Henry Dixon that she hadn't thought of in years. He had tucked her into him when they slept. Now, of course, she and Al slept in a huge bed, far enough away from one an-other so that their separate sides of the bed were warmed only by the tiny, futile attempts of Eileen. But Henry Dixon had kept her close to him and it had been comforting and safe. How lonely had she been since then, since Henry Dixon? So lonely, she thought, that she had made a whole world of it. And she burst into tears.

Well, she cried and cried. She smeared her makeup and disarranged her hair and got herself wet, all the time knowing that she was feeling very sorry for herself. Loneliness, even saying that's what she was feeling, was as common as air, was the necessary cost of autonomy, was it not? It was lonely at the top, it was lonely at the bottom, it was lonely in between, it was lonely in a group or not. Loneliness was something, she realized, that you always felt, but some-times, for a while, forgot about. So, if you always felt it, then there was no rea-son to make this tremendous spectacle about it. But she did anyway. She cried some more, then pulled herself together, then cried some more, then pulled herself together again, even going so far as to take down her hair, comb it out, and pin it up again, and then, when she was putting in the last pin, she started crying again, as if it were possible for all of her bodily fluids to empty them-selves through her tear ducts. She cried until she had forgotten almost entirely about Henry Dixon, and was just a self-perpetuating crying machine, and then she cried some more, until a voice very nearby said, "Och, don't be wiping your face on your skirt, dear. You'll never get that out of the fabric. Here, I've got quite a large hankie with me, and it's clean, to boot."

Rosalind sat up. Next to her on the bench was a woman of about her own age, but not so well preserved. She had dark, dull hair, with streaks of gray, and she was wearing a shapeless gray sweater over another shapeless pink sweater and a mackintosh thrown open over that. She had on a pink wool skirt, and dark-brown shoes. She smiled and said, "Crying in the park. Don't I know all about that? Maybe I've cried in one park or another every day of my life. Does you good."

"Do you think so?"

"Och. Of course it does. Keeps things moving at the very least. Myself, I find it relaxing. I go home a more patient woman than I was when I stormed out of the house."

"I don't think I've cried in years."

"Must have hurt you to do so now, then."

"Maybe. I don't know. I'm a mess, I'm sure."

"Yes you are. You're soakin' wet, you are. But it's a sunny day today. You'll soon dry."

Rosalind had expected the woman to offer to take her home, perhaps, and let her clean up there. A shuddering sigh came up right then, and Rosalind sensed that it was the last one, and she was done crying for now. She yawned. The woman said, "There you go. You'll be takin' a nap soon, if you don't watch out."

"I do feel a little sleepy."

"No doubt."

"I thought maybe I had forgotten to marry the man I really loved. That's why I was crying."

"Must have felt lovely, then, a good cry over a vain regret like that. That's a grief to be cultivated, because you can come back to that one every time you need relief."

Rosalind laughed.

"Och, it's true. The lovely young lad, so handsome and true, the lovely young lass, yourself, of course, always perfectly dressed and pretty and sweet, and the life they would have had, aging gracefully and kindly, not so much the harridan you've gotten to be married to the tyrant you've made of your old man. Was he Irish, this fellow you should have loved?"

"Maybe. Most people in America are in some way or another. He was charming."

"You know that I am one of twelve sisters?"

"No, I—"

"Twelve sisters. And I myself have ten daughters, and each of my sisters who isn't a nun has eight daughters or more. They wrote about us in the newspapers. No one in the family has had a son in a hundred years, and we've given it quite a go. My husband, he said we eat those y-chromosomes for breakfast, us O'Malley girls. It's a joke now, really. But I'll tell you something I know from watching all these dozens of girls."

"What's that?"

"It never matters who you love or who loves you. Your fate is your own after all. And it doesn't matter a whit if you celebrate it or if you bemoan it. It's yours anyway."

"That sounds very bleak."

"Does it?"

"Right now it does."

"Well, maybe. But maybe you'll see it differently sometime." The woman got up. She said, "You may keep the hankie. I've got piles."

She went off, and that was that. Rosalind sighed and stood up. She felt emptied out now, as if the floor had dropped out of the containment building and everything inside had drained away. She began to walk.

PERHAPS IT WAS the moon that awakened her. Certainly when she opened her eyes it was right there, framed by the drapes and the window sill. It was good to see it, and to recognize it, because she didn't recognize anything else. The room was large and ornate in a well-taken-care-of but dated way. There was a door to her left, a door to her right across the room, and a pair of French doors at the end of the bed. There was a telephone next to the bed. She recognized that, too, a hotel phone. She picked it up and pushed the "0." When a voice answered, in English, she said, "Where am I?"

"Ah, good evening, Mrs. Maybrick. You are at the Royal Ireland Hotel in Dublin, Ireland."

Rosalind thanked him.

When she stood up to close the blinds, she had no clothes on, and she saw that her clothes, much wrinkled and very dirty, lay on the floor between the bed and one of the doors. Without closing the blinds, she sat down on the edge of the bed and picked up her skirt and a shoe. The skirt was soiled everywhere, and her shoe was muddy, too. Rosalind looked at them in wonder. Then she stood up again and looked into the mirror. Her hands went immediately to her hair, which was still partially pinned up. Sleep, or something, had put it into a terrific tangle. There were leaves and grass in it, which, looking in the mirror, she began to pick out. The light of the moon was that bright. She recognized that this was an unusual way for her to be, naked and disheveled, but, in fact, it didn't worry her. She looked at her watch. Her watch was gone. She knew that, whatever had happened to her, nothing had happened to her. She was safe and warm in her hotel room. She could see no cuts or bruises in the mirror, and she felt no pain anywhere. She put her arms above her head and stretched. She felt good. Rested and alert. She bent down and picked up her clothes—stockings, the other shoe, camisole and slip, jacket. Bunched in the pocket of the jacket was a large handkerchief. Her handbag was beside the door. She opened it and looked inside. Everything was there. She folded her clothes and set the pile on the desk. Now she lay down on the bed again, and applied herself to remembering what had happened to her between the departure of the lady who had given her the handkerchief and right now. Had she gotten lost? Had she fallen asleep somehow, laying her head on leaves? Had she met anyone else? Her mood as she asked these questions was only interested, not disturbed, and that, plus her freedom from any evidence of injury, reassured her that whatever had happened it was benign enough.

But it was a mystery. She could come up with nothing.

She held her hands up in the brilliant moonlight, and looked at them. They were clean. She looked first at the palms, then at the backs. Even her nails were perfect and unbroken. Fine. But her hands were interesting, pearly in the moonlight. She placed her palms together, then looked at them again, then put them to either side of her face. They were cool and comforting. Of course they were. People often remarked upon that, that her touch was comforting. Al sometimes asked her just to put her hand on his head to see if he had a fever. He never did, but he felt comforted. Dick, too. Her stepchildren and her stepgrandchildren. That was funny, something she had noticed over the years without realizing. Her hands offered something whether or not her intentions were involved. Well, that was a pleasant thought. She rested her face in her hands. Ah. Yes.

Her face. Well, Rosalind didn't have to look at her face in the mirror to know all about it. She had looked at her face in the mirror enough times over the years. Probably she would never have to look at it again. She removed her hands and turned her face toward the moonlight. Perhaps she felt it, little grains of silver light gathering on her cheeks and forehead and nose and chin, collecting on her lips and eyes, congregating on her neck, scattering through her tangled hair. Right where all those quanta of light lay clustered, there was her face, as in a mask. She could feel it tingling, the tiny interval between her self and what the light revealed. That was what you could not look past, wasn't it? They told you that in school—when you looked at something, really you were looking at reflected light. There was no way to look at the thing itself, at least with your eyes. Eyes were made for this world, with this sun and moon and all their imitators. Perhaps, Rosalind thought, there were other worlds inside this one that eyes were not made for. Even so, she did not touch her face, not wanting to disturb the granules of light shimmering there. Rather, she stood up and let the light cascade down the rest of her body, over her shoulders and breasts and belly and hips, thighs and knees and shins, and ankles, a dry flow of infinitesimal beads, almost audible, if the ear could hear such a lovely sound, note falling upon note, a torrent of harmonies, setting her vibrating from the crown of her head to the soles of her feet. She stood very still, so as not to interfere with this vibration, and held her arms away from her body. Still her eyes were closed, but the light of the moon was so bright that she could see everything perfectly well.

This feeling, Rosalind thought, was not unlike orgasm; it had that richness. She supposed that, if it was not orgasmic, then it was not any feeling she had ever had before; perfectly new. The sensible thing, of course, was just to stand there and feel it, quit questioning it, and so she did. And as she did, her skin diffused and the motes of light heavy upon it went suddenly into her and began vibrating within, except there was no within and there was no without. She had been invaded from all sides, taken, penetrated, removed, replaced, done for.

There was no climax, no movement upward or downward. The feeling was present, and then she sighed and sat down again on the bed and the feeling was gone. Nothing came after it, no longing, no sense of loss, no fear, only another sigh. And then she slipped between the sheets of her Irish bed and slept without dreaming until the fragrance of scones and lemony tea awakened her in time for her plane, even though the hotel dining room was four floors down and at the other end of the building. But in Ireland, it appeared, anything was possible.

52 / LIQUIDITY

Now," said Mary Lynn to Deirdre, "what I really appreciate about Thoroughbreds is how liquid they are."

"You mean asset-wise," said Deirdre.

"Oh my God, yes," said Mary Lynn. "In comparison to the house, the beach house, the boat, the art, and the old cars, and all the junk Skippy's bought over the years, my God, it's going to take us years to sort that out."

Deirdre gathered that she was not leaving him for the guy from Microsoft but, rather, on general principles. She no longer wanted to be the doer of good works married to a Washington power-broker. Which element was the worst—the good works, the marriage, the power, or Washington itself—defied analysis, but none of them held any appeal any longer, and since Skippy didn't know how to do anything in the world other than power-broking in Washington, there was no shifting him, and so—

Deirdre sensed that she was expected to provide some female solidarity on this. That was why they were not out at the track, but having lunch in a restaurant. She sensed this because, just before she left the track, George had said to her, "I bet it's a divorce, darlin', so be sympathetic." All through the barley soup and the potted shrimp on a bed of bitter greens with aromatic vegetables, Deirdre had been biting her tongue and reviewing her female experience for some sort of sisterly feeling, but in fact it appeared that she had no relevant female experience and she was incapable of sisterly feeling. On the other hand, she was surprised to note, she was not either enraged or terrified. It was she herself who had gotten rid of most of her owners, and so it was she herself who had put all her eggs in the Hollister basket. When the Hollister horses (who even now were running well and making a profit) had liquefied and flowed away, she would have six horses in her barn, three allowance horses who had earned her maybe twenty thousand dollars in the last year, and three claimers, who, of course, were only passing through. And, of course, the miracle mare and her divine daughter were as liquid as all the others, and would pass on, too. One of her perfect daughters, a three-year-old, had won a stakes in California, enhancing the mare's value yet again, and thereby pricing Mary Lynn and Skippy's half well out of Deirdre's range.

"You know," said Mary Lynn, "Skippy keeps saying, 'But they won't remove him from office! They don't even have a simple majority! I don't understand why you're leaving me! Wait till after the vote! Wait till after the election!' Well, just you wait. This isn't the first or last marriage for which this whole thing was just too much."

"I'm sure," said Deirdre. "But this can't be just about that."

"You know it isn't," said Mary Lynn, "and I know it isn't, but Skippy thinks everything is about that. So what I say to him is, *they* have to stay married, but the rest of us don't."

Deirdre ate her dessert—lemon tart with a raspberry sauce—and she did not splutter. Neither did she curse, neither did she wail, neither did she gnash her teeth, neither did she tear her hair, but only thanked Mary Lynn for their long association and wished her well.

LATER, WHEN SHE ASKED George about why she had gone so quietly, he said, "But, Cousin, you were not having a near-death experience. You were having a death experience. Against such a thing, protest does not avail."

Deirdre had always assumed that a death experience would be sudden, or at least quick enough, but this one happened a drop at a time, giving her plenty of occasion to wonder why giving up something she had such a beef with was so painful. First of all, George decided to leave and go back to Ireland. He had his reasons for this, but they were, as both of them knew, only excuses. Money, employment, preferences, really, he just wanted to be back in Ireland, and his experience with her might help him to a job at a stud or with another trainer there. Tiffany didn't like this idea at all. "Now, in the first place, George, things aren't over here, so you don't have to be buying your ticket home right now. And in the second place, even if Deirdre took a little vacation from training and went to, say, Tahiti, for a long break, and the horses went to other trainers, you could find yourself another job, and this would be a very good time for you to better your position by taking a job in California or up in New York. I bet Dagoberto would—"

"That sounds like quite an effort, darlin'."

"Well, of course it does, but—"

"My plan is to float to the top, not to swim there."

"Now, I'll tell you something about that," said Tiffany. "I saw on the TV that men are heavier than water, and so you better not be thinking you're going to float to any top of anything."

George laughed.

"And trainers are leaving the business in England all the time. I read that in the *Thoroughbred Times*. Even the trainer for the Queen of England is leaving the business because he can't make money racing in England, and—"

"In Ireland you don't have to make money, darlin', you just need something to do to keep you occupied during the day—"

"And the sheiks are moving their whole operation to France because the bookies in England won't give back more than one percent of their take because they can always get out of horse racing entirely and stick with football—"

"You've been reading those racing magazines in your spare time!"

"Well, of course I have, you should, too. Now—"

"I'm thinking I need to find my level, Tiff. You need to find your level, too, you know. I just have a feeling your level is several stories up from mine."

"Well, if I had your experience and knowledge, I wouldn't be going back to Ireland!"

"Oh, wouldn't you, now? Well, don't you know that's where you soak it up? In Ireland, it comes right into you with the air you breathe. You should go with me, dearie. They'd eat you up like sweet buns in Ireland."

Ah, well, Deirdre's heart flipped over on that one, but Tiffany tossed her tiny braids and said, "No, thank you."

And so George made his reservations, and they all knew he was just happy to go back and be another Irishman among Irishmen.

And then Helen came to Deirdre one morning, and said, "Deirdre, honey, I just want to tell you my plan, because, even though I'm going to keep doing your books and all, I'm going to do them from home, because, you know, I've gone into the consulting business."

She held up an ad. It read: "Which phone company? Which cellular? Which computer? Which Internet provider? Which insurance plan? And where should I go for lunch? Let me arrange your life. I know ALL the details, and what's more, I've read the fine print! LET'S GET GOING, Helen Vanden Plas, 1-800-876-5432."

"What are you charging?"

"Seventy-five dollars an hour."

"Gotten any calls?"

"Twenty-six so far. Ten jobs."

"Want to buy a racehorse? It's a good tax deduction."

"Ah, sweetie, don't I know it. I'll still see you, honey. I'll come out and have lunch with you."

Maybe she would. But it was nice to know she would think about it.

Two days later, the van came in and picked up Mary Lynn and Skippy's horses. Two were going to New York, one to Kentucky, and the other three to California. Deirdre watched as Tiffany wrapped them. She wrapped the chestnuts in green, the gray in red, the bay in yellow, and the brown in electric blue. She did a good job, even all the way down, not too tight, not too loose. Then she led them up the ramp one by one and clipped them into their stalls. The van guys lifted the ramp, and then they were gone with a puff of diesel exhaust. Now, of the six non-Hollister horses, there was only one horse left, because she had told all her owners she was leaving the business. That horse was racing that afternoon, and would surely be claimed. If not, his owner, who was a bettor who claimed and lost a horse maybe once a year, had said he would take him off the next day, and that would be that.

Only Tiffany remained.

Deirdre had told her to go back to Dagoberto, who was in Florida. With her five months' experience working for Deirdre and some persuasion from Deirdre herself, not to mention the fact that Tiffany's horses had won $114,000 since August, over $200,000 altogether, Deirdre was sure Tiffany could write her own ticket with Dagoberto. Tiffany didn't say anything one way or another, and Deirdre didn't say anything more, either, because the best thing about her day every day, and the one thing that made her the grateful, mild-mannered, and accepting woman she had miraculously become, was the sight of Tiffany in her jeans from the Gap and her Australian boots and her cowboy hat and her tiny little braids and her orchid-colored polo shirt from Lands' End. Tiffany's position in Deirdre's barn was flexible, especially now that there was only one horse. What she elected to do on this, his last day, was groom him three times, top to bottom, and clean his bridle, and make sure, it looked like, that all the straws in his stall were oriented in the same direction. Deirdre said, "You'll be rubbin' the hair off the poor beast."

"There's nothing to do. I stripped the other stalls yesterday. And I cleaned the feed room, too. He can use a bit of affection. He seems like he's gone without it. I think that makes them a little dull."

"Darlin', a poorly bred horse who's only won three out of thirty starts *is* a little dull."

"Maybe a little affection would wake him up and give him some reason to, you know—"

"Win a race?"

"Well, yes."

"You are a sentimental thing, I must say."

"The horses like me."

"Yes, they do. Tiffany, you could be rubbin' some nice animals—your own."

"You said you wouldn't have them here."

"Your livelihood is of importance to me, especially as you are a young woman with a significant horse habit. As I am paying you such a pittance, and that is about to end, you need—"

Tiffany always hated this line of talk, and interrupted her at once. "What's the most horses you ever had in your barn?"

"Racehorses? About forty. That was three or four years ago."

"Before the wreck."

"Long before. But I had sixty horses in my barn when I had the jumpers, for about five years there. It was a fair operation for a twenty-four-year-old girl to take on. I didn't know what I was doing, which was a fine thing, and the best way to be with horses, if you ask me."

"How many did you ride every day?"

"Six or eight. I didn't groom them, though. I had a couple of young men just for that. Young in the sense that they were unmarried, but they were older than I, och, everyone was older than I then. It was a full-time job just sending in the show entries and keeping track of the show tack and equipment. During the show season, you could run your fingernails against their skin and come up clean, and that was horses who had turnout every day and did their best to put themselves in a mess."

Tiffany sighed.

"That is not a desirable life, Tiffany, my girl."

"You would still be doing it if you hadn't broken your back."

"Let's talk about you. Now, I had a little chat with Bill Trout, and he's got a couple of horses for you to rub, two allowance winners and a two-year-old with some good breeding. He said if you groomed for a bit and he saw how you worked with the horses he would—"

"Deirdre, I've got five horses in Florida. If I got them here when they were going north, my expenses would be a lot less—"

"Now, darlin', here's something I'm going to tell you, and I'm only going to tell you this one time, so I want you to stop picking apart that horse's mane and listen."

Tiffany lifted her head and turned her splendid gaze toward Deirdre.

"I'm done with this business."

"Cakes are done, people are finished."

"Thank you for correcting my usage. I am finished with this business. I've told you all along it's a bad business, and I understand that you and I don't agree about its merits relative to dealing drugs, litigating anti-trust cases, working in the federal government, spending your life in the prison system, recording rap music, cooking Italian food, working at Wal-Mart, singing in the church choir, or selling real estate. I accept your views, dear, but I am burnt to a crisp by this business. I have had enough."

"You know so many things that I may never learn—"

"Last night, I lay awake and I estimated how many horses have passed though my hands in the last thirty years. I came up with thirty-five hundred. Thirty-five hundred horses that I have laid hands upon, ridden, contemplated, dreamt about, decided the fate of, lost, hurt, broken down, misjudged, wondered about."

"Learned from," said Tiffany.

"Gotten futilely attached to," said Deirdre.

"Do you remember all their names?"

"No, but I bet I could remember something about each one if I were reminded."

Tiffany came out of the stall. She said, "I know you care more about this than you're letting on."

"Do you?"

"I know you are sad."

"Then you know more than I do, Tiffany." Deirdre looked at her watch. It was about an hour and a half until race time, and that was late, since the horse was running in the last race of the day. Tiffany stepped right up to Deirdre and put her hands on her hips. Deirdre looked up at her. She said, "You know, Deirdre, no one ever has asked you what *you* are going to do now."

"And why do you think I would tell you?"

Tiffany smiled mischievously. "Because I'm the last one around and we're alone?"

"I am a cross-grained woman and I never do what's expected of me."

"You always say that, but I don't see it, frankly. I think you're sweet."

"Mother of God." Deirdre crossed her arms in front of her chest. "I'll never be able to hold my head up around this place again."

The horse, who had been eating some hay, lifted his head and put it over the stall guard and pricked his ears at her. He was a run-of-the-mill four-year-old chestnut with a run-of-the-mill white splotch on his forehead. She had claimed him for the owner about three weeks before and run him once since then. She would not have claimed him, but the owner was a faithful believer in form, graphs, numbers, and thought he was due for a bounce. He had lingered without bouncing, dwelling, as Deirdre told the owner, in his lusterless pedigree. He surely would not be one of the thirty-five hundred equines that Deirdre would remember. Even now she wasn't quite sure of his name. And yet, though he was forgettable and she was burnt to a crisp with it all, the sight of those inquisitive eyes and those alert ears in that long face (A horse went into a bar; the bartender said to him, "Why the long face?" A horse went into a pub; the landlord said, "Why the long face?" This was a universal joke) tickled her.

"What do you *want* to do?" said Tiffany.

"Well, now, that's the difficulty, isn't it? I know what I don't want to do, but I don't quite know what I do want to do. But there's the opportunity, isn't it? Horses was what I wanted to do, and horses have made me . . ." Her voice trailed off.

"With me," said Tiffany, "the problem was knowing what there was to do."

"Ah, well. Now, I never learned to cook nor sew nor please a man nor please my teachers nor read a book nor watch television, so you see— Och, I'm going across to the cafeteria for a bite. You rub that horse again—I see a speck has landed upon him from above—and when the owner gets here, you practice your people skills upon him, because, darlin', everything you know about the horses is for naught if you cannot make their owners feel important."

And she turned on her heel and walked away.

IT WAS AMAZING how quickly it had all boiled away, those thirty-five hundred horses, those friends she had taken into her heart. This afternoon, with luck, it would all be gone, and by bedtime tonight she would be a forty-one-year-old woman with nothing to show for years of effort. All over the track, she knew, there were trainers going under. Trainers went under. That was part of their job description. You lost your barn of stakes and allowance horses at Belmont, and then you turned up a while later at Charlestown or Fingerlakes, and you had a horse or two, and you lived at the track and cooked on a hotplate. Where had you been all those months? Or you lost your own horses and went to work for someone else, rubbing their horses. If you were young enough and little enough, you rode their horses. Or, if you had some presentability, you went to Kentucky or New York or California and worked on a studfarm or a training farm. At least, thanks to the wonderful mare and her splendid filly, she was breaking even. That didn't always happen. But Deirdre wasn't mistaken about being finished. She was finished. George was right about her, she had taken it all too much to heart, and now what she couldn't explain to Tiffany was that she couldn't stand it anymore. The drama that still delighted others had worn her out.

And, after thirty-five hundred horses, could there be another one who could get to her? Who could say, I am interesting enough for you? She dared him, or her, to come along. She dared him or her to seek her out in that retail-outlet mall or that office or that coffee shop or that car dealership where she, Deirdre Donohue, planned to renew her existence and seek her fortune.

53 / MARVELOUS

AFTER NEW YEAR'S, Residual came out of her layoff like a debutante swathed in golden tulle. She won the Artemis Stakes (G2). She had her picture in *The Blood-Horse*, galloping home alone on a hand ride. People stopped saying "Breeders' Cup" and started saying "Kentucky Derby." Buddy felt the old familiar surge of ambition, and he felt it in the old familiar way, as something soothing and accustomed, a nice on-ramp that the Lexus turned onto of its own accord, that led clearly and unequivocally to a named freeway and a known and desirable destination. He had a revelation—all the wrestling with his conscience, or with Jesus, or whatever, that he had been doing in the last year was something he could choose not to do. It was that simple. And then, of course, Deedee revealed her condition.

Buddy knew perfectly well that Residual wasn't the sort of filly who could get used to another exercise rider—Deedee, he thought, was a flake, but, horse-wise, an exceptionally tactful flake. Buddy took her aside, behind the barn, far out of the earshot of anyone, and he whispered to her in a very low voice, so low that perhaps even Jesus could not hear. Certainly Deedee could not hear. She said, "What?"

Buddy murmured, "Have you considered terminating the pregnancy?"

Deedee sniffed.

"You and Leon are very young still."

Deedee looked off into the distance.

"Kentucky Derby."

"I already told my mother."

That was that.

So there was a delay with Residual while they tried to find another exercise rider she liked. The problem was subtle. She was never disagreeable or reluctant, but even when the rider liked her, and they all did, it was clear that she couldn't find her rhythm the way she had with Deedee. Finally, Buddy persuaded the jockey to turn up every morning, but even he didn't have quite the touch Deedee did. It was hard for him to put away the last little competitive bits and attend completely to the filly. He was good enough, though Buddy in general didn't like jockeys' exercising horses. When the jockey got on, that was meant to be a signal that something different was taking place, and Buddy thought it was confusing to a horse when the jockey got on in the morning. And then the jockey broke his wrist on some cheap claimer (to tell the truth, one of Buddy's own cheap claimers) and was out two weeks. Buddy tried raiding the exercise staff of some of the other trainers, and that was when he understood that no one wanted to work for him, even to ride the fabulous filly.

MARVELOUS MARTHA was in her fifties, anyway. No one knew where she came from, and she wasn't saying. One rumor was that she had been married to the famous Jimmy Williams for a week or so at one time or another. Marvelous Martha wasn't saying anything about that, either. But she was such a legend that, a long time ago, a guy had named a filly after her, and the filly had won several allowances and a stakes, and then gone on to produce nine foals, seven runners, six winners, and one stakes winner. Marvelous Martha lived in Berkeley and worked as a free-lance theatrical art director in the Bay Area in the afternoons and evenings. In the mornings, she exercised horses at Golden Gate. She had no other duties—she didn't clean tack, she didn't make conversation, she was paid in cash, and since she didn't drive a car, a taxi had to be sent for her. She was expensive. Buddy flew up to San Francisco and went to her house in Berkeley, where she received him skeptically. He described his dilemma.

"Mary Bacon rode until her baby was born. What's wrong with this girl?"

"She won't do it."

"I hate L.A." She poured a cup of chai and pushed it across the table to him.

"I can move her out to Santa Anita for the duration."

"Put me up at the Ritz?" She got a twinkle in her eye.

Buddy gulped.

Marvelous Martha laughed. "That's okay. A short-term lease on an apartment will do."

"You'll come and try her?"

"I always get along with the horse. I'm sure I'll get along with the horse."

"Good, then—"

"No bute, no steroids, no turndowns, no toegrabs. We work the first set every day. No press. I don't talk to anyone at any time. And when I get off, you have a glass of spinach-and-wheat-grass-and-carrot juice waiting for me. I go home every Saturday afternoon and come back Monday night. You pay. Including my taxi ride to and from the airport in Oakland."

What could he say? Besides, he would put it on the owner's bill.

And she was marvelous. Of course she had been married to Jimmy Williams; even at fifty-something, her look on a horse was sexy and magical. Residual looked happy and relaxed, and turned in a bullet work. Buddy nominated her for the Delilah Handicap (G1), to be run February 7, which would be, he thought, a nice warm-up for a race against the boys.

The elderly owner kept saying, "Is this all right for her? Is this going to hurt her? She's such a sweetheart. She doesn't have to go to the Kentucky Derby at all, Buddy. I don't care about that."

But Buddy did care about it. He had had several potential Derby horses over the years. None of them had gotten to the starting gate. This filly had as good a chance as any one of them. When he went to church with his wife—he still did that, he was keeping his doubts to himself—he promised that he would get back to Jesus when the Triple Crown was over.

———

AND THEN the owner died. It was all over the papers when he woke up one morning. Azalea Warren, the last of the real Warrens, after whom mining towns all over California had been named, the great-granddaughter of Frederick Warren, the granddaughter of Senator Ezra Washington Warren, the daughter of, the cousin of, the sister of, the niece of. But not the mother of. Miss Warren had no issue. A banker called him the very next day and told him that the horses were to be sold at auction. Buddy pointed out that the best auctions were months away. Could they, the banker asked, be mothballed, as it were?

Buddy explained that a racehorse was a dynamic rather than a static asset. You had to keep it moving forward, both literally and in its training. In fact, he got rather eloquent, for him, expounding on the temporary and unpredictable nature of a racehorse's value. He used Residual as an example. Here she was, hot as a firecracker, worth seven figures at least, but she could die tomorrow, and then she would be worth nothing, since Miss Warren had not believed in insuring her animals. The banker afforded Buddy a lengthy silence, during which Buddy stared out the window of his office. The blinds were open. Out in the barn aisle, horses came and went, exercise riders threw their tack over the tack bar and cleaned it, the vet Curtis Doheny walked by, two jockey agents approached, and then all the people and animals parted and Buddy saw her. The banker said, "How would I sell her, then, while she is still valuable?"

"I can do that for you, for a standard ten-percent commission."

The banker understood the concept of standard commission quite well. Buddy tried to be helpful. "She would have to be appraised, of course."

"Who would do that?"

"A horse agent."

"Do you have some names?"

"I can supply you with two or three."

"Fine."

"Sir Michael Ordway is one." As he gave Sir Michael's number, Buddy continued to watch her come, sashaying down the aisle, sunglasses in her hand, cupidity in her face. Andrea Melanie Kingston. Buddy finished with the banker and hung up as the door to his office opened. When she came in, saying, "Oh, Buddy!," he said, "Mrs. Kingston, today is your lucky day." After that, it was too easy. He took Andrea Melanie to Residual's stall. The filly was eating her hay. When Andrea Melanie said, "Oh, Buddy!," the filly lifted her lovely head and turned her liquid eyes and looked deeply into Andrea Melanie's countenance. When Buddy mentioned the words "ten-percent commission from the buyer," Andrea Melanie nodded enthusiastically, as if such a thing would be a distinct privilege.

THE SALE WAS COMPLETED two days before the race, and on the day of the race, Buddy thought, everybody acted like they were going to a wedding. Andrea Melanie wore a cream-colored suit and a shiny little hat. Jason Clark Kingston, now Residual's owner, so recently relieved of $1.4 million, wore pinstripes. Marvelous Martha went home and turned up in this pink outfit. Leon had on a navy blazer, and Buddy himself had on his usual charcoal gray. And then, in the morning, Buddy's wife called and said she was coming out, and here she came in robin's-egg blue, with the shoes to match. Deedee decked the filly out with a couple of braids. The jockey wore burnt orange. It was a sunny day, and the filly looked gold-plated. When the jockey was put up and they followed the horses out of the walking ring, Buddy saw that fans were reaching out their hands toward her, saying, "Hey, filly! Hey, Residual! Hey, baby!" And then they shouted at him, "Good luck, Buddy!" "You gonna win, Buddy?" "Great filly, Buddy!"

Buddy himself was not happy. It was like being at a party where they'd planned too long and spent too much money and they expected the fun to arrive any minute now. In fact, it was like being at a wedding. In fact, it was like being at every one of the weddings of his children. It was bad luck to plan like this. It closed the box. It left no room for the unexpected. The filly was carrying 117 pounds, but it might as well be two hundred, thought Buddy, with the weight of everyone's expectations.

He put on a happy face, held the hand of Andrea Melanie, looked deep into her eyes, reassured her of his faith in the filly, but even as he said the words, he felt himself get smaller and farther away. On the way up to the box, he veered off and placed his bets, and he placed his bets with confidence, but not with joy, sorrow, or fear. He said, "Give me a hundred dollars on number four across the board in the seventh race," and then he knew he was having the worst moment of his life. He knew it was the worst moment of his life because all the other worst moments went over him in an avalanche—every time his father turned away from him, shaking his head in disappointment, all those moments when he waited to grow taller than five feet five and didn't, all the times he realized that he was angry and his anger was expanding around him. Horses dying, breaking down, getting claimed or not claimed, owners leaving. You name it. If it was a bad moment, he relived it now, in the worst moment. And the way he knew it was the worst moment was that there was nothing wrong at all. Everything was as good as it could get in this world for him, and that told him that there would never be any relief. He took his ticket and moved away from the window. His ticket looked strange to him. The betting hall looked strange to him. All of the other bettors and race-goers swam around him and he had no energy left. He nearly sank down, but instead he put one foot in front of the other and managed to get to his box, where the wedding guests were watching the bride parade to the gate. He put his head in his hand and thought, "I don't know what the fuck I am doing."

The race was a mile and an eighth, so the gate was at the top of the stretch. He saw the horses go in, he heard the bell clang, he saw the gate open and the horses break. They ran past. Residual was there with them, but it was meaningless. The horses headed into the first turn. Residual had moved up and taken the lead, but it was to no avail. Buddy didn't think this filly, or any other horse, would ever get a rise out of him again.

But of course he was wrong. As the horses entered the backstretch, it impressed itself upon him that there was something not right about the track, and then, a split-second later, he realized what it was. The gate had not moved, was not moving. It stood stationary across the width of the track, as if it had been built there. Buddy looked away from the horses, and came alive at the same moment everyone in the stands came alive, in time to watch the guy who normally drove the tractor that towed the gate off the track stand up and wave his arms. Right then, the announcer began shouting, "Jockeys! Hold your horses! Jockeys! Stop your horses!" Half the grandstand, half of Buddy's companions, rose to their feet. The other half pushed themselves back in their chairs. It was a sunny day. The horses kept running. Residual was still in the lead, now by a length and half. They came into the second turn. The announcer was now screaming, "Jockeys! Heads up! Alex! Chris! Stop your horses!"

Stop your hearts, thought Buddy. He glanced at Andrea Melanie. Tears were pouring down her cheeks. Jason Clark Kingston was blanched to the roots of his hair. The horses were bunched and focused, the arrow had left the bow, the bullet had left the barrel of the gun. No turning back now. That was what everyone was thinking.

But no. They were horses, not missiles. Through his binoculars, Buddy saw the filly's head go up, and then the heads of the others, and then the smooth stream of speed broke up, eddied, spun this way and that, and then there were just individual riders and mounts scattered about the track; the race was over, the danger was past, the thought that something bad might happen was wrong, and nothing was lost except the betting pool.

That night, Buddy knelt beside his bed, his habit, and he gave thanks, full-hearted thanks, not his habit, the way you do when you have seen a possibility that you never want to see again. The fact was, he felt a little saved again. Not inspiringly saved, but a little saved, the way he had felt as a boy when his father said, "I'll give you one more chance."

54 / EPISTEMOLOGY
AND HERMENEUTICS

A T Belmont Park, Epic Steam came to hand very quickly. Yes, in the barn he was surrounded by mares, all of whom were on progesterone and emphatically never in season. Yes, they used a stud chain on him, and whenever Luciano worked on him he was twitched, and Frankie came to Dick and asked him to pay for a big life-insurance policy for the duration, but there was no bolting, no rioting in the starting gate, no attacking other horses. Dick knew that the stewards were watching, and that the starter was *really* watching, but there was nothing the horse could be accused of. Dick was watching, too, watching insatiably. He couldn't take his eyes off the horse. Every stride entranced him. Privately, Dick thought that he was seeing the return of Ribot or Nearco, both of whom appeared in his pedigree more than once, and both of whom had been unruly in their day. There was no petting the horse or making up to him. But you could watch him all day and never get enough. You had to keep him tired, though, just for safety's sake. He worked three-quarters, seven-eighths. He galloped or trotted on his days off, and in fact, had no days off. When Herman Newman, having had unauthorized conversation with other owners who had their own opinions, questioned the program, Dick got a little firm with him. "Citation! You know Citation worked a mile! They had to work two horses with him, one at the beginning and one at the end, to keep him sharp! This is your first horse, Mr. Newman, so you don't realize how remarkable he is, but he could be a legend!" And then Derby Derby Derby, just to keep the guy a little off balance. It was worth not going to Florida, changing his whole mode of operation, to keep the horse at Belmont and Aqueduct, where there was plenty of space, just to watch the animal.

In fact, the colt was working quite nicely, and Dick had him ready for a race. The colt was working so nicely that Dick was tempted to imagine himself as a genius—a person who understands the few simple elements of any process that will propel it forward where always before it has been fatally retarded. And now that the colt was working so well, a lot of people were looking at him in a new way. His quirks, like viciousness, appeared to have been taken care of. No longer did his unpredictability serve as a disincentive, and Dick knew that Herman Newman was the belle of the ball.

They talked every day. Herman Newman was a nice man, but you had to tell him everything over and over. What was a blinker again? What were rundowns again? Tell me again what Legend is? How do you mean, prophylactic? Arthritis in a three-year-old? Tell me again, is a three-quarters work a minute, eight seconds good? Tell me again, what should I say to this reporter? There were lots of apologies—Herman Newman was always saying, You know, I take this, what is it, ginkgo biloba for my memory, and maybe it is getting worse, but I don't know. I've always liked to be reminded right now of what I already know. It drives my wife crazy. But, you know, you don't know the same thing today as you did yesterday. Every day, the sun comes up all over again. And so-and-so called me again.

So-and-so. Here was Dick's deepest worry, the paradox of his existence. Herman Newman could be seduced at any moment. Horse agents called him all the time, French, English, sometimes American. Then he would call Dick for advice. This guy Tommy Ormond called. His buyer was a quiet man, didn't like his name in the papers. "Japanese," said Dick.

"The Japanese don't have any money anymore," said Herman Newman.

"They do at the top," said Dick.

"Why won't he tell me his name?"

"There's a lot of secrecy in horse racing," said Dick.

"Tell me again why that is."

"Because there's a lot of money at stake, especially on the betting side."

"Should I sell the horse?"

"Don't ask me that," said Dick.

"Who can I ask? I don't know anyone but you. Tell me again why I shouldn't sell the horse."

"Because he's a great horse. He can win for you and make you a lot of money."

"Okay."

And then, later in the day, "Hi, Herman Newman here. This guy called me, Simon St. Melbourne. What is he, Australian?"

"English."

"He has a buyer."

"From Hong Kong, I bet. He has Hong Kong connections."

"There's still plenty of money in Hong Kong. Some of it's Chinese, too. You think Beijing is interested in this horse?"

"I have no idea, Mr. Newman."

And then, "Herman Newman here. This guy Gustave Galopin or something like that called me."

"Arabs. They haven't had much of an interest in American racing until lately."

"Tell me again—"

In fact, there was no reason for the man not to sell the horse. Herman Newman was not a horseman, and seemed uncomfortable in his new role as owner. All over the world, on the other hand, there were deserving men who had spent dozens of years and millions of dollars without ever coming close to a horse like Epic Steam. Why should Herman Newman, a man who couldn't remember what a blinker was from one day to the next, run a horse like this one, when men who knew horses, who had horses in their blood, who in some cases believed that they had been horses in previous lifetimes, had no chance at him? Ah. Well. Of all the things in the world that were unfair, ownership, that simplest of them, often seemed the unfairest of all.

There was only one reason for Herman Newman to own Epic Steam, and that was that Dick Winterson wanted to train the animal. Of course, if he put him in a good race and the horse won, which Dick was sure he would, then the pressure on Herman Newman to do the right thing would only increase.

EPIC STEAM was ready to run. More important, Herman Newman was ready for him to run. "Tell me again why we missed this Count Fleet Stakes? Tell me again why you scratched him, is that the word, from the Whirlaway Stakes? It's all right with me if he gets shipped somewhere. Whatever it takes. Tell me again why you don't want to ship him?"

"He's hard to handle."

"Didn't you tell me he seems to have turned over a new leaf?"

"Yes, I did."

"Don't you trust him?"

"I'm starting to trust him."

"Tell me again why you don't want to put him in a race."

"I do want to put him in a race. But I want it to be the right race."

"What would be the right race?"

One that no one in the world was looking at.

"I think maybe the Paumonok Stakes."

"Have I heard of that race?"

"No. It's a prep race. If he does well, he can go in a famous race."

"Okay. Tell me again when they run this race?"

"In a couple of weeks."

"Should I be there?"

"Yes, you should, Mr. Newman."

"You just remind me what to wear and do."

"You're very game, Mr. Newman."

"I'll tell you something. I don't mind looking like an idiot. I never have. People who are worried about appearances don't get anywhere. They're always checking themselves out. That takes a lot of time that, at my age, I don't have. So I look like an idiot, so what, you know what I mean?"

"I do, sir. The Paumonok Stakes. I will keep you informed."

"Tell me again what that race is worth?"

"About a hundred thousand dollars to the winner."

"That's a nice piece of change."

"Yes it is, sir."

IT WAS ONLY on the morning of the race that Dick realized that he had never actually run Epic Steam before. He had worked him and read about his previous races and fantasized about every named race there was and obsessed day and night about the horse, but when it came to actually knowing what the horse would do in a race, or, for that matter, in the saddling enclosure, in the test barn, under the stands, out on the track with ten thousand people looking at him and yelling, well, that he didn't actually know. An oversight of some magnitude.

To Herman Newman, he said, "The horse is well prepared and fit. He's been training superbly. I think he's as ready as he's gonna be." Whistling in the dark.

To himself, he recited all his own statistics—horses trained, races won, money earned, blah blah blah. But it didn't matter. Every step out of the barn with this horse was a blindfolded step toward the edge of a cliff. You didn't know where the drop would be. Actually, the training had been going fine, and for the last two weeks they had even trained the horse with a four-year-old gelding, to accustom him at least a little to the proximity of another horse. The gelding was a big self-confident turf horse, a little on the phlegmatic side. His exercise rider was big and phlegmatic, too, and a couple of times when Epic Steam pinned his ears to bite his partner that guy gave him a cut across the face with his whip to ponder at his leisure. It wasn't something Dick liked to do, but that, too, worked well enough.

Dick wondered why sometimes all the evidence in the world that everything was fine wasn't enough to convince you.

Frankie took a different attitude toward the whole thing. He just shrugged and said, "Look, boss, my opinion? Stop making a special deal out of this horse. Put the jockey on him, tell him to run, and leave it at that. You're giving yourself a heart attack trying to figure this horse out. Bottom line? He's a fucking horse."

And so Herman Newman showed up, and so his wife showed up, and she was the sort of wife Dick would never sleep with, which was a relief, and so his sons and their wives showed up, and the same went for them, and it was like showing a vanload of tourists around. One of the sons was in toys, also, and another was a professor of something like medieval Russian history and the third was a rabbi. Yes, a real rabbi, with the hat and the coat and the long curls. Dick had never seen a rabbi at the track before, but he was glad. Maybe, he thought, that was the secret to Herman Newman's run of luck. He made a point to brush against the rabbi and then touch the horse with that hand, since he didn't dare invite the rabbi to endanger himself by approaching the horse.

The Newmans stood in a circle around the horse, at a safe distance, contemplating him. What's more, as they contemplated him, he put aside his busyness for a moment and contemplated them. At this moment, Dick took the opportunity offered and threw the jockey into the saddle. The jockey exchanged a glance with him. The glance said, So far so good, here goes.

Dick shepherded the Newmans through the betting hall and up to his box. It took a while, because the Newmans were amazed by everything they saw. Even Herman, who had been here a couple of dozen times, seemed freshly amazed. By the time everyone was seated, Epic Steam had picked up his pony and was out on the track. The rabbi, who upon perusal looked to be rather young, leaned around his wife and touched Dick's sleeve. He said, "This equine of ours seems to me to have a rather intransigent quality."

"You're not the first to notice that, but I'm surprised you noticed it so quickly."

"Would this be a good quality in a racehorse?"

"Within certain limits, yes."

The man pressed his fingers into his beard and regarded the track. He said, "Highly ritualized."

Dick said, "It's the same every day, everywhere, all year round."

"I like that," said the rabbi. "I might come back."

"You don't see too many rabbis at the track."

"What are those numbers on that display there?"

"Those are the odds. The odds on our horse are three to one. He's had lots of good races, but he hasn't raced for a long time, so the bettors like him, but he isn't the favorite."

"This is a strange thing for my father to do."

"Why is that?"

"All his forebears were revolutionaries. I'm the black sheep of the family. My grandfather would have died to see his grandson a rabbi. He nearly died, or said he did, when my father revealed he was investing in the stock market. When he told us he bought a racehorse, my mother took him to his doctor. She really did. But now we don't mind. I'll tell you something. My father is a man of perfect innocence, at least as far as I've ever seen. He never manufactured a toy that had to be recalled or was even rumored to be unsafe. But that's not what I mean by innocent. That's just not guilty. It's more like every experience is new to him, no matter how many times he's done it before."

"I've noticed that," said Dick. Epic Steam went into the gate, then backed out, then went in again, then backed out again. Two men closed in on his rear. He kicked out but missed both of them. Then he went into the gate and stayed there. Dick said to the rabbi, "There they go."

The big dark horse broke from the third slot and bounded forward. For Dick, he alone was distinct in the swirl of horseflesh. It wasn't even voluntary. His gaze simply picked out Epic Steam and focused on him and the others disappeared. The horse was not in the lead, but about four lengths back in the third lane, running forward like a normal racehorse. It went on like that. Dick began to think he was a genius again. Thinking he was a genius felt like a sort of inner melting—gravel turning to molasses. Or maybe that was just the feeling of relief. The horses came out of the first turn, Epic Steam as crystal clear as the moon on a dark night. Dick could see his tail streaming, his muscles stretching, the hand of the jockey on the rein, holding but not pulling. "Every horse is trainable." That's what he would say to the press when they asked. There were other good horses in the race, horses people were talking about in only positive terms. Dick couldn't make them out. Down the backstretch, Epic Steam went a little wide, into the fourth lane, and then the fifth lane. The horses went into the second turn. The leaders, three of them, were bunched on the rail. Epic Steam was fifth. But he was wide.

The rabbi said, "The horse seems to be awfully far to the outside. Geometrically, isn't that unwise—"

"Watch this," said Dick.

The big dark horse swept around the turn, far away from the others. And then they were in the stretch. Epic Steam was in the middle of the track now, all by himself, and Dick realized that this was how he had to run, way to the outside. It was the only safe way. But, of course, the horse was fit enough to climb Mount Everest. And here was the payoff. With nothing to distract him, the horse bolted for the finish line, passing so far to the outside of the other animals that they didn't see him and so didn't hook on and catch fire. Maybe even the other jockeys didn't see him. He was a stealth bomber. The jockey didn't even have to go for his whip—in fact, it looked like, the guy just had to hold on tight and hope he could stop the horse in time to get to the winner's circle. The horse won by a length. It was only then, sitting there for a moment, that Dick felt the depths of his own fear, all that fear he had been covering over for God knew how long. Then he stood up and shepherded the Newmans down to the winner's circle. They, of course, were amazed.

While they were standing there with the photographer and with the actress who was to help the track president give out the trophy, waiting for Epic Steam and his jockey and his groom to return from the next borough, Dick said to the rabbi, "Your father really deserves this."

"You may think so," said the rabbi. "Sure he does. But the wonderful thing about my father is, he never even thinks about what he deserves."

Dick wondered what Herman Newman would possibly talk to other owners about, should he find himself engaged in such a conversation.

And here came the horse, exhausted but still alight, his neck arched, his nostrils flared, all his veins standing out, full of himself, and, you might say, happy. Herman Newman, forgetful of every warning Dick had ever given him, went up to the horse and embraced him around the neck. And then they drew up in a line and the cameraman clicked the photo, and Dick remembered that in horse racing, always and forever, luck was better than genius. And that's what he told the guys from *The Blood-Horse* and the *Thoroughbred Times* when they asked him.

55 / PARK MIN JONG

JESSE OFTEN WONDERED whether his thoughts influenced events. For example, his mother had just called him to dinner, and he was walking toward the table and noticing that she had made eggplant parmesan and thinking that he didn't like eggplant parmesan when the front door slammed open and Leo burst in. His mother said, "Oh, Leo, there you are, I just put—"

But Leo ran into the bedroom. Jesse went to the doorway of the bedroom, and saw that his dad had a gun in his hand, and was loading bullets into it. Jesse had never seen a gun before, except in the movies or on television.

Leo was jamming bullets into the cylinder. Jesse turned and went out, went over to his mother, who was sitting quietly at the table. He sat down in his place. She didn't say anything, didn't even seem to notice him, but then, when Leo came into the room, she startled. Leo said, "I'm going to Park Min Jong."

This was a park that Jesse had never heard of. "Why are you taking a gun, Dad?" said Jesse as Leo snapped the gun into his shoulder holster and then slipped his arm into the strap. "Are there gangs there?"

"I'm just going to make sure. I won't use it unless I have to, but I'm going to make sure."

"Make sure of what, Leo?" said his mom, quietly, more as if she had to say it than as if she really wanted to know.

"Well, it's simple. I called that bookie yesterday at eleven-thirty. I can get the phone-company records to back me up. And I said, 'Give me fifty on the sixth horse in the first race and fifty on the third horse in the second race.' The odds were eight to one on the first horse and six to one on the second horse. I know those were the bets, because I remember the feeling I had—six one three two—you know, that was the address of that apartment we lived in that time, remember that?"

"That was six one three three," said Jesse's mom.

"Well, exactly, but you can't make the daily double on the third race. It's got to be on the second race." He looked at her with fond irritation, and said, "You know, I don't understand why you can't get a grasp of that thing. That's the simplest thing in racing, what the daily double is. Anyway, those were the bets I made. Do I have to record myself now? Keep some kind of unimpeachable record? I mean, what is happening to this country? When Mickey Cohen ran things, well, my dad would tell you, they ran pretty well, but that's because, between you and me, they were run by Jews."

"Where are you going with the gun, Leo?"

"These Korean bookies have their own boss, you know, they all do. That's what happened to this country. Every ethnic group has its own boss. It isn't like when I was a boy, Jess, when things were more centralized. Now you've got to be schlepping down to Korea Town, or—" He broke off. His hair seemed to stand on end. Jesse always had this feeling, that when his father got angry his hair stood on end. "What the hell am I wasting my time here for? The God-damned payoff on that bet was over fourteen hundred dollars, and if I don't get it, there's going to be a payoff, let me tell you!"

"Leo—"

But his dad was out the door, throwing on a jacket, before his mom finished her sentence. She got up and went into the kitchen without looking at him. Jesse sat down at the table and focused on the eggplant parmesan. It was red, with white cheese over the top, and there were orange streaks of grease on the cheese, blackish crusty things around the sides. It had a strong smell, probably not a bad one—he could imagine its even being a good one if you were in a certain mood. But he wasn't in that mood. He knew that he should look away from the eggplant, that he was making the eggplant look worse to him than it had to, but he just kept looking at the eggplant anyway.

His mom came out of the kitchen with some bread in a basket and a smile on her face. She set the bread down and then sat down herself, and pretty soon a big spoon went into the eggplant, and a big lump of it went onto his plate. Steam rose around it like a ghost. A big lump of it went onto his mom's plate. She was still smiling. Jesse knew all about that smile. It was a smile she was doing a good job at, and it was all she could manage for right now. As Jesse incorporated most of the eggplant into his system, he thought about the jockeys at the track, their stomachs, and he thought about the eggplant going around the knot in his own stomach, just sliding around it, and it got down okay. After they had finished, she said, "I'll clear this up, honey. It isn't much. Why don't you go do your homework right now, and then maybe we'll play a game before you go to bed."

He didn't have any homework, so Jesse read a few chapters of an old *Goosebumps* book that he had under his bed. Then he cleaned out some of the stuff under there—there were lots of candy wrappers, some popcorn, and a couple of withered apple cores, as well as shreds of this and that. He didn't understand how things under the bed got shredded like that, but okay. Finally, because his mom seemed to want him to, Jesse came out of his room and walked across the living room and sat down beside her. She smiled instantly, and then said the very thing that Jesse had refused to say to himself all evening: "I hope your father doesn't get hurt."

"I didn't know he had a gun," said Jesse.

"Let's play Uno Stacko."

"Okay."

She went over to the shelf and got the game, a tall stack of red, green, yellow, and blue plastic pieces shaped like I-beams. The point was to try and remove the lower beams and place them on top of the stack, until you had a very unstable tower that suddenly fell over. Leo would always give him a dollar if it fell over on his turn. But, then again, Leo would always take a dollar from him if it fell over on Jesse's turn. Leo was a believer in justice rather than mercy. He had said that over and over for years, since long before Jesse knew what either justice or mercy was.

She carefully set up the stack, aligning it with the cardboard piece that came with it, then she handed him the dice. He rolled a two and pulled one of the number-two pieces out of the middle of the stack, then set it on top. Then his mom pulled out a four, and so on and so forth. He was terrified that she might say something about Leo, but when she started talking she said, "I called up the place tonight, and I'm going to learn to drive."

"You are?"

"He said it would take longer because I'm thirty-five, but I think now's the time."

"Why?"

"Well, sweetheart, I don't think I'll ever get back to New York, you know?"

"I never thought we would get back to New York, Mom. Dad grew up here, and he hates Aqueduct."

"I'm joking, honey. I know we won't get back to New York. I wouldn't want to go, either. But I'm going to learn to drive. It's kind of exciting, really." She had two turns, and pulled out a one and a three. Jesse pulled out a four. They kept going quietly, and Jesse felt himself get a little into the game. A long time ago it had been his favorite game, say when he was four and five. He'd found the growing tower almost scary, but he'd been quite proud of the stillness with which he could place those I-beams. He was really into the game, which was why it surprised him when he himself said, "There's something wrong with Leo." He didn't say "Dad," either, he said "Leo," just like he didn't know his own father very well.

"Oh, Jesse," said his mom.

"There is. I think he's got a brain tumor."

"Why is that?"

"Because there's something wrong with him. The things he says don't go together right."

"I don't think he has a brain tumor, darling."

"But you do think there's something wrong with him."

"I do."

"Tell me what it is." Jesse thought sure she was going to use some word he didn't understand, some kind of disease word, but she said, "He's just so full of longing."

"What does he long for?"

"To stop longing for things, I suppose."

This Jesse understood perfectly. In the first place, he knew what longing was, and in the second place, he could easily imagine this endless circle of longing to be freed of longing. He said, "Do you think Leo is handsome?"

"Yes."

"Me, too. Is that why you married him?"

"Maybe. He was different then. He was only twenty-two. None of this stuff had taken hold. And I was only twenty. The thing is, Jesse, Leo needs someone to tell him that he didn't do anything bad."

"But he did. He's done lots of bad things."

She sat back on the couch and looked at him. She said, "I know, Jesse. That's the problem I can't solve." She looked at him. She said, "You can't solve it, either, honey." Jesse said, "I know." And he did know. So many times, he had said, "It's all right, Dad," but Leo had never believed him. Here was the thing, Jesse thought: On the one hand, there was the track—money, signs, horses, getting out of school, sunshine, and a general nice feeling to begin with that could get better or worse by the end of the day. Jesse knew all about that. But now, on the other hand, there was a gun and the will to use it and the men who might have to have it used on them. And it was all the same thing. What was Jesse supposed to think about that? He said, "Are you scared, Mom?"

She nodded, and then she said, "Not all of the time, though," and Jesse understood that all along there had been more going on than he had known about, that all along he had been in a car in the fog on a winding highway, and he was the only one in the car who didn't know that sometimes, maybe quite often, the car veered toward the edge of the road and only just kept going out of luck.

Fortunately for everyone, whatever had happened with Park Min Jong, it had been all right, because Leo was in a terrific mood when he got home. He came into Jesse's room and got him up and sat down on the bed and told him some things he had to know. Jesse's mom came to the doorway, and one time she said, "Leo, it's two a.m.," but Leo said, "When a boy has to learn something about how the world works, it doesn't matter what time it is, honey." Leo never spoke to Jesse's mom in any voice but a loving and kind one.

The first thing Leo did was take the gun out of his shoulder holster and lay it on Jesse's bed, carefully pointing the end of the barrel away from everyone, toward the corner of the room where stood Jesse's clothes tree with Winnie-the-Pooh on the top. "Son," Leo said, "I'm going to tell you what happened tonight, because I want you to know exactly the kind of man I am. If you're going to judge me, and all sons judge their fathers, that's part of life, then you need to have the whole story."

"Okay," said Jesse.

"Now, son, there was once this guy named Henry David Thoreau. He lived near Boston, but they didn't have Suffolk Downs then, so he wasn't a racing man, but he said some good things anyway, and one of the good things he said, well, not good in the sense that it is a *happy* thing, but good in the sense that it is a *right* thing, was that the mass of men live lives of quiet desperation, and of course he meant women, too, since in those days 'men' meant women and men and children. The first real racetrack in the Northeast was Jerome Park, you know, that was started by Winston Churchill's grandfather—"

Jesse thought it was safe here to show interest by asking who Winston Churchill was.

Leo said, "Winston Churchill was a British politician who was short enough to be a jockey, but of course he couldn't keep his weight down. There's a famous picture of him with two other guys, Franklin Roosevelt, who was our president, and Joe Stalin, who I don't believe was a racing man, either, but all sorts of interesting new information is coming out of Russia now, so we could be surprised. Anyway, that's beside the point."

Jesse decided it was better to keep his mouth shut.

"My father lived a life of quiet desperation, and this is why. He let the bookies walk all over him. I can't tell you the number of times my father came home and the bookies had changed the odds on him, or failed to pay him off, or even just ignored him by not taking his bets. You know, when a bookie dies, they always write in the paper, 'Joe Schmo made his fortune in questionable investments.' That's a fact." He turned to Jesse's mom, who was still standing in the doorway, and said, "Did you know that, Allison?"

Jesse's mom shook her head.

"I always thought that was funny. I mean a funny phrase, but the way that they try to skim money isn't funny at all, and is very like the way that rich and powerful people in general try to take more than their share. You know, speaking of Joe Stalin, I just remembered a funny thing. Once I was thinking about Joe Stalin for some reason, this was back in the East, and right there on the program for some race was a horse named 'Marxist,' so I put a hundred bucks on his nose to win, because I was thinking of Joe Stalin, who was a Marxist, of course. Do you know what a Marxist is, Jesse?"

Jesse shook his head.

"Well, they don't have Marxists anymore, but they weren't all wrong, you know, because they knew about how money works, and bookies work, and how the track always gets too much of the bet pool, and another thing, too, which is that power always comes from the barrel of a gun. Marxism, you might say, was a whole philosophy about the vig. You know what the vig is? It's the takeout, what the middleman gets, and how the little fish always pays the vig and the big fish doesn't."

Meanwhile, everyone was looking at the gun on the bed.

Leo sighed. "Anyway, son, that Marxist horse paid off thirty-to-one that time, so I always had a soft spot in my heart for Joe Stalin, who came into my mind just at the right moment for me to go with one of the best long shots I ever bet."

Jesse wasn't quite sure where all of this was going, but he didn't want to introduce any other possible digressions, so he kept his mouth shut. Leo continued to stare at the gun. Jesse's mom finally stepped into the room and sat down at the end of Jesse's bed.

Leo went on, "I made up my mind when I was your age that I wasn't going to live a life of quiet desperation like my dad. Now, that is saying that I *judged* my dad and found him wanting. I know that, and may I be forgiven for that, but it is a natural thing to do, and someday you will do it, too, and you will be forgiven for it, too. Today, when I went to see Park Min Jong, I had that in mind. That I had judged my father, and that, in order for me to be justified about that, I had to act on my judgment. So, you see, when I ran out of here, I was doing that for you, son. And for my father. And for your mother, too. Now, here's another thing. Korean society is a very patriarchal society. Do you know what that means?"

Jesse shook his head.

"That means that the father rules the roost and everybody pays attention to him. And when I went to see Park Min Jong, and I had my gun with me, I had all of these things in my mind, and also my fourteen hundred dollars. If there is fourteen hundred dollars coming to my family, that I have earned for them, then, as a man and a father, I have to get it, you know."

Jesse hazarded a nod.

"That's one of my principles. And"—he drew a wad of cash out of his pocket—"I got it." It was a biggish wad, so Jesse thought he must have gotten it in small bills. Leo peeled a five off the outside of the wad and laid it on the covers, on Jesse's knee. He said, "There's something for you, son."

"Thanks, Dad."

"I learned a lesson with that money, son. Ask me what it was."

"What was it?"

"I learned that the Koreans will respect you if you stand up to them. The Chinese won't, and you never want to stand up to a Russian, you know, just stay away from a Russian bookie, no matter what. The Jews are still the best, taken all in all, and I don't say that because we're Jewish, you know. It's just all lessons. Life is a set of lessons, and if you pay attention every day, you'll learn them." He stood up. "Got that?"

Jesse nodded.

"You're a good boy," said Leo. And he pulled Jesse's mom up by the hand, and put his arm around her waist. She said only the second thing she'd said all night, which was "Don't leave the gun, Leo."

Leo turned and picked up the gun, looked at it, weighed it in his hand, and said, "Son, when you come to judge your father, remember that I had the guts to take it, but I wasn't dumb enough to shoot it, okay?"

"Okay."

Leo hit the light as he went out of the room. After a moment, when he knew his parents' door was closed, Jesse got up and opened his curtains, but there was nothing to see, no moon and no stars. He lay down again, on his back, and pulled the covers up to his chest. Leo didn't have to tell him anything more about Park Min Jong in order for Jesse to know for a fact how it had gone there. Leo, of course, thought that when the bookie gave him the money he was also giving him respect, but, Jesse realized, how could that be true? Right then, in the middle of the night, it was as if he saw Leo through the bookie's eyes, small-time. All the talk. The whole system. The racetrack itself. Everything about it was very small-time. All the theory in the world, and even all the money in the world, couldn't change that.

56 / CHICKENS

NOW THAT ROSALIND had realized that her function in life was simply to follow instructions, she had many fewer problems. One offshoot of the Information Revolution was that instructions everywhere abounded, and most of the time you could follow them in any one of three to ten languages. And, then, people came into the gallery, workmen, artists, other dealers, customers, friends, and they were full of instructions, too. Artists, for example, were paragons of instruction. Following their wishes on exactly how and where to hang each of their pieces was a Zen exercise in discipline, futility, patience, and, finally, removal of the self from the material plane of existence. Friends and other dealers were full of instructions on how to deal with various artists, and Rosalind noted them all. The telephone rang all the time, and voices from all over the world told her where to pick things up, what to pay for them, where to ship, how to wrap, what to expect. Rosalind nodded and smiled and knew exactly what to do and what spirit to do it in.

It was with this practice under her belt that she was standing in her gallery toward dusk one evening, appreciating a moment of calm comfort (the February weather on Madison Avenue was gloomy and chill, therefore the gallery was bright and warm), when she answered the phone, and was instructed by

Krista Magnelli to go out to Belmont the next morning and see Limitless. "He's been at the track for two months now," said Krista. "I just have a niggling worry. For one thing, I don't like to call your trainer and pry, and for another, I'm sure nothing's wrong."

The fact was that Rosalind knew exactly how to follow this instruction. She had driven out to Belmont Park countless times. No consultation with any authority in any language was at all necessary. But it was a good thing she had been following instructions so carefully for such a long while, because otherwise she would have felt her heart jump at the thought, and not for joy. She might even have reeled backward a centimeter or two at the very idea, or had to shake her head to clear any small fog that settled there. But because she was so practiced now, she just said, "Well, Krista, it probably is time for me to check on things out there. Thank you for reminding me. Al has been back and forth to Russia so much, and I've been—"

"You know," Krista said, "it's not like I've had a bad feeling or anything, I mean, no more so than the usual bad feelings that I get about everything."

"We certainly would have heard if anything were off with the horse. I'm sure he's fine."

"Well, the thing is, I *don't* have a bad feeling."

"I'll be happy to go see the horse."

"It's very reassuring to talk to you, Rosalind."

"I'll take care of whatever needs to be taken care of."

"Thank you so much."

The important thing to understand was that, if you were simply going out to see your former lover because you wanted to or needed to, then of course you would be uneasy, but if you were going out there because you were instructed to, then there was no need to be uneasy, because your instructions, as they evolved, would also include instructions about how to know what to say and do in your former lover's presence. And so there was nothing to worry about.

Eileen, who had been sleeping in the broom closet, nosed open the door and came into the wide space of the gallery. She stretched deliberately backward, then deliberately forward. She seemed to propel every mote of stiffness from her tail through her shoulders, then out through her upraised black little nose. Then she shook herself vigorously and looked at Rosalind. Rosalind hardly spoke to her anymore, at least not to give her commands. Each of them had taken full measure of the other and arrived at a permanent understanding. Eileen would not under any circumstances give up certain modes of expression that she deemed necessary to her well-being. On the other hand, she would come, sit, stay, lie down, be quiet, be affectionate, and respect Rosalind's belongings without being prompted. For a Jack Russell, Rosalind had been told, this verged on sainthood. Rosalind picked up her coat. Eileen came over and sat down beside her. Rosalind turned out the lights in the office and the storeroom. Everything else was buttoned up tight. Eileen followed Rosalind's clicking heels down the stairs, out the door, down the street. At the restaurant where Rosalind had agreed to meet friends, she paused outside the door, leaned down, and opened her totebag. Eileen jumped in, lay down, curled up. Rosalind opened the door and walked in. Of course the maître d' had seen the dog get into the totebag, of course the totebag bulged suspiciously, but the maître d' said nothing except "Let me show you to your table. Your party is already seated."

Rosalind knew that everything about her was a topic of conversation among her friends, several of whom faithfully repeated all the gossip about her to her. They greeted her so enthusiastically, even affectionately—Darlene and Max, Wanda and Fred, Danielle and Isaac—partly because they had been discussing her just moments ago. She set the bag of dog gently in the corner and went around the table, kissing and smiling and exclaiming. She *was* glad to see them. She didn't mind that Max snapped at Darlene, Darlene whined at Max, Wanda laughingly exhibited Fred's failings to everyone, Fred drank, Isaac's voice could be heard all over the restaurant, and Danielle brought out a little scale for weighing her portions and talked only about grams of fat on the menu. She didn't mind that they speculated about her, that they doubted whether she could make the gallery go, that they thought Al's new business interests were keeping him away from home a *lot* of the time, that her attachment to Eileen seemed eccentric. She didn't mind that they guessed she had had, was having, an affair, but no one could figure out with whom.

She ordered the risotto with saffron and bay scallops and the crispy zucchini with flecks of arugula and chanterelle mushrooms for herself, and a half-order of mashed sweet potatoes for Eileen ("Hold the mint"). And then it only took her a minute or two to grant everyone's wishes. Fred exclaimed, "My God, they've got a Badia a Coltibuono. It's seventy-eight dollars, but I've always wanted a taste of that." Max picked up Darlene's hand and put it sweetly to his lips; Darlene said, "I know where I can get that money for those geezers. Rosalind, don't you know someone at the Rockefeller Foundation?" "I do," said Rosalind. Wanda said, "You know, my shoulder was aching all day from this weather, but it feels fine now." Isaac said to the waiter, "Are there onions in that dish?" And the waiter said, "No, sir." And Danielle said, "Oh! Bon! The ladies' room has come free. I've been waiting at least twenty minutes!" This happened all the time now. As soon as Rosalind gave the signal, and she herself didn't know what that was, the wishes of everyone around her were satisfied at once. Actually, it was a good indicator—only about 10 percent of any group were wish-free at any one moment. Rosalind was rather surprised at that, especially now that she herself was one of the wish-free ones.

The granting of wishes did not have a prolonged positive effect, but it was good in the short term, as a form of relief. It was like when Rosalind used to smoke, in her twenties. Smoking had not made her feel good, only feel the cessation of the desire for a cigarette. Wishes coming true, she noticed, did not make her friends feel good, only feel the cessation of that particular wish, and the more she noticed that, the fewer wishes she herself had. Her meal was set before her. She tasted it. It was good.

Max said, "Think about it. Here we are, seven spouses accounting for, what, eighty or a hundred years of marriage all told? I was listening to my daughter talk on the phone to her fiancé. First she talked about where they were going to find an apartment, then she talked about how they were going to furnish it, then a restaurant she wanted to go to, then she told him how to go about doing something that she had decided she wanted him to do, then she told him about another friend of hers who was getting engaged, then she went out of the room, and Darlene and I talked about her, then we talked about something we were going to buy, then we talked about a vacation we were going to take, then we talked about the Morrises, you know she has filed for divorce, then we talked about something Darlene wanted me to do."

"And he said, 'Isn't it better just not to talk at all?'" said Darlene. She turned to him. "I do not agree with you that marital conversation is more or less like having the TV going all the time."

"What is it, then?" said Max.

"I don't think this is a safe topic," said Wanda. "Farting in marriage is much safer, if you ask me. At least when you talk about that you aren't revealing anything personal to everyone."

"The Morrises always had great conversations, you know," said Isaac. "Wide-ranging, erudite, smart, funny. You could sit and watch them converse for hours. It was like a movie."

"But think," continued Max. "What's the last actual topic you discussed with your spouse? Not a grievance, not a plan, not the children, not an assigned task, not gossip, not checking up or ordering around. Just something of general interest."

"Last night," said Wanda, "I told Fred about a guy in a sex column in a magazine who wanted to hook up his girlfriend to his stereo system by the rectum and give her a buzz."

"The author of the sex column said there was specially made equipment for that. News to me," said Fred. "We talked about that for a half an hour at least."

"Fred remembers it today, too," said Wanda.

"We talk about Clinton every day," said Isaac.

"Oh my God," said Wanda. "That's pathological."

"Sometimes Mitterrand," added Danielle.

"We talk about God," said Darlene.

Rosalind looked at her.

"Every day," said Darlene.

Rosalind looked at Max.

Max looked startled for a moment, as though his cover had been blown. Then he said, "What do you and Al talk about, Rosalind?"

"Horses."

"Art?"

"Al doesn't like art. I talk about art with other people."

"Talking about art is all opinions," said Danielle. "Or gossip. Very boring. God is much more interesting. I would not have thought this of you, Max."

"I didn't know you were religious," said Wanda. "You don't seem religious."

"It's not religion," said Darlene. "It's God himself. You know, what are his qualities and preferences. Why does he do one thing and not another, or does he do anything, and if he doesn't do anything, then why does he allow certain things to be done. Does he take sides, that sort of thing. If you pray for a Mercedes, could he give it to you, would he, should he."

Everyone ate. Eileen poked her head out of the totebag and ate the sweet potatoes off their plate. After a while, Isaac said, "Pure speculation."

Then Max said, "What is there to say about horses?"

"What are their qualities and preferences." Rosalind smiled mischievously at him. "Why do they do one thing and not another."

"You're teasing me."

"You shouldn't be offended," said Wanda. "As soon as you start talking about God, everyone gets offended."

"I'm not offended at all."

"He's not," said Darlene.

"Plus whether they're going to win or lose."

"You know," said Wanda, "I personally feel that it is not acceptable to do it under the covers."

Yes, Rosalind thought, they had revealed their marriages—not so much by what they said as by how they sat, how they looked at one another, how they moved in tandem. If Al had been here, what would these friends have perceived about them? At any rate, what she was embarrassed to tell was that she and Al talked mostly about his complaints, or, rather, he talked, and she was silent. She would nod or make a noise or suggest something, but how these others talked to each other, even Max and Darlene, whatever they said, she and Al did none of that.

She looked around the table. The marriages of New Yorkers always looked different from the marriages of her parents and relatives in the Midwest—more voluntary, more arbitrary—and as she recognized this, she also recognized that she was perfectly set up now to slip into singlehood. That state would be much like this state—the gallery, a restaurant, Eileen, lively comings and goings, the way she had been in her twenties, but enlarged by money and sophistication. Al as her ex-husband would be much the same as Al in Uzbekistan. All divorce would be, it seemed to her, was walking out of Al's house in Westchester County and locking the door behind herself.

BY THE NEXT MORNING, when she was on her way out to the track in the Mercedes with Eileen beside her, she had progressed a bit, toward compassion. Poor Al, decades of shooting off his mouth and no one daring to stop him. And he liked to be stopped, didn't he? He was demanding because he didn't know how else to be. She thought of herself sitting at the table with him, eating calmly. What it felt like to her was being a stone, rolled over and over by the relentless surf of his complaints, but maybe what it felt like to him was being in an empty room, having to shout louder and louder just to see if there was anyone there. Because who was there inside her containment structure, anyway?

They got out to the track in no time, found a parking spot right away, passed through the gate. It wasn't a pleasant day. Riders and horses were bundled and huddled against the cold wind. On the other hand, no sleet, no snow. Rosalind hadn't thought much about it when Al told her that Dick wasn't taking the horses to Florida this winter, since Aqueduct had year-round footing, but now that decision seemed to her evidence of masochism. Even Eileen, snapped into her little coat, found nothing to fascinate her today.

And here was a line of horses in Dick's colors, crossing to the entrance of the track and passing through. They were lovely, weren't they, long-legged and tight-bellied, dressed up in blue quartersheets to keep their haunches warm, steam blowing out of their nostrils and rising around their heads and ears. The riders wore gloves and hooded sweatshirts and looked even more dedicated than usual. The first horse in Dick's line reared as he went onto the track. Its

rider leaned forward, and the horse came down bucking and kicking up. Rosalind and Eileen found Dick.

She did not go up to him right away. For one thing, he was staring intently
at the line of horses. He shouted, "Let him trot off, Frankie. Try to contain
him, but don't try to stop him." The horse leapt forward, and Frankie went
with him.

"Who's that?" said Rosalind.

Dick spun around.

"Oh, you scared me!"

"Sorry."

"That's a horse named Epic Steam. He won the Paumonok Stakes the
other day. He's a monster."

"Big."

"Huge."

"What about Limitless?"

"Look right over there. He's working with that chestnut. I'm glad you
came. Did Al come? They're going to do an official work, the colt's second."

"How's he doing?"

"I don't know."

"Well, he's been here a couple of months, Krista said—"

"Watch."

The two horses, bay and chestnut, picked up a canter, very slow and
easy, and made their way along the outside rail to the other side of the track.
Rosalind could hardly see them, they were so lost in vastness and activity.
They went along in front of the grandstand, Limitless slightly ahead of the
chestnut. At the seven-eighths pole, they turned toward the inner rail, making
their way carefully across the track. Then they stood for a second at the pole,
and then they were out of there. The chestnut was on the rail, Limitless was
beyond him.

"Look at that," said Dick.

"What?"

He handed her the binoculars. She put them to her eyes. He said, "The
reins are practically flapping."

"So what?"

"You can't run a horse like that. It's dangerous. The horse is liable to do
anything. If all he did was veer across the path of the horse beside him, that
would be enough to have him disqualified."

"Does he veer like that?"

"Not so far. So far he runs straight."

"Then why worry about it?"

He didn't answer. Eileen went over to him now for the first time, and sniffed his shoe. Then she came back and sat down in front of Rosalind and looked up at her.

The horses were coming out of the turn. As they approached, it was clear indeed to Rosalind that Limitless could tolerate nothing from the rider. She said, "He taught himself how to run. I'm sure he doesn't want to get in another horse's way. Don't you think he has a plan? I do." Dick pressed the button of his stopwatch and said, "Wow!" Then he put the stopwatch in his pocket and said, "But I always say wow with him."

"The breeder called him that, Wow."

"Excuse me, just a minute." He took the binoculars from her and put them to his eyes. She followed his gaze to the far side of the track again. The big black horse was moving now. Even from this distance he stood out. His edges seemed to vibrate. They were into and out of the turn in no time. They ran past, and then into the second turn. Then they ran around that turn. Dick said, "Could be bolting. Maybe not. I told Frankie to give him a little extra." The horse seemed to eat up the oval. Dick said, "All I want in this life is to get that horse to a grade-one race without a mishap. The Gotham would be perfect for him."

"All you want?"

"All I want."

"Hmm," said Rosalind. Possibly this was within her powers, but she couldn't decide, and then the moment passed.

The dark horse floated to a trot, trotted for several ground-covering strides, then floated to a walk. Dick said, "You know, when they sent me this guy, I thought he was a bad mover. But he just had a broken leg."

Rosalind laughed.

But she saw how he looked at the horse. That was something maybe only an old mistress could see, too, that half-believing disbelief, here she is, here it is, I've been waiting for this all my life, please may I not screw it up. It was not so much a look of desire as a look of alertness. It said, this is the one, all the others are all the others. Rosalind sniffed. Limitless was nearby, and she looked at him, but Dick didn't. Rosalind did not want to be miffed by this, by this simple false thing of having her horse overlooked in favor of someone else's horse. Limitless and the chestnut came to a halt below them, sideways to the track, and waited. Rosalind regarded her horse. His haunches, of course, were covered by the quartersheet, but she could see his legs. They were very long for his size, a little cow-hocked. The exercise rider sat calmly on him, one hand tucked in his armpit, the other on the buckle of the reins. The horse turned his head and neck to watch other horses galloping on the rail. He had a long neck, a long head, and long ears. The reins sloped from the bit in a long graceful curve, and lay along his shoulder. Was that it? That leather curve? When the two horses turned and began to walk away, she saw that the horse had the back, too, that dipped just behind the withers, then swept under the tiny saddle toward the point of the croup. And underneath him, his four legs looked limpid with speed. She said to Dick, trying to get a rise out of him, "Look at my horse. Doesn't he look exactly like one of those English racing paintings— Mill Reef walking along, or someone like that?"

Dick glanced at him. "He is fit." And then he looked back at the big colt, who was shaking his bit in his mouth. Dick shouted, "Hey, Frankie! Everything okay? He was a monster!"

And then they followed the horses back to the barn. Eileen stayed close to her heels. Rosalind chose her words. She said, "You like this horse, then? You think he's got something?"

"He's got it all. Size, breeding. He's won five races already, I—"

"No, Limitless."

"Oh. Well, sure. I mean, he's come along since the summer. I'm thinking of putting him in a race in about four weeks or so. He's fast and he loves to run. We just have to show him how it's done."

What was unexpected was that she, or, rather, her body, had absolutely no reaction to his. He could have been anyone. He had gone back into the smooth fabric of the world. Sometime and in some way since last she saw him, he had returned to being not of compelling interest. One of her friends who had had several husbands and lovers always said, in fact, "Oh, I don't know. There's always that moment when you look at him and say, So what?" However, it was amazing to experience it. Her eyes went to her horse's glittering ankles ahead of them rather than to Dick's face.

It was true that she didn't have Dick's experience. Perhaps there wasn't much that was special about Limitless (though doubting her own esthetic judgment was not customary with Rosalind), but there was an elastic quality to his whole being that concentrated itself in the movement of his hind legs as he walked back to the barn. She didn't have to use any of her powers on him; he had powers aplenty of his own.

She went to Limitless's head when the groom took him for unsaddling. He was friendly, too; obviously Krista had loved him. He pricked his ears and sniffed her sweater and hands. She stroked his neck and under his chin, scratched his forehead. She called him sweetheart in a low voice. Those eyes. Arresting, kind. The eyes of horses, Rosalind thought, always told you something a little bit beyond your comprehension. They always asked of you more than you were able to give. But even in that context, Limitless's eyes were uniquely beautiful, long-lashed, prominent, calm, self-aware. She said to the groom, "Do you like him?"

"He's no trouble. Good horse." That was all.

She followed Dick into his office. Eileen, she noticed, hesitated and then crept in, without her usual self-confidence. Rosalind picked her up. After she had closed the door, he said, "So—how are you?"

"I'm fine. I don't have a lot of time, because I want to get back to the gallery before noon. How are you?"

"I've moved. I found a place in Queens that's quite beautiful, really. Louisa likes it."

"How is Louisa?"

"She's doing well. She's been doing some recitals. They love her in the *Times*, you know. I went to two of them. We're friends."

"Look, Dick, I'm moving the horse to another trainer."

"Rosalind—"

He stared at her and she stared at him, and a lot of information passed between them, but she wanted to tell him why, anyway, so she said, "The horse is not getting through to you."

And he said, "No. I see what you mean. I'm not getting through to the horse, either. Who are you going to send him to?"

"I don't know. I suppose I'll have a vision."

"I suppose you will."

A bit later he walked her to her car.

THAT EVENING, she conjured up a fellow at a party. He came in the door, handed over his coat, and made a beeline for her, where she was standing by the smoked whitefish pâté. She could tell that he didn't even know why he wanted to talk to her, but he introduced himself anyway, Sir Michael Ordway. She said, "You look like a horse person of some sort, a horse agent, maybe?"

He laughed at what he thought was a coincidence. "Have you horses, then?"

"A few. Only one at the track right now."

"You know, that's so intriguing, really, because I know of a horse, fine animal—"

"I'm not looking to buy a horse."

His face fell, then brightened again. "Oddly enough, I have a very dear friend whose name I am not at liberty to divulge, who is always in the market for—"

"I don't want to sell any of my stock, either."

"It would be quite a coup, and quite profitable for you—"

"Sir Michael, here's what I would like. I would like for you to do something utterly disinterested and benevolent, for which there would be no payment of any kind, and possibly even no credit given. Nothing at all but a thank you."

Sir Michael stared at her, looked away toward the far corner of the room, then gave her a cheery smile. He said, "That would be an interesting change. What would it be?"

"I need a good trainer."

"Who's your present trainer?"

"Dick Winterson."

"Ah. Brilliant. His father trained in England quite a bit. Why not stick with him? He's won a lot."

"His plan for the horse and the horse's plan for himself are too different."

"And, of course, he has that Epic Steam horse now. There's an animal that fills your agenda."

"That, too." Rosalind took a sip of her champagne.

"I have lots of friends."

"I would like you to disregard that fact."

"Build up my credit in heaven rather than here on earth, as it were."

"I think we understand each other perfectly."

"May I call you?"

WHEN AL CALLED from Lithuania late that night, he began at once. His feet were killing him, and there were these pains shooting from his knee to his groin, they weren't constant, but he would be walking along and all of a sudden, bam, he was nearly doubled over, and you couldn't get a good cup of coffee in this country, even though the hotel was supposed to be the best, European standards, ha, the hot water ran out before you were even wet and the roads, he had a headache from the moment he woke up in the morning, it must be the ventilation—

"Al."

Maybe he should have brought those other shoes he had. He could never decide what shoes to pack. He hated to fucking pack, anyway. Why had he gotten into a line of work where he had to actually leave his house and go to these godforsaken—

"Al."

And the heating. It was all steam-radiator heat, and it dried your sinuses right up. He'd brought along the whole medicine chest she'd sent, the Sudafed and the chlorine, what was that stuff, but it was so dry inside, your brain felt like a shriveling walnut rattling around in—

"Al, would you like to call me back later when you have something more fun to talk about?"

"What?"

"You're complaining."

"Well, of course I'm complaining."

"I can't do anything about it."

"I just want a sympathetic ear."

"What for?"

There was a long cellular pause, then, "Well, I don't know."

"What do you really want?"

"A laugh, I guess."

Rosalind reflected that she had never given anyone an actual laugh.

There was an even longer cellular pause. Al sighed, no doubt beginning to meditate again on his complaints.

Rosalind closed her eyes, her mind a blank. How could this be so hard, giving Al what he wanted? She gave everyone else what they wanted. Having nothing to lose, she opened her mouth: "You know, my dad knew this guy back when I was a girl. A guy who lived in Milwaukee. He heard that if he went into chicken farming the government would give him fifteen hundred free chickens, so he got himself a little plot of land, and called the Department of Agriculture, and asked for his chickens. He was really determined to make a go of this, so when the chickens arrived he and his wife spent days digging the holes about a foot apart, planting the chickens. They watered them a couple of times, fertilized them, everything. But it didn't matter, the chickens didn't come up."

Al was silent.

"So they called up the office for chickens again, told them the chickens had died, and asked for another fifteen hundred chickens. The chicken guy quizzed them—had they fed the chickens, watered them? Oh, yes, of course they had. Well, he said, try giving them more of each. So the chickens arrived, they planted them again, but this time they watered them every day and dug the fertilizer right into the soil. Still no go. Not a chicken came up. So they called the office again, and this time they said they'd send a man out to analyze their operation. Fair enough—they'd done everything they knew how to do."

Al cleared his throat.

"So the guy comes out, and they show him the chicken field, and he walked around. They see him dig up a chicken or two, shake his head. He's there for the whole morning. Finally, he comes in, and he says, 'Well, I'm going to authorize fifteen hundred more chickens, but this time, be sure and plant them farther apart.' "

Al laughed.

Rosalind laughed.

Al said, "So, uh, Rosalind. What have you been doing today?"

57 / THE RETURN OF THE DEMON

WHAT IT FELT LIKE, as far as Joy was concerned, was forgetting one life and remembering the other. What she forgot was something about her day. She remembered getting up in the morning, going with Farley to the track, grooming, riding, doing things for horses, going with Farley to the cafeteria, gossiping with other trainers, getting horses ready, going in races; you name it, she remembered almost all of it. What she didn't remember was how she had done it, what it had felt like, what gave her that energy and then made her want to expend it. What she remembered was what she had known before committing her most recent big mistake—she had known that a small room, limited contact with others, and a heavy schedule of routine work enabled her to pursue her goal, which was to live in a small room, have limited contact with others, and pursue a heavy schedule of routine work. Her most recent big mistake had been to think she could move outside those parameters. But it was not that she missed the ranch (What was there to miss? Nothing in retrospect or prospect looked more or less appealing than anything else), rather it was generally considered better to function than not to function, and so it probably was. She was not functioning. It was not good.

She heard Farley's steps come into the room. Since the onset of her recent depressive episode, she didn't get up at all. Sometimes she did put her head out from under the covers. She did that now. She said, "What day is this?"

"Saturday."

"How long has this been going on?"

"Eleven days."

"Are you hankering after signs of progress?"

"Trying not to."

"Is this affecting your expressed love for me?"

"I don't think of this as you."

"What if this is the real me?"

"I choose not to believe that."

"You know, my father told me a story when I was a kid about a hog he saw at a fair one time. It weighed twelve hundred pounds, and couldn't get up on its trotters any longer. His dad told him that it never slept or woke up. It always just existed in a sort of semi-awake twilight zone. Does that sound appealing to you?"

"No."

"It does to me."

"What's appealing about it?"

"No movement."

He sat down on the bed, smoothed the hair out of her face, and took her hand in his. Then he put his other hand on her elbow, and began moving her arm up and down, back and forth, while stroking it gently. He was smiling at her. She let him do it. He set her arm down. It tingled nicely. She said, "You have to go to the track. Tell me about it."

He ran down the list of horses and what they were doing today. Froney's Sis was not on it. Froney's Sis had gone back to the ranch. Her departure for the ranch had coincided with the onset of this thing that had happened to her. That looked like cause and effect, yes, but it wasn't. This thing that had happened to her had no cause, never had. Elizabeth said that it could not be accounted for with reference to this lifetime, that she had another lifetime or two that she was experiencing simultaneously with this one. Events in the other lifetime(s) were resulting in feelings in this lifetime. Perhaps in her other lifetime, right now, she was very ill. Perhaps, Joy suggested, she was dead. When Joy told her mother Elizabeth's theory, she did not dismiss it out of hand, which surprised Joy, for her mother was a fervid believer in psychotherapeutic drugs. Sometimes Joy thought that if she could just get them all going at once—Farley manipulating her body, Elizabeth investigating her past life experiences, her mother altering her brain chemistry, Plato putting her into her proper socio-economic and cultural context, and Mr. T. conceptualizing her inner being—then that would be enough to hoist her over the edge and back onto the plane of well-being. She said, "You really have to go."

"I know."

"Do you have infinite patience?"

"I have enough for right now, and that's all I need."

After he left, she recollected that he did have infinite patience. Look how he had been with Froney's Sis.

That thought was enough to start the crying again.

SHE WOULD BE crying again, thought Farley as he pulled onto the 210. Three weeks ago he would have said that he had come to a remarkable place for him, a place that he valued. It was more than the fact that he was with a woman most of his waking and sleeping hours with whom he felt comfortable and had no conflict. It was more than the fact that when she leaned into him, and touched him, he wanted to pull her closer and closer. It was more than the fact that their conversation was an unceasing duet, harmonious and measured, sometimes resting, sometimes quickening, a song of many movements. It was more than the fact that he exerted no effort to be good with her, but felt patience and kindness and warmth drawn out of him without fear (he would like to have been always what he was with her now). Around Christmas he had thought about this a good bit, that, looking back, conflicting desires and expectations, mounting disappointments and misunderstandings had compromised every relationship he had ever had, a sack of junk tied to his foot that he had dragged forward with every step. But this he did not have with Joy. They were too grateful for there to be resentments. Even now that this thing had happened to her, he was still grateful—grateful for her nearness, grateful for her soft voice, grateful for the sight of her face, grateful for her willingness to let him wrestle with her depression for her, by touching her, bathing her, moving her this way and that. He was grateful to her that she had given herself up to him, let him take care of her and express love to her rather than isolating herself and going apart. But still.

As he pulled off the 210 at Baldwin, he flinched away from that thought.

But then, as he went into the horsemen's gate, and looked at his watch (it was seven exactly), he made himself look at that thought.

How long?

The way to think about it, said Barney, his regular vet, the only person he had really confided in, was that she was on stall rest. Thirty days of stall rest. Thirty days of stall rest was something you had to make provision for, but nothing terrifying. "And," said Barney, "thirty days of stall rest does wonders."

He found his spot and parked.

He thought it was interesting that, having finally moved his barn permanently to Santa Anita, he now did not know, no one knew, what was going to happen to Santa Anita's backside. It was only now that he had become fond of the place. What he had once seen as ramshackle inconvenience he now saw as homely charm. As he walked to his barn, he looked around, studiously avoiding the next question, but of course, when he got there, the question presented itself. There it was, his narrow, intelligent white face hanging over the stall door, undoubtedly looking for Joy. Farley walked up and gave Mr. T. the one permitted pat on the cheek before the horse turned away. Oliver spied him at once and came over. Farley said, "How'd it go with the first set?"

Oliver told him.

"What else?"

Oliver ran down the vet list.

"What else?"

"Somerville called again. He said you never called him back yesterday."

"I didn't."

They exchanged a look that Farley understood perfectly. Oliver was imploring him. Two of the biggest owners on the West Coast had offered him three horses each, two three-year-olds and four two-year-olds. The three-year-olds were ready. The two-year-olds would be ready in about three weeks or so. He had not yet said no. But he had not yet said yes. The fact was, he had no stalls, and he couldn't get any more, at least for right now. The barns at Santa Anita were smaller than those at Hollywood Park. Everything was more crowded. Oliver wanted him to move some horses to Hollywood Park, and put him, Oliver, in charge of them, but Farley didn't like the footing there. He didn't want to train there. A stall could open up, though, the stall behind them, Mr. T.'s stall.

Mr. T. did nothing now that the filly had gone back to the ranch, and he did not have the prospect of doing anything. In ten starts, the filly had had one win, one second, and one third. She had earned twenty-one thousand dollars. She had been unsound off and on. The fact was, she wasn't a racehorse and she wasn't coming back. Mr. T. didn't quite have the temperament for a pony horse. He didn't like male horses to be inside his personal space and he was well mannered but not in the least phlegmatic, the way a pony horse needed to be to be utterly reliable. And his experiences over the last six months, galloping, running, breaking from the gate from time to time, had accelerated his aging process. He was stiffer, crankier, harder to ride. He had no usefulness as a horse at the track, and the track wasn't a good place for him to be now. No grass, no friends, no turnout, nothing to do. Time to go home; he still belonged to Mr. Tompkins, and Mr. Tompkins, of course, would make a place for him somewhere. Except, of course, how would Farley, how could Farley, possibly break this news to Joy? Right now, on day eleven of her thirty days of stall rest? His friend Barney the vet said he couldn't. Her mother said he couldn't. His own conscience said he couldn't. A friend of his who had gotten through a serious depression said that he couldn't even tell her he was moving the horse somewhere like the L.A. Equestrian Center, which wasn't all that far away, because for Joy the thought of the horse in a new place, having to adjust, be lonely, be away from familiar surroundings, be by himself, be among strangers— Did Farley get the picture? Farley did certainly get the picture.

So, in addition to "How long?," there was "What will it take?"

Oliver said, "You should at least call him. He seemed a little annoyed."

And then there was this, his own revisitation of old demons. "I will," he said, "after this set." And here they came, eight horses and eight grooms and eight riders converging, allowing him to put it off.

But this was his greatest temptation, the thing he had that matched Joy, the thing that had done him in before. Of course he could call Somerville; his cellular was hanging from his belt. And in some remote way, he wanted those horses in his barn, all six of them. There were two Salt Lakes, a Vice Regent, an A.P. Indy, a Strawberry Road, and, of all things, a Sadler's Wells filly Somerville had bought in Ireland. He had cheap horses he could send to Hollywood Park, horses who would do fine in spite of the footing. And Oliver could handle it. If he called Somerville right now, and then after him the other guy, Maraniss, they would be setting things up for this by the time the fourth set was finished training. If he didn't call, the horses would go to Frankel or Hofmans or Mandella—there was no shortage of good trainers in southern California, and Somerville and Maraniss had used most of them.

No one was around him. He could put his hand on his phone and make the calls.

He should at least say no. To fail to call at all was openly rude, and owners, all owners, even those not routinely accustomed to being fawned over, recognized rudeness.

He had done himself in like this before; toward the end of his marriage, he had simply stopped using the phone entirely for about two months. He did not answer, he did not call, and he allowed his message machines, at home, at the barn, to fill up until anyone calling him just got endless ringing. The foundation mare had been more than angry, more than frustrated. She had been confirmed in the knowledge she had had all along that he could not be understood, reached, appealed to rationally. Was he willing to destroy everything, she said, their family, his career, the last lingering shreds of feeling between the two of them, his own self-respect? Somehow yes was the answer. Actually, it was something of a miracle. You could explode your life into unrecognizable fragments just by not answering the phone and not returning calls. Two months in Bali, two months on the moon would have done a far less thorough job than he had done by not answering the phone.

And what was he doing the whole time? He was wondering why he didn't want to answer the phone. Horses vanished from his barn without warning— if he had answered the phone, he would have reassured the owners and not lost the horses, or at least known that they were being moved. As it was, various grooms and assistant trainers would show up, or even van drivers, and ask for the horses, and he would let them go. Finally, there were nine cheap horses in his barn, and then other horses belonging to other trainers came into his stalls, or what had been his stalls. He didn't question that, either.

It was a strange episode that gave him a sense of kinship with drunks, suicides, plagiarists, anorexics, self-destroyers of all kinds. When he looked back on it, he seemed to himself to have been paralyzed, or even enchanted. There had been a stillness about the whole period. Outside, the tempest raged, in that everyone he knew was justifiably angry with him, and some still were, ten years later, but inside everything was quiet, and eventually the phone didn't ring at all. After some period of silence, he couldn't remember how long, he made the first call of his new life, to the manager of an apartment complex who he saw in the paper had an apartment for rent.

Taken all in all, he had no regrets, but he didn't want to do the whole thing over again. But by the time he was out at the track, he was even less inclined to make the calls. "Hey," he said. "How's it going? Hey. Hey, baby." It was a pleasant day. No smog. The ridge of the mountains across the track seemed etched in light. His associates, three of them, stood together in comfortable fellowship. A couple of owners were there, too. You could always tell them by their ignorant alert self-consciousness.

His horses appeared on the track, jogging around to the other side or heading to the back of the chute for gate-training. He thought, I need help here, and then the phone at his waist began to ring. It rang three times. All around him, feet started shuffling. It was noisy and uncomfortable. It rang a fourth time, and he knew that the messaging system would pick up. He could hear it perfectly: "Farley Jones is not available at this time. If you would like to leave a message, please do so at the beep." Except that the phone rang again and again. Someone, Farley didn't see who, said, "Shit." Then Buddy Crawford turned around and said, "Farley, answer the God-damned phone, because if you don't I'm going to throw it out onto the track."

Farley answered the phone. As he did so, he heard one of the other trainers say, "Hell, Buddy, nice to see you're back to your old self."

"Tell me about it," said Buddy.

"Farley?" said a Brit from deep in the cellular universe.

"Hey," said Farley.

"This is Sir Michael Ordway."

"Hey."

"May I make an inquiry?"

"Of course."

"Have you room for another horse? Rather a mystery horse, if you ask me, but interesting owners."

"I'm sorry, I don't have a stall available, and it's so crowded here, I don't know when I can get one."

"You're not keeping horses at Hollywood Park anymore, I understand."

"Haven't for several years."

"Too bad, then."

"Sorry," said Farley.

"Indeed," said Sir Michael.

OLIVER KNEW THAT he should not pick up the ringing phone, but he did so anyway, because he couldn't help it, because he always picked up the phone before he realized what he was doing and because he thought it might be someone with a nice horse to send to Farley, or perhaps Farley himself calling from the track, telling him he had changed his mind about sending him over to Hollywood with his own string, that wasn't so unusual, was, in fact, quite usual. But it was his girlfriend. She started in right away. "Did you talk to him?"

"There wasn't really time. He was a little late—"

"There's always time if you make time."

"I'll make time. I told you I would make time."

"I don't want to go to Tokyo and Kyoto and Kuala Lumpur and Hong Kong and Bali and Fiji with thirty-seven Mitsubishi dealers and their wives for twelve fun-filled days and have to think about your situation out there the whole time. Honey." She remembered to soften the last word.

"He isn't necessarily going to see things my way. He's already said—"

"What did we say last night, Oliver?"

"I have certain needs. Career needs."

And here came Farley, opening the door and walking right into his own office with a smile and a look of inquiry. Oliver lifted his finger, but didn't actually look at his boss.

"Yes, you do, sweetie, and you need to attend to them. I can't do that for you, you know that."

"Yes, I do."

"Now, tell me again what you're going to ask for."

"I can't really do that."

"We went over it last night, honey."

"I know, but—"

"This is an avoidance problem on your part, darling. You have a real thing about giving bad news. But that just means things slide and slide. I think it would be really good for you to just run down the list right now, the five action points that we went over, and get them clear in your mind."

Farley was getting himself a cup of coffee from the coffeemaker.

"I know what you mean, but that's not what I'm—"

"Oliver, sweetheart, you know, back home, when the team is, say, forty points down and none of the boys are trying any shots or getting any rebounds?"

"Yes." Her dad was a high-school basketball coach.

"And at half-time, they all go into the locker room, and they huddle together, and they have a come-to-Jesus meeting right there?"

"Yes."

"Well, that's where we are right now. Come to Jesus. Up or out. Bottom line. You and him. You and me."

"I know what you're getting at, but—"

"Hand him the phone. I know he's standing right there. I'll talk to him myself."

Ah, well. And just because anything could happen, Oliver held out the phone to Farley, and said, "It's for you."

Farley sat down in his desk chair and put the receiver to his ear. Oliver turned away from the desk and looked at the bulletin board of win pictures from the last year or so—Garden Variety winning the Santa Luisa Handicap; Garden Variety again, this time in the Willard Scott Stakes, Parson Jack winning the MGM Handicap, Duly Noted winning the Judy Garland Futurity. Oliver glanced at Farley, who was stroking his beard thoughtfully. Oliver figured that she was being rather forceful. He turned back to the win pictures. Sterling Silver winning the Calistoga, Panettone winning the Hitchcock at Del Mar, Duly Noted winning the Cardiff. Farley put the receiver back in its cradle. He said, "You're fired."

"I am?"

"She said that being fired would be exactly the opportunity you need to get out of your career rut and rethink your life plan. She said that, between us, you and I encourage one another's natural passivity, and though that's fine for me, at my age, approaching retirement and with all of my children grown and no real financial commitments, assuming that my condo is paid for—"

"She said that?"

"Yes. You, on the other hand, are just starting out, and it's clear to her that a kick in the pants could change your life, she was intensely grateful for every kick in the pants she herself had ever received, had I ever heard the expression 'Every knock's a boost?,' and so, all things considered, you're fired."

"I'm sorry she talked to you like that. She doesn't realize that she's being rude—"

"She wasn't rude, she was logical and forceful, and she made some very good points. So there you go."

"But I don't want to be fired."

"Best thing for you."

"I think you're joking."

"No, I'm not joking."

"You mean, I'm really fired?"

"For your own good, yes."

"Who's going to be your assistant?"

"Joy, I guess. She's the obvious candidate."

"She's going away for twelve days with some car dealers."

"Well, my advice is to have a new job, or at least a career plan, by the time she comes back."

"I still think you're joking. You're smiling."

"I'm smiling because all my problems have been solved."

"What do you mean?"

"Well, I got rid of Sir Michael Ordway, so Mr. T. doesn't have to go. Joy will have something to do to keep her up and about. And I don't have to worry about you, because you are going to take care of yourself."

"I don't want to take care of myself." But that sounded weird, so Oliver said, "I mean, I do want to take care of myself in the normal way, but—"

"Here's something to remember. If you wait for the feeling in order to act, you'll never act, but if you act, the feeling will follow."

"It will?"

"The third set is ready. I would say, be out of here by tomorrow. How does that sound?"

"I thought you liked me! I thought we got along!"

"I do and we do, but if you're fired, you're fired. There's a structure to the whole situation."

He got up and walked out of the office. Oliver immediately picked up the phone and dialed his girlfriend's office number and cell number, but she could not be reached.

JOY COULD BE REACHED. Even after what had happened to her, she still didn't mind answering the phone. In fact, it felt functional and virtuous to answer the phone, and so on the first ring she stopped crying, on the second ring she swallowed and wiped her eyes, on the third ring she sat up, threw off the covers, and noticed that the sun was shining, on the fourth ring she found the phone under the pillow, and on the fifth ring she said, "Hello?"

"Hi," said Farley. He didn't have to make an effort to soften his voice. Talking to Joy softened his voice for him.

"Hi," she whispered.

"Are you available for employment?"

"In what sense?"

"Can you show up here and be my assistant trainer, starting tomorrow?"

"Assistant racehorse trainer? Is Oliver moving to Hollywood Park?"

"Oliver's girlfriend and I agreed that I would fire him."

"You did?"

"It was me or her, she said. She sounded like she meant it. And she made a rather good case for it being me and not her."

"That's so weird."

"So I need you."

"I can't, I—"

"For right now. There's lots to do."

"Hire him back."

"No."

"It doesn't interest me. I have no faith in it. It'll make me crazy. It'll be like it was back at the university. I'm afraid."

"But you know how to do it and I need someone to do it. The barn is full. Put one foot in front of the other. That's all."

"Do you have infinite patience?"

"Will you return all my calls for me?"

"Yes," she said.

"Yes," he said.

"Done deal?"

"Done deal," said Joy. And she hung up. And she burst into tears.

IN HIS OFFICE, Farley put down the phone, closed his eyes, and blew out a noisy sigh. What it felt like was nothing so much as reaching out and grabbing her at the last minute, just as she went over the edge. It was not so clear whether he could hold her, convinced as he was, now more than ever, that she would slip away in the end. He had his methods and his resources, didn't he? Patience. Stoicism. Keeping at it. The same old same old, virtues tried and true. Hiding out, the foundation mare would have readily, and even triumphantly, called it. Ah, yes, hiding out was always a temptation for a man of dignity and reserve such as himself. And so he had made a little contract with Joy.

Barney had told him about that. A guy he'd read about in a book made a contract with his wife, every year, that she wouldn't commit suicide that year. One year she could handle. And they had lived together thirty years, one year at a time. He got up and went around the desk. Outside, it was high noon and quiet. The horses who had worked that morning were eating or dozing. Only Mr. T. popped his head over the door and looked at him. Farley hadn't thought a lot about their earlier association. It had lasted less than a year. In the fifteen years since, hundreds of horses had passed through his barn. But of course it was odd that the animal should turn up again, and bring Joy along with him, a Fairy Godgelding, no matter what this mumbo-jumbo of Elizabeth's was all about.

"Hey," he said.

The horse pricked his ears.

"You tell me what to do next. You tell me and I'll listen. Done deal?"

Mr. T. looked at him intelligently.

58 / JUSTA CLAIMER

OVER VALENTINE'S DAY, William Vance let his girlfriend persuade him to take her to Florida on some of Justa Bob's winnings, and then he talked her into going out to Gulfstream. And then he saw this horse by Skip Trial, the sire of Skip Away, out of a Secretariat mare, who'd been dropped into a seventy-five-thousand-dollar claiming race, and so he put up the cash, and the horse won, only his third start, but he came out of the race off behind, and then, when William got him X-rayed, it turned out he had a coffin-bone fracture—just a fragment floating there in the hazy picture—and with a special shoe, he might be ready to go again in the late summer. Right then, William had this feeling that he was due for a bad turnaround, but he didn't pay attention to it, and when he went back to New Orleans to finish up and head back to Chicago, he was still in a pretty good mood. Two days later, though, his four-year-old colt tied up after a work, knotted up so hard you thought if you smacked him he would ring like a gong, right out there on the track. They didn't dare move him, and had to trailer him fifty yards back to his stall. His urine was nearly black. The other four-year-old, a good solid allowance mare, just hadn't liked the footing in Louisiana and hadn't run a lick since the beginning—"too good," said William to Romero when he called to tell him all about it. "She can't get a hold of it. She looks dazed out there." Even then, William kept having that feeling that everything was going to be all right in spite of the coffin-bone fracture and all, until a few days after the tie-up. At first they thought that, even though the colt's urine was coffee-colored—a very bad sign—there was some chance that he would—well, what?—come back to his old form? William gave up that hope pretty quickly. Come back to the track at all? Two days, three days, four days passed. The horse stood in his stall, unmoving, his eyes half closed, unable or unwilling to eat, the fitness and even the flesh passing off him like a dream. Then William thought, well, he was a colt, good-looking and not that badly bred, someone could stand him somewhere like Wisconsin or Minnesota, but then, about a week after the incident, a big lump appeared over his croup, maybe a foot long and four to six inches wide. The vet came out and poked it. He shook his head. You hardly had to twitch the horse, he was so listless, but they sedated him and incised the lump. Black-brown fluid with some strands of something oozed and dripped out. William had never seen such a thing, but he knew what it was before the vet told him. "William," said the vet. "That's necrotized muscle tissue."

"He's done for," said William.

"I'm thinking he is," said the vet.

They euthanized the horse ten minutes later. William went out to his truck and cried.

BUT, OF COURSE, he still had Justa Bob. Justa Bob had finally lost, and done it twice, last place and second-to-last place in a twenty-five-thousand-dollar allowance and a twenty-two-thousand-dollar allowance. He was tired. William's plan was to take him back to Chicago and let him slack off for several months. He called Romero. "The thing is," he said, "I shouldn't have claimed that Skip Trial colt. He's standing here in the barn."

"They come back from coffin-bone—"

"I don't have the money to pay some of my bills or get back home. The vet bills—"

"Run him." William knew he was talking about Justa Bob.

"He's too tired for the company. There's a bunch of fresh horses coming in."

"Run him. Someone will claim him for sure."

"I know they will, that's what I'm afraid of."

"Are you attached to that horse?"

"Well, of course I am. I—"

"You're the one who always says you get attached and you're dead."

"I know, but Justa Bob is different."

"None of them are different if you can't get home."

WILLIAM GOT Justa Bob ready for the race himself. He went into the stall, and cleaned him up and put a couple of braids in there, just for fun. He curried him and brushed him and rubbed him all over until the animal's brown coat looked like walnut veneer. He separated the hairs of his tail and smoothed them out one by one, sprayed on a little silicone spray. He wrapped and taped his back legs, put yellow polos on the front. His silks, just a yellow shirt with white sleeves, looked good on this horse, too.

Justa Bob stood there, calm and alert. By now he had started fifty-four times, and he knew everything about it. When the time came for the fourth race, William walked him to the receiving barn and out to the saddling enclosure himself. He was wearing clean khaki trousers and a white shirt. He looked good. They both looked good. Of course horses were everywhere, and trainers, and jocks and grooms and owners. Some in every category were very high-class, especially among the three-year-olds who were taking this route to the Derby rather than the New York route, the Florida route, or the West Coast route, but William thought Justa Bob stood out, anyway. No, he wasn't all that fast, and he wasn't all that pretty, but he had hung on and for a long time and never failed to cooperate, and never failed to give it, whatever it was, everything he had. William wished that guy from the *Times-Picayune* were around right now, because he wouldn't be tongue-tied. He'd know exactly what to say. William looked at his watch. Time to go out there.

Yes, this whole thing had a sort of funereal quality to it, and to be honest, you never knew until after the race whether the horse had been claimed, but if not, then. If not this time, then another time. As usual in racing, money and sentiment had gone off in different directions, and here he was.

So he put the jock up, a young kid who needed the experience, and he said, "Just hold on and let him run his race. He knows more about it than any horse out there. At the end, don't go for the whip. If he's got gas, he'll give it to you himself. And don't be afraid if he gets you into a bunch at the finish line. That's the way he likes it."

The jock nodded.

William didn't go up to his seat, but stood down on the rail with the bettors. Justa Bob had drawn the number-one position, which was okay in a nine-furlong race like this one.

Okay until the number-two horse came out of the gate and bumped Justa

Bob toward the rail, and dislodged the young jockey, who slipped to the outside. Then Justa Bob staggered a step, maybe from the uneven weight. And then the other horses were past him, and he was alone in the rear. Then he veered to the outside, and the rider righted himself and took hold. And then Justa Bob took off. Normally, William knew, he was a stalker. He liked to be just off the pace, saving himself for his only move. And he was old. If his only move didn't work, he didn't have another one—that was the key to his losses. But now he ran like a different horse, full-bore, head down, body flat. He ran down the horses in front of him one by one, two by two. William was sure the jockey had nothing to do with it, was just sitting there. It was mesmerizing. One, two, three, four, five. He shot them down one by one and kept going. William wasn't sure the jockey was even looking where they were going—from this distance it looked like he had his face buried in the horse's neck. They were coming around the second turn and there was one horse left, a chestnut four-year-old by A.P. Indy, a well-bred and once expensive animal who'd had some good wins lately. In the homestretch, Justa Bob blew past him as if jet-propelled, and crossed the finish line a good three lengths in front. "God damn," said William Vance to himself. "And here I thought I knew that horse."

He ran out on the track to meet them when they came back a few minutes later. The jockey's face was blanched. He said, "Hey, Mr. Vance. That was kinda scary."

"How so, Eddie?"

"Well, I nearly fell off there at first, but he kinda hoisted me back on, somehow, or that's what it felt like, then he took the bit in his teeth and ran like hell."

"Were you watching where you were going?"

The jockey licked his lips, then said, "Well, no, sir, not for part of the way."

"Well, it's over now. And you won."

"Yes, sir, we did. I'm sure I'll be happy about that later, sir."

William led the horse to the winner's circle and had the picture taken with just the three of them; then, of course, it happened. The steward came out with the red tag and hung it on Justa Bob's bit, and there he was.

So he cleared twenty thousand dollars on the race, with the purse money and the claiming price. That was plenty to get him out of here and back to Chicago, Justa Bob's parting shot, parting blessing. Later, when he was reporting the race to Romero, kind of down in the mouth, Romero said, "You know, the first time you ever saw him, man, the horse was almost dead."

Six months ago, thought William. Only six months ago. Hard to believe.

And then he let himself say the thing he had been trying not even to think. He said, "When they led him away, I thought he was a little off."

"Well, then, lucky thing you got rid of him, eh, man?"

"Sure," said William. "Never too soon to sell one, you know." He guffawed—yes, he did, the way you do, lucky for sure. But if he was so lucky, why didn't he feel all that good about it?

MARCH

59 / WESTWARD HO

NOW THAT ROSALIND was an art dealer, she discovered that she had fulfilled one of her accountant's dreams, 100-percent deductibility. Everything she bought, every plane ticket, every hotel stay, every meal out of town or with an artist, every use of her automobile for art-buying purposes, every car rental, you name it, if she spent it, she could deduct it. There was even a reasonable expectation that she could deduct expenses for maintaining her personal appearance, since she had a certain image to uphold. The accountant's goal of reducing her tax bill to zero was not quite the same as Rosalind's goal, no doubt a relic of her Midwestern youth, of living a responsible life. There were, after all, plenty of goods and services that the various jurisdictions she sojourned in provided—roads, street lighting, police, flood control, air-traffic control . . . Rosalind found herself running dry in the face of her accountant's look of amusement. In defense, Rosalind closed her eyes and granted him a wish. A moment later, he opened his desk drawer and pulled out a pack of cigarettes. "Go ahead," said Rosalind. "I don't mind."

Full deductibility, though, was something you could only really appreciate once a year, and for this year, the last in the millennium, Rosalind had already appreciated it. Even so, it gave an extra bit of comfort to the first-class flight to Los Angeles that she took just after her meeting with the accountant. She had some money to spend and some space to fill in her gallery, and she was on her way to meet several artists who were eager to fill it. She also had the name of three trainers at Hollywood Park and Santa Anita whom she planned to interview for Limitless. She had no idea what to ask them. She who had once been an owner-in-law, an addendum to the breeder, the wife who came along, was now the responsible party. But, as always now, she figured something would come to her. Or to Eileen, who was nestled quietly inside her carrying case underneath the seat in front of Rosalind. The flight attendant went by, looking a bit harried. Rosalind glanced at her, then granted her a wish. A moment later, the head of the guy in seat 1C, a guy whom Rosalind had recognized as Pete

Rose, dropped forward into a heavy sleep. The flight attendant noticed this, too, and visibly relaxed. Rosalind wondered if this power of hers had a time limit or a use limit attached to it, and where it came from, and then the sunshine blasted her through the window, and by the time she had closed the shade, she was back to her normal condition of not wondering about anything.

Her plane landed just after 10:00 a.m. She was on her way to Santa Anita by eleven. She who had been to Belmont Park, Saratoga, Churchill Downs, Newmarket, Chantilly, Longchamp, Cheltenham, Gulfstream, in some cases time after time, in suits and hats and lace and silk and every kind of expensive shoe, had never been to Santa Anita, but she saw immediately that it was her kind of place. It was across the street from an arboretum and not far from the gardens and the collection at the Huntington Library. It was painted green and buff, there was topiary in the courtyard, there was art deco running the entire length of the grandstand, there were mountains setting off the track, and there was a shopping mall across the parking lot for rest and recuperation. She had the strong sense of having arrived at her home racetrack, and she crossed off her list the name of the trainer who was based at Hollywood Park.

The trainer, who was famous and already in the Racing Hall of Fame, was to meet her at the front entrance, and she expected to recognize him, because she had seen his picture, but the man she recognized first was the tall fellow who had fallen upon her at Saratoga last summer. Well, staggered into her. He recognized her, too, and came up to her with a warm smile, and took both of her hands in his all of a sudden, not as if he did this all the time, but as if he couldn't help himself. He had a kind look and a friendly voice. He looked more like a teacher or scientist than a horse-trainer, but he also had that air of unlimited patience that good horse-trainers always seemed to have. Rosalind said, "I'm supposed to meet Richard Case here. I think I'll recognize him." They looked around. But he held off, and Rosalind said, "You're a horse-trainer, too."

"Yes."

"Do you have any room in your barn? I have a horse—"

She saw that he hesitated, but then he looked right at her and he said, "Well, yes. In a way. Would you like me to call Richard for you?" He put his hand on his cellular. Rosalind closed her eyes. Surely there was something a person in the wish-granting business could do about a socially awkward situation.

There didn't seem to be. Richard Case came up a moment later, and he was a perfectly acceptable world-famous horse-trainer, the son of a legend, the nephew of a legend, and well on the way to being a legend himself. He was handsome and articulate and had gone to Oxford and, moreover, had room in his barn. He had met Al once and liked him. He kept his hand firmly on Rosalind's elbow as he guided her up the steps to his box so that they could talk at leisure and watch a race or two.

The race was five furlongs, for two-year-old fillies. There were ten horses running, and the *Form* made it clear that they were top-class company—A.P. Indy, Seeking the Gold, Mr. Prospector, Holy Bull, Affirmed. Southern California was where the money was, so here was where the best horses gathered to sort themselves out. Eileen sat on a separate chair. As always, she put her forepaws on the railing, and looked alertly down at the track. Rosalind said, "I told you my horse is a homebred, and he hasn't done much in his three two-year-old starts. On paper he doesn't look at all like these fillies."

"He's not fashionably bred," said Richard Case, "but I'm familiar with his sire. He had his first crop last year, and they haven't done much, but he himself was—"

"Himself. That's what they call him at the farm."

"—a late bloomer. He was bred in Europe and ran mostly in Europe. The Europeans loved him. The horse is inbred to Ribot through one of his European sons on the top line and through Tom Rolfe on the bottom line. I always thought it was odd that the old man brought him to this country, but he was a funny old man. Once he wrote a piece I saw about upgrading Thoroughbred stock by breeding to classic European bloodlines. Very old-fashioned in some ways. Didn't go over big with the Kentucky boys."

"My husband chose the stallion. I never knew why. But the horse has a lovely stride." One of the fillies in the race was named "Avarice." Rosalind gave her the win. She found another gear in the homestretch, covered the last two furlongs in twenty-two and a quarter seconds, and came in at thirty-three-to-one. Even her jockey looked astounded. Richard Case laughed cheerfully and said, "That was nice. Shall we go around and look at the horses?"

But Rosalind felt as though she were on someone else's date. The prospective mate was as desirable as could be, and she could claim him at any time, but he had "no" written all over him. As they entered the path to the barns, Rosalind saw Farley Jones in the distance, with his girlfriend, who took his hand and kissed him on the cheek, and nestled into his armpit, while Farley himself seemed to expand a bit, as if the girlfriend's proximity opened him up. She was little and blonde, built of much the same materials, Rosalind thought, as Eileen. Richard Case was saying something charming and knowledgeable. Rosalind nodded, but hadn't heard a word. Win percentages, training philosophy, footing at the track, racing in southern California in general, the meet at Santa Anita was ending, Hollywood Park, then Del Mar, had she ever been to

Del Mar. It was a pleasant sound, like the burble of a fountain. Then it fell silent. Rosalind came to understand that she was supposed to say something. She said, "The horse is quirky. I want him to do what's easy for him and to have a purpose in life. My husband cares about winning, not about the money but about having that jolt. We just retired a good filly who gave him that jolt on a regular basis. He misses it. But it's more important to me that the horse enjoy his work. If he doesn't like racing he can do something else, but he's fast. Everyone agrees about that."

"Of course," said Richard Case. When they got to his barn, she saw that it was perfectly clean, beautifully decorated, a model of order and system. Farley Jones's barn was the next one over. While Richard Case took a call (that was a thing that every horse-trainer did, you couldn't hold it against them), she spied. They went in and out of the office. The little girlfriend went over to one of the horses, a white one, and stroked his ears and nose, then kissed him. There was a head hanging over every stall. Richard Case said, "Excuse me just one more second, if you don't mind," and took another call. That was when Rosalind bolted.

When she got to Farley, she said, "It's funny. I know I haven't known you before this, but I feel like I've missed you anyway."

FARLEY NEVER GOT to say anything to Rosalind Maybrick about that time in Saratoga. Maybe he had made too much of it by now, and so he thought it would sound silly. She was a pleasant warm woman and what she wanted from him for the horse was a nice change from the usual. Their conversations were friendly, about plans for the animal's shipment and supplements and extras Rosalind wanted to be sure the horse received, but there was nothing personal in any of it. Even so, her presence reminded him forcibly of something he still could not label or define. What it was closest to was some sort of electrical process, where she made contact at one point and contact at another point and the molecules between the two points straightened themselves out. What Elizabeth had said was "She crossed your heart."

What did that mean?

"Well, that's how you get electrocuted, you know. You have one live wire in one hand and another live wire in the other hand, and boom. People don't always die from electrocution. Sometimes they just get put in order."

Well, maybe.

At any rate, a stall opened up as if by magic, and when the horse arrived a week later, Farley looked at him a long time with Joy. Rafael held him and they walked around him and around him. There was a way in which he looked like just a horse. He was bay with a touch of white—a tiny star on his forehead, and a little triangle on the inside of his right hind fetlock. He had a long narrow head, dished, and long ears. He was plenty fit—the previous trainer had conditioned him perfectly. His belly was tucked up and his neck was slender and muscled even though he was a stud colt. He was long in the back, long in the leg, long in the forearm.

They watched him go out, they watched him come back. Farley said, "Try that again, please." They watched him go out. They watched him come back. It was hypnotizing. Joy said, "That must be an eighteen-inch overstep."

"He's—what would you say?—sixteen hands, maybe sixteen one? But he's got the hind legs of a seventeen-hand horse."

"Who's going to ride him?"

"I don't know. Why don't you get on him and walk him around and get a feel of what his manners are like."

When he threw her on top of the horse fifteen minutes later, she said, "I don't know that I've ever felt anything like this. It's not exactly power." She walked off, around the end of the shedrow. A few minutes later, she reappeared at the other end of the shedrow. She was grinning. She said, "I don't want to get off."

"Don't, then. Walk him out to the track and give him a little trot."

It was late in the morning, and the track was hardly in use. The horse walked calmly along, turning his head this way and that, taking everything in. He was calm. When another youngster suddenly reared up some fifty yards away, Limitless stopped, watched, moved on. That is, he flowed to a halt, flowed through it, flowed back into a walk. They entered the track, turned to the left, and flowed into a trot along the outside rail. Farley noticed that Joy had maybe a finger's contact with the horse's mouth, and then she let off on that. The horse continued to trot, his strides big and supple, his head up, his body balanced. They went once around the track. When they got to the gate again, Joy reined him up and he threw up his head so high that he nearly knocked her out of the saddle. "There's the problem," said Farley, standing at the rail.

"But that was my fault. I didn't need to do that. He was coming down on his own." She patted the horse and let out the rein. The horse dropped his head. He continued around the track again, walking that walk.

When they put him in the stall they had set aside for him, his whole demeanor changed. He was no longer happy or calm. He wouldn't taste his hay, took no drinks of water, sniffed his oats and turned away from them. Farley watched him, but he showed no signs of settling, and ignored Farley when he approached and spoke to him. His eyes were up and out. After a couple of hours, Farley exchanged him with a horse in an outdoor pen, away from the darkness of the shedrow. Things in the pen were marginally better, in that he would grab a mouthful of hay from time to time, and he did take a drink, but clearly confinement was not his cup of tea.

THE NEXT MORNING, Joy called Elizabeth, who, it turned out, was negotiating the contract for her three books, which were out to twenty publishers. They were in the middle of the auction. So far, six publishers had come in with offers ranging from $250,000 to $475,000. Elizabeth was very Elizabethan about it. She planned to take the highest offer, whatever it was, and place half of it with Plato's friend in commodities and half with Mr. T. She would then observe the relation between her sense of what was about to happen to the money and what did happen to the money. After that she expected to train herself to view the future as the past and the past as only one possibility of the many that woulda shoulda coulda happened. "For example," she said, "and if I take a call waiting while I am explaining this, I apologize, let's say that you and I disagreed about something that happened. Let's say that Nathan Zada and I disagree about every single thing that went on in our marriage. Well, that could mean one of three things. One of them is that neither of us was there to witness the disaster. Another is that two separate things happened that bear no real relationship to one another. And a third is that nothing happened at all. He was dreaming his dream, I was dreaming my dream. Am I going to tell him that he dreamt the wrong dream? Actually, I told him that for years, but I forgive him for that now."

"For dreaming the wrong dream?"

"No, for eliciting that kind of bullshit from me. Anyway, it's a complicated subject. Suffice it to say that the past is as variable as the future, otherwise we wouldn't disagree about it. How is Mr. T.?"

"He's good. I want you to ask him about a new horse here."

"Honey, is this an emergency?"

Joy looked across at the horsepen, where Limitless had put his head down and was beginning to weave. She said, "Yes."

"My mind is awash with money and sex. I can't fit a horse in there."

"Sex? I thought you were having this auction."

"Yes, but Plato is walking around priapically naked as a kind of living offering. It's very ritualized, but the sums of money offered do keep getting bigger. Anyway, ask him yourself. You can. Or ask the new horse. What's his name?"

"Limitless."

"Oh, there they go. I have to take this call." As she hung up, she heard Elizabeth say, "Plato, sweetie, turn a little more toward the sun there—"

She went over to the new horse and stood beside the pen. He was looking off into the distance, but after a second he turned toward her with his ears pricked. She opened the door and stepped inside, cupping her hands down by her waist. He arched his neck to investigate them. After he smelled her hands, he sniffed the front of her shirt, and then stuck out his tongue and licked her a couple of times. Then he turned to look again. Farley came up to them. Joy said, "I'm going to take him for a walk."

Farley said, "Honey, you be in charge of him. Do whatever is the easiest thing to do. There's no pressure with this horse. You're going to be riding him, too."

"I am?"

"Yes," he said, kissing her on the top of the head. "You are."

"You are sacrificing this horse to me. I can't ride him."

"You rode him."

"I can't gallop him and work him."

"I think you have enough experience for that now. You've galloped a lot of horses in the last six months."

"Give him to Angelica. She has a nice way."

"Yes, she does. But you have a nicer way. Angelica fits herself to the horse and she's good at that, but you get the horses to want to fit themselves to you. I've told you that before."

"I have no energy."

"This horse has enough energy for both of you. Look at him. He's made of energy."

Joy put the halter over the horse's head and led him out of the pen. He perked up immediately.

FARLEY OFTEN WATCHED them together, more than he had to, more, even, than love, or curiosity about this particular horse, would require. When he assigned the horse to her, he had lied a bit. She wasn't quite experienced enough—there was a wider margin of potential danger than he liked—but, frankly, it was possible that he could pin her down this way, through both pleasure and obligation, possible that he could give her enough to do and to think about that what she called "her thing" would stay in abeyance each day, day after day, that she would stick with it, if not with him. For himself, he remained doubtfully nonchalant. He pretended that he wasn't noting every sigh, eyeballing the angle of her shoulders, awakening in the night with her. He pretended he wasn't waiting, wasn't looking for signs, wasn't heaping things upon her—tasks, affection, attention, thoughts, touches, looks, overreactions to her every move and word. A man of lifelong reserve, like himself, could perfectly mimic reserve, could quell panic any time he wished to. In the meantime, the horse was something else.

AFTER HIS TWO required works, some ten days after his arrival, Farley ran him. The race was a thirty-two-thousand-dollar maiden allowance race for colts and geldings three years old and up. Farley went out one morning and came back an hour later. When he came back, he said to Joy, "I found Roberto Acevedo."

"What did you ask him?"

"If he could ride a horse with a silk thread."

"What did he say?"

"That he would like to try."

After the race, which Limitless won by two lengths, Roberto said to Farley, in Joy's hearing, "He's got a homing device on his nose. All he has to do is leave the gate. I would have had him on a looser rein, but I was afraid of snatching him by mistake."

That evening, Farley called Rosalind, who was in Istanbul, and told her the news. She thanked him and said, "Send him to a farm for two weeks. One with lots of big pastures." It was all very easy and routine. Farley's considered opinion was that the horse might turn out to be a useful animal.

IN ISTANBUL, Rosalind hung up the phone and lay back down on her bed. It wasn't yet dawn, but outside her window, the shouting, noisy business of the city was well begun, and she was wide awake. Eileen leapt up on the bed and nestled into Rosalind's armpit. Rosalind wondered, what is the sound of a nick? Bold Ruler approaches Somethingroyal. Polynesian approaches Geisha. Pharos approaches Nogara. The mare stands still, flips her tail to the side. The stallion leaps, the deed is quickly done. The assembled men are occupied with leadshanks and leather capes and fleece boots. There is noise, yelling, encouragement. The mare is made much of. These are the sounds of ignorance and hope. Twenty or fifty years later, Secretariat, Native Dancer, Nearco, the products of these matings, cast the light of good luck back over these routine events. No Thoroughbred is conceived without intention, but these transcend mere intention, they transcend wish, they transcend dream. The most assiduous and dedicated breeder feels in his bones undeserving of their genius and beauty. It is a pure gift. It must be a tone, thinks Rosalind, a dark, sonorous, resonant tone for Nearco, a liquid pure middle C for Native Dancer, a bright ethereal note for Secretariat. The sound of a nick would be music as quiet as a thought, but lingering, audible even now to those who could hear it. It was after 6:00 a.m. in Istanbul, and so after 6:00 p.m. in Los Angeles. The day's racing would be over, the barn would be quiet, with the horses standing in their wraps, eating hay. Rows of horses, clean, well fed, rustling in their straw, grunting, snorting, shaking themselves, switching their tails, whinnying from time to time, and all of them sounding several of those silent notes, the Nearco note harmonizing with the Princequillo note, the Seattle Slew note harmonizing with the Buckpasser note, the ancient Teddy note still harmonizing with the Fairway note. The hum around Limitless was unusually delightful. Rosalind knew that as well as she knew anything beautiful. And there was a nick with the trainer, too. The trainer brought his own music that was partly intuition and partly knowledge and partly intention and partly desire. All those things mattered to the owner. But what mattered to the horse, Rosalind suspected, was something else, some consonant vibration that relaxed him and focused him and allowed him to play his own song, the song of the DNA, all the innumerable measures and bars of A T G and C that unreeled themselves within. The phenotypes lifted their heads, pricked their ears, pawed, looked at one another. The genotype swirled through them all, a full score of nicks playing itself in a thousand stalls. Thank you, thought Rosalind. The golden cup has come around to us now, Al and me, Farley and Joy, Roberto and Rafael. Better to recognize it and receive it with care.

She turned back to the phone and picked it up. Al was but two hours ahead of her, though she was hazy about his exact location. She tried his cellular number, and he picked it up on the first ring. He said, "Yeah."

She said, "Hello, dear."

"Rozzy." His voice softened. But, then, his voice always softened. It struck her there for a moment that Al really did love her.

"The horse won his race."

"Well, maybe he's not such a useless animal after all."

"I don't think Dick was the right trainer for him."

"Nah. Nah, he wasn't."

Now there was a very long pause. At the end of it, she knew that he was thinking about the last year, and she was thinking about the last year, and he knew that she was thinking about the last year, and she knew that he knew that she was thinking about the last year, and so, when she said, "Forgive me, Al," he could say, "Ah, I already did, Rozzy. I was just trying to figure out a way to tell you that."

"I, um—"

"We don't need to talk about it, Rozzy. Anyway, until sometime when we can barely remember anything about it."

"All right, Al."

There was another pause, into which she felt it was expected, but not desirable, to insert some information about what would happen next. Better, she thought, to close that space for the time being, so she said, "How's it going?"

"They don't have a thing here except the ore. Talk about infrastructure. You can't talk about infrastructure. If I had any brains, I would forget all about it. Jerry keeps calling me, every day, and telling me to forget all about it. It's not like I'm known for my social conscience. No brains, no social conscience, I can't stand a lot of these guys, either, and Maybrick Industries is not made of money—"

"Come home."

She surprised herself, saying this, especially since she herself was nowhere near home.

"Nah," he said. "Nah. It's kind of fun in a way. At least I get to blow my stack a lot and they don't mind. Blowing your stack is the way you do things here."

"I—" But did she? Did she miss him really? Enough to say it?

"Yeah," he said, "I miss you, too."

"I—" Her tongue was completely tied. She knew that for an absolute fact, but he said, anyway, "Yeah, honey, I love you, too." After he hung up the phone, she looked at it for a moment before setting it in its cradle.

THE NEXT DAY, Joy called up Mr. Tompkins and asked if Farley might send along a horse belonging to another owner, just for a vacation. Mr. Tompkins, of course, said yes, what was one more horse among hundreds, and so Limitless found himself in the center of the world—a hundred thousand beef cattle on one side, a South Pacific paradise on the other, Hollywood and Arabia over the way, almond groves and peach orchards and mares and foals and alfalfa fields stretching everywhere, and the bright hard glare of the central-California sun burnishing all creatures from above. He lived outside, day and night, for two weeks.

APRIL

60 / KENTUCKY DERBY (II)

YOU COULD GET to the Derby for six hundred dollars if you put your money down by the beginning of February. Of course, between the beginning of February and the beginning of May, keeping the horse on course cost about twenty thousand dollars, so that six hundred didn't seem like much, which Buddy thought was a pity, since almost four hundred owners had put down their six hundred dollars. It was like the start of some marathon somewhere that you saw a picture of in the paper, a nation of runners bunched and nobody looking special or anointed. Buddy saw in *The Blood-Horse* that Lukas had twenty-one, Baffert had sixteen, and this kid from New York had twelve. Buddy had one. He might have had two if he hadn't let that crazy black horse go. That crazy horse, not seeming crazy at all, had won a stakes race in New York. Maybe, Buddy thought, he was the one who had been crazy, all those thoughts about Jesus when he should have been training horses, getting to races, going with his instincts. Yes, you could say, as he had said to himself, his instincts were suspect, morality-wise, but he kept coming back to them. That had to be for a reason, if only for the reason that he wasn't smart enough or young enough to get himself any better ones. At any rate, that way Jesus had wanted him to train horses, that way was too laborious for him. He hadn't the energy both to get his work done and to wrestle with his conscience. It had to be one or the other.

There were seven other fillies nominated. The most fun, Buddy thought, would be an all-female Kentucky Derby, but of all the unlikely things that might happen in racing, probably that was the most unlikely. Three fillies had won the Derby in 125 years. But Residual had beaten all the other fillies based on the West Coast at one time or another, though each of the ones she had beaten had also beaten her, so she wasn't a shoo-in. Last summer, when he had had two shoo-ins, he hadn't even enjoyed it. Well, it all went to show you that introspection just ended up with things like you sleeping the sleep of the dead in some dripping jungle treehouse in Hawaii while the best Breeders' Cup day ever went on without you.

Never again, thought Buddy.

Never again, vowed Buddy.

Residual, on steroids, progesterone, and regular shots of hyaluronic acid to her joints, was running like a machine. She was feeling like a machine, too. What everybody said was that she had matured. Certainly she had grown an inch and put on about a hundred pounds. Her coat was nearly as fine and shiny as it had been—she was very similar to that former filly—but what it felt like to everyone was that, rather than adding something, maturity had taken something away from her. Maybe it was that running was now her vocation, whereas it had formerly been her avocation. Her former vocation, affection, was now just an occasional hobby. She came forward for her carrots, she let herself be petted, she nickered at this one or that one, but she was altogether more reserved. She worked every five days, always giving the satisfaction of a job well done. Marvelous Martha enjoyed riding her, and considered her a good filly, but she and Deedee had never compared notes. She thought Deedee was a little self-indulgent (had she herself not ridden Grand Prix at Indio when she was six months pregnant?), and Deedee was speechless with envy that the filly she considered her own, just on loan to Martha, might get all the way to Churchill Downs, and so hadn't ever mentioned the day when that crazy colt chased them and the filly found a whole easy, happy, insolent realm of speed that felt like greatness to Deedee. Not knowing it was there, Marvelous Martha didn't think to try and find it.

Now that Buddy was back to his old self, Leon, assistant trainer to Buddy and husband to Deedee and prospective father to Alana Marie, thought not at all about the risks you had to take to get your own future stable of racehorses and more about keeping his job. He was respectful, anxious, and easily intimidated. The only creature around the barn who still really liked him was the filly, but even though she only had eyes for him, he only had eyes for Buddy.

Every time the Kingstons came out to the track, Buddy made so much of them, and showed them and told them so many things, that even Jason Clark Kingston seemed pleasantly confused. Andrea Melanie was gaga. Whereas Jason seemed to take the idea of running his filly in the Kentucky Derby as his due, and therefore not surprising, Andrea Melanie's mind seemed blasted. When Buddy looked at her and said, "Derby Derby Derby," she just looked at him and nodded nodded nodded.

But the fact was that, whereas once everyone had agreed that Residual was an astounding, wonderful, unprecedented filly, now they all agreed that she was a very good filly, one of the best, and certainly something like the Derby was possible for her, you never knew.

THE THING WAS, Buddy thought, to get the filly to Keeneland. The Keeneland meet lasted fifteen days, the shortest meet in horse racing, but in fifteen days they gave out something like seven or eight million dollars in purses. Every race was worth plenty, and everyone who could take it was there, training their horses, eating in the clubhouse dining room, gossiping, going to parties at night, eyeing all the three-year-olds, and feeling the field for the Derby jell around them. When Keeneland was over, you moved up the road to Louisville. Buddy had gotten to Keeneland once before, but his horse had popped a splint there (such a little thing, fatal to nothing but Derby hopes) and he had never gotten up the road to Louisville.

Certainly everyone in the barn was willing, and even eager, and even desperate to get to Keeneland. The jockey saw the size of those purses in all those races that he might be able to find a ride for as a blue-chip investment in his pension plan. Marvelous Martha, for all her experience, had been to Keeneland only once, and then as a pedestrian. To go as the fifty-two-year-old exercise rider of a Derby hopeful, and a filly at that, would be a story to catalogue right beside the time she jumped a horse over a five-foot course in a muddy farmer's field in Ireland, after dark, lit only by the headlamps of two cars and a horse van. Didn't have a single pole down, either. Leon was well aware that no one in Keeneland knew him at all, so he could get a fresh start there on being the sort of person he had always meant to be. Deedee just wanted them all to get the hell out of southern California and give her some peace.

Andrea Melanie, who was to convince Jason to foot the bill, thought they were all still traveling blissfully down the freeway toward her own starring performance in the greatest winner's circle in America.

Buddy reminded himself several times that Keeneland was a destination rather than a goal. First you called Tex Sutton horse transport, then you put the filly on a van with her groom and her stuff, then she walked up the ramp onto the plane and was led into her stall. The back of the stall was set in place, and eleven or so other three-year-olds, some of them less famous than Residual and some of them more so, were led on, stalled in. The grooms got out their sleeping bags and their coolers and their magazines and their Diet Cokes and arranged themselves in the aisles between rows of horses.

After considering her personal requirements with regard to accommodations and nutrients, and weighing those against the chance to do yet another new thing in the world of horses (she had flown FedEx and KLM, but never Tex Sutton), Marvelous Martha decided to go along, and it was a good thing she did.

Residual, of course, loaded onto the van calmly, unloaded calmly, stood at the bottom of the airplane ramp calmly, and loaded into the plane calmly. She was wrapped like a birthday present, green fur over her poll and around her nose, green wraps around her legs and tail, a soft, light, green sheet covering her from withers and chest to tailhead. She was the third-to-the-last horse on, against the far wall, just in front of the ramp. She hadn't needed to be tranquilized, but Marvelous Martha had a couple of syringes in her purse, just in case. Of course it was an essential rule of horses that time is not of the essence, but they were loaded and taxiing down the runway by 9:00 a.m., only an hour and a half after the scheduled takeoff. As soon as they were in the air, Residual and her two companions began nosing their hay nets full of timothy, and Marvelous Martha took out her cooler and opened it. She had a banana-raspberry smoothie with apple-blossom honey, two slices of raisin challah with fresh cream cheese, a small thermos of cranberry juice, some water crackers, and a jar of gefilte fish. She set these out. For later, she had an individual quiche florentine, a cold liter of sparkling apple juice, and a fruit compote. To read, she had a copy of *A Chakra and Kundalini Workbook,* by Dr. Jonn Mumford. The other grooms and exercise riders were about half her age and not similarly equipped. She had just opened the book to the chapter on solar-plexus charging, something that would certainly come in handy in any horse-related activity, when she heard the first clang. She didn't think anything of it. Above and to her side, Residual flicked her ears and went back to eating. A clang came again. Marvelous Martha looked up. Some of the other humans and all of the other horses were looking up, too, up and forward. The clang came again. Marvelous Martha took a bite of her challah, then packed everything neatly back in her cooler and closed it. She was a methodical person. She stood up, gave Residual a pat on the neck, and strolled forward to the front row of stalls. She did not like what she saw there, which was a bay colt tossing his head and rolling his eyes and trembling. Every time the metal stall partitions between himself and the horses to either side of him made a noise or even vibrated, the horse flinched and jumped. The pilot had the curtain open between the cockpit and the cargo area, and he was speaking to the groom. The groom was saying, "Yeah, I gave him the shot."

"Give him some more."

"I don know, boss, he might fall down. I don know."

"Are you the only person with the horse?"

"Yeah, boss. The horse always good before. Never like this."

Some other grooms were standing around. They parted when Marvelous

Martha came up behind them. Even the pilot was younger than she was. She said, "May I help?"

"This horse has got to calm down," said the pilot.

Marvelous Martha went to the horse's head, and he noticed her, which was a good sign. She stroked him along the neck and head, took his ears in her palms, fingered their tips. He let her do it, but when the metal partition creaked again, he jumped again. She asked the groom if she could give the horse another shot. He shrugged. The pilot said, "Give the horse another shot." She gave the horse another shot.

But it was no good. Even after the few minutes it took for the tranquilizer to have its effect, the horse was trembling and rolling his eyes. Marvelous Martha couldn't tell if it was something about the sound or something about the vibration or something about the metal itself. She stroked and talked: "Relax, sweetie. It's all right. You're a good boy." The horse reared up six inches and caught himself against his tether. That frightened him even more, and he reared up again. The horses on either side of him were now moving restlessly, and the horses behind him were paying close attention. The interior of the plane suddenly seemed very small, very crowded, and very fragile. They were an hour into the flight, somewhere in Arizona. The horse's own groom now leaned over and threw up.

"Oh, God," said the pilot, closing the curtain.

The horse's groom sat down, put his head between his knees, and closed his eyes. Marvelous Martha said, "What's your name?"

"Maurilio," he groaned.

"Maurilio, look at me. Take your wrists in your hands like this and press your thumbs against this spot, and you'll feel better."

He did so.

"Feel better?"

"Sí."

"Now clean that up."

But the horse was snorting and stamping now, and throwing his head. You could take your pick, thought Marvelous Martha—an angry horse, a stubborn horse, a fearless horse, and a panicked horse. The one you never ever in your whole long life with horses wanted to see, as mean as some of them could be, was the panicked horse. She held tight to his halter as he threw his head, and he lifted her right off the ground. You could feel the strength of the adrenaline pumping through him in that one moment alone. She pulled back the curtain between the horse and the cockpit, and she said, "He's getting out of control. What do you usually do?"

"Shoot him or land."

"Are we to that choice yet?"

"You tell me."

Marvelous Martha regarded the horse. Sweat was pouring off him. Stamping around had caused his wraps to slip down under his feet, and two of them were flapping, but of course there was no going into the stall to fix anything. He was jerking at his ties now, and the two horses beside him were beginning to sweat, too. Panic could shoot around a herd in a heartbeat; in fact, panic did shoot around herds in the pounding of hearts. The quickest information passed between any two horses was always: Time to flee. He reared up again. She said, "Time to choose."

The pilot said, "I'll land, then."

They landed in Texas, West Texas, on a runway barely distinguishable from the forbidding sagebrush prairie around it. The wind was blowing. Steers were standing on the other side of some rusty barbed wire, chewing their cud and staring. Dismembered pickup trucks lay here and there. It was hot, midday. There was no water. All of the horses had to be unloaded, all of the stalls taken apart. The panicked horse had to be left behind with his groom; providing for him took an hour on the phone. The other horses had to be led around. They wanted to try out the grass, which was at least green, but they couldn't go into it, because it was full of holes and metal junk. Frustration and bad behavior ran through them, and even though Residual was the best behaved and the best provided with caretakers, she was the one who got kicked, right in the left hock. Later, when she told Buddy about it, Marvelous Martha did not tell Buddy she had seen it coming, but she had. One of the fillies was backing up toward another horse, yards away from Residual. Residual was minding her own business, but her groom, a good groom, decided to get a little farther out of the way, so he led her off, and here came that angry filly, dragging her groom, and she went right up to Residual and she whipped around and laid one on her. If that wasn't karma, Marvelous Martha thought, then what was?

61 / A NIGHTMARE

ONE THING Dick had noticed over the years, say forty-five of them, the length of his life, was that there was often some little thing that you hadn't paid much attention to at the time that rose up to destroy you later. He knew that "destroy" was a strong word, but it was the word he chose. What happened was, on the day after the Paumonok, the starter came to him and said, in a mildish tone of voice, "That Epic Steam horse needs some more gate-training. He delayed the race yesterday, and I don't want that anymore."

Dick, of course, had nodded. Horses sometimes needed more gate-training. The gate was a frightening, dangerous thing, a technological answer to the second-oldest question in horse racing—after "Who's the fastest?" you got "Did they get off at the same time?" To use a starting gate with fit, lively, youthful Thoroughbred horses was emphatically to make the best of a bad situation. Horses fell down in the gate, fell over in the gate, fell backward in the gate, and even if none of those things happened, when they jumped out of the gate, the stress on their spines, pelvises, and hips of leaping from a stand-still to a gallop was something neither God nor nature had provided for anatomically. And Dick's understanding of this was all very well, but it did not make Epic Steam one whit more willing to go into the gate.

With a perfectly tuned sense of his own leverage in any situation, the dark colt used the attention that his associates were paying to this dilemma to demonstrate the many ways in which he was not in sympathy with their plans for him. Dick tried to listen to Frankie, who, of course, was the person most often in the gate with the horse. Frankie said, "If he's gonna go in, he's gonna go in. If he's not gonna go in, he's not gonna go in." Dick recognized this as a tautology, but at the same time it had the ring of truth about it. The question was, how many times did you try it out, to see if he was gonna go in? On the one hand, each try irritated the animal. On the other hand, the first principle of horse-training was that if you allowed the horse to succeed in having his way he would understand all the more clearly his strength relative to yours, his ability to intimidate you relative to your ability to intimidate him.

As a result of this being the first principle of horse-training, it was a principle that had been applied to Epic Steam since birth. He understood it perfectly as the first principle of survival—every time a human ratchets up the pain, the horse must ratchet up the resistance. There is never so much pain that resistance is impossible; rather, the more pain there is, the more resistance is necessary. Epic Steam was a well-trained animal. He always took pain as a sign that something was coming and he'd better get ready.

Thus it was that, on the very first day of gate-training, when Frankie urged him just a little harder than usual to get up to the gate, he pricked his ears and propped his forelegs, and refused take a step some five or six yards back from the open doors.

Frankie waved his whip.

The horse rolled his eyes and tossed his head.

Frankie said, in a rough voice, "Get up there!"

The horse backed up a step.

Frankie bethought himself before bringing the whip down on the horse's haunches, and called to a couple of assistant starters. He said, "Okay, start over." He turned the horse in a circle to the left, then a circle to the right. He walked away from the gate, walked around the gate. The men opened the gate front and back and stepped away from it.

The horse was not fooled. As soon as Frankie got the idea "gate" in his mind, the horse stopped dead. Frankie chirped to him, gave him a little kick, closed his eyes, and tried to relax. The horse bucked.

Frankie hit the ground.

Frankie was unhurt.

The horse ran off a half-dozen steps, then stopped and turned around.

Just this, just this single evidence of interest in him, prevented Frankie from losing his temper. He got up, waved off the other men, and went over to the horse. He took the reins over his head and led him back to the open gate, then walked him through it.

Someone threw him up on the horse, and he walked the horse through the open gate again, this time mounted. After that, he said, "Okay, that's enough. I'm not going to press my luck."

Frankie, Dick thought, had done a good job. But that didn't change the fact that the horse was further behind in his gate-training after the first day of gate-training than he had been after the race.

FIVE DAYS LATER, Dick and Frankie and Herman Newman were in Dick's office with the door closed, discussing what had happened. At this point, Herman Newman looked more confused than unhappy. Dick knew that that would change. He said, "So the result is, I'm sorry to say, that the horse has been ruled off the track."

"Tell me again what that means," said Herman Newman.

"Epic Steam isn't allowed to train or run at Belmont. He savaged a man."

"I don't see how his behavior was exactly savage; I mean, I understand what he did, but—"

Frankie piped up. "I had a good grip on his mouth. I just had the feeling that he was thinking something, so I had a good grip on him, but he jerked me right out of the saddle—"

" 'Savagery' seems so strong a term—"

"It's just a word we use. I mean," said Dick, knowing he was lying, "we don't know that the horse had savage intentions."

"So tell me again. The guy—"

"Assistant starter."

"In the gate with him."

"Yes, holding his bridle."

"And you were there, Frankie."

"I was waiting for the gate to open."

"He reached over and grabbed the guy by the shirt."

"He took a piece out of his chest, too," said Dick.

"And he pulled him down under his feet. Or the man slipped down."

"Sir," said Dick, carefully, "I believe that he pulled the man down."

"But we don't know that. We can't read the horse's mind."

Yes, we can, thought Dick.

"And then he stepped on the man and broke his leg at the ankle."

"Herman," said Dick. "Mr. Newman—"

"He stomped him," said Frankie. "A colt or a stallion, that's something they do. He stomped him and he was not intending to stop. He was stomping him good—"

Dick gave Frankie a look. Frankie said, "Well, he was."

Dick said, "Entire male horses can be quite aggressive, sir."

"Entire?"

"Horses with their testicles."

"Oh, that. So it's a sexual thing."

"Yes." Dick felt a moment of clearing.

"So let's remove his testicles and fix that."

"But he's been ruled off, sir. Even if we geld him, they won't let him come back."

"But if we know what the problem is and fix it, I don't understand—"

"Maybe, sir, we should have done that before. But now it's too late. He savaged an assistant starter. That's black and white as far as the track officials are concerned."

At last, Herman Newman's face fell. The three of them sat there quietly.

Herman Newman said, "Let me see. Now, Dick, was there something that you weren't telling me about this horse, I mean, about his state of mind?"

Dick looked up quickly, then away, then back. All those things he had said about the horse leapt to the tip of his tongue. Unpredictable, talented, quirky, not friendly, don't try to pet him, don't give him any carrots or treats. He could defend himself like that, and for a moment he was aching to do so. But he said, "You know, I don't think, sir, that I communicated clearly the scope of the horse's temperament problem—"

"He is one son of a bitch," said Frankie.

"We did think, for a while, that we had him under control," said Dick.

"I'm disappointed," said Herman Newman. And Dick knew that he was, and that his disappointment had nothing to do with the Derby or the Triple Crown or the money, but that it was a personal disappointment having to do with Dick himself. His shame at this was sharp and painful, but, then, at least it wasn't ambiguous. Then he told him the really bad news. He said, "It's likely that the horse won't be allowed to train or run at any other good track, either. There was an incident at Hollywood Park last summer."

"Tell me again—"

"I don't believe I told you the first time, sir."

"Was anyone hurt in that incident?"

"No."

"Well, that's a relief."

"At any rate, the thing is, Epic Steam is a famous horse. He's won several races, including the Paumonok, he was a good Derby prospect"—amazing how he could put this in the past tense and still say it so calmly—"and so other tracks are going to not want him to run or train there, either."

"Not want him to? Like they don't want him to but he can?"

"No. Like, they don't want him to, and he can't."

"That seems harsh, not to give him a chance."

"Oh," said Frankie, "that horse has had plenty of chances. He is one son of a bitch, that horse."

"You said that," said Dick.

"I'll say it again," said Frankie. "However, it don't mean I don't like him. I do like him."

"It's so black and white," said Herman. "Surely there's some sort of appeals process."

"There isn't," said Dick. He looked Herman Newman right in the face. In fact, he almost took his face between his two hands. He said, loud and clear, "The horse is finished, sir."

"It's so hard to believe," said Herman Newman.

Ah, thought Dick. Ah.

"What do we do now?"

"Normally, an owner would sell him. He's got good breeding, and he's won some good races. Studfarms are used to dealing with these sorts of animals. You could realize most if not all of your investment—"

Herman Newman stared at him. This, thought Dick, this is a man who's never sold a bad toy to a little child. What could he possibly be doing in the horse business?

62 / JUSTA FAVOR

Back in Chicago, his horses pleasantly installed in the new stabling at Hawthorne, with spring just around a corner or two, the Skip Trial colt healing nicely, and his horses making money, William Vance couldn't quite recall the state of mind he had been in down in Louisiana. It nagged at him, the way he lost Justa Bob like that, a horse everyone in Chicago asked him about as soon as he got back. The thing that nagged at him the most was how off the horse had been after the race. Had his guilty conscience magnified the horse's lameness? Had it minimized his degree of lameness? Had the horse been bobbing his head or not? Had the coffin-bone fracture his new horse came up with given him the idea? The more he thought about it, the less reliably he could remember. His new state of mind convinced him that, whereas not so long ago he had found himself unable to keep hold of a horse he already owned, now he would be able to find a horse that had disappeared.

The horse was no longer at Fair Grounds. A week's phone tag with the racing secretary there told him that. Nor was he at another track in Louisiana— not Louisiana Downs, or Delta Downs, or Evangeline Downs, where horses might be training even though there were no meets. And William couldn't remember the name of the trainer who had claimed the horse—something French maybe, a Louisiana name like Delahoussaye or Desormeaux, but not one of those. A "D" name? He woke up at night trying to remember.

In this project, his own success was no help. He had thirty-two horses in his barn now, and they were running well and winning. He had owners to talk to and riders to direct and jockeys to hire, and it was exactly the sort of busy, enjoyable flurry that distracted you from that nagging worry that only returned when it was quiet, and everyone you might call or contact was away from the office. He put small ads in *The Blood-Horse* and the *Thoroughbred Times:* information wanted, brown gelding, seven years old, named Justa Bob,

by Bob's Dusty, out of Justa Gal, by Rough Justice. Five hundred dollars
reward.

FIVE HUNDRED DOLLARS was something that Justa Bob's new owner,
R. T. Favor, né Robert Biddle, would have taken a genuine interest in, but he
was not a reading man, or a subscribing man, and though he thought of himself as a horse-trainer, and claimed a horse from time to time when he had
some money, he was not at the moment associated with any particular track.
He had the horse at a run-down stable outside of Houston, and the best that
could be said for him was that he was not actively abusing the horse right at
this time. He was feeding him, watering him, housing him, and cleaning his
stall whenever he remembered to do so. R. T. Favor was a man of many aliases
(for example, he had claimed the horse under his Louisiana owner's-license
name, Ronald de Montriere), and a rap sheet as long as a short novel, but
under every one of them he had displayed a hot temper and a penchant for
drink. He was, therefore, not of an investigative turn of mind, and Justa Bob's
lameness, which was a slab fracture of the right knee, did not present itself to
him as an occasion for.veterinary attention—for example, X-rays, which, like
all investigations, tended to reveal more than R.T. cared to know. So from time
to time he buted the horse, but most of all he espoused the efficacy of stall rest,
which was just as well, since the stable where Justa Bob lived had no turnout.
Justa Bob's lameness was just typical, R.T. often said, of what was always happening to him—bad luck with horses, wives, girlfriends, parents, bosses, partners in crime, even though he himself always did the best he could. And how
could he train the horse, anyway, when he had these deals he was trying to put
together?

Justa Bob himself was not displeased with his circumstances. The stall was
confining and the provisions were suspect (he ate what seemed wholesome and
left the rest) but every broken slat and missing board allowed him to impove
his acquaintance with R.T.'s other horse, Doc's Big Juan, a five-year-old quarterhorse gelding, a burly chestnut with a bald face, a blue eye, and considerable
joint deterioration in his ankles and knees (Wouldn't you know it? remarked
R.T., philosophically). The two horses often stood nose to nose or nose to
withers, nibbling each other here and there, avoiding the nailheads, wire ends,
and broken boards all around them. They dozed. They kept an eye on the
goings-on, such as they were, around the barn, they avoided, as much as possible,
the unquiet presence of R. T. Favor ("God-damned horses don't even like me,"
observed R.T., without taking it personally). Would Justa Bob happily give up

Doc's Big Juan in order to return to better circumstances in Chicago? Hard to say. The depth of attachment between horses is hard to gauge, as is its worth in relation to other forms of equine well-being. But it could not be said that Justa Bob felt unhappy. He was only a horse, after all, but he could understand a trade-off just as well as the next guy.

ALL OF R. T. FAVOR'S deals fell through. He couldn't believe it. Some stuff he was getting from a guy turned out to be completely the wrong thing, and he had to eat it. Then a guy who had some money of his and said he was going to pay him back didn't show up, and when R.T. went to the motel where he was, the guy had checked out. Then his girlfriend said she was going back with her old boyfriend, and she was keeping his mattress and box spring, a perfectly good set from Sears, until he gave her back some stuff of hers that he had sold to a friend of his without telling her two months before. It was time, R.T. thought, to get back to training horses. He appeared at the stable early one morning—suspiciously early, as far as Justa Bob was concerned—and he had tack in his arms. He looked over the stall door, said, "Hey, you guys, time to earn a living," and threw the tack down on the ground and went looking for a cup of coffee.

He came back two hours later. It was now broad daylight, and R.T. was a little irritated because he had gotten into this thing with a waitress. That sometimes happened when you were just looking for a cup of coffee and minding your own business. You got to flirting with the waitress, and she was kind of a bitch, and that egged you on, and you tried teasing her a little bit, just harmless, and then it turned out that you couldn't get out of there until you got a smile out of the bitch, and sometimes that took a while.

So it was hot. R.T. kicked the tack to one side and haltered the red horse and pulled him out of the stall. He was fat. R.T. couldn't remember how long it had been since he had gotten the horse. Wasn't that sometime in January, when he had that money from that deal? Well, nothing like two, three months of stall rest. The horse moved away from R.T.'s unquiet presence and R.T. gave the horse a jerk. Justa Bob was watching them. R.T. tied up the red horse and brushed him down, then he picked out his feet and tacked him up. Then he went over to the other side of the barn and found this guy named Lex, who was an exercise rider, horse behavioral consultant, and experienced cowboy, as it said on some cards he'd had printed up, and he brought Lex over. There was no reason on earth why they shouldn't team up, thought R.T. It was meant to be.

As Lex trotted Doc's Big Juan out to the arena they had at this place (when he got some money, he would move the horses to a regular training center), Justa Bob whinnied after him. R.T., who wasn't especially annoyed with Justa Bob in particular, picked up a brush, threw it at the stall door, and snarled, "Pipe down!"

The abuse had begun.

63 / IT'S ALWAYS SOMETHING

S AM PULLED on a long vinyl sleeve, moved the mare's tail out of the way, and buried his arm almost to the shoulder in the mare's anus. She took a little step to the side, but was otherwise patient. Krista couldn't help looking away.

"Nice follicle," said Sam. "My guess is she's ready."

"Okay, then," said Krista.

Now Pete came out with Himself on a shank. Maia, thank goodness, was with Krista's mother at the grocery store. Krista's mother had agreed to help them by babysitting during all the breedings, and sometimes she also helped them by buying a few groceries.

What a nice mare, Himself seemed to be thinking. His ears were up, his tail was up, his neck was arched. He seemed to spring off the ground in elastic little steps. The mare was winking like crazy, flopping her tail over to the side, dropping her haunches, and so, when he bumped her with his nose, she seemed to say, Oh, yes, indeed. Ready ready ready.

Still perfectly gracious and well mannered, Himself stretched his nose and wrinkled his upper lip. "I saw a giraffe do that once," said Sam. "At the St. Louis Zoo." The mare lowered her haunches another centimeter, and Himself began to quiver all over. Krista thought he looked splendidly beautiful. "This fellow does give new meaning to the word 'stud,' " Sam muttered, and then the stallion leapt, needing no handlers or penis man, doing it all himself. The mare stood receptively, but Krista couldn't help looking at her back pasterns. She jerked and held with the thrusting. In Kentucky, she knew, three or four guys would be pushing up against her chest, helping her stabilize herself. Krista counted three and then four thrusts and stepped toward the mare's head, expecting Himself to dismount, but the thrusting continued, five, six, seven. Pete and Sam shared a glance. Eight, nine. Pete said, "I've never—"

Sam went up behind Himself and put his hand between the horse's back legs. Ten, eleven. Twelve. Twelve thrusts was a lot. The stallion's thighs were shaking now, not an eager quiver, but with fatigue. What if he fell? Krista checked Himself's eyes to see if they were rolling back in his head, but he was looking straight forward, staring, as if to encourage himself. He was grunting and thrusting, grunting and thrusting.

"No thrill," said Sam.

"I would say not," said Pete.

"That's a technical term. No ejaculatory thrill. Here." And he put Pete's hand between the horse's legs. "It's a pulsing of the urethra."

No kidding, thought Krista. On Himself's back, the skin corrugated into a pattern, and she couldn't help thinking of large structures, like bridges and roads, fatiguing, breaking apart. She closed her eyes.

But the horse simply dismounted, though awkwardly, his erection shooting forward from his back legs to his front, pale and smooth. He looked disturbed and confused. The mare groaned with relief and Krista stroked her neck.

"Walk her around," said Sam, thoughtfully, "she'll be okay."

But it still seemed like another thing to Krista. Did every strange thing in the world have to happen to them?

Himself looked more surprised than anything else, that and tired. He shook his head impatiently.

Sam said, "Ejaculatory incompetence."

"Is that a disease?"

"No, just an event. Okay. Okay. I'll do what I once saw your grandfather do." He went over to his truck while Krista and Pete kept the animals moving.

Sam brought back his stainless-steel bucket, the twitch, a coil of rubber hose, the mouth pump, the funnel, and a pint bottle of a clear liquid. In a moment he had twitched Himself, and had Pete holding the twitch. Himself stood there with his head forward, his eyes half shut, that look on his face of a twitched horse, half pained, half pleasured, all lost in space. He might be being treated for colic. Only his erection showed that there was something else going on. Sam fed the tubing down the stallion's nostril coil by coil. Himself did not object. Then the vet put the mouthpiece in his own mouth and cleared the hose. Finally, he poured the clear liquid slowly down the funnel into the hose and into the horse's stomach. It was so quiet Krista could hear the birds singing and the maple leaves sighing. Krista sighed herself. In a moment, Sam was finished, and he eased out the tube. Pete untwisted the twitch. Himself came to, and bent his head down to rub his lip on his knee.

"What was that?" said Krista.

"Gin," said Sam. "He was just a little overexcited. We'll wait a few minutes for the medicine to take effect."

"A pint?" said Pete.

"Basically a shot and a half, at his weight. We'll see."

And they did see. And it was pretty good, Krista thought; if not that, then at least a relief. The mare was cooperative, the ejaculation was thrilling. Later, when Krista came out from putting the mare away, giving her a bag of carrots and a nice big flake of grass hay, Pete and Sam were drinking shots of their own, but of bourbon, not gin.

Krista came up to them. "Why gin?" she said.

"Well," said Sam, "your grandfather used to say racing is an English sport of long tradition. Gin would be the traditional remedy. I think of it as a kind of veterinary heredity, just like, and parallel to, all these horses descending from Eclipse." He regarded his glass for a moment, one of the ones Krista and Pete had gotten for their wedding. Then he said, "Let's make this a courtesy call. I always wanted to try that gin cure. Bottoms up."

64 / PEACE AND QUIET

FARLEY THOUGHT it was always rather peaceful in California during the Triple Crown. Hollywood Park was open and the horses were running, but it was sleepy—only a few stakes races, and the best of those for turf horses. What it was, was that the press was elsewhere, and so were the Industry Leaders. The Industry Leaders had made it their personal mission to bring horse racing to the attention of the general public, with the NFL as their model and television as their medium of choice, which was fine with Farley, though his own view was that horse racing out at the track, newspaper reading, still photography, placing bets in person, and writing thank-you notes by hand were all related activities, and football, ESPN, video, on-line betting, and not writing thank-you notes at all were another set of related activities. In short, with everyone who was young, up-to-date, well dressed, and ambitious away in the East, the dedicated horse-players had the track to themselves. And the dedicated horse-players, in their quiet way, liked Limitless quite a bit.

After a cold winter, the weather in Pasadena was everything that those who had paid to live there expected—balmy, bright, hopeful. Farley was hopeful, too. He and Joy got up every morning after sunrise and went to the barn. His forty-six horses were wide awake and ready to work, and they were working well enough. Every day or two, he shipped a couple over to Hollywood and ran them. After the races he shipped them home. Or not. Claimers were always coming and going. He was starting to like that game again, too. Joy devoted herself to Limitless. He came back from the ranch just as fit as when he left. Farley did not put him on a regular work schedule, but let Joy decide, when she got him out to the track, whether he felt like running or not. At first this was scarier than Farley had thought it would be—here he had always considered himself sensitive to the needs of individual horses—but when Joy said that the horse was ready to run two days in a row, and then again on the third day, Farley balked. The horse was young and foolish. He didn't know how he was stressing himself. For his own good—

"The thing is," said Joy, "he is having a really good time. I don't like to say no to him. I really think—"

"When Rosalind said to let him do what he wanted, I didn't think he was going to want to do so much."

"You're the one who's always saying racing is in their minds."

"And I'm the one who keeps thinking soundness is in his bones. What if he—"

" 'What if' is my line, not yours. That's when they start you on Prozac, you know, when you say 'what if' all the time."

"Oh, yeah?" Farley loved a joke from Joy. "Let him go, then. We'll pretend no what ifs."

She took him to the seven-eighths pole and let him run. He blistered the track for half a mile, then trotted around with his ears pricked as if waiting for a round of applause. In the afternoon, she took him out and walked him. Sometimes they were gone for a couple of hours. He let himself say, as if his fear that she would slip away from him was just generalized cautiousness, "I don't like you wandering away. What if—"

She smiled.

He shut up. On the one hand, there was the truism that if you visualized a bad outcome your own expectation would cause it. On the other hand, there was the truism "Be prepared." Surely by this time in his life he should have drawn some sort of conclusion about the relative merits of these truisms, but they seemed equally possible, along with "Speak of the devil and the devil doth appear," "Least said, soonest mended," and "Leave no stone unturned."

Three weeks after the horse's first race, Farley put him in another one; the purse this time was forty-eight thousand dollars. Still allowance company. Roberto brought him in cruising, three lengths in front. Farley said, "Okay, you've ridden him twice. Tell me how he likes to run."

"You can see, boss—"

"I can see, but you tell me."

"Well, he's a closer. He likes those easy early fractions. You know, most of the time when we're back there in the last group, I don't get the feeling he's thinking about things at all. It's like he's just enjoying himself. Scoping out the others, you know. He doesn't put in a lick of work the way you think of work."

"He's got quite a stride. You should see him as well as ride him someday."

"It's easy, boss. Just slippery. Then, about the three-eighths pole, he kind of wakes up, looks for a hole, and goes for it. I don't get the feeling that he's look-ing at the other horses as horses at all. Like, you know, most of them, they get their eye on a horse coming up on the outside, and they just hook onto that, and that makes them want to put themselves out there. I've seen that so many times when I'm coming up on a horse. His eye rolls and you see the white, and he's looking at your horse and saying, 'No way, buddy.' But this guy, he doesn't even think of them as horses or something."

"Maybe he's looking for a better class of company."

"I think so, boss. But the one thing is, besides his mouth, he doesn't like to go fast early. I wouldn't like to push him if you had horses that were going to eat him up in the early fractions."

So he sent him to the farm for a week, then moved him up ten days later to sixty thousand dollars, but still in allowance company. For this race, Rosalind showed up. Al was in Uzbekistan again, but Rosalind expected him home sometime soon. The morning line on Limitless for the race was three to one. By post time he was the favorite, two to three. Joy sat next to Rosalind and glanced at her from time to time. What she admired about her was the subtle smile that burnished and lit her up as she gazed toward the starting gate. On the other side of Rosalind, Farley said, "The trouble is, he's running out of conditions. If he wins this race, I'm going to have to put him in a stakes race."

"That sounds good to me," said Rosalind. "Don't you think he can do it? He's posting great works."

"And a lot of them," put in Joy.

Farley stared out at the track, stroking his beard with his hand. Joy contin-ued, "But it's like having a present to open. Sometimes you just want to put it off a little longer. At least, that's what I say." She reached around behind Rosa-lind's chair and found Farley's hand. He grasped her fingers. He said, "That's not what I say."

"What do you say?"

"Bit by bit over the last few weeks with this horse, I've dropped all these big chunks of what I knew about horse-training."

"Like what?"

"Like that you shouldn't work too often, that long slow gallops are better for the horse than frequent works, that the jockey rides the horse, and asks for this here and that there, you know." He smiled. "That a horse lives in a stall at the track twenty-two hours a day." He grinned. "That I know what is going on with this horse."

"Not even Elizabeth and Mr. T. know what's going on with this horse," said Joy.

"Who're they?" said Rosalind.

"Mr. T. is that white horse in the stall by the office and Elizabeth is our animal communicator."

"What do they say?"

"Well, Elizabeth says that Mr. T. does not recognize Limitless. She can't pin him down on what he means by that. When he streams a picture of Limitless to her, his outlines are only semi–filled in."

Rosalind looked at her. She said, "How funny."

Farley said, "Do you buy this animal communication, too?"

"I don't know, but his breeder said to me his eyes looked to her like the eyes of a woman about to let her silk robe drop to the floor."

"And, you know," continued Farley, "I always thought that a big horse had a big personality. A multitude of quirks are supposed to be a sign of intelligence and self-respect in a horse. But he's, oh, I don't know, sort of colorless."

The horses approached the starting gate. Joy saw Limitless enter the fourth slot on a loose rein. The other horses entered like horses, that is, with some urging on the part of their jockeys. She said, "He's not affectionate. When he sees me, he never nickers, he just paws to get out until I put the leadshank on him. I think he would have a personality if he wasn't so absorbed." One by one the back gates snapped shut. There was silence, then clanging turbulence as the front gates opened. "And it's a fine start," proclaimed the announcer's voice upon the quiet air.

Rosalind thought that exerting her powers with her own horse would constitute a conflict of interest, and so she refrained from giving any signals at all, but sat in her chair with a space in her head and her hands folded in her lap. She made no wishes. Next to her, Farley said, "Easy enough." One furlong into the seven-furlong race, the number-one horse had taken the lead, with the number-ten horse right on his heels. Then four more were bunched. Limitless was next, with three horses strung out behind him. She remembered how she had felt about racing for so many years—all races were the same. Some horses ran. Most often, the ones toward the end of the line came up and won. Or the horse who started out in front stayed in front. Over and over, the same pattern worked itself out, number one through number fourteen, in various shades of earth tones. Owners, trainers, jockeys, bettors exulted or sighed or cursed or cried, and then it was time for the next race, and the pattern worked itself out again. However personal every interested party considered the outcome to be, it was not personal—the numbers had to come in in some order or other; the pattern had to work itself out in some way or another, eight or nine times a day, week after week, year after year, decade upon decade. How boring she once thought it, never quite believing it was the grand opera or the great adventure that others saw. Now, though, she had grown sensitive to the variations on the theme. You didn't have to have a big-stakes race or designated great runners for the race to be beautiful and compelling. You didn't even have to have a betting interest. All you had to do was pay attention. Every race formed itself as a picture, or as a story, or as a design. In this case, the picture was of two chestnuts at the front, neck and neck, and Limitless drawing to the outside, passing the second group, and taking a bead on the leaders. The story was of the timing of his move. He had not been paying attention for several furlongs—you could see that without binoculars—and then he dug in, closed on the second horse, who, perhaps tired from the early fractions, bumped him in the stretch, startling him. The design was adagio, vivace, rest, adagio, as Limitless recovered from being bumped, but not quickly enough, and ran third. And then, of course, another way of looking at it was introduced, as the sign "Inquiry" flashed on the screen, and Farley jumped up to run down to the track, and the race became a piece of litigation.

"He doesn't like physical contact at all, I've noticed," said Joy. "It doesn't surprise me that he was offended at being bumped."

The numbers went up, and Limitless remained in the show position. Rosalind and Joy went down to meet the others on the track.

Farley was shaking his head. He said, "He wasn't bumped. He thought he was going to *be* bumped."

"Touch me not," said Rosalind.

The jockey, Roberto his name was, glanced at her and nodded.

"I told you he was awfully opinionated," said Rosalind.

Farley looked at her as they followed the horse and his groom under the stands. He said, "All the great ones were. But mind you, that's not a promise."

"Just let him do what he wants," said Rosalind. The next day she left for a week in Sri Lanka, although her gallery was pretty full already, but she loved making it look crammed, like a treasure chest. Limitless left for the ranch.

AFTER THE HORSE had been at the ranch for a week, Farley thought he would sneak him up to San Francisco for the California Derby. It was a stakes race on the grass but not a graded stakes; the press was in New York now, clamoring for the Belmont. The trip was an easy three hours or so from the ranch. The purse was $150,000 added, and it was Rosalind and Al, through Farley, who added another $22,500 late fee. The weather was rainy and the turf was soft, a first for Limitless in his four California starts.

And the horse was particularly restive in his stall. When Joy took him out and walked him around and around, a small, drenched figure in her long dark raincoat, Farley almost hadn't the heart to go on with it. But he was interested to note that the horse didn't mind the heavy mist. When Rosalind called him from Capri to find out what was going on with her animal, she said, "Oh, I meant to tell you, he was out all last winter, at the training farm in Maryland. Rain, sleet, snow. You name it, he's stood out in it."

That was the key to it. All through the race, while the other horses, mostly Cal-breds, seemed to be staring down at the turf in disbelief, Limitless galloped home double-time. "I think," said Joy, bundled up in a coat and a horse blanket, "he's just happy to be out of the shedrow."

Farley called Rosalind in Nice, and Rosalind called Al in Helsinki.

"AL," SAID ROSALIND. "I think we're in the same time zone."

"Oh, yeah? Where are you, Rozzy?"

"I'm in Nice. Remember that hotel we stayed in with your kids that time? I'm there." She had come there just because her other hotel was overbooked, but just then it seemed like a fated coincidence, that she should be reminded of a pleasant time they had had.

"That was a decent place. That was a fun trip, wasn't it? There wasn't so much yammering all the time. What time is it?"

"It's just before seven."

"I guess I'm supposed to get my wake-up call pretty soon, then."

"This is your wake-up call, Al."

"So wake me up."

"Well, let's see." Rosalind was hesitant. "I guess that I am turning over and snuggling up to you—"

"Can we throw that hairy dog out from between us?"

"We can remove her gently and set her on the floor."

"All right. I can do that. So you're kinda pressed up against me. I got these silk shorts on you got me. That's all I got on. What do you have on?"

Rosalind was naked. She said, "I have on an antique silk nightgown that I bought in Paris last week. It's ecru, with some lace at the collar."

"Ecru is kind of off-white, right?"

"Yes."

"So how long is it?"

Rosalind thought a moment. Then she said, impulsively, "It's short."

"Mmm," said Al. "You got anything on underneath that?"

And even though she was naked and had been married to Al for twenty years and she had started this and she was lying, to boot, she blushed. But then she went on with it: "Well, no." And that was the truth.

"Now I got my arm around you, and with my other hand, I'm fiddling with your hair. You know, Rozzy, you've got great hair. It's nice."

"It is nice. And I like the smell of your neck. I think your chin is a little bristly." Saying these things reminded Rosalind of how familiar Al's fragrance and texture were to her. That was valuable after all, wasn't it? The world was so full of new things; you were always looking for and looking at new things. Eileen, disturbed, woke up, snaked her way out, and jumped down with a little plop. In her ear, Al said, "My chest is so hairy and your skin is so, so, so—"

"Not hairy?"

"Well, yeah. I always liked that for some reason."

Rosalind laughed.

"There's my wake-up call. I can hear them trying to click through on the other line. I got to meet this guy."

"Me, too."

"But just for a moment, put your leg over mine. I'm turning toward you a little bit, and I'm putting my hand on your face."

Rosalind closed her eyes, seized unexpectedly by the thought of his desire.

"That's good," said Al. "Ah, Rozzy."

Rosalind turned onto her back again. Eileen jumped on the bed and came right up to her face and stared at her, ears pricked, little black bean eyes, little black bean nose. Rosalind admitted to herself that she felt uncomfortable. Something new was happening. She actually seemed to be remembering why she had fallen in love with Al in the first place. She said, "Say, the horse won the stakes. The California Derby. Very soft turf. They almost moved the race onto the dirt."

"I wish I'd seen that."

"Me, too."

"I wish we'd seen it together. What'd he win?"

"About a hundred thousand."

"What do you know. Is this my Breeders' Cup horse?"

"I don't know, Al."

"You know, I deserve a Breeders' Cup horse."

And then he hung up, and Rosalind hung up, but after that, she thought all day, as she was buying art and meeting artists and eating soupe au pistou and roasted chicken with sweet red peppers, What do you know. What *do* you know?

———

IN THE VAN on I-5, heading back to the ranch, Limitless was looking out
the window. The van, though confining (he was in a four-by-eight-foot stall,
his head tied next to a net of hay that he sometimes could grab a bite out of
and sometimes could not), did not make him feel that same jumpiness that a
regular stall did. For one thing, he could feel the movement of the whole vehicle over the highway pass up through his hooves and ankles and legs. If he went
with it, and it never occurred to him not to, the gentle shaking lulled him. For
another, he recognized perfectly well that the passing scenery was passing—
that he was moving through the landscape in a similar way to his movement
on his own feet, and that was reassuring, too. He was Limitless. There had
never been a moment in his entire three years of life when he hadn't intuitively
felt movement to be good and right.

In addition to these basics, he recognized the landscape—hot, flat, golden-
brown below and bright blue above. It was the landscape of freedom. Sometime in this landscape, the van would stop, the ramp would go down, the
tether would come off his head, and he would find himself in a place of utter
comfort, which, for him, had nothing to do with heat, cold, rain, shelter,
hunger (though there was a shelter and plenty of the best possible food), and
everything to do with being able to move at will, walk, trot, canter, gallop,
buck, kick, rear, roll, graze. Like every genius, and he was a genius, as his race
record would eventually prove, he had not so much a plan as a specific, over-
riding aim. His nature was out of balance in this way, whether through brain
chemistry or as a result of organization of the nervous system as a whole. His
aim was to run. And he was in luck. Not only did he mean to run, he could
run; perhaps, though, the cause and effect were reversed—he could run, and so
he meant to run. The feedback loop hummed endlessly—he could, he did, he
wanted to, and he could. For him, as for all geniuses, the aim was insistent,
the prompt was immediate and strong. The three-year-old never forgot that he
wanted to move. Eating, sleeping, regarding fillies with interest, socializing in
general with humans or horses, having to stand for a bath or another procedure, all of these activities only momentarily distracted his attention from his
real aim, which he felt in his body, his mind, his heart—move move move.
Like all geniuses, he had no perspective, could get no perspective, did not even
seem to understand that there was such a thing as perspective.

And so he recognized the ranch as a place where he was happy, or at least
almost entirely in the state of relief that comes from doing all the time what it
is that you aim to do.

JUNE

65 / NOT IRELAND

THE BROCHURE for the cruise that Deirdre got from the travel agent in Silver Spring mentioned the picturesque mountains, the magnificent fjords, the charming and lively gold-rush town nestled between the mountains and the sea. There were also Russian churches, fabulous wildlife, splendid northern lights, and, of course, nightly entertainment and world-class cuisine. It did not mention the very best thing about the whole two weeks, which was no horses of any kind. No horses on the airplane, no horses on the cruise ship, no horses in Juneau, no horses where the face of the glacier broke off into icebergs and floated out to sea. You could take horses to the Arctic, and even the Antarctic—that Brit, Scott, had tried to take ponies to the South Pole, wasn't that a typical Brit thing to do—but horses in the Arctic were such an entirely futile enterprise that only a person with a uniquely strong sense of self-destruction would attempt it. Deirdre hoped not to meet any of those, and so not to see, hear, touch, or sense with any sixth or higher sense the presence of an equine for two whole weeks.

On the other hand, she saw, they were building a racetrack in Hanoi.

Another thing the brochure advertised was plenty of fun with the other passengers and a friendly and convivial staff. Deirdre took this as a signal that she should, as an embittered and antisocial woman, carry with her all possible resources for entertaining herself. After scouring the bookstores in her local mall, she came up with four books whose combined total number of pages came to 7,123, which was 123 more than she would need if she read twenty-five pages an hour, twenty hours a day, seven days a week for two weeks. These books were *The Complete Works of William Shakespeare, Modern Literatures of the Non-Western World, Civilization and Capitalism,* and *Economy and Society.* She had not, she told Tiffany, heard of any of the authors, but they were probably as good as any. This was not entirely true, but Tiffany believed her anyway. On the ship she discovered that, what with her habitual rising time of

5:00 a.m. and the time change, she was wide awake, in spite of Max Weber, Fernand Braudel, and all the others, at 2:00 a.m., and sound asleep by dinnertime. The good thing about this was that it further reduced her opportunities for contact with others.

Her cabin was on the inside, about one-half the size of a stall. She had hung her clothes in the closet, stacked her books next to the bed, and set her shoes beside the door. The room was just small enough to remind her of an anchorite's cell she had seen once back in Ireland. What you did was have yourself walled in when you were, say, thirteen, and then have yourself carried out seventy years later, after you died. You spent all of those years praying for the souls of those who had walled you up in there in the first place, and who was to say it wasn't as full a life as any other?

She lay back on the bed and realized that she had for some time been feeling the soundless roar of the ship's engines, and that now the ship was moving. She overcame the impulse to go out of the cabin and up to the deck. She reached over and turned out the light. The cabin was now dark. She closed her eyes and opened them. The cabin was equally dark both ways. She closed her eyes again and opened them again. She wondered if it took the entire seventy years to erase thought from the mind.

It was generally considered wise and good, Deirdre knew, not to mention agreeable to others, to look upon the bright side of every experience. The experience had not been found that did not have a bright side that could be looked upon. Death, for example, widely considered a negative experience, had an infinite number of bright sides. At every funeral and every wake the mourners vied with one another to be the most optimistic, if not about the dead person's life (so-and-so was an unredeemed and dedicated sinner with no charm and ugly to boot), then about his death (well, it was about time his relatives and friends gained some relief), and if not about that, then about the provisions for the funeral (at least there's caviar, or chicken, or perhaps tuna, or maybe only just beer, but it's wet), and if not even about that, then about the possibilities for his afterlife (God is merciful, after all; if God is not infinitely merciful, then who is?). Bright sides were everywhere. They had especially abounded at the racetrack, where bolts from the blue devastating to dreams and pocketbooks were continual and unrelenting. The tedium of looking on the bright side had worn her out, had it not?

There was something quite nice about this rumbling darkness, she thought.

But there she was, looking on the bright side again, even her. Yes, she was bored on this ship, and tired, and cramped, and her buyer's remorse about spending $2,345 on this cruise to Alaska was vivid and hot. Even so, no matter how tenaciously she held on to her real regret at yet another useless and expensive decision in a long life of same, she automatically did that "at least" thing. At least the stuffy little expensive box they had her in was embedded in a large-ness of movement and noise that had a sort of fugitive excitement.

Appalling. Whatever the degree of conviction that you bring to your desire to witness the true reality of things, you cannot keep yourself from looking on the bright side.

Deirdre sighed and turned on the light.

It was a relief to be away from Tiffany, who had been persuaded to go to work for Bill Trout, but who had only two horses to rub, and so had plenty of time to take an interest in Deirdre's cruise. That was another tedious exercise, her own unstoppable attempts to decipher the meaning of Tiffany's attentions. Tiffany called her every day to ask her some question she could have easily asked Bob Trout. Tiffany took her to the mall and caused her to buy some at-tractive garments. Tiffany looked at the brochures with her and uncovered the best deal. Tiffany gave her a new handbag to replace the twelve-year-old job that had been like another hand to her. Tiffany picked her up, took her out to breakfast, and drove her to the airport. Tiffany kissed her good-bye. Deirdre was the first to admit that she didn't understand the customs of Tiffany's mi-lieu of origin, and so she had gone to a movie where a black woman played the star's best friend, and she had come away feeling that perhaps the extraordinary warmth of Tiffany's friendship was in part gratitude and in part a relic of Tiffany's upbringing, and so she remained cautious. Since she considered her-self naturally cautious, she could not understand why her present caution was so difficult. However, perhaps the difficulty was owing to the fact that she adored Tiffany with an adoration that was as permanent as a rock. This adora-tion partook of all forms of human love that Deirdre was familiar with, and she knew their Greek names, too, because she was educated to do so. There was philia—that was friendship, such as she had felt with George. There was agape—that was a charitable, expansive sort of feeling, larger and more pas-sionate than kindness, but of the same order. And there was that kind of love that you felt for horses—a holy wonder at their beauty and courage and purity—Tiffany's physical perfection brought that out in her. And, too, there was, indeed, eros. That would be desire, wouldn't it?

Well, then, her cousin George was gay as they came, and who could say which of the many other cousins of all degrees were of the same persuasion, and who could say that she was not? No man who had ever tried to date her, and there were a few, though only a few, would be surprised. A couple of them had been handsome fellows, too, well formed and good-humored and even, Mother of God, affectionate, and there had been the odd incident of sexual in-tercourse here and there, and what she had always thought was that she had taken after her mother in seeing the whole thing as a trap, a ruse played upon a woman by her own RNA, which sought to extend itself into the future no matter what the cost. Her mother, the saint, had three children and no more, and never said a word to Deirdre in all of her childhood about marriage.

Tiffany's effect upon her was like the effect of a finger upon a lump of clay. Every word she spoke, every gesture she made, every smile, every touch, every moment of her presence changed Deirdre's inner shape. She retained her usual expressions and habits on the outside, but inside she was plastic, taking one impress after another. Perhaps alone in this little room, far away from Tiffany and all her communications, she would find some knowledge or resolve that would harden her to Tiffany's presence and prepare her for Tiffany's inevitable departure. And if you looked on the bright side of that one, well, you were a fool, weren't you?

Deirdre got up and put on her shoes and opened the door into the corridor. It was narrow and fluorescently lit. The engines were less apparent here. Not far down the corridor, a staircase went up to the right. She went to it and mounted. Her back hurt. That was familiar. The staircase came out upon another corridor like hers, and she saw an open door to the left, a door with a high sill, through which she felt a fresh breeze. Beyond the door, of course, was the deck and the sea and the skidding foggy clouds, mere veils rent into rags, revealing both three-quarter moon and stars. There were others on the deck, though it was, by her watch, about 4:00 a.m. Alongside the boat, lit by cabin lights perhaps, the wake was illuminated in edges. She did not think they were far from land. She could see widely separated dots of light in the distance. And now that her eyes had adjusted, she realized that the darkness wasn't truly dark. Off the stern of the ship, just on the horizon, night was already gone. Of course, that was an attraction of this particular cruise—less and less night until, finally, no night at all. Deirdre turned right and began traipsing sternward on the deck, her left hand on the rail. It was not unlike making your way along the outside of the racetrack to the three-quarters pole, where your rider would turn you, bring you to the rail, and stir you up into a work or a gallop. Remember that, she thought. Remember that feeling when you were a tiny girl of being the horse and the rider all together, of trotting on your own two feet, then cantering and prancing, jumping little jumps, reassuring yourself when you got spooky or wild with a little pat on your own rump. Toward the end of the afternoon, when you got tired, you would carefully cool yourself down and put yourself away, not forgetting to comb your mane and give yourself a carrot. Hadn't her mother been good about that, giving her bits of carrot and apple and even lumps of sugar as treats for the horse in her, telling her that, no matter how her horse misbehaved, he always deserved a treat in the end, because the misbehavior wasn't meant, it was just a little mistake, and tomorrow would be another day, would it not? It was good advice never to put a horse away when you were mad at him, but always to give him some words of praise and a bit of something and a scratch about the head. You did that, and no matter what had happened, you felt better and were off on a good foot for the next day.

Deirdre could and did say for herself that the horses had liked her, that they did a good job for her, that, whatever they represented in terms of disappointed hopes and failed expectations, they themselves welcomed her into their company, approached her, greeted her, watched what she was doing. Once upon a time that had been enough, more than enough. You got up, threw on some clothes, ran out to the barn, and, whatever you were feeling, sleepy, anxious about money, achy, fearful, hard, they plucked you right out of that with their pricked ears and big eyes and open nostrils. Of course they were looking for their feed—some would be rattling their feed buckets, or kicking the doors, knowing like clocks that you were late—but only a fool thought a horse was purely a processor of hay and oats. Ah, well, she missed them a bit.

She came to the stern of the ship and looked down. It was light enough now, and the waters of, what was this, Puget Sound or something like that, were clear enough for the screws of the engines to be visible, turning and churning. Big spruces and evergreens made a dark shadow across the distant hillsides. The moon was faded, and the stars were gone. A grand flotilla of seagulls had taken their place, crying aloft. Mother of God, this oceangoing was a noisy enterprise indeed. She turned and headed forward, westward, still dragging her hand upon the rail. Three passengers, bundled in blankets, lay attentively in deck chairs. Nature-lovers, no doubt, connoisseurs of natural beauty. Her uncle, George's father, had been such a man. Once wild, he had become a farmer like all the others, he was the one who would stand and watch the sunset, go out and look at the stars of an evening, take the children to see some waves breaking on the shingle, just for a lark. Perhaps he had needed solace for something. He would have been much like George, no doubt. George, still her loyal pal, had been back in Ireland for two months now, and he had written her often to tell her all about working at Coolmore, telling tales upon her, feeling sanguine all around, happier. Happier than what? She had not thought he was unhappy, but there you were. He had needed solace for something and he had got it now.

The worst part was to go on being yourself. Everything you had learned, all those conclusions you had drawn, crusted you over. You had thought it was so good to learn each lesson—each lesson prepared you for something, it seemed, or else how could you bear the pain of the lessons—but in the end, all the bits and pieces added up to no sensible curriculum, and what you had made of it all was contradictory and confusing. You saw horses like that all the time. A horse was trained by a rider with a heavy hand, and the horse concluded that it could not stretch into the bit, and therefore its neck curled over, it stepped short behind, it refused to jump, the rider whacked it with a stick, the horse got caught between two promises of pain. And all the time you were noticing this in your friend's horse, she was noticing that, every time your horse spooked and you tensed, you were teaching your horse that there was something to spook at, and he was getting spookier and spookier. The very thing that you were, or your friend was, was the very thing that your horse learned to misbehave from, despite your intentions, your wishes, or your willpower.

Better, even though you were forty-three, to throw in the towel, to admit that all the looking on the high, bright side, all the efforts to benefit from your experience, had resulted in only this—you were all the more confirmed in being yourself and all the more tired of it.

But, still, her mother had cut up bits of apple and carrot, and put them into her hands, and sung, "The pony goes to his little stall, the cart gets put away, we've had a lovely ride around the verge of Corwyn Bay. Now I lay me down to sleep, the hounds all curled around. The moon hangs o'er the grassy lane, and the fox has gone to ground."

IN MARYLAND, Tiffany and Ellen were standing in the center of Ellen's largest riding arena as Audrey trotted around them on Ellen's equitation pony, Moses. It was early, so they were the only ones around besides Ellen's two grooms, who had just started cleaning stalls. Tiffany said, "She was reluctant to load." The two women looked at each other and laughed.

"Did you have to use a whip?"

"Only to get her to buy the clothes."

"That must have been something."

"Girl, I showed the patience of Job, as my mama would say."

Ellen shook her head.

"I want to gossip about her. I think maybe it's safe now that she's four thousand miles or something like that away," muttered Tiffany.

"She always finds out. Especially if you meant well."

Tiffany shook her head. The pony traveled in a limber circle once, twice, three times. Ellen said, "Okay, Audrey. I'll set up a cross-pole."

"A cross-pole!" exclaimed Audrey.

"Even Michael Matz starts the day with a cross-pole!" Then, "Aren't you going up to New York today to watch your horse run?"

"As soon as I leave here. I just wanted to—"

Audrey and her pony trotted over the cross-rail, then stopped, turned, and went back the other way.

Tiffany said, "Does she like me? I think she does, but then she won't talk to me for four days or something, and I don't know. I worked hard for her."

"After she came out of the hospital with her back, she didn't talk to me for a year and a half. I went to see her in the hospital every day. I took her things, I cleaned her house, I took care of the horses. As soon as she possibly could, she stopped speaking to me."

"How did that make you feel?"

"I missed her, but, you know, I kind of expected it. She wasn't ungrateful. She thanked me, and she meant it. But there're some people, you know, they always think about things in terms of deserving them or not, and the more you give them, the less they feel they can take, because they've used up what they deserve. Unless they can give you something back, they don't deserve anything more, and so they shut you off."

Audrey trotted back and forth over the cross-rail again, then Ellen walked over to the standards and dropped one end of a red-and-white pole to the ground and lifted the end of a blue pole onto a jump cup, making a small vertical jump. She called out, "Now take this at the trot, also!"

Seeing the jump being raised from its minimal cross-pole height, the pony livened up considerably, pricking his ears and lifting his tail. He trotted smartly to the base of the fence and hopped over it. Audrey pushed her heels down and put her hands in the pony's mane. A couple of steps after the fence, she brought him to a halt and turned him around, and Ellen said, "Okay, do it again." Then, "Believe me, Tiff, she likes you. No doubt she loves you."

"Did she say that?"

"To me? What do you think? She'd take a kick in the head over admitting something like that. Go back and forth over it, Audrey, until you and the pony are really comfortable."

Tiffany, watching, could see Audrey relax and concentrate. What a thing this was, she suddenly thought, to finish with her two charges at the track, then to come here and watch this, then to get into her car and drive to Belmont and watch her filly run in a race that she well might win. How strange it was that you had said yes and why not and I'll try that, and you got someplace where there were horses behind you and horses in front of you and horses all around you. She said, "But if she likes me— I mean, when I like someone, I can't get enough of them. Or something. It's like with the horses. I had one, and then I wanted another one, and now it's just about all horses all of the time. But it seems like, when she likes something, she right away starts going off about it and backing away from it."

"Does that bother you?"

"Not really, no. I just don't understand it. I mean, nothing about her bothers me. She's funny, and all that stuff she puts on, you can see right through it, and the last thing she would ever do is hurt somebody."

"You know what?"

"What?"

"People love her. Horses love her. She always always always has your best interests at heart, and she puts herself out to make sure you know what your best interests are, even if they conflict with hers. When she had the jumpers, I remember, people would come around and want to buy horses, and she would say, 'Now, darlin', you won't be wantin' this lad. He's got osselets and he won't last ya a year!' And then she would wonder why she had all these horses standing in the barn. When she got to the track, she did better, because at least she would get her horses claimed, and that paid a lot of the bills at first. You know something?"

"What's that?"

"Just a second." Ellen went to the jump and raised it a notch, so that now it was about two feet high. "Okay, dear," she said to Audrey. "At the trot, please." She came back to Tiffany and said, "In all the years I've known Deirdre, I have never one time been angry with her. I can't say that about anyone else."

"I've never been mad at her, either. And I never saw George get mad, really, though he pretended a couple of times."

"There you go. But she's a conundrum."

"What's that?"

"A riddle."

"What did you call that?"

"A conundrum."

"I like that. Conundrum. That would be a good name for a horse, you know. A filly by Secret Hello. You know, what I really need is to get myself a nice broodmare, say twenty-five thousand dollars or so, and breed myself a commercial weanling. If you sell them as weanlings, it's almost pure profit, Bill says. Conundrum."

"You are obsessed."

"Look who's talking."

"I'm ready!" exclaimed Audrey. "Can I do a course? With that triple combination? Not too low!"

"Who's obsessed?" said Tiffany, nodding toward Audrey and the pony.

"We have set a very bad example for Audrey," said Ellen. But she was grinning.

IT WAS DAYLIGHT NOW. The gray dawn was blueing up toward a bright, breezy morning, and Deirdre was of two minds. The sunlight had an irrepressible good effect upon her, just the sort of biological knee-jerk reaction that was so burdensome to the free play of the intellect, and so she was tempted to go back to her stall and lie down next to her books. And she was tempted to have something to eat. The cruise line advertised twenty-four-hour-a-day victuals, and perhaps it was time to put them to the test. The ship was still heading west. She was no longer alone in her perambulation of the deck, however, for several early-morning joggers were doing their laps. One of the ship's personnel was about to hoist the flag over the stern.

Before he left, George had taken her out to dinner and fed her all of her favorite dishes—some very nice crab cakes, a salad of baby greens with a balsamic vinaigrette, a veal piccata nestled on the plate with braised fennel and leeks, and a felicitous lemon-ginger mousse. For her part, she had given him something, a black-and-white photograph she had found in an art gallery, of six male athletes, naked, from behind, a baseball player, a marathon runner, a basketball player, a jockey, a soccer player, and a pole vaulter. Though the collage was seamless, all the figures had been blown up or reduced so that they were equal in height to the marathon runner, who was six feet tall. All were nicely burnished, too. "I consider this a purely educational graphic, George," she had said, "and I expect you to hang it in the kitchen."

"Who do you think that is?" he said, pointing to the jockey.

"Could be anyone perfect," she had replied. "Your eye does go to that one, does it not?"

"They're the first to tell you they're the most fit."

"It does look that way from this photo, doesn't it?"

They had gone on about the picture for at least a half-hour, then he had taken her in hand. He said, "You've done everything for me, Cousin."

"You've earned your pay, George. You've done your work and kept your sunny disposition and never incurred the wrath of the officials or the owners."

"You must accept my gratitude, anyway."

She had sniffed, then said, "Well, I do. And you must accept mine, for giving me a laugh now and then. I'm going to miss you."

"Yes, you are, so I am going to do you the favor of telling you all over again that you are a prideful woman. You don't think much about the seven deadly sins, no one in this country does, but even so, they're still about."

"You can accuse me of gluttony, George." She had taken another bite of her mousse. Lust she kept to herself. "But if you ask me, life is the deadliest sin, as it always ends in death no matter whether you sleep in every morning or not. Personally, I think insomnia is—"

He went on, "The priest at my church calls them 'the seven deadliest self-imposed punishments.' "

"That's very California of him. No wonder you're going back to Ireland."

"You've imposed a considerable burden of pride upon yourself, Cousin."

"Have I?"

"Pride is the hardest burden to bear, the number-one sin, the one that separates you from God."

"I knew that name was going to come up."

"God loves you, sweetheart."

"Ah, George—"

"All these years, I've given in to your pride and not talked to you about God at all, but now's the time."

"Why?"

"Because it is. You are rejecting the love of God, and look at you. You may call yourself an embittered woman all you wish, as if saying it will make light of it, but it's true and it doesn't make you happy."

"And the love of God will make me happy?"

"Here's how it works, Cousin. First you admit it exists, then you admit you can see it, then you admit you can feel it, then you admit you want it, then you return it, and then it fills you. Then you are happy."

"Seems like a lengthy process, George."

"Pride makes a grand thing small, darlin'."

And then they had stopped talking about it, and she had taken George to the plane the next day and put him on it, and that had been two months ago. He had nailed her good, and they both knew it. Her own pride had made every grand thing she'd ever experienced small, and then smaller. Wasn't she right now among the nature-lovers, busily making all this grandness about her—this ocean, these mountains, this light of day—as small as she could so she didn't have to admit that she couldn't experience it, didn't know how, was immune to it?

But, then, did she know how to make anything large anymore?

By now the scene around her was bright and animated. The deck was full of people, first-day-of-vacation people, who were oohing and aahing at the scenery they had awakened to discover. How they had slept, how hungry that sea air made them, how happy they were to be here, it wasn't like this back in Columbus, how nice it was to make a change. Many of them smiled at her and said "Good morning." She smiled back. Even to speak, she thought, would be to cast a cloud over their pleasure.

Tiffany she had made large, so large that she had had to run a third of the way around the world to cut her down to size. What had she said to George, in passing, as if it didn't matter, just for something to say? That she was tired of making a big deal of everything. "What have I gotten from bringing my passions to bear on everything, George? Exhausted. That's what." But it was all too true. The horses had done her in; Tiffany might do her in.

She went around to the stairs and mounted to the next deck, the promenade deck. It was much fancier up here, with great windows all along the deck, and polished wooden doorways and gold and all. She turned and entered the dining room, which was already, at, what was it, five-thirty, set up and aglitter with glassware and place settings and napery. She walked down the long buffet table, upon which men in white were setting out platters and chafing dishes. Bagels. Cream cheese. Another sort of cream cheese, onions, smoked salmon. Another sort of smoked salmon. A tiny dish of capers. She lifted her gaze. Dishes by the dozen, piled and mounded and stacked with food, all of it fresh, all of it made into a picture. She took a deep breath, and felt that biological rebound set in again—daylight, food, beauty, luxury. Were they not the simplest things to fall for? And yet. She went to the end of the buffet table and picked up a plate.

TIFFANY WENT AROUND the barn with Ellen and followed her down a path that led to the back of the property, to a wooded pasture screened by trees from the rest of the paddocks. The day's mid-Atlantic heat and humidity were gearing up, but there had been plenty of rain and the grass was green and thick. Groups of horses, grazing in twos and threes, looked up or came over to the fence. It was a scene Tiffany was utterly familiar with now, but it always pleased her. She was reminded of something. She said, "I meant to tell you. My mama was talking to her cousin, and she said that they had a great-uncle who was a horse-breaker in North Carolina back around the twenties and thereabouts. He didn't have any children, so the cousin didn't know much about him, but now my mama doesn't think this is all so crazy anymore. Or, I guess, better crazy in the family than crazy out of it."

They came through the trees. Standing at the far end of the two-acre rect-angle was a large black horse. He lifted his head, but he did not approach, not even one step. He looked at them for a minute or two, then bucked, kicked, farted, and set off galloping. He ran toward the fence, ducked, pivoted, kicked up his heels, and ran in the other direction. Tiffany, whose runners had given her a good eye, said, "He's fast!"

"Look at him turn. He can pivot on one front toe or he can rock back on his haunches."

He reared, and his forehand was in the air for what seemed like five min-utes. Ellen said, "Made to jump. But you can't touch him or approach him."

"Why did you buy him?"

"I didn't. They gave him to me."

"Who gave him to you?"

"Barry Jordan, at Patch Creek Stud Farm, up by Chesapeake."

"Is he a stallion?"

"Not anymore. That's why they gave him to me. His owner had him at the track up in New York, and he won some big race, but then he got ruled off for savaging someone, so they sent him to the studfarm to see if that would calm him down, because, you know, sometimes it's the stress of racing that makes them bananas, but he was still bananas, and when the stud manager said that they preferred not to stand him, the owner had him gelded."

"You know what Deirdre says."

" 'Geld him now and improve the breed.' "

"So you said you would make him into a riding horse?"

"I said I would. We'll see. It takes a month for the testosterone to clear. It's been two weeks. But I took all the mares out of these back paddocks. We'll see."

"What's his name?" said Tiffany.

"You know what? They wouldn't tell me. And they wouldn't give me his papers. All I know is what I told you. Of course, I could read his tattoo and call the Jockey Club, but I can't get close enough to him to read his tattoo at the moment." She was smiling, perfectly happy. Nothing ever daunted Ellen, or, rather, nothing about a horse ever discouraged her. "We'll name him some-thing when we think of it."

This horse was a discouraging sight. He was rearing and running around and kicking up and pinning his ears now, and two times he ran toward the fence as if his bad intentions were personally directed at them. At the same time, he was obviously beautiful and talented. Tiffany said, "Ugh. I don't like him."

"He is a bad bad boy," said Ellen, but she said it fondly. "Maybe when he's less of a boy, he'll be less bad. We'll see."

They turned and walked away, down the path and into the trees. Epic Steam stopped expressing his opinion of them and stood still. After they disappeared, he put his head down to graze, but then he began trotting the fence line. As for his testicles, they were gone but not forgotten. The fence was four feet six inches high, white boards, with a live electric wire running around the top to discourage wood chewing. Epic Steam was not nearly bored enough to chew wood—he was much too interested in the mares and fillies he could smell in the distance. One of these days, though no one yet knew it, he was going to discover his greatest talent. It was just a matter of time.

JULY

66 / ALL FEMALE

ALTHOUGH LEON was fully equipped, with beeper, cellular phone, and voice mail, when Deedee went into labor at the Safeway in Arcadia, there was no one available to take her call. Right there between tortellini on one side and herbs and spices across the aisle, she lost her waters with a splash. But she who had once weighed 102 and now weighed 152 was well beyond embarrassment. The first thing she did was look in her grocery basket. Best not fool around with the frozen foods. She moved those to one side. That left a bag of potatoes, some oranges, two loaves of bread, a box of Team Cheerios, a jar of peanut butter—oh, what the hell. She took her purse out of the baby seat, knowing that the next time she saw one of these seats she would be using it, and left. Her goals were changing by the second. First it was shop for groceries, then it was at least buy the basics, now, as a result of feeling the first labor pain of her life, it was make it to the van in the parking lot.

She stood still. Underneath her maternity T-shirt, she saw as well as felt the contraction. It unfurled upward like a sustained gripping sensation, held her tight, then eased off. After it was gone, she began to count and walk at the same time. The Lamaze teacher had said the initial contractions would be about ten minutes, give or take a minute, apart. Deedee gave and took eight minutes. The contractions were two minutes apart. She had the second one right by the door and the third one about halfway to the van. She tried Leon again, left him another message, looked at her watch. It was eight-forty-two. She could not contract, walk, count seconds, and talk on the phone at the same time, so the message she left was, "Oh, shit, Leon, where are you?"

The first contraction in the van lasted thirty-six seconds, which left her just over a minute to turn on the ignition and pull out of her parking place. Then she sat there for another thirty-six seconds, gasping, while cars lined up waiting for her to move. They weren't honking yet, though. Then she thought she was going to faint, so she put down her window, but since it was hot outside, that didn't help much. She put her head down on the door of the van and closed her eyes. That's when the waiting cars started honking. Sometime later, in the midst of the noise, a voice said, beside her ear, "Deedee? Is that you?"

She lifted her head. It was Marvelous Martha. Deedee said, "The contractions are two minutes apart. How did Residual work this morning?"

"We just jogged. She did a half in forty-four and a half yesterday, though. Move over." Deedee moved over. "What hospital are you in?"

"Arcadia Methodist."

"I should have known."

Deedee put the seat all the way back, which didn't help all that much, since the baby, a nine-pounder according to her doctor, now straddled all of her internal organs. She lifted her feet and put them on the dashboard, then said, "Don't make me put on my seatbelt. Ohhhhhhh."

It came to Deedee that she might well die in the next five minutes to five hours, and so it would be best to make a confession. She said, "I'm sorry I didn't like you. I was envious and angry."

"That's okay, dear."

"And I've been a bitch to Leon. I mostly got pregnant to focus his attention."

"It seems to have worked, sweetheart. He's much better at his job now."

"I was sorry I got pregnant. I thought about having an abortion."

"Most people do, honey. Thinking about it isn't the same as doing it."

"Ahhhhh."

"Did they teach you how to breathe?"

"Heeheeheehaahaahaaheeheehee."

"There you go. The baby doesn't know what you're thinking, either."

"I wish I'd done better in high school, and then gone to college."

"You still can."

"I was so awful to my mother. And she did this for me. I took money out of her purse for something."

"What was that, Deedee?"

"Heeheeheehaahaahaaheeheeheehaahaahaawheeeeew."

"It won't be far now. We're almost there."

"It was for a jumping clinic with George Morris. I took it out of her purse a little at a time for three months when I was fifteen."

"At least it wasn't drugs. You can pay her back after the baby's born."

Should I live so long, thought Deedee. But she said, "Leon told me something."

"What's that, honey?"

"He told me that he saw Buddy and Curtis Doheny standing outside

Residual's stall. When they saw him, they walked on down the aisle very casually. Ahhhh. Heeheehee. Here we are. Oh, God!"

Marvelous Martha pulled into the emergency entrance and glanced at her watch. The attendant was right there. She said, "I think her contractions are less than a minute apart."

The attendant opened the passenger door of the van while another attendant brought out a wheelchair. The two of them helped Deedee out of the van. Marvelous Martha went around and took Deedee's hand. Deedee said, "Can you find Leon?"

"I'll try."

"Thank you for being at Safeway."

Marvelous Martha smiled and said, "Is your conscience clear now?"

"Mostly."

"Then go have a baby!"

But then, after she got back into the van and pulled it out of the emergency entrance, she decided to park and go in, just to see.

Inside the emergency-room door, they had already stretched Deedee out on a gurney. One nurse had hold of one leg and another nurse had hold of the other leg. A woman doctor was leaning forward, looking at the opening of the birth canal. Just as Marvelous Martha approached them, she stood up and said, "Baby's crowning. Let's do it. What's your name, Deanie?"

"Deedee," said Marvelous Martha.

"Deedee. Well, Deedee, give us a push."

"Hunnnnnhhhhhhhhh," exclaimed Deedee.

"Good one," said the doctor.

Marvelous Martha took Deedee's hand.

"HUUUUUNNNNNNNHHHHHH!" exclaimed Deedee.

"All right! Here we go! Yes!" shouted everyone all at once, including several patients waiting in the emergency room to be treated.

"One more for good measure," said the doctor.

"OOOOOOOOOHHHHHHHHHHHHHAAAAAUUUUUNNNNNH!" ululated Deedee.

All over the emergency room, "Yeah! Go! Wow! Yeah! Yeah!"

"Here she is," said the doctor.

Marvelous Martha stroked Deedee on the forehead and then leaned down. Deedee's eyes closed briefly. She was panting. Before she could say anything, Marvelous Martha whispered in Deedee's ear, "It's a filly."

———

BUDDY AND LEON had gone to New York with a horse who was running in the Dwyer Handicap, and Marvelous Martha was supposed to follow a week later with Residual, who was entered in the Coaching Club American Oaks. The filly was working well, and seemed, Marvelous Martha thought, to have rededicated herself to pure speed. In four starts since January, not counting the race that ended prematurely, she had won twice, run third once, and run fifth once. With each race she got tougher and faster. Getting kicked in Texas had hardly set her back, except for the Derby. The top fillies, especially on the West Coast, were very fast company this year, much more interesting than the males, and Residual herself wanted to keep up with them. They had gone from being debutantes to being M.B.A.'s in one year of racing. They ran for the finish line with their eyes rolling and their ears pinned, the vigorous daughters of mares who ruled their pastures, and Marvelous Martha, who had ridden many a tough mare in her day, admired the filly's willingness to learn what it took. In fact, she was enjoying herself so much, with Buddy and Leon gone and Deedee cocooned in her condo with Alana Marie Taylor-O'Connor, that she forgot anything could happen, and then something did. She got out to the track for her daily session, this time a jog after the previous day's work, and the filly had a big soft swelling, warm and painful, in and around her right knee. She was off but not hobbling. It was easy to guess the problem—it was a common racehorse problem, especially with a speedball. The question was not whether she had a chip in her knee, it was how many. The groom put the filly back in her stall while Marvelous Martha went into Buddy's office to find the vet list.

After putting in a call to Karen Busher-Sysonby, D.V.M., whose work she had seen and admired, Marvelous Martha called Andrea Melanie Kingston, who was right there beside the phone. Marvelous Martha reported that the horse probably had a chip in her knee, and would Jason mind coming out to the track and speaking to the vet. Andrea Melanie said, "Jason is in Europe."

"Well, if she wants to do a surgery, which she probably will want to do, she should talk to the owner about it."

"Really?"

"I think so."

"Is Buddy there?"

"No, Buddy's in New York."

"Are you going to consult him?"

Marvelous Martha pondered that word, "consult." If the horse had a chip in her knee, that was a pretty cut-and-dried matter, upon which little consultation was needed. Besides that, the authority Marvelous Martha most often consulted was her own intuition. Limiting her consultations in this way resulted in a much more productive use of time and much less interpersonal conflict. And in addition to that, she had noticed over the years that everyone more or less agreed about a fait accompli. She said, "Well, let's talk to the vet. You can make up your mind."

"I can?"

"Of course you can. Though, of course, Buddy and your husband are readily available by phone."

"And computer link," said Andrea Melanie. "We can send any pictures or other information to Jason's personal computer."

"There aren't really any decisions to make in this case. She's got a chip in her knee. It has to come out. We can thank God that we have a vet to do it. You know, I had a boyfriend once, this was when I was very young, who was a real cowboy, and one time I saw him build a fire and stick his big pointed knife into it, and I said, 'Lester, what are you doing?,' and he pushed his chaw of tobacco to one side and looked up at me and said, 'Honey, I'm gonna take that chip out of that horse's knee.' And he did. Once he pulled his own tooth, too."

"He was your boyfriend?"

"Not for long after that."

"Have you had a lot of boyfriends?"

"Yes, I have, and we can talk about that, but why don't you come on out here and talk to the vet with me." And so she did and so there was no further discussion of telephones or computer links.

Although Karen Busher-Sysonby, D.V.M., was scientifically trained and also excelled at objectivity, she was not unaware of the circumstances of the present surgery. The horse was beautiful and famous; the trainer, whom she had worked for only once and who did not have the best reputation, was out of town; she herself had more credentials than experience; the owner of the horse was not herself a horseman; the guiding hand here, Martha Someone, was assuming more responsibility than was hers by right; and the horse's bloodwork showed a slightly elevated concentration of red blood cells. All the same, the X-ray showed a simple, dime-shaped chip on the distal aspect of the radius, right front. You could get in and out of that in forty minutes, and looking to others who were older and male for permission to do the obvious was a characteristic of women that Karen Busher-Sysonby did not like, especially in herself. You could float teeth and give vaccinations all your life, or you could go ahead and do what you had been asked to do, and Karen Busher-Sysonby had not gotten through vet school by refusing to go ahead and do what she was asked to do.

Now she had the horse on her back on the table in the surgery, her right front leg propped on a pole, the knee bent about thirty degrees. Her anesthesiologist, Portia Vedette, looked half asleep, as always, and the technicians were talking to one another in low voices. Karen scrubbed the knee three times, and made two small incisions for the arthroscope. The interior of the knee joint appeared suddenly on the TV screen beside her, and she began making the subtle movements with the scope that would enable her to find the location and dimensions of the chip—here was one edge—a new monitor would be nice in this surgery, she knew a guy who was working for sporthorse people, and he had much better equipment, you'd think that the richest track in America, if not the world— Portia said, "Huh," and she followed around the edge, it was very thin, but seemed to be— Portia said, "Uhhhh, shit." Karen looked at the EKG monitor, and the oscillating line depicting Residual's heartbeat was flat as the Pacific horizon. She looked at Portia. Portia was wide awake, and the technicians had stopped talking and started gawking. Portia said, "Atropine," and gave the filly a shot. The line began to oscillate again.

Karen said, "How long was it flat?" She was breathing hard.

"Only a few seconds, twenty, maybe. Where are you?" She was breathing hard, too.

"I was finding the perimeters of the chip."

"Well, grab it and take it out, because this operation is over."

Looking back at the TV monitor, Karen inserted her forceps, found the chip, and eased it out of the incision.

"Close it up," said Portia, and Karen began suturing two small incisions. On her second stitch, Portia said, "Dead again."

Karen looked at the EKG monitor. The flatness of the line was absolute. She tied the suture, removed the drapes, and Karen had administered another shot of atropine, and still the line was laser-flat. "How long has it been?"

"About forty seconds at this point."

"What now?"

"Oxygen. Prayer."

Behind them, one of the technicians, Dorothy, said, "Come down, baby. Come down, sweetie." Karen glanced at her. She was staring up into one corner of the room. She said, "I see you up there, floating around, trying to decide. It's up to you, Mama. Your life has just begun. You've got a lot of stuff to do, Mama. You've got to win some more races and all of that." Now the woman closed her eyes and rocked her head back and forth, and said "Yes, filly-girl. Yes, filly-girl, yes, filly-girl." She was almost keening. Karen looked at Portia, who tore her gaze away from the monitor long enough to shrug a tiny shrug. The technician crooned, "There we go. There we go. Come on, little darling. Who are those babies going to go to if they can't find you? Come on down, sweetheart."

Portia said, "She's started again. There. It's pretty strong, too."

The technician hadn't heard. She was still rocking her head. She blew out her breath, snorted, and cried, "Come back, little girlie, little filly-girl!" Karen touched her on the shoulder. She said, "She's started again." The technician stood still and nodded, but she didn't look at all embarrassed. She said, "Good. It worked."

"Something worked," said the other technician.

"The horse," said Karen to Marvelous Martha and Andrea Melanie about half an hour later, "cannot undergo another surgery. She's, let's say, allergic to the anesthetic halothane. A certain percentage of horses are. It causes cardiac arrest."

"Oh my God," said Andrea Melanie.

"She did arrest on the operating table," said Karen.

"I knew we should have told Buddy," said Andrea Melanie.

"I doubt that he would have known of her allergy, unless she's had surgery before."

"No, she hasn't," said Andrea Melanie. "She arrested? What exactly does that mean?"

"She died," said Marvelous Martha.

"Yes," said Karen. "She did. She died for about thirty seconds, and then she died for about a minute."

"Oh, Jason would kill me if she died!" exclaimed the owner. "Is she awake yet?"

"No. We're waiting for that. There's one thing you should know," she said.

"She could wake up an idiot," said Marvelous Martha.

"There is a chance she'll have the equine equivalent of cerebral palsy, yes. Why don't we all go in and watch her for a bit."

The filly was still stretched out in the recovery stall when they entered it, an IV into her neck. The two technicians were squatting beside her. One was stroking her head. Marvelous Martha went and knelt beside her and touched her on the ears. There was no talking. After a minute or two, the filly opened her eyes and lifted her head. She sighed and looked around, then, a little hesi-tantly, she rolled up on her sternum and looked around again. "She's quiet," said Karen. "That's a very good sign. If she was flopping around, that could mean there's brain damage." But it was clear to Marvelous Martha that the filly continued to be herself—calm, well disposed, sane. All she did was sigh a cou-ple of times and shake her head and ears, the way you would. She passed her tongue over her lips, yawned, looked at everyone. Then she stuck out her forelegs and levered herself up.

"Did you get the chip?" said Marvelous Martha.

"I got the chip," said Karen Busher-Sysonby. "And now I have another surgery. Please call me if there's a problem." Everyone nodded. As she left, Karen hooked her finger around the sleeve of Dorothy, and urged her toward the door. Dorothy gave her a look, an intimidated look. Karen leaned over her—the technician was rather short—and whispered in her ear, "You can work with me anytime. Thank you."

Scientific training and a natural bent toward objectivity were all very well, she thought, but with a filly worth over a million dollars, you had to play all the angles you could find.

LATER THAT NIGHT, after she had returned to Berkeley, Marvelous Martha placed a call to Karen Busher-Sysonby. She said, "Did that filly die of natural causes?"

"Ask me if she revived of natural causes."

"What do you mean?"

"One of the technicians called her back. She said she was floating in the room and asked her to get back into her body."

"I know someone that happened to. Her kids called her back."

"This was a horse."

"Well, you know, doctors always doubted acupuncture until they saw it work on horses."

"Maybe."

"But what killed her?"

"Oh, as I said, sensitivity to halothane isn't uncommon."

"And everything else was normal? All the pre-surgical workup and everything?"

"Oh, yes. I mean, within the range. Her red blood count was high-normal, but that was all. Why do you ask?"

"I ride her every day. I'm fifty-three years old. I want to make sure she has four legs, a heart, and a brain before I get on."

"Well, you won't be getting back on for four months, anyway, so, when she comes back to the track, let me know, and I'll keep an eye on her."

A WEEK LATER, after Buddy was back and the filly had gone to the farm to recuperate from her surgery (Buddy was angry that he hadn't been consulted, but what could he do, it was a done deal), Marvelous Martha came down to San Diego from Berkeley for the day but did not go to the track. Instead she took a cab out to La Jolla, and paid a call on Andrea Melanie.

Marvelous Martha was brown and stringy—all her flesh, of which there had never been much, looked welded to her bones. Her hands and her shoulders were large and powerful, as if leased from another body. Her hair and her blue eyes had lightened in the sun. Andrea Melanie was intimidated, the way you got looking at the desert horizon. She could not imagine how a person, a woman, could do such a poor job of taking care of herself. She was therefore somewhat distracted while Marvelous Martha was talking to her. On the one hand, sun damage was sun damage, not easy to repair, the best policy was always prevention. On the other hand, a peel, or even a dermabrasion, worked wonders, especially the first one. You didn't have to do it over and over and get that look you sometimes saw of a sort of incandescent fish-belly white. She said, "Excuse me?" Marvelous Martha repeated, "Deedee made some childbed confessions, and one of them was that Leon had seen Buddy and a well-known crooked vet standing outside Residual's stall."

"Who is Deedee?"

"The old exercise rider, who got pregnant."

That reminded Andrea Melanie that Marvelous Martha had mentioned boyfriends. That was interesting, given her looks. Andrea Melanie's deepest conviction was that once your looks were gone there were to be no more boyfriends, and so you had better consolidate your assets early and hold on to them. She, for example, was eighteen years younger than Jason. His first wife was his age, and his second wife was only six years younger. His fifth wife, she thought, would be thirty or forty years younger.

"I just have a feeling."

"Excuse me?"

"I have a feeling something unethical is going on. The vet said the filly's blood count was a bit high."

"Well, she's off at some farm for a while, and, frankly"—Andrea Melanie leaned close to the older woman—"I'm kind of relieved. Everything was getting rather exciting and distracting. Now we're going to the Derby and now we're not and now we're running in a race and now the race is stopped and now we're going to New York. I don't know. It's much too much like some kind of Hollywood movie, all these twists and turns in the plot line. You know, after we bought all that art a couple of years ago, the art didn't then do anything. Horses keep doing things."

Marvelous Martha had to admit that she left La Jolla less hopeful than she had been upon arrival, especially since, after everything she said, Andrea Melanie seemed more eager than anything else to press upon her an unopened bottle of La Prairie something for putting on your face.

Andrea Melanie, however, in spite of the distraction of having to deal with Marvelous Martha's weirdness, understood fairly well that Buddy was doing something to the horse in order to get her to the Breeders' Cup. But, she thought, wasn't that his job? At seventy-five dollars a day apiece for the five horses Jason had in his barn, profitability was not necessarily required, but fun was, and Andrea Melanie had been in racing long enough to know that the Breeders' Cup was the most fun of all.

67 / SWAPS

THE PLAN was that all of Limitless's connections were going to meet in Los Angeles to watch him run in the Swaps Stakes, his first Grade One race. The race was for three-year-olds, the purse of five hundred thousand dollars would certainly be worth more what with late entries, and the population of three-year-old runners had been nicely winnowed down by the rigors of the Triple Crown. Elizabeth and Plato were finishing up their week on Kauai ("All I can say," she told Joy, "is that, for true sexual enlightenment, you have to give up everything you think you know about sex, including who is the man and who is the woman." "How do you do that?" said Joy. "I'll say no more right now," said Elizabeth) and flying in the night before the race. Al was flying from Japan to Rio de Janeiro with a twenty-four-hour stopover in Los Angeles. Rosalind was coming in from Edinburgh. Krista and Pete were coming, too, though only from the East Coast of the United States. They also planned to arrive the night before. Mr. Tompkins, who had taken an interest in the horse, was flying himself and ten employees down in the DC-3. Roberto was riding several races on the undercard, so all he had to do was walk out of the jockeys' room. Farley had to come in from Arcadia. The only one Joy doubted the timely arrival of was herself. She had to find the sense to come in out of the rain.

What she had done was, she had moved out of Farley's condo without telling him she was going to about four days before the race. She did not then explain herself, because she didn't know how to explain herself, or why she had moved. She had simply felt a longing for isolation. Her guesthouse up at the ranch had been perfect, she thought. Barricaded behind piles of horse magazines, tack, boots, stable equipment, work clothes, and riding gear, she had found herself with just enough to do, nothing, and the exact number of people she could handle to do it with, which was no one. She recognized this state of mind perfectly, having dwelt within it for almost all of her years in California, and though she didn't welcome it, she saw that it was hers and claimed it. It was perfectly relaxing in its way, because by contrast the elevated degree of sociability she had been striving for since getting to know Elizabeth seemed exhausting. Everything was exhausting. Mr. T. was exhausting, Limitless was exhausting, Farley's love and kindness were exhausting. They must be, because she was exhausted. The day after she moved out of the condo, into a motel in Ontario, she slept for sixteen hours.

Once she had slept for sixteen hours, that is, through the night, through the morning, through the afternoon, and through her normal dinner time, there came to be a kind of languorous ease to not revealing her whereabouts, or even admitting to herself that she was "gone." She wasn't "gone," because she was here, right where she knew she was, and she was fine, and another nice nap, she thought, would do her a world of good. But first, a bath. She went into the motel bathroom, a soothingly tiny and windowless space, with the bathtub stuck behind a damp, dark shower curtain. She ran the water, took off her T-shirt, and closed the door. The mirror steamed over immediately. She locked the door. The telephone was out in the other room, and she didn't want to look at it. The tub filled and she climbed in.

FARLEY WAS STANDING in the one place where he could see both Mr. T., in his stall, and Limitless, in his pen. Both horses were eating their hay, but both horses looked at him from time to time, the old horse turning his long white, dished head toward him, elegant and classic; the three-year-old popping up to regard him, his profile more unusual—not Roman-nosed, but long and straight, with those huge eyes and those nostrils round and open like the blossoms of a foxglove. It had been twenty-four hours since Joy's departure, and he felt caught here, on this exact spot, as if, should he stand here long enough, she would materialize at the one point on earth where her three great loves—old horse, young horse, old man—intersected. He could also see the door to his office, upon which "The Tibetan Book of Thoroughbred Training" hung, grimy with the dust of years of horses. "The Tibetan Book of Thoroughbred Training" was not so easy to follow when your sweetheart had disappeared without a word. Now, at the twenty-four-hour mark, everything in the world, it seemed, urged you in an anti-Tibetan direction. "Do not pay attention or investigate" surely meant "Do not call the police." "Do not see any fault anywhere" surely meant "Do not allow fear to turn into anger or despair." "Do not take anything to heart" would mean "This is not something she did to you." "Do not hanker after signs of progress" encouraged patience. And then there was "Do not fall prey to laziness." Well, laziness would be letting this rise up and close over him, a fear so large and enveloping that it could render him thoughtless, moveless, hopeless. And a state of constant inspection was forcing himself to observe it all, to take an interest, to see what would happen. He gave himself one more minute to follow the Tibetan way, and then another minute after that. One minute at a time was about all he could manage. In that minute, and again in the next minute, he would try to listen to his intuition that, though everything was not all right with Joy, she was safe somewhere, thinking something through or feeling something out that he could not help her with.

It goaded him to look at Limitless, though. She rode him, groomed him, walked him for hours a day. At the least sign of restlessness, she put the shank on him and led him out. She knew that Mr. T. could take care of himself, that he, Farley, could do the same, but only she could take care of Limitless, and that had turned out to be true. All day, the horse had been anxious and worried, suspicious of other handlers, including Farley himself. As Farley watched him, the colt's head popped up again. At every sound, the colt's head popped up. It didn't matter whether the horse wanted Joy because he was attached to her, or whether he wanted her because he wanted to get out, it was clear that he wanted her and was expecting her. Of course, should she not come back (Farley observed that, as he thought this thought, he gave out an involuntary little moan), the horse would accustom himself to others, but with the biggest race of his life only three days away, something like this could make all the difference.

Farley turned away and walked down the shedrow. Walking down the shedrow gave him the illusion of looking for her, as if he would turn a corner and there she would be, rolling wraps or dumping a bucket of water or coiling a hose. But there she was not. He walked down the shedrow anyway, with each step listening to his intuition, with each step doubting himself and longing for advice. It had been a long time since he had wished so thoroughly to give himself away like that, to put himself in the hands of some authority and be told what to do. That would be the relief of calling the police, wouldn't it? Or calling her mother, or calling Elizabeth. But her mother's alarm would outstrip all but the most extreme situations, and Elizabeth, Farley still didn't entirely trust.

He got to the end of the shedrow, looked down at his feet, looked around, turned around, walked back. The six rules of "The Tibetan Book of Thoroughbred Training," he realized, invited exactly that, and that above all, trust. Trust that you don't need to ask questions, trust that there is no one and nothing to blame, trust in the fact that you are not the center of the universe, trust that events will reveal their true meaning on their own, trust that you will not be overwhelmed, trust that you can see and understand if you have the calmness to do so. It was not that he had to trust Joy, but that he had to trust life itself. And how could you do that, after thirty years at the racetrack, where shock, surprise, and amazement were the daily fare?

And yet there he was, Mr. T., nineteen years old now, standing in his stall, looking at him. Farley knew that it was hard enough, when your human children were eighteen or twenty, able to read, write, balance a checkbook, drive a car, and listen to reams of advice, to send them off to do what they wanted to do, which was to go off—and his own kids had been a little adventurous, one in Australia, one in Jamaica, the other two well-traveled. How much harder was it to walk a horse up the steep ramp of a horse van and watch him head into the unknown—unknown to you, but, more profoundly, unknown to him? There was no preparing a horse to go, no describing to him what he would do, what the people would be like. There was no reassuring him that there would be plenty of hay and oats or grass. Sometimes you didn't know that there would be. You could not prepare him to communicate to his new associates that he had certain preferences and desires and needs, and that if those were accommodated he would be a good, cooperative horse. Sometimes horses went away from you happy and calm and came back full of vices and fears, hard to handle and nearly broken down. Sometimes horses that you had trained as two-year-olds went to someone else, and you were right there in the grandstand watching when the horse shattered his foreleg as a four-year-old, and you knew that wouldn't have happened if you were still training the horse, knew it even though it was not true and you were wrong to think so. Farley went over and put his arm around Mr. T.'s nose, stroked the horse on the cheek and forehead. The horse had been on his own for nineteen years now, finding himself here and there, and even though he was picky about his food and cranky at times and nervous about certain things, here he was, fit and shining and healthy, able to get along and even thrive in a world that had not been made with him in mind. No one had planned this life for the horse—most likely his breeder had planned for him to be another Nearco, a successful racing stallion with a lifetime sinecure at a studfarm in France or Germany. But here he was, he who had been around the block and had lived, according to Elizabeth, to tell about it. If you wanted to, you could look right at Mr. T. and see trust written all over him, whether you believed in his betting system or not. And so Farley laid his cheek for a moment against the cheek of the horse, and said, "Okay."

BACK IN BED and unable to go to sleep, Joy tried to remember the longing that had brought her here. She could summon up the images she had obsessed over, the quiet, the stillness, the piles of stuff that never moved, the darkness. But those images had been memories of her place at the ranch. Hadn't she known that, wherever she went, that was not what she was going to find? Wasn't she that sane, sane enough to know the difference between memory and desire? What she could not summon up was the feeling itself. It must have been very strong, but now that she was here, by herself, lying alone on a bed in a room, she felt neither the feeling nor the satisfaction of the feeling. Instead, she felt lots of other feelings, none of them paramount. First, of course, there was what you might call the unease of disobedience. She had certainly done wrong to abandon her responsibilities without a word, to cause the man whom she loved and who loved her fear and worry. Now that she was no longer overwhelmed with longing, there didn't seem to be a whole lot of justification for doing that, or for walking away from Limitless, whom she had made, selfishly but steadily, entirely her own over the last four months. And she longed for them, too, now that she had separated herself from them. Was this her besetting sin, that, when she had the thing she wanted, she could not appreciate it, or even feel it? Last night, it had been easy. She had been asleep, luxuriously asleep, and perfectly happy, for sixteen hours. No dreams, no wakings, no life at all, just a boatload of sleep drifting down the dark river. As in the past, though, her body's disappointing inability to sustain that had left her right here, wide awake and regretful.

She got up and went into the bathroom, where she looked at the bathtub for a moment, thinking she might take another bath, but her fingertips were still pruny from the last bath. Instead, she brushed her teeth, then flossed, then sat down on the toilet seat and clipped her toenails. When in doubt, groom.

The fact was, though she was always calling herself depressed, and her condition depression, she didn't truly know what depression felt like. Sometimes it felt like longing, sometimes it felt like grief, sometimes it felt like fatigue, sometimes it felt like confusion, sometimes it felt like stupidity. When she had been on the Prozac, it had felt like all of those things but made less important, as if there were a buzz of interference on the line between those feelings and her. What if, she thought, instead of saying that she was depressed, she said that she was tired or confused? Wouldn't she then take a nap or seek clarification? How about discouraged? How about self-hating? How about afraid? How about separated from what was going on in the world and lost in herself? What would be the antidote to that? Some instructions to follow? On the one hand, it was easier just to say she was depressed. On the other hand, all the remedies they had for depression seemed not to make much difference. The depression was nearby or a little farther away. Maybe a more specific approach, though time-consuming and perhaps overdetailed, would actually work.

At the moment, her depression felt like pure adolescence. Here I am, looking in the mirror, she thought. I look lifeless and unpleasant. My skin is pasty and my eyes are dull and my hair is dirty and I have no appeal. Moreover, I have no desire to please. Relieving my beloved's worry is as easy as calling on the phone, and yet I don't want to. I don't want to express that minimal fleck of love when, over the past six months, I have expressed love with every look and gesture, hour after hour, day after day, week after week, so that I thought the expression of love was an unbreakable habit.

Well, yes, she could trace the onset of her depression to moving in with Farley. That was another thing she had longed for, to be in his steady, kind presence all night long. What she hadn't reckoned with was the fact that she didn't sleep much when she was with him. They liked to sleep entwined, and so she was aware of his presence all night long, aware of her love for him, aware that any moment he could turn over and embrace her and kiss her and give her that gift of his own desire and pleasure, aware that she could do the same. She woke up and looked at his face, woke up and kissed his arm, his chest, his shoulder, his cheek, whatever part of him was nearest. However light her kiss, however designed not to waken him, he responded with a touch or an appreciative squeeze. As a result, she had been in sleep deficit for weeks, and here it came, fatigue, a lowering of spirits, a sense that she could not do what she craved to do, which was simply to sleep entwined. But, then, the last time she moved in with someone, with Dean, at the university, depression had set in there, too, almost immediately. Then she'd thought that her depression was owing to Dean's frantic quality. He had no peace in him, day or night. Even sitting in front of the TV, he rustled and twisted and creaked and talked and sought reassurance and made plans. There had been so little that was lovable about Dean that she had stuck with him for years, getting more and more depressed. But now she saw that there was always a story about the depression, but the underlying fact was that she couldn't be with anyone, not even quiet itself, kindness itself, love itself. What it was that she seemed to aspire to was very small. A single room with a small bathroom, and in a dark little corner of that, a bathtub with a heavy dark curtain to block out the light.

OVER IN ARCADIA, Farley wasn't getting much sleep, either. It was hard enough at the track, where there was plenty going on, to maintain a level of sanity that was partly willpower and partly business, but here, in his condo, in his bed, between the sheets that still carried her scent, it was a challenge. He was a guy with procedures, a guy with rules, a smart guy. Everyone said that about him. The first rule was "Keep cool" and the second rule was "Pay attention" and the third rule was "Think before you act." Of course, the foundation mare had misinterpreted these rules, and frequently offered her critique of them. According to her, his first rule was "Retreat," his second rule was "Watch instead of act," and his third rule was "No spontaneity at any time." That he should have ended up at the racetrack was a continuing source of amazement to her, since he was a natural for, let's say, accounting or teaching biology at a very quiet convent school in a rural location. Of course, since the end of their marriage, she had apologized for her more colorful characterizations of him, but, then, she hadn't taken them back, she had just shifted her relationship to them.

He was certainly not following his first rule, since he was sweating profusely and had a steamroller headache. And when he got up to pace around the room, setting Joy's things in order, he stumbled over everything, and when he came out of the bathroom, he actually ran into the door in the dark and bruised his forehead. And as for thinking before acting, he couldn't think at all, so it was a good thing it was the middle of the night and no action was required.

Of course, there were several actions he could take. He could get in his Yukon and drive frantically around, looking for her the way you would look for a lost dog. He could go to the police, which seemed all the more attractive now that its being the middle of the night gave everything the quality of drama and panic. He could call or, better, drive to every emergency room in southern California and look into the face of every female patient. If he could not find Joy, then at least he could begin eliminating each one of the three or four million women in southern California who were not Joy. Or he could bellow like a wounded bull. Or he could pound his head against the wall, put his fist into the wall, go into the kitchen and pick up a frying pan and beat some dishes to death with it. The very thoughts made him pant and sweat all the more. He went back into the bathroom and turned on the shower.

Ah, he was so much better at this other thing, this removed, detached, floaty thing, where the horses worked and ran and won or did not win, where the owners came and went, and you viewed them with amusement, where you were detached and funny and enigmatic and steady and agreeable. At not expecting the worst or the best, but just going along. He was so good at being good with her—responsible and thoughtful and reassuring and witty—and now she was gone anyway, in spite of all his efforts, and it was very much like that time he had collapsed at Saratoga, just keeled over, and Rosalind Maybrick had set him right again, just by touching him. That, he thought, was who he should call, but he had no idea where she was. Somewhere in Europe, not really reachable, and so he, who always took care of himself, had to take care of himself again, and it was unfair, all of this taking care of himself, taking care of horses, taking care of Joy, taking care of his staff and his children and his owners and the foundation mare's monetary needs. The sweat was pouring off him and his head was exploding, so he got into the shower and it pounded down upon him, into his hair and beard and eyes and mouth, over his shoulders and belly and down through his body hair and over his penis and testicles and down his legs, first hot, then warm, then cold, then very cold, until his skin was throbbing, and he got out exhausted, toweled off, went back into the bedroom, and changed his sheets. While he was doing this, he felt better. He stretched the corners of the contour sheet over the corners of the mattress, laid the top sheet neatly down, pushed the pillows into their crisp cases, and then lay down naked, cool, and dry. And then he reached over and picked up the sheets he had taken off and dropped on the floor, the ones impregnated with her scent and his scent, and he put them over his face and wept.

IT WAS ONLY about eight o'clock Eastern Daylight Time when Joy's mother answered the phone and noted that it was Joy on the other end of the line, sounding very morose. She was not surprised that Joy was up by five; Joy had been getting up by five since she was born, which was part of the problem between them which Joy's mother no longer blamed herself for, because she no longer believed it was possible to bring a child into this world and prevent it from experiencing legitimate suffering or its surrogate, neurosis, or both. She was rather surprised, though, when Joy said, "Why am I like this?," because Joy had never asked her that question before, and her mother's repeated offers to answer that question unasked had been spurned, which Joy's mother no longer blamed Joy for, because she no longer believed it was possible to tell anyone anything, especially something that they needed to know.

Nevertheless, she was prepared for this question, having rehearsed and refined the answer countless times over the years. She said, "Because you want to be."

"I want to be tired and confused and isolated and anxious and full of self-blame and disoriented and unkind and resistant and joyless?"

"In comparison to something else, yes."

"In comparison to what?"

"I don't know what else there is, dear."

"A great guy, a great horse, a good job."

"The man could leave you."

"He won't."

"You could leave him."

"I won't. I mean, I have, but I wouldn't."

Joy's mother decided not to touch that one. She said, "Why not?"

"Because there's nothing not right between us. What's not right is in me."

"In comparison to what?"

"In comparison to him. In comparison to you. In comparison to what's normal. Why am I like this?"

What a tempting question that was. Had not Joy's mother and her sister and her best friend gone over this chapter by chapter, verse by verse, more times than she could count? Did she not have all the theories at her fingertips, nature, nurture, brain chemistry, lack of willpower, tragic view of life, mutation, bad luck, unwitnessed trauma, surge of hormones in the womb, environmental influence, unremarked-upon head injury, curse? But she said, "The question isn't 'Why?,' Joy, it's 'What now?'" And then she decided to try a different tack that didn't often work with Joy. She said, "What do you want to do, dear?"

"I don't know. I only know what I long for."

"What do you long for?"

"Right now I am longing for Farley and the horses and the track."

"What were you longing for?"

"A little dark room, peace and quiet."

Joy's mother licked her lips and consulted her own experience. It wasn't like she wasn't an expert on introspection, retrospection, regret, and second thoughts. She took a deep breath and did something scary, still scary—she spoke honestly to her only daughter. She said, "You mean a coffin, right? You mean a tiny space where you can lie down and close the lid over yourself and never see or hear or think again, where you can stop breathing and stop wondering and stop being afraid and stop feeling your heart beat and blood coursing through your veins and things changing every minute, every second? You mean that, right? You were longing for that."

There was a long silence on the other end of the line, and then Joy said, "Yes."

"Do you think you will be happy with that when you get it?"

Joy said, "No."

And her mother said, "Then it's time for you to figure out how not to get it, because it seems to me that you can only ask for it so many times before your request is granted."

"Will you call him up and tell him I'm okay?"

"What's his number?"

———

FARLEY, having gotten up at last, was still at home when his cellular rang. It was Joy's mother, her voice flat, giving away only one thing, "She's okay. She called me."

"Where is she?"

"I don't know."

"Is she coming back?"

"I don't know."

"What's she doing?"

"I don't know. Stop asking questions."

"Why?"

"Because you keep raising the threshold. I bet that before I called you were saying to yourself, 'As long as she's safe, that's all that matters.' "

"I did say that, actually."

"Well, there you are. Don't ask for any more right now."

Farley, who was used to thinking of Joy's mother as kind of a ditz, stood corrected.

WHEN HE GOT TO THE TRACK, tired as he was, he sorted things out at once, and the day went along quickly enough. He had horses in two races, a maiden special weight for three-year-old fillies and an allowance race for colts and geldings. That was Bernard Baruch. Lorenzo de Medici was running in Kentucky, and Ivan Boesky was in foal to Wild Again. The brothers had two other fillies with him now, Carl Icahn and Billy Sol Estes, a pair of two-year-olds by Seeking the Gold, but the brothers didn't come out if it wasn't a stakes race. Billy Sol Estes had considerable promise. By the time Bernard Baruch, who won his race, had finished up in the test barn, it was late, and when he got back to his office, Elizabeth had left a message on the machine for Joy, that they had been bumped from their flight in Lihue and could not make the race. After he had checked the horses one last time and left instructions with the night man, he went back into the office for his briefcase, and there was a call from the Maryland people, to say that they were staying home because the baby was sick. Then he went home and fell into bed, only to wake up at 4:00 a.m. to a call from Al Maybrick, at Narita Airport. "Listen," said Al, as if Farley had any other choice. "I got to go right now to Murmansk, and skip Rio altogether. I don't care about that, but I haven't seen Rozzy in weeks. You tell her I'll meet her in Stockholm a week from tomorrow, okay?"

"Okay," said Farley.

"That horse gonna win that race?"

"I understand there is a tip that he is. He looks very fit, Al."

"Whose tip?"

"Someone knowledgeable in the barn."

"I've heard that one before. I don't suppose they simulcast to Murmansk."

"I doubt it."

"Well, next one, maybe. Breeders' Cup, maybe."

"Good night, Al."

Then he got up, though it was two hours until he had to, and went to the track.

Santa Anita was wide awake, and Buddy Crawford's first set was already out there, though it was still dark enough for the lights to be on. If Joy went off, Farley thought, I could go back to this, to these earliest, coolest, purest hours, the kind racetrackers kept if they cared about nothing else in the world but racing.

When he came in after the second set, there was a call from Rosalind, saying that her plane had been delayed on the tarmac by a terrorist bomb threat, and even though it was over now, she couldn't possibly make the race, and so she was going to go on to Caracas. He gave her the message from Al. Her voice softened. She said, "He said he'd be there?"

"Yes."

"It's very hard to dial Murmansk on the cellular, so, if he calls to find out the results of the race, tell him I'll meet him in the hotel lobby at noon Saturday."

"Right."

Then he had a note from the front office that Mr. Tompkins had lost an engine just outside of Fresno, turned back, and landed safely, but would not make the Swaps Stakes. Put down five dollars to win on the horse Limitless and he would pay him back later. The morning wore on. The morning line on Limitless was five to two. He was the second favorite. It looked like his audience for the race would consist of Farley and eleven thousand strangers. At about three o'clock, Rafael pulled the horse out of his pen and led him over to the receiving barn. Farley lingered and lingered, but the phone didn't ring and the footsteps did not come. Finally, he went to the saddling paddock alone. Limitless and Rafael were standing there in position five, calmly and alone. It was a good big race, eight colts and two fillies. Baffert had two in, Lukas had one, MacAnally had one. Owners were everywhere. Limitless stood quietly while being saddled, but on his toes, his ears flicking back and forth. Rafael held him while Farley pulled his forelegs out one at a time, then Farley held him while Rafael smoothed his tail and toweled his face again. His odds were down to two-to-one, and he was still the second favorite, after one of the Baffert entries.

The paddock judge stirred them up, and as Roberto approached, there were plenty of well-wishers and hopeful bettors leaning over the barriers. He threw Roberto onto the horse, and as Roberto picked up the reins, ever so delicately, Farley felt anticipation perk the colt up. He followed him under the stands. Both of the Baffert horses looked terrific. He went to a betting window and bet five dollars for Mr. Tompkins. He saw as he came up the stairs to his box that the horses and their ponies were trotting. Limitless's pony was hard put, as always, to keep up with his big trot.

She was sitting in her usual seat, and when he came up to her and sat down, she put her arms around him under his jacket and laid her cheek upon his chest. He put his hand on her head and pressed it into himself, and they sat like that until the horses were in the starting gate. Then, because it was a Grade One race, Limitless's first, they sat up and watched, but Farley held Joy's hand tightly in both of his.

The horses broke evenly and well, and around the first turn, Limitless and General Challenge settled together in the back of the field, which was not good for either one of them, since both preferred to dog it alone while the front horses spent themselves. But now they were pushing each other; and they both had so much speed that they could not help moving up on the main group. Farley glanced over at Baffert, who had his binoculars pressed to his face. Down the backstretch, the two horses simply mowed down the company in front of them, matching stride for stride. Through his own binoculars, Farley could see that McCarron had the big chestnut gelding on a tight hold, while Roberto had Limitless nearly on a loose rein. It was impossible to know what Limitless's reserve was, but General Challenge seemed to have plenty. Into the second turn, they were just behind the two leaders, who were both on the rail, one about a length in back of the other. Farley saw Limitless pull out to go wide and he said, "I think Roberto's forgotten who he's racing against."

Joy said, "Limitless doesn't care."

The other horse stuck to him as if tethered and they went around the second horse and took aim on the first. Farley saw Roberto glance at McCarron, and then he saw McCarron ask the big gelding for a little more. They were at the first horse's shoulder, nose to nose, stride for stride. They hit the eighth pole. Limitless's reins were flapping, and Roberto had his hands in the horse's mane. McCarron lifted his left hand with the whip in it. The jockey of the number-one horse had already whipped the animal twice, and he raised his arm again. At that moment, Limitless switched leads, flattened, pinned his ears, and pulled away from the other two. He crossed the finish line a neck in front. Farley ran down to the track, taking no chances and pulling Joy with him.

There was nothing like a Grade One stakes win to set things right. A little serotonin and a few endorphins always cleared your head and made you see that whatever you were thinking that was dark and fearful, well, that was wrong—enlightening, perhaps, in some way, but a divergence from the truth. Everything about a Grade One stakes win was reassuring, from the look on the horse's and the jockey's faces of excited accomplishment to the smiles in the grandstand to the shouts of congratulation as you lined up for the win picture. After the excitement, there was the pleasurable moment in the test barn when the horse stretched his hind legs back, lifted his tail slightly, dropped his penis, and urinated into the jar, and then there was the afterglow of the walk back to the barn, the various ministrations of bathing, walking, wrapping, massaging, through which you demonstrated to the horse what a good job he had done and how grateful you were for him and to him. Farley had a rule—never talk about or listen to any fantasizing about future races—no dreams allowed. This win, whatever it was, was good enough to enjoy right now. And so, thanks to Limitless, Farley found himself sitting up in bed at about two in the morning, wide awake, holding Joy against his chest, feeling her warm and affectionate softness. They had been asleep, and had coasted back up to consciousness. She said, "You know, sometimes I find the State of California personally overwhelming."

Farley laughed.

"I love your voice," she said.

"I know you do."

"My mother said that I wanted to die, but right now it doesn't seem like it was as true as that, that it was more like a pretense. Or like I was substituting something fake for something real that I couldn't remember. I just couldn't remember."

"What?"

"This. I couldn't remember this. I couldn't remember how to feel your presence."

"Do you feel it now?"

"Yes."

"Me, too."

"That's enough, then," she said.

AUGUST

68 / SELF-IMPROVEMENT

THE REASON R. T. Favor never got Justa Bob and Doc's Big Juan back to the track was that he had this accident with his truck where he went off the road one night on the way home from a bar, and even though it was no big deal, he just ran it into the ditch, it got caught up on a stump or something, and he couldn't rock it off, so he couldn't get it out of the ditch, so then he did something that really had him laughing, he got his shotgun off the rack in the back window, and he shot the damn truck in the driver's-side door, blam blam, the thing was dead, that's what made him laugh, that the engine was dead and so he shot it, and it was dead in two ways. Just a joke, a pun, harmless, but there was this sheriff's deputy who lived in a house nearby (wouldn't you know it?) and he woke up and came out, and even though R.T. knew he hadn't shot the truck more than a couple of times, the fucker gave him one of those blood tests that you get when you piss some cop off for no reason, and what happened after that was R.T. ended up in jail! R.T. had noticed in the past that he never met up with a cop who wasn't in a bad mood, and then they look at your record and it all starts over again.

It was August, and so the owner of the stable, whose name was Angel Smith, was keeping an eye on the horses, even though all the boarders did their own work. You couldn't let them run out of water, that just caused you yourself more problems, so he made sure R.T.'s horses had water, and then, the next day, he gave them some of his own hay, because they had nothing in front of them. The day after that, he did the same thing. Well, the day after that, R.T. finally came out there. He'd been out of jail for a couple of days, but he'd been feeling a little under the weather from the whole experience, and, besides, his truck was impounded for non-payment of parking fines, and it wasn't easy to get out to the stable. When he got there, no one was around, and he looked and saw that someone was watering the horses and giving them some hay, and then he turned around and walked away. His conscience was clear. If they were being taken care of in his absence, then, well, that was that. R.T. was getting tired of Texas, anyway. It was hot. His truck never would have gotten him any-where else, but his thumb could. So he walked out to the road and stuck it out, and pretty soon he had himself a ride, and the fact was that he would be some-where far away by the time of his court date, and that was an old habit that had stood him in good stead over the years.

After a few more days, Angel noticed that R.T. hadn't shown up in a week now, so he approached Lex about picking up R.T.'s board bill and taking care of the horses, but Lex respectfully declined, so, while he was deciding what to do with the two animals, whom he called "Amigo" and "Frank," he put them in a pen together so that he could rent out the stalls. The pen was about twenty by twenty, wire mesh. It was in the lee of the barn, facing the road, and had some shade at noon from the overhang, and in the afternoon from the barn it-self. The footing was the same as the driveway—hardpan. There was a shallow depression in the middle of it that filled with water during storms. It was not comfortable to lie down in, but that wasn't what bothered Justa Bob. It was one thing to have Doc's Big Juan in the next stall, putting his head through the window. A large grassy pasture would have been even better than that. But in a twenty-by-twenty-foot pen, Justa Bob found that he had no place he could call his own. The old man just threw the hay over the top, so that it landed in one spot. Justa Bob really didn't care for eating what was already scanty enough in close proximity to another gelding, and so their friendship came under some pressure. There were squeals and bites and kicks. For his part, Doc's Big Juan felt much the same way, that good fences make good neighbors. And he was a little younger and quicker than Justa Bob, so he managed to avoid injury, while also laying one on the other horse from time to time. Soon Justa Bob had three good bites—one on his haunches, one on his neck, and one on his back. For his part, he had managed to kick Doc's Big Juan in the knee, which swelled up. The barn owner thought that, compared with some he'd put in the pen, they were doing okay and would get used to one another.

IT WAS ALSO HOT in Maryland, where Epic Steam, now known as "Sud-den Intuition" or "Toots," continued to hold solitary court in his own two acres of grassy pasture. Ellen took care of him herself, and everyone else had strict instructions to leave him alone. It was an old cowboy trick for taming a bad actor. The first thing you did was isolate the horse from all social contact with horses or people. For a week, she didn't even get out of her truck to feed him, but threw supplementary hay over the fence as she drove past. When he was lonely enough, he would greet her, and, sure enough, on the seventh day he did—he nickered at her. She immediately got out of the truck and went over to the fence, threw in the hay, and spoke to him kindly, but only briefly, and she didn't attempt to touch him. The next morning, he was standing at the gate looking for her. She threw most of the hay over the fence, and spoke to him again, but this time she showed him a carrot, and then dropped it onto the hay. When he approached it and ate it, she spoke to him again, in a calm, friendly, but not fawning voice. Then she got in the truck and drove off. For the rest of the day and night, some twenty-three hours and forty minutes, Toots was alone.

Having achieved his lifelong goal of separating himself from the company of tedious and punishing humans, Epic Steam did not now know quite what to do with himself. He trotted and galloped around the pasture, reared, squealed, bucked, and played. He kicked the fence, sometimes repeatedly, as always enjoying the sound of the impact. Often he stood in one spot or another, alertly listening to the sounds of horses and other creatures that came to him on the breeze. There were storms, an uncomfortable novelty since he had no shelter, so he got wet and windblown. He grazed. The grass was delicious, and there were plenty of other little plants that he sampled by the way, as he did the bark of the trees in the pasture, but not the fencing, since he didn't care for the sting of the electric wire that ran along the top board. He dozed. He slept, most often in the heat of the afternoon rather than at night. With only himself for entertainment, he got a little dull, and then a little duller. He experienced the ebbing of testosterone as the ebbing of a certain kind of frustration, but that was a slow process, for his testicles had been quite well developed and part of his problem all along had been their efficiency in promoting his masculinity.

Toward dawn one morning he had what could only be called an idea. He was standing in the corner of the pasture closest to the woods. Though the leafy hickories and oaks and hackberries hid his view of the other horses, they did not interfere too much with either their scent or their sounds—he often heard them whinnying, and often whinnied back to them and they back to him. Now he trotted over to the fence and pressed his chest against the gate. The gate gave a little bit, which was encouraging. He pressed against the gate again, and it gave again, because the chain holding it was loosely snapped. Now he trotted away from the gate and then back to it, butting it with his chest. He liked the play in it. It gave him hope. So he tried it again, this time from a bit greater distance. He was a bully and strong—it came naturally to him to push things down. Part of his problem with people was that they were always yelling at him and poking him when he crowded them. He'd had elbows in the ribs countless times, handles of mucking forks and shovels, the occasional hoofpick, a twitch handle. So, for the third time, he trotted away from the gate, intending to come at it again and hit it a little harder this time. He made a circle.

But, standing back from it, he saw something else about it—that the space beyond it was just like the space in front of it—grassy and open. The gate itself had a bar running across the bottom, right along the ground, and a well-defined bar along the top, and three bars in between, about a foot apart. You could, he realized, look over it, through it, at it. It was not, he realized, a wall. He trotted toward it, then he turned and trotted back toward the middle of the pasture, then he turned toward it again, picked up a canter, and did the obvious thing—he jumped out of his pasture.

Later, when everyone realized what had happened, no one was surprised. He was a young athletic horse, his pedigree riddled with Nearco and Nasrullah blood. Damascus, Raja Baba, Blue Larkspur, all the Thoroughbred jumping lines. The gate was only four and a half feet high, and he was a seventeen-hand horse. Nor was Epic Steam surprised. It took him only once to find out that jumping came naturally to him, that once you could jump you could not be confined, that four and a half feet was easy for him, and that once you were in the habit of jumping out of pastures there was no end to the havoc you could wreak.

The first thing he did after congratulating himself upon his escape was to trot through the trees and investigate the other pastures and paddocks. Of course the other horses were much enlivened by the sight of him—he so obviously was out of bounds. He riveted their attention and distracted them from the daily wait for morning hay and grain. Soon he had them all galloping about. Also, since he was a troublemaker by nature, he visited with all of them over their fences, and issued various challenges having to do with dominance and masculinity. And all of them were ready to take up these challenges. He was a new horse. Every horse in the herd had some sort of instant opinion of him. And there were so many horses turned out on these summer nights that he had plenty to keep him busy.

It was by now about seven-thirty, and all would have been fine if it hadn't been Sunday morning, when Ellen's feed girl gave herself an extra half-hour in the sack. She was asleep in the apartment above the barn, with the windows closed and the air conditioner on high. Just as she turned over, glanced at the clock, and decided to allow herself another fifteen minutes, Epic Steam was deciding to try that jumping thing again, and within seconds he was just where he had wanted to be for so very long, in a paddock with four mares. Something this exciting for the four mares hadn't happened in years, so they stood stock-still, ears pricked, tails up, staring at him. He took this as encouragement, and lifted his own tail, arched his neck, and progressed in a beautiful *passage* around the perimeter of the pasture, picking his feet up as quick and high as if the ground were strewn with hot coals. All the horses in every other pasture looked on and occasionally whinnied encouragement. After displaying himself to his own satisfaction, Epic Steam lowered his head and snaked it toward one of the mares, a little bay. He approached her. She moved away, toward the other mares, and he paused, but then approached again. Manners do not come naturally to a young stallion, and did not come naturally to Epic Steam in any event. Her retreat aroused some of his inherent aggression, and he went after her. He thought he might bite her. Intent upon this thought, he did not pay attention to his position relative to the other mares, and so did not realize until it was already happening that they were kicking the stuffing out of him.

At this point, the feed girl got up, yawned, went into the bathroom, peed, and brushed her teeth. Then she found her jeans and paddock boots, a T-shirt, and a Diet Coke. She put on her baseball cap that was hanging by the door, and went down the stairs. First she went into the barn, and noticed that the stalled horses seemed a little restless. She fed them, which took about fifteen minutes. Then she loaded up the feed and hay into the bed of the farm pickup, pulled it out of the feed shed, and headed toward the back of the property, past the arenas and the first turnout. She stepped instinctively on the gas when she saw that almost all of the pastured horses were trotting around. Her first thought was that a pack of dogs had gotten into one of the paddocks, which had happened once, and she felt that adrenaline rush of fear. But there was no barking. Only over where those mares were—

And there he was, the great Epic Steam, his intuition having failed him, standing in the corner of the pasture by the gate, his head down. The mares were grazing peacefully, having seen the threat and dealt with it. The feed girl didn't know whether to call Ellen first or to try to get the horse out first—he was a dangerous animal, she knew. But then she went up to the gate, and he looked so forlorn that she took one of the halters hanging there and went inside. He put his head in the halter, and, with the mares looking on with interest, she led him, limping, out of the gate and down the path, back to his own peaceful spot on the other side of the woods. She spoke to him kindly and pityingly, and he didn't mind it.

WILLAM VANCE DECIDED to give up on finding Justa Bob. The Jockey Club gave out information only on who had owned a horse for his last start, and that was William himself. The new owner hadn't started him again in six months. That was a bad sign—all William could think that that meant was that the evidence of lameness that he remembered was pretty bad—a bowed tendon most likely. What he imagined was that the new owner had him at a farm somewhere, rehabbing him. If it had been six months, then the horse could come back anytime, so he could turn up, but the national racing magazines only gave the results of stakes races, and Justa Bob was a claimer. William began to lose hope, to pay less attention to the whole deal, but his conscience still ached every time he walked into his office and saw those eight photofinish win pics, sometimes with Justa Bob on the outside, sometimes with Justa Bob on the inside, always with his head down and stretched, his nostril flared. Short of going down there and asking around, he had done his best, he thought. Probably he should just put it out of his mind.

AUDREY OPENED THE DOOR of her closet, took out her suitcase, and laid it on the floor of her room. Then she went over to the dresser and reached into the top drawer, took out a pair of pink underpants, and unrolled them. Inside them was the key to her suitcase. She unlocked the suitcase. Out of that she took a ratty teddy bear, Arnold. His back seam was open. She stuck two of her fingers into the bear's stuffing and felt the edges of the money, a nice wad, the three thousand dollars she had won hitting a twenty-to-one long shot that Deirdre had told her had no breeding, no record, no speed, and no hope when they'd gone to Pimlico for the last day of the meet. On the other hand, he was gray, so she bet him anyway, and now she had enough money to buy a horse, and, more than that, her mother's permission. She pushed the money back into the teddy bear, locked the teddy bear in the suitcase, hid the suitcase in the closet and the key in her underwear. She was thirteen and going into ninth grade, old enough to put her money in the bank, as her mother had pointed out, but having the money in her room felt like having the horse, whoever he or she was, very close at hand.

A car horn beeped, and Audrey looked out the window of her bedroom. It was Deirdre's sedan. Audrey grabbed her helmet off the bed and ran for the front door, not forgetting to shout good-bye to her mother as she slammed out. As soon as she was in the car, Deirdre began. "Now, Audrey," she said, "I have been shamed into taking you on this jaunt on the score that I have nothing better to do, which is not exactly true, but true enough. My own purpose is to make sure that you don't get on anything your own grandmother couldn't ride and to talk you out of every animal either on the grounds of conformation or on the grounds of temperament."

"Thank you." Audrey was serene in the assurance that they would find something at either the first or the second barn.

"Have you ever haggled for anything, darlin'?"

"You mean, tried to talk the price down?"

"I do indeed."

"No."

"Well, I hate to lay this curse upon you, Audrey, but you are a natural horsewoman, who can read the *Form,* place a bet, pull a shoe, and jump a triple combination. If that is your fate, then you're bound to be broke unless you can buy them cheap and sell them dear."

"I don't want to sell him. I want to buy him."

"Your horse is not your boyfriend, Audrey. If you want to learn what they have to teach you, then you must let them come and go, and always make a profit out of the back end."

"Okay," said Audrey, a little deflated. She saw that they were almost to the turn of Marshville Road. That was where the first two prospects were. She put on her helmet. They turned down the gravel road, and Audrey thought, This is it. We are almost there. I am going to see him very soon. She saw that every fencepost and telephone pole and flying bird was very significant. They went over a hill and there was the barn, red and white, and he was in there, probably already standing in the crossties. She bounced up and down in her seat. They turned into the parking lot and pulled up to a sign that said "Riders Park Here." Here he had been living. These were familiar scenes to him. Every day, he would walk out of the barn and across this very parking lot to the jumping ring. He was thirteen years old (both of the geldings they were planning to see here were thirteen years old).

But in fact he wasn't here. The horses shown to her were heavy and dull, just horses. One was brown and one was chestnut. She tried to be enthusiastic about the chestnut, but when she got on him, his gaits were choppy and hard to ride. The brown didn't even jog sound, and Deirdre said to the owner, "This one needs a vet, darlin'. He's got heat in his foot and a digital pulse," and that was that.

That was that all day. They looked at ten, she rode six. In addition to the one with choppy gaits, there was one with only one eye, one who couldn't switch leads behind at the canter, one who bucked and spun when he passed other horses in the arena, one with an ugly head, and one who was very big and jerked her right out of the saddle about every three minutes.

As they drove away from the last barn, Audrey said to Deirdre, "You guys made a plan to teach me a lesson."

"Did we, now?"

"Yes. You took me out to see all these horses because you knew I wouldn't want to buy any one of them."

"I suspected, yes. But, Audrey, these are horses in your price range. The unfortunate circumstance here is that you don't ride in your own price range."

"That one was okay. He just had an ugly head. He had nice gaits and he jumped well."

"Yes, he did. But, you know, you want to be glad to see that face every morning, not be saying, 'He's fine enough but he's got a head like a coffin without handles.' Believe it or not, someone is going to come along who thinks that's a pretty head, or a handsome head, or a head with character. That's the one who should own that fellow."

"I need to win some more money."

"That's when you don't win it, when you need to. You keep that cash in your sock or wherever you've got it, and your horse will turn up."

"How about a horse off the track?"

"We'll see."

That night, Audrey wrote a letter to Miss Joy Gorham, at the Tompkins Ranch. It read,

Dear Joy Gorham,

You don't remember me, but one time I wrote to you, and you rescued a horse that I had taken care of in Texas. His name was *Terza Rima, and you wrote me back about him. I hope he is still healthy and happy. Since that time, I have learned to ride and also learned to bet, and I now have some money to buy a horse. Since you live on a big studfarm and racing farm, I wonder if there is anything there that might be appropriate for me. I am a good enough rider so that I teach lessons at my barn. I show hunters, three feet and three-six. I won seven blue ribbons in equitation this year. I am about five foot four and I weigh about 115 pounds. I have three thousand dollars to spend. I would give a horse a very nice home.

Yours truly,
Audrey Schmidt
1245 Hopewell Drive
Morristown, Maryland

She enclosed a picture of herself on Moses, taking a very flowery three-foot-six oxer at an A show. That pony was for sale. Ellen expected to get forty thousand dollars for him. She sealed the envelope, gave it a little kiss, and put it in the mailbox. Then she did what her mother was always telling her to do, she tried to forget about it.

WHAT WITH THE TRIP to Kauai and going through the galleys of the first volume of her three-volume *Spiritual Housework: An Astrolabe for the Next Millennium,* and overseeing her investment experiment, which meant being in constant communication with Mr. T. (so far, the return on her investment in the commodities market was running at about 23 percent annually, while the return on her investment in the Hollywood Park market was running at about 22 percent), Elizabeth was rather overextended. Even so, she had time to notice that someone was falling in love with her, and that someone was Mr. Kyle Tompkins, owner of Tompkins Racing and everything else in the entire world. One of the things that Elizabeth had discussed at length in her work was the future of monogamy. Monogamy, she pointed out, had a very checkered past, and at the beginning of the present millennium was purely a property arrangement. Whatever one's theory of male sexuality, she went on to say, it only seemed to fit intermittently and with unease into monogamous marriage. When women were not tied down by pregnancy and child-rearing, there was much evidence to support the notion that they were not monogamous, either. Her own experience, which she related in detail, demonstrated that developing one's sexuality took discipline, focus, money, and time, and should not be considered the recourse of mere idleness. Thus it was that she had an entire theoretical framework in which to fit the fact that Kyle Tompkins was married, and not only married, but California married, which meant that impulsive or passionate actions on his part would have many tedious legal ramifications and could dislocate a significant number of innocent members of the working class, shifting the wealth that was now filtering down to them in an orderly fashion into the coffers of the parasitic legal class, who were, even in quiet times, always circling the Tompkins fortune like moths about a lightbulb.

Which was not to say that Elizabeth was unaware of the fact that Kyle Tompkins' wife was forty-two years old, whereas she, Elizabeth Zada, was sixty-two years old, that Mrs. Tompkins was and had been all her life a beauty, whereas she, Elizabeth Zada, had graduated from a plain childhood to a gawky adolescence and thence, to the outspoken relief of her mother, to the best wifehood that she had been able to manage at the time, to Nathan-may-he-rest-in-peace-in-spite-of-all-those-animals-he-murdered-as-a-furrier Zada, no prize himself. Her passion with Plato was a project joyously conceived and carried out with relish, but the fact was that never had she aroused actual longing in any man until now, and it had a potent effect upon her. When she opened her e-mail every day to the compositions of Kyle Tompkins, it was with anticipation rather than disapproval. Nor had she as yet shown them to Plato, though he would have plenty to say about them, for he was always eager to exploit his interpretive skills.

Plato was ready for marriage and fatherhood. Elizabeth had been telling him this for several months now. He was thirty-three and secure in his vocation. Though his tendency to theorize at length might not be every woman's cup of tea, he had plenty of money, plenty of self-knowledge, lively convictions, habits of kindness and patience. If he was not as well prepared for domestic life as any man in America, Elizabeth couldn't imagine who was, and Plato was inclined to agree. They had done well together, but a change was in the wind, and Elizabeth was preparing to add a chapter to volume two *(Twin Suns: Relationships in the New World)* called "So Let Us Melt Us: How to Choose to Flow Apart."

Kyle Tompkins was a man her own age. He had actual memories of Elvis. He had seen *Rebel Without a Cause* in the theater. He wrote, "I want you." It made her feet cramp to read it. He knew enough to woo her with desire rather than money, looks, intelligence, accomplishments, or promises of good times. She did not delete it, but clicked "keep as new." And every time she looked at it, it did seem new. At last she went out of her Internet server, put down her mouse, and got up from the desk.

In his office, Plato had his jeans off, his head back against his chair, and his hand in his shorts. She said, "Hi, honey. May I talk to you for a second?"

"Of course."

She went over to him and knelt beside his chair, and put her own hand into his shorts, covering his. He had a nice erection, but he was only casually stroking it. She kissed his paunch. He put his other hand on her hair. He said, "What's up?"

"Is our critique of monogamy a felt thing or a theoretical thing, do you think?"

"I think the best way to look at that is to observe how many rules there are that maintain monogamy. The more rules there are, then the more the institution enforced is a social convenience rather than a natural impulse. Look at capitalism, for example. Capitalism is based on the natural impulse of greedy self-interest. It functions robustly without rules—all the rules exist to limit and contain its functioning. But without rules, habits, and customs, monogamy doesn't function at all."

"But how do we feel about it?"

He looked at her, then said, "I think we understand the relationship between freedom and jealousy, in that, if we view love and affection as a zero-sum endeavor, then what someone else has of one of us, that is what the other of us has lost. On the other hand, if we view love and affection as a self-creating and renewing endeavor, not bound by concepts of scarcity, then any love that accrues to either one of us accrues to both."

"In what sense are we using the word 'love'?"

"I think we agree that love is not a feeling in the same way that, say, sadness, gladness, desire, anger, and fear are, but, rather, a condition of existence that each individual has greater or lesser tolerance for, depending upon what he associates from his past with feelings of attachment. We've seen ourselves that past associations can be removed from the concept of love, thus raising our tolerance for its condition much higher than we think possible."

"Mr. Tompkins wants me."

"You sound surprised."

"I am, a little."

"Well, look at it this way. Mr. Tompkins is accustomed to indulging in a taste for the unusual. You are certainly the most unusual woman in his circle right now. It's not surprising that he should locate you as the next venue for a habitual pattern of behavior. Or, dear, you can look at it this way. You are a fine piece of ass, and it shows, and any guy who can see it is a wise man."

She put her arms around him and nestled her face into his neck. He said, "When we find ourselves entering into a transitional period, the support of intimate friends is an invaluable consolation, because it encourages us to create new neural pathways and new patterns of pleasure-redundancy."

She said, "I know that, honey, but thanks for reminding me." They looked square at each other, both knowing from their training that this was a preliminary biological and cultural signal that some form of sexual activity was acceptable to both of them. Elizabeth licked her lips, another signal. Plato's hand moved inside his shorts, and Elizabeth saw it. She inhaled sharply, and then they both moaned, closed their eyes, and slowly cocked their hips. They were well trained. Desire leapt up instantly, hot and full. Elizabeth closed her eyes, and Plato leaned forward and kissed her lightly but lingeringly on the lips, nothing hungry or sudden, but slow and then slower, inducing a state of both mental and physical concentration. Elizabeth put her hand over his. His erection, now firm, long, and thick, had its usual Skinnerian effect upon her. Having never suffered anguish in her relationship with Plato, having never known anything from him but kindness and care, she had no past references to restrict her response to his manifest desire. (She had written about this in her book.

"The penis," she wrote, "should not be asked to lift the burden of repeated un-kindnesses from the relationship. Grievances dealt out and endured are the surest route to impotence.") She felt her nipples rise. "Mmmm," said Plato.

"Ahh," said Elizabeth. She stretched out on the Oriental carpet.

DOWN IN TEXAS, Angel Smith's grandson asked him if there was a horse he could ride. Angel got out Justa Bob, put an old bridle on him with a long shanked bit, and threw the boy up. He walked him around and around the arena, kicking him in the sides when he wanted to stop and practicing various moves. Pretty soon, he was turning around in circles as they walked, riding backward, lying down on the horse's croup. He must have had him out for three hours, which was a good thing, because the horse had been developing a stress-related impaction colic, and the movement relieved both the stress and the impaction. Angel told the boy if he would come out every day and ride the horse he could be his. The boy said that he would, but vowed to himself that trotting, a jolting gait hard to sit and easy to fall off of, was out of the question.

IN MARYLAND, Epic Steam, or Sudden Intuition, had decided to allow Ellen to hose and doctor the gashes and bruises the mares had given him. He even let the vet drain the hematoma on his chest. He stood quietly, his head down, without a shank over his nose or a tranquilizer in his system. Ellen said, "When he feels better, he's going to go back to being a bad boy, but I don't mind giving him a taste of kindness while we can."

IN CHICAGO, William Vance's son, who normally had no interest in horses at all, said, "I'll help you."

IN CALIFORNIA, Audrey Schmidt's letter was put in Mr. Tompkins' box, because Joy's forwarding-address card at the post office had expired.

ALSO IN CALIFORNIA, Elizabeth Zada e-mailed Mr. Tompkins to say that she considered "friendship" to be a large relationship category, into which all sorts of behaviors naturally fell, and that she certainly felt considerable friendship for Mr. Tompkins.

SEPTEMBER

69 / BIG TIME

BUDDY CRAWFORD had 110 horses in his stable now, and was more successful than he had ever been. He had fifty at Hollywood Park, thirty at Santa Anita, and another thirty at Del Mar for the Del Mar meet. His win percentage was up around 20 percent, and the press interviewed him almost as often as they interviewed Baffert. He wasn't a funny guy like Baffert, but they always said he "is peppery and straightforward," "pulls no punches," "tells it like it is." Everyone was eager for Residual to get back from the farm and back into training. In her absence, she had gone back to being a great filly—one of the best if not the best of a great crop of fillies, obviously the kind to mature into a terrific four-year-old. Real racing men were always connoisseurs of the older horse, unlike the Derby-crazed general public. Look at Kelso. Look at Forego. Look at Cigar. Look at Stymie. Unlike Secretariat, they were revered by men who knew something about horses and racing, something more than pretty pictures.

His staff had grown. Leon had the horses out at Santa Anita, and he had an assistant trainer of his own. Two guys he had hired from the East were watching over the horses at Hollywood Park while he was running the ones at Del Mar, but even so, there was a lot of driving that San Diego–Pasadena–Inglewood triangle. He had not only his cellular but his car phone, in case someone should be trying to get in touch with him while he was talking to someone else, and the car phone was attached to a fax machine. He also got an assistant assistant, Lanai her name was, whose only job was to drive with him and answer the phone in the car and tell him who it was, so that he could choose who he needed to talk to more, the one on the cellular or the one on the car phone.

As a result, he was sleeping like a log, which was the best thing to happen to him in thirty years.

One thing that he had gotten over was the notion that he had to know much about all of these horses he had, including their names and breeding. So he kept in his mind the names and breeding of the most expensive ones—the Mr. Prospectors and the Deputy Ministers and the Unbridleds, whose owners were the most likely to demand results. He let the assistants keep track of the others. He also had gotten rid of all his claimers. If you were driving and flying somewhere all the time, then you couldn't keep an eye on everyone's horses in the same way that was natural when you were out in the trainers' stand every day, and so for Buddy claiming had become a game played blind and for not very high stakes, not worth it anymore. Buddy felt the loss, though, especially since he didn't feel very comfortable in the constant company of the rich, the well-educated, the well-born, and the essentially non-horsey.

In spite of what they all agreed about Residual, the filly didn't excite him all that much anymore. Finally, her career had so many ups and downs and strange events that he had backed off from her in some way. Still, it would be nice to get the filly back from the farm so he could put her back into training. She had a whisker of a chance to get to the Breeders' Cup, and if she got there, she had a pretty good chance to win it, since the distance was right for her, and her times were consistently as good as the best who Buddy suspected would get there.

Buddy had never spoken to the girl vet who did the surgery, and had not taken the occasion to use her again. Sometimes he saw her around and he didn't really acknowledge her. So she recommended 120 days off. His own vets, who hadn't seen the symptoms, the X-rays, or the surgery, didn't have much to say about the whole thing. A hundred twenty days out of training was standard, ninety was okay in certain circumstances, and sixty? Well, there were trainers who brought horses back into training sixty days after a chip surgery. No one had done, say, a follow-up study to show that breakdowns occurred more or less frequently, but the anecdotal evidence, well—

She looked good. Her coat was all shined up again, she was in good flesh, her eyes were bright, and her manner was alert. Well oxygenated, as always. It was nine weeks to the Breeders' Cup. If the filly trained well, it was marginally enough time to get her there. That was another reason to bring her back to the track—the longer she languished out of work, the less fit she would become, and the longer it would take to get her back into racing fitness. Buddy had never been a big believer in letting the horses down. They were Thoroughbreds—they thrived on work and running. It was a mental thing. If they couldn't do what they were bred to do and enjoyed doing, then they got restless and developed vices. A chip was a chip, not a fracture or something like that. It was something that broke off, not something that broke. What was left was perfectly fine. Well, there were all sorts of reasons to bring her back, and not many reasons not to, but even so, he was glad Deedee was riding again and that Marvelous Martha had packed up her bags and her opinions and returned north. Marvelous Martha had lots of opinions and couldn't be intimidated, it seemed like. Buddy didn't want her back, so he even did Deedee the favor of putting the horse in Arcadia, close to home, so that Deedee could bring the baby, ride the horse, and go home.

The first morning, when the groom tacked her up and Deedee took her out to the training track just to walk around for a while, she bucked and crow-hopped all over the place, which she had never done, and which gave Deedee to think of her new responsibilities as a mother, but then she settled down in her usual way, and anyway, she was never a dirty bucker or a dirty spooker, sneaky or determined to dump the rider. She was just happy and energetic and reactive. When she had quit bucking, she walked around alertly, with big steps, but relaxed, too, just the way Deedee liked her. It did seem vaguely to Deedee that the filly had had a surgery and was coming back rather quickly, but she decided that Buddy would know best, and anyway, many sleepless nights and sleepy days had compromised her sense of time. As they were walking around, Deedee reflected happily that the filly felt fine and she, Deedee, was glad to get back to work, too, especially since Buddy was being so accommodating about Alana Marie. When all was said and done, the thing she had been afraid and annoyed about, missing the big time, hadn't happened at all. The big time was yet to come, and she was right there for it. Everything had worked out all right in the end. And Buddy had told her that, when she was ready to ride a few more, he had some good ones for her, some easy rides on class horses, and there was nothing wrong with that. All in all, she thought as she rode the filly back to the barn, things were about as fine as they had ever been for her. She was married, employed, still riding horses, and not even close to being a waitress at McDonald's out in Bakersfield, where her parents now lived.

The next day was Sunday, and Buddy told everyone that he was instituting a new policy with the Santa Anita horses, that on Sundays they didn't have to be at work until six. He didn't know if it was permanent, but he thought he would try it and see what happened. If it worked out okay and nothing got overlooked, then he would try it at Hollywood Park when all the horses moved back from Del Mar. There was no one who did not welcome this idea and think it was long overdue, and everyone remembered not to get up at 4:00 a.m. except Buddy himself, who was there as usual, wondering where the cars belonging to his staff were when he pulled into the parking lot at a quarter to five. Only Curtis Doheny was there, and when Buddy got out of his Lexus, Curtis got out of his Ford truck and came over to him.

About the only thing Buddy was not sure of was how to guarantee Curtis Doheny's silence. When Curtis had approached him in the early summer, he had been in a different mood, hadn't really thought about that part of it, had been swept along by Curtis' enthusiasm. Before her last pre-surgery race, they had given the filly three shots of Epogen, Curtis' helpful suggestion. Surprisingly, Buddy had not known about Epogen. What happened was, Curtis Doheny had asked him one day if he remembered that colt that Brit trainer Colin Gallorette had had, that had won so many races back in the late eighties, before the guy went back to England and kind of disappeared. Buddy had said, "Yeah. That was about the only good horse that guy had."

"Well, you know what?"

"What?"

"That horse's owner's kid was some kind of long-distance bicyclist, and he persuaded the owner to try something all these other bicycle riders he knew were trying. Builds red blood cells nine ways."

"Geritol?" Buddy had said.

"Something that really works," said Curtis, "enhances the number of red blood cells, and carries more oxygen to the muscles, and the horse runs faster and longer. It's like a bigger heart."

"What does it do to the horse?"

"Nothing," said Curtis.

"Then why isn't everyone using it?"

"They will be, in ten years. It'll be just like Lasix."

Buddy had thought this was just the thing for Residual. It was not an item he put on the Kingstons' bill. Not, you might say, a currently legal item. She had run very well. He thought he could see a difference in her fractions—maybe only two-fifths of a second, but every fifth of a second was a length.

"How ya doing," Curtis said now, not a question. "That filly's back. You must be thinking Breeders' Cup or you would have left her on the farm another couple of months."

"Bad for 'em to let down." Buddy directed his steps toward his barn, and Curtis fell in beside him. Buddy remembered that he had given everyone an extra hour. Why had he done that? It was far better to get up every morning at the same time, no matter what. Curtis Doheny was a big, fat, awkward man, and Buddy never liked how he loomed over him. It made Buddy feel like something was going to fall, that something was Curtis, and maybe he would fall on Buddy.

"Is there something I can do for you this morning, Curtis?"

"I thought I'd have a look at that filly. See the outcome of the experiment, you know. Do a little science."

This, Buddy knew, was bullshit. What Curtis wanted was to be seen with people, even if there was no one around to see him. He said, "Curtis, right now, I think maybe you should go your way and I should go my way, and then maybe we'll get a cup of coffee later."

Curtis didn't take his suggestion, and came along after him, sort of flapping his feet and rolling along. The thing about Curtis, for Buddy, was that he always made him conscious of his own size, which was short and thin. Curtis pulled out a large handkerchief and loudly blew his nose. Then he said, congenially, "So—you got some good ones in the barn these days, Buddy. That's what everybody says."

"Then it must be true," said Buddy.

"Nah. I saw you had three winners down at Del Mar the other day, and two the next day."

This was common knowledge, so Buddy wondered where these platitudes were going.

"The thing is, I'm thinking of buying an interest in a couple of horses again. I'm back on my feet now, pretty steady, and I got some money to spend. You got any owners who are looking for a partner?"

"I might," said Buddy, disconsolately. The only hope of keeping Curtis quiet was keeping him isolated, or giving him partners who could speak no English. In southern California, those kind were few and far between.

"Yeah, I put together about two hundred grand."

Buddy's head had to swivel in Curtis' direction.

"No shit," said Curtis complacently.

"Why don't I take you to the sales in Keeneland next week and get you a couple of yearlings of your own, then?" said Buddy. This was a brilliant idea.

"Nah. I want to buy into a couple of better-class horses and not have to foot all the training bills myself. Makes more sense."

Yes, unfortunately, it did. Buddy decided to test the depth of Curtis' resolve. He said, "Have you talked to anyone else about this?"

"Nah. You got the best horses."

This was not in fact true. Several other trainers had horses that were as good as Buddy's or better. The other half of the sentence was "of all the crooked trainers." Buddy felt himself actually squirm. He said, "That's good saving, Curtis."

"Ah, I put together a couple of long shots, let's call it that." He laughed. Then he said, "So listen. I like this colt Fuzzy Minister. He's got a couple of wins. And that colt who just got back from a lay-up. Hickory Dickory. My bet is, he's hotter than a pistol."

Buddy saw right there where the ground lay. What he had assumed was an idle thought on Curtis' part was a well-conceived plan. The groups who owned these particular colts were large and convivial, on the young side, and not very knowledgeable. Curtis planned to get in with them for some reason still unclear—perhaps it was only to have friends and associates he could pal around with. He said, "I can ask if they're looking for more partners. You know, a group gets too big, and the winnings aren't much."

"But the horse gets syndicated and goes to stud and there you are."

"Those are two nice colts. Deputy Minister and A.P. Indy. Just what everybody wants."

"I think so, too. You see that article in *The Blood-Horse* in the spring? Said A.P. Indy was the top stallion in the world. You and me, we keep that guy running and winning, and we got it made. These guys who own him are going to kiss our feet. Looks like a sure thing to me."

"Curtis, you've been around the racetrack for twenty-five years or more. Don't you know that the only sure thing is that a sure thing is never a sure thing?"

"Hell," said Curtis, jovially.

What made Buddy especially leery of this deal that he now felt tightening around his neck like a noose was Curtis' well-known chattiness when he was drinking. The man would brag about anything if he had a drink or two under his belt and an ear in his vicinity. He said, "So. Let's talk about something else. How are you otherwise, Curtis?"

"Never been better."

A very bad sign.

One thing you needed if you were a crook, Buddy had always thought, was a well-developed sense of right and wrong. Without that, you couldn't keep track of your sins and keep them to yourself. That was one thing Jesus had done for him, shown him black and white. Now when he had a choice to make, he knew what it was. That was part of his new level of success, and also a sort of containment procedure for the sins he continued to commit. Since he was better able to keep track of them, he knew he could deal with them sometime in the future all in one fell swoop, you might say. When Curtis was in his cups, he had no sense of right and wrong at all, and would report everything he did, right or wrong, in the same semi-whining, eager-to-please tone of voice. Buddy cast about for a neutral question to ask, but Curtis had no wife or children. He had drinking or not drinking. Other than veterinary medicine, that had been his whole occupation as long as Buddy had known him.

"Say," said Curtis.

"Say what," said Buddy.

"I heard that you did some Jesus-freak thing."

"Oh, yeah?"

"Yeah."

Now the looming seemed larger than ever. Buddy said, "I had what they call a midlife crisis, I guess."

"Kind of a religious thing?"

"You might say that."

"So where are you now on that?"

"What do you mean?"

"Well, you know."

"I guess I think this is kind of a personal subject, Curtis."

"Well, yeah. I see that, but if you got it, flaunt it. That's what it says in the Good Book."

"It does?"

"Sure. It says that Peter denied Jesus three times. So I take that to mean that if you've got religion it's the same as Peter denying Jesus if you pretend that you don't."

"I've never heard you talk like this, Curtis."

"Oh, I know a lot of scripture." They were almost to the shedrow. The horses were looking for their morning hay. Some of them looked up as the two men approached. Buddy found his throat constricting at the idea of talking about his personal relationship with Jesus to Curtis Doheny, especially since Jesus had gotten a little remote in the last few months.

Curtis went over to Fuzzy Minister with a proprietary air. The colt was a beauty like his sire, blood bay with a perfect white stripe down his nose, a shining mahogany coat, and an elegant head. His dam was by Nijinsky, and he was a good example of the precept that the best racehorses were the best in every way—best-looking, best-tempered, best-bred, easiest to train. This was a precept that was often observed in the breach, but when you looked at a horse that had been a million-dollar yearling, like this one, it was nice to remember it. Curtis said, "Yeah, this is the best two-year-old in your barn. I fiddled around with racehorses before, you know. I had shares and claimed a few and all that, but this time I said to myself, Nothing but the best. I deserve nothing but the best."

Buddy wondered what the deserving part referred to.

"We gonna push this filly a little bit?"

We? "What?"

"Looking at that filly, I say go for it."

"Yeah." Buddy went into the feed room, and Curtis followed him to the doorway, where he stood, blocking the light and scratching his balls. He said, "You know, I could do a lot of work for you. I could work only for you. Who you got now? Barton? Couple others? Why don't you just employ me, and I'll just work for you. We can make a deal. I can work all three tracks for you. I think it's a good idea."

"Maybe."

"You got a lot of maybes today."

"Well, I don't feel I can make a decision on all this stuff right now." Buddy didn't really have anything he needed to do in the feed room, and what he had thought of as a refuge, he saw, had turned into a trap. Curtis continued to stand in the doorway, now with his feet more or less planted and his hands in his pockets. Buddy reckoned his height at about six three. That would make him ten inches taller than Buddy and maybe twice his weight. Buddy elected not to push his way out, but all the same felt a considerable urge to bend down and snake between the guy's legs. Instead, he said, "Somehow, Curtis, I feel that you are threatening me."

"You know, Buddy, we've been friends for a long time, and with all due respect for your intelligence, I've got to tell you that I am. Between you and me, I've got a lot of plans. I've had one of those midlife crises myself, just this summer, and what I came up with was that I deserve better. Better treatment, just in general a better life. And, you know, everyone knows that no one's going to give you what you haven't got the guts to go out and get for yourself, so I made up my mind to go out and get it, you know what I mean?"

"Yes, I do," said Buddy.

"So, Buddy, you're my first stop on this train. We've been friends a long time and we've done a lot of business. So, if I want to turn my life around, you're the obvious place to start. My bet is that we're going to be spending a lot of time together. What's your bet?" He smiled for the first time this morning, and Buddy noticed that his voice had lost that eager-to-please quality.

"I bet we are," said Buddy. For all the fact that Buddy knew that Curtis Doheny was a loser and maybe worse than that, that the man was ugly, damp, disheveled, gross, and did not seem at the moment to have his, Buddy's, best interests at heart, there was something, oh, don't you know, relaxing about being with him and going along with his program. Though Buddy wouldn't have thought of introducing him to any of his owners or of having a closer relationship with him twenty minutes ago, well, the fact was, why not? Curtis could be useful to him, but that was the least of it. And Curtis could hurt him, even physically, though that seemed unlikely. The fact was, it was kind of nice to be with someone who knew what he wanted. At least what he wanted was specific and clear. And he really seemed to want it. That was something, too, something to appreciate and observe. Buddy stepped up to Curtis and looked up at him. Behind him, he could see that the lights had gone on in the office, and that Danny and Raoul were heading down the shedrow, a couple of Diet Cokes in their hands. He said, "You know, Curtis, I'm sure we can work something out."

Curtis grinned pathetically, suddenly transformed from angry to happy, like a kid, Buddy thought. He stepped back. He said, "You know, Buddy, I don't mean to get that way. But let me tell you, things haven't been easy for me," and as they went out of the feed room and walked down the shedrow, Buddy saw that maybe this was to be his penance, on the principle that no kindness goes unpunished—to listen, hour upon hour, to Curtis' life story.

70 / PRÉ CATALAN

AFTER LIMITLESS WON the Del Mar Derby, Grade Two, nine fur-
longs on the turf course, and added $267,000 to his previous winnings,
Rosalind, who was there for the win, called Al, who was in Helsinki, and said,
"Honey, where are you going to be the first weekend in October?"

Al liked it that she had called him "honey," even though she often called
him "honey." He checked his virtual calendar and said, "I have a meeting in
Berlin on Friday evening, and one in London on Tuesday, but I haven't got a
plan for the weekend itself. Is he running that colt in the Breeders' Cup? I want
him to run that colt in the Bree—"

"How about Paris?"

"Ooh," said Al. "Are you making a date?"

"I am."

"Where are we staying?"

"How about the Georges Cinq?"

"Where are we eating?"

"Well, Sunday night at the Pré Catalan."

"Didn't we eat there once before? Isn't that quite a romantic eatery?"

"On our honeymoon."

"Did we have a honeymoon?"

"Yes, Al, we did. And maybe we're overdue for another one. But I thought
I would invite some friends to come along."

Al wondered if Rosalind had positive memories of their honeymoon.
There were those, he knew, who would doubt the very idea, but with Rozzy,
you never knew. He said, "Not too many, okay? And make sure I know them
all."

"I will."

"I leave it in your hands, honey. But you tell him—"

"I know what to tell him, Al." Her voice was very sweet, which reminded
Al, Another month of this and I'm done. It wasn't quite possible to know yet

how many men and women now unemployed or marginally employed would soon be making primally heavy and large metal objects in factories now being built by Alexander Maybrick Industries International, but when all was said and done and everyone had expressed their opinion about the Information Age and the shift from manufacturing to service industries and ascendancy of bioengineering over plain old engineering, large and heavy metal objects were still going to come in handy as long as people were intent upon reproducing themselves and then piling up air miles, land miles, sea miles. He had been home for sixteen days out of the last ten months. He had seen Rosalind four times, though he talked to her almost every day. Truth to tell, he could have been home more, he could have seen her more, but he had been trying it out, being without her. And when all of *that* was said and done, after she did something to you and you did something to her, and you were resentful and hurt and you had all these other feelings you couldn't quite name, what you had to decide was very simple—with her or without her? When you were thirty or forty, maybe without her seemed rather attractive. But when you were sixty-five, without her seemed like a life sentence, and a short one at that. So, he then thought, the horse could run on dirt and turf, sloppy and fast. So, he thought, the horse has won three-quarters of a million dollars in a couple of months. I'd like to see the damned animal race. I'd like to see the damned animal race in the Breeders' Cup. All well and good, but Al could hardly remember what the colt looked like. Bay, probably. Most of them were.

In the meantime, Rosalind was placing another call, from her hotel, the Ritz-Carlton in Pasadena, to Farley's office at Del Mar, where Farley was overseeing the morning's training. Rosalind said, "Well! Good morning! How is the star this beautiful day?"

"He's fine. Legs are ice cold, attitude is pleased and proud, but not arrogant."

"What does Elizabeth say?"

"Well, she says that, all things considered, he prefers the turf and what's next?"

"What are you thinking?"

"Well, there's something of a layoff until the Oak Tree meet. He can go back to the farm, though it seems a shame right at this point. Eight lengths over the best turf horses on the West Coast, and hardly breathing hard, is pretty fit—"

"Al has his heart set on the Breeders' Cup."

"That's a definite possibility, though with it at Gulfstream this year, I don't know. Racing in Florida sometimes comes as a shock to a California horse. One race in between—" said Farley, but while he was speaking, he got an entirely distinct, non-Breeders'-Cuppish tingle of anticipation. Maybe it was the tone of evident delight in her voice. He only had time to recognize that his heart was already pounding when she said, "I think I'll give a party in Paris the first weekend in October, three weeks from now. I think Limitless will be the guest of honor."

Farley didn't say anything. It was as if she had read his mind, but not his present mind, the mind that understood the exigencies of real life, that rather dreaded shipping the horse to Gulfstream, even for the Breeders' Cup. The mind she was reading was a mind he had given up sometime ago, that still thought anything was possible. He said, cautiously, "You know, Rosalind, the one American-raced horse ever to do anything in the Arc was Tom Rolfe, and he only finished fifth."

"Then there's nothing to lose. Besides, isn't Tom Rolfe somewhere in the horse's pedigree?"

"Tom Rolfe was Lake of the Woods' broodmare sire. He was a son of Ribot, who won the Arc twice. Lake of the Woods has Ribot on his sire's side, too."

"And Limitless's dam has all that other stuff."

"Yes, the Nasrullah and Hyperion and Mahmoud breeding. But the course at Longchamp is usually really deep in the fall—"

"Didn't he win that race in northern California on a soft course?"

"Yes, but there's also a long hill at the end of the race. It's very punishing—"

"The horse doesn't know how to be punished. He'll run his own race and we'll see what happens."

"It's a mile and a half."

"Well, what can happen? If he can get a distance, he can get a distance. Wasn't his broodmare sire a steeplechaser?"

"Yes. Bold Ruler's older brother, Independence."

"Don't steeplechasers have to get a distance?"

"Very much so."

"Well, then."

"Well, then."

She said she would be out later, and hung up. The Grand Prix de l'Arc de Triomphe! Farley had to sit at his desk awhile, his head spinning, before he could get up, go out, and tell the others.

THE HARDEST THING to do, Joy realized, was to maintain your routine. The first temptation was to move Limitless back to Santa Anita and start training him a little harder, thinking of that distance and that long hill before the finish line that American horses weren't used to and all the rest of it. But when the van came to pick the horse up two days after the race, as usual, Joy put him on it, and watched it head in the usual direction, back to the ranch. If the horse was used to a week at the ranch after a race, then a week at the ranch he should have. The second-hardest thing to do was to attend to business as if nothing were happening. In fact, nothing was happening. The Del Mar meet was ending, the horses were moving back to Santa Anita. The vast quantities of equipment that went with them had to be organized, cleaned, packed, loaded, and sent. And of course there were other arrangements to be made, too, but they were just arrangements. She got on the phone to the only travel agent she knew, Oliver's girlfriend, and she asked for four tickets to Paris, France, for September 28 to October 5, and one, for Roberto, the jockey, September 30 to October 3. Hortense, up at the ranch, had already told her that she would handle the arrangements for Mr. Tompkins, should he decide to go. And Limitless's groom, Rafael, and his hot walker, Lupe, would go with the horses on the horse jet.

Oliver's girlfriend said, "You're all going to Paris? How perfect."

"Farley has a horse running in a race there."

"Oliver's in sales now, you know."

"I heard that."

"Toyota sales."

"Really."

"He's doing very well."

"That's great."

"He sold twelve cars last month, including two Land Cruisers."

Joy had no way of telling whether this was doing well or not. The woman said, "Oh, God," and started to sniffle.

Joy said, "What's wrong?"

"I don't want him to be a car salesman."

"Maybe there's something else he could do—"

"Take Oliver back! I don't want to be married to a horse-trainer, either, but he wants to *be* a horse-trainer."

"I'll talk to Farley. We would need someone to manage the horses while we were gone."

And so she bought the tickets, and the girlfriend gave her a very good deal. Then she called Tex Sutton.

AT THE RANCH, they gave Limitless the biggest pasture there was, one of the ones set a little back toward the hills. It rolled a bit, the way pastures did in the East. Three days later, there was a freak rainstorm, two inches in four hours. Limitless galloped.

ONE NIGHT at the dinner table, with two of his older brothers there and three of their kids, and a nice pork stew with garbanzos that his mother had made sitting in front of them and Roberto thinking that he could eat maybe a garbanzo or a chunk of the pork, but not both, he said, "So, Dad, where is Paris, France, anyway?"

He wasn't quite sure what he meant by this. Certainly, he had heard of both Paris and France, in the same way he had heard of semiconductors and Bob Dole and DNA, while at the same time not knowing as much about any of these things as he did about riding racehorses, buying sports cars, and investing his winnings in mutual funds, which his father insisted upon. He was reaching for the serving spoon to the pork stew, but hadn't quite grabbed it yet when his father exploded into a torrent of Spanish, reached across the table, and knocked him out of his chair. While he was on the floor, his two brothers jumped up, grabbed his father, and sat him down again, the kids started crying, and then his mother said, in English, "I will not talk about this until you have apologized to Roberto, Huberto!"

"He should apologize to me!"

"For what?" And now she went into Spanish, and they had a furious argument that Roberto, whose English was better than his Spanish, couldn't quite follow, but he did notice that he was being referred to more than once as an ignorant, stupid, horse-riding idiot who would never make anything of himself in spite of all their efforts, and was this their reward after seven children, to hear that his son did not know where the most famous city in the world was?

This led to going into the back storeroom and finding all of Roberto's old school records, and then his grades for ninth grade, where they had taken world history, and according to the grade report, Roberto had gotten a B in the class both semesters, although, to be frank, he couldn't remember anything much about the class, even the teacher. But his father forgave him for not knowing where Paris, France, was in the present, since it appeared that he had known where it was at one time, before these damned horses drove everything out of his mind, and wasn't that always the way, and so his father made him a list of four places to go to, the Eiffel Tower, the Louvre, the Champs-Élysées, and Notre-Dame, and told him that he could not come back into the house without some proof of having visited these places while in Paris, and Roberto nodded and agreed, and family peace was restored. At the same time, it was also true that Roberto had eaten two big helpings of the pork stew while all of this was going on, and so, when he got up in the morning, he had gained a pound. But there was no racing, anyway.

LIMITLESS CAME BACK from the ranch, with no apparent loss of fitness or readiness to run. Joy had him out of his pen almost all the time she was at the track now, but that wasn't because of any plans they had. He was just so bursting with go that confinement was a torture to him. Thus it was that when Elizabeth wanted to talk to her she had to come to the track, which was okay, because she wanted to see Mr. T. in person, anyway, and thank him for some recent tips which would make it possible for her to do some important shopping during her own sojourn in the City of Light. She found Joy and the horse wandering around at the far end of the barn area. She gave Joy a hug, and got right to the point. She said, "Mr. T. raced at Longchamp."

"Yes, he did," said Joy. "He won two stakes there. What a good boy he was."

"He wants to go back."

Joy had a sinking feeling. She said, "You mean, to advise us? How does he know we are going?"

"When something is in your mind, it's available to him." Yes, thought Joy. Like refusing a jump or bucking. Why not this, too? "He just wants to go back. He keeps streaming me pictures of turf like I've never seen in California."

Joy assembled all the negatives as best she could. "It's thousands of dollars, and he's never been a part of Limitless's training routine like he was with Froney's Sis. I don't know that we can persuade the Maybricks to pay for something like that. Anyway, I gather they don't keep a lot of horses at Longchamp, so that means finding him a place in Chantilly, you know. And he's old. Travel like that is hard on a horse." Joy wasn't quite sure why this idea was getting more and more upsetting for her.

"He wants to go. If we're there for a few days I bet I can win his airfare back. Or, rather, he and I can."

Joy regarded Limitless, who was putting his nose under the fence and trying with his upper lip to reach a tuft of grass. She said, with glum certainty, "He wants to stay there."

"He's not saying that. He doesn't understand time. But returning to the scenes of childhood is always a powerful impulse, maybe even for horses."

Joy felt the tears come up.

"Or I'll get Kyle to front the money."

"Kyle?"

"Mr. Tompkins."

"You call him Kyle now?"

"As a matter of fact, I do. I'll tell you about it sometime."

Joy felt the tears dissipate, as a result of mere curiosity. Elizabeth said, "I'll work on it. Now I have to go." She gave Joy a kiss and a hug, and walked away. Really, Joy thought, she looked awfully good for a woman of her age. It was right out of her book—the chapter she had shown Joy called "Transformation as the Ultimate Cosmetic."

A while later, she put Limitless back in his pen and went over to Mr. T.'s stall. She hadn't ridden in him two weeks now, even though everyone knew that, to keep an old horse going, you had to keep him going. He turned from his hay as soon as she approached and nickered. She palmed a piece of carrot between his lips and stroked his ear while he crunched it. Their last ride hadn't been much, either, only a walk around the backside and out to the parking lot. It was clear even to Joy that he had to go somewhere, but how she could let him go there without her was not clear at all.

PLATO OPENED the mail center, and scrolled up to an e-mail he had gotten about a week before. He opened it, read it, then wrote in reply:

Dear Dominique,

As I mentioned to you before, some friends and I will be in Paris at the last of September and the beginning of October. We are coming for a horse race. I must say that I have been reading the book you sent me about fifth-, sixth-, and seventh-dimensional statistical calculations as a way of understanding phenomena that don't seem to fit into our three-dimensional world. I wanted to refer you to an article I read last year about bee dances as a possible example of a larger-than-three-dimensional phenomenon that appears as a two-dimensional shape, namely a hexagon, in our world. I also found much of interest in the chapters on time. While there were some points made about sequentiality/non-sequentiality that I myself had been working with in my attempts to "predict" economic patterns, there was much else that was new to me and that I failed quite to grasp. It would be helpful to me to perhaps meet with you and discuss these ideas, while at the same time, of course, enjoying a good meal and a glass of wine.

I note in the author information in the back of your book that you are not yet thirty! I am impressed! You have a much firmer sense of all these concepts than anyone I've met before. Let's do get together.

As he was clicking "send," he thought, And she's pretty, too. But that was something you didn't mention until you had a good sense of whether the woman was a follower of Cixous or Naomi Wolf or even Camille Paglia. Feminism was a house with many mansions, and it didn't do to open any of the doors without knocking.

AND SO THEY FOUND themselves installed right there at Longchamp. What with string-pulling on all sides, they didn't have to stay out in Chantilly, but were allowed to bring the horses right to the track and train there. France-Galop was happy to have an American horse there, even one whose wins were rather obscure. And since the horse was only going to be there for a few days, the track officials let Mr. T. come, too, as his pony, and Elizabeth swore that the old horse knew perfectly well where he was and was grateful to be there. Joy didn't know who paid, and didn't ask. It was a grand comfortable luxury to have him along, to watch him look around, take everything in, switch his tail back and forth in lazy appreciation of this and that new thing. Or remembered thing. He was mannerly, calm, and companionable. Joy prevented herself from saying too often, Oh, look at him, isn't he good? Isn't he beautiful? Isn't he smart?

Even on Thursday, the first morning after his arrival, Limitless was unchangedly alert, eager, happy. As long as he was on the move, he seemed to recognize no significance in the landscapes wherein he found himself located. The French officials gave them an extremely civilized time to train, nine-thirty, which meant that Joy and Farley woke up, stretched, ordered room-service petit déjeuner, made love, answered the knock at the door, ate, kissed, showered, dressed, read the English papers, which had a lot about racing both here and at Newmarket, snuggled, called for the car and driver, went over to the track, and were almost awake by the time Joy was ready to be mounted.

Of course the horse was a great galloper—that was his trump card, his ace in the hole, his bottom line, his safety net, his genius—but as a devotee of dressage, what Joy most appreciated was his trot. Limitless balanced himself between the rider and the earth, his diagonal pairs of long legs springing him upward and forward, the delicate ovals of his four hooves only tapping the ground. From ears to tail, his spine was supple and open. Joy knew this in her own spine—she had twisted and lifted a bag on the plane and stiffened herself up. As soon as she rode Limitless the first time, the looseness of his back had loosened hers. His mouth and his tail were the indicators. His mouth carried exactly the weight of the bit, a few ounces, his tailbone flowed out of his spine, then curved gracefully downward, and the breeze picked up the silken hairs and completed their metamophosis into effortless motion. Crouched just over his heart, she posted a light allegro 4/4 rhythm, her hands carrying only the weight of the reins. His trot was never a containment, always an expansion. Each time it was new. She thought she remembered it, but because it was so pure and uncontaminated by any wiggling or failures in rhythm, it was not rememberable. She had had a dressage teacher once who had told her something impossible, that he could feel the horse's every breath. But with Limitless, now, there were times when she could feel not only his every breath but his every heartbeat, at least at the trot, when his heart rate would have risen from its usual forty beats to something like sixty or seventy. When Farley flagged her down and told her that was enough for today, she said, "Oh. How long have we been trotting around?"

"About forty minutes. The horse looked so good I didn't stop you. He—"

"Did we actually move around the course?"

"Sure. You started here, went over there and then there, and now you're back here."

"Limitless would be a great, great dressage horse." And now her feet were on the ground again, and here was Mr. T., standing with his ears pricked, taking it all in. Rafael took Joy's saddle off Limitless and put it on the white horse, and Farley said, "Go ahead, stretch his legs a little bit. See what he remembers. Everyone here is eating out of Rosalind's hand. You can do whatever you want. The colt looked good. Tomorrow and Saturday he can gallop a little; then, the morning of the race, he can rest a bit."

And he tossed her onto the big horse. An image came into her head of a pigeon flying into the coop, home at last. The feel of Mr. T.'s familiar walk replaced the vanished sensation of Limitless's vast trot. Her hips swayed back and forth, her pelvis rocked gently. She stilled it. He halted. She relaxed. He walked on. In front of her, his long white neck ended in his tapered white ears, now pricked with interest. There were a few other horses about, probably other foreign animals, from England or Ireland or Germany. There was the huge crème-colored grandstand by the finish line, there were white fences threading the turf, and there was the turf itself, as brilliant under the overcast sky as if the sun were within it, shining out green. That was a beautiful word, Joy thought, "turf," a word full of thickness and moisture and nourishment and color. Of course Mr. T. wanted to come back here. A horse removed from turf, his natural bed, his preferred food, his earliest playground, must certainly be the definition of exile. She urged him into a trot, but instead he began to canter, and rather than rein him in, she let him go forward. He did what she thought he would do, easy canter on a loose rein, ta-dum, ta-dum, ta-dum, the three waltzing beats of a creature who had nothing to flee or to seek. He had won at Santa Anita and she had ridden him there, but riding him here, where he had won his stakes races, was much more delicious, put her in mind of the host of others who had galloped and raced here for two hundred years, thousands of horses, all related to one another, all incarnations of the same invisible force, each one the center of a tempest of speculation and conversation, but each one silent and mysterious. Everyone acted now as if through Elizabeth they knew the royal road to Mr. T.'s unconscious, but in the best of circumstances, everything she said would only be an approximation, and so he, too, whatever the success of his betting system ("The proof is in the pudding" was what Mr. Tompkins always said as he plunked down quite large sums at the betting windows and sent Plato to pick up quite larger ones at the payout windows), was still only what each of them made of him. Joy supposed that what Mr. Tompkins made of him was just another facet of his own money-magnetism. What Froney's Sis had made of him was a large, steadying presence. What Farley made of him was the reassurance that what he did as a trainer was harmless and even of some value. What Plato made of him was the model of all the orderly forces of the architectural and dynamic universe. What Joy made of him was simple innocence and love, a horse to ride into the world upon, though the world frightened and dismayed her, a beloved and reassuring large presence. But what did Mr. T. make of himself? She had to admit she would never know. What had he told Elizabeth once? That he was a horse, not a prophet. And a horse needed to graze the rich turf with some equine friends, stroll leisurely from spot to spot, find some shade during the middle of the day.

He gave up his canter and came down to a trot, then a walk. Then he stopped and rubbed his nose on his knee, sighed, and moved off at the walk, once again pricking his ears, looking around. Perhaps, Joy thought, this would be the last time she would ever ride him. If he wished to stay behind after they left, his wish would be granted by Rosalind. The horse sighed. Joy sighed. She saw that everyone, including her own better self, expected her to leave him behind.

"NOW," SAID FARLEY to Roberto, "they haven't had rain so far this week, and there's no rain predicted for tonight. Longchamp is *always* deep and holding for the Arc, but it isn't this year." They were way out on the course, near the starting gate, so far away from the grandstand that it looked compact, like the bull's-eye of a target. Farley walked toward the right-hand rail, the inside rail in France, and drove his heel into the turf. Roberto came along behind him. Roberto was still a little sleepy, and having a hard time listening. Farley said, "Don't be surprised if the horses are bunched right around you. European races tend to be more tightly bunched at the beginning."

"He hates that," said Roberto. "He's gonna trot if he has to, to let them get ahead of him."

"That would be very unorthodox," said Farley. "Don't let him do that."

"I was joking, boss."

"This is new to me, Roberto. I've thought about this race for thirty years, and watched it five or six times, but being out here, this is new to me. The fact that the turf is as firm as a California turf course is in our favor. The fact that they're going to bunch very tightly on the turn is not in our favor."

"You know, boss, I think about this over and over, but I don't have any-thing to think. You shoulda got Stevens or McCarron or someone like that."

"Bottom line, Roberto? Stay on him, keep going, and see what he wants to do."

"I know how to do that, boss."

EILEEN CRAWLED OUT from under the covers. Rosalind was already up, sitting at a little table. Not far from her were Eileen's little dishes, one full of kibble, the other full of water. It was nice to know they were there, but not an issue of great urgency. Eileen jumped down off the bed, and spent some time stretching and yawning, pointing her back toes one at a time, especially flexing and extending her hips, stretching and curling that essential canine muscle, her useful tongue. When she tightened her little tail, she could always feel it there, much longer than it really was. That was the one lasting riddle of Eileen's life, where the rest of it had gone. Ah, well. Now she stood foursquare and regarded Rosalind. She had to admit that Rosalind looked good lately, as good as any dog you could name. Her fur was glossy, her eyes were bright, her blood coursed robustly through her flesh (something Eileen, as a predator, was quite sensitive to). Her flesh itself was warm and soft. Eileen recognized that, too. There had been a down period, a period of what had seemed to Eileen to be a sort of chill. During that period, a dog could nestle into Rosalind all she wanted and never warm up. Why else had she barked at Rosalind in those days? Wake up, fix this, I don't like it. Now, though, you could wake up pant-ing in the middle of the night just from lying next to Rosalind, inside the covers or out.

"Time to get up," said Rosalind.

Had the woman not noticed that she was up?

"I thought Al would be here by now." There was a sigh.

Al. Here. Eileen had thought he was gone for good. She had thought, in fact, that they were pretending to be looking for him, the way you pretend to look for a tennis ball, rather than really looking for him, the way that you look for a rat down a hole, and that, after going through the motions for some length of time that only Rosalind would know, they would end that activity and go home and do something else.

Rosalind picked up the phone and said, "Ah, bonjour, monsieur. S'il vous plaît, je veux téléphoner un restaurant par le nom Pré Catalan. Ah, merci." She patted her lap and smiled, and Eileen went over and jumped into it. Rosalind rolled her over and tickled her on her stomach. Then she said some things about their plans for later in the day. Wherever they were, Eileen liked it. There were dogs everywhere, little, interesting dogs with many many opinions that had to be corrected by her, Eileen, and there was no getting into bags or crates or being ashamed of oneself as a dog. Wherever it was they were, dogs were held in high esteem here. Rosalind said, "You need to go out. I'm almost ready." But they waited, still, and Rosalind looked several times at her arm, and got up several times and went to the window. Eileen came to feel that lifting her leg on the foot of the radiator was very tempting.

Eileen investigated her kibble, but what need of it was there? Here, she had noted with satisfaction, dogs sat on chairs at tables and ate from spoons, and what they got was not kibble by any stretch of the imagination. "Okay," said Rosalind, at last.

They went out the door, into the elevator, out of the elevator. Eileen knew at once that there were several dogs in the lobby, but she pretended not to notice them for the moment, only puffed herself out a bit and lifted her head. Rosalind said to the man across the desk, "I expected Mr. Maybrick early this morning, and I can't wait for him any longer. I have to get out to Longchamp. Please be sure he gets my note when he arrives."

"Of course, madame."

"Merci." Still she lingered, and then they walked out into dog heaven.

ROSALIND HAD NEVER SEEN such a crowd for a horse race. Cars, cabs, vans, buses already congesting the arteries and side streets of the whole west end of Paris, as if every citoyen were deserting the ville for the bois. Buses had plates on them from every country in Europe, and metropolitan buses were frequent and teeming as well. She snapped Eileen's leash on her collar, but then carried her anyway—there were too many feet. You could not say the weather was good—dry but overcast, as it had been since their arrival. It was good weather for having lots of pensées, and Rosalind had been having her share. She had not really gotten into any sort of exuberant or even lighthearted mood yet, though she had spent two pleasant evenings with Farley and Joy and the others, as well as some artists and artists' agents she knew. She had eaten well, passed time at the Pompidou Center, had her hair cut, and bought some underwear that cost as much as outerwear. She could not even say what her pensées consisted of, and the others seemed subdued, too. But she went from activity to activity, not in the state of merry pleasure that she had expected when she came up with this idea, but in a state of suspension. This food was all very well, this wine was excellent, these paintings were first-class, but they were not reaching her, and so it was with the crowds at Longchamp. They streamed past her and gathered around her and fragmented and streamed away, and were apart from her in more than just their conversations in a language she did not understand well. Perhaps it was simple. Perhaps she missed Al.

Certainly, she had made the wrong plan for meeting him. Thoughtlessly, she had brought along the pass that would get him into the owners' enclosure. If she went in there with it, then he would not be able to get in there himself. She should have left it at the hotel, but she hadn't been sure he would go to the hotel if he were really late. Now, standing among the regular patrons of the track, she saw that it would be astounding if he found her. She made her way over to the walking ring, which was built like a theater in the round. Tiers and tiers of staring faces looked down upon the horses they were just bringing out for the first race, and the horses looked like alien beings, as they always did if the crowd was very big. There were a lot of horses in the first race—twenty or something like that. Rosalind picked out the winner at once—number seven, brown, two white hind fetlocks. Her powers had modified themselves recently. Instead of bestowing wishes, she now seemed to recognize those upon whom wishes had already been bestowed. It was something of a relief. She scanned the tiers of faces, but Al's wasn't among them.

By the fourth race, she had given up looking for him, and decided that, if there was finding to be done, it was Al who would have to do it. In this state of suspension, the looking was exhausting her, and anyway she wanted to see the horse and Farley and the others and be taken into the enclosure of privilege and given a glass of wine and a warm greeting. Eileen, who did not like the crowd at all, shivered against her, and that reminded Rosalind that it was cold here. The other dogs had coats on, which made Eileen look even more like a barbarian than she was. No doubt about it, even though she had been to Paris many times and felt quite at home there, Longchamp, where she had a horse running in the Arc, where she was about to take her rightful place at the privileged center, made her feel very Appletonian. Instead of watching the fourth race, a sprint, she presented her pass, went through the gate and out the other side, toward the barn. Then she remembered never to assume anything, especially that Alexander P. Maybrick would not be able to enter any enclosure he might wish to enter, and that gave her a moment of hope, but when she got to Farley and Joy, they hadn't seen him, either, and were surprised that he wasn't with her.

What a silly thing to do, she thought, looking at the others, to bring four people and a horse who had won a few minor stakes races to a place like this. What in the world were they doing? She could tell by looking at the others that they didn't know, and they could no doubt tell the same thing by looking at her. All of this was based on the idea that they had nothing to lose, but it felt like they did have something to lose, even if it was only pride.

And then Farley went to get the horse, and this Elizabeth person showed up with Kyle Tompkins, who owned the ranch Limitless vacationed at after every race. Kyle was wearing a beautifully cut seal-gray English suit with a pink tie, and on his feet, equally beautifully cut cordovan cowboy boots, burnished to the color of an Irish setter, like classic oxfords, but as pointy-toed as a pair of boots with feet inside them could be. The very sight plumped up her confidence. "Pleased to meet you," he said. "That's quite a horse you've got there." Rosalind noticed that she wasn't the only person breathing a sigh of relief now that Kyle Tompkins was here. The feeling was general. He was a gust of dry, sun-bright, Central Valley, California, air blowing right through the Bois de Boulogne.

And then the horse came out, one of fifteen, and then the jockeys came down. Roberto looked enameled in his bright-blue-and-gold silk shirt with his incandescent white pants. He said to Joy as they followed the horse, "These jockeys are pretty big here. Taller than me." Joy put her arm around him and squeezed him, and then Farley hoisted him on. No ponies came out. Roberto had to ride the horse out to the starting gate. By the time Rosalind and the others had placed their bets and made their way to their box, horses were already cantering down there. She saw that Farley had Joy by the hand, and he was squeezing tight. But he sounded calm, saying, "You know, it's easy enough. A wide, long run. The turf isn't as deep as I thought it would be, since the rain's held off. The trouble will come if they start too slowly and he forgets this is a race and his mind wanders. But I told Roberto only to get on the lead if he has to; it's a long long way home." And then Rosalind took his other hand, and he gave her a squeeze. Rosalind said, "Maybe we should just look upon this as a good field trip for Roberto and a way of furthering his education."

Farley looked at her, then kissed her on the cheek and said, "Maybe we should just look upon this as the chance of a lifetime, given to us by a woman of great kindness and wisdom, for which we will always be thankful."

Rosalind blushed.

GETTING FIFTEEN HORSES into the gate was even harder than it looked. Limitless stood, calm but alert. It was Roberto who was beginning to feel himself space off. This one backed out, that one wouldn't go in, three or four gate officials closed in on the hindquarters of this other one. And then they said something to him in French and Limitless walked in happy, and Roberto was just feeling the pleasure of that when the gates clanged open and there they were. It was a little sunny now, and every horse was pouring toward the rail, but slowly, ever so slowly. Limitless's long stride took him to the front, and Roberto woke up and pushed his hands into mane up the horse's neck, forbidding himself even to think about the unthinkable, touching the horse's mouth. He felt the horse flinch under him as another horse got very close, and then Limitless stretched a bit and pulled ahead. The herd of animals oozed around the turn. Limitless's ears were flicking forward and back as he looked for a comfortable and familiar place to be. Roberto crouched even more tightly into his neck. All around him, the European jockeys were almost standing in their stirrups, going up and down, yo ho heave ho, it was rather disconcerting. You know, thought Roberto, I am only eighteen years old. I have only been doing this for two years. How much new input is too much new input?

The straightaway extended before them, the longest, widest, greenest straightaway Roberto had ever seen. The traffic to his immediate left thinned, and then, three strides later, disappeared. Roberto shifted his weight to the outside and gripped the horse's mane a little tighter. Limitless, ever sensitive, moved left. The bunch to his right, on the rail, began to accelerate, and there appeared another bunch to his left, way over, some group of horses that were so far from the right-hand group, they seemed to be running in a different race. And they pulled ahead, too. Roberto saw Limitless glance at them, then glance at the group to the right. Roberto knew he was a good jockey now. Two years' experience had given him strategy as well as horsemanship, ideas as well as tact. Now he had an idea, a very small idea. His idea was to stop thinking about the bunch of horses to his left and to stop thinking about the bunch of horses to his right, but only to raise his head slightly and focus his own eyes on the middle tier of seats in the distant grandstand.

EVEN WITH HER BINOCULARS, Rosalind could see next to nothing. Since the course was a long J-shape, the start was something like a mile away, and the turf muffled the sound of the hooves. For a minute or two, there was nothing exciting about it—only a turbulence of equine shapes in the dim distance. And then, suddenly, they were visible, two groups, one rather to the outside rail beside the grandstand, and one rather to the inside rail, away from the grandstand. The announcer was shouting in rapid French, not helpful, and Rosalind had a head-on view. She could not even see her horse, or feel the excitement of watching him run. She knew nothing of this sort of racing, not even how to feel.

That is, until a solitary animal shot through the parting between the two groups, and the shirt curled at his neck was blue and gold and the cap on his head was blue and gold, and Rosalind saw. He was running hard and straight, by himself, not part of a group or hooked onto anyone, just the way he liked to run. His ears were pinned and his nostrils wide as trombones and his front hooves up by his nose. Where was he? She could not tell. His position bore no relationship to either of the groups. And then there were about three seconds just before they crossed the finish line when it looked for all the world as though he was in front by half a length, and then his number went up on the tote board, and what she did not feel that she had seen happen even though she was right there, was true.

Pandemonium shook the grandstand, that an obscure horse from California who had gone off at twenty-to-one odds should win the Arc! Rosalind smiled. Of course, Limitless had not known of his own obscurity. The inability of horses to read the sports pages, Al had always said, was one of their advantages as a sports investment.

FARLEY'S MIND went blank as the horse crossed the finish line. He was yelling, of course, throwing his arms around, hugging Joy and kissing her all over her face, saying things like, "Oh, no! Oh my God! Look at that! Wow! Wow!" But the thing that happened was so much bigger than his preparation for it that he balked at taking it in, at seeing it, hearing it, knowing what came next. He was beyond incoherent. It was more like he was disassembled. His body stood there, laughing, hugging Joy and listening to her, but what was really the case was that he was waiting to be put back together. The herd of horses and jockeys was still cascading across the finish line, and continued to do so, a thousand horses making a storm of noise, and he stood there. After a century, he turned his head, just a little to the left, and there were some horses coming back toward him, this time at the trot, and, just as in the race, how strange was that, déjà vu all over again, the horses parted, and here came Limitless, head up, reins flapping, his chest as wide as a barn door, his legs as long as sapling trees. Farley ran for him. Roberto was shouting for everyone to hear, "Boss, look at him, he could do it all over again, look at him, look at him! He's a running machine, boss! He's a monster! He only tried for a moment there!" Farley reached for the horse's bridle, but the horse wasn't looking at him, he was looking at a hundred thousand screaming faces, his neck turned elegantly, his gaze attentive, his ears pricked, and Farley was struck, he told Joy afterwards, not by his speed or his grace or his beauty—those qualities in him they appreciated every day—but by his dignity. And then the horse noticed him, and lowered his head, and Farley stroked him on his neck and said, "What a fine young fellow you are!"

AFTER HE WATCHED the race from the rail with a hundred thousand other nobodies, Al gave up trying to get to Rosalind or his horse or anyone else he knew. He couldn't speak French, and he couldn't get anyone to listen to him, and his temper was rising, which was the wrong way to celebrate a win of this magnitude by a horse he himself had bred (though admittedly on a whim, not out of any advanced knowledge of pedigree). So he did what Harold the Proctologist, whose instructions were ever and always in his mind, would have told him to do, he vacated the situation, knowing that he would just fuck it up somehow if he stuck around. For the last twenty-four hours, it had been one thing after another, and all of it crowded, jostling, anonymous. Plane delays, train delays, a strike of some kind and a sympathy strike, and then at the hotel they had lost Rosalind's note, and Longchamp itself, a place he had only been to before as an honored and wealthy guest, was considerably different when you were just a guy and had no access, and whether they understood who you were or not, they could always stonewall you for not speaking French. And the contrast between this and, say, trackless forested waste, where he had been just sixty hours before, was more than a little unnerving.

And then, by the time he had ridden a bus (two guys got into a fistfight in the front), hailed a cab, tried to communicate in German and English, and made his way back to the hotel, only to discover (Rosalind had telephoned in another message) that he had to go back out to Longchamp to find the restaurant, all he wanted to do was take off all his clothes and get into the shower for the rest of the night. Really, he was kind of pissed off. He had told them over and over that he wanted to go to the Breeders' Cup. How many times did he have to say it? Were they deaf or something? What was up with Rosalind, anyway?

The horse was a runner, though. He had seen the horse as he came through the other horses with that look on his face. He was the best runner Al had ever bred. This thought made Al stand stock-still in the shower, and blasted away all his other complaints. Somehow, he had failed to think this thought until right now. Maybe he was a better runner than a lot of guys had ever bred. That was a new thought, too. Wow, thought Al. I did that. I sent that mare to that stallion. If I had not done that, it would never have been done. You couldn't really say that about anything else he'd done in his life except fathering his children and marrying Rosalind and, okay, breeding those other horses who had been nothing much in the larger scale of Thoroughbred breeding. Al shivered and turned off the water. When he came out into the bathroom, there was Rosalind's message on the counter. He stepped over and picked it up. The address of the restaurant, the phone number, the time they were to meet, and then, "Love, Rosalind." She had told the hotel operator to put that there, "Love, Rosalind." Fact was, he didn't have to be without her for that short life sentence. He could be with her as much as he chose. Al hiccupped and began to dry himself very quickly. Something was happening in his body. As fast as he rubbed, this sensation came on, a tingly but melty sensation, not unknown, but no everyday deal with him. He rubbed faster, and then began to rub his head and face. The sensation came on all the more strongly. Then he recognized it. It was gratitude. Al began to laugh, or something like that, something convulsive and big.

AT THE RESTAURANT, Al could see them at their table from the entrance to the dining room. Farley, his girl, a tall woman, a hairy guy, the little jock talking like mad to a pretty woman with a French look about her, and a man of about his own age who was ordering wine. And Eileen, sitting on a chair. She was the one who saw him, but she didn't bark. She just noticed him and looked away. No Rozzy. Her chair was pushed back and her napkin folded upon it. No food as yet—they hadn't started to eat. He turned around, disappointed not to have seen her at the moment when he expected to see her, needed to see her. He walked to the top of the stairs and looked down.

Here she came. She was dropping something into her purse and closing it. She was wearing a peach-colored suit and her hair was coiled at the nape of her neck. She was looking over the railing of the staircase. She was sighing. She was not looking where she was going. She was sighing again, and looking at her feet. Up she came. Al was placing himself. Al was holding out his arms. She was turning her head, but not quickly enough to recognize him. And then she was walking into his arms, and he was embracing her, and she was saying, "Oh, Al, I was just calling the hotel again," and he was saying, "I love you, I love you, I love you," and he was kissing her and lifting her up and feeling her arms tighten around him as if she really meant it, really was glad to see him, really did love him still and again after all these years, whether he deserved it or not.

71 / HAPPILY EVER AFTER

LOOKING AT those two horses dozing in the shade of the overhang reminded Angel Smith of how hot it was in South Texas, even in the middle of October. But these days he was feeling so bad that it didn't take much to remind him. He could barely drag the hay around to his own animals, and he for sure couldn't watch out for any of the boarders, so he'd told 'em all. This was the last month. Everybody had to go by the first of November. He was retiring and closing the place up. His own horses, seven of them, were going to the auction yard, that included Amigo and Frank. It was funny, he thought, that, of all the horses he had had in his day, these were the ones he would end up with, none of whom he had chosen, seven hard-knockers for whom this was the end of the line.

But he had to sit down. It was pretty amazing when you thought about it, one day you could get up at 5:00 a.m., muck out twenty pipe corrals, eat breakfast, ride your cutting horses till the weather got hot, then go into town and make a couple of deals, come back out, and there was still time before dark to work another couple of cows, then you ate supper, got drunk, went to bed, and when you got up twenty years later, you could barely walk across the parking lot, you were so weak and sick. So he sat down. The chair creaked, and he saw the horses turn their heads to look at him, one brown, one chestnut, and then he closed his eyes.

Justa Bob shifted his weight from one hind leg to the other and yawned, then blew the dust out of his nostrils. Doc's Big Juan was right beside him, but he didn't mind that anymore. He didn't mind much of anything anymore. He had dropped two hundred pounds since William Vance knew him, and with the weight had gone many of the opinions he once held. He was seven now, but he looked seventeen—long whiskers, prominent ribs and withers and hips, harsh coat. Doc's Big Juan looked a lot better—as a quarterhorse he was bred to get by on lower-quality forage and less of it. Doc's problem was that he couldn't walk. The arthritis in his ankles and knees bothered him every day, and so he hobbled around the pen as little as possible, stiffening himself up still further. Justa Bob looked terrible, but he was sound, and the intermittent attentions of Angel's grandson, Dino, kept him that way, since Dino loved to ride, but was afraid to do anything but walk. So Justa Bob got out of the pen about three times a week, and spent several hours walking around. Since Dino was too lazy to put the bridle or saddle on the horse, and didn't care whether the horse followed any accepted protocols, Justa Bob could always spend at least part of his time grazing what little grass grew around the stable area.

Both horses continued to watch Angel Smith in his chair. Angel Smith was by no means fast on his feet. The horses had been with him for eight months, and they knew how he moved. Between the time the hay was given to the first horse in the morning and to the last horse, there was a prolonged period of shuffling and resting on Angel's part. They were familiar with that. But now something was different, and it was no challenge to an observant animal like a horse to notice it. The challenge was to care. Justa Bob was depressed and Doc was achy and the weather was hot and the sun was bright and the hay wasn't very good and the two of them were half asleep anyway. But still. Justa Bob yawned again, and then Angel slipped a little farther down in his chair and fell out of it.

Doc whinnied. No one knows what a horse is communicating by a whinny, except maybe "hello." "Hello" is a safe bet, and perhaps that was all Doc was communicating. To Justa Bob, he communicated a discomfort that Justa Bob already felt. He whinnied again, and then Justa Bob whinnied. Once they started to get themselves worked up, it was easy enough to go on with it. Justa Bob whinnied again. Pretty soon, they were stamping around the pen, whinnying and whinnying. The horses they couldn't see, inside the barn, heard them and responded—and perhaps all everyone was doing was saying hello, hello, hello. But they were making quite a ruckus. Angel Smith lay still. And then his wife opened the back door of their house and heard all the noise. She saw that Frank and Amigo were stampeding around in their pen. She came out a little farther and looked around for Angel to see what was going on, and then she saw him. When she ran over to him and bent down beside him and discovered that he was unconscious but still breathing, the horses stood still and watched her. That was okay, then, they thought, and it was, because for the rest of the day, what with the ambulance and the people coming and going and the relatives and all of the commotion, there was so much to look at that you didn't even notice the heat.

———

WHEN MR. TOMPKINS got back from Paris, he didn't quite know who he was anymore. Before he left, he had known exactly who he was—a man with vast agricultural assets, plenty of power in the state legislature, and a headache every day that grew right out of who he was like a tomato plant in a compost heap. When he got back from Paris, and five days in the bed of Elizabeth Zada, the headache was gone and the real property had assumed an unprecedented vagueness in his mind. His son and his secretary had to keep saying to him, "Dad?" "Mr. Tompkins?" Nor did he know who Elizabeth Zada was. On the one hand, there was this big old woman with a loud voice and an uppity manner and a way of talking about regular things like marriage and love and housework and even food and taking a shit that was weird to the point of incomprehensibility, and on the other hand, there was the magic she did to him that made him think thoughts he had never thought before and have erections like he had when he was sixteen, except that when he was sixteen they would shoot up and pop off as soon as he, or some girl, touched them, and now they came and stayed and seemed to get bigger and harder, and in all his years as a man of wealth and privilege and sexual appetite he had never heard of anything like it, not nude Asian women, not girls girls girls, not Hollywood Madam, because it had nothing to do with youth, nothing to do with looks, nothing to do with money, nothing to do with equipment. So of course it must have to do with love, though Elizabeth said that was the advanced course, and he was not allowed to tell her that he loved her, though he tried to slip it in.

Mr. Tompkins went into his office and closed the door, then picked up a secure hard-line phone and dialed Elizabeth's number in Fresno. When she answered, he could think of nothing to say except "I love you," but he dared not say that, so he just waited, feeling about twelve years old. Finally, her wonderful voice said, "Kyle?"

"Yes."

"I'll see you Friday, as we planned. Don't do anything."

"I won't."

"Here's an exercise. Open seven letters. Just take the first seven right off the top and say yes to every one of them. It's perfectly safe, and you can afford it."

"I know I can."

"I'll see you Friday."

"All weekend?"

"All weekend."

"Okay. I—" But she had already hung up.

"I'VE GOT A JOB," said Deirdre. "And I like it."

"I'm not trying to interfere with that. I just need you to tell me something," said Tiffany.

"Ask me over the phone."

"You have to come out and see."

"See what?"

"Just come out."

"I'm in quarantine. I can't look at any horses except with Audrey."

"Audrey will be there."

"Send me a videotape."

"I, Tiffany, want to see you. I haven't seen you in three weeks."

Deirdre laughed. She said, "How are your horses runnin', darlin'?"

"I still don't have a stakes winner, but Somnambulist ran third in the Kelso Handicap. How's your job?"

"You know, Tiff, I don't see how you can go wrong in Washington real estate if you have the right attitude. What you do is, you take your dullest clients to your strangest houses, and you say, 'I don't really think this is right for you, possibly a little, I don't know, uncomfortable, but I thought you would like to see it, because so-and-so lived here,' and pretty soon they want to show themselves that they're just as cool as so-and-so, and anyway it's different from what they had back home, and why else go to Washington in the first place?"

"It was nice of Mary Lynn to give you that house to list."

"She set up this whole real-estate thing. I always said the best thing you could do was put yourself right into her hands. She told me how to sell it, too—she calls it Maison Billing Gates, for all the hours Skippy's law firm billed to Microsoft."

"Please come out."

"There is a listing out that way I would like to see."

"Thank you. Tomorrow."

"Call me tomorrow and I'll tell you."

After hanging up, Tiffany turned to Ellen. "Sometime tomorrow."

Ellen nodded. She said, "We'll keep him in until just before she gets here."

DICK WAS WATCHING Luciano massage a two-year-old filly. Luciano was working on her gluteals now, and the filly was grunting very softly. After a moment, she sighed. Then Dick sighed. Luciano said, "Ah, well, you know, that's horses."

"That's not horses as we know them. No American horse has ever won the Arc before. I didn't see it."

"Did he have it?"

"I don't know, I didn't see it."

"Blinded by the Derby."

"That's right. I wouldn't have thought of the Arc in a million years."

"Well, there you go. You couldn't have trained the horse, because the horse was going to win the Arc, and you weren't going to get him there, so he had to find himself another trainer."

"I bet Rosalind got the trainer to send him there. No California trainer would think that up on his own."

"You don't know that."

"I believe it, though."

"What if Rosalind had said to you, 'This horse is going to the Arc'?"

"I would have ignored her."

"You loved her."

"Yes, I did. Probably that's why I would have ignored her. I told her everything she knew about horses, and whenever she said anything about them, I didn't listen because I'd heard it all before." Dick sighed again. The filly sighed again. Luciano was gently pulling her tail, first left, then right, then down and back. "I met my ex-wife's new boyfriend. He's a sound engineer. They were very affectionate together."

"You got a girlfriend?"

"Nah."

Luciano came around the filly and started at her head again, this time on the right side. After a few moments, he said, "You want to go have something to eat? It's about that time. I found this place where they make a great paglia e fieno. You know what that is?"

"No."

"Your ex-wife's got a boyfriend, your ex-owner's horse won the biggest race maybe in the world, you don't have a girlfriend and you also don't know what paglia e fieno is? May I have your attention? May I tell you a few things? May I give you a little bit of help here?"

"I wish you would, Luciano."

"Okay, then," said Luciano. "The first thing you have to know is that paglia e fieno means 'straw and hay,' but what that's referring to is the pasta, okay?"

"Yeah," said Dick.

———

Dear Gustave,

Please forgive me for not writing this letter in French, but your English is far better than my French ever was. This is a letter of reference for the American jockey Roberto Acevedo, who, as you know, rode our horse Limitless to the win in the Arc. Roberto has informed me that romantic considerations have led him to decide to settle in France. I am writing to the trainers and horse agents I know to introduce him. He is an exceptional rider, from an exceptional family of riders. He is rather taller than is usual for an American rider, and maybe a kilo or two heavier, but he has a wonderful sense of pace and as good a pair of hands as I've seen. He is especially good with sensitive horses, like our Arc horse. I hope you will give him a try. He can be reached in care of Mlle. Dominique Lalande-Ferrier, 14 Rue Donegal, in Paris (tel. 98-73-46-50). I have also suggested that he call on you personally, and I think he will do so. Roberto and Mlle. Lalande-Ferrier have indicated that her position at the Sorbonne will not prevent their relocating to Chantilly.

Yours truly,
Farley Jones

When Elizabeth picked up the phone, she thought the party on the other end of the line was going to be the interviewer from *The Independent*, whose call she had been told to expect by her English publisher. Instead, it was Joy. She sounded blue. She said, "Can you read Mr. T. from here?"

"You mean in France?"

"Yeah."

"Sequentiality and locationality make no difference in this context."

"What's he doing?"

"Ask him yourself."

"I don't know how."

"Yes, you do. Close your eyes if you have to. Just bring him into your mind."

"You mean remember him?"

"Start that way."

"Then what?"

"Well, start now and see."

"Do it with me."

"That wouldn't do any good. It's not like lifting a box, where we both take an end. It's more like looking into each other's faces. We're both there, but we aren't seeing the same thing. Just bring him into your mind."

Joy was silent for a moment, then said, "Oh."

"What?"

"Well, when he came into my mind I wasn't looking at him. I was looking from him. The first thing I saw was lots of green close up, but also the horizon curving around that, and other horses between the close-up green and the horizon, but they weren't very distinct to look at. I felt them, though. It was like some were resonating with me and some weren't."

"That seems familiar," said Elizabeth.

"Is that what you see?"

"Something like it."

"I don't know whether to believe this."

"You've always said that, then you've always acted as if you believed it, and what's been the result?"

"The best relationship I've ever had with a horse."

"Why question it, then?"

"Because maybe I'm making it up."

"What if you were?"

"Then I would just be deluding myself."

"By what standard? Doesn't it make you happy to bring him into your mind?"

"Yes."

"Well, if you ask me, the happiness that you feel when you bring him into your mind is your own self expressing love. That's your only evidence that love exists. When Farley embraces you, your mind recognizes love in his embrace. It isn't there unless your mind recognizes it. So, even when you think you are feeling Farley's love for you, what you are really feeling is, once again, your own mind expressing love, but defining it as coming from him to you. You could drop that definition, though—all those definitions that have to do with location and time—Mr. T. was here and now he's there, for example. Farley is apart from you, for example. One day we lift the box. We are weak and the box is heavy, and it's hard to lift. Two weeks later, we've gotten stronger, and the box is light. We don't ever feel the actual weight of the box. We only feel the ease or difficulty of the lifting. One day we feel unloved and alone. A week later, we feel loved. The difference is that we've remembered how to feel love, not that our circumstances have changed."

"I never told you about the time I ran away, when you were in Hawaii."

"You ran away?"

"It was exactly like that. I forgot how to feel his presence and love."

"The easiest thing for me when that happens," said Elizabeth, "is to do what we just did. Bring him into your mind and say, 'I love you.' "

"Okay, I understand that," said Joy.

"And?"

"Relaxing, isn't it?" prompted Elizabeth.

"Well," said Joy. "Yes. Yes." She sighed again.

"Oops," said Elizabeth. "There's call waiting."

"How much did they give you?"

"A million pounds."

"What are you going to do with it?"

"Start a boutique publishing house in England, specializing in futurology. Plato is going to be the editor-in-chief. I want to try my system against the bookies there. We've had enough of Fresno. Got to go."

———

Dear Audrey,

Some weeks ago you wrote a letter to a former employee of mine, Joy Gorham, and because her forwarding address had expired at the post office, and my secretary knew I would be seeing her, the letter was put with my mail. I never saw it, and so I did not deliver it to her, and then, when I was opening some mail, I opened it by mistake. However, I am glad I did, because before I realized it was for Joy I read it, and saw that you are in the market for a horse. I believe I have just the horse for you, and it is a horse that Joy spent a lot of time with, caring for and training. Her name is Froney's Sis, and she is a gray Thoroughbred filly, three years old, about fifteen hands two inches tall, pretty and sound. She went to the track, had one win, and then came home because racing did not suit her. Since then, a couple of the cowboys around here have worked with her, and she is very well broke to do just about anything around the ranch, but both of them feel that they are a little big for her, and that she would make a good youngster's horse. She is, they say, quite affectionate. Sort of a one-girl horse. We have, among other things, a vanning company, and there is a van leaving for the East Coast in a couple of days. I am going to put this horse on the van for you. The van will be in Maryland, Virginia, and Pennsylvania for four days after they drop the horse with you. If you do not care for the horse, just give the boys a call, and they will bring her home again.

Also, the horse you inquired after, *Terza Rima, has been retired to France, to the studfarm Haras Chamossaire, near Deauville. You may e-mail them if you would like news of him, at Vatout.Firdaussi.Chamossaire@aol.com.

> Thank you very much for your letter,
> Yours truly,
> Kyle Tompkins,
> Tompkins Perfection Enterprises International

Mr. Tompkins sat back and read over the letter he had written, then turned to the page beside it and crossed off number five. Two to go. He began another one,

> Dear Senator Boxer,
>
> It may be that I got on your fund-raising list by mistake, since I have always been a donor to Republican causes. Nevertheless, due to unforeseen circumstances, your name has come up, and although I have many reservations about your views and your performance in Washington, I am sending your PAC a check for fifty thousand dollars. Thank you very much for this unusual opportunity.

Then, as hard as it was, he signed his name and wrote the check.

IT WAS ALL VERY EASY for Deirdre to say that she just had to be honest with herself, that she did not want to see Tiffany, and best admit it, but as soon as she was honest with herself and admitted it, well, then, Mother of God, she wanted to see Tiffany more than anything. The thing that she did want to see about Tiffany was her beauty and her friendliness and her enjoyment of life. What she didn't want to see about Tiffany was her own conflicts about that very beauty, friendliness, and enjoyment of life. And so, to be honest, she wanted to see Tiffany more than anything else in the world, and so, to be honest, she didn't want to see her at all, ever again. Selling real estate was ever so much easier. She was a contrary person, she fit sideways into a contrary market, and she didn't feel nearly the qualms of conscience consigning an innocent, well-meaning domicile into the hands of knavish owners as she had selling horses.

She turned into Ellen's access road, and glanced into the big front paddock just in time to see a large black horse canter toward the paddock fence in a leisurely manner, fold his legs, and come down on the other side. Then he turned and headed directly for her car, only sliding to a halt as she herself skidded to a halt. Horse and car were now nose to nose. Deirdre sat back and adjusted her seat belt. It had happened so fast that she hadn't had time to react, but now she did. Her heart was pounding, though whether from the sight of the horse jumping or the possibility of hitting him she did not know. The horse, however, did not look startled. He put his nose down to the hood of the car, then turned himself about and trotted away from her, tail up like a flag, head swiveling this way and that. Deirdre laughed. The thing that she was laughing at was that the fence in this front paddock was five feet high. She had built it herself. She was enough of a horsewoman to know even without having paid close attention that the horse had jumped it effortlessly from an easy canter. She followed him as he turned and headed toward the barn. She saw Ellen come out to receive him, followed by Audrey. Ellen sent Audrey back in. Then Deirdre saw that he had a halter on, and that dangling from the halter was an eight-inch length of rope, which Ellen caught and held on to, though the horse tried to pull away from her. Difficult beast, she thought.

A half-hour later, Deirdre, Ellen, Tiffany, and the horse were in the arena. Audrey had strict instructions to stay out of the way. The horse's name was Sudden Intuition, or Toots. Ellen was riding him, Deirdre was standing in the middle of the arena, and Tiffany was sitting with her feet up in a plastic chair. The horse was huge and strong—seventeen hands and twelve hundred pounds or more, and still a three-year-old. You might worry for his future soundness, but he had ten inches of bone—his legs were like telephone poles and perfectly correct. He was, no doubt about it, a prize.

Of course, he ground his teeth, jerked his head around, wrung his tail, got behind the leg, did not care to participate or cooperate, a story as old as man and horse. Ellen was a good rider, and strong. She got him on the bit—which wasn't hard for him, since he was built well—and she moved him into a big, expansive trot. No problem. He went five or six paces like a metronome. Then he used his big strong old neck and jerked her forward, and no power of human arms or back was going to hold him. And she already had a fairly severe bit on him—anything harsher would eventually inure him to pain and make him worse. Only when he was jumping did the horse behave. Then he galloped forward over the jumps, and responded almost entirely to balance and seat. Deirdre said, "What are you planning to do with him?"

"Make a jumper out of him."

"He's good at it, but you don't have much control. You'll be tempted to take him to A shows and all that."

"Why not?"

"Because the courses are getting more technical all the time. There isn't so much room for just a big jumper. He's got to make a tight turn over a spooky vertical on flat cups to a giant Swedish oxer, then turn again to a big triple combination. He's not adjustable like that."

"But—"

"Never will be. He's a brute. It's global with him. You've got to watch out for him in the stall, he's not friendly or eager to please. The things he likes to do he likes to do for himself."

"He's so young—"

"He's had a whole career, darlin', and he busted out of it. I see the whole thing. He's a gelding now, and he's still opinonated. He must've been a force of primal fear when he was a stud colt. You know, Gunther Gabel-Williams said he would rather face a roomful of tigers than an angry stallion, and I always thought he was the one who should know."

"What can he do, then?"

"Go for a 'chaser, that's what I think. You just point him down the course and let him run till he's tired, two or three miles later. I see him at Cheltenham myself, eating up that valley with those big feet."

"Do you think so?"

"It's a dying sport, love."

"Every horse sport is a dying sport, except there are more horses in the world being ridden for pleasure than ever in the history of mankind. Who's going to train him?"

"Jonathan Sheppard's good. Someone like that."

"You," Ellen said.

"Me? I never trained a 'chaser."

"Don't you want to?"

"No, of course not. No more of that."

And then Ellen turned the horse in a circle, put him into a gallop, and jumped all the fences along the side of the arena, jumped out of the arena, crossed the road in one stride, jumping into the pasture, galloped, or rather swept, across it, jumped the far fence, turned, galloped down the road, and disappeared. Deirdre turned to Tiffany and said, "What in the name of all the saints is she doing?"

"Showing off, I guess. She's never jumped him like that before."

"She used to have one grain of sense, doncha know. She's lost it now, though."

"I'm glad you came out, Deirdre."

"Are you? I'm sure it's horses all the time with you now, darlin'."

"Can't stop, can't turn around, can't go backward, can't think about anything else." They looked at each other, and Deirdre saw that Tiffany was deadly serious. Her life was full, no room for anything else. Deirdre sighed, then realized that it was a sigh of relief. She said, "Och, what a shame."

"I wish you would help me again."

Horse and rider returned, not down the road but across another set of paddocks, jumping in, jumping out, jumping in, jumping out, and then they jumped right back into the arena and came to a halt in the center, in front of her. Over by the barn, Audrey was shouting, "Yeah! Yeah! Wow! Yay, Ellen!" Ellen was panting. The horse was blowing. She said, "I'm the rider. You're the trainer. Tiffany's the owner. What do you say? You can't say he's not good enough for you or that Tiffany can't afford it or that it won't be fun."

"Did you plan this?"

"No. No, though we wanted you to see him. But it wasn't until we were all sitting here, right in place, that I saw how it would work."

"It'll work," said Tiffany.

"Me, too!" shouted Audrey. "I want to do something, too!"

"You can be the cheering section!" called Tiffany.

"It'll work," said Deirdre, and after saying that, she knew it would— jumping, steeplechasing, friendship, and all the rest of it.

So this guy Angel Smith knew, named Horacio Delagarza, trailered five of the seven horses over to the auction yard and put them with the other auction horses in the corral. Then he went back for the last two, the two in the pen. They were the sorriest pair, one hardly able to walk and the other one just skin and bones. When he got back with them, it took a while to get the cripple off the trailer and into the corral, and he saw the guy watching, the guy with the double-bottomed livestock trailer parked in the back of the parking lot. The guy with the double-bottomed trailer was the slaughter guy. He came every week, and he always had enough money to go off with a full load, horses on the top shelf and horses on the bottom shelf, all bunched together, their heads down by their feet. It was a sight that Horacio hated to see, even though he wasn't otherwise a pussy. After he unloaded the cripple, he untied the skinny one and let the bar down behind him. The skinny one backed right off the trailer and pricked up his ears and looked around.

The other five of Angel's horses each had something going for them, but these two, well, who was going to buy them? thought Horacio. He sighed.

This skinny one was a friendly sort. He rubbed his head on Horacio's shirt, and then, when Horacio turned around, he bumped his head into his back. Mostly horses ignored you if they didn't know you. And then, when Horacio turned around, the guy looked right at him, right in the eye. "Yeah," said Horacio, " 'Save me' is about right. Except you should have gotten someone to do that before now. It's too late now." He put the horse into the corral, and the guy went over to the crippled horse and stood beside him. Lots of horses were milling around. The dust was unbearable, so Horacio got himself a Coke, found a seat, and wiped his face all over with his handkerchief. He had told Angel's wife he would stay until the horses were sold and bring her back the money. She kind of hoped there would be several thousand dollars, even seven thousand dollars for seven horses, but Horacio couldn't see it. Two or three maybe.

From where he was sitting, he could see all of Angel's horses. The skinny one wasn't knocked out like the cripple, nor was he scared or agitated like most of the others. He was looking around. He was right there, looking for a good home, thought Horacio. Good luck, buddy.

The buyers, even the ones who weren't buying for slaughter, were a hard-bitten, unpitying bunch, Horacio thought. They were looking for useful animals who could get down to work right now. No pets, no projects. Horacio looked away from the corral. It was a bad lot in the corral. The slaughter man would fill up his truck for sure.

The auctioneer came out and started peeling off the horses like cards from a deck. The lots were random. Good ones came after bad ones. They were led in, walked around, trotted around a few steps, then stood up. The auctioneer said something about each of them that was obvious to anyone looking on—here's a nice palomino, this one trots good, three white stockings on this one, pretty head here. It was just patter, didn't mean anything. Every horse had a buyer, and half the time the buyer was the slaughter man, whose voice rose out of the silence at the end of any bout of unsuccessful bidding and offered a couple hundred dollars. Bang, down came the gavel, and the slaughter man's boy walked in and led the horse out to the double-bottomed trailer.

When they brought in the chestnut who could barely walk, it was so obvious that he would go to the slaughterhouse that there was only a moment of silence while the auctioneer looked at the slaughter man and the slaughter man said, "Ten dollars," and the auctioneer said, "Anyone got fifteen?," and no one said anything, and the horse went for ten dollars, and as they led him away, the skinny one, Horacio saw and heard him, let out a loud whinny, and so, on the principle of the squeaky wheel, he was next.

Justa Bob came into the center of the ring and looked after Doc's Big Juan, whose tail was disappearing into the crowd. This whole situation did not look good to Justa Bob, and Doc's departure looked the worst of all, so he whinnied again. Some horse out somewhere whinnied back, but it wasn't Doc, and Justa Bob pulled against the leadrope attached to his halter, then turned in a circle around the man holding him. "Quit!" said the man, and Justa Bob quit. Although things had not always gone well for Justa Bob, this was the first time he had ever been treated purely as an agricultural commodity, which he read in this way—there were people around him, and they were looking at him, but they had nothing to do with him. Were he to attend to their body language and attempt to connect with them, he would become confused and fail. And so he didn't know what to do, and so he lowered his head and stopped paying attention.

Someone bid twenty bucks for him. Fifty-four starts, twenty wins, seventeen seconds or thirds, lifetime winnings $172,000. There were horses at stud who had won less. The auctioneer asked if anyone had thirty, and there was a long silence. Finally, the slaughter guy said, "Well, there ain't much meat on those bones, but I'll take him off your hands for thirty." The auctioneer looked at the first guy, who shook his head. Horacio put his hand in his pocket. But what in the world would he do with a horse? He didn't need a horse. The slaughter boy led him out of the ring. Ever himself, Justa Bob nuzzled his back pocket as they walked away.

Some of Angel's horses brought a fair amount, and when all of them were sold, Horacio had $3,766 to take home to the Smiths. He walked out of the auction yard to the parking lot, and did up the back of the trailer, got into the truck, and turned on the ignition. Right there in front of him, right in his windshield like a big second thought, was that double-bottomed cattle truck, now crammed with horses. The boy was bringing another one out. He opened the bottom door and shooed him in with the others. Then he turned to walk past Horacio, who rolled down his window and said, "Hey."

"Yeah?"

"What if I wanted one of those horses?"

"You had a chance to buy it back there."

"I didn't take my chance. I want to take my chance now."

"Too late."

"Too late for me, maybe. Too late for the horse. But not too late for you."

"Yeah?"

"Yeah." Horacio got out of the truck. He said, "Look. Your guy paid thirty bucks for the horse. I'll give you thirty to give him, plus another hundred and fifty to unload the horse and give him to me."

"Yeah?"

"Yeah."

The kid's lethargic manner vanished. He said, "Yeah. Which one do you want?"

Just a brown horse, Horacio thought as he walked across the lot. How would he remember or distinguish? Skinny, that was how. But in the end, he didn't have to sort or distinguish. Justa Bob was standing at the door with his ears pricked, knowing there had been some mistake. A double-bottomed cattle trailer was just not his type of conveyance at all, not at all. When the kid opened the door, Justa Bob came down the ramp and gave Horacio justa bump in the chest.

72 / OR NOT

WHAT BUDDY realized was, all you had to do was make up your mind, and he had made up his mind. Making up your mind did not involve wishing for something. It involved having it, but recognizing that there were two forms of having it—after a while there would be the general knowledge that you had it. But before that, and necessary to it, was the private knowledge that it was already yours. First the inspiration, then the incarnation. Thus the knowledge that Residual was going to win the Breeders' Cup Distaff made way for every step on the road that would get her first to the finish line. Generally, this sort of certainty was considered bad luck at the racetrack, asking for trouble, but, then, that must be why, Buddy thought, everything was so up in the air at the track. There was general agreement that anything could happen, and so anything could happen. If more trainers simply claimed what was theirs, and bettors, and owners, and jockeys, you name it, well, then, things would organize themselves a little more clearly.

The best thing about knowing something was yours was that from that knowledge followed every other thing that you needed to know. For example, when, after about two weeks in training, the filly's knee puffed up a little bit, Buddy knew he didn't have to report this to the Kingstons, because the Kingstons had gone to Bermuda for a couple of weeks on vacation and didn't want to be disturbed. And then Curtis, who was checking all the horses every day now, gave her a little Adequan and a little bute, and the swelling went down. Then they backed off on her training for a few days, which was fine, because she was pressing them hard, and maybe the knee was a sign that she didn't know what she was doing as well as she might.

They had her training with another mare, a four-year-old, the kind of mare who never forgot who the boss was. She won about every three times, and purely on determination, since she didn't have all that much speed. When she trained with Residual, the filly and the mare goaded each other. The mare found some speed and the filly found some grit, and who was the boss was an issue they never settled. Buddy stalled them far apart from one another. He didn't want them settling things to their own satisfaction during their time off. Perhaps for this reason, Deedee complained to Buddy that the filly was harder to handle now, a little irritable, putting in a few bucks and a spin from time to time. Buddy knew what was his, and so he just looked at her and said, "Can you handle it if you have to?"

"I hate to take a firm hand with her, because she's never liked that before—"

"She's toughening up. She's not a baby anymore that you have to coax along. Fillies turn into mares."

"I know, but—"

"You have to have what it takes, too, Deedee."

Couldn't be clearer than that, thought Deedee. You could muddle around outside the big time, or you could pay for your ticket and enter the tent. After that, she managed the filly as well as she could, the way you would manage a horse whom you didn't like very much and whose point of view you did not pay much attention to. And once she got used to that, it turned out that she didn't like the filly or think about her as much as she used to. And anyway, there was Alana Marie, always Alana Marie.

Leon was standing there one morning when Deedee was about to enter the track and the filly reared right up. The mare was behind her, and at the sudden delay, she put in a buck or two herself, and then went around Deedee and Residual and walked out onto the track. Residual followed her. But Leon had a moment, he sure did. He remembered right there why up until Deedee he had dated only waitresses, college students, receptionists, and one elementary-school teacher. Right then, what had looked like a dynasty in the making looked like a potential tragedy. Deedee was such a good rider, so supple and strong and athletic, that Leon had forgotten that anything could happen at the racetrack. So he thought of Alana Marie himself, took a little dip in the lake of fire, and watched the filly start down the track, shaking her head and pinning her ears. By the end of the work he had not quite forgotten about it, but he had tagged it for future reference and put it away. Just had to get to the Breeders' Cup. That was all.

The next day, Buddy was there at five and Curtis Doheny was there, too, not as he was always there, just to be there, but with intent. Buddy went up to him, to save himself the sight of Curtis huffing and puffing and rolling and flapping across the parking lot to him. Curtis said, "Time for a little insurance. Say, that guy called me last night. Thanks. I bought into Fuzzy Minister. We got to run him now. It's been six weeks since his last race, and I saw his last timed work was pretty good. I thought maybe the Sorry Charlie Handicap would set him up for the Oak Tree Invitational."

"I haven't been thinking much about that, but—"

"You concentrate on this filly, and the other stuff will get done, right, Buddy? That's the way, baby. My suggestion, just for the prophylactic effect, we inject that filly's knee. Regular weekly injection, a little acid and a bit of cortical steroids, and it'll just bathe that baby in something very soothing."

"She's probably ready for that."

"Ready or not, here we come," exclaimed Curtis, laughing. He had the stuff with him, and so they did it right that morning. No one was around. Another example of, when the problem comes up, the solution is right there for you, Buddy thought. You've just got to know what you want. And the next thing that happened was that the Kingstons came back from Bermuda, and drove out to the track to watch the filly work, and the filly was as good as gold—sound and cooperative and affectionate. As they walked back to the barn, Jason Clark Kingston said, "You know, with the Internet gaming possibilities, a place like this might be a good investment."

"It was just bought," said Buddy. Jason gave him a look that told him, in the software universe, saying that something might not be available was like saying you planned to retire those dollar bills in your pocket. Buddy commented, "You know, Mr. Kingston, since you enjoy racing so much, maybe you would enjoy bringing some of your computer-oriented friends into the game—" Ahead of them, as they entered the barn area, Curtis Doheny stepped right up to Andrea Melanie and introduced himself. Andrea Melanie held out her hand, and Buddy saw Curtis nearly melt over it—he took it and bent down and was laughing foolishly and all that. Buddy had to turn away from Jason Clark Kingston just as he was suggesting that he and Sir Michael Ordway might be able to find the time to accompany a group from San Jose to Keeneland in November for the sales, and go around to another aisle and do something. Watching Curtis Doheny was like watching someone get something on someone else, spill coffee or something slick. It just made you uncomfortable, even though it wasn't your business.

Fifteen minutes later, after he accompanied the Kingstons to their Lexus 470, Curtis came to find him, all excited. "You know, I didn't think I had the guts to ask her, but I did, I asked her if she would let me buy into this filly, even though I made it a point not to buy into fillies when I started this, but this is such a good filly, and the turnaround if she were to get sold in January could be very quick. She said no, but at least I asked. That was the thing for me. I'm always afraid to ask, you know. Ask and ye shall sometimes receive, do not ask and ye shall never receive. So I have to practice asking. The great thing is, I didn't take it personally."

"What did she say?"

"She said, 'My husband is kind of a lone gunman and I don't like to share anything.' "

Buddy cleared his throat at this, then said, "I wish that you wouldn't approach my owners without talking to me about it first."

"Yeah?" replied Curtis. "But that's just the thing. I've spent my whole life thinking I had to get permission. I'm not going to do that anymore—pardon me for asking, but, hey . . . I made up my mind and I know what I deserve."

"What do I deserve?"

Curtis swept his arm around in a big gesture. He laughed. "Hey, Buddy, you've got it all. You've got what you deserve. I'm not trying to take anything away from you, Buddy. I'm trying to give you more! This is a win-win situation, Buddy. But at the same time, I have to do what's right for me, don't I?"

"Yeah," said Buddy. He always agreed with Curtis, because talking to Curtis always finally reminded him of what was true—if you knew it was yours, then it was yours.

The weeks went by rather quickly. There was a big to-do when that horse of Farley Jones's won the Arc over in France. Winning the Arc had a certain novelty appeal, and there was a lot of talk about it. Every trainer on the track had seen that horse train and run, and those who had predicted something like this always seemed to be talking to those who had known all along that something like this was impossible—must have been a fluke, he was a good horse, but . . . That sort of conversation. But look at the Breeders' Cup. The European horses had come in force last year, and had come to the track they liked best, Churchill, and they hadn't even taken home the Mile or the Turf, their very own races. That just went to show you where European breeding was these days. Buddy opined that all those big European races weren't even the equivalent of American Grade One stakes anymore—ten years, even five, and it would all be the Breeders' Cup, the Dubai World Cup. Europe was fine while it lasted, but things were different now. Even so, when Farley got back, everyone was all over him, and two of Buddy's owners switched their horses, that was six horses in all, and there was a lot of speculation about when Farley would run the animal next. He was set up perfectly for the Breeders' Cup, both the Classic and the Turf. Buddy would have thought it was a straight shot, done deal, no-brainer, but Farley was deep, and didn't say anything about it, not even to Curtis Doheny, as Curtis himself told him when he came to give the filly another interarticular shot.

"He's not my type, really," said Curtis. "Kind of cold, and keeps to himself, though his staff and his owners seem to like him. I called a couple of them, just kind of on a dare to myself, to see if any of them wanted a partner, but they weren't very friendly, so I said to myself, Curtis, you don't need this, you deserve better. I even called that guy Maybrick, who owns the Arc horse, but he was kind of gruff with me. Hell, my money's as good as anyone else's."

"You don't want to get overextended."

"Ah, this colt's going to make a quick buck. He wins the Breeders' Cup after the Arc and they'll syndicate him for ten, fourteen million even if he doesn't have a four-year-old season, and I said to Maybrick, A four-year-old season is a big risk at this point. You have to weight your economic interest against your fun."

"How long did you talk to the guy?"

"Not long. But I gave him the benefit of my experience at the track. That's all I could do, you know?"

"Yeah," said Buddy.

All the other stuff they needed to do just fell right into place. Arrangements at Gulfstream, arrangements for shipping, Buddy's own travel arrangements. Even his wife did the right thing and begged off going, because she hated Florida. He had a bunch of winners every week. Time flies, he thought, when you are having fun. Andrea Melanie called him and asked whether she should make arrangements for a big party. Buddy said yes. "Friday night or Saturday night?"

"Saturday night," said Buddy.

"Oh," said the owner. "I love you, Buddy. You are so perfect. Now, you tell Deedee and Leon that I got them a suite so the baby can have a room of her own. They are such a cute couple, and so nice. I will make all their arrangements, like for a babysitter for Saturday night. This is just the sort of thing I love to do best."

"You're good at it," said Buddy.

"We all have our niche," said the woman, "and yours is pure horse-training genius."

The next morning, the filly was just a hair off. Curtis didn't even notice it, and neither did Leon, but Buddy, cursed with an eagle eye, did. So he gave her a little bute on his own, a gram in her evening feed and a gram in her morning feed, and she was fine. The knee looked just like the other knee, almost.

Knowing what was yours and what wasn't was what enabled you to sleep. Buddy was sleeping soundly every night, and taking a little nap every afternoon, during whatever race he didn't have anyone running in. Sometimes he walked through the aisle of his barn at Hollywood Park and looked at his two-year-olds, wondering which one would win the Kentucky Derby. All he had to do was pick one, but he had to pick the right one. That had been the problem when he was having all those dealings with Jesus, he thought. He didn't know what he wanted, and so he was tormenting himself all the time and not getting anywhere. If you wanted two things, then really you didn't want either one. You were always turning this way and that way, trying to make up your mind. Well, those days were gone, and here he was, sleeping, winning, busy as a beaver. And anyway, the other thing about Jesus, according to everyone, was you always had another chance with him. And you didn't always have another chance for the Breeders' Cup.

The Breeders' Cup! The Breeders' Cup! The words themselves got him a little agitated, a little sick to his stomach. He started yelling more. After those two owners went to Jones, he saw that he had to spend time with all his owners, even though Andrea Melanie was calling him four times a day, and Jason once or twice. Sometimes when you got a big horse in the barn, and were dragging it around here and there, the owners of the other horses got a little miffed, and you got home from the big race, and there you were, barn empty. So he had to keep rolling the whole ball of string all at the same time, picking up this end and picking up that end and tying each little knot. He was on the phone a lot.

Ten days out from the race, Curtis showed up again, this time to give the filly the first of this series of Epogen injections. Buddy was a little nervous about shipping her around these injections, but, of course, you had to do what you had to do. Curtis wasn't daunted. He said, "You got my plane ticket to Florida, didn't you?"

"I don't know," said Buddy.

"What do you mean, you don't know?"

"I mean, I wasn't thinking about it. I don't think—" He looked at Curtis, who did not look either happy or eager to please, and went on, "You know, I'm running around like crazy. You don't want to get all the other owners comparing themselves to the one who's got the big horse, so—"

"How the hell did you think this filly was going to get her injections, if there wasn't any ticket for me? You got all the other tickets, and not mine? Let me tell you something, Buddy, I go in the first row. A jock you can find, an exercise rider you can find, an assistant trainer you don't really even need, but me you need."

"You're right, Curtis—"

"I wouldn't want to show you who you need and who you don't need. You should be able to figure that out on your own."

"It was an oversight—"

"You heard of Freud?"

"Yes."

"Well, you know what a Freudian slip is?"

"I—"

"I'll tell you. A Freudian slip is something that looks like a mistake, and everybody says it's a mistake, but there isn't such a thing as a mistake. My feelings are hurt, Buddy, and you know how I am these days. I've made up my mind that I deserve better."

"What can I do? I'll buy you a ticket."

"You all going first-class? Lukas always goes first-class."

"We were going to go first-class, yes."

"Great!"

In fact, they had all been slated to go to Kentucky in Jason Clark Kingston's personal jet, but Buddy so recoiled at the thought of Curtis and the Kingstons in close personal contact for two or three hours that he bought five first-class tickets and a seat for Alana Marie's baby chair. That was something like ten thousand bucks, but his share of the pot for his Breeders' Cup was something on the order of three hundred thousand dollars, so what the hell, he thought. Of course, four days later, when he was sitting next to Curtis and Curtis was leaning over him to get a look out the window, damp and panting and heaving around in his seat, he saw the downside to all of this, but then he made Leon change places with him. For the next two hours, he saw Curtis talk and Leon nod, and had more and more second thoughts. Booze was free in first class, Leon had no idea about the Epogen, and there was no guarantee that Curtis was sticking to his life story, or, rather, at any time he could go into that part of his life story that involved doping horses so they would run no matter what. Eventually Buddy could stand it no longer, and he traded places with Leon again. By this time, Curtis was stinking like a pig. Buddy felt like he was being crushed against the wall by some heavy horse, like a Percheron, the sort with a small brain and a big ass and no real connection in between the two.

In Florida, they waited a day for the horse, and she arrived in good enough shape for the most part. Her knee was a hair swollen and she was tired and annoyed. She tried to bite her groom and then kick him, but the reporters were all over the place, and so no one said anything, and Buddy told the Kingstons not to come out until the filly had rested and started eating again. Except she didn't start eating again. This was not unusual. Horses ran the gamut, like people. He'd had this one horse, back in the seventies, who sometimes didn't eat for days, and would drop a hundred pounds and put it right back on again. If you'd had enough horses over the years, you would have seen just about everything, so the filly's not eating didn't mean a damn thing, Buddy and Curtis agreed. She put in a good work, seemed to like the track, and that was all that mattered.

There were parties everywhere, and Buddy decided that the better part of wisdom was to keep Curtis with him as much as possible. He could introduce Curtis to the people he knew, or have Curtis introduce himself—those seemed to be the alternatives—so he made sure Curtis didn't feel left out. The problem was, Curtis' demands got bigger and bigger. At first an introduction was enough, but after that, he got so he wanted to be in the conversation, and then so he wanted to be doing all the talking, and then, when people started avoiding him (and why not, thought Buddy), he wanted to know why, and what Buddy was going to do about it. "I'm a friendly guy," he kept saying. "I want only the best for these people. You know, when I'm talking to a guy and he walks away from me, I see that as rude. I got something these people need! I can be a little enthusiastic, but I don't mean anything by it. You'd think— Well, I'm not going to think about that. Positive thinking is the key, you know. Know what you want and go for it. Where are you going?"

"To the can."

"Good idea." And so Curtis followed Buddy into the men's room, and kept talking even while they were taking a leak.

The very thought of all the time he was going to be spending with Curtis was so disheartening that Buddy decided to take it just one day, or even one moment, at a time. The moments did indeed crawl very slowly by, and Buddy was really glad that, back in southern California, Curtis at least had a place of residence that was nowhere near Buddy's house. At the same time that the time was passing so slowly, though, it was flying by. They gave the filly her second Epogen injection, another injection into the joint capsule of her knee, and her third and last injection of Epogen, and that meant it was only forty-eight hours until the race. What with the press and the hoopla and the fraternizing and the deal-making and the constant chatter, it was very hard to remember what belonged to you. The press and the oddsmakers thought things were undecided, and it was an extraordinary temptation to fall into that trap, the trap of thinking the race was wide open, when in reality it had already happened, as it were, but this was another way that they tried to sway you and shake your certainty. The way Buddy knew they were wrong was the déjà vu. From the moment they gave the filly that injection, he knew he was only seeing what he had seen before—every stride of her gallop the day before the race, including her little tiff with Deedee, where Deedee had to smack her once with the whip to get her to go forward, including the sight of his own hands opening the filly's mouth and pasting her with two grams of bute that afternoon, just for good measure, including the groom saying that once again she hadn't cleaned up her feed, including himself saying, of all the horses who had shipped in, show him who had cleaned up, show him the *fillies* who had cleaned up, including himself ranting on about fillies, why would he do that, except that he had done it before, they were sensitive and picky and strange and they always had some deal, including Curtis standing here and standing there, always with an eager grimace on his face, always catching Buddy's eye and giving him the high sign.

And at last, there they were in the gate, all closed up and quiet. What a relief that was, a moment of pure peace, and thank God it was the first race of the day, so still that Buddy nearly jumped out of his skin when the bell clanged and the gate opened, and, my God, horses were running down the track yet again. How many? It didn't matter. Some. More than a few, fewer than a lot. It made Buddy's head spin to see it happen again. It happened so many times it was hard to keep every time separate in your mind. They were bunching, and then they were expanding, and then they were bunching again, and the people next to him were leaning into him from both sides, pressing on him like a fever, until he started coughing. There was a lot of screaming all around him, and he had no idea what was going on, except that he was in hell and he wanted to get out, but some fat guy was leaning on him, holding his arm, and his own screams, which had nothing to do with the race—here he was, looking right at it but not seeing it—couldn't even be heard, there was no one to save him now, it was terrifying, how did he get this small, and then he was running with the others down the steps and out onto the track, and the fat guy said, "I told you, no problem. What a team we are!," and it was embarrassing for a winner like Buddy to be so out of it that he didn't even know that he had won! So they led him into the winner's circle, and they all lined up, and it was the Breeders' Cup, and they took the win photo, and then the reporters were all around, and Buddy kept smiling, but all the time the only thing he could think about was the look on the filly's face when they brought her back. She was beyond exhausted, beyond afraid. She was done for.

Seven more races; the day lasted forever. Buddy locked himself in his hotel room at six o'clock and went to sleep. At some point, the phone rang, and then a whining female voice said, "Oh, Buddy! I am giving such a fabulous party! Everybody's here!," and Buddy said, "I'll be right over," though he had no idea whom he was talking to. He slept the sleep of the dead until four, when the ringing of the phone awakened him again, and it was Residual's groom and the vet, whom he had called. The groom said, "Boss, this filly was just standing here with her head down. When I put the feed in her tub, boss, she didn't even look up, then she just lay down, boss, so I called the vet."

Then the vet got on, and said, "Mr. Crawford, we've got a real problem here. Maybe you should come out here, because, as far as I can see, this filly's got a raging case of pleuropneumonia, and I'm not sure I can save her."

What had Buddy's father always said to him? Oh, yeah. It was, Who do you think you are?

EPILOGUE

T HE MORNING AFTER the Breeders' Cup, it was training as usual in
Chicago. The weather wasn't any good, either. William Vance wasn't feeling so terrific. He thought he was coming down with a cold, maybe. He went
over to the hotplate and set on some water for tea, this herb tea that his girlfriend gave him. He sniffled experimentally, trying to decide if the tickle in his
throat was worse than it had been five minutes before, and the phone rang. He
picked it up, and said, "Yeah?"

"Mr. Vance?"

"Yeah?"

"My name is Angel Smith, down here in Texas. I had this heart attack
about a month ago, but I'm okay now, as long as I stick with my diet and get a
little exercise, and my wife stays on me about that. Anyway, I was going to tell
you that, the day I had this heart attack, I was feeling really bad, and I sat down
in my chair and I went out, you know, I think maybe I actually died, you never
can tell, but at any rate, the horses started raising such a fuss—"

"Do you have a horse you're interested in training, Mr. Smith?"

"Nah. I'm too old for that. Anyway, I got your number from track information, because I called the Jockey Club—a friend of mine told me how to do
it, after I checked the tattoo on the horse's lip, and you were—"

"Do you have Justa Bob?"

"Well, I call him Amigo, but yeah. I got him. He nearly went to the
slaughter, but—"

"You know," said William Vance, "if I hitch up the trailer right now, I can
be down there sometime tomorrow I think. Tell me where you are?"

"The horse don't look too good, Mr. Vance. I ain't got much money to
keep a Thoroughbred like that—"

"I don't care. I got plenty of feed. You tell me where you are. I've been
looking for that guy for months."

———

In California, very early, still dark, Jesse woke up from a dream of Residual. It wasn't like the race they had seen the day before on the simulcast at Hollywood Park, where she had been whipped, and stumbled at the end, and almost gotten beaten by that big filly, and then come back to win, and all the guys who had bet on her (and that was everyone, including his dad) were screaming and cursing. It was some other race, where she was just running, ears up, nose out, and her jockey wasn't whipping her at all, but just giving her the reins and floating along the way she had done that time he picked her to win in her very first outing, when she was just a baby and Pincay had ridden her. In his dream, everything was quiet and he was standing there and the filly ran and Pincay turned his head and looked at him, Jesse, and smiled, and then the filly won, and even though she was the favorite, she was a long shot, and everyone in the stands went home with lots and lots of money, as if the bet pool never had to be shared, but was bottomless, and nothing about the race-track was mysterious or dangerous. Jesse lay awake after that, while the room began to lighten, and he thought of the money he had made, seven dollars on a five-dollar bet, and he thought that he would just keep that, his Residual money, something to fall back on in case he ever needed it. And then he sighed and turned over and went back to sleep.

Al was on his cell phone with Farley Jones. Right next to him, still under the covers, Rosalind was on the regular phone. Eileen was sitting on the end of the bed. Al knew for a fact that she was contemplating barking, but hadn't made up her mind yet. It was Sunday morning, about ten o'clock. With her free hand, Rosalind was tickling his palm, and then she winked at him, but she was speaking in a very businesslike voice. She said, "Yes, Sir Michael. I'll tell him. Just a minute." Al lifted the covers just for a glimpse of Rosalind. She had on a beautiful silver lace nightgown, bunched up around her thighs. Al dropped the coverlet. She said, "The buyer is Japanese. Sir Michael says he thinks it's Matsuo Oku Stud."

Al repeated this into his cell phone. Farley was silent for a moment, then said, "I saw that place once. It's unbelievable."

Al said to Rosalind, "He's been there."

Rosalind put her hand over the mouthpiece. "Ask him if they take good care of the horses."

Al put the question. Farley laughed. He said, "Not like anyplace you've ever seen, Coolmore, Gainesway, you name it. The Oku stallions get regular exercise, and their paddocks are scattered in with the mare pastures. It's the closest thing I ever saw to a natural situation. Horses live forever there."

Al nodded emphatically. Rosalind was still tickling his palm, which was making him forget that this was a business deal. Just to remind himself, he said, "They said seven million. What do you think?"

Farley said, "Well, Al, I know this sounds strange, given what we've just been through, but my instinct is to be realistic about this. His breeding was odd before the Arc, and it's odd now, not something that appeals to the American bloodstock market. Breeders look at the animal's broodmare sire, and though Independence was a great steeplechaser and the full brother to Bold Ruler, he ran in 1954. About six guys in the world even know who he was. You could run him for another year or two and make more money racing, but that's always a risk, and could hurt his value rather than enhance it."

"Not to mention accidents," said Al.

"Do not mention accidents," said Rosalind. Then the plummy voice on the other end of the line said, "Accident? Has the horse had an accident?"

"Certainly not, Sir Michael," said Rosalind. She moved her hand up Al's arm, lightly, on the inside, non-hairy part.

Al glanced at her. He was ready for this negotiation to be over.

Al said, "I hate to take him away from you right now. Your gal out there seems to like him, too."

Rosalind said, "They said we could visit him as much as we want. They have a guesthouse."

Sir Michael said, "I quote Mr. Nakadate, 'It would honor us so highly to receive the former owner and trainer of Limitless, that we would certainly be happy to bring them to our small island, at our studfarm's expense, anytime they might choose to do so. Their friendship is our foremost aim.' "

Rosalind said to Al, "I guess we all have a new place to vacation."

Farley said to Al, "I like Japan very much, as a matter of fact. I was there for the Japan Cup once."

Rosalind's fingers arrived at Al's cheek and forehead, where they traced a little pattern. It made his scalp prickle. He said to Farley, "Looks like a done deal to me."

"Me, too," said Rosalind. She traced the figure again, then ran her index finger down his nose and chin and hairy chest. She was smiling at him.

"That all?" said Al. "Hey, Farley."

"Al."

"Thanks," said Al.

"Good-bye, Sir Michael," said Rosalind.

He pressed "end." She put the phone on the cradle. Eileen barked one time, practically a command. But it was no good. They weren't paying a lick of attention to her. Well, that was fine. She jumped off the bed and went out of the bedroom. She surveyed her domain. Free at last. She trotted down the long, familiar hallway into the kitchen, jumped up onto the counter, and trotted over to the sink. There, she noted with deep satisfaction that the plug had been left out of the garbage disposal.

FROM *The Thoroughbred Times:*

Breeders' Cup Distaff (G1) Winner Residual Out of Danger

Residual, the flying filly who only two weeks ago won the Breeders' Cup Distaff, fighting off a late drive by smooth-running mare Beautiful Pleasure, has been declared out of danger by the veterinarians at Rood and Riddle Veterinary Clinic in Lexington, where the filly was airlifted two days after the race. A spokesman for the clinic said that the filly had been in critical condition for almost ten days, but that she was now comfortable, and headed for full recovery. Trainer Buddy Crawford, for whom the Breeders' Cup win was the culmination of a lifetime in racing, said, "I never thought she wouldn't recover. It just never crossed my mind. She's a fighter. Of course, she's a lover, too. But first and foremost, she's a fighter."

The filly's owner, Andrea Melanie Kingston, wife of California software magnate Jason Clark Kingston, told the press that the filly would be retired to one of the Kingstons' newly purchased farms, possibly Alhambra Farm outside of Lexington, and that a breeding was planned to Skip Away in the spring. In ten starts, Residual won six graded stakes, including the Grade One Breeders' Cup Distaff, the Grade One Bette Midler Handicap, and $2,214,000.

Of their plans as owners and breeders, Mrs. Kingston said only, "Whatever my husband does, he does in a big way. Wherever he is, he expects to be a presence, and he is. And we just love Buddy."

Quote of the Week

"The party officials couldn't have been more helpful. I think the outlook is good, myself, and personally, the change of scene will be welcome. Any new project is wonderfully exciting. I can't tell you how I am looking forward to it." —Sir Michael Ordway, British horse agent, on the announcement of his appointment by Vietnamese officials as the first racing secretary at the oval being built outside of Hanoi.

"Certainly," said Krista into the telephone. She shifted Maia to her other hip and wrote down the number. "I'll fax you a contract today and we'll expect the mare at the end of the week. Thank you, very much." She clicked off the handset and set it down on the desk, then she looked at the note she had made—Storm Cat, out of a stakes-winning mare by Pleasant Colony. The mare herself had won something like three hundred thousand dollars and already produced a stakes winner out of four foals. And they were sending her to Himself, the sire of the legendary Limitless, first American winner of the Arc, ever. And they were paying seventy-five hundred dollars to do so. And they thought they were getting a bargain. And the guy had said, "I saw a mare you bred last year. She came home looking like a million bucks."

"Oh, sweetie!" she said to Maia, who laughed in return. Storm Cat! Seventy-five hundred bucks, thirty-eight mares booked for the spring so far. Krista had already ordered a year's worth of hay, a grass mix, and stored this vast treasure in the hay barn. She carried Maia out of the office and stood there under the eave of the mare barn.

Across the way, Himself, dirty as a pig already, was rolling joyously in the cool mud, writhing this way and that, flopping onto his right side, then onto his left, hooves waving in the air. He got up, shook himself, snorted, then he leapt and kicked out. After that he galloped across the paddock, bucking and snorting. Yes, Krista noticed, the mares were watching.

Nothing had happened—no disasters, no destruction, nothing unexpected that couldn't be fixed. She felt Maia's hand on her neck and she looked into that darling face. "Down!" said Maia. Krista bent down and stood the little girl on her feet, then she laughed. "Thank you," she said. "Thank you, thank you, thank you."

AUDREY SET DOWN her *Thoroughbred Times* and stood up. Ellen had asked her to clean the office, and that's what she had meant to do, but there was the magazine, and of course she had to read it cover to cover, all the races, all the veterinary articles, all the letters to the editor and the opinions and the articles about great sires and great mares. Oh, she thought. Oh. What a lucky girl I am. She pushed the sleeping corgis off the couch and straightened the cushions and pillows, then she picked up the paper coffee cups and threw them away. Now the corgis were standing at the closed office door, whining, so she opened it and let them out. There she was, across the aisle, looking at her, her beautiful gray mare from California, Chantilly. Such a neat, trim little mare, so quick and bright. Audrey stood in the doorway, transfixed with love, and the mare gave a deep, affectionate nicker.

A NOTE ABOUT THE AUTHOR

Jane Smiley is the author of nine previous works of fiction, including *The Age of Grief*, *The Greenlanders*, *Ordinary Love & Good Will*, *A Thousand Acres* (for which she was awarded the Pulitzer Prize), and *Moo*. She lives in northern California.

A NOTE ON THE TYPE

This book was set in Adobe Garamond. Designed for the Adobe Corporation by Robert Slimbach, the fonts are based on types first cut by Claude Garamond (c. 1480–1561). Garamond was a pupil of Geoffroy Tory and is believed to have followed the Venetian models, although he introduced a number of important differences, and it is to him that we owe the letter we now know as "old style."

Composed by Creative Graphics,
Allentown, Pennsylvania

Printed and bound by Quebecor Printing,
Fairfield, Pennsylvania

Designed by Cassandra J. Pappas